THE SIXTH BOOK OF UNEXPECTED ENLIGHTENMENT

GUARDIANS OF THE TWILIGHT LANDS

Praise for the Books of Unexpected Enlightenment

"The action is non-stop, with child's play, schoolwork, and danger all churned together. Lamplighter introduces many imaginative elements in her world that will delight...."

—*VOYA*

"The British boarding school mystery meets the best imagined of fantasies at breakneck speed and with fully realized characters."

—Sarah A. Hoyt, author of *Darkship Thieves*

"L. Jagi Lamplighter, a fantastic new voice and a fabulous new world in the YA market! Rachel Griffin is a hero who never gives up!
I cheered her all the way!"

—Faith Hunter, author of the *Skinwalker* series

"*The Unexpected Enlightenment of Rachel Griffin*, a plucky band of children join forces to fight evil, despite the best efforts of incompetent adults, at a school for wizards. YA fiction really doesn't get better than that."

—Jonathan Moeller, author of *The Ghosts* series

"Rachel Griffin is curious, eager and smart, and ready to begin her new life at Roanoke Academy for the Sorcerous Arts, but she didn't expect to be faced with a mystery as soon as she got there. Fortunately she's up to the task. Take all the best of the classic girl detective, throw in a good dose of magic and surround it all with entertaining, likeable friends and an intriguing conundrum, and you'll have *The Unexpected Enlightenment of Rachel Griffin*, a thrilling adventure tailor-made for the folks who've been missing Harry Potter. Exciting, fantastical events draw readers into Rachel's world and solid storytelling keeps them there."

—Misty Massey, author of *Mad Kestrel*

OTHER BOOKS BY
L. JAGI LAMPLIGHTER

For an up-to-date list, see http://ljagilamplighter.com/works.

THE BOOKS OF UNEXPECTED ENLIGHTENMENT
The Unexpected Enlightenment of Rachel Griffin

The Raven, The Elf, and Rachel

Rachel and the Many-Splendored Dreamland

The Awful Truth about Forgetting

The Unbearable Heaviness of Remembering

Guardians of the Twilight Lands

The Young Angels' Society (*forthcoming*)

... and more to come.

THE PROSPERO'S CHILDREN TRILOGY
Prospero Lost

Prospero In Hell

Prospero Regained

THE SIXTH BOOK OF UNEXPECTED ENLIGHTENMENT

GUARDIANS OF THE TWILIGHT LANDS

L. JAGI LAMPLIGHTER

BASED ON THE WORKS OF MARK A. WHIPPLE

ILLUSTRATIONS BY JOHN C. WRIGHT

Wisecraft Publishing
A publishing company of the Wise

Published by Wisecraft Publishing
A publishing company of the Wise

ISBN: 978-1-953739-16-2 (print)
       978-1-953739-17-9 (ebook)
First edition
Revision 1.0.2 2023-09-04

Edited by Jim Frenkel

Cover art by Dan Lawlis
https://danlawlis.wordpress.com

Interior illustrations by John C. Wright

Typeset by Joel C. Salomon

Cover design by Danielle McPhail
Sidhe na Daire Multimedia
http://sidhenadaire.com

The text for this book is set in Alegreya, created by Juan Pablo del Peral of Huerta Tipográfica, and licensed under the SIL Open Font License, Version 1.1; see https://fonts.google.com/specimen/Alegreya and https://github.com/huertatipografica/Alegreya for details.

Chapter headings are set in RM GINGER, © 2009 Ray Meadows, licensed under Creative Commons' CC BY-ND 3.0; see https://fontstruct.com/fontstructions/show/258661 for details.

CONTENTS

Staked for Her Troubles 1

Awakened by Joy 7

Encircled by Barghests 19

The Difficult Art of Keeping Promises 31

Dear Your Majesty 41

A Tad Creepy, Even to Me 49

The Unexpected Enlightenment of Rachel Griffin 63

The Silver Sandal Caper! 73

Damaged Souls 81

Twelve Pairs of Gloves 91

A Very Influential Fairy 101

With Intent to Deprive 111

To Cast a Cantrip 123

Adventures in Slumberland 133

Gasp, Dare, and Firehawk 143

Three Coat Racks and a Steeplechaser 155

An Exchange of Birthday Presents 167

For He's a Jolly Good Fellow 179

Do You Know Him, Too? 189

Have Prince, Will Travel Again 201

The Overly-Ample Homecoming of Sigfried Smith 209

The Cry of the Dart 219

Dart, Dart, Cruel Dart 229

The Lord of Dartmoor 237

Guardians of Lost Worlds 245

Half an Hour Too Late 255

Immortal Memories 267

Twilight Excursions 281

Morthbrood on the Moors 295

Peers of the Round Table 305

Needle and Dart 317

The Fourteenth Birthday of Lady Rachel Jade Griffin 331

A Long-Awaited Conversation 343

Guerre du Coeur — 357
More Ghosts Than You Could Shake a Stick At — 367
For I Am with Thee — 377
The Foothills of Heaven — 385
The Door to Saving Everyone — 395
April Fool's Day — 409
The Gryphon Knight — 421
Return to Roanoke — 433
The Day Before the Celebration — 443
May Day Eve — 453
The King of the Daoine Sidhe — 465
The Fastest Game on Grass — 479
The Heart of Dreams — 493
Wraith Attack! — 501
Facing the Dragon — 511
The Walls Come Tumbling Down — 521
More Powerful Than Sorcery — 533
Breaking Through the Clouds of Gloom — 547
Last Sunrise—of Freshman Year — 561
Short stories that take place during *Guardians of the Twilight Lands* — 570
Cast of Characters — 571
Glossary — 579
Acknowledgements — 583
About the Authors — 584

DEDICATION

IX

This book is dedicated to:
Officers Vicky Armel
and
Michael Garbarino

And to all who have died in the line of duty.

ONCE THERE WAS A WORLD

THAT SEEMED AT FIRST GLANCE MUCH LIKE OTHER WORLDS

YOU *MAY HAVE LIVED IN* OR READ ABOUT,

BUT IT *WASN'T....*

CHAPTER ONE:
STAKED FOR HER TROUBLES

RACHEL GRIFFIN PAUSED ON THE SEVENTEENTH STEP OF THE STAIRCASE leading to the boys' side of Dare Hall. It was four in the morning, and she was dressed like a cat.

It was Sunday, February twenty-fifth. She was still in her Year of the Dragon Ball costume, a black bodysuit with white spots and a tail wired to stick out behind her. Her hair was twisted into two tight cat ears atop her head, and smudged black grease pencil whiskers meandered across her face. Her nose was a smeared dab of black makeup.

In one hand, she held a speckled feather given to her by the Guardian of the World.

Was it the next step that had a loud squeak? Despite her exhausted state, she thought back, precisely recalling the last time she had climbed this staircase. She did not want to accidentally wake the boys in the nearest dorm room.

Rachel stepped over the noisy stair and continued creeping upward. She was so tired; her sight kept blurring. She had been up all night. She longed to return to her room and take off her costume, which she had been wearing for almost ten hours. This task had to be done tonight, however; or her friends would make her promise not to share secrets, and she would not be able to keep her word to the Prince of Transylvania. She just had to make it to the fourth floor and find Wulfgang Starkadder.

She nearly tripped on the rug of the second landing. Only by wind-milling her arms did she avoid a fall. She almost tried to catch herself with the hand clutching the feather. Frightened of damaging it, she pulled the pouch she wore around her neck from under her bodysuit and slipped the feather into its bigger-on-the-inside space. To her relief, it fit.

Then, right hand on the railing, she continued up the stairs.

As she climbed, her fatigued mind wandered, drifting, in a kind of nigh-delirious shock, over recent events. The previous day had been the best and the worst of her nearly fourteen years, and she was still having trouble taking it all in. Wonderful things had happened: a delicious Lunar

New Year's celebration, her first masquerade ball, her first dance with her boyfriend—though that was not the dance lingering in her memory—and, most importantly, her first meeting with her eldest sister, Amber.

But terrible things had happened, too.

From the moment she had learned that a daughter had been stolen from her parents, she had longed to meet this lost sister. Only, reality was nothing like what she had imagined. While tiny and childlike on the outside, Amber had been raised to be a killing machine—a "death doll." She was also completely uninterested in being a member of the Griffin family.

Rachel swallowed, a lump forming in her throat. Grasping the banister more tightly, she sped upward, almost as if in a dream. As she recalled the dire events of the previous night, however, it felt less like a dream and more like a nightmare. She and her siblings had taken Amber to England to meet their parents. They had learned that, while everyone else's memory of the stolen baby girl had been erased twenty-two years earlier, her mother's perfect memory had not been touched. For more than two decades, her mother had suffered the agony of her first child having been stolen—without being able to speak about this to anyone.

Tears filled Rachel's eyes. Thinking of it tore her heart—what a lonely existence.

Then, on their way back, Amber had altered the lives of the students at Roanoke Academy for the Sorcerous Arts forever.

When Rachel had first arrived at school, Stony Tor, rising to the north of Roanoke Island, had been the prison of the Heer of Dunderberg—a storm goblin who had terrorized the Hudson Valley for centuries, casting lightning bolts and sinking ships. The Roanoke Covenant, which governed the relationship between the Academy and the many fey who lived on the once-floating island, relied upon the school keeping the storm goblin imprisoned. In return, the fey had promised not to trouble the mortals—the magical Wise or the mundane Unwary.

Last November, the storm goblin had escaped into the Hudson Highlands. Over the last four months, he had remained at large, attacking the school with storms and boulders. Yet, Rachel had held out hope that he could be captured and the Covenant restored. Last night, that hope ended abruptly—when her death doll of a sister captured the storm goblin and casually killed him.

Now, all bets were off.

With Roanoke Covenant permanently disrupted, the local fey were free to wreak havoc upon magical and mundane alike. To counter this, the Wisecraft had sent Agents to patrol the campus and protect Roanoke's students. But who would protect the ordinary Unwary who lived on either side of the Hudson River?

As she climbed the stairs, Rachel recalled Tommy Check, an Unwary teen who had been the victim of an ogre. She gritted her teeth, grateful that her blood brother, Sigfried Smith the Dragonslayer, had killed that ogre. *How many more like Tom Check will there now be?*

Quietly, alone on the staircase, dressed like a cat, Rachel Griffin vowed to find a way to restore peace to the fey and the mortals.

Reaching another landing, Rachel abruptly returned her attention to the present. Had she climbed three flights while reminiscing? Or four? Ordinarily, she would check her perfect memory, recall each motion of each leg, and count how many times she had moved from stair to stair, but she was so weary. This mental act, usually so simple, daunted her. She had been climbing this staircase forever. Surely, this was the fourth floor. Reaching the landing, she crept down the hall.

She stopped at the third door on the right and opened it a crack. Inside was pitch black. The curtains were drawn. She could make out nothing. Down the hall, a door closed—the loo, if she guessed correctly—and footsteps sounded, coming toward her. Rachel ducked inside the dorm room and pulled the door closed behind her.

She crouched low, moving slowly so as not to disturb the will-o-wisps in their nighthoods. If she had guessed correctly, the bunk on the right was Wulfgang's. She crept forward, one hand outstretched, until she felt the window, thankful that no one had left shoes or pieces of costumes on the floor to trip her. She pulled back the edge of one curtain, trying to peer at the faces of the sleeping boys. A sliver of pure silvery moonlight pierced the darkness, illuminating the dorm room.

Rachel dropped the curtain as if it were hot. She stood motionless, listening to the pounding of her own heart. Closing her eyes, she recalled the moment when the moonlight lit the room, examining the boy in the bunk on the right. The dark hair was similar to Prince Wulfgang of Transylvania. It could be him.

Now all she had to do was wake him up, tell him all the secrets she knew—secrets that could destroy the world—and her part would be done.

She would have kept the promise she had made to him last night. In return, Wulfgang had promised to befriend Nastasia Romanov, the Princess of Magical Australia. Nastasia desperately needed a friend of her own class, one with whom she could feel free to discuss the secrets that she knew.

Rachel drew a deep breath, grateful to have completed this obligation. Then she paused, her heartbeat taking off like a galloping horse. How was she going to wake him? Crown princes probably had martial training. If she tapped his shoulder, would he punch her in the face? *Oh, why had she signed up for this?*

Rachel put out her arm and began inching forward in the darkness, stepping where her memory told her the floor was open, avoiding a stack of books and a dropped suit jacket that lay just beside the bed. Two steps more and she would reach the bunk.

She never made it.

A sudden motion knocked her to the cold wooden floor. Something sharp poked into her chest, pushing against her breastbone. A weight pinned her legs. The curtain she had disturbed earlier swayed. In the flicker of silvery moonlight, she caught a glimpse of her captor. An older boy in pajamas straddled her, pushing her down. Dark, shoulder-length hair fell around his face. His free hand pressed a wooden stake against her chest, its sharp point above her heart.

Rachel recognized him. It was Abraham Van Helsing.

"Little vampire wanted a snack before sunup, eh?" growled the leader of the Dare Hall Vampire Hunters Club. "You picked the wrong room, vixen!"

Boy, was he right about that! Wrong floor, even!

Terrified, Rachel croaked out. "I *am* in the wrong room. Sorry! Please don't stake me!"

"Aww, poor little vamp, begging for her life, is she?"

What now? Should she call Vladimir Von Dread on her black bracelet? No one else could arrive in time. The thought gave her pause: What was the Prince of Bavaria doing with her sister Sandra in London? She was not entirely sure of the nature of their relationship. If Rachel called and Vlad jumped here to save her, *would he be wearing pants?*

A crackly voice from another bed said, "Guhhhh. Abraham, who are you talking to? What time is it? Can't you and the Ferret Brothers or the

Colts, or whatever crazy animals your friends are named after, have your crazy meeting in their room?"

The door swung open.   Above her, the domestic will-o-wisps whooshed out of their nighthoods, filling the dorm room with light. After total darkness, even their soft, buttery glow seemed blinding.

An older boy's voice snapped, "What are you doing, Abe?"

"What's it look like? Staking a vamp."

"Isn't that Peter Griffin's little sister? I thought she came in here. Get off the poor girl!"

The crackly, sleepy voice, asked, "What would Pint-Sized Griffin be doing here?"

Abraham growled back, "Looking for a snack. She's a freaking blood-sucking vampire. Why else would she be prowling around on the night of a full moon, peering at sleeping people? Full moon's their favorite snack time. Like werewolves."

The older boy in the doorway replied, "Um, maybe she's *looking for her brother?*"

Rachel lay on her back, still fantasizing about what the expressions on the faces of the boys might be were Dread to suddenly appear in their bedroom, but she could not do that to Sandra. The newcomer came over beside her and kneeled down. She could see now that it was Pete Komarek, her brother Peter's best friend. He must have been the person whose footsteps she had heard coming down the hallway. His midnight trip to the loo may have saved her life.

He put two fingers lightly against the side of her neck. "Abe, she has a pulse. And a normal body temperature. She is not a vampire. If you hurt her, not only will you be murdering a living human being, but you'll also be dead as soon as her family finds out. You know her oldest sister is Sandra Griffin, right? She could turn you into a pinecone."

Abraham put his hand on the side of Rachel's face.   He frowned. "Yeah. Okay, Pete. She's not a vamp."

Rachel let out her breath. It came out in a huge *whoosh* of relief. Van Helsing grunted in disgust and climbed off her legs.

Pete smiled down at her. "Are you okay, Rachel? Are you looking for Peter?"

"No. Very sorry!" Rachel squeaked in her proper English accent. "Wrong room."

Pete smiled kindly at her. "Hey, cute outfit. Have you been up all night? You should get some sleep. And avoid Abe here and his whacko friends."

"Or you could try knocking," growled Abraham.

He climbed back into his bed, grumbling to himself.

Rachel rose and gave a wobbly curtsy. "Thank you very much. For not staking me." To Pete, she blurted out, "Thank you for saving my life, Mr. Komarek. If you ever need anything—your life saved? A cup of tea?—you have but to name it. Good night!"

She turned and ran.

Abandoning her Wulfgang plan—she would have to try again in the morning—she ran down the steps to the foyer and headed for the girls' side. She made it upstairs, gathered her night things, and took a quick shower, during which she tried in vain to scrub the grease paint off her face. Then she fell into bed and slept.

Chapter Two:
Awakened by Joy

"Wake up, sleepyhead!" Joy O'Keefe shouted right next to Rachel's ear.

Rachel struggled to open her heavy eyelids. Strands of dreams still entangled her, trying to draw her back into slumberland. *Surely, it could not be morning already.*

"It's after eight!" cried Joy. She was a bubbly young woman with mousy brown hair. "And there's an Agent here to see you."

"To see *me?*" Rachel echoed blearily.

Was it only eight in *the morning?* That meant she had received less than four hours of sleep. She had intended to sleep until noon, possibly all day. Who in their right mind would wake someone up early on the morning after a ball, and how could Joy be so cheerful when she herself had not even left for bed until after one in the morning?

Rachel's thoughts moved sluggishly, trying to work out why an Agent might wish to see her. Was she in trouble for sneaking into the boys' side and nearly getting staked? Did Roanoke Academy send Agents of the Wisecraft for such offenses? That seemed harsh.

"Who—?" She struggled to sit up, eyes not quite open. Her cat, Mistletoe, lay curled up against her side. The black and white cat purred softly. "Did you recognize the Agent?"

"Nope. Don't think I ever saw him before," Joy announced cheerfully. "It wasn't Darling or Standish or someone famous."

Rachel yawned and rubbed her eyes. "So it's a he? What did he look like?"

"He was very tall and wonderfully handsome." Joy giggled and spun in a circle, spreading her arms. "I wouldn't mind being interrogated by that Agent!"

"Tall and...." Rachel closed her eyes, thinking.

From her perfect memory, she brought up the faces of all the Agents in the Wisecraft—well, all of them as of last summer. It was possible they had hired new ones. The Agents, the law enforcement of the Wise, were perpetually short-handed. It had been that way ever since Aaron Marley and the Terrible Five had slaughtered all of the Agents in one stroke, nearly twenty-eight years earlier. The Wisecraft had never entirely recovered.

Reviewing the Agents, she looked for candidates who were unusually handsome and tall. Most Agents were healthy and athletic, but a few stood out as particularly stunning. Agent Michael Garbarino, with his dark, intense eyes, was astonishingly handsome. Rachel happened to know the young man was a selkie who spent his downtime as a seal; however, Garbarino was not tall. James Darling was dashing, and Rachel secretly thought the dark-skinned, dreadlocked Dorian Standish—the Agent from Prester John's Kingdom—was the most handsome of all; however, Joy knew both of them by sight and had already declared it was not either of these. The unusually observant Agent Sherlock Moth of London was startlingly good-looking, probably the effect of his elf blood, but he was not especially tall either. Agent Rupert Larson, also of London, was strikingly tall, but, while not unpleasant, Rachel would hardly have called him "wonderfully handsome." The same went for Agent Bridges. That left....

Rachel's eyes flew open. She made an impatient noise in her throat. Jumping out of bed, to the dismay of her cat, she rifled through her trunk until she found her green photo album. Opening the album, she held it up for Joy to see.

"Did he look like that?" she asked, pointing at a picture.

"Yes. That's him!" cried Joy, clapping her hands. "How did you come to have that picture? Do you ogle it in your free time? Does Gaius know? If I had a boyfriend, I don't think I would want him to know I was ogling Agents. Can I have a copy?"

Rachel rolled her eyes. "That's my father."

The look on Joy's face was priceless.

Four minutes later, Rachel bounded down the staircase. She had nearly run down in her nightgown, but it occurred to her that while it was perfectly appropriate for a young girl to greet her own father in her night clothes, she might be seen by others. In the interest of propriety, she had changed into her black academic robes and had gathered her normal accoutrements: her neck pouch, the necklace her brother Peter had given her that protected her from the paralysis hex, and the silver wand that had been her grandmother's. She had paused before the mirror on Nastasia's vanity, wiped the sleepy sand from her almond-shaped eyes, brushed back her black shoulder-length hair, secured it with a hairclip sporting a red bow, and donned her mortarboard cap, pushing the black tassel to one side. She started to climb under her bed to grab Vroomie, her bristleless, but decided against it. It was unlikely Father had come to take her flying. Finally, she grabbed her red wool duffle coat, in case he wished to take her out of the dorm. Her coat matched her hair bow.

A few crimson-wrapped Korean treats remained from the Lunar New Year's festivities. She stuffed them into her pockets. Then she ran all the way down the four flights of stairs.

Ambrose Griffin stood in the foyer of Dare Hall. Tall and calm, he had dark hair and implacable hazel eyes and wore the uniform of the Agents of the Wisecraft—a tricorne hat, an Inverness cloak with its half cape, and a medallion bearing an image of a lantern surrounded by stars on a chain around his neck. A fist-sized diamond tipped his fulgurator's staff. He rested the staff against the wall and caught his youngest daughter around the waist, swinging her in a circle. Rachel laughed and smiled back at him, but she wished he would put her down. Much as she usually enjoyed this greeting, operating on less than four hours of sleep was making her feel dangerously close to nauseous.

"Hello, little dart," the Duke of Devon said in his elegant British accent as he placed her on her feet. "I am sorry to wake you so early after our late night, but we have some questions that no one else seems to be able to answer."

"Of course," said Rachel, taking his hand.

He led her out the door and across campus toward the docks, making her grateful she had taken time to dress.

"What shall we do about the loss of the Heer?" she asked, hoping the Wisecraft had a simple, clear solution. Her sister Sandra had mentioned that Father had a plan. She probably meant that he had arranged to send the Agents who were now crawling all over campus, but Rachel hoped he had an actual fix. "How do we reinstate the Roanoke Covenant?"

Ambrose Griffin shook his head sadly. "I do not know. That remains to be seen."

Rachel bit her lip, disappointed.

She and her father walked across the snow-covered campus, along the tree-lined path, through the ruins, and down the stairs of Bannerman's Castle. Instead of continuing to the docks, her father headed south, across snowy fields. Rachel looked around. Then she remembered back, allowing her perfect memory to reveal anything that might have been obscured. The only difference was an Agent's tricorne hat and Inverness cloak draped between two of the boulders near the shore.

"Who left a hat and cloak?" Rachel asked, gesturing at the garments.

Her father had to squint hard to see them.

"Michael's in the river talking to Old Man Hudson," he replied, "but even the river himself claims he cannot make heads or tails of it. Can you tell me what happened last night?"

Rachel pressed her lips together. Dazzling sunlight reflected off the snow, pristine except for a few animal tracks. Rachel, in her sleep-muddled state, kept blinking. She shaded her eyes and gazed over at the dark waters of the river.

She knew what had happened. She could tell him, but should she?

"Didn't Sandra tell you?" she asked hopefully.

Her father nodded. "She told me what she knew, but there were things she could not explain. What happened to the river? Did it attack Amber and Andre the Second? Did you see a monster? Was it Hudson himself? Tell me in your own words what happened."

The river? *Oh.* She sighed. There was no particular reason not to tell him, especially since her brother Peter also knew what had occurred.

"No. The river was not involved. I tried to kill the Master of the World. Then I changed my mind. If you doubt me, ask Peter," she answered gravely.

"*You* tried—" Her father's voice rose. "You tried *what?*"

She met his gaze stoically. "He did such terrible things to our family. Mummy said she thought about killing him every night. Peter and I thought his death might make her happy. At the last minute, however, the Comfort Lion objected, so I forgave him."

"You forgave the Comfort Lion?"

"No. I forgave Andre the Second. I don't hate him anymore."

Her father frowned at that. "I don't know which is more disturbing, that my thirteen-year-old daughter was considering committing murder or that you were willing to forgive him. He did us great harm."

Rachel said seriously, "I discovered a trick that does tremendous damage. It required lightning imps. There were some about, so I tried it. Then I changed my mind and deflected the attack into the river. It caused... a bit of a splash."

"You can say that again," murmured her father under his breath. Aloud, he explained, "We received complaints from Cornwall-on-Hudson —" He gestured toward the town on the west bank of the river, northward of where the Roanoke Glass Hall stood on the far bank, beneath Storm King Mountain, and then behind them, toward the eastern shore of the Hudson River. "—all the way to Cold Spring. Apparently, the houses near the shore on both banks were pelted with water."

If she had been less tired, she would have nodded gravely. Instead, to her horror, she giggled. She pressed her fist against her mouth, hoping that would stop it, but it did not.

"Sorry about that."

"You did that?" he asked, incredulous. "Truly?"

She nodded. Not meeting his eyes, she admitted, "I made the crater on the Tor, too."

He lifted his hat, ran a hand over his hair, and then returned the tricorne to its place. "I heard about that. Might I ask how you did it?"

Rachel opened her mouth and froze. "Um. The spell I used... is confidential."

"Confidential to whom?" Her father frowned.

"Ouroboros Industries."

His eyebrows shot upward. "O.I. is teaching freshmen proprietary spells?"

"No. William shared it with me, and I... modified it."

She did not add that she had shared the secret of this crater-causing spell with her second cousin, Blackie Moth. He was building a rail-gun for O.I. that had been commissioned by the King of Transylvania. Why the King of Transylvania wanted a garlic-shooting *rail-gun* to fight vampires, no one had explained.

"Ah. That's a pity. Though I really think you...." Suddenly, he straightened and looked toward the bare trees of the forest to the east. "What was that?"

Rachel saw nothing. She thought back. The corner of her eye had caught a dark shadow. She examined the memory, making out the shadowy shape of a large dog.

"Barghest," she said warily, moving closer to her father.

"Can't be." He shook his head, still scanning the tree line, though he put a protective hand on her shoulder. "There are no barghests on Roanoke Island."

"It was a barghest. I remember the shape clearly. I've fought a barghest before."

"You have?" He looked at her sharply. "Why was that not in my reports?"

Rachel shrugged and answered his first question. "Back in September, at Beaumont."

"In Transylvania?" He casually pointed his staff at the spot where the shadow had appeared. "Was that the time some students fell out of dreamland and ended up there? I... had not realized you were part of that group. Did I know that before I lost my memory?"

"I don't know." Rachel shrugged again. "But about Beaumont...."

Her father swung around suddenly and fired a stream of bright sapphire sparks at a dark shape that sprinted across the snow-speckled rocks by the shore—on the opposite side of them from the first shadowy shape. Rachel breathed in the scent of freshly cut pine that accompanied her father's enchantment. The canine shadow sank behind the rocks, barely avoiding the hex.

"They're behind us! That's not good!" He touched the lantern in the middle of his medallion and announced clearly, "Agent under attack. Help needed south of the docks!"

Grrrrrrr. Five smoky canine shapes slipped out from the rocks and the forest both, flanking them. Rachel's father pulled her close to him and then swung his staff in a circle. Sapphire sparks shot out towards some shadowy figures. Glowing, golden Glepnir bands flew toward others. One golden band entrapped its prey. The other went wide. Three of the creatures were hit by the paralysis hexes; the remaining one vanished behind the rocks.

"Why are they here?" Ambrose mused calmly, alertly watching for the last barghest. "They are a European menace. The foreign creatures on Roanoke Island all arrived over a century ago, back when the island still floated. Barghests were not among them. Who would import barghests to America? Could these be some native variety?"

Rachel was impressed by her father's aplomb, considering the number of menacing creatures. On the other hand, he had disposed of them easily. Maybe five barghests were nothing to him; maybe he fought off a dozen every morning, just to keep in shape.

"These are British barghests." She pointed at one of the frozen creatures. "See how they have snouts like Irish wolfhounds? I recognize them from Daring Northwest's drawings in his book *Barghests, Black Shucks, and Other Menaces of the Moors.*"

"You're right." Ambrose frowned. "That makes their presence even more puzzling."

"Morthbrood!" father and daughter exclaimed simultaneously.

"That's not good," murmured Agent Griffin.

From overhead came a glitter of green. Rachel blinked against the glare of the sky. It took a moment for her tired eyes to resolve the falling green object into Dorian Standish's boots.

Agent Standish dropped from the sky, his Inverness cloak billowing around him like dark green wings. One hand gripped his staff; the other held his hat. With a sound no louder than the footfall of a moccasin, he landed upon his famed magic boots, bending his knees deeply.

Dorian Standish, who hailed from Prester John's Kingdom, a West African Country of the Wise, had skin the color of dark coffee, thick black hair that fell to his shoulders in tight, oiled curls, and a neatly trimmed beard. He was quite pleasing to the eye, but it was the mischievous twinkle in his gaze and the promise of laughter about his lips that really charmed Rachel. He looked as if he knew a secret and was eager to share it with her.

She liked people who shared secrets.

Standish crossed to stand behind her so that Rachel was sandwiched between her father's standard-issue, dark-charcoal Inverness cloak and Dorian's non-regulation loden-green.

"What have we here?" asked Standish in his lilting Prester John's Kingdom accent. He looked warily back and forth across the snowy land-scape.

"Barghests," said Rachel's father.

"Possible Morthbrood attack," added Rachel.

Standish made a noise of surprise. "Morthbrood? Weren't the last of them rounded up this fall along with Dr. Mordeau? If they are stirring again, that bodes not well."

"Nettle cake?" Rachel's father asked tersely.

Agent Standish shook his head. "All out. Used the last this morning."

Rachel's father swore under his breath. "I only have enough for two."

Inwardly, Rachel sighed. If this had been yesterday, she could have pulled out hers and seemed resourceful indeed, but she and Peter had eaten her last piece of nettle cake last night, to protect themselves from the lightning imps and the Heer.

"Morthbrood, for real?" asked Agent Standish, his gaze scanning the treeline. "People are always calling 'Morthbrood! Morthbrood!' but it turns out to be something else. I thought they had finally been wiped out."

"They're an ancient order," replied Ambrose Griffin. "They existed even before they became the followers of Morgana La Fay, back in King Arthur's day. I wouldn't put it past them to maintain their organization underground." He paused. "Or above ground, in Bavaria."

The two men spoke casually, but they were both fully alert, watching the forest and snow-covered fields with an eagle eye.

"That's right. Didn't quite a few of them retreat there after their defeat?" asked Agent Standish. He shook his head. "Hard to imagine the Terrible Years were twenty-five years ago."

"The twenty-fifth anniversary of the Battle of Roanoke is on May Day," volunteered Rachel. She, too, peered at the forest. "There's going to be a big celebration."

"Could they be gearing up for that?" asked Standish.

"I wouldn't put it past them," murmured Ambrose Griffin, his gaze on the tree line.

A shiver went through Rachel. The twenty-fifth-year celebration would be taking place here, on campus. Was Roanoke Academy in danger? On top of the wild fey, who now felt free to ensorcell students, fear of an imminent attack by the Morthbrood might be enough to prompt the Board of Visitors and Governors to close the school.

Aloud, she said, "The spriggan who lives on Stony Tor believes that the Morthbrood had something to do with the attack on the skating party —when Sigfried killed the ogre—but it would not say how they were involved."

Her father raised a skeptical brow. "Who told you such a thing?"

"The spriggan."

Agent Standish grunted in surprise. He leaned down towards Rachel, squinting one eye and glaring at her with the other, the look he called The Eye. "And by what strange chance did wee Lady Rachel come to speak to the spriggan of Stony—"

Awwwwooooo! Barghests poured from shadows and crannies, a whole pack. They loped across the snow; the shadowy figures blending into one another, making them hard to count. Straight-legged with heads down, they circled the Agents. Then, with growling snarls, they attacked.

The dark beasts leapt at the Agents. Rachel stood between the two men, trembling. Ordinarily, supernatural enemies did not unnerve her, but this was far closer to fifty shadow hounds than to five, possibly many more. So many approached at once that a seething, shadowy blackness carpeted the snowy fields. *How many barghests could the three of them hold at bay?*

Her father and Standish aimed their staffs, firing off a cascade of spells. Glittering sparkles of red, blue, and silver swooshed through the air, accompanied by bursts of music and mingled scents—pine, vanilla, bonfire smoke, and others. The attacking hounds variously froze, fell asleep, howled in pain, slowed down, turned tail in terror, were caught in glowing golden Glepnir bands, or suffered other unpleasant fates. Yet dozens more nimble avoided the attacks.

The three foremost shadow canines rushed forward, growling and snapping. The rest fell back, circling at a greater distance. Rachel watched the shadowy beasts warily, her wand ready in her hand. These barghests struck her as more dangerous than the one at Beaumont. That had been someone's pet; it had acted like a big dog. These were like wild wolves, ruthless and so fast she could barely track them. She regretted not having brought her broom.

"Wish I had brought Askia," murmured Standish, speaking of his familiar. He pointed his staff at a hound. It shrank to the size of a house cat but then shook itself and swelled up again. As it escaped his spell, he made a noise of disgust, adding, "I left her guarding Roanoke Hall. She would enjoy this."

Rachel's father nodded grimly as he fired a stream of something that looked like lightning but moved like water. It obliterated one hound but merely pushed a second one backwards. "It would be useful to have a cheetah at our side. Can you call her?"

"I can, but that would leave my post at the school unguarded," Standish replied.

Two more shadow dogs ran forward, growling and yapping. The Agents froze one and repulsed the other back with a blast of silver sparks.

"Wards stop them," Rachel called, helpfully. That was how she and her friends had kept them at bay in Transylvania, but Xandra Black had been with them and had come prepared.

"No good. Not a warder," replied Agent Standish, "but I can do this."

He gestured with his staff in each of the cardinal directions. Transparent, giant shields shimmered into existence. Rachel recognized the *bey-athe* cantrip. She knew this cantrip stopped only spells, not material objects, but then barghests were merely made of shadow stuff. Maybe it would work on them.

The pack rushed forward, coming at them from many directions. Two leaping shadow hounds bounced off away where the *bey-athe* shields hung. Standish spun his staff and clonked one of the fallen shadow dogs on the nose. The staff passed partway through the insubstantial barghest before causing any damage. Finally, the beast let out a painful howl. Rachel's father blasted several barghests with a stream of spells from his staff. Rachel shot two of them with *turlu*, hoping to stop them in their tracks, but the cantrip had no effect on the insubstantial canines.

Suddenly, a barghest sailed over the nearest *bey-athe*s, leaping at her father's back. Another ducked under one of the large shimmering shields and lunged directly at her, teeth bared.

Chapter Three:
Encircled by Barghests

R ACHEL'S HEART BEAT SO VIOLENTLY THAT HER RIBCAGE SHOOK, BUT SHE refused to let fear paralyze her. The creatures moved rapidly, but no more rapidly than Ethan Warhol with his *quickstep* cantrip. She had beaten Ethan in a duel more than once.

She cast two paralysis hexes. Blue sparkles swooshed from her lips and from the diamond tip of her silver wand. They swirled around both attacking barghests, freezing in place both the one targeting her and the one leaping for her father. Rachel drew a shaky breath, breathing in the fresh scent of evergreen that accompanied her hex. Her father shot her a quick glance, and Agent Standish grunted in approval. Rachel had begun to feel quite pleased with herself when the first barghest slipped free of her hex. It turned tail and ran.

"Oh, it got away!" she cried.

The second also slipped free. She whistled again. The shadow dog dodged the blue sparkles, its ears perking up. It cocked its head and stared at her face. It sniffed, scenting the air, and then it let out a short howl and lunged. Its shadowy jaws closed on her arm. The creature seemed insubstantial, but the teeth sinking into her right forearm felt like jagged needles.

Rachel screamed, a high, ear-piercing shriek of sheer pain.

Her father stabbed his gem-tipped staff into the dark body of the barghest. Multi-colored light exploded from inside the beast, flying outward, like a hound-shaped firecracker. Rachel rubbed her arm once. It stung terribly but she saw no blood. Drawing a ragged breath, she called upon her mother's dissembling technique. It was meant to hide emotions, not pain, but it worked. Her arm burned with pain, but it was now buried inside, as if far away.

The shadow hound lifted its head and howled. All the other barghests had turned their heads and looked at her. The hair on the back of Rachel's neck stood up.

Rachel took a stumbling step back. *They're after me!*

She dismissed the idea with a shake of her head. It was ridiculous. The barghests could not be here to target her. No one could have known that she would come today. Still, she was shaken by the eeriness of their strange regard.

Rachel, her father, and Agent Standish hurled spells nonstop, the Agents doing a great deal more damage than she did. Standish focused on one opponent at a time, but her father cast spells that obliterated whole swaths of shadow dogs in an instant. The pack had diminished by a third. The shadowy bodies of frozen and sleeping hounds littered the snow; however, a great many still circled them, or perhaps more were still appearing. Rachel began to fear that her wand would run out of stored spells before they ran out of enemies.

Another barghest charged at them. Dorian Standish blasted it with silver sparkles that picked up and threw its shadowy body thirty feet. On the other side, Ambrose Griffin struck their attackers with a constant stream of silver-white fire. The pack retreated, circling again.

Rachel's father's attention was on the fight, but he spoke calmly, "You need more strength behind your enchantments to hold such insubstantial creatures. A few have even slipped my hexes. Glepnir bands are working, but I don't suppose they've taught you to cast that yet."

Rachel fired off three Glepnir bands at the shadowy dogs. Her injured arm shook. Only one of the glowing golden rings hit, encircling the creature's tail, not impeding it. Rachel sighed.

"Solid technique," stated Agent Standish, as he snared a barghest with a glowing golden band. "Aim needs work."

She nodded, though Dorian could not see her. Neither of the Agents seemed aware that she had been bitten. They must have thought she screamed from fear. She pulled down the sleeve of her coat to hide the injury; no point in distracting them in the midst of the battle. Luckily, barghests were not known to carry diseases as kelpies did.

The shadow dogs were still watching her with their beady eyes, or at least, she imagined they were. Perhaps she was particularly tasty? But the barghest that attacked her had howled and alerted the others before it bit her. The whole thing was mildly disturbing.

On the other hand, maybe it was her imagination; maybe her father and Agent Standish each thought they were eyeing him, too.

With a splash, a seal leapt out of the Hudson. It harrumphed across the shore, ducking between the two boulders over which hung the Inverness cloak. The feyishly-handsome Agent Michael Garbarino stood up in his tricorne hat and his charcoal Inverness cloak and grabbed his fulgurator's staff with its huge amethyst tip. Immediately, he sent out a blast of wind so powerful that all the shadow hounds in front of him scampered away. Then, he sprinted down the newly cleared path. When he reached them, he stood with his back to the other two Agents so that the three of them now formed a triangle, with Rachel in the middle. She breathed a little easier, gripping her wand tightly in her hand.

Her father turned to Agent Garbarino. "Nettle cake?"

The younger Agent nodded. "Plenty to spare. But will it help? They're insubstantial. They'll probably just zip away and come back again afterwards."

"If only we could make them substantial," said Agent Standish.

"The only thing that usually does that is blood, and that's never a good idea," replied Garbarino. "Let me try this first."

Agent Garbarino tapped his staff against the ground. A fountain of golden glitter exploded from the tip, floating around them with an accompanying burst of beautiful classical music. A ring of golden sparkles encircled their group. Half a dozen barghests ran at them, but not a single one broke through the *Sacred Ring*.

"Only four minutes," Garbarino said with quiet intensity. "It's my last one."

"Let's use it well," replied Rachel's father, blasting more barghests.

Safe inside the *Sacred Ring*, Rachel felt light-headed—partially because of her injury but also due to lack of sleep and hunger. The last she could do something about. Sticking her free hand into her pocket, she pulled out a leftover Korean treat. She unwrapped the *taraegwa* from its red napkin, shoving the sweet, ribbon-like confection into her mouth. Across the snowy field, one of the shadow dog's red eyes tracked her movements. It loped across the snow toward her, but this time, it was clearly eyeing the treats. She aimed her wand and shot off a wind blast. Her own attempts at weather enchantments were pathetic, but this charge had been played by Sigfried. The rousing notes of his trumpet rang out from her wand, along with an accompanying swoosh of silvery sparks that pushed the creature back twenty feet.

The three Agents fought harder. They had impeccable aim, but many of their spells and cantrips had no effect on the semi-immaterial beasts. Dozens of glowing golden bands held immobilized barghests, but the rest of their attacks had only temporary effect. For four minutes, Rachel and the Agents fired nonstop, the lovely classical music of the *Sacred Ring* playing in the air. Rachel froze a few barghests and tossed a few more. Agent Standish put shining golden Glepnir bands around the ones she paralyzed.

"And... that was my last Glepnir," Dorian exclaimed. "I can cast fresh ones, but that's less efficient. Or I can...."

Agent Standish touched himself with his staff and then planted it in the snow, so that it stood straight beside him, its fist-sized emerald glinting at the sky. He began casting Glepnir bands, moving so rapidly that his hands were a blur. Rachel realized he had cast the *quickstep* cantrip upon himself. Before it ended, he had captured dozens of shadow hounds.

The lyrical music ended, and the golden sparkles of the *Sacred Ring* winked out. The barghests lifted their heads and howled, an eerie, blood-chilling sound that made the hair rise on the back of Rachel's neck. Swallowing, she pressed against her father. The shadow hounds backed away and began to circle again. About a third of the original number still stood. Though, from the number of beasts scattered across the snow, the pack might have grown beyond the original number.

As before, two or three of the smoky beasts rushed forward, snarling and snapping, and then fell back again, joining the circling pack.

"They're attacking like wolves," said Agent Garbarino. "Worrying their target in the hopes of separating us. As long as we're not intimidated, we should be okay. A single elk can hold off a wolf pack if it stands its ground. It's when they run that they become prey."

"Don't split up," Dorian Standish nodded. "Understood. Anything else?"

Garbarino shook his head. "That's where their resemblances to real wolves ends."

"A pity we can't make them more substantial," murmured Ambrose Griffin.

Rachel rifled through the library in her memory. Surely, there must be something more effective than shooting off hexes that did not hold or cantrips that did not hit. Old legends? Stray comments by tutors? Had Daring Northwest mentioned anything in his books? What did she know about barghests? About fighting insubstantial creatures?

Oh! She did know something! Watching their spells not have the effects they should struck her as familiar. Hadn't she found herself in this very situation two weeks ago, when she and Vlad's people had fought the water horse? *Could the solution they used there work here?*

There was no time to gather a Lark and a Thorn or to lay out a complicated trap, but she knew the song that her ancestors, the Wyllt women, had used to lure barghests on the moors, and she knew she had something that had drawn the interest of one of the shadow beasts.

Rachel slid her hand into the pocket of her coat and drew out a red-wrapped treat. She slowly unwrapped it and snapped it in half. One of the creatures had eyed her last one. Maybe this would work. Holding the two pieces of *taraegwa* out and waving them in the air, Rachel opened her mouth and sang.

> *On the cold moors surrounded by fog,*
> *I lost my love to a heartless bog.*
> *One moment, he was courting,*
> *And then he was drowned!*
> *And all around me, the hounds did howl.*
>
> *Oh, my love, come back to me!*
> *The hounds encircle and won't let me be.*
> *The break of morn I never shall see,*
> *Unless you should come back to me.*

The Agents shot her quizzical glances over their shoulders. Rachel kept singing, the notes soaring as she sang the ballad about the young woman alone on the moors with the Black Dogs of Dartmoor. Her voice was euphonious and sweet, her ability to hit and sustain the high notes a testament to her years of singing lessons and diligent practicing. A few of the barghests paused, listening.

She met the red eyes of one of them, holding the treat up for it to see, moving it back and forth like a metronome. The creature's eyes tracked her movements. Then, a second beast began to track her hands as well.

"It's no good," Agent Garbarino gasped. "They keep escaping us and returning. One just leapt out of my Glepnir band! I've never seen that before. Moved so fast, it escaped before the band contracted. If we don't try something new, they'll wear us out."

"Any ideas?" asked Agent Standish, who was panting.

Rachel reached the end of the ballad.

"Shoot these two..." she cried, throwing half a *taraegwa* each at the two attentive shadow hounds. To her delight, both of them lunged for the snacks. The hounds' shadowy mouths closed around the food. They swallowed. Their coats grew darker, more substantial. Their fangs began to gleam white. "... now!"

The Agents fired. Agent Standish hit one with a fiery blast. Her father struck another with an unknown cantrip. Both barghests died.

"Yes!" Rachel cried. "Here, I can try again!"

Her father reached into his cloak and pulled out a little nettle cake muffin, which he thrust in her direction. "Eat this first."

He turned to Agent Garbarino. "Michael?"

Agent Garbarino nodded and pulled out a nettle cake, which he shared with Standish. His looked more like a pancake. Rachel ate hers, grateful to have more to eat. The Agents gulped down their own nettle cakes.

As she swallowed the dry muffin, she noticed the shadow dogs paid no attention to it. Their eyes only tracked the Korean treats. Rachel crumbled the remaining *taraegwa* into small pieces. When her throat was clear, she sang the ballad again. The remaining shadow hounds began to track the movements of her hands. This time, when she reached the end of the ballad, she tossed the crumbled treats into the air and then struck them with one of Siggy's wind blasts. The silver sparkles scattered the crumbled pieces. The pack howled and descended on the crumbs, fighting among themselves.

Why barghests would be interested in Korean Lunar New Year treats, Rachel had no idea; but they were, and she was grateful.

The Agents raised their gem-tipped staffs toward the sky. There was an odd crackling noise and a growing odor of ozone. The moment the shadowy hounds grew more substantial as they ate, Rachel's father barked out, "On my word: three, two, one. Now!"

Simultaneously, the Agents lunged forward. They swung their fulgurator staffs down to strike the ground.

Lightning rained from the heavens. Jagged, electric-white bolts snaked across the snowy field, evaporating snow and shadow dogs alike. The entire pack yowled. The more physical barghests lit up and then charred. The shadowy ones leapt lithely away, though the few that were hit directly dissolved into puffs of smoky nothingness.

Watching the decimation of the pack, Rachel was not surprised that the fulgurators were the most prestigious and feared of all the armed forces of the Wise.

Boom!

Rachel clapped her hands over her ears. The noise was tremendous. Her head rang. She wondered if the strange conical helmets, with their long flaps covering their ears and necks, worn by fulgurators helped protect their hearing from the devastation of their art.

The lightning continued to crackle and leap. Electricity so bright it left lavender afterimages on her vision crawled over her limbs, producing a tingly sensation. After a few seconds, blackened earth showed through huge channels of melted snow, and the only evidence of barghests nearby were charred remnants of canine corpses.

With a high-pitched yowl, the still-insubstantial shadow dogs turned tail and fled. Only they chose the wrong direction. As they sprinted northward, a tawny blur barreled down the stairs of the ruined castle and into their midst, sending them sprawling like nine pins. Agent Standish let out a shout of joy.

The lithe and fearsome Askia leapt atop the lead shadow hound, piercing both its sides with her claws. The hound howled. The barghests turned tail. With the cheetah attacking from behind and the Agents in front, the rest of the barghests were subdued.

It was finally over. The remaining shadowy beasts, as solid as wolves, were scattered all over the snowy field. Dead.

"Good work, my friends!" exclaimed Standish, dropping to a squat and reaching out his arms to Askia, who sauntered over and rubbed her cheek against his.

Rachel smiled, happy to have helped.

As the Agents began to discuss what to do next, Rachel's gaze fell on a lone shadow hound at the edge of the forest, now as solid as a dog and leaving footprints in the snow. The barghests ordinarily had a sly, crafty gleam, but this one looked confused, even terrified.

It met her gaze, pleading. She should have shouted out, drawing the Agent's attention, but the entreating look in its eyes touched her heart. She remained silent.

A moment later, it had slipped among the trees and was gone.

Rachel joined the Agents by the riverbank, where Agent Garbarino sat on a large stone lacing the knee-high boots he had leapt into when he came out of the river. His hair was just damp enough to make him look dashing, and his eyes were so intense that Rachel lowered her lashes demurely.

"I see you whistle like your mother now," her father noted approvingly.

"It's quite useful," Rachel replied casually as if people could whistle up enchantments every day. Secretly, she was very pleased he had noticed.

Dorian Standish still squatted down, rubbing his head against that of his cheetah. Rising again, he let out a deep belly laugh and came over to ruffle Rachel's hair, causing her to realize that she had lost her cap in the fray. Askia circled around them, butting her head against her master's leg, nearly knocking Rachel over.

"Good to see you, Lady Rachel." Dorian smiled down at her, his eyes twinkling. "That was some fine wandwork back there. A little more oomph and you will be a formidable sorceress! No baddie will dare face you!"

"Enough about wandwork! That was some excellent enchanting!" Agent Garbarino looked up from where he had finished lacing his boots. "I've never seen enchantment done without visible magic, outside of we selkie. We have a similar kind of singing for calling fish, but I have never seen it used on the fey. Amazing."

It took her a moment to realize that Agent Garbarino spoke of her singing. She ducked her head shyly, flustered, as always, by praise and attention. "It's been handed down for generations in our family."

"Goes all the way back to Merlin," Dorian added.

"Truly?" Agent Garbarino looked to Ambrose Griffin for confirmation. When Rachel's father nodded gravely, Garbarino added thoughtfully, "Myrddin Wyllt was a friend to selkie. He may have learned it from us."

Agent Griffin brushed the snow off a boulder and sat down, resting his staff on his knees. "What did you discover, Michael?"

"Yes!" Dorian Standish leaned on his staff and grinned at Garbarino. "What did Old Man Hudson have to say?"

"He claimed he had nothing to do with it," replied Michael Garbarino. "Said something fell from on high."

Agent Griffin glanced at his daughter before saying, "He's correct. I will give a full report when I get back to the office. But first, I need to escort my daughter back to campus."

Michael Garbarino shook his head in amused chagrin. "Can't believe you solved the case while I was down there talking to Hudson, Ambrose."

Standish chuckled. "It's why Griffin is a big boss, while you and I, Michael, are grunts."

Ambrose Griffin shook his head. "Bridges is currently in charge. I am just one of you."

Agent Garbarino, who worked for the Shadow Agency in London and knew of Rachel's father's memory loss, nodded solemnly, but Agent Standish's eyes widened.

He said, "I had heard talk along those lines, Ambrose, but I thought it was rumor."

Ambrose Griffin shook his head. "I hope to be back within six months."

"On-the-job injury," explained Agent Garbarino.

Rachel squirmed, looking down. That was not exactly true. Her father's memory loss was more of a family-related injury. She wished she could blurt out that it was all her fault; however, as that was a dire secret, she kept silent.

"You look in good form," Agent Standish looked the duke up and down. "I trust you've recovered?"

"Magical injury," Garbarino murmured softly. "Memory loss."

"Ah. That's harsh."

Rachel shivered. She felt about memory loss the way another person might feel about the loss of a limb. Anyone's memory loss disturbed her, her own father's triply so.

The Agents' conversation turned to matters of logistics. As Rachel shifted her weight, she felt her eyelids drooping. The bite on her arm ached painfully. She waited for a lull in the conversation so she could show it to her father.

She was flattered by the kind things the Agents had said to her, but the pleasure this brought hardly balanced the chagrin she felt at how poor her performance had been compared to the Agents. After all the battles she had fought in the last six months and the duels she had won at Knights of Walpurgis meetings, she had begun to feel pleased with her skill at sorcery. Watching the Agents severely reduced her opinion of her own prowess.

She spotted her square black cap in the midst of the snowy field. She ran and fetched it. As she was returning to the others, a motion across the Hudson caught Rachel's eye. Her heart tripped and then took off at a gallop. On the dock near the glass hall was Captain Zephy, the proprietor of the *Pollepel II*—the ferry that brought people back and forth from Roanoke Island. The good captain stood talking to a familiar figure who towered over him. Annoyed at her heart's waywardness, Rachel took a deep, calming breath. Then, she raised her good arm and waved. Across the Hudson, Vladimir Von Dread waved back.

Touching her black bracelet, she murmured, "Vlad, are you heading back to school?"

Dread's voice sounded clearly in her ear. "Presently."

"My father needs to go back to the office. Could you escort me back to campus?"

"Certainly. As soon as my business here is complete. Give me a moment."

A sweet feminine voice rang out in mid-air. *"Emergency. All possible Agents to the New York Wisecraft offices. Emergency. All possible Agents to the New York Wisecraft offices."*

Rachel's father and the other two Agents tapped the lantern-and-stars amulet they wore around their necks, and the voice ceased. They glanced at one another, their expressions calm, yet alert. She pulled the sleeve of her red wool coat further down over her wound. She did not want to distract her father if he needed to leave. She could go by the infirmary.

"You'd better go ahead." Agent Griffin stood. "I must see my daughter back to campus."

Rachel ran forward. "Please don't wait on my account, Father. I have my own escort."

Her father shook his head. "It'll take longer for someone to come here than for me to walk you back."

Vlad's voice spoke in Rachel's ear. "I have completed my business. Call me when you are ready. I'll come immediately."

Rachel opened her mouth to explain to her father and paused. The previous night, after she had convinced Vlad to dance with Princess Alexis of Magical Australia, she had thought smugly to herself that not every thirteen-year-old could snap her fingers and produce the Prince of Bavaria. This seemed too fantastic an opportunity to waste.

She raised her good arm and snapped her fingers. "Dread."

A brilliant column of light formed on the far shore of the river, stretching up into the sky. It winked out and then formed at her right shoulder, coalescing into an imperious young man clad entirely in black. Vladimir Von Dread towered over everyone except for Rachel's father. He looked magnificent with his black swan-feathered cloak streaming from his shoulders, his face stern beyond his years. It was as if some elfin knight had stepped out from Underhill purely for the purpose of escorting her home. Rachel lowered her lashes, smiling.

When it had become apparent that Rachel's finger snap was resulting in someone jumping in, the three Agents had looked pleasantly intrigued. When the beam of light coalesced into Dread, Garbarino and Standish took rapid steps backward, thunderstruck. Even Rachel's father's eyes widened minusculely. Out of the corner of her eye, Rachel saw him tense and straighten.

The Crown Prince of Bavaria inclined his head regally toward the Agents. "Your Grace. Agent Standish. Michael."

"Your highness," the duke acknowledged coldly. He crossed his arms.

"Prince Vladimir!" cried Agent Garbarino in a mix of delight and awe. "What a pleasure to meet you here, so far from the Rhine!"

"Bavaria!" murmured Dorian Standish, his voice rising in surprise. He glanced at Rachel and wiggled his eyebrows. Holding one hand up as if to shield his gesture, he pointed at Vladimir from behind it, mouthing, "That's a *prince!*"

Rachel pressed her lips together to stop herself from laughing. She nodded regally as Dread had done. Dorian looked openly impressed. It occurred to Rachel that even Agents seldom met royalty, much less royalty who also happened to be world-famous for having won Olympic medals. She recalled how impressed Agent Standish had been, back in September, with the aplomb that the Prince of Bavaria had shown when questioned under the *Spell of True Recitation*. She also could not help but notice the familiarity with which Vlad and Agent Garbarino had addressed each other. She had heard there was only one Agent of the Wisecraft allowed into Bavaria. She suspected she now knew which Agent that was.

Rachel turned graciously to Vladimir as if princes appeared out of mid-air to squire her about every day. She asked sweetly, "Shall we go?"

"Of course, Miss Griffin." Vlad offered her his arm.

As they departed, arm-in-arm, Rachel overheard Agent Standish murmuring to her father, his voice full of wonder, "Where did your daughter learn *that* spell?"

Chapter Four:
The Difficult Art of
Keeping Promises

Vlad walked Rachel through the ruined castle, down the tree-lined path, and past the security detail of Agents flanking the bench where the wall of trees opened onto the campus. After answering the guards' questions, they continued by the lily pond and the Memorial Gardens, towards the campus proper. Rachel filled him in on all that had happened: her father's questions, the fight with the barghests, and the emergency call the Agents had received.

"Barghests." Vlad frowned. "I do not recall them among the fey denizens of Roanoke Island. I make no claim to a memory such as yours, but matters of security seldom escape me."

Rachel nodded. "They're not local to Roanoke. These were British barghests. Father and I think this might indicate Morthbrood activity."

"Ah, Morthbrood." Vlad was silent for a few steps.

"Don't you have former Morthbrood members living in Bavaria?" she asked casually, though in truth she was very curious about these persistent rumors.

"Father accepted refugees from among both Veltdammerung and the Morthbrood after the Terrible Years. They had to agree to severe security restrictions, but they had nowhere else to go, so a number did accept his terms."

"Can you ask him about this?" asked Rachel, congratulating herself on holding a full conversation with him without once feeling afraid.

"I will inquire," Von Dread replied, "though today may not be the best day to ask."

"Why is that?" asked Rachel.

He pursed his lips. Rachel feared he would not answer. When he did, she almost wished he had not.

"My father is less than pleased by the news that his heir and the heir to the throne of Transylvania nearly came to blows on a ballroom floor."

A lump formed in Rachel's throat. So much for a fear-free conversation. That event was entirely her fault. Did he blame her? Between the treatment he received from her parents the time he walked her home and Princess Alexis Romanov throwing herself at him when, at Rachel's request, he asked her to dance, she feared Vladimir would not want to do her a favor again.

There were other things she would have liked to tell him, but the lump in her throat took up all the room, leaving no space for words.

Vlad escorted Rachel as far as Roanoke Hall. She thanked him and headed to the dining hall, where she reluctantly joined her friends after they spotted her. As her excitement wore off, lack of sleep caught up with her. Whether it was fatigue, that sick sensation that followed an unexpected burst of adrenaline, or the aching bite on her arm, Rachel began to feel quite ill.

The scent of cinnamon and warm bread usually made her hungry; now she just felt queasy. She sat down, gripping the table tightly with her left hand, cradling her injured arm on her lap. *She had stayed up too late. She should go back to bed.*

To make matters worse, the main topic of conversation at the table was: that beastly tyrant, the Prince of Bavaria. Joy O'Keefe and Princess Nastasia Romanov were angry at Von Dread for manhandling Nastasia's sister on the dance floor the previous night "in such a brutish fashion as to make her cry." Rachel longed to jump to Vlad's defense and explain what a fine gentleman he had been when Alexis put him on the spot by asking him to marry her, so as to save her from her engagement to the boorish Crown Prince of Transylvania; however, in her sleep-sodden state, she could not think of a way to explain how she had overheard this private conversation without revealing the existence of her black bracelet.

She forced herself to swallow a few bites of oatmeal and orange juice, her thoughts turning in circles. She should go back to bed. She should look for Wulfgang. She should go to the infirmary and see to her arm, which hurt even more now and occasionally oozed blood. All those things, however, required standing up.

Sigfried Smith lounged beside her in all his boyish glory. His breath-stoppingly handsome face was smeared with jam, and bits of scrambled egg adorned his golden curls. His familiar, Lucky the Dragon, swam through the air beside him. An Asian *lung*, Lucky had golden fur and ruby stomach scales. His long koi-like whiskers, his horns, and the fluffy dorsal ruff that ran down the length of his back to the puffy tuft at the end of his tail were all a brilliant crimson. Lucky's shape was surprisingly elastic. His sinuous, ten-foot-long body could stretch to as long as twenty feet, and he could slither along the ground like a serpent or straighten his golden legs and rise to the height of a large dog. He could also snake through the air, as he did at the moment, carefully removing the crumbs of egg from his master's hair with flicks of his long ruby tongue.

"I was keeping that egg for later," Siggy announced, "but, for you, Lucky, anything."

Rachel did not even bother speculating about how the egg might have come to be there.

The conversation about Dread's shortcomings dragged on. Siggy scowled, annoyed someone was bad-mouthing his hero. He retaliated by engaging in his favorite pastime of "taunt the princess." This, too, contributed to Rachel's growing headache. To distract him, she leaned over and whispered the story of how she had nearly been staked by Abraham Van Helsing. She thought the whole story to be rather funny. To her surprise, Sigfried did not take it that way. He grew genuinely distressed that his blood sister had been threatened and declared angrily that someone should "punch Van Helsing in the mug."

"Really, Sigfried, it was entirely my fault," she objected.

"Your fault? What if he'd *killed* you? You could have ended up *dead*," Sigfried replied. "Then you'd spend the rest of eternity flitting here and there in darkness, like a bat! Without ever having properly grown up." He shivered. Ghosts were the only thing that scared him.

"I don't think the afterlife's that bad, is it?" objected Rachel, but she frowned.

She liked to think the people she knew who had departed from this life were living in the Elysian Fields or some other pleasant place; however, it was possible many of them were in Hades's kingdom or Annwfyn or some other drab existence—or worse, the place of torment to which Remus Starkadder had been dragged. *That was a disturbing thought.*

Siggy's girlfriend, Valerie Hunt, joined them, balancing her tray on the camera slung across her shoulder as she cleared a spot on the table to deposit it. She was sharp-eyed and golden-haired, with a squarish jawline.

She paused to snap a picture of them all, preserving Rachel's queasy, half-asleep state for posterity.

"Why are there Agents all over campus?" Valerie asked as she sat down. She rapidly spun her knife around her fingers and then stabbed it into her pancakes. Sigfried and Lucky looked on, fascinated.

"She does that like a right criminal!" Sigfried said, awed.

"That's why we love her," Lucky cooed back.

"For her criminal mind," Siggy sighed contently.

"And her golden hair," Lucky added dreamily.

Rachel replied, "With the storm goblin dead, the Roanoke Covenant is broken. The fey are no longer bound to leave us alone; so the Agents are here to protect us."

"The Heer is dead?" Nastasia Romanov, Princess of Magical Australia, looked up from where she was eating an English muffin with knife and fork. Her perfect features and cascading blonde ringlets gave her an un-earthly beauty. The breast of her black school robes was embroidered with a golden emu. "I heard no such report."

"*Someone* else *killed the storm goblin?*" Sigfried jumped to his feet, shouting at the top of his lungs.

The rest of the dining hall stared at them. Rachel ducked her head, suddenly shy. Valerie grabbed her boyfriend by the arm and yanked, try-ing to get him to sit down. Sigfried resisted, his face seething with hot rage. Rachel recalled how eager Siggy had been to test his mettle against the storm goblin. That was how she and he had met.

Under her breath, Rachel murmured, "Amber killed him."

Nastasia's perfect brow was still knit. "That was most unwise of Miss Praetor. She has caused us no end of difficulties."

"Amber killed him?" Siggy's eyes grew wide. He let Valerie pull him back into his seat. "Wish I could have seen that! If it couldn't be Lucky and me, I guess Amber's the next best. Did she use her eye-beams? That must have been awesome. Did he flail much? Did he scream?"

Rachel remembered how the Heer's child-like face had become old and gnomish as Amber squeezed it. She shivered and did not answer.

Zoë Forrest lounged across two chairs, eating French toast, her short pixie hair and her long forelock braid the same cinnamon-and-buttered-toast brown as her meal. She used to look like a fourteen-year-old, but ever since she had been rescued, after falling into the darkness between worlds, she had been growing taller. She no longer looked like a child. If

Rachel had been required to guess her age, she would have said twenty. Also, Rachel noted suddenly, her ears, which used to be rounded, were looking decidedly pointed, almost as pointed as those of William, whose mother was a Moth from Underhill, a.k.a. a fairy.

Zoë had not really been paying attention. Now she sat up and interrupted Nastasia.

"Enough about this," she drawled in her light Kiwi accent. "Who cares whether the storm gobbledygook lives or dies or whether Vladimir Von Dreamboat is a total jerk. Aren't they all? Save Siggy here." She rolled her eyes toward where Sigfried was now urging Lucky to light his breakfast sausage on fire, in honor of Amber toasting the Heer. "Can we finish our discussion from last night? I am not sure why we had to stop. We were talking about sharing information. Specifically, how we're not going to do it. Sound good to everyone, right?"

No. Not this again!

"You are so obsessed with this!" Joy objected, giggling. "Really, is it so important?"

"Blabbing could break the Wall that protects our world—the thing that keeps the monsters and demons Outside from devouring us alive," Zoë countered. "Believe you me, having seen it, I don't want the *Out There* to get in here."

Rachel desperately tried to think of some way to postpone this discussion. She still had not spoken with Wolfgang. Her already queasy stomach began to churn as if the oatmeal she had eaten had gone into rebellion and was trying to make a break for it. The room swayed.

"I think I am going to be ill," she squeaked. "Again."

She jumped up and ran for the loo.

After vomiting, for the second time in less than twelve hours, Rachel sank down and leaned against the cold wall of the stall, shivering. Her head had begun to pound. She held it with both hands, trying to soothe the pain. This only aggravated the ache in her wounded arm.

The outer door opened slightly, and an otter slipped into the girls' room, sniffed in her direction, and ran out again. Rachel blinked after it.

There came a knock as the outer door swung open. A girl's voice called, "Miss Griffin? Are you okay? It's me, Mylene Price. I saw you run out of the lunch hall. Are you feeling sick?"

"I don't feel quite myself," Rachel whispered. "Could you find my boyfriend?"

She could have called Gaius, of course, but the nice upperclassman wanted to help her. Rachel had helped Miss Price twice: once, during her first week of school, when Mylene was being attacked by a wraith, and a second time, after she recovered her health, when Rachel, in her role as the gym teacher's assistant, had given the Dee Hall upper school junior private classes on how to fly a broom. Due to the wraith that had been secretly hidden in her shadow, Mylene had been too ill during her first two years at Roanoke to learn properly.

"Yes, I can." Mylene pushed open the door to the stall where Rachel was sitting on the floor. Her otter peered around her leg, nose twitching. Mylene's pale red pigtails bounced as she held out a little vial filled with a clear liquid. "I can also give you this.

"It's good for upset stomachs," Mylene continued. "And it's very mild. It's like magical ginger. Believe me when I say, I know about feeling sick. Though thanks to you and Mr. Smith, I haven't felt ill once since you two discovered the wraith that was preying on me!"

Rachel looked at Mylene carefully. Was this an attempt to humiliate her? No, she saw only a desire to help. Rachel knew what that felt like, wanting to help someone who helped you.

She gave the other girl a wan but hopeful smile and accepted the vial. "Thank you."

Mylene looked pleased. "I'll go get Gaius."

She ran off. Rachel opened the vial and sniffed. The odor was similar to an elixir her mother made that was about as medical in nature as drinking cola syrup to calm a stomachache. Deciding to trust Mylene's good intentions, Rachel drank it. Immediately, she felt better. Her head and arm still ached, but the nausea was receding.

Gaius's voice sounded just beside her ear. "Rach, on my way."

Rachel leaned against the cold steel wall of the stall, her eyes half closed. It was strange, and yet a huge relief, that her fascination with Vladimir in no way diminished her affection for her boyfriend. Gaius was so funny, so handsome, and so very good to her. His company brought her comfort and joy. She did not think she could have made it through the school year without him. Her life had been peaceful and quiet before coming to Roanoke

Academy; in contrast, in the last six months, she had experienced more disturbing events than many people saw in a lifetime.

The worst had to be the discovery that her stolen sister—already an upsetting concept in itself—disapproved of their family connection. Perhaps this was due to Amber's false belief that her parents had given her up willingly. Now her sister knew the truth. Rachel hoped that next time they met, Amber would embrace being a member of the Griffin family.

As she sat there, too weary to rise, Rachel kept picturing her new eldest sister—tiny and delicate and yet entirely mission-oriented and devoted to military discipline. Apparently, being snatched from her family and raised in a barrack had allowed her to develop the abilities needed to pass some dreadful test and gain a power that had allowed her to kill Belial, the Lord of Lies. Rachel was glad that her sister had destroyed this terrible enemy, but she could not help noting that killing the demon in charge of lies had not resulted in a reduction of lying. She herself now lied a great deal more than she had before she came to school.

She used to be a truthful girl.

Rachel contrasted Amber with the other Griffin siblings: Sandra, Laurel, and Peter. Sandra the Spy was elegant and competent, and she had a quick sense of humor that Amber lacked. Peter could be a bit too serious, but he was kindhearted and had a heightened sense of family responsibility that contrasted dramatically with Amber's lack of interest. The most extreme difference, however, was between Amber and Laurel.

Laurel, the family wild child, was rebellious and spirited and full of fun. She was not the sort of person to which any military leader would give a second look, and yet, she had something, a quality Rachel wished she could put into words, that now seemed inexpressibly dear. Rachel would much prefer her family members to be free to be like Laurel than to be forced to be like Amber.

After all, not everyone could be Sandra.

She pulled up her legs and lowered her head, resting her forehead on her knees. Wasn't she being incredibly selfish? Amber had a great destiny. She had fought wars, saved lives. Weren't those lives worth more than some ineffable quality that Laurel had and Amber lacked? Rachel acknowledged sadly that this was most likely true. With that acknowledgment, a darkness settled over her heart, weighing her down like a cold and sopping wet blanket.

Mylene stepped through the outer door of the girls' bathroom, looked to see if there was another girl present, and stepped out again, calling cheerfully, "All clear. I'll stand guard."

Gaius Valiant burst into the girls' room, his normal carefree expression replaced by one of concern. His chestnut hair, normally pulled back into a neat queue, had escaped its tie, long strands falling across his cheeks. His teak and brass fulgurator's wand clacked against the door as he rushed through. Gaius was short for his age, though he still towered over Rachel. He had been growing recently; however, so his old patched robe was too short for him.

Rachel sat on the floor of her stall, shivering. Her legs felt wobbly, so she did not try to rise. She just looked up at him and managed a half smile.

"I never did find Wulfgang last night," she said apologetically, "and I'm afraid I wasn't as careful as I promised either. I almost got staked by the leader of the Dare Hall vamp-fighting gang. I was lucky. One of my brother's friends saved me. Also, I was bitten by a barghest."

Gaius blinked. "I am glad I asked you to be careful. Had I not, no doubt you would have caused Dare Hall to explode. Was the barghest in the same room with the vampire hunters?"

Rachel giggled, but it was a weak giggle. She recalled how the barghests had seemed to eye her and shuddered. No doubt that had been a trick of the light.

Gaius sat down beside her and rubbed her back. In the presence of his calmness, her thoughts grew less chaotic. She began to feel a little bit better. Still, she turned her head away, embarrassed. She must smell awful.

"I did think of calling Vlad," she murmured, shivering in spite of her attempts to stop. Gaius pulled her closer, which felt wonderful. His body was firm and radiated warmth. "I thought it would be fun to see their faces if he jumped in, but I didn't want to do that to Sandra."

She did not mention her concern about pants.

"Could you help me over to the sink?" she asked plaintively.

"Most certainly," Gaius replied, jumping to his feet. "Milady's wish is my command!"

He helped her up. She cried out only once when he put pressure on her right arm. She moved slowly to the sink where Gaius helped her to wash her face. Then she rinsed out her mouth and drew back the sleeve of her coat to wash her wound. The sight of the deep bites, purple and bruised, startled her so badly that she began to feel lightheaded. Spots appeared before her eyes. Gaius's breath escaped with an audible hiss.

"That's it, young lady!" He scooped her up in his arms. "It's the infirmary for you!"

He carried her across the commons and up the brick stairs into the infirmary. Rachel rested her head against his shoulder and smiled slightly, as happy as her pain and nausea would allow. She felt immensely grateful to have a strong and attentive boyfriend.

Within the brick building, the pale blue walls were adorned with arcane symbols traced in silver. Overhead, an orrery hung beneath a periwinkle-blue domed ceiling, painted with fluffy white clouds. Its clockwork sun and planets rotated independently, allowing the nurse to adjust the celestial influences within the room for healing purposes.

Nurse Moth met them by the gurgling fountain in the center of the room. She was nervous and bird-like with a large aquiline nose, dressed in the white-on-white habit and wimple of a nun of the Order of Asclepius. She insisted Gaius set Rachel on her feet and examined her with a critical eye. Then she made shooing motions toward Gaius and put Rachel in the same bed as on her previous visits.

"Don't send Gaius away!" Rachel reached out toward him, upset.

The nurse gestured for Gaius to return. He did so, standing patiently beside the bed. The nurse pulled the flame-orange curtains half closed on either side and sat down beside Rachel.

"*Chérie*, you are very thin," she noted, concern in her voice. "Much thinner than last time you were here. You're already slight for your age. Have you been sick and not come to see me?"

"I... I wasn't sick. I just wasn't very hungry," Rachel admitted, not bothering to add that the issue had since resolved itself. "I made up for it, though, at the Lunar New Year Celebration yesterday." She was certain she had eaten enough during that one event to make up for all the meals she had skipped a few weeks earlier.

"Child, you have been worrying, *non*? I heard about your father. Is that it?"

Rachel nodded fervently, telling a lie with the silent motion of her head. Then, she regretted this because it caused her temples to throb. Only, was it a lie if, at the time, she had thought she was upset about her father's memory loss? She dared not look at Gaius. It still unnerved her that she had missed all those meals because she had been angry *at him*, only she had not realized it. He had criticized her loyalty to the Raven. The thought of Gaius siding with her father against her still stung if she thought about it. So she did not.

"Father's memory loss has been hard on my family," she said truthfully. "My mother has been upset, and normally, she's the calm one."

Gaius's face filled with concern. Shoving stray locks of chestnut hair out of his eyes, he spoke to the nurse. "Miss Griffin had an appetite when she ate with us."

Rachel fixed her gaze on the purple and green dragon-vein agate set into the headboard of the bed, still unwilling to meet her boyfriend's gaze. Gaius could not possibly have noticed she was eating less, because the one time each day she had eaten normally had been when she ate lunch with him.

The nurse clucked like a mother hen. "*Chérie*, if you keep too much inside and don't get things off your chest, they'll eat their way out, leaving you very thin indeed. Your young friend here seems more than happy to keep you company. I am sure he'd be willing to lend an ear. It can help to talk about a problem, even if it cannot be resolved."

Rachel ducked her head, blushing. "I'm always happier when Gaius is here."

Gaius was the last person in the universe with whom she could discuss this matter, especially now that she had forgiven him. Besides, she had already discussed it with Vlad. She did not feel the need to discuss it further. Still, she was very happy for Gaius's company.

"Is that why you came?" the nurse asked. "Because you have not been eating well?"

Rachel shook her head, sending her shoulder-length dark hair flying, and then again wished she had not. The pain in her head flared, temporarily blocking out the capacity for speech. She stifled the moan that tried to escape her lips.

"She was bitten by a barghest," explained Gaius.

The nurse cried in nigh-comical concern. "*Zut alors!* Why did you not say so at once?"

Chapter Five:
Dear Your Majesty

Nurse Moth retrieved her scrutiny sticks, two lengths of wood carved with runes and set with precious gems, and ran them over Rachel's body. Gems flashed, and the nurse gestured for her to remove her coat, which she did with help from Gaius. Then Nurse Moth pulled up the sleeve of Rachel's robe to reveal the bites, bruised and caked with dried blood.

"Trés mal, chérie!"

The nurse bustled off. Left on the bed with her wounded arm out-stretched, Rachel felt faint. She purposely looked away from the ugly bite marks and bruising. Gaius sat on a chair beside her. He squeezed her good hand and gave her an encouraging smile.

The nurse returned with a tray upon which sat a steaming mug of broth, a thick bar of Icelandic chocolate, and a glass of water that she had drawn from the fountain in the center of the infirmary. The broth smelled of savory medicinal herbs. Rachel did not think it would be wise to eat much, but she nibbled obediently on the corner of the chocolate. It was tarter than she had expected, but tasty. She offered some to Gaius. He shook his head, peering at her with concern.

Nurse Moth left again and returned with a long, slanted wooden trough filled with warm water and floating dried flowers that emanated a sweet floral perfume. Rachel recognized chamomile and lavender, among others. The nurse gestured for her to lean forward and arranged the pil-lows against the headboard. As Rachel leaned back again, Nurse Moth placed the trough across Rachel's lap and washed her wrist and forearm carefully with a sponge and a green liquid that smelled minty. When she was done, she lowered the injured arm into the warm, scented water, ar-ranging it so that the wounds were submerged.

"Can't you just wave your wand and heal the cuts?" asked Gaius, watching everything carefully. "I thought wounds were easy to heal."

"Regular wounds," Nurse Moth replied, "but barghests are half in this world and half in another. They wound the spirit. This water—from our healing fountain—will draw out the ill humors and heal the damage to her soul. After she soaks, I will spread a poultice on her arm to help regenerate her spirit. We should be able to heal the physical wounds in the morning."

"What would happen if you healed the physical wound now?" asked Gaius, curiously.

"She would experience phantom pains in her arm. Perhaps for years to come."

"That doesn't sound good," murmured Rachel.

"*Mais non, chérie*, it does not." The nurse eyed her severely. "So keep your arm in the medicinal bath until I return."

She looked Rachel over, tutted once, and departed.

Once she had gone, Rachel leaned forward to whisper urgently to her boyfriend. Pain shot through her head. She gritted her teeth and soldiered on. "Gaius, I need your help. I'm about to either have a huge fight with my friends or to have to lie to them. Neither option makes me happy."

Gaius pushed his wayward chestnut locks from his face again and frowned unhappily. "We should really try to *reduce* the amount of lying we do to our friends. Not that I lie to my friends, but I... haven't been completely forthright with Vlad for some time. I think it's justifiable, but that doesn't keep me from feeling guilty."

"Gaius, you can tell Vlad anything you wish—except the thing the Guardian of this world told us not to repeat. I don't mind if you share the other secrets I've told you. I trust him."

Gaius leaned against the chair back and whistled. "Well, that's a relief."

His locks fell into his eyes yet again. With a noise of impatience, he untied his black velvet hair ribbon, letting his chestnut hair fall loose over his face and shoulders. It made him look dashing and untamed. Rachel drew in a quick breath, hoping that he would lean over and kiss her. But he disappointed her by merely retying the ribbon that secured his short ponytail.

"I am glad." She smiled. "It's not my friends who worry me. It's keeping my word to Wulfgang."

"Wolf... who?" Gaius blinked, thoroughly confused. "Oh! Starkadder the Seventh."

The chocolate tasted surprisingly good. She tried a sip of the broth, holding the hot mug with her left hand. It had a pleasant savory taste. When a swallow or two did not increase her queasiness, she leaned back against the headboard and slowly drank the whole thing. She shot her boyfriend a warm, sideways smile, but he still made no move to kiss her. She considered moving closer in the hope that he would take the hint, but with her arm soaking, the logistics proved impractical.

"Siggy and I agreed privately to share our secrets—the non-super-duper-secret secrets—with him. We wanted to help his bid to befriend Nastasia. She needs a friend, and she won't accept any friend who doesn't already know the secrets." She thought but did not add aloud, *Maybe if she has a friend of her own, she will stop requiring so much of me.*

"Right," Gaius nodded. "I remember now."

"Only now, my friends are breathing down my neck. They want me to promise not to share info with new people, ever again." She looked up at him, pleading. "Could you do it?"

"Promise your friends?"

Rachel giggled. "No, silly. Talk to Wulfgang. I can advise over the bracelet."

He smiled, his eyes twinkling. "Ah, finally something I can do to help relieve all these burdens you carry. Yes, I'll go tell him. And no, I won't stop, even if you ask me. So you can tell your friends it wasn't your doing."

He rose and, leaning over, gave her the lightest of kisses on the top of her head. Then, he pulled the curtains closed and walked away, whistling cheerfully.

Rachel finished her broth and lay back, the light from the healthful green flames in the glass ball hovering above her bed shining on her face. She did not know if it was the chocolate, the healing broth, the warm floral-scented water on her arm, or the emerald flame, but her arm did not hurt as much, and the throbbing in her head had finally begun to recede. As her physical pain ebbed; however, her mental agony grew. The darkness that had settled over her heart while she sat on the cold floor of the loo seemed to be growing heavier. The images of Amber and Laurel hovered side by side before her mind's eye, taunting her.

Fierce as a tiger. Calm as a lake in August. And cool as ice—when you are not as fiery as a furnace. Her beloved grandfather approved of sacrifices for the greater good. At least, that was how he treated his soldiers—and himself. Would he have felt the same way about his family? Would he have approved of sacrificing a girl like Laurel to get one like Amber?

Amber won wars; Laurel did not.

The nurse came back with a bag filled with supplies. She dried Rachel's arm and smeared it with a medicinal poultice that smelled of menthol and yarrow. Rachel gritted her teeth as it was rubbed into her wounds. It smarted and made her eyes sting. After a moment, however, the pain faded. Nurse Moth then bound the arm in gauze and bandages.

"There, *chérie*. That will complete the necessary healing and removal of unwanted humors. In the morning, we can remove the bandages and heal the wounds, *mais oui?*"

"*Oui*," replied Rachel, with a faint smile.

"Get some rest. You will feel better when you wake."

The nurse waved her scrutiny sticks over Rachel's body, gave a Gallic shrug, and cleared away the empty mug. She dumped out the now-warm cup of fountain water and brought Rachel a refill, which she drank eagerly. The cool water from the fountain tasted sweet and refreshing. Nurse Moth looked her over once more, gave an approving nod, and departed.

Rachel settled back into her pillows, her eyelids closing. Just as she was drifting off, Gaius's voice spoke beside her ear. "Er, so, I found Starkadder. Took me a while to hunt him down. About to approach him," he drawled cheerfully. "As I go—unable to be stopped by you, no matter what your friends say—could we review again what it is I am telling him? Generally?"

"Of course!"

They talked for a few minutes, deciding which secrets could be shared: the existence of the Outside and worlds beyond their world; how so much of the new magic that had been discovered of late, came from Outside; how Wulfgang himself and his family came from Outside; the existence of demons; the existence of the Guardian of the World; the identity of the Master of the World and the extent of his powers, including his power over the Guardian.

"I think that will do it," concluded Rachel.

"That's quite a bit. It's a lot to take in." Gaius paused. "Um... it has to be Starkadder, right? Sorry, I am not a big fan of his brother Romulus. His sister Freka's sweet. You've been around Wulfgang enough to tell he's not like his prig of a brother, right? I am going on your intuition. I would not want someone like Romulus in our circles."

Rachel snuggled down into her pillows and sighed, "When did my life become so complicated, Gaius? I made this agreement with Wulfgang *before* Vlad and Romulus almost ended up in a duel—which I feel bad about, even though I didn't see it coming. The last thing I need is someone else in my group that doesn't like Vlad!

"But Wulfgang seems all right," she continued. "More importantly, he likes Nastasia, or I think he does, and Siggy likes him. So, yeah. It does have to be him. Sorry."

She could almost hear Gaius shrug. "Eh. Life's complicated. No point in worrying."

Rachel said, "Romulus acted like an *eejit* yesterday. Wulfgang may allow Siggy to get petrified and then use him as a shield, but he doesn't strike me as a cad."

Gaius chuckled. "Well, I can't blame Starkadder for that! I don't see how anyone could resist the temptation to use a petrified Mr. Smith as a shield. Good man. I shall attempt to explain."

"Thank you." A huge weight lifted from Rachel's shoulders. "Have I mentioned you are the best of boyfriends? I'll have to think of some good-girlfriendy things to do in return. The first is: when you are done, go square things away with Vlad. Tell him whatever you've been keeping from him for my sake—save what the Guardian told us not to repeat."

"Will do," he replied cheerfully. She heard a noise that might have been Gaius giving a mock salute. "Valiant, over and out!"

Rachel slept. After a few hours, she awoke and lay in bed, staring at the orrery over the top of the flame-orange curtains, watching Venus and Saturn revolve on their clockwork orbits. She thought about her morning. Each time she recalled the reactions of her father and the other Agents to Dread's sudden appearance, a wave of giddy delight broke over her. She kicked her feet with glee, tossing her comforter up and down. They had been so impressed by the sudden appearance of the crown prince. Their expressions had been so funny, and Vladimir's behavior had been so proper and so chivalrous.

A warm flush crept through her. She pressed her palms against her hot cheeks. *This was not good.* She should avoid anything that heightened her awareness of Vlad. Gaius was the best of boyfriends. Even if he had not been, she could hardly date Vladimir Von Dread, six years her senior and in love with her sister. Yet, thinking about him made her feel wonderful…and miserable. She wished there was someone with whom she could discuss how she felt. But who?

Not Nastasia. The princess disapproved of Vladimir. She would never understand. The Princess of Magical Australia was supposed to be Rachel's best friend, but she was proving disappointing in many ways. Last night, Rachel had decided Nastasia no longer qualified to be her best friend. She was now searching for a replacement. But, again, who?

She could not tell Joy or Valerie or Salome. They were not loyal to her. There was no assurance they would not blab her secrets to the world. Or worse, to Gaius. Zoë was even worse. She had started out as Rachel's friend, but nowadays, everything out of her mouth seemed nihilistic or outright mean. Astrid? Rachel was fond of her other roommate. She was even mentally auditioning her for the role of new best friend, but she did not know the other girl well enough for such intimate confessions. Rachel's mother? Her mother did not even approve of her dating Gaius. Sandra? What would she say? *"Oh, by the way, I'm in love with your boyfriend?"*

Telling anything personal to Laurel was right out.

The person she really wished she could talk to was dead, killed by Rachel—or by the Heer of Dunderberg, depending on how one looked at it. Illondria, the beautiful, seven-foot-tall Queen of the Lios Alfar, would have listened attentively and offered kind advice.

Rachel missed her Elf.

Thinking back to brunch and how Nastasia had jumped to entirely wrong conclusions regarding last night's events, Rachel realized there might be something she could do to help Vlad, and thus, indirectly, Gaius, by aiding his boss. Sitting up, she asked the nurse for paper and ink and penned a letter.

> *To His Royal Majesty, Andre III, King of Magical Australia,*
> *Dear Your Majesty,*
>
> *You might wish to know about an event that happened yesterday at the Year of the Dragon Ball. Your daughter, Her Royal Highness, Princess Alexis, spent the entire ball sitting by herself. I thought it was odd that her brothers were not standing up with her, so I went over to talk to her.*
>
> *She did not respond at first but merely looked at His Royal Highness, Prince Romulus. I think magical rays came out of her eyes and scorched his back. Or at least, they would have had she had such rays.*
>
> *Princess Alexis then said that it was okay. Her brothers were busy. She was fine sitting there looking pretty while her fiancé danced*

with other girls. She said it very properly, but I felt she might be sad. So, I offered to arrange for a line of boys to come by and ask her to dance —in hopes that this would lead to her fiancé taking more note of her. She declined. So I promised to send by one extraordinarily important boy—thinking that Prince Romulus might value her more if he thought she was of interest to a rival who was his equal. (Boys can be like that.)

I sent His Royal Highness, Prince Vladimir of Bavaria, explaining to him first that if he would ask Princess Alexis to dance, she would say no. He agreed.

Princess Alexis did not say no.

I happened to be in a position to overhear them, so I can assure you that the prince did not do or say anything to distress her. He praised her sweetness, her beauty, and her intelligence. He then offered to fight a duel to free her from Prince Romulus because, his words: she should not marry the boy if he did not treasure her.

Princess Alexis said that would not help, and she started to cry.

Seeing that she was crying, Prince Romulus came to take her back. He thought Prince Vladimir was harassing her and came to her rescue. I thought this was a good step. It boded well for their future. Boys enjoy rescuing girls, and girls enjoy being rescued.

Only, Prince Romulus did not do it correctly. He did not comfort her, speak kind words to her, or hug her. He yanked her away roughly, or would have, if Amber had not come to her aid. Then he went off to dance with other girls. Again.

I thought you would want to know. Particularly, if it might forestall an international incident with Bavaria.

With love,
Your daughter's friend,
The Lady Rachel Jade Griffin

There, it's done, Rachel thought primly. Recalling Lucky's comment the previous night about her fate should she be atomized and his newly coined term for such a fate, she added mentally, *I hope he will not Vapor Rachel me for my impertinence.*

Chapter Six:
A Tad Creepy, Even to Me

Rachel lay back on the pillows, her arm resting gingerly atop the comforter. The longer she remained, however, the darker her thoughts grew, as the events of the last few days caught up with her. Her heart bled for her mother, who had endured so much—two decades of thinking about her daughter without being able to tell a single soul. The pain of this was almost too much for Rachel to bear, and she was merely thinking about it. She had not had to live with it secretly for twenty years. *How had her mother endured the experience?*

Then there was her sister Amber, so martial and stern. Everything in Rachel wanted to reject this person who treated her so coldly, but if she did, the forces that had ripped apart her family would triumph. Rachel had forgiven the Master of the World for taking her sister, but that did not mean that she did not wish to repair the damage.

Her thoughts drifted to the wishes she had made on the first three stars of evening a few weeks earlier, and her subsequent discovery that some stars were evil. The very notion that there were bad stars disturbed her. How much control did they have over the lives of mortals? Was it evil stars that had separated Amber from the family? Were they the true guilty party in the death of her Elf, Queen Illondria of the Lios Alfar?

The Guardian had promised she would discover what she should wish upon, since stars were not safe. She wondered what this might be.

This thought reminded her of Siggy's comment about the dead flittering like bats and sent an icy chill down her spine. Where was Illondria? Nastasia had returned her shade to Hoddmimir's Wood, but what had become of her since? Elves were nigh immortal. Was she flitting like a bat in Hades' kingdom, or did they get their own afterlife? What about the Heer of Dunderberg—the original storm goblin? Did he still exist? Did many people meet such an end—mingled with a fey and transformed into a monster? Is that how the Egyptian sorcerer Mambres turned into an ogre? Would this happen to anyone she knew? To her?

What did happen to people after death? Some became ghosts; Rachel had met quite a few. Some who had died were dragged down to a place of eternal torment. She had seen this happen to Remus Starkadder. But what happened to good people? Did they really flit about like bats? Old Thom had disappeared in a brilliant beam of light. So had John Colman, the Dutchman who had merged with the storm goblin to form the Heer of Dunderberg. Perhaps she had misunderstood, but she thought she had seen his friends beckoning to him from on high.

Where had these two ghosts gone? A beam of glorious light hardly sounded like Annwfyn. Could they have gone to the Elysian Fields or what the Irish called the Fortunate Isles? The early Greeks had believed that only those related to the gods achieved this honor, though later poets had expanded the citizenship of Elysium to include the heroic and the worthy. But who judged which souls were worthy? Rhadamanthus, Minos, and Aeacus? According to lore, Saturn was the ruler in Elysium, but Saturn had fallen and become the gruesome demon Moloch, who demanded child sacrifices. Was he the one who decided who could enter the pleasant afterlife? That did not sound promising.

Where was her grandfather? Rachel shivered. During the first week of school, her math-tutor-turned-evil-fire-breathing-dragon had implied that her beloved grandfather's final resting place might not be a pleasant one. Could he also have been dragged down like.... Rachel covered her head with her good arm. That thought was too terrible to finish.

A dark shape winged by the infirmary window. Its shadow fell over Nurse Moth's face where she sat at her desk near the back wall, but she did not look up. Rachel thought back, reviewing her memory. The corner of her eye had caught a glimpse of an unusually large black bird, a Raven with blood-red eyes. She waved in the direction it had flown.

"He is a tad creepy in his Doom of Worlds form," Rachel murmured aloud, "even to me."

The nurse rose and went into the back room, leaving Rachel alone. She ran a finger over her black bracelet but decided not to trouble the Guardian. She did slip out of bed, however—despite the throbbing in her temples—and thew open the glass pane, just in case he decided to fly back this way.

The chimes hung by the window rang in the cold February breeze. A swirl of green healing sparkles blew from the chimes toward where Rachel stood. The fresh scent, like newly-mown grass, cleared her head a bit, making her feel a little better.

No sooner had she lain down again than the Raven flew in the window and landed on the side of her bed. Her heart leapt with joy. He cocked his head, and the windowpane slid down, blocking the cold winter air.

"Little one," the black bird croaked, "did you see others such as myself last night? Creatures with wings and crowns of light?"

"Does my *remembering* seeing wings count?" asked Rachel.

He ruffled his feathers. "Did you see one who appears in the guise of a female?"

"With peacock wings?" Rachel asked with a shudder as she recalled the sultry, seven-foot redhead who had fled the moment she recognized St. Michael.

"No. Not her," the bird said dismissively. "Was she there? That was unwise. I will have a word with her if she returns. No, this one would have been an elegant being, white-winged with very blue eyes." He ruffled his feathers. "One of my bright sisters was here last night. A great one. She talked with one of your fellow students. I know not which. She was strong enough to hide under my nose but not strong enough to cover her scent."

"You have a sister?" Rachel breathed, curious about everything to do with him.

"We are neither male nor female," replied Jariel, "being but thoughts of the Altogether Highest; but we take on appearances in keeping with our roles. Those among us who customarily appear feminine, we, as a convention, refer to as our sisters."

"That makes sense." Rachel thought back. She recalled a young man with brilliant blue eyes and white wings who had danced with her and spoken for a time with Nastasia, but not a woman. She shook her head.

The Raven croaked, "It is saddening. I know many of my brethren do not wish to speak with me. Having this sister ignore me is another thing altogether."

"I am sorry," Rachel whispered, her heart breaking at his sorrow. "There were a great many angels... and other things... here during the hour when you left with Amber."

The bird's black head bobbed. "They came to see where our Father had spoken."

"Your father?" Rachel asked, puzzled.

"Through your sister Laurel."

"At the skating party? When light came out of her eyes? She said such beautiful things!"

"Indeed. It is not often that our Father comes down and speaks so directly. The effect of His growing closer was felt all across Sideria. The chaos calmed. The demons retreated. Wars they were causing ended. Peace broke out in many places, on many worlds." He still looked like a bird, but his voice was now melodic and beautiful, the voice of an angel.

"Wow!" Rachel breathed in wonder.

She recalled the vision she had seen after the incident with Laurel. In it, golden light had fallen from heaven, lighting up everything, and the bubbling darkness below the universe had receded. She also recalled that the voice speaking through her sister had told her not to despair. *Why was that message so hard to remember?*

"Across Sideria?" she asked. "I've heard that word before. Amber mentioned it, and so did my Elf, back in October. What is it?"

It amused her to refer to the ancient, ethereal queen as "my Elf." It was not like claiming a possession so much as acknowledging a relationship, similar to "my teacher" or "my mother."

"It is the name of the universe hanging upon the World Tree," said the Raven.

"The *universe* has a name?"

"It is the sidereal universe."

"Oh, you mean sidereal, as in pertaining to distant stars?" Rachel cried.

"Correct. The Starry Universe. Sideria is the name the Wayfarers use."

"Wayfarers?" Rachel tipped her head back. "I've heard that before, too. Death used it, in Nastasia's vision of Dread, when he realized she could see him—right before he read her mind. He said, '*A child. An interloper. A Wayfarer, perhaps? Let us discover what she knows.*'"

"It is a name for the divine gift that grants the Romanovs the power to travel between worlds." The bird's black head cocked to one side. "Death? Ah, the Horseman, in Chartres. Yes." He paused then added, "And, before you ask about Wayfarers, that is a topic upon which I am forbidden to speak."

"Ah. Of course." Rachel sighed.

The Raven shimmered and changed into his eight-foot-tall form, dressed in a loose tunic and trousers of black poplin. His feet were bare. She appreciated that he had gone to the trouble of wearing a shirt this time. He pulled off his golden halo and laid it on the bed. Then he stretched his enormous black wings, which were far too large to fit properly in the room, and folded them behind his back, where they appeared to form a feathered cloak. He glanced at the chair, which was suddenly taller, straighter, and sturdier, and sat upon it.

Rachel smiled at him. Then she straightened up, startled by a thought. "Was he here last night, Death? Was that the same Death with whom I danced?"

The Raven turned and stared off into the distance. "No. The Four Horsemen were driven from Sideria, though at a terrible price. The one who attended the ball was another Guardian of the Twilight Lands. It is his wont to take that guise instead of that of a heraldic animal."

A shiver of wonder ran from the top of Rachel's head to the bottom of her soles. Her lips parted. She scrambled out from under her comforter and knelt atop it, staring at the Raven.

"Are there *more* Guardians?" she asked him, astonished.

The motion of rising to kneel caused her head to throb. She held still, waiting for the pain to subside. Jariel reached out and brushed his fingertips across her forehead. Suddenly, the pain vanished. Rachel smiled in gratitude.

"Many worlds here in the Twilight Lands have Guardians," he replied.

"The Twilight Lands? Is that the same as Sideria or different?"

He contemplated this. "It is both the same and different. 'The Twilight Lands' is the name my brethren use for what lies below the Heavenly and above the Infernal."

Rachel was not sure what some of those words meant, but she asked about the most important part. "Many worlds have a Guardian," she clarified, "but not all?"

"Guardians are assigned. Not all worlds have had one assigned."

"Assigned by whom?" Rachel pressed, fascinated.

Jariel considered for a moment. "This is well known and can hardly be considered a secret. Guardians are appointed by the emperors. Both the Eternal Emperor and the now deceased Holy Emperor were able to assign Guardians."

"Who assigned you?" she asked.

He opened his mouth and closed it.

Rachel sighed and climbed back under her comforter, leaning on the pillows propped against her headboard. *Guardians of other worlds,* the very thought filled her with a supernatural awe. She longed to ask more questions, but she did not wish to press Jariel on subjects upon which

he seemed reluctant to speak, lest he depart. She considered asking him about the land of the dead but felt strangely reluctant. Finally, she forced the words from her throat.

"Jariel, where do we go when we die?"

He bowed his raven-dark head. "Of that, I am forbidden to speak."

"What? Why? Who would forbid such a thing?"

The Raven looked off into the distance. Then, he addressed Rachel, "Would you like to see a secret? One you may share with your friends but, perhaps, not with the Romanov...."

Rachel nodded, her eyes wide. Would he show her the answer to her question or something about other Guardians or angels or secrets of Sideria? She trembled with anticipation.

Gently, he picked her up and cradled her in his arms. He smelled of strong winds off the ocean and yet also of warm summer breezes. The world around them seemed to melt and reform. When it returned, the edges were blurry.

The vision showed Rachel's dorm room. Within the hazy edges, a short young woman who vaguely resembled Rachel's mother leaned against the wall by the door. It took Rachel a moment to realize it was Amber without her hood.

"This is a memory," said the Guardian. "You can speak aloud. No one here can hear you." He pointed. "She would not have been visible. She was concealing herself by her arts."

Rachel glanced at the angle of the shadows. "This was yesterday, while Nastasia was dressing for the ball, wasn't it? I was in the bathroom, getting into my black jumpsuit."

The Raven nodded.

Amber looked tired and sad. Then, suddenly, she glanced around. Reaching into her pocket, she pulled out a square of silver glass the size of an old-fashioned calling card. She stepped outside the room and stood in the hallway.

Rachel started and leaned forward. She compared it in her memory to the glass in Beaumont Castle. They were the same shade and intensity of silver—the color of moonlight.

Amber said softly, "Who is it?"

An image formed in the card. It showed the head and chest of a man. He wore a white robe trimmed in silver. His long black hair had been drawn through a delicate silver hair crown on top of his head and then spilled down his back. His eyes were shaped much like Rachel's or her mother's. He was handsome yet stern and exquisitely calm.

He spoke in a voice that was simultaneously strict and comforting. "Hello, disciple."

Amber's voice replied, "I am not a student of Kunlun Mountain, Chiang Long."

"You are still my student, are you not?"

She nodded expressionlessly.

"The emperor is curious how you are faring. Did you discover who was calling you?"

Amber nodded again. "I can give a full report, but I do not believe this method is unobserved."

Chiang Long was silent. Then he said, "The local Guardian is monitoring us. I can feel its presence. That is proper, as moon glasses form a bridge between worlds, and it is a Guardian's duty to maintain the world's wards. Our Guardian here on Mount Eternal, the Firebird, is also aware of us. I detect no one else; nonetheless, I sense your hesitation. You can give your full report later. I shall let the Emperor know you have completed your primary mission."

"Moon glass! I knew it!" Rachel cried. "The glass in Transylvania, the one through which Daring Northwest disappeared? That was the moon glass Dr. Mordeau asked Valerie about!"

Jariel nodded wordlessly.

Amber gave another curt nod.

The robed figure said, "I sense pain in you, young one. You have not felt this conflicted in a long time. I warned you about finding your family, did I not?"

She nodded again.

He shook his head in disapproval. "My order takes us from our families at a very young age, right after birth. We do not concern ourselves with those we came from any more than we would with anyone else. I have explained to you why this is."

Amber nodded.

Rachel cried out as if in pain. "He's trying to take her from us all over again!

Chiang Long continued, "Family can be used against you. The Powers of Darkness will use such connections to edge their way into your heart. Fear, Hatred, Jealousy, Sadness. These are tools of the Darkness. You must be above and apart from them."

"Yes, Master Chiang Long," Amber said obediently.

He continued, "You are a weapon of our Emperor, and you are quite sharp. Demons fear you because you are pure, and you cannot be corrupted. Do not let others do their work for them. Repeat after me....

Chiang Long began to chant. "All things are empty."

Amber replied, "Nothing is born; nothing dies."

Rachel whispered to the Raven, "That's the *Heart Sutra*."

"How do you know this?" asked Jariel. "It is not from your culture."

"I read everything," replied Rachel, leaning forward to listen.

Chiang Long and Amber continued, taking turns:

"Nothing is pure; nothing is stained," *he intoned.*

"Nothing increases and nothing decreases," *replied Amber.*

They continued for a time, ending with:

"There is no suffering; no cause of suffering."

"No end to suffering; no path to follow."

"There is no attainment of wisdom," *he chanted.*

"And no wisdom to attain," *she finished.*

Chiang Long gazed at her fondly. "Amber, you are still quite young. The path we walk is a lifelong journey. It is hard, but you shall be strong. I've seen it already."

She gave him a wan smile and nodded again.

"Now, meditate," *he said.* "Clear your mind. Use what I have shown you. Find the cause of your conflicting emotions and examine them as if apart from them. Take their power from them, and you shall be balanced once again."

"Yes, Master Chiang Long."

"Very well, my quiet little one. Meditate upon what I have said. I shall see you soon."

The image of Master Chiang Long flickered and vanished, and Amber slipped the square silver mirror back into her pocket.

Hot tears ran down Rachel's cheeks, tears she had hidden from Amber. She wrapped her arms tightly around Jariel's neck and laid her head against his shoulder. That robed man, whoever he was, wanted Amber not to be a Griffin. He was deliberately undoing Rachel's hard work.

The Raven said gravely, "I thought it might interest you to see that."

Rachel wept, but she managed, "Thank you."

He put a black-feathered wing around her; its softness was more comforting than any blanket. She wept harder. She had been hoping that meeting her family would be enough to bring Amber back to them.

She had not realized they had an adversary actively working to convince her lost sister to cut herself off from them. Now that Amber had gone back, away from their father's kind wisdom and their mother's gentle love, would she remember what it had been like, that moment when she had been one of them? Or would she again fall under the sway of this Chiang Long and rip her family from her heart?

Presently, Rachel wiped at her tears. "But he is wrong. That is not what family is."

Jariel smiled sadly, still cradling her in his arms. "The Order at Kunlun Mountain has many strange beliefs. They are under siege by the denizens of Wicked Canyon and rightfully fear that good things can be twisted by my fallen brothers. They are correct that demons play upon such emotions quite skillfully."

Rachel sniffed. She snuggled against him, breathing in his ocean scent and feeling the softness of his feathers against her cheek. A heat radiated out of him, warming her whole body.

"My family seems so precious," she whispered. "So full of something I wish I could put into words. Something Amber lacks. Every time I notice this, it hurts—because I know she would have been different had she grown up with us. Even worse, I don't think Amber has noticed that anything's missing. Whatever the missing quality is, it's not of use on a battlefield."

She leaned against the Raven, wishing she could explain this precious thing.

"Perhaps," he mused, "having something that isn't useful is part of its preciousness."

"Maybe," she sniffed softly.

"Take heart, dear one." He stroked her cheek with a wing feather. "I foresee that these matters shall be resolved in time. Patience will be a great friend to you."

Patience. Rachel sighed. Patience was not her strong suit. And yet, the gentleness of his words, the kindness of his touch, worked upon her soul like a balm.

"I love my family." She struggled not to cry again. "Discovering that a family member had been ripped from us—it's like discovering a gaping wound where the limb you didn't know you were supposed to have is missing." She wiped her eyes with her sleeve. "But thank you."

The Raven nodded. Still cradling her, he rose as easily as if she were a kitten and placed her upon her bed. Rachel settled upon the mattress and rearranged her blankets, pulling them up to her shoulders. Then, she lowered her lashes, a tiny smile haunting her lips. She rested there, afraid to speak, afraid even to breathe, lest the happiness of having him sit beside her turn out to be a dream.

Thinking of the vow she had made to do her best to find a way to bring peace between the mortals and the fey, she raised her head and met the Raven's gray eyes squarely.

"Jariel, this matter of the Roanoke Covenant. Can you do anything to help us?"

"No. I may not interfere in internal matters."

"Oh." She looked down at her comforter. "I knew that." Looking up, she tried again. "I know you can't interfere directly, but can you do *anything*? I don't want the school to close."

He glanced off far to the east. "I foresee a solution may be found in the spring. Do you wish to be part of it?"

"Oh, yes!" She bounced twice on the mattress with excitement. It felt good to bounce without pain in her head. Her arm ached only mildly.

He looked eastward again. "There. It has been set in motion. Whether you choose to act when the opportunity presents itself, I leave in your hands. I have not bound your free will."

"How will I know when it happens?" Rachel asked.

The Raven shook his head. "That I cannot tell you, Rachel Griffin. Only my Father knows the true shape of the future."

As he would say no more, Rachel changed the subject. "Amber seemed to think that the Master of the World doesn't know exactly what's going on here. Is this true? Are you doing things he doesn't know about? Or is it just that he has not told Amber?"

Jariel replied gravely, "I cannot think of a way to answer your question and not break prior agreements."

"Then don't." She lay back on her pillow. While she wanted to know, she feared to press him to talk about things that were forbidden to him. The pained look on his face when his oath of silence put pressure on his heart always frightened her.

The rhythmic patter of raindrops sounded on the roof. Listening to them was making Rachel sleepy. The sky had clouded over. Through the window, she caught a glimpse of her friends hurrying to get out of the rain. There was a tutor walking with them. No, that was Zoë.

Turning her head, she gazed up at Jariel. "What about Zoë? Why is she growing tall?"

The Raven turned to regard Zoë. "I have not observed her for some time. Does she remember her past? That is... troublesome. Particularly with her."

"Oh, I know!" Rachel sat up suddenly. "Zoë's remembering her past, like Sakura did the time we don't talk about. Is that why she's grown so tall? Will the world be damaged?"

"I hope not," Jariel murmured thoughtfully. "She does not have Miss Suzuki's ability to impose order and undo my work, so her remembering is less dangerous to the Walls. Still.... What I did to her was complex and powerful. If it is broken to this degree, it must have been done by another power. I do not think she has the ability to do it herself. I foresee the cause will not turn out to have been a pleasant one...." He frowned.

"Bad things happened to her when she fell into the dark," Rachel whispered.

"I fear so," he replied softly, adding, "I had hoped that none of them would remember, except in a distant way, at least until they were grown. Perhaps the trauma of what occurred when she fell brought back her memories. Or perhaps it was Him, breathing upon her."

"You mean the Comfort Lion?" Rachel asked.

Jariel nodded and then said, "I did not destroy the people they used to be. I made that life as if they had dreamt it long ago. I do not wish to change their spirits—except in certain specific cases. But even there, I merely offered a better path forward. I never forced. Some have accepted; some have chosen to reject—but I also did not want them to pine for the old lives that are lost to them. Do you understand my dilemma?"

"Yes," Rachel said slowly. "It is a hard thing, but I think you have done amazingly well."

"Buried memories are like ghosts. They haunt the person who cannot remember them. Some people resist their lure better than others," he said. "I can help Zoë without touching her memory." He raised his head and peered out the window. Outside, Zoë suddenly changed direction, parting from her friends with a little half-wave.

Jariel stated, "She will be here soon. I will speak to her. I foresee there is little chance she will not be frightened. If you comfort her, it will help."

"I will try," Rachel said gravely.

Chapter Seven:
The Unexpected Enlightenment of Rachel Griffin

THE FRONT DOOR OF THE INFIRMARY OPENED, AND IN WALKED ZOË FOR-rest. Her hair was a dark green and dripping from the sudden rain. She came and sat beside Rachel on the bed, one hand resting on her tiger-spotted quoll—an orange beast with white polka dots, vaguely the size of a possum—that watched bright-eyed from her shoulder. Rachel recalled a quoll familiar gave its master the gift of lucid dreaming and that this one bore the incongruous name of Aardvark.

Zoë did not seem to notice the eight-foot-tall man with gigantic black wings sitting beside the bed. She opened her mouth to speak, but Rachel stopped her by touching her hand.

"Don't be afraid, Zoë," she said, "but the Raven wants to talk to you."

A boy now sat on the Raven's chair beside the bed. He had tattoos on his face, and one shoulder was hunched and raised above the other. He smiled a toothy smile at her.

"Hello, Zoë Moth."

Zoë looked at him and blinked. Confused, she blurted out, "Nikau? How did you get out of the Tower? Or, wait. Didn't I save you? But if so, why are you still hunched?"

"I'm not really Nikau," the boy replied. "I look like Nikau, so that you will feel calmer. I want to talk to you about your memories, and the changes they are causing in your appearance."

"Um…." Zoë swallowed. "Okay…."

"I am the Guardian," said the boy, "The protector of this world. I can make you an object that will lock your appearance as it should be. I shall cause it to be extremely hard to detect, even by the strongest sorcerers."

Zoë frowned. "You look like Nikau but you're not. That is really weird."

The Raven stood and rippled, turning back into his eight-foot-tall, winged form. Zoë tensed noticeably. The quoll ran from her left shoulder to her right and back again.

The Raven asked, "Is this better?"

"No." Zoë shook her head.

Jariel actually rolled his eyes. "I shall assist you as I have stated. Or, if you wish, I can change your memories again. I can make much of what happened outside my world seem as if it were a dream from long ago. It is your choice."

Zoë looked at Rachel, who squirmed. Changing memories made her extremely uncomfortable. She was not the right person to come to for advice.

Rachel asked, "Do you want to remember your other life or have it seem like a dream?"

Zoë shrugged. "It's hard to say. I remember the old life as if it happened a long time ago. Before I was little. On the other hand, it's hard to think of myself as fourteen now. I was already fourteen once. It's crazy to think I have to do it again. I don't want to have my memories messed with again, though." She looked up at the Raven. "Could you please not change them?"

He nodded and laid a hand upon her shoulder. Then, he put his hands together, and, when he opened them, he was holding a black, lacy necklace, the kind that fit snugly like a collar. It had a pendant hanging from it, a small golden disk containing a black *Ehwas* rune, which resembled an *M*. He handed it to Zoë. She examined it and smiled.

"I like it," said Zoë.

He nodded with the slightest of smiles. "I thought you might."

Zoë dropped the quoll next to Rachel and fastened the necklace. Rachel and the quoll gazed at each other speculatively. As she closed the clasp, Zoë suddenly shrank. She grew shorter and slenderer until she looked about fifteen or sixteen rather than twenty. Also, the tips of her ears were rounded again. Once in place, the rune disappeared, leaving a simple golden disk dangling from the lacy black collar.

Zoë came around to the other side of the bed and flopped back, lying on the pillows next to Rachel. She scooped up her familiar and put the orange polka-dotted creature on her chest. It grunted a noise that reminded Rachel of wood chimes and scratched its side with a rear leg.

Zoë asked, "Uh, so, what's his deal? Does he...work for you?"

"No!" Rachel gave a short, shocked laugh, painfully embarrassed that Jariel had overheard such a hubristic notion. "I work for him."

"What do you do for him?"

Rachel shot the Raven a wistful look. "So far, he hasn't asked for much. I wish he would."

Jariel gazed thoughtfully at Rachel. "Is that so?"

She returned his gaze, her eyes shining with hope. "I'll do anything you ask of me."

The Raven reached out and touched Rachel's cheek, his gaze tender and his caress extremely gentle. Rachel leaned her cheek against his palm. They gazed at each other with fond affection. Zoë looked away, slightly embarrassed.

"Oh!" Rachel cried suddenly, as Jariel drew away.

From the pouch around her neck, she drew out the missing feather and extended it to Zoë.

"My feather!" Zoë cried, grabbing it. She hugged it to her chest, displacing the quoll, who let out a short, hoarse bark before wandering down to curl up between its mistress' feet.

"Is it...?" Zoë peered at the feather carefully, examining both sides. "Yeah! It's mine. I know it so well, every spot and dot. Where did you get it?"

Rachel pointed at the Raven. "He gave it to me."

"Thanks," Zoë whispered to Jariel, her cheeks slightly pale. She hugged the feather to her, rocking back and forth slightly. Then, she put it back into its customary place in her forelock braid. As she ran her hands over it, it turned a mottled green to match her dark green hair.

"Thanks. I will never forget this. Never."

The Raven nodded. Then, he looked out the window at the pouring rain, though Rachel suspected he was looking at something far beyond the sight of mortal eyes. She lay back, resting against her pillows. Zoë's weight leaned against her. From the steadiness of her breathing, Rachel realized that the other girl had fallen asleep.

"That was fast," Rachel murmured, gazing in surprise at the sleeping girl.

Jariel turned back to regard her. "Do not be disturbed. I wanted to speak to you of her condition without her hearing."

Startled, Rachel realized he had made Zoë fall asleep. Even more startling, he must have caused her to come here, too, "made it likely" as he put it. There was no other reason Zoë would have turned away from the others and walked to the infirmary. She probably had not even known Rachel was here. That he could by an act of will bring Zoë here or make her fall asleep was also creepy. Rachel forgave him.

That must have been how he had drawn Amber here. He made it likely, and she could sense that, so she came to investigate. That was what the Master of the World had asked him to do to her parents; only he had found no probability where her parents agreed to surrender Amber, so he had been asked to change them and make them into people who would agree. That part, she laid squarely upon the Master of the World. She did not hate him any longer, but she still felt strongly that he had been wrong to make such a request.

The Raven said, "I have not, sadly, helped her as much as you may think. The damage done to her is deep. She has seen great darkness and has a wound I cannot heal. A wound in her heart. It will take time and care for her to be whole again. It shall be up to you and your compatriots to do this. I stand apart and cannot be as a friend to her."

Rachel balked. She did not have a very good track record of helping people. If anything, she seemed more suited to disturbing them. Was there a need for that? Surely, she was well on her way to becoming an expert.

She nodded obediently, but she felt she should give the Raven fair warning.

"Poor Zoë." She sighed. "I want to help people very much. I keep trying, but I mess up. Sometimes, what I think of helps. More often, it makes things worse. But I won't give up."

"Indeed," said the Raven. "You should not."

Rachel smiled and folded her hands atop her comforter. She felt both rather grown up, talking to the Guardian of the World, and at the same time cherished, like a small child in the presence of loving parents.

"You say you will do anything I ask," Jariel asked, gazing at her gravely. "Is there any command I can give you that will lead to you having a lighter heart? The future is unclear."

She lowered her lashes shyly. "If you want me to be happier, I'll try."

"If I told you to release yourself from the obligations you have placed upon yourself, would you listen to my command?" he asked.

Rachel did not answer. She wanted to obey any order he would give, but inside, she felt only sadness. Her devotion to saving the world was what kept the darkness and despair away. Everything she did, everything she practiced, even her classwork, folded together in her mind into one coherent whole—her effort to be prepared to save the world.

If the Raven asked her to give that up, she would. He was the only person whose orders she felt she could follow—other than the Lion—because he was the only one whom she believed knew enough of what was truly going on to give wise orders. Everyone else seemed to know less about the current situation than she did, even her father, now that he had lost his memory. If they did not have proper information, how could she trust them to ask her to do the right thing?

If the Guardian were to ask her not to listen to him, on the other hand, that would be a tragedy. She would have no one left she could obey, which was a bad place for a nearly fourteen-year-old girl to be. If he ordered her to stop saving the world, she foresaw the rest of the school year being like the two weeks before the skating party: sleeping all the time, not eating, not caring about anything. Without a greater purpose, it was as if she had eaten fairy food. One could depart from fairyland after eating their food, but if one stayed in the mortal world, one would sicken and die. *She was not capable of going back to being an ordinary girl.*

The Raven gazed at her, his eyes full of compassion. "Rachel Griffin. I would never wish you to be unexceptional."

Rachel's head shot up. She gawked at him. How had he known what she was thinking? Could he see alternate possibilities where she spoke her unvoiced thoughts aloud? That was disturbing. And yet, his words brought her comfort. Suddenly, she flushed with shame.

How could she be so vain? What did it matter whether *she* was ordinary or extraordinary? Was she so shallow as to believe this was about *her?* It did not matter if she were happy or unhappy. That was not why she protected the world. She fought to save it because it was worth saving, because she loved it, because it tore her soul in half to contemplate parents watching their children die, beautiful landscapes crumbling away into nothing, and all the terrible destruction that would come, were the world to be lost.

Rachel recalled standing in front of Beaumont with Mortimer Egg's wand in her hand. All around her, like the dark shadows of dragons, were the *tenebrous mundi*—beings that maintained the Wall protecting her world from the darkness Outside. If she had been under a geas, as Egg believed, her next actions would have caused those strange shadowy beings to tear down that Wall. Her whole world—everything and everyone she loved— would be gone now. She had come so close to losing everything that mattered. She never wanted to come that close again.

"I want to help!" Rachel cried from the bottom of her heart, staring into the face of the Guardian of the World. "I don't want anyone to be lost if I can prevent it!"

The Raven gazed at her, his eyes gray as a cloudy sky above the sea. He said nothing, yet Rachel sensed that he approved. A sense of burden began to lift. She felt lighter, more joyous. Was it okay to let go of her concerns? Or was she shirking responsibility? She recalled Jariel's earlier comment about a thing being precious precisely because it was not useful.

Could such a thing be? Nastasia believed the ends did not justify the means. Rachel's grandfather and the Master of the World believed the opposite, Vlad, too. Her beloved grandfather, with his practicality and his willingness to make sacrifices for a greater good, certainly would not have agreed with the princess.

Had Grandfather approved of Andre the Second taking Amber? He must have known about it at the time, before the Raven made him forget. Was that why her mother disliked him? Because he sided with yielding Amber? But if he had, had that idea come from him? Or had he been changed by the Raven as her father had?

All of a sudden, it occurred to Rachel that she was wrong about her grandfather. General Blaise Griffin had not believed everything was duty-bound. He had believed that *soldiers* could be sacrificed—that *he* could be sacrificed—but he did not put civilians into that category.

She knew he did not, for he had often spoken of this. He had written about it extensively as well. Rachel had read many of her grandfather's journals, particularly from the Second World War. She now saw something in his writing that she had not previously grasped. Her grandfather had been fond of a quote by the American Founding Father, John Adams: *There are only two creatures of value on the face of the earth: those with the commitment, and those who require the commitment of others.* Reading her grandfather's journals, she had always assumed that he was thinking of himself as someone in the first category—a creature of value due to his commitment to do what must be done. *But the quote had two parts.*

If Grandfather truly believed it, then he must have also believed in the second *creature of value—those who required the commitment of others*, whose safety made all the sacrifice worthwhile. Surely, the women of his own family would have fallen into this second category. Surely, Grandfather had felt that her grandmother, her mother, her sisters, and, yes, even she herself, were creatures of value—worth protecting. Even Laurel with all her foolishness.

Laurel! Rachel bolted straight up and grabbed onto the headboard. Suddenly, it all made sense, as if she had been walking in darkness and had been unexpectedly enlightened.

"Oh, my!" She gripped the mattress more tightly. "I've just had the most astounding revelation!"

Jariel still sat beside her. He tilted his head inquiringly.

"All this time, I've been wrong," she spoke softly. "I assumed we should all act like Grandfather, like Vladimir—at all times. But Nastasia's right, isn't she? About the ends not justifying the means?"

He did not say anything, but he watched her face intently.

"I keep thinking that if all were right with the world, Amber would be more like Laurel. Or at least, more like Sandra or me. But I couldn't put into words why this would be good."

He nodded, "I remember."

"Amber's a death doll. She saves lives by killing monsters, right?" she continued. "Maybe she's saved thousands of lives. Isn't that good? Isn't that worth losing a sister? Doesn't the end of all the good she's done justify the means of taking away my parent's child?"

The Raven continued to watch her face attentively.

"Yet, as I said before," Rachel continued, struggling to put her sudden realization into words, "in my heart, I kept thinking that whatever frivolous, silly Laurel had that Amber did not, it was a thing worth having. I couldn't find any words to explain it, but if I were to try, I think it would have to be a word like *joy*. A joy worth having—not because it accomplished things or won battles, but just in and of itself."

"Joy is a thing of many splendors," stated Jariel.

"But who in their right mind would agree with me?" Rachel asked, still filled with awe at her new understanding. "No general or emperor would acknowledge that this lost, ineffable *something* was so valuable that it would have been better to let Amber to have become a person who had it than to have a sharp weapon against the enemy, as Chiang Long put it, right? The Emperor, the Starry Universe itself, might look at me and ask coldly, *'Would you have wanted all those she saved to have died?'*"

Rachel met the Raven's gaze, her eyes shining. "But no matter how many people Amber has helped, I bet it is not even a tenth, not even a hundredth, or possibly even a hundred-thousandth of the good done by the sudden calm that your brothers and sister came to investigate last night —by the demons pausing and being pushed back. Right? You said wars stopped."

Jariel cocked his head and then nodded slowly.

"And whose doing was that?" Rachel cried triumphantly. "*Laurel's!*"

The Raven's gray eyes grew more piercing. The feathers of his black wings rustled.

"The daughter who stayed with my parents," Rachel continued, "the daughter who was frivolous but who had that joy—that *je ne sais quoi*—she may have done more good for this war effort than Amber. By being exactly who she is and nothing more."

Jariel's face filled with sorrow. "Yes, there is wisdom in what you say."

She leaned toward him, serious and fervent. "I vow to do what's in my power to protect that joy, to make the world a place where the good and beautiful can flourish." Rachel raised her right hand as once she had seen Von Dread do and declared solemnly, "So swears Griffin!"

The Raven smiled. "So witnessed."

Rachel's eyelids fluttered closed. When she opened them, Jariel was gone. Next to her, Zoë jerked awake. She looked around frantically for a moment and then shivered and sighed.

"He left, and I'm not a rabbit or a block of wood. Hooo!"

"Nope." Rachel gave her a hug. "Though he did leave you a nice necklace."

"That he did." Zoë hugged her back. Then, she lay for a bit, fingering the black lace around her neck.

"How are you feeling?" Rachel asked.

"Could be better," Zoë shrugged. "Could be worse, too."

Zoë pointed her toes, stretching. Her quoll waddled up from where it had been sleeping. It climbed up her body and sat on her face. Zoë sighed and slid it to one side, where it curled up beside her ear.

"What happened at brunch after I left?" asked Rachel.

"We all promised to not to share information outside of the Die Horriblies," said Zoë.

"Good grief!" Rachel scowled.

Zoë drew away from her and peered in surprise. "I thought you'd be the most gung-ho about this? Don't you want to protect the world?"

"I do, but it's... complicated."

"Complicated how?" pressed Zoë. "The Lion told Sigfried that his telling me about that elf, without taking safety precautions, was what killed her. An elf who was older than spoken language, much less sliced bread. Is it bad that I don't want anyone else to die because of me?"

Rachel gritted her teeth. What was it with her friends? People were always putting her off, refusing to answer questions by saying something that indicated that they did not want to say more, and she was left stewing. When she tried it, however, her friends continued to badger her. They never just let her be. It was one reason, she realized suddenly, that she had taken to lying.

When she lied, they left her alone.

Chapter Eight:
The Silver Sandal Caper!

"Zoë," Rachel sat up in bed, "what happens to us after we die? Do we flit like bats?"

"Bats? Flit? What?" The other girl snorted. "Of course not. Where'd you get that from?"

Rachel lay back again. "In *The Odyssey*, when Odysseus seeks advice from a dead sailor, everyone in the land of the dead is a shade that only gains substance and recalls itself fully after feeding on blood. Otherwise, they are like forgotten memories, empty husks of what they once were. Are you sure that's not our fate?"

"'Course not, mate!" Zoë insisted. "What a waste that'd be. After we die, we come back again. As someone else. Get born as a baby. Or maybe a turtle or a bug if we've been real jerks in this life. Nothing to it."

"So we stop being us?"

"Only to a degree. We lose the specifics of who we are now, but we keep our core."

"But...." Rachel made a face. "How does that even work?"

Zoë shrugged. "It's like what happened to me when I came here. I've forgotten the specifics of the person I used to be, the things I used to do—good and bad—the relationships I used to have. Many people we know have gone through this: Seth, Misty, Prince Von Dreamboat, Cutie-pie Gaius, Valerie. Salome was *dead* before she came! Many of us don't even have the same parents here we did before—I definitely don't.

"We don't seem to have suffered too much for the experience," she concluded. "Being reincarnated's like that."

Rachel shivered. The thought of forgetting one's life horrified her. Before she could reply, however, the door to the infirmary swung open, and in clanked Seth Peregrine in his hockey gear. He had been rather short for his age back in September, but in the last month or so he had shot up and now resembled a beanpole. He had warm brown eyes and wavy strawberry-blond hair. He was friendly with Zoë and Siggy, but he was the only member of Rachel's core-group—the students with whom she shared all her classes—with whom Rachel seldom spoke.

As he clanked over towards them, Zoë lit up. *Oh!* Rachel's mystic girl powers—as her father called them—tingled. Zoë *liked* him!

Seth slouched into the chair beside the bed, explaining that he had seen Zoë enter the infirmary and not emerge again, so he had come to check on her. He asked if she was okay and how she was doing. Zoë answered nonchalantly, but Rachel got the distinct impression that she was very pleased. He didn't stay long, but Zoë had an unusually big smile after he left.

As he departed, he passed Marta Fisher, the daughter of their science tutor. She was a studious young woman with straight blond hair. A copper-hilted dagger stuck up from a sheath on her hip, the symbol of membership in the Brotherhood of the White Hart, a secret organization devoted to the safety of the World of the Wise. Marta was one of only five Roanoke students who had been deemed worthy of membership.

Marta paused at the fountain, spotted the two girls, and walked over to their bed, frowning slightly. "Hi, Rachel. Hi, Zoë. How are you two feeling?"

"A bit better." Rachel broke off a piece of her chocolate bar and held it out to her.

"No, thank you," said Marta.

"I'll take that." Zoë snatched it from Rachel's fingers and gulped it down. "Ah, chocolate. The good stuff." The quoll watched its mistress eat with great interest. Zoë flicked it fondly on the head. "Sorry, no chocolate for you. I don't know if chocolate is good for quolls."

Marta said, "Rachel, are you here because Abraham Van Helsing hurt you?"

"No." Rachel drew out the word, puzzled.

"Which Van Helsing?" Zoë muttered. "The vampire-hunting college kid? Or the one from the novel *Dracula*? Is this a Transylvania thing? If so, this time, it wasn't my fault."

"Um, okay, but..." said Marta. "Rachel, did you ask Sigfried Smith to punch Abraham?"

"What!" Rachel cried, sitting straight up.

"Did he?" Zoë grinned. "Wish I'd seen that!"

Rachel cried, "Certainly not! I was the one at fault. Why would I ask someone to punch Mr. Van Helsing? Though, really, Abe might want to think about hexing his vampires in the future and only staking them after he confirms they're undead."

Marta's eyes grew wide. "But I thought you said you weren't hurt. He didn't stab you with a wooden stake, did he?"

Rachel's slid her mask of calm over her face. "He did not hurt me."

Marta looked even more concerned. "Rachel, it's important you don't go into another student's room without knocking. You know that, right?"

"It was dark, and I was very tired. I was on the wrong floor."

Marta said, "You should still knock, even if it's your brother's room. Other boys live with him. You might… surprise someone."

"Okay," Rachel said, chagrined. "I-I was trying not to wake up the other boys."

"I see. Please be careful in the future, okay? You shouldn't be on the boys' side at night. I'll give you a pass—because it was the Year of the Dragon Ball—but see that it doesn't happen again. As for Abe, I'm going to have to report his attempting to stake a student to the dean."

Marta gave a little wave to Zoë and left.

Rachel sighed. She was truly embarrassed, and yet she could not but help feel touched and a tiny bit amused that Sigfried had gone to such efforts for her sake.

Aloud, she said, "What was Siggy thinking?"

Zoë shrugged. "With Sigfried? Who can tell? So, um, did you find who you were looking for on the boys' side? Were you looking for Siggy? Why didn't you use the calling cards?"

"No. I never did. I went to bed." She paused only a millisecond before lying blithely. "I thought the card wouldn't work because Siggy would be asleep. If it was loud enough to wake him, it would wake his roommates as well."

Zoë snorted. "I think some of the boys here might… *might*… be slightly high-strung."

"Yeah…" Rachel giggled, "especially the vampire hunters on the night of a full moon."

"Rachel? Wake up, sleepyhead. We need your help for nefarious purposes." For the second time the same day, Joy's voice woke Rachel from a deep sleep.

Rachel opened her eyes. She felt rested and more like her normal self. It was dark outside. She could still hear the rain, the wind, and the window chimes. Inside, the emerald light from the healing globes illuminated Joy, who stood by her bed, and cascaded over Valerie, Sigfried, Lucky, and Zoë, who was no longer lying down. At the bottom of the bed stood Valerie's best friend, the sultry Salome Iscariot, her long blonde hair glinting green in the glow of the globe.

"The princess just had another vision!" Joy cried excitedly.

"Really!" Rachel struggled to sit up. "What was it about?"

"We're not sure. She's gone to talk to the dean." Salome's large, luminous eyes sparkled with excitement. "Students sneaking away from the ball last night, maybe? Nastasia said the kids in her vision were in costume. They rowed somewhere. To the Glass Hall? Very mysterious."

"Do we know more than that?" Rachel asked, puzzled.

"No, but we will." Valerie sat down on Rachel's bed and swung her camera on its red strap in front of her. She took off the lens cap. "As soon as you help us with our little caper."

"Dastardly scheme," corrected Sigfried, who was sporting a black eye. "We're going to commit a crime. We didn't want to leave you out."

Rachel wanted to speak with him about Van Helsing, but it was not a conversation to be held in front of an audience. She decided to wait.

"Technically," said Lucky, in his gravelly dragon voice, "only I get to commit the crime. The rest of you are just abetting."

"What exactly is this about?" Rachel looked back and forth between her friends' faces.

"We're going to—" Joy began, bursting with excitement.

"Shhh!" Valerie interrupted. "The less said the better. If we don't tell her the details, she can't be implicated for her part."

"My part?" Rachel smoothed her shoulder-length hair, which had gone every which way. She reached behind her head and wondered vaguely what had become of her red hair bow.

An eerie horripilation traveled through her. This vision, this scheme, could it have anything to do with the solution to the problem with the fey that Jariel had set in motion? There was no reason to believe these two things were related, yet she felt certain they were.

Valerie moved to the chair and began adjusting her camera. "Rachel, you can remember Zoë's sandals, right?"

"Of course."

"How well?" drawled Zoë. "Can you remember the soles? The insides?"

Rachel tipped her head back. The soles were easy. She had occasionally been behind Zoë and seen the bottoms as the other girl walked. She had also seen the sandals on the floor in Joy and Zoë's room, so she knew what the inside of the shoe looked like. The only part she could not remember was the lower side of the upper straps.

"Not all but reasonably well. Why?"

"Can you conjure them?" challenged Salome.

Rachel started to laugh, but the others all looked at her expectantly.

"Conjure them?" she cried, pointing at her own chest. "Me?"

The whole group nodded.

"A-ask Sigfried," Rachel cried. "He's a much better conjurer."

"We did." Valerie made a face.

"What happened?" asked Rachel, looking curiously from friend to friend.

Siggy reached up, his fingertips coming together to form an upward beak, the gesture for the cantrip that accompanied conjurations. "Come on, Lucky! Let's make more! How about sandals with wings? Sandals with pointy toe-knives! Oh, I know! Sandals with high-powered heel-rockets attached! They're much better than simple silver sandals!"

"Sandals with dragon scales!" crowed Lucky, flying in a loop and then, as he came around, fixing his eyes on a spot just above Siggy's head.

"*Muria!*" Sigfried cried, pulling his fingers down.

A pair of winged sandals that looked nothing like Zoë's fell down out of a puff of mist in mid-air. Lucky caught them and held them up lovingly. They were both left shoes.

"Our first pair!" the dragon cooed.

"Maybe they can fly," cried Sigfried.

"Shh!" Valerie elbowed him. "You'll wake the nurse."

"I don't think she's here," said Joy. "I saw her talking to Mr. Chanson down by the gym."

"But Siggy, those don't look anything like Zoë's sandals," Rachel said, confused.

"So?" Sigfried shrugged. "These are better."

"See what I mean?" asked Valerie, pointing at her boyfriend.

Rachel sighed. *Boys.*

She closed her eyes and pictured the sandals. She recalled watching Zoë walk and stand. She recalled seeing the sandals lying at rest. Then, biting her lip nervously, she pulled her fingers into a beak and reached up. *"Muria!"*

She pulled the sandals in her mind's eye into the world. As something fell into her hands, she opened one eye and peeked. A perfect copy of Zoë's sandals rested on her hand, except there was something blurry about them, something coming from the lower part of the upper straps. Rachel opened both eyes and looked more closely.

Mist poured from the sandals, dry mist with a faint scent of lilacs and plaster of Paris.

"Mayday! Mayday!" shouted Valerie. "Conjuring mist!"

Everybody panicked. Salome shrieked, jumping up and down. Valerie scampered backwards, falling over Payback, her Norwegian elkhound, who had been behind her. She barreled into an orange curtain. It gave way, dumping her onto the next bed. Joy shrieked, too, but as she was next to Rachel, she breathed in a lungful of the mist and slumped over, asleep.

Zoë shouldered past Joy, her coat over her mouth, and muscled open the window. Siggy grabbed the sandals from Rachel and threw them into the rainy night. Before they hit the ground, Lucky shot forward and breathed a plume of fire. The conjuring mist ignited, burning a weird violet color that emitted a darker smoke, and raindrops sizzled when they met the flames.

With a cry, Rachel dispelled her conjuration. The ball of purple flame with accompanying black smoke burned brightly for an instant and then winked out. Terrified, she checked Joy to make sure she had not been hurt. Wounds taken in conjuring mist could not be healed by magic. There was no sign of damage on the sleeping girl.

Valerie climbed to her feet, pulled the flame-colored curtain back into place, and brushed herself off. "Okay, that could have gone better. I admit it," Valerie said, soothing the agitated Payback. "But you were close. Try again."

"Yeah, nah," Zoë turned back from the window. Something moved strangely under her coat. Pure terror jolted throughout Rachel's body—until she realized it was the quoll. "Maybe this is a bust." She leaned over and shook Joy's shoulder. "Wakie, wakie, sleepyhead."

Joy continued to sleep, her head on Rachel's bed, and she began snoring softly. Rachel was tempted to yell in her ear, revenge for the two times

Joy had woken her, but decided against it. Revenge was petty and did not become a lady.

"That was awesome!" cried Siggy. "Why did you send it away?"

Salome took a deep breath. "Okay, that was almost not boring! Let me move farther away before you try it again." She backed up to the cot across the chamber from Rachel's. "Ready!"

"Are you all bonkers?" cried Rachel. She pulled off the comforter and knelt on the bed. "Except for Zoë's lone sane voice. You want me to do that *again*?"

"We need a conjured pair," Salome explained, "otherwise, we can't commit our crime!"

"We're going to liberate Zoë's shoes," said Valerie.

"Because we need Zoë's shoes if we wish to see Nastasia's vision?" Rachel asked, catching on. The others nodded.

"But...." Rachel threw up her hands. "The idea is crackers from the beginning. Even if I could conjure a solid pair, they would only last twenty-four hours. What good would that do?"

"You underestimate the complexity of Goldilocks's cunning plan," said Sigfried.

"Overly complicated cunning plan," Lucky stated proudly, snaking back to wrap around both Siggy's and Valerie's shoulders.

Valerie held up her camera. "Conjure them and put them on the windowsill. I only need them long enough to take pictures. Worst comes to worst, I send the photos to my friend Wally Wren, and he photoshops out the mist."

Rachel had no idea what she meant, but she had heard of trick photography. She took a deep breath. "Okay. I'll try again. Everyone, step back."

She closed her eyes, taking a moment to calm her jitters. Then, she pictured the silver sandals, the straps over the foot, the wrapping that went to above her ankle. She pictured the unseen parts with the same rough leather as the inside of the back strap. Once she could picture it, she put all the parts together to form a composite whole.

"Okay. Here goes." She crossed her fingers for luck with her left hand and formed the gesture for the cantrip with her right. *"Muria!"*

She opened her eyes. Silver slippers appeared and fell to the bed. Everyone jumped backwards, but no mist issued from them. The shoes bounced on the mattress, glittering in the emerald glow from the globe of healing flame.

Valerie snatched them up and placed them neatly on the comforter. Then, she took pictures of them from every conceivable angle. Her brilliant flash lit the chamber, glistening off planets and fluffy clouds.

"Got 'em!" Valerie announced. "Rachel, you can de-conjure them."

Rachel tried. Nothing happened. "Can't. It's been more than ten minutes."

"On it!" cried Lucky.

He swooped forward, snatched up the sandals, and dropped them in Siggy's hands. Siggy threw one and then the other out the window, shouting, "Pull!"

Salome ran forward again, watching eagerly. Each time Sigfried threw, Lucky incinerated the sandal with a blast of red-orange flame.

Salome clapped at the end. "Bravo! Bravo! Encore! I'm sure we can find other things to incinerate. My math manual? Belladonna Marley's stupid poodle?"

"I'm game," announced Lucky.

"What now?" Rachel asked Valerie and Zoë, ignoring the fire show. "How are photographs going to help?

Salome turned to Rachel. "That's where I come in. Valerie will develop the photos, and I will send them to my parents' shoe factory. The foreman adores me. He makes me anything I ask. He'll make us a pair of sandals that look exactly like Zoë's!"

"That's where Lucky comes in," Siggy announced. "He's going to sneak into the dean's office, all invisible-like, and switch the fakes for the real ones. I know the dean can normally see him, but if he takes an elf-herb chameleon potion, uses his natural invisibility, and makes sure she's not there, it should work."

"As long as sandals are there, the dean isn't likely to notice the difference," said Valerie.

"Wow." Rachel considered. "That's actually brilliant."

"That's my Goldilocks!" Siggy put his arm around his girlfriend's shoulder.

Joy lifted her head sleepily and yawned. "Sorry, what'd I miss?"

Chapter Nine:
Damaged Souls

The next morning, Nurse Moth removed the bandage from Rachel's arm. Fetching her flute, she played a lilting tune. Green sparkles played over the wounded area, accompanied by the scent of freshly baked bread.

The wounds closed. Rachel lifted her arm, running her hand over the newly healed skin and kneaded her flesh where the barghest had bitten her. There was no pain and no scar. The only scar on her arm was on the side of her right wrist, the one she had received from the blood-brother ceremony with Siggy. Rachel was still grateful to Nurse Moth for making that cut form a scar. It was important for blood siblings to have matching scars from where they cut themselves during the ceremony. Had the nurse used magic to heal that wound perfectly, it would have ruined everything.

When the nurse finally released her, Rachel trudged back to her dorm through the cold drizzle. The driving winds blew sideways, so that the large black umbrellas that hung brim-to-brim in a continuous line over the gravel pathways hardly protected those walking beneath them from the elements. She felt sorry for the proctors and Agents stationed outside on guard duty, watching for wayward fey. When she saw her favorite proctor, the handsome, young Mr. Fuentes, standing with his collar turned up against the cold and a single, silver-rimmed umbrella floating over his head, she dashed into the dining hall, poured a mug of hot chocolate, and brought it out to where he stood close to the edge of the forest near Dare Hall. He thanked her gratefully, blowing on it and warming his cold hands against the hot mug.

Arriving home more wet than not, she fed Mistletoe and took a shower. Then she set out to breakfast and onto class. The day remained dark and rainy. Lightning danced overhead in balls and forks, lighting up the otherwise dim campus with brilliant white flashes as the lightning imps expressed their displeasure at the death of their lord. In the bright moments, Agents could be seen standing guard all over the campus, their tricorne hats, Inverness cloaks, and fulgurator's staffs singling them out from the tutors and proctors.

The next few days passed slowly. The weather remained bad; lightning and thunder became constant companions. The huge floating umbrellas seemed to have become a permanent fixture over the walkways. In Language, they learned *Argos*, the Glepnir Band cantrip, which Gaius had already taught Rachel. Since the class was Language, with an emphasis on early writings and some Shakespeare along with a bit of the Original Tongue, what she most wanted to know—how to improve her accuracy with that cantrip—was not discussed. They also learned *Kefwyth*, the Word of Summoning, and *Endro*, the Word of Revealing, a cantrip that revealed hidden things, such as concealed doors. Rachel wished there were a cantrip that would reveal the answers to questions that stumped her.

Right when Music was becoming nightmarish for Rachel, who was falling behind because of her resistance to practicing her flute, Miss Cyrene began instructing them in the bedazzle hex. Hexes were short, just three notes, and Rachel was good at them. What was more, she already knew this one. Hard times would come again when they moved on to summoning Asrai, but for now, Rachel felt like a condemned prisoner who had unexpectedly received a reprieve.

In Art, they began a section on how to conjure hollow objects, like boxes or simple teapots. It was exactly the skill Rachel could have used the previous day for the sandals. During free time at the end of class, she folded an origami griffin out of gold foil paper. At dinner, she gave it to Pete Komarek as a thank-you for having saved her from Abraham Van Helsing. He received it graciously.

In Geometry, they were finishing *Book VI* of Euclid. They also learned how throwing down seeds, such as flax or peony, compelled many kinds of vampires or undead to pause and count them. Rachel, Siggy, and Zoë exchanged smiles. They had proven this one the previous fall when they used a packet of peony seeds to stall the attacking child skeletons in Tunis.

In Science, they were still on quicksilver shoes. Siggy was running down the halls at high speeds, and Nastasia and Joy now had slippers that moved a third faster than normal, but Rachel could get only one of her shoes to work, which left her moving rapidly in a circle.

Wulfgang Starkadder normally did top-notch work in class, but instead of working on his shoes, he kept bursting into laughter, as if some cosmic joke had just been played and only he knew the punch line. Wednesday afternoon at lunch, Rachel mentioned this to Gaius.

Gaius pursed his lips. "I am not sure Starkadder took the information very well."

Rachel sipped her juice. "Maybe Wulf's suffering from Metaplutonian shock. Too much strangeness too quickly. Maybe he'll end up as crazy as Sigfried."

Gaius nodded. "Maybe. It was a rather large amount of information."

"Siggy should talk with him," Rachel said thoughtfully. "They're kind of friends, and Siggy has been through it before—discovering the world is much stranger than he'd thought—since he was raised Unwary and only learned about the existence of magic recently."

"That might help," Gaius agreed, "though the idea of Mr. Smith making any situation calmer is a bit hard to swallow. As to Wulfgang, I am not sure if the Wise have a more flexible worldview or less. You'd think it would be more, all things considered. But he is royalty. He was raised differently, I assume. I have no idea how much of an impact what I told him will have."

Rachel sighed. "Why is everything much more complicated than it needs to be?"

As she was preparing to leave the dining hall and return to class, Sigfried grabbed her arm. His grip was so tight it hurt. She turned to scold him, but her words died on her lips when she saw his face. His expression looked odd. Valerie was with him. She was as pale as a sheet as she stared into her calling card. The ordinarily intrepid reporter girl looked unnerved.

"Siggy? What's wrong?" Rachel asked, suddenly frightened.

He moved close to her and growled in a low voice. "Look at your calling card."

Lucky snaked around the group of them, looking this way and that as if trying to catch an assailant or perhaps protect them from ambush. Rachel pulled out her own calling card. The green glass cleared, showing a conversation in the open courtyard behind the dining room, an image of what Sigfried watched with the magical all-seeing eye amulet he wore hidden beneath his robes. In the picture, Agent Standish spoke with Agent Caldor, from the New York Wisecraft office, and Maverick Badger, the grizzled head of security at Roanoke. Agent Caldor had fought Veltdammerung with them in September and nearly died. Rachel was glad to see he looked well.

"... come here?" Standish was saying in his lilting accent. "That was what she did last time, but, of course, we weren't onto her yet."

"How long has she been free?" grunted Badger.

Agent Caldor replied, "She escaped Sunday morning. Overwhelmed her guards and vanished into New York City. She had outside help."

"Agent Browne and the Strega kid went with her, you say?' asked Badger.

"Yes to Browne," said Caldor. "They paused to break him out. The Strega kid we had already let go. Mordeau insisted she had him under a geas, so we couldn't press charges. Not sure who authorized releasing him, though. The Grand Inquisitor was in a fine state when he found out. He'd wanted to grill the kid."

Badger scowled. Rachel received the impression he was scowling at Jonah Strega, for the terrible things he did, not at Cain March, for wanting to interrogate the terrifying young man.

"Mordeau seemed obsessed with finding the person who helped Dean Moth catch her," said Caldor. "Did you all ever figure out who that was?"

"No luck there," growled Badger. "No one ever came forward."

Rachel swallowed. Mordeau was obsessed with finding *her*? Luckily, as far as Rachel knew, there was no way for her to do that. Unless Gaius tattled, which he would never do, so she was safe. Though the memory of how the barghests had looked right at her, as if she were their prey, sent a shiver down her spine.

Agent Standish shook his head, dreadlocks flying. "Mordeau's bad news."

"If she comes here, we'll be ready for her," growled Maverick Badger.

The three men parted ways. The surface of the card returned to a green-tinted glass. Rachel slipped it into her robe, her heart pounding.

"Dr. Mordeau's free?" she whispered, shocked.

This must have been the emergency that had called her father and the other Agents away after the barghest attack. But why had no one told the students? She understood they did not want to spread panic and that parents were already concerned about the loose fey. But shouldn't a person such as herself be notified so that she could be alert? After all that had happened in September, Dr. Mordeau now disliked Rachel personally. It might be nice to know of the possible danger.

On the other hand, there already were Agents all over campus. Would it really help to have the student body more anxious and starting at every shadow?

With a shiver, Rachel glanced around the dining room and thought back, matching people's bodies to their shadows, looking for Dr. Mordeau's wraith-shadows. She did not see anything out of place.

Aloud she said, "Strega was not geased. He did those things of his own free will."

"I have some business to take care of," said Sigfried, his voice cold and hard. "I'll be back tomorrow, or in a week. Come on, Lucky."

Lucky wrapped around his master like a war scarf. He looked fierce and resolute.

"Boyfriend of mine, no, you don't!" commanded Valerie.

"I have to... do my laundry," Siggy said, trying to look innocent, "with my knife." He made a stabbing motion over and over.

"Sigfried Smith," Valerie said, her blue eyes steely, "I need you to do something for me."

"I am about to. Kill the bastard who hurt you!"

"Not that."

"Then what?"

"I need you to make me a promise."

"What about?" Siggy looked wary. He reluctantly lowered his imaginary knife.

"That you won't try to hunt down Jonah Strega."

"Oh, I won't *try*!" Siggy's eyes glinted dangerously.

"Siggy, I am serious! I want you to promise to leave him alone. Not to seek revenge."

"Why?" Sigfried had a crazy gleam in his eye that Rachel did not like.

Valerie's bottom lip wobbled. Rachel suspected that she knew how the other girl was feeling. Valerie did not want her boyfriend to get hurt. She could not tell him that, however, because he would take it the wrong way and rush off and do something inexpressibly foolish.

Valerie looked right and left. She grabbed Sigfried's wrist with one hand and Rachel's with the other and dragged them out of the dining room, down a hall, and into an empty room beneath one of the spiral staircases.

"Look, I didn't want to say this in front of Rachel," she began.

"Me?" Rachel squeaked, shocked.

Valerie continued, "Because—well, we all know how she feels about changing memories but...." She took a deep breath. "Right now, I don't remember what happened."

Oh. Rachel swallowed. Maybe Valerie had been right not to tell her. The hallway swam in her vision. She took a deep breath and pushed her discomfort aside. This was about Valerie.

"What do you mean?" Sigfried asked.

"My parents had a long talk with the Wisecraft. My father pointed out that it was their fault I remembered the...." Valerie's voice caught. "... the rape part. I wouldn't remember if it hadn't been for their stupid truth spell. So he asked them to make me forget again. He thought my having to think about it was... too much for a teenage girl.

"The Agents explained that I couldn't forget forever. If I tried, problems could develop. At some point, I will need to process the experience and deal with it, but... they could make me forget for a time. Until I turn eighteen. I realize I'm putting off the inevitable, but my parents and I felt I might handle it better later. So it seemed like a wise idea."

"Okay," Sigfried scowled. "That makes a stupid kind of sense."

Rachel did not trust herself to speak. She hated the idea of tampering with memory with a visceral hatred. In this case, however, could she blame Valerie?

"However," Valerie continued, "and this is the kicker: if anything traumatic happens involving... anything related—*like if my boyfriend goes to jail for killing him*—it will break the memory seal and bring it all crashing back.

"So, for me, I want you not to do anything that might bring that son-of-a..." she paused and swallowed, "back to my mind." Her eyes flashed with unexpected heat. "Promise me!"

Defeated Sigfried raised his hand, palm out, as Rachel had done when swearing before the Raven. "I will not hunt down... the vermin. So swears Smith."

Broom practice on Wednesday was held in the gym due to the poor weather. Rachel aided her boss, Mr. Chanson the handsome P.E. teacher, by sticking with the stragglers while he organized relays for the faster kids. The group of stragglers was much smaller than it had been in the fall. Rachel had successfully helped a number of them to become decent fliers.

After work, Rachel stayed behind to discuss an idea for Gaius's birthday present with Mr. Chanson, who promised to help with her plan. Again, he complimented her on how well she flew for someone who had only been flying for two years now, come the end of March. Once that was done,

Rachel headed to her dorm, trudging along beneath the umbrellas, nodding occasionally at someone coming the other way. The silvery glow from the J-shaped handles and from the umbrella rims lent an eeriness to the deepening twilight.

As she trudged, she contemplated her boss's compliment. When he had said something similar back in September, she had not taken it very seriously. But now that she had been assisting in teaching flying for eight months, she could see clearly that most of the really good flyers had considerably more experience than she did. For the first time, she herself began wondering why it was that she had picked up broom flying so quickly.

She was quite lucky to have Mr. Chanson as a boss. He was such a kind and mild-mannered man. She felt grateful that she had not had trouble obeying Mr. Chanson's order not to fly in and out of windows. She admired her boss and did not want to hurt his feelings. Still, she wished she could retreat to her hexagonal room with the sofa, or at least slip in and retrieve the plushy lion Sandra had bought for her during her visit to London. Rachel had considered landing on the roof and climbing in the window, but now with so many eyes keeping a watch around campus, she feared her chances of doing so unobserved were slim.

The temperature was dropping, the rain turning to driving sleet. Rachel picked up speed, eager to get inside. Two of her fellow classmates whizzed by her in their quicksilver shoes. Rachel sighed. She could put her one finished quicksilver shoe on, too—and move very quickly in a circle—but that would not get her home any quicker.

Ivan Romanov came across the grass, sleet pelting onto his spiky, dirty blond hair, as he held his mortar cap with its bronze tassel under his coat to protect it. A lanky young man with a rather well-formed jaw, he slid to a stop just in front of her.

"Mini Griffin! This is for you."

He handed her a letter sealed with pink sealing wax, exactly the same color as Magical Australia's money. In the flash of the next lightning bolt, she could see that the seal pressed into the wax formed a wombat.

"It's from Father," said Ivan. "No idea what it's about."

"Oh. I wrote him a letter," cried Rachel.

"Did you? How enterprising. Good things, I hope."

"I think so. I was trying to help."

"I have no idea what Father has to say, but while I have you here, I wanted to thank you."

"Oh, what for?"

"For being such a good friend to Nastasia. It can't be easy. She was always a bit... stiff-necked, but ever since her injury.... Well, I'm sure you understand. Either way, I just wanted to let you know that I appreciate it. Alexis and Alex do, too."

Rachel squirmed, feeling guilty. She had been planning to demote Nastasia from best friend to something much lower on her loyalty totem pole. Hopefully, he would blame her reaction on the cold weather.

"I don't know what you mean... injury?"

Ivan peered at her face. "She was burned by phantom fire. You were there, right?"

"Yes, I know about that, but...."

"Don't you know what phantom fire does?"

"It causes terrible pain, right?"

"That's not the half of it. Don't get me wrong. Pain is bad, but it ends. When it's over, it's over," Ivan explained. "But phantom fire's not like that. It causes pain because it damages your spirit—your soul."

"What?" Rachel cried.

Thunder cracked across the sky. The umbrellas overhead trembled.

Ivan nodded grimly. "It eats at the soul and leaves spiritual burns. Souls do recover, but it takes time. Before they recover, the person has less spiritual flexibility. Nastasia was always a bit... prim, but the effect of the phantom fire has made that far more pronounced. She's more of a stick-in-the-mud than she used to be, less able to adapt or change."

"Oh," said Rachel in a small voice She recalled that Gaius had told her, back on that first Friday in September as they tried to get back into Drake Hall to save her friends, that phantom fire burned the soul. She had thought that just meant that it hurt more.

"That's why we're so grateful you put up with her. This kind of injury can make a person rather... wearing."

"I... am glad I can help," Rachel whispered in a small voice. "I wish I could do more."

Ivan touched her fondly on the shoulder. "You're doing just fine."

Upon reaching her room, Rachel saw that she still had an hour before she needed to meet Gaius to study advanced algebra. It was so kind of him to teach her the more advanced mathematics. She loved the chance this gave her to spend time with him. Still, it would be a while before she had to leave to meet him. Sitting down on her bed, she opened the letter Ivan had given her. It read:

> *Dear Lady Rachel,*
> *Thank you for your thoughtful letter.*
> *It seems everyone and his sister wants to inform me of how poorly*
> *Romulus has treated Alexis. You would be surprised by how many*
> *people have brought this to my attention.*
> *Nonetheless, I appreciate your concern for my family.*
> *Your friend,*
> *Andre III, King of Magical Australia*

Rachel smiled, folded the letter, and stuck it among her books. She was touched by the signature: *your friend*. It made her very glad that she had written; however, it also made her feel even worse about the news she had just received. Nastasia was injured—less resilient and more stiff-necked—*because of her*.

It had been Rachel who had insisted on running into battle; Rachel who had wanted to follow Dr. Mordeau to save Gaius. Nastasia had not wanted to go. It had been Rachel, again, who had left her friend in danger-ous Drake Hall while she flew away. True, she had done it to warn people and may have saved lives—she had definitely saved Mr. Fisher's life.

Still, Nastasia would not have been injured were it not for Rachel's recklessness. Nastasia had wanted to obey the tutors and remain in the infirmary, but Rachel would not listen. So Nastasia had come along, out of friendship. And become of this, the princess had been attacked by the now-dead Remus Starkadder and had become the annoying, over-bearing, rule hound she was today.

Rachel hung her head and sighed. She could not, in good conscience, abandon Nastasia now.

Chapter Ten:
Twelve Pairs of Gloves

Thursday was Leap Day, and the next day would be Kalends. Classes ended at noon, and the afternoon was given over to festivities and games, or would have been, were it not for the threat of rogue fey and the terrible weather that lightning imps had been throwing at the island for four days—not to mention the danger of Dr. Mordeau seeking revenge, which still had not been announced. After talk of canceling the festivities, it was decided they could be held in the gym.

The Knights of Walpurgis meeting that evening had also been canceled, to Rachel's dismay. She did note that the next meeting would fall on March seventh, Gaius's birthday. They would finally hold the elections for second-in-command, the position they had nominated candidates for at the very first meeting she had attended, back during the first week of school.

She hoped Gaius would win. It would make a fitting present.

Freed from the need to run the Knights that evening, Vlad had invited his people to lunch in New York City and had obtained permission for them to go. Rachel, who had not been invited, ate with her classmates. The dining hall had been hung with laurel boughs in preparation for Kalends—technically, the Kalends of March. There were no Vestals and no Eternal Flame at Roanoke, but all the hearth fires would be extinguished and relit. A special holding pen had been prepared in the menagerie for the hearth salamanders, where they could cavort together. They would be gathered up from the dorms and taken to the pen tonight. Everyone was hoping the weather would remain on the warmer side for one more day.

If it fell below freezing, with no hearth fires and no salamanders, it would be one cold night.

In the morning, a real Vestal Virgin would come from Rome and rekindle the fires. If they were lucky, she would come very early, and the heat would be off for only a short time. If they were not lucky, it would be a very cold day.

The Die Horribly Debate Club discussed this over lunch, amidst the booms of thunder. Kalends was a sacred day, even among the Unwary; so even Sigfried and Valerie knew it marked the beginning of the nineteen-day pilgrimage of the monks of the god Mars. These monks might choose to join the Vestals and visit the school, or they might not. Every year, their travels were different.

Rachel returned to the kitchen for a second helping of French toast. On the way back to her table, she stopped off to say hi to both Agent Standish and Mr. Fuentes, but neither of them had received any update as to what the Wisecraft intended to do about the failure of the Roanoke Covenant. She paused with the gentlemen for a few minutes, chatting with Carlos Fuentes about the final outcome of the recent Winter Olympics. She considered surprising them by revealing that she knew about Dr. Mordeau's escape, to try and finagle additional information out of them, but decided against it. With a sigh, she returned to her friends.

Rachel, Siggy, and Valerie, by silent agreement, had not mentioned the escape of Dr. Mordeau to their other friends. Rachel had shared the information with Gaius but had been a bit disappointed when he told her that Von Dread already knew. Not only was she disappointed that she had missed out on the pleasure of revealing this astonishing bit of news, but also it smarted that Vlad had learned the information, most likely from his father, yet neither he nor Gaius had seen fit to share it with her.

When she sat down again, her friends were still discussing Leap Day and Kalends.

"Isn't it funny," Joy asked the princess, "that all the big holidays whose names have to do with the calendar are in March? My sisters and I always laugh about that."

"I'm not certain I perceive your meaning," the princess replied amiably as she sipped her tea. "Can you elucidate?"

"If that means *make more clear*, yeah. If it means elude something, probably not," Joy quipped back. Then, she grinned. "Just kidding. I know what *elucidate* means. Yes. Kalends is a holiday we celebrate on the first of March, but it really means 'the first of.' In the old days, like Roman times, every month had a kalends."

"It's also the origin of the word *calendar*," interjected Rachel.

A bolt of lightning jagged by the tall windows, illuminating the dining hall, followed by a clap of thunder. When they could hear again, Joy nodded. "Then there's Ides. Ides means the middle of the month, so every month also had an ides. But we only celebrate the Ides of March."

"Ah, so true!" Nastasia said. "I believe you and your sisters are onto something." She gave a sweet smile. "Perhaps it's a plot."

"A plot by March!" cried Joy, delighted.

"Is that Cain March?" asked Valerie. "If so, he may be a bit older than I thought."

"Cain March, the Grand Inquisitor?" Zoë asked, sitting with her chair tilted back and her feet resting on the table. "The final authority for all law enforcement in the World of the Wise? Yeah, nah. I bet he's secretly immortal. He's certainly scary enough."

"Now, now," Nastasia admonished gently. "Mr. March is a family friend. I would prefer you not disparage him."

"I doubt the Grand Inquisitor would think saying he was scary was disparaging," countered Zoë. "He clearly works at it."

"Works… as in standing before a mirror and practicing looking bone-chillingly terrifying?" asked Valerie, mimicking gazing into a mirror.

"Exactly," replied Zoë with a decisive nod.

"I don't think he's so bad," said Rachel. "He's my father's boss. And his wife is very nice. Remember, we met her in dreamland when we were escaping from the Veltdammerung cultists at Beaumont."

"Oh, we did." Zoë shuddered. "At the time, I didn't really make the jump from Eve's mom to 'Wife of the *Grand Inquisitor.*' I had other things on my mind—like that I might be *dying.*"

"Speaking of the Ides of March." Valerie stood up and took a picture of them. Zoë caught sight of the camera and threw her hands up in front of her face. Her chair came down upon all four legs with a bang. "Isn't that the first day of spring break?"

Rachel nodded. "Roanoke Academy Spring Equinox Break begins at sundown before the Ides and runs through Fey New Year, which is known to us mortals as April Fool's Day."

"Best day of the year," quipped Siggy.

"It's the boss's birthday," explained Lucky.

"We'll have to do something special for your birthday, Siggy," Rachel cried happily. "You are coming home with me for the break, right?"

"If you are sure you have the room—for Lucky and me and our gold," said Siggy.

"Yeah, can't leave our gold behind," said Lucky.

"Oh, we have the room," laughed Rachel.

Rachel's older sister Laurel sauntered by their table. Instead of her usual subfusc uniform, she was dressed in a red knit sweater that hugged her curves and a white poodle skirt with a bright scarlet petticoat peeking out beneath. In her hand was an English-language issue of *La Bougie du Sapeur*, the French satirical newspaper released only once every four years, on February 29th.

Rachel gawked at the red petticoat. "Are you planning to propose to Charlie?"

Laurel, who was brimming over with good spirits, rolled her eyes. "Certainly not! He has to ask me—when the time is right. But I could use twelve new pairs of gloves." She surveyed the lunchroom. "Whom should I ask?"

"Oh!" Rachel looked around, too. Lightning outside played a pale light over those dining. "It has to be someone who will say no. Otherwise, you'll find yourself in no end of hot water. And it has to be someone who knows that if he says no, he has to buy you gloves. Otherwise, he will just think you've lost your mind."

Laurel tapped the newspaper against her palm. "I could ask... or maybe.... Oh, what about.... Hmm. If I ask more than one boy, would you like some? I hardly have room for twenty-four or thirty-six pairs of gloves."

Thunder shook the glass in the windows.

"No. It's all right." Rachel resisted the urge to giggle. "I don't want your blood gloves."

"Blood gloves?" Siggy cried. "Are those gloves that have been drenched in blood, or gloves made of blood?"

His girlfriend quipped, "I think they're blood gloves like blood money. Am I right?"

Rachel nodded.

"Okay, I give," said Valerie. "What are the gloves for?"

"There's a rule in the World of the Wise—in some mundane places, too," Rachel explained, "that a girl is allowed to propose on Leap Day. But she has to wear a red petticoat, and if the boy turns her down, he has to buy her twelve pairs of gloves."

"Why gloves?" Valerie frowned.

"To cover the shame of not wearing a wedding ring." Laurel held up her hands and wiggled her fingers. "Okay, I've picked my first victim, er target. Wish me luck. Ta, ta!"

"Your sister is strange." Zoë now lay stretched across several chairs, her arms crossed behind her head. "And coming from me, that's saying something."

"She thrives on chaos," Rachel replied mildly, watching Laurel saunter over to some poor unsuspecting schlub. "I wonder if Vladimir left campus precisely so that no one could propose to him. Were he here, he might find himself buying a great number of gloves."

Zoë shrugged. "Eh, Bavaria can afford it."

As the group of friends walked under the floating umbrellas and onto the bridge that crossed the reflecting lake, Nastasia asked, "Whatever happened to the plan to go to dreamland? I wanted to show you all my vision."

"Oh! That's right!" Rachel cried, careful to stay beneath the silvery rims of the umbrellas as the rain poured down in torrents. "I never did get to hear about it."

"That's because when I went to tell the others, you were nowhere to be found," the princess said tartly.

Rachel nearly abandoned her new resolve to be nicer to Nastasia. "That's because I was in the infirmary. I had been bitten by a barghest!"

"Bitten by a barghest!" Siggy cried. "Did you fight barghests without me? Why didn't you call us?" He gestured from himself to Lucky. "We missed out on stakings and bitings?"

"My father took me to the river to ask me some questions about the death of the Heer—"

"I missed out on that, too!" Sigfried exclaimed.

"—and we were attacked. Agents Standish and Garbarino were with us."

"And they let you get bitten?" Zoë asked disapprovingly. "Some defenders of the weak."

Lightning lit the sky in long, jagged, branching lines. By mutual consent, their group began walking toward the gym, where the Leap Year festivities were to be held.

"I don't think they knew I was bitten. There were dozens and dozens of barghests. We had to fight them for a long time."

"Worse and worse!" moaned Siggy.

"Oh, Siggy, you're so funny!" giggled Joy. She gave Sigfried a light punch in the arm.

"And what about you?" Rachel demanded, turning on her blood-brother. "Why did you punch Abraham Van Helsing? What were you thinking?"

"I was thinking I wanted to punch him, really hard," Sigfried replied simply.

"I was thinking that, too," said Lucky.

"Why?" cried Rachel.

"He tried to stake my blood-sister. What kind of blood-brother would I be if I couldn't protect my tiny miniature, minuscule sister? A stake-wielding interloper will think twice before he has second thoughts about attacking us! We're a team!"

"A trio!" agreed the dragon, nodding his head in time with his boy's. "Three sides of the same coin!"

"But he didn't know it was me because it was dark," objected Rachel, struggling to follow their logic. If they were the head and tails of the coin, did that make her the tiny rim?

Sigfried crossed his arms. "That's no excuse."

A thunderclap rolled over the landscape. It was so loud that Rachel and Nastasia grabbed each other in surprise. Valerie grabbed Siggy. So did Joy, which earned her an arch glance from Valerie. Chagrined, Joy let go of Siggy's arm and grabbed Zoë.

"About your vision?" asked Rachel, when the sound of driving rain could be heard again.

Nastasia nodded serenely. "I had a vision the afternoon of the twenty-fifth, the day after the ball. In it, the students were in costume. I don't remember those particular costumes from the ball, but I would know them if I saw them again. They stole one of the rowboats with eyes and rowed across the river. Only in the vision, the shore looked different. High and rocky. That's neither here nor there," she added. "The important thing is: They had the Kadderstar."

"What?" Rachel cried, stopping in mid-stride. This caused people behind her to bump into her and nearly knock her over. Siggy grabbed her and yanked her out of the line of foot traffic—and into the rain. This saved her from a bruising but got her wet. "Are you sure?"

"Not entirely," the princess admitted. "In the vision, the gem looked silvery; but it was exactly the same size, shape, and cut. I have never seen another like that."

Rachel stepped back under the umbrellas and followed her friends. She thought back and exclaimed with surprise, "I have."

But the others were not listening.

"Do you think someone stole the Kadderstar?" Valerie asked, eyes bright as they stepped off the bridge onto the commons. "That huge purple gem Romulus Starkadder wears? That would be the story of the year! Isn't whoever has it officially the heir to the Transylvanian Throne?"

They continued under the huge black umbrellas along the gravel path to the gymnasium.

"I jump to no conclusion, but it's possible," Nastasia replied slowly. "That was the night of the altercation between Romulus and Von Dread. I didn't recognize the students in the vision, so they might be from Drake, as I have had the least interactions with those from that hall."

Joy jumped up and down, brimming over with excitement. "And you think that Von Dread sent his thugs to steal Romulus's ring of power and carry it away?"

Nastasia said primly, "I make no accusations."

Rachel objected, "But didn't you say the vision happened the night of the ball? Vladimir was at the dance, right? In plain sight."

"The vision took place at dawn, the next morning. At least, the sun was rising," said Nastasia. "You would not be aware of this because you had departed, but he and Mr. Valiant left the ballroom immediately after you, and they did not return. Plenty of time to pull off a caper."

"But that'd bec—." Rachel clamped her mouth shut.

She started to say they had left to listen over the bracelet so they could come to her and Sandra's rescue if anything went awry—which must have been what they were doing since the bracelet was vibrating and yet they were absolutely silent. If they had been dancing or talking, she would have heard—but explaining would mean revealing the existence of the black bracelets, which she was loath to do.

"I only report what I observed," Nastasia replied placidly. "You place far too much faith in Mr. Von Dread. He has already proven himself to be unscrupulous once."

Rachel scowled. She did not believe for an instant that Vlad had instructed his minions to steal the Kadderstar. There would have been rumors if Transylvania's irreplaceable purple jewel had gone missing. Besides, she recalled once having seen several other gems with exactly that cut. One had been purple, the exact shade of the Kadderstar, but another had been silver.

Nastasia continued, "Auriel told me that my visions would...."

Rachel leaned forward. "Who?"

Nastasia looked surprised. "Oh, didn't I tell you? During the ball, I spoke to Auriel, the angel who is responsible for sending my visions."

"No." Rachel blinked. "You didn't."

"The angel appeared as a very young man in a domino mask with remarkably blue eyes."

"I... danced with him," Rachel murmured, startled.

Why hadn't this Auriel spoken to her? Embarrassed, Rachel ducked her head. She refused to stoop to coveting her friend's good fortune.

The princess continued, "I was told that it was my upright moral character that led to my being chosen to receive these visions and that Heaven was pleased with me."

"Heaven?" asked Valerie.

The princess shrugged. "A place? The sky? A person's name? It was unclear. What was clear was that some beings in some upper place were impressed by my devotion to duty, loyalty, honor, and truthfulness."

Great, Rachel thought glumly. *Now Nastasia was going to be even more insufferable.*

Arriving at the gym, Rachel excused herself to go to the loo. Instead, she slipped into the broom closet. Away from prying eyes, she touched her black bracelet and murmured, "Jariel, what was the name of your sister? The one who was hiding from you?"

The Raven's voice sounded beside her ear. "Auriel."

"Nastasia says she talked to an angel named Auriel. Only it wasn't a girl. It was a young man in a domino mask. He had very blue eyes and gull wings. I danced with him, too."

"Ah. I thank you, Rachel Griffin," Jariel said, a touch of amusement in his voice. "I am gratified to learn that my sister was not hiding from me."

"What do you mean?" Rachel asked curiously.

"It was a masquerade, was it not?" He sounded almost merry. "She came in disguise—as one of our brothers."

The rain fell steadily, punctuated by lightning and thunder. Despite this, the afternoon was spent in pleasant entertainment, mainly board games and simple group activities. The Dee Hall students won at Scrabble, and the MacDannans beat everyone else at chess.

At dinner that night, Laurel strolled by the table and handed Rachel five pairs of ladies' gloves and one pair of warm winter mittens. The gloves were in a range of colors: white, cream, red, blue, and tan. The white and the cream were long evening gloves. The rest were short. She gave Rachel a casual wave-salute and sauntered off, carrying her own pile of gloves, which looked to Rachel like far more than a dozen, possibly more than two dozen.

Ivan Romanov dropped by the table where Rachel and her friends sat eating to talk to his youngest sister. While he was speaking with Nastasia, Freka Starkadder strolled up to him. The Transylvanian princess had an almost feral beauty. Her straight oak-brown bangs hung over her intensely brown eyes. She brushed them to one side.

"Romanov, a moment of your time?" Freka practically purred.

"Ah, Freka." Ivan glanced up from where he had been standing beside his sister, one leg resting on an empty chair. "Looks like we won't be related after all," he said cheerfully. "My father nixed our younger siblings hooking up." He patted Nastasia on the head and gestured at Wulfgang, who sat at a nearby table with Seth Peregrine and Enoch Smithwyck. "And my mother nixed Romulus marrying Alexis—for which, I must say—we are all grateful."

"Yes. About that." Freka voice was low and inviting, her wolfish eyes dancing. "And I have an idea. Our parents are so eager for an alliance, and it is, after all, Leap Day."

"I beg your pardon?" Ivan straightened up, surprised. He accidentally kicked the chair under his foot, which fell over with a bang.

She batted her wolfish eyes. "Ivan Romanov, would you...."

In one motion, Ivan leapt forward and pressed a finger against her lips, silencing her.

Freka's face crumpled. Her complexion grew blotchy. Rachel felt bad for her. Clearly, she felt she was being humiliated. She took a step backward.

"Oh, right!" Freka snapped, her voice cutting, "Magical Australia's too poor to pay for a pair of gloves, much less twelve. That's why your parents came crawling to us. Your currenc—"

Her voice trailed off, because Ivan was standing very close to her. He loomed above her, staring down into her eyes with an unnervingly steady gaze. Reaching out, he took both of her hands into his. She looked rapidly from his hands to his face, confused and a little frightened.

"My dear Freka," Ivan spoke elegantly in his Magical Australia accent, "no future queen of mine need do the proposing. Assuming our families agree—which we know they will...."

In front of the entire dining hall, Ivan Romanov, Crown Prince of Magical Australia dropped onto one knee before the eldest princess of Transylvania, still holding her hands in his. Freka gasped, her face now very pale. Her chest rose and fell with the rapidity of her breathing.

"Princess Freka Starkadder,"—he gazed steadily up into her eyes—"will you do me the honor of becoming my bride?"

Freka gasped with joy. She cried out an answer, but it could not be heard over the cheering of the crowd.

Chapter Eleven:
A Very Influential Fairy

THE NIGHT WAS COLD, WITH NO HEARTH FIRES OR SALAMANDERS TO WARM the dorms. Rachel lay shivering even with her comforter. She pulled Mistletoe under her covers and tucked them close around them, trying to build up some heat. Finally, she had to slip out of bed and find a pair of sweatpants to put on under her flannel nightgown.

That worked, a little.

The next day was dreary and icy. The majority of the Kalends activities were canceled, though some intrepid souls did bundle up and go out in the sleet to wait for the Vestal Virgins. Rachel spent the morning reading and drawing pictures. She had been keeping up with her drawing during her classes, whenever the tutors reviewed material she had already memorized, and she was pleased with her progress; however, there were things she could not seem to master. She resolved to speak to her Art tutor about them at her next opportunity.

Around noon, just when she was thinking of going out for lunch, the lockdown warning began pealing out from the six bell towers atop Roanoke Hall. She caught only the briefest glimpse of four Agents in their Inverness cloaks squaring off against a giant winged and tailed frog before the shutters slammed closed. Rachel sighed.

Really, they *had* to do something about all these fey.

If the Agents could not solve the problem, the students would have to take up the matter themselves. Despite her vow the night she was nearly staked and her conversation with Jariel, Rachel had been secretly hoping the Wisecraft would solve the problem without help from her, but, alas, that had not yet happened. She made up her mind that as soon as the lockdown ended she would go to the library and see what she could learn about covenants with the fey.

Late that afternoon, the Vestal finally came. Despite the driving sleet, Rachel joined the crowd gathered on the commons. She had seen Vestals many times. The Duke of Devon was responsible for distributing the newly kindled fire to one-eighth of Great Britain. Thus, Gryphon-on-Dart was a stop on the Vestals' procession. Before she came to Roanoke, however, she had not known that her grandmother had been a Vestal Virgin before Amelia Abney-Hastings quit the order to marry Rachel's grandfather. The event now held more significance for her.

The Vestal Virgin floated upon a flying umbrella platform held up by two white umbrellas, the rims of which gave off a faint golden glow. She wore a long white pleated *stola*, her hair covered by a white shoulder-length shawl with a fringe of red tassels—the same garments sacred virgins had worn since time immemorial—and held before her a simple Roman terracotta lamp that burned with the gold-tinged white fire of the Eternal Flame.

Rachel eyed the small, flattish lamp with interest. There were two such lamps in her house, one carved in the shape of a dragon with a duck on its back, the other bearing the image of a man riding a gryphon. As children, she and Peter had pretended these were Aladdin's lamp and rubbed them in hopes of producing genies. One time, her grandmother had caught them at it, snatched the lamps away, and chased them from the drawing room. Only now did Rachel realize these objects must have been keepsakes from her grandmother's former life.

As she shivered in the rain, she imagined being a grandmother—once the children she and Gaius would have had grown up to have children of their own—and finding her grandchildren playing with the mementos of her life as an adventurer librarian of the Library of All Worlds, or whatever her future held. She liked to think that she would be kinder to her future descendants.

Beside the Vestal on the floating platform, an acolyte carried a second earthen pot with coals from the sacred fire in the Temple of Vesta that the Vestals had extinguished during Candle Dark in December. It had been relit the next morning using a specially shaped brass pot that gathered and magnified sunlight, focusing it on a single spot where dry kindling could be laid—by law, the Vestals were not allowed to relight their fires from ordinary household hearths but must use pure flame, lit anew from sunlight. This brass pot, or one like it, had been used to rekindle the sacred fires for nearly three thousand years.

Around the floating platform marched bodyguards, four fighting monks of the Temple of Mars, their spears gleaming. Over their Roman armor, the *Flamen Martialis* wore wolfskin cowls, the upper scalps of the wolves resting upon the crowns of their heads, forming eyed-and-eared hoods with fangs.

The procession made its way through the hemlock forest, north of De Vere Hall. Master Warder Nighthawk and his assistant, Urd Odinson, escorted them to the primary hearth of Roanoke, on the ground floor of the Warding Tower. Carrying the Eternal Flame, the Vestal circled the tower, with Rachel and the rest of the shivering crowd behind her, and then joined her acolyte in relighting the hearth flame from the coals they had brought from Rome.

Once the new fire grew into a blaze, warding students from De Vere gathered brands and coals and ran them to primary hearths in other campus buildings. After this, the Vestal and her entourage departed. To Siggy's disappointment, none of the monks of Mars turned out to be this year's pilgrims.

Once the primary hearth fires were lit, Flora Towers Skaife, the Mistress of the Beast, and Umberto Sarpento, the custodian, led a second procession returning the salamanders to their hearths. Slowly, the drafty old buildings began to grow warm again.

Once the formalities ended, Rachel darted across the freezing commons toward the library. As she entered Roanoke Hall, she encountered her Language tutor, Mr. Tuck. He was a large heavyset man with a short brown beard, dressed in the black and green robes of a canticler. A green tassel hung from his square, black scholar's cap.

"Miss Griffin," he said mildly, "I believe I never properly apologized to you for not believing you back in September—about the wraith."

Rachel smiled, startled and yet pleased.

"In my defense," he stated, "students say a great many things that don't turn out to be true, especially late at night. Still, I should have investigated before dismissing your claims. Due to my negligence, students were injured, which I deeply regret. In the future, I hope you will feel you can come to me. I promise to take you seriously."

Rachel curtsied. "Thank you, sir. I appreciate it."

He nodded ponderously and then added thoughtfully, "It was a strange affair, a wraith supping undetected for years upon the daughter of Canada's foremost wraith hunter. It is a pleasure to finally see Miss Price with rosy cheeks, now that she is free from this parasite. She is doing better in her studies as well. I never did hear anything about why this predator was able to slip by our normal methods of detection. A disturbing matter, really."

"We have wraith detectors?" Rachel murmured, more to herself than to him, but the tutor answered kindly.

"Indeed. Indeed. The campus is warded against many types of super-natural ills. Ordinarily, a wraith would be unable to enter. But this year, these defenses were evaded twice: once by the wraith targeting Miss Price, which you and Mr. Smith so valiantly yet foolishly assaulted, and once by the wraith-like spirits that apparently made up Dr. Mordeau's cloak—an alchemical talisman unlike any of which any I have previously heard. We have increased security significantly, but without another cloaked wraith to study, we have no idea if our new defenses are satisfactory."

"Does Mylene's father know anything?" Rachel asked. "As a wraith hunter, I would guess this was his bailiwick."

"A good question," Mr. Tuck intoned. "A good question indeed."

Rachel continued onto the library. Roanoke Hall had been the first build-ing relit after the Warding Tower, so when she entered, she found herself warm for the first time all day. The librarian, Mr. Poole, in the long owl-feathered robes of a monk of Athena, sat behind his desk going over some accounts. When she asked him where the books on legal covenants were, he pointed the way without even looking up.

Any question about why the librarian had treated her request so ca-sually vanished when Rachel reached the section. The shelves were bare. With the exception of three gigantic tomes on the top shelf, every single book on covenants and law of the Fey was missing. Rachel gawked at the empty shelves, peering upward in the semi-darkness. It was daytime, so only a few lights were on. The windows high above should have allowed her to see here, but the sky was so overcast that it was as dim as twilight.

Rachel frowned petulantly at the empty section. Why was it empty? Had someone stolen the books to keep the school from solving the prob-lem with the fey? If so, who? A fey? Someone who wanted to close down Roanoke Academy? With a sigh, she started to turn away, when a bolt of lightning flashed by the window, bathing the shelves in brilliant light.

Rachel looked up at the window and screamed. Something hung in the air between her and the wall. It was as big as a human, with a wash of silver light spreading out behind it, filling the space between the two stacks. A second girlish scream echoed from above her. Then, both cries were lost in the crash of thunder. Very close by, a dog barked excitedly.

In the aftermath of the lightning bolt, the library seemed even darker. Rachel grabbed her wand and pointed it at the form, which now stood on the floor. It was slightly taller than her. Then, it bent down, and a feminine voice whispered, "Hush, Angelo, hush! This is a library."

The dog stopped barking, and the figure straightened up. "Rachel Griffin? Is that you?"

Rachel's vision finally adjusted. Before her stood Marlowe Hall college freshman, Iolanthe Towers. Her long, straight, black hair was held back by a bright turquoise headband. She had Japanese features but spoke with a Midwestern accent. Silver fox ears extended from her head, and a silvery fox tail tipped with a puff of white swished behind her. When she saw Rachel was looking at her head, the fox ears and tail vanished.

Between the two girls, Iolanthe's Australian Shepherd—part tan, part spotted black and gray—cocked its head and gave two quick, sharp barks. Then, it panted happily.

"Quiet, Angelo," Iolanthe whispered again, rubbing the dog's head. "Sorry, Rachel, I didn't mean to scare you. You startled me. I didn't realize anyone else was here."

"Me, too." Rachel nodded her head rapidly.

"What are you doing in this section?"

"Looking for books on how covenants with fey are made, but they're missing."

"They've all been checked out," said the upperclassman.

"By whom?" asked Rachel.

"Everybody," Iolanthe laughed. "All the college students have been given assignments to study covenant law and make recommendations on how to solve the current problems. Juniors and seniors at the upper school, too."

"Oh," murmured Rachel, who suddenly felt very foolish for having thought she might have something to contribute.

"Why were you looking?" asked Iolanthe, with interest.

"I-I wanted to help—figure out how to solve the problem."

"That's sweet. It wasn't assigned?"

Rachel shook her head.

"Why you?" asked Iolanthe. She seemed quite keen on the answer. "I mean, why did you come here personally if it wasn't an assigned question?"

Rachel bit her lip. Then, she told the truth. "It was my fault the Heer got killed. I just wanted to see if I could help undo the damage."

Iolanthe started to smirk. Then, her face grew serious. "It really was your fault?"

Rachel nodded. "He was killed by Amber—my sister—only she was stolen away as a baby. She noticed the Heer because of something I did."

"Wow. That's... wow." Iolanthe was quiet for a time.

"How about you? Are you here because you were assigned the topic?" Rachel asked.

Iolanthe shook her head. "I was assigned the topic, but I read these books all the time. That's what I want to do when I graduate—go into law and become a mediator."

"Truly?" Rachel asked, intrigued. "How did you come to choose that field?" She squatted down and started petting the dog. Its fur had such beautiful colors.

Iolanthe flashed her a mercurial smile. "I come from a rather illustrious family."

"Could it be that you're related to a very influential fairy?" Rachel asked, smirking.

Iolanthe grinned. "That very influential fairy, about whom Gilbert and Sullivan wrote their operetta, is my great-great-grandmother. Or rather, both the character of the fairy Iolanthe and the character of the fairy queen were based on her. Gilbert and Sullivan took a lot of liberties."

Rachel nodded. "My family was attached by marriage to one of her knights, once upon a time, so I am aware that the reality bears little resemblance to the operetta."

"That's my father's side of the family," said Iolanthe. "My mother is Kuzu no Ha."

Rachel shot up to standing. Her jaw dropped. "*The* Kuzunoha? The most famous kitsune in the world? You're the younger sister of the great *onmyouji*, Abe no Seimei?"

"Much, much younger sister, yes." Iolanthe straightened and gave Rachel a pixie-sweet grin. Silver fox ears popped out of her hair and twitched as if listening and then vanished again. This set her mortarboard cap and its white tassel bobbing.

"Didn't he live over a thousand years ago?" cried Rachel.

"He did. And that only scratches the surface of the secrets of my parentage." Iolanthe winked.

"Are you related to the kitsune girl in my class?" Rachel asked. "Kris Serenity Wright?"

Iolanthe nods. "Her mother is my niece."

"Wow," Rachel breathed. "That's quite a pedigree."

"That's why I want to go into mediation," Iolanthe said. "You know how fey are, always looking to slip in loopholes. It's very helpful, when forming agreements with them, to have someone present who they are reluctant to push. The great-great-granddaughter of an influential fairy, who also happens to be the daughter of a famous kitsune, is exactly the type of person to whom the average fairy or salamander or oread will give less guff."

"That's really wonderful." Rachel's eyes lit up. "In fact, that's even better than if the books had been here. You're an expert! You can sum it up for me, can't you? A beginner's primer in fey law. What do I most need to know?"

"What's your goal?" asked Iolanthe, torn between skepticism and amusement.

"I want a new covenant between Roanoke and the local fey—so that no one will get hurt, particularly not the Unwary. They have no idea they are in danger. I would h-hate for one to get hurt because of my mistakes."

Iolanthe regarded Rachel thoughtfully. "I suspect you are taking too much onto your shoulders. You're not responsible for someone else's actions. But your motives are good. Okay, here it goes: Kit Tower's Primer: Fairy Law in a Nutshell.

"All covenants with the fey need a focus, a reason. There are three main reasons: First, force. By which I mean: violence. The Wise beat up the fairies and force them to sign, and if the fairies break their word, they beat them up again.

"The problem with this one: there are some mighty powerful fey here and a lot of them. The Wisecraft might win a straight-out battle, but they might not. Even if they did, there could be many casualties, particularly among the Unwary population along the Hudson.

"Second, trade. The fey want something. We give it to them so long as they continue to keep their side of the bargain. Fey are good about keeping to the letter of anything they've agreed to, but they won't make a lasting agreement for a one-time gain. So we can't offer them, say, a pile of chocolate or Turkish delight and then expect them to keep a long-term agreement, unless we provide more every first of the year or on Ladies' Day or whatever.

"In the previous covenant, keeping the Heer bound was what the Wise were offering in return for the fey keeping their side of the bargain. Right now, Nighthawk and the Grand Inquisitor are searching for something to offer in place of the Heer.

"Problem is, there doesn't seem to be any easy, meets-everyone's-needs thing that the many different kinds of fey want. One could carve out individual agreements with different fey, but that's chancy because some sprite or other always feels it isn't part of the groups addressed and won't obey."

"What's the third reason?" asked Rachel, fascinated.

Iolanthe waved a hand. "That one won't work here. It's a treaty."

"Treaty?"

"Yes, the Wise make a treaty with an existing authority, like a fairy king or a high lady."

"Like when Underhill sends Sir Calidor Moth to a Round Table Meeting?" asked Rachel.

Iolanthe nodded. "I don't know much about the British Round Table —it's your ruling body of the Wise for England, right? Oh, wait! You're Sandra's little sister. Your father is a Peer of the Round Table, isn't he?"

Rachel nodded.

"It's similar," said Iolanthe. "Let's say—I assume this is the case—that there is one ruler over all the fey in your area, or at least one that many acknowledge. And this ruler sends this Moth knight to negotiate. Then if you can make a treaty with that ruler, all the lesser fey have to obey."

Rachel nodded. "Why can't we use that here?"

"No ruler. Too many separate parties. There's the native spirit beings. The fairies who came over with the Dutch. Those who came with the English. On top of that, there's all the fey who live on Roanoke Island, who all recognize very different authorities."

Rachel said, "So if we could find an authority they all agreed upon, that might work?"

"Yes, but the chances are nigh zilch. It would have to be someone the fey considered to be one of them, but who would protect and look out for us humans? Someone really big, like King Auberon or Queen Titania or King Finvarra or Erlkoenig, that kind of figure. Right now, Master Warder Nighthawk's the closest thing we have, but he's a go-between, not a ruler."

Rachel nodded slowly.

"My hope, my wish,"—Iolanthe hugged her arms and spun in a circle—"is when they finally come to an agreement, I'll be allowed to watch or even participate in a small way."

Rachel smiled at her. "Well, if I should figure out an answer, I will be sure to invite you."

"Yes." Iolanthe laughed gaily at the serious little freshman. "You do that."

Rachel straightened up. Suddenly, everything she had not been saying came spilling out of her mouth. "You laugh. You think I am too young? Too small? Then I suppose you think I couldn't keep Mortimer Egg from destroying the Wall protecting our world; or paralyze the demon who was about to sacrifice my mother and me long enough for the… well, I'm not supposed to say, but I helped; or stall the ogre so it didn't abscond with your cousin. Or…" she swallowed, "get the Heer killed."

She did not add that she had murdered an Elf.

Iolanthe's pupils widened. "Did you do all those things?"

Rachel nodded solemnly.

"Wow."

"And you never can tell what I'll find out," Rachel replied, absolutely serious. "Information loves me. It comes and finds me."

"Well, if you figure out how to solve this, promise me you'll call me. I want to be there."

Rachel lifted her chin and held up her hand, palm out. "So swears Griffin."

They smiled at each other. Iolanthe clicked her tongue at her familiar, and the upperclassman and her dog departed. Only after the older girl left did Rachel realize that she had not asked Iolanthe what she had been doing in mid-air.

She thought back, trying to determine what the swath of silvery light behind the other girl had been; however, her memory offered little help. Whatever it was had been partially blocked by the next bookshelf as Iolanthe came around the corner, so Rachel could not determine the shape of it. Was it a cloak that Rachel had not noticed afterward? An optical illusion caused by the brightness of the lighting? There was no way to tell, but Rachel could not help thinking, as she walked away, that it had looked remarkably like wings.

Chapter Twelve:
With Intent to Deprive

"They look so cute together," Joy sighed on the following Monday, as Ivan and Freka strolled hand-in-hand across the commons. The couple walked beneath a large red umbrella that floated, seemingly of its own accord, above their heads.

Joy and Rachel stood under one of the rows of huge black umbrellas with glowing silver rims, gazing out at the pouring rain, along with Zoë, Valerie, and Sigfried. The princess stood four giant umbrellas away from them, speaking kindly to an admiring student in need of advice. The last of the snow had been washed away days ago, except for tiny piles that had once been Snow Lucky and other works of winter art. The temperatures were below freezing; however, the lightning imps sent constant rain, so everything was covered with a thin layer of ice. The new couple's footsteps crunched as they walked across the frozen grass.

Rachel agreed with Joy. Before she could comment, however, Salome ran up to their small group, breathless with excitement.

"They're here! The silver slippers," Salome crowed. "We can commit larceny tonight!"

"Shh!" Joy looked over her shoulder at where the princess still spoke with another student. "Nastasia will hear you."

"What's wrong with that?" Rachel asked, shocked that Joy, of all people, wanted to keep something from the princess. "I thought this was so she could show us her vision."

"Yeah, nah," said Zoë, "you know how the princess is about the dean. She'd turn us in."

Oh! Joy must have been willing to go behind Nastasia's back because it was for Zoë. Rachel noted with interest that Joy now put her loyalty to her roommate above her devotion to the princess. She doubted that would have happened a few months earlier.

"True." Rachel frowned thoughtfully. "In fact, when we spoke about stealing the shoes once some time ago, the princess was strongly against it. How are you going to explain suddenly getting your sandals back?"

Zoë reached behind her head, stretching. "I may have happened to mention that the dean would be giving them back to me."

"So, what do we need to do?" asked Rachel.

"First step." Valerie pantomimed driving her fist into her palm. "Ditch Nastasia. Any ideas?"

Rachel thought about this. "Wednesday nights, nearly everyone's at the Young Sorcerers' League. The princess goes, and afterwards, she does private training with her siblings. That's the only time I can think of when she's regularly busy with someone other than us."

"Oh, that's good!" Valerie nodded. "In fact, doing it when the campus is nearly empty sounds wise. Why don't we slip out a bit early and do it Wednesday night?"

"If we slip out early, the princess will notice." Joy wilted. "I don't want to hurt her feelings or leave her alone."

"Hang on," Zoë said. "She won't notice—or care—if Valerie, Salome, and Sigfried leave, and Rachel's not in the YSL. Why don't you and I take princess-distraction detail? If they aren't finished once Nastasia goes off to practice with her brothers and sister, we can join them."

"I guess so." Joy drooped further, disappointed to be left out of the action.

"Second, we need a lookout," said Valerie.

"That's me," said Sigfried, tapping his chest, where his amulet lay beneath his robes. "Only I'll need a broom. Can't risk trying to get into the building at night and getting caught or even having to talk to someone, which would distract me from looking out for Lucky. I can watch from outside, but I want to be close, so I can see more of the building."

"You can borrow my broom." Rachel regretted the words the moment they left her mouth. She pictured Sigfried in the dark trying to figure out the complicated levers of the steeplechaser. For months now, he had been practicing occasionally on Vroomie and could fly the steeplechaser decently on a nice balmy afternoon, but night flying was a different situation. "Or I'll borrow one for you from the gym."

"What?" Valerie asked, leaning forward. It was hard to hear over the pounding of the rain on the heavy cloth of the umbrellas.

"Broom!" Rachel began. "Oh, never mind. We'll work out the specifics later."

"Finally," said Valerie, raising her voice over the rain, "we need people to run interference. There are two directions people can approach the dean's office from. So we need two people."

"Oh, me! Me!" Salome raised her hands and wiggled her fingers. Her nails were painted purple and white with gold stars. She batted her long eyelashes. "I am *purr-fect* for that role."

Rachel said, "Why don't I take the other end of the hall? If any of the Agents come by, I can talk to them, and I know some of the proctors, too."

"Then it's decided," said Valerie. "Wednesday night: distract the princess; lookout to keep an eye out for Lucky; two people to run interference. That's it. I'll go with Sigfried and fly the broom, so he can concentrate."

"You're good at this," said Zoë.

"As my father the cop is so fond of saying," Valerie quipped, "I spent my youth among the criminal element."

A lightning bolt cut across the sky and struck the tallest tree on the commons, illuminating the entire campus with an eerie brilliance. Everything seemed frozen as if caught in a painting. Then, the air ripped itself apart into a *kaboom*. It was not as loud as the fulguration attack on the barghests by the Agents, but it still shocked the eardrums and made it hard to hear afterward. Rachel and quite a few of the others clapped their hands over their ears. Siggy shook his fist at the heavens, shouting something, but the words were lost in the thunder.

Then all was silent. Flames danced in the upper branches of the tree.

For a moment, none of the students around the commons moved. Then, Wulfgang Starkadder pushed by Rachel. He strode from under the umbrellas into the rain. He was handsome in a brooding fashion, with wavy dark hair, a very straight nose, and a strong chin. Ordinarily, his charm was marred by his constant, superior sneer, but now he looked resolute.

Reaching the middle of the rain-soaked lawn, he raised his arms toward the rainy sky and shouted: "Enough!"

"What is he doing?" Zoë asked. Rachel could hardly hear the other girl's voice. It seemed to come from far away. "Swearing at the sky?"

"Maybe he's gone bonkers," Joy whispered. "He's been laughing like a madman in class all week."

Rachel had to tamp down the desire to giggle. Poor Wulfgang: his madness, too, was no doubt her fault. Then she realized that she did have an inkling as to what he might be doing. His sister Freka had mentioned her younger brother had a special gift involving weather, but that it had been useless due to the greater strength of the Heer. *But the storm goblin was gone.*

Rachel looked around. Sure enough, the pouring rain seemed to be lessening. She watched to see what he would do next, fascinated.

"*Hagalaz*," commanded the young Prince of Transylvania, spreading his arms wide.

The rain stopped. The dark gloom of the day lightened. Directly above his head, the sky opened, and a single beam of sunlight broke the clouds, striking only Wulfgang.

Wulfgang bowed to the gathered crowd, facing left and right. Then, he walked off, whistling jauntily. Around the commons, students, tutors, proctors, and Agents began to clap.

"*That* was exciting," said Salome, watching him go, "for the minute and a half it lasted. The Starkadder princes do have an undeniable appeal. I wonder if I should get myself one."

"Like you're going to dump Ethan," smirked Valerie.

"Hey, a girl can dream." Salome made shrugging into a sensuous motion. Sigfried pantomimed sticking his thumbs into his eyes, so as to blind himself against having to glimpse such a display. Valerie snorted and shook her head, and Joy shot Salome a dark look.

"Hang on," Rachel said suddenly.

Ordinarily, stealing back Zoë's shoes would be the sort of caper she loved. Now, suddenly, she felt uneasy. The memory of her conversation with the Raven, about the ends not justifying the means and the preciousness of joy, came back to haunt her.

She said slowly, "Are we really certain we should be committing theft?"

"What have you done with the real Rachel Griffin?" asked Sigfried.

"If this isn't the real one, boss, can I eat her?" asked Lucky.

"Just for the record," said Valerie, "it isn't theft."

"How do you figure?" drawled Zoë.

"Theft is taking the property of another without consent and with the intent to deprive the original owner permanently of its use," Valerie explained. "The sandals do not belong to the dean; they belong to Zoë. So it is not the crime of theft."

"Bah!" Sigfried exclaimed. "How boring. If it's not a crime, I don't want to be involved."

Valerie laid a calming hand on his arm. "Don't worry. It's at least trespassing."

"Robin Hood is not known for being the world's greatest trespasser," objected Siggy.

"Look," said Zoë to Rachel, "the dean spoke to me three days ago. She promised she would give my sandals back at spring break—she thinks I'm going to take them home and leave them there. Sorry. Pzzt. No such luck. But the point is, we're merely borrowing them two weeks early. If it makes you feel better, I promise if she changes her mind and doesn't give them to me for spring break, I'll have Lucky here put the real ones back."

"What crime is it? Taking back something confiscated by the dean?" asked Sigfried.

Valerie thought about this. "Well, it's at least rule-breaking."

"Oh, I like that!" Siggy's eyes shone.

"And disobeying an adult," added Valerie.

"That's good, too!" cried Siggy.

"You are so predictable, Siggy," giggled Joy. "Like a contrary machine."

Siggy turned to Lucky, "Is that enough mayhem for us?"

"Disobedience to adults is our sacred duty!" crowed Lucky.

The dragon and the boy bumped fist to clawed talons. Rachel sighed.

The cloud cover had begun to disperse. Beams of sunlight broke through, glittering off the ice that coated the campus, transforming it into an elfin wonderland. The sunbeams looked almost solid as they sliced through the gloom. Rachel was reminded of her first day on the island, when a beam of sunlight had led her to the winged statue—or rather, the statue that, back then, had had wings. A little bit more of the darkness that had surrounded her heart lifted, as if a single ray of sunlight had pierced that gloom as well.

"Is there another option?" asked Rachel. "Could we use the thinking glass in the Warding Tower instead of going into dreamland?"

"How would we get everyone up there without being noticed?" asked Valerie.

"Couldn't we fly…?" Rachel paused. "Does my promise to Mr. Chanson not to fly in and out of windows include the open arches in the Warding Tower? That's… rough."

Salome and Joy sighed together over the handsome gym tutor. "Mr. Chanson!"

"Women!" Siggy rolled his eyes.

"This Mr. Chanson is beating your time, boss," Lucky said hurriedly. "He's stealing your harem girls. Should I burninate him?"

"Lucky," Siggy put an arm around Valerie's shoulder, "as I have told you many times, I am a one-woman man, and Goldilocks here is that one woman."

Valerie gave him a friendly punch in the bicep. "You better believe it, slugger."

Siggy turned to his dragon. "Besides, if Mr. Chanson can survive being thrown through fifty feet of solid earth and stone, he might survive burnination, too."

"Survive burnination?" The very idea horrified Lucky.

Valerie chuckled. "I wish Lucky had been with me back in middle school. There are a number of guys who cried out for burnination. Dick Morgan's drug-dealer friend—he was bad news. That old guy who used the metal detector on the south part of Goose Rocks Beach. Mind you, I don't object to old guys on beaches. Or metal detectors, but this guy, ugh. He used to leer at us girls. He so deserved some burninating. Oh, and that smelly guy who peed in one of the trolleys at the museum, and they sent Wally and me to clean up after him. Definitely him."

She shook her head. "I grew up in one of the safest cities in America. Definitely the safest in Maine. Former presidents and their families live there. Your chance of coming upon a crime is seventy-three percent lower than in any other Maine city—official numbers!—but I encountered every creep in the entire place."

"So you are a criminal magnet?" asked Zoë. "Like a weirdness magnet, but for crime."

"Indeed," Valerie nodded.

"Explains why she got Siggy," giggled Joy enviously.

"Wait. I have a question." Zoë raised her hand. "You keep talking about your checkered past. How did you hang out with the criminal element if your town didn't have one?"

Valerie chuckled. "My dad, the cop, worked in Biddleford, about twenty-five minutes away. Biddleford's the second most dangerous city in Maine. I used to go down there after school to report on things. That's where I met the real criminals. But even my safe town had boys who smoked behind the school. I investigated them, too."

"That crime-magnet thing even happened to you here," said Joy. When Valerie smirked at her, Joy added, "No. I don't mean Sigfried. Didn't Egg come here looking for *you*?"

"Yes. Yes, he did," said Valerie, glowering.

Rachel's heart went out to Valerie. She wondered what it would be like to be the object of such malice. Then she remembered the intent gaze of the entire pack of barghests and shivered.

"What did the dean say to you," Rachel turned back to Zoë, "when she took your shoes?"

Zoë shrugged. "She just said, 'I'll take those,' and carried them off."

"That's all?" asked Rachel.

"Every single word," replied Zoë. "Besides, the point of her confiscating them was to make sure I don't lose more students. But I have a new plan that will make it 100So there's nothing to worry the dean."

The sun was coming out everywhere. Blue sky spread over the island for the first time in over a week. The whole campus now glittered like an ice sculpture. Rachel had not realized how much of the dimness of the afternoon came only from the overcast sky. A few weeks ago, it would have been nearly dark at this time, but it was finally March. The days were growing longer.

"Hmm," Rachel sighed. "Okay, I'm in. They're your sandals, but if she doesn't give them back, I do think we should return them."

"It's a deal," agreed Zoë. "Now, let's get rocking!"

Wednesday evening, Rachel found herself loitering in the hallway of Roanoke Hall. She leaned against the wall of a first-floor corridor. The dean's office lay in the hall behind her on the left. Farther down, at the other end of the hallway, Salome lounged, chattering happily, whether to herself or to some student she sought to distract, Rachel did not know.

Rachel was dressed in her red coat and snowman hat, her calling card tucked in an inside pocket. From there, Sigfried's voice occasionally drifted up as he gave various instructions, warning when people approached or describing things around corners or through closed doors. Siggy himself hovered outside on Vroomie along with Valerie, who was controlling the bristleless. Rachel had wanted to borrow a Flycycle for them, but Valerie was afraid of being questioned by the proctors as to why she was flying a school broom at night. She assured Rachel that she could control the steeplechaser.

Rachel was less sanguine.

Pulling out her calling card, she peeked at it. To her relief, she saw that Sigfried and Valerie had mastered hovering. They floated above the chilly waters of the reflecting lake about ten feet from the dean's window. The surface of the lake beneath them was covered with a veneer of ice, too thin for skating. The reflection of the starry sky above twinkled on this icy surface below.

Since Wulfgang's performance on Monday evening, the weather had been crisp and clear, almost balmy, for which Rachel was grateful. Between the bad weather and the Agents discouraging people from going outside, Roanoke Hall had been crowded the previous week, even the normally seldom-used fifth floor. The building was so full of people that her private hallway—the one she used for practicing cantrips and hexes—had not been private.

"Okay," Siggy's voice came over the calling card. "Lucky's in!"

The image coming from Siggy's All-Seeing Amulet shifted. Rachel could see the dean's office: her large cherrywood desk with its black ink blotter, the arcane tomes and jars of specimens lining the shelves, and the stand made from a young tree upon which the dean's familiar often rested. Rachel's heart skipped a beat. She had not thought to tell Siggy to make sure the eagle was not there before Lucky entered the office. Fortunately, the perch was empty.

The image flickered. Hallways and other rooms flashed by. Then, the card showed the dean's office again. Rachel thought back, examining the brief glimpses in more detail. She was surprised to come upon Zoë's friend, Misty Lark, alone with a drum set in one of the soundproofed practice rooms around the corner beyond where Salome stood. Everything in the room except the drums—books, extra drumsticks, a music stand— was floating in mid-air. So this was why Siggy had asked when they would learn to make objects fly around as Misty did. Rachel had no idea how Misty accomplished such a feat.

Siggy's voice continued, "See the closed door on the back wall of the office, to the left of the dean's desk? The confiscated items are behind that door. I can see Zoë's slippers, high up on a shelf to the right. Lucky, time to go!"

Rachel could not see Lucky, who used two types of invisibility, but the second door slowly opened. Rachel held her breath. If the door were warded, it might set off an alarm.

Nothing particular happened.

"Lucky's in!" Siggy crowed again. "Or should have we assigned code names? Goldilocks, what's a good code name for Lucky? Burninificator?

Skywatch Two? Snakulon?"

"Lucky is fine, dear," Valerie replied. "Let's get what we came for and get out!"

"Hurry!" Rachel bounced up and down on the balls of her feet, hoping to jar the butterflies in her stomach. "Don't dawdle for anything! We don't want to get caught!"

The calling card flickered again as Siggy checked the hallways. Then it showed the inside of a second room, behind the dean's office. It included comfortable chairs, an end table, a tea set, filing cabinets, bookshelves, and a long closet to the right, in which many objects were stored. Rachel could see Zoë's sandals up on a high shelf. They looked exactly like the false copy.

The fake slippers suddenly appeared, sitting on the high shelf. The real slippers vanished, now concealed by Lucky's invisibility. Rachel held her breath, afraid to move, lest some kind of alarm go off now that he had taken them.

"Mission complete!" crowed Sigfried.

"Wait!" Rachel squeaked.

"What's wrong?" asked Valerie, tersely.

"They're not in the right place," Rachel said, comparing what she was seeing with her memory. "Lucky, the other pair was closer to the door, and the left shoe was at a slant."

"Does it matter?" asked Valerie.

"I don't know," Rachel replied, still bouncing nervously. She wanted Lucky to get out of there before anyone discovered him. There were people on campus who could see through both his kinds of invisibility. "We don't know what the dean might notice."

"Fix 'em, Snakeasaurus Rex!" instructed Sigfried.

The sandals jerked to the right. Rachel gave precise instructions until their position exactly matched the one in her memory.

"Should I look in the filing cabinets, boss?" came Lucky's gravelly voice.

"Hurry back," Rachel urged. "Let's not push our luck."

"Might as well look," replied Sigfried, casually. "Nice to know what's there. At least, crack open the drawer. I can't read the files if there's no light."

The viewpoint flickered around, passing Misty Lark, with her flying books and drumsticks, and then Salome and then Rachel in their spots in the hallways again, returning to the dean's second room.

"No! Hurry out!" Rachel objected, peering around the corner. She glanced from the closed doors of the library on her left to the empty corridor running toward the main doors on her right. Then, she ducked back around the corner again. "Someone could come any minute!"

"If they do, I'll see 'em," said Sigfried. "There's no one there now."

One high drawer slid open, followed by the sound of sniffing. The drawer was filled with very old folders, yellowed and brittle.

Lucky sneezed. "Nothing here, boss. Just some old papers, very musty."

"Very well, Lucks, let's get...."

"Pull out a folder," asked Valerie. "Let's see what these records are."

"We've done what we came for," Rachel insisted. "Lucky, get to safety while it's safe."

The drawer moved again. A folder slid up into view. It flopped open, and the calling card showed a student's records from a long-ago age.

"That's boring," complained Siggy. "I thought there'd be treasure maps. Or loot."

The view in the calling card flashed over the hallways and then back to the back room so that the names on the old, dusty files flicked into view. Then, the viewpoint flickered elsewhere, but Rachel stayed with her memory of the file names in the filing cabinet, reading them.

"Wait!" she cried. "Lucky! Go back!"

"I thought you were the one in a hurry," Valerie's voice stated wryly.

"I saw my grandfather's name!" Rachel said. "I don't suppose Lucky could...." She sighed. "I guess that's too much to ask."

"I'm on it!" Lucky announced.

The folder marked *Blaise Griffin* gently eased itself from the drawer and floated over to the coffee table in the middle of the room.

"What should I do with it, boss?" asked Lucky.

Rachel said excitedly, "Just show me the pages. I can read them later."

"On it," said Lucky's growly dragon voice.

"Why'd you want to see them?" asked Salome. "Not objecting. Just curious."

"My father told me that my grandfather was expelled, but, eventually, he came back. I have no idea why," said Rachel. "I'm curious about the whole thing."

Valerie murmured, "I didn't know they let you come back once you were expelled."

The fragile papers slowly flipped over, one after another. Rachel gazed at each one raptly. She wondered how Lucky was moving the delicate papers so easily. There seemed to be a damp spot on some of them. Was he using his tongue?

"Expelled! There it is!" Her voice rose in surprise. "For... *theft?*"

"That seems like an ill omen, doesn't it?" murmured Valerie.

"At least they let people come back later," replied Sigfried.

"Some people," Valerie observed, wryly. "Maybe. Two hundred years ago. Whose fathers were dukes. Who knows if it would happen today."

More hallways flashed by. A walking feminine figure flickered by so quickly that even remembering back, Rachel could not make out the location.

"Someone's coming!" cried Sigfried. "Quick! Get out of there, Lucky!"

Lucky stuffed the file back and shut the drawer. "You forgot my code name, boss."

Chapter Thirteen:
To Cast a Cantrip

"My side or Rachel's?" asked Salome, yawning. "I don't see anyone coming."

"Rachel's. An Agent. Female."

"I'm on it!" Rachel announced. "Going calling card silent."

She tapped the card, turning it off, and slipped it into her pocket. This was chancy; now Siggy could not alert her when Lucky was safe, but it was better than having an incriminating voice emerge from her pocket at just the wrong time. She regretted not having invited Gaius along on their heist. He could have talked to her over the black bracelet without anyone else hearing. She also regretted missing out on seeing the rest of her grandfather's file, but, hopefully, the pages she had viewed but not read yet would reveal interesting information.

Okay. Show time. Rachel stepped around the corner. To her surprise, the Agent walking toward her at a very determined clip was Michael Garbarino's partner, Vicky Armel, here from London. The Agent strolled down the hall, her Inverness cloak flowing behind her. Underneath it, she wore a coat of sable fur, a short skirt, and a pair of high black boots. Rachel could not think of a time when the lovely, dark-haired Agent had not been dressed in fur. She occasionally wondered if Vicky Armel were a magical animal, like her partner the selkie. What better place to hide an enchanted animal skin than in a closet full of fur coats?

Rachel gave the Agent a cheerful smile. Agent Armel had always been kind to her. The first time they met, Vicky had given her Splashdown the Dolphin, one of Rachel's favorite stuffed animals, who still occupied a place of honor on the trunk at the foot of her pink canopy bed. It had been her fourth birthday, soon after Agent Armel joined the Wisecraft.

"Hallo, Agent Armel." Rachel waved.

"Hallo, Lady Rachel," Agent Armel replied, the heels of her boots clicking rhythmically against the marble floor. "What are you doing here so late?"

"Coming from a practice room," Rachel lied blithely, gesturing back towards the soundproof rooms where Misty played the drums.

"Diligent in your studies. That'll take you far." Agent Armel gave her a fond, approving nod, adding, "Lovely to see you but can't talk. Must investigate a matter."

Rachel's heart fell. *Agent Armel knew.* Vicky Armel worked for her father—well, currently for Agent Bridges—as the Shadow Agency's warder, which meant a disruption in the wards had been detected. Rachel had been hoping their adventure would go unnoticed, but she should have known better. Still, maybe she could stall the Agent long enough that no one would ever know the disturbance had been caused by them.

"Has there been a fey sighting?" Rachel asked innocently.

"Nothing so exciting." Agent Armel threw Rachel a quick smile, but she continued to move forward in a determined manner.

Rachel's sense of dread grew. As the Enochian of the Shadow Agency, the Agent herself was certain to be warded in ways that might allow her to see through both of Lucky's invisibilities. Even if he had left the dean's office, Armel might see him hurrying down the hall with the sandals.

This was bad. Dire action was required. Rachel planted herself directly in the path of the oncoming Agent, put her hands on her hips, and spoke the only words she could think of that had a chance of stalling an Agent.

"Agent Armel, why didn't anyone warn me that Dr. Mordeau had escaped?"

"Dr. Mordeau?" the young woman asked, startled. "What makes you say that?"

"She did escape, did she not?" asked Rachel.

"Lady Rachel, I don't have time to discuss this now."

Rachel had not wanted to *ever* admit her part in Mordeau's capture, but she could not think of anything else that might delay the Agent.

"She did, did she not?" asked Rachel, raising her chin. "What if I'm on her kill list for my part in her capture? Shouldn't I have been warned that she is loose?"

"You should have—? Warn you, personally?" Vicky Armel asked, flustered.

"I was the one who froze her, allowing the dean to take her down. What if she saw me?"

Agent Armel's eyes narrowed. "How did you know someone froze her? The dean specifically did not share the information about how she was helped—so she could question anyone who came forward and learn if they were telling the truth."

"Because I'm the one who froze her." Rachel wondered how that had not been clear.

Vicky Armel laughed kindly. "Lady Rachel, I don't think even Sandra could have hexed a tutor during her first week of school, much less a powerful sorceress, such as Dr. Melusine Mordeau. Why are you saying all this? Did you have a tiff with your father? If so,"—she raised her hands pleadingly—"please don't drag me into it."

"You don't believe me?" Rachel asked, astonished.

"No," Agent Armel said gently, giving Rachel another fond smile. "I'm afraid I don't."

"You think I am too young to pull off a decent hex?"

"I do," Agent Armel shrugged with an apologetic smile.

Indignation seized Rachel. Here she had kept this secret for so long, despite the dean's efforts to find out who had helped her. Now that she finally admitted her part, she had not been believed. This filled her with fury. There was one way to prove the truth!

Rachel whistled. Blue sparks flew toward the Agent, who cried out in surprise. They surrounded her far too rapidly for her to block or defend herself. Rachel smiled triumphantly.

The lantern and star amulet that the Agent wore over her sable coat glittered. The blue sparkles bounced off of Agent Armel and flew back toward Rachel. When they came near her, they spun oddly and winked out. Rachel put her hand on the amethyst of Peter's necklace and smiled, relieved not to be frozen by her own spell.

That would have been embarrassing.

"Lady Rachel, that was rash, but no harm done." Agent Armel ruffled Rachel's head affectionately. "But let's not hear anything else about freezing Dr. Mordeau, shall we? Your hex didn't even freeze you. I know you want to know everything, pumpkin. But some things we need to keep secret for reasons of our own, and one of those things is that Dr. Mordeau is free. I don't know how you found out, but please keep it to yourself."

Rachel slid her dissembling mask over her face. It rankled terribly to have her competence at the paralysis hex, of all things, questioned, especially by someone whose good opinion she valued. She considered removing her amethyst necklace and whistling again, so that the spell would freeze her, and the Agent could see how well it worked—but then she would be standing in the hallway, frozen. Who knew what indignities that might lead to?

Agent Armel gave her a final wave and departed. Her heels clicked against the floor as she rounded the corner toward the dean's office. Rachel closed her eyes, fighting frustration. There were many things in life she had not mastered, but there were two things she was good at: flying and paralysis hexes. Yet thanks to her wonderful amethyst necklace, the Agent now thought she was a pathetic little girl who was unable to cast. Worse, she had *finally* come clean about having helped the dean against Dr. Mordeau, but she had not been believed.

It was so unfair. Opening her eyes, she took a deep breath and headed outside. She hoped her humiliating herself in front of the Agent she admired had given Lucky the time he needed to slip away.

Outside, Zoë waited on the bridge across the reflecting lake, grinning. It was dark, but the other girl stood in the pool of light from one of the tall lamp posts, her hair and feather as black as the cloudless and moonless night. In the lamplight, a bulge was visible under her coat that Rachel assumed was, again, Aardvark the quoll, until she noticed the familiar sitting on Zoë's head. Rachel started and then laughed with relief. Of course, the bulge was the sandals.

The mission had been a success.

Rachel sagged against the waist-high, solid stone balustrade that ran along the side of the bridge and laughed. "It worked?"

"We did it!" Valerie exclaimed with delight from where she sat on Vroomie, hovering above the lake about twenty feet away.

"Crime committed!" Siggy whooped, punching the air.

His exuberant motion jarred the steeplechaser. Valerie quickly worked the levers. To Rachel's relief, she did the right thing in the right order, and the broom steadied.

"Okay, Siggy," Valerie said, "let's get to solid ground before…. Whoa! Whooooa!"

The steeplechaser wobbled. Valerie grabbed the cast iron and brass handles, trying to steady the device. Rachel bit her lip, wondering if she should shout out instructions or if that would make things worse. *Hold steady. Left lever one notch. Kick the tail fan to fold it in manually.* The words echoed through her head. Only Valerie could not kick the tail fan. Sigfried was in the way. Rachel fought her desire to cover her eyes and drew her wand.

Valerie slowly straightened up, steering the broom toward the shore. "Okay, I got—"

Her sleeve caught the right lever. Rachel opened her mouth to cry out, but it was too late. Vroomie went into a spin. Its motion resembled a roasting spit—if Vroomie were the spit, Valerie and Sigfried were the roast, and the ice-covered lake was the cookfire. Valerie held on for dear life until the broom righted itself, but Siggy had been leaning backwards.

As the steeplechaser spun him upside-down, he fell off, plummeting like a stone. He crashed through the thin layer of ice and into the freezing waters of the lake. Then, he was gone.

"Sigfried!" screamed Valerie and Rachel together.

Lucky dived into the freezing waters, his long serpentine body plunging straight down. His head disappeared almost three seconds before the tuft of his tail finally sank beneath the surface. Wand in hand, Rachel climbed up on the balustrade and peered down into the chilly waters, searching the black lake and the jagged hole in the ice for some clue of her blood-brother. Her heart thundered so loudly that she could hardly hear anything else.

Zoë pelted across the bridge to the stone walkway at the edge of the water. Valerie landed the steeplechaser near her, leapt trembling from the broom, and ran to the edge, where she joined Zoë in peering into the blackness of the lake's depths.

"Siggy!" Zoë cried. Turning back towards Rachel, she shouted. "I don't know what to do! It won't help for one of us to go in there! Where is he? Where's Lucky?"

Salome sauntered out of Roanoke Hall. "Well, that went swimmingly. Could have been more exciting—what's wrong?"

"Speaking of swimmingly," Zoë pointed at the lake, her finger shaking, "Siggy just took you up on that!"

"What, he...." Her pretty face caved, and her voice broke. "Siggy's in the water? Like Lilly Pfeiffer? Valerie! Wha-what should we do? Should I go for help? What if he gets sucked into the tunnel that runs to the moat?"

"Get a proctor! A teacher!" cried Valerie. "Siggy can't swim! He can't swim!"

Rising panic choked Rachel. She fought back. *Cool as ice*, she reminded herself fiercely and then winced. Her grandfather's choice of words seemed unfortunate. Cool as ice was exactly what she did not want Siggy to be.

She had to act! Rachel stretched out her arm. *"Varenga*, Vroomie!"

The steeplechaser lay on the walkway near Valerie, who was leaning dangerously over the edge. The bristleless leapt across the short distance into Rachel's outstretched hand. Then, she was on the broom and over the break in the ice, her wand pointed downward.

What to cast? Would the vine cantrip produce vines in the water? If it did, would they help Siggy up or pull him down?

"Get Agent Armel!" she shouted to Salome. "Tell her to call Agent Garbarino if he is on campus. He could go down there. Seals aren't afraid of cold water!"

Salome ran back into the building. Zoë spun and dashed across the commons toward the nearest proctor in the distance. Valerie stood on the edge, screaming Siggy's name over and over. Her face was absolutely white. Twice, she started to turn away, most likely to go for help, but fear and anxiety kept drawing her back to the lake's edge, scouring the waters for any sign of her boyfriend. Rachel suddenly remembered that Valerie had once found the dead body of her other best friend—the aforementioned Lilly Pfeiffer—floating in water.

No wonder Valerie and Salome were panicking.

Rachel kept peering downward, ignoring the way her racing heart shook her body. "Does anyone know the cantrip to stop cold?"

She could ask Gaius or call Vlad for help. She had opened her mouth to call one of them when the water beneath her trembled. Rachel pointed her wand at the spot. With a loud splash, Lucky's head broke the surface. He flew upward, clearly straining, the rest of his long body trailing into the water. Beneath the water, in the dim light from the lamp, Rachel thought she saw the top of Siggy's head.

She activated a *tiathelu* cantrip and yanked upwards. Lucky rose from the water more quickly, but he and the water-logged teenage boy were too heavy for Rachel's current skill level. She fired off two more *tiathelus*, using the combined effort of all three cantrips.

Siggy and Lucky shot into the air. They tumbled, head over heel. Siggy ended up in mid-air, head down, feet upward, with water pouring from his mouth. *Oh no! That was bad, right?*

Rachel yanked him toward the edge of the lake. She and Lucky worked to turn his head upright. They rushed him toward the shore and lowered him to the ground. *Should she try to lay him down? Was he still conscious?* That had been a lot of water! Was he still....

He couldn't be dead! He couldn't!

Siggy jumped free of Lucky and landed on the ground, arms outstretched in victory. He was shivering, but his face broke into a giant grin of glee. Valerie's body hit him like a speeding arrow as his girlfriend wrapped her arms around his dripping body. Tears poured down her cheeks. He gave her head a pat and threw his hands upward again.

"I can breathe water!" he shouted, his voice reverberating through the cold night.

"Wh-what?" Valerie shivered, her teeth chattering.

"I can breathe water! I went down into the freezing abyss of darkness. My chest seized up. Couldn't move it to breathe. Then, I did, and all this water rushed into my mouth. Didn't bother me a bit. It was like breathing air."

"How...how could that be?" Valerie looked at the others, who shrugged and shook their heads to indicate that they did not know.

Rachel swooped down and landed. Leaning Vroomie against the bridge, she cast the cantrip Gaius had used back in September to take the orange juice off her robes. She had managed it once, the time Eunice had deliberately thrown juice at her.

"*Silu varenga. Taflu.*"

Oh! She understood it now. They had not learned *silu*, but she knew it had to do with water or liquid. Vlad had used it the first week of school, the time he brought the moat water to life. *Varenga* meant return. *Taflu* pushed something away. She smiled, pleased, at her greater understanding. Sadly, however, her cantrip did not work. The water trembled slightly and sloshed a bit, but it did not move off Sigfried's body and form a ball in the air.

Behind Rachel, a cheerful feminine voice said, "Let me do that."

Agent Armel's boots clicked on the stone of the bridge as she came toward them, along with an ashen-faced Salome, who was yanking on the Agent's arm as if to get her to move faster. Vicky Armel came up beside Rachel and cast the same cantrip.

The water on Sigfried's body swooshed into the air and formed a ball. The Agent used the *taflu* gesture to send the water back into the lake.

Rachel sighed. It would be Agent Armel who saw her fail at yet another spell.

"I bet it's because of Lucky!" Rachel said, as they tromped down the staircase in Roanoke Hall that led to the Storm King Café and hot drinks.

"What is because of Lucky?" asked Salome, her luminous eyes wide. "Did Lucky push Siggy into the water?"

"No! Breathing water," Rachel said. "We've been wondering what kind of a familiar gift came with Lucky. *Lungs* are water dragons. I bet Siggy can breathe water because of Lucky."

"I saved the boss!" Lucky beamed with joy. He was wrapped tightly around both Sigfried and Valerie, since the latter would not let go of her boyfriend. "Hey, did you hear that, boss? You can breathe water 'cause of me!"

"Wish I could have done that when I was younger," Sigfried said. "It sure would have come in handy back in the orphanage, particularly the time Punker and Banger stuck my head in.... Well, never mind about that. Not for the ears of girls."

Remembering another gruesome story Sigfried had told involving Punker and Banger, Rachel shivered.

They clattered down the spiral staircase, breathing in the smell of apple pie and grilled cheese. The café closed at nine-thirty on weekdays. They still had twenty minutes.

Rachel slipped up beside Zoë. "Now you have your shoes. You can help the urisk."

"The who-what-now? Oh! That little goat-legged guy from the Masquerade Ball," Zoë ran her hand over her hair and braid, so they matched her silver sandals. She turned her feather moonlight-colored mottled with black specks. "Sure. I can help him, but how do I find him?"

"Wasn't he going to hide out in the ogre's empty cave?" asked Rachel. "Let's send Lucky to ask him to come to the opening of the tree-lined path, as that's as far as the proctors let us go."

"Yeah. That'll work," replied Zoë.

Rachel whispered to Lucky and, after a word to Sigfried, the dragon slipped away.

At the café, Xandra Black and Fort Thorn, the young man who worked at every job on campus, were behind the counter, little paper hats atop their heads, or—in Xandra's case—atop the hood that covered half of her face. Rachel and her friend gave their orders. Their drinks came quickly because the café was nearly empty; most of the students were still at the YSL meeting. Upon receiving their hot chocolates, the group of friends crossed the black and white checkered floor and sat at a table far from the other customers. They chose the spot beneath the Heer of Dunderberg on the mural that took up the back wall and portrayed the battle between the Heer and Captain Vanderdecken.

Zoë placed the silver slippers on the table for all to see. Then she covered them with her leather jacket.

"Where's Joy?" asked Salome, looking around.

"With the princess," replied Zoë. "The YSL meeting isn't over yet. I snuck away. Said I had a headache."

"So, what's the plan now?" asked Valerie. A bit of color had returned to her face.

Zoë leaned back, propped her feet on the table, and gave them all a slow, lazy smile. "Be ready tonight."

CHAPTER FOURTEEN:
ADVENTURES IN SLUMBERLAND

IN HER DREAM, SHE WAS RIDING HER PONY WIDDERSHINS ACROSS THE moors, racing against a horse made out of cloud. Next thing she knew, Zoë Forrest walked towards her; her pixy-short hair and her long forelock braid a deep purple glittering with tiny silver stars. The feather, in its spot of honor in Zoë's braid, resembled the Milky Way.

Zoë waved, a silvery light shining around her. "Hey, Rachel, wake up! Er... rather, don't wake up but... lucid up?"

Rachel blinked, disoriented. She had not intended to fall asleep. She had lain down to review the pages from her grandfather's file and had drifted off after only the first page. Now, she felt awake, but she was still standing in the scene from her dream: The moors stretched out before her, but if she turned and looked behind her, she could see the forest that grew in the dreamland of Roanoke Academy.

"Did it work out? With the urisk?" she asked, looking around.

Zoë shrugged. "It was a bit tricky, with the Agents and all. But between Sig and me, we managed it." Zoë gestured and began walking. "Let's go. We have a lot to do tonight."

Rachel followed her a short distance to where Joy and Nastasia waited among the trees of the dream forest. Together, they wandered up and down the undulating wall-like ribbons of mist that ran through the landscape, peering into the oxbows and eddies at individual dream dioramas until they found Valerie. In her dream, she was standing in a swanky gentleman's club interviewing fellow classmen Solomon and Solon Drake, sons of a famous judge. As soon as Zoë's silvery light fell on her, she grew lucid. Zoë asked her if they should look for Salome, but Valerie shook her head, saying that her friend had not gone to bed yet and thus would not be dreaming.

As they searched for Sigfried and Lucky, Rachel saw a dreamscape that looked a bit like home. This person was also dreaming of wind-swept moors. Suddenly, she recognized the farmhouse in that dream. It appeared in a painting that hung in Roanoke Hall.

"Wait!" she cried, grabbing Zoë's arm. "This is Gaius! Can we take him with us?"

"Sure. No skin off my incisors," Zoë replied casually.

Joy hooked her arm through Nastasia's. "It's your vision, princess!"

Nastasia gave Rachel a sympathetic smile. "I believe young Mr. Valiant has proved himself, and I have already given my consent to his joining our expeditions. Let us wake him."

Rachel gave her friend a grateful smile, but she could have cried with happiness. Zoë strolled to where Gaius knelt fixing a device Rachel was pretty sure was called a tractor.

"Wait!" called Valerie. "Princess, didn't you say you suspected your vision was of Von Dread's minions stealing the Transylvanian heirloom? Don't get me wrong. I think Valiant's all right, but what if Dread's the perp? Won't having his henchman here make things awkward?"

Nastasia thought for some time before answering. "I believe it'll be all right. If I am wrong about the vision, then to exclude Mr. Valiant based on false pretenses would be most unfair. If I am right, and Mr. Valiant was in on the crime, then he can explain himself. If I am correct, but Mr. Valiant knew nothing of it, perhaps it will open his eyes to the true nature of cretin to whom he has chosen to pledge his allegiance."

"Sounds good to me." Zoë tapped Gaius on the shoulder.

Gaius started. "Rach. Zoë. What's... where am I?" He stood up. "Ooooh. Dreamland."

He brushed dream hay off his dream overalls. Both the hay and the overalls dissolved into mist. He now wore his black academic robes, patches and all.

"Would you like to come with us?" Rachel asked, holding out her hand to him. "We're going to see the princess's vision."

"I rather would." He grinned and took her hand, squeezing it. "This should be good fun. Hello, Miss Romanov, Miss Hunt. Miss O'Kee—" Gaius's voice cut off, and he turned his back to the girls, holding his free hand up beside his eyes as a blinder. "Um... Miss O'Keefe?"

Rachel and Nastasia wore their long, flannel, Victorian nightgowns. Zoë, who had walked up here from the waking world, was in her street clothes, and Valerie wore her bright yellow *Hello Kitty* pajamas. Joy, however, wore a cute peach and cream teddy. The short, silky garment covered very little of her.

Joy looked down at her exposed body and gave a little shriek. Rachel blushed. She would not have wanted Gaius to see her dressed thus, much less a boy who was not her boyfriend. Perhaps she should have been jealous, but she merely felt amused at Joy's expense. With Zoë's help, Joy's teddy became her favorite baby blue pajamas. When the all-clear was given, Gaius turned back. Joy was still bright red.

"No harm, O'Keefe," he gave her a fond wink. "I didn't see anything. I swear."

"Not anything worth looking at anyway," quipped Zoë.

Joy punched Zoë in the shoulder. Gaius wisely stayed silent.

They found Siggy in the midst of a cave. The cave had a hole in the top. Through it, a single beam of sunlight fell upon an impressive-looking sword with twin dragons—one of silver, one of gold—wrapped around the hilt. A voice came from the sword, crying out: *"Come find me—if you are worthy."*

A shiver ran through Rachel. When Siggy had described this dream to her once before, she had imagined the sword calling out in a noble voice, but this voice was disturbingly creepy. It did not sound like the voice of something Rachel would want to find.

Siggy's eyes focused on Zoë, and he shook himself. A moment later, Lucky popped into the dream. The creepy voice continued to call out from the sword.

"That's weird." Zoë pointed at the sword. "That's not an ordinary dream. It's...."

The cave, the sword, and the voice all winked out. They stood in a gray, misty void.

"Did you do that?" Zoë demanded of Siggy.

"No." Siggy shrugged. "I didn't do anything."

"Yeah, nah," she shivered. "That wasn't a dream."

"What was it then?" asked Valerie.

"Excalibur!" sang Sigfried. "It says I am worthy and should come find it! Maybe if we find it, we can find King Arthur. Do you think he'd be upset if we woke him up a little early?"

"I've always wondered," replied Lucky, "why England's Darkest Hour? Wouldn't it make sense to wake up a bit before that in, say, England's Mid Evening, England's A Little After Dark, England's Dim Twilight, or even

England's Late Afternoon Just After Tea, and avoid falling into the darkest hour altogether?"

Gaius and Rachel, both being British, snorted with laughter.

Valerie, however, merely repeated acerbically, "I meant, what did we just see that winked out like a light switching off? You said it wasn't a dream. What was it?"

Zoë shrugged. "A vision? A sending? Don't know."

"Creepy!" sang Joy. She shivered. "Stop scaring me, Siggy!"

"We're all here." Nastasia put her free arm through Rachel's. "Shall we go see my vision?"

"Wait! This is my dreamspace, right?" Siggy squinted, and something exploded. Rachel had no idea what, but there was an enormous boom and a gigantic blossoming of fire. "Ace! Okay, I can control the space here. Before we leave, I want to show you something. This happened the night of the dance...."

"The Year of the Dragon Masquerade Ball!" Lucky corrected, proud of his connection to the event.

"The Fear of the Dragon Masquerade Maul," agreed Siggy. "Lucky saw this—happened just before all that lantern stuff—and he showed it to me. Now I am going to show it to you. Lucky, help me with this."

"I'm on it, boss!" promised Lucky.

A dream version of the campus commons at night appeared around them, along with bright paper lamps shaped like red dragons and orange goldfish. The images were murky and out of proportion, but they became more realistic as Siggy and Lucky squinted at them. A dream image of Amber walked across the grass. A second Lucky, not the one currently wrapped around Sigfried, crouched in the shadows.

From the dream, Siggy's voice said, "Shadow the girl and see what she does, where she goes. She is very wary and very dangerous, so abandon the chase the moment you even begin to suspect she might see or sense you."

"You got it, boss." Almost immediately, Dream Lucky said, "Yeah, busted."

Amber turned and reached out her hand toward Lucky.

"This happened that night? I mean, it's something that really happened?" asked Joy.

Sigfried nodded and gestured at the scene playing out before them.

"Come here, little one," called Amber.

Dream Lucky slithered through the night and began walking alongside Amber. Rachel wondered if her sister realized that Sigfried could see anything Lucky could see. Amber walked down the tree-lined path and out onto the docks. To Lucky, she said, "I'm sorry, little one. I don't think that you will be able to keep up with me when I fly. Though I may be wrong. If you wish to come with me, you'll have to let me carry you in my arms."

Dream Lucky's mouth did not move, but his voice was audible, saying, "Boss, why is she being nice? Should I blast her?"

Dream Siggy's voice replied, "Do not blast any member of the Griffin family. Miss Griffin is a member of my harem, and this is her sister. Her name is Amber."

"What?" shrieked Joy with a giggle. She let go of Nastasia and came and elbowed Rachel in the side. "Rachel, are you two-timing Gaius?"

"Not with Siggy!" Rachel cried, horrified at the idea. She pulled her arm free of Nastasia to defend herself from Joy. Her cheeks suddenly pinked. "Or anyone else!"

"Should I be worried?" Gaius addressed Sigfried with an airy gesture.

"It's just Lucky talk," said Siggy, dismissively. "It's what he understands."

Dream Siggy continued, "Amber was kidnapped from her brainwashed parents as a baby and raised in her world's version of St. Dismas's—and then brainwashed to think having your family life taken from you is good. She thinks of her corps as her mother and father. She also is a Metaplutonian creature, as powerful as Mordecai Egg, or more so."

"Mortimer Egg," whispered Rachel.

"St. Dismas's?" murmured Gaius.

Rachel whispered back, "The orphanage where Siggy grew up."

Dream Siggy resumed, "Her boss is the Master of the World, and he commands the Raven, who can reshape reality and re-write history at whim. In other words, her boss is the guy who orders around the guy who controls reality. She also is the only possible lead to finding our father (or uncle, or whatever) since apparently, we have relatives among the Metaplutonians.

Rachel watched her friends surreptitiously. Siggy and Gaius already knew about the Master of the World, as did the princess; however, it was new to Joy, Zoë, and Valerie, all of whom stared open-mouthed at the news that someone ordered around the Raven.

"We?" asked the dream dragon.

"Come on, Luckster. We're brothers. My uncle is your uncle. I'll share."

"Got it, boss," replied the dream dragon's voice.

"Talk to her," said Dream Siggy's voice. "Ask her if she can have you back here, safe and sound and sane, before dawn. If so, go ahead and go with her. At the mo-

ment, there is no reason to mistrust her. As best I can tell, she's an enemy of Egg and his crew, and the enemy of my enemy is my ally. I hope. Also, don't panic if we lose our mental contact. She has some sort of ward around her that stops magic."

Dream Lucky's voice said, "You got it, boss! No blasting her."

The dragon turned to Amber and spoke out loud. "Okay, I'll come with you if you can have me back by dawn. Also, no being all sneaky and taking over my brain."

Amber smiled slightly. "I promise I will return you before dawn, unless I am dead. And I will not take over your brain, in a sneaky manner or directly."

She picked him up in her arm. Lucky wrapped around her like a feather boa. He made himself smaller than his usual size, so as not to knock her over. Amber then lifted gracefully up into the air, high above the commons. She did not use a broom or any device. She just went upward, as if she could fly by thinking.

Rachel's jaw dropped. Her sister was *flying!* Flying without a broom. Happiness and a strange tightness warred in her heart. She wanted to do that!

Up in the sky, Amber looked into the distance. Her eyes began to glow as if with reflected starlight, though too bright to be from the stars. Starlight-colored butterflies fluttered from under her cloak and gathered in front of her. The butterflies formed a cloud and then dissolved into glitter, which gathered into glowing points directly in front of her eyes. Jagged starlight-colored beams, crackling like electricity, came from these points and zig-zagged into the distance.

Caw! The noise was so loud and raucous that Joy jumped, and Valerie grabbed Siggy's arm. Though the Raven did not unnerve her, Rachel took advantage of the other girls' reactions to step closer to Gaius. He casually put an arm around her shoulder and pulled her against him, which earned him a grateful smile. The princess frowned slightly but said nothing. Whether it was the *caw* or Gaius's arm that made her frown, Rachel could not tell.

Soaring beside Amber in the night air was a Raven the size of an eagle. Even in the darkness, its eyes glowed blood red.

It croaked, "Again, I ask you to not use that power while you are here."

"Guardian," Amber replied serenely, "I am not reaching outside the world. There is little chance anything will notice."

The Raven croaked, "For what do you search?"

"The demons," replied Amber. "Will you take me to them? I can find them on my own. Their stink is so strong that I can smell them across the world. But they're behind defenses set up by the local population. I am sure I can break them or slip by

them, but, if you were to help me, I could just be there, could I not? No one needs to be disturbed or alarmed."

The Raven hovered silently for a moment. "Very well."

The black bird became a winged man, eight feet tall with a circle of light above his head, which he took off and held in his hand. He held out his other hand to Amber. As soon as she took it, the three of them vanished.

"At this point, I panicked," said Siggy, casually.

"You told me not to panic!" objected Lucky.

"Yeah, I told *you* not to panic. I didn't say anything about me!" said Siggy. "It was really weird not having you in my head!" To the rest of them, Sigfried said, "About an hour went by."

"It was twenty-seven minutes, exactly," Lucky corrected. "Super-death-doll-girl Amber said so. I'll do the next part. The boss wasn't there."

The scene before them now showed the secret chamber two levels beneath the Ouroboros Industry's degossamerization dome in Detroit, the very same chamber that had required so many security precautions before Rachel and Gaius had been allowed to see it. High above was a giant iris, fifty-feet in diameter. Just in front of them stood a huge pentagram of a hardened, semi-transparent, umber-colored substance, ten or fifteen feet high and a hundred forty feet across. Inside, trapped like spiders in amber, were Mortimer Egg, Serena O'Malley, and the giant bull with the face of a man—the demon Morax.

Gaius's arm tightened around Rachel's shoulders, and she felt him catch his breath. Aloud, he drawled airily, "Ah, well. So much for the ace up our sleeve. Any objections to me informing William about this as soon as we get back? Or, er, wake up? He'll need to report this breach of security to O.I."

"Fine with me," answered Siggy, "and it was my, er, Lucky's memory, so you don't need anyone else's permission."

"That's right. If the boss says yes, then yes is yes," declared Lucky.

Valerie whispered, "Lucky, that makes no sense."

"Sense is overrated," Lucky replied serenely. "Right, boss?"

"That's right," agreed Sigfried, high-fiving Lucky.

Valerie rolled her eyes and snapped a picture of the two of them, nearly blinding everyone else. She added, "This is such a frustrating way of gaining information. If only we could interview the figures in the visions."

"Don't talk to dream images!" Zoë warned. "It can go badly."

"Besides," said the princess, "we are asleep. That's not a real camera."

"Oh, right," Valerie murmured, chagrined.

"I'm sorry," Rachel whispered to Gaius while the others were distracted. She rested her head on his shoulder. "We were hoping to keep O.I.'s new demon-trapping technology secret."

Gaius brushed her forehead with a very light kiss and shrugged. "It's disappointing. I won't say it's not. I had hoped we would have an advantage that we could keep hidden from the Master of the World." He gestured with his free arm, "But what can we do?"

Ahead of them, Amber, with Lucky still wrapped around her, approached the umber block of demons, her eyes still sparkling with starlight. The eight-foot-tall angel with black wings stood silently behind them.

"This is very clever, Guardian," she said. "They're alive, and their minds are functional; but they're not asleep or awake. The demons are trapped within. They can't even influence the local dreams. They can't act. It's ingenious, almost as if they are frozen in time. How did you make this?"

The Guardian spoke in his melodious angel voice, which caused Amber to give him an odd look. "I did nothing. The device is designed by the locals. Very, very intelligent locals. A mixture of magic and technology."

Amber slid her hand across the umber substance. "Alchemy and Star Yard tech? And extremely elegant at that. I thought they could not function together. Even Hank Rake would be impressed."

Beside her, Gaius sucked in air, no doubt recalling that Star Yard was the name of the space station he had accidentally destroyed in his former life, at least, according to Amber and to the fetch that lived in the china doll of Rachel's classmate, Magdalene Chase. Rachel stepped even closer to him. His former life scared her. It was an enemy she did not know how to face. If he ever remembered it, might he turn into someone else? *Someone who didn't love her?*

Gaius leaned down and whispered into her ear, "Who is Hank Rake? Isn't that the name of the guy with the super mech suit in the comic *Hellraker*?"

Rachel shrugged. "No idea."

Amber gestured at the demons. "Why are there demons here at all? The purpose of closing off this world was to bar them from entering. Our information promised that if we removed all the followers of the master of the angels, the demons would not enter the world either."

"That is what your emperor told me." The Guardian's expression was unreadable.

"But it didn't work?" asked Amber.

"They were gone for a short time," replied the Guardian. "But mortals have free will, and they desire the forbidden. Despite all precautions, a clever but unwise sorcerer devised a way to summon a demon."

"That's unfortunate," Amber said.

The Guardian gazed down at Amber, his face impassive. "His first action was to send the fiend to slay your family It murdered your aunts and uncles and your grandfather's first wife."

"My family?" Amber raised her chin sharply. "Why? Were they trying to stop the prophecy—stop my destiny?"

"That is one possibility," replied the Guardian.

Amber tapped on the umber substance. "This is ingenious but dangerous. Why have you not destroyed these demons? They can be reduced to halos and turned over to the emperor."

The Raven looked at Amber with a gaze that Rachel was glad he had never turned upon her. "Doing so would force me to change the memories of many people. I refuse to do so without direct orders. And even then... I would not test me."

Amber cocked her head and looked at him for a time.

Siggy chuckled. "She looks just like Rachel when she does that."

Nastasia tossed her golden curls and laughed, a silvery sound. "That she does."

Rachel sighed. She could not see the resemblance.

Finally, Amber said, "I think my emperor doesn't understand you. We have so few Guardians like you, and things have been so hectic. So few worlds are left, and many of the Guardians have been in their role for so long they have begun to act like the animals they resemble. I think my emperor should come and speak to you, no? Perhaps learn what you want and what you need in order to do whatever it is you do here?"

The Guardian replied, "I tire of manipulating minds. The sorcerers here do it, too, but that is not by my hand. I would prefer if it were no longer asked of me, except to fight against evil such as this." He waved his hand at the demons in their umber prison.

She nodded. "Changing memories has been done for so long and so casually, no one stops to think about the people who are affected. No one, that is, except for you." Amber turned back to the demons. "That one, the woman, is not possessed. Why is she contained within?"

The Guardian replied, "Because they are not sure if she is possessed or not. It is sad; her mind is fractured. One part of it is not evil at all. Just scared and trapped. Perhaps, in the future, she will be released and healed."

Juma's mother! Rachel shivered, recalling the young man and his miniature elephant, Jellybean, and how she and her dream unicorn had saved him from being sacrificed by Morax. Could his mother be saved? That was a heartening thought.

Amber's gaze fell upon Mortimer Egg. "They need a Trempetta. A shame they're all lost."

The Raven said nothing. His eyes glittered in the dim lighting.

Amber scratched Dream Lucky under the chin. "I've seen enough."

Amber and Lucky were on the docks with no sign of the Guardian.

Lucky unwrapped from Amber. "Uh, thanks for the ride."

"You are welcome," said Amber.

Dream Lucky flew off. As he headed back to campus, he announced, "Boss, I'm okay. And I am not a servant of the super-powerful ninja girl. I think, at least."

"I will still love you even if you are the brain-slave, butt-monkey of super-ninja-Griffin-girl from beyond space and time," Dream Siggy replied loyally.

CHAPTER FIFTEEN:
GASP, DARE, AND FIREHAWK

"MR. SMITH, THERE ARE LADIES PRESENT!" NASTASIA SOUNDED MORE AStonished than indignant.

"Lucky!" Sigfried chided, "You should not repeat such language in front of the girls. Girls don't like words like monkey. Or maybe it was a different word."

"Just telling it like it is, boss," Lucky replied loyally. "Goldilocks told me that a reporter has to be accurate."

Valerie grinned and gave Lucky a thumbs-up, unfazed by his choice of words.

Nastasia spoke with gentle dignity. "We have before us a perfect example as to why we should always comport ourselves with decorum, even in private."

Joy piled on. "Yeah! That was super rude. I'm ashamed of you!"

Above the girls' heads, Rachel caught Gaius and Sigfried exchanging a look, as if both silently agreed that expecting boys to talk like girls when they were alone was absurd.

Aloud, Gaius asked, "What's a Trumpetta? A little trumpet?"

"Don't know," Valerie quipped back dryly, "they were all lost."

"I bet there's one on our world," Gaius said thoughtfully. "I bet the Raven saved one."

"Because of the look on the Raven's face?" Rachel nodded. "I wonder who it is."

Nastasia replied, "I did not take the Guardian's reaction to mean that he knew where one was. Rather it seemed that he had nothing further to add upon the matter."

Gaius shrugged. "Could be."

"I think the more interesting question is," the princess continued, pursing her perfect lips, "Who told my grandfather that if he removed all the followers of the angels, the demons would leave? And, more importantly, what other actions might he have taken based on this faulty information source?"

"That's a very interesting question," Rachel said slowly. "Could the prophecy that led to the kidnapping of my sister have come from the same source?"

"I don't think so," replied Joy, "because your sister really did kill the demon she was prophesied to kill. With her eye beams. I bet she killed him with the same eye beams she used to murder that poor red cap!" Joy's lip trembled slightly.

"Red caps are murderous fiends," replied Valerie. "They're called that because they dye their caps in the blood of their victims—human victims. I wouldn't feel sorry for those perps."

"I'd like eye beams," mused Sigfried in a dreamy voice. "Just thinking of all the things I could murderify with eye beams transports me with joy."

"I'm transported all the way to murder heaven," murmured Lucky.

Valerie thumped Siggy on the shoulder. "I think murder heaven is called Valhalla."

Siggy grinned. Gaius nodded, acknowledging her point.

"I must say," Valerie continued, "it felt good to see Egg encased in that caramel stuff, safely locked away where he can't hurt humanity. Or kidnap my father again." She sighed. "Wish they'd lock up Dr. Mordeau and her creepy assistant, too."

Siggy reached for his knife and then frowned when it was not there and then grinned when the dreamstuff provided him with an even larger knife, which then poofed into cloud stuff.

Valerie snorted. "Let me show you how it's done, champ." She reached down and drew a knife, from where, Rachel could not tell. The knife remained solid. She made a few elegant cutting gestures with it.

Siggy watched her perform these actions, sighing with dreamy delight. Then he perked up. "Teach me to do that!"

"Not now, slugger," Valerie replied. "It's Nastasia's show now."

Meanwhile, Rachel looked to Zoë expectantly. She knew the other girl had recovered some of her previous memories. Zoë yawned and stretched. Rachel continued to gaze plaintively.

Zoë scowled. "Oh, all right. Trempetta are a kind of ghost-hunter who can dispossess people. I've never met one, so I can't tell you if any are around." She turned to the whole group. "Enough dilly-dallying. We're going to a spot where Nastasia can *finally* show us her vision, but first I want to establish the rules."

"Don't spread out, or we fall out of dreamland?" asked Joy. "I know that one by heart, and I have the scars to prove it!"

"Nope." Zoë shook her head, forelock braid flying. "New rules. I didn't walk you up here. I 'woke' you out of your own dreams. I made you lucid. This means that you *cannot* fall into the waking world. In fact, if you tried to follow me down to the waking world, you all would vanish before I got there. You can't fall out of here. You're just dream stuff."

"That's not creepy," murmured Gaius, patting his chest to see if he was substantial.

"However, there are still issues," Zoë continued. "See this silver light around me? It's what keeps you lucid. If you wander too far from me, you will—most likely—fall back into a dreaming state. It won't hurt you. You will still wake up whenever you would normally wake, but you will be gone from our scene, and we might not be able to find you again. So, stay close."

They left Siggy's dream and walked through the dark evergreens, following Zoë. It was eerily quiet. Their footfalls made no sound. A slight mist clung to the trees, smelling as always of lilacs and plaster-of-Paris.

"This should do." Zoë led them into an unoccupied eddy of the ten-foot-high ribbon of mist that held the sleepers' dreams. "Princess, it's showtime. You're on."

Nastasia interlaced her fingers and stretched as if prepping for a sporting event. "Gather around. I will do my best to recall...."

The princess's perfect brow furrowed slightly. A forest appeared around them. Only it was murky and unfocused, and many things looked out of proportion. Rachel began to feel an unpleasant sensation, much like carriage-sickness. She grabbed Gaius's arm and closed her eyes.

Nastasia's voice said apologetically, "At least, there aren't any emus or white ibises. One never knows what might pop out of one's subconscious after years of living with my father."

"You keep bin chickens at your palace?" Zoë asked. "I would think that a royal residence, at least, could be free of scavenger pests."

"Firstly," the princess said mildly, "the white ibis is a beautiful bird, once worshipped in Egypt. It's not their fault humans leave tasty morsels in rubbish bins. And, secondly, not only do we have them, but also my father knighted one and made him the minister of trash collection."

Rachel opened one eye. Things were still distorted. She shut it again and gripped Gaius's hand more tightly. He squeezed back, firm and comforting.

"Did they collect the garbage?" asked Valerie, interested. She reached for her notebook and then sighed as she remembered that it would not help to write anything down here.

Nastasia sighed. "Well, they did eat out of the bins, and Father declared that to be a success. For all I know, it was Father's doing that they moved into cities and became such a bother to begin with. With him, one never knows."

"They moved into the urban areas in the nineteen seventies," said Zoë. "That's what my cousin the barber told me. They became a nuisance in New Zealand about a decade later."

"Then perhaps, it's not my father's fault, but really, I would not put anything past him. Let us begin," Nastasia concluded serenely. "Ah! The angel Auriel told me that I can request help to remember my visions. Auriel, I would appreciate assistance. There we go."

Rachel opened one eye. The individual leaves were now so crisp and sharp that it hardly seemed like dreamland at all. She opened the other eye.

"Much better." Valerie looked around, still gripping her dream knife. "What're we looking at?"

Rachel examined the rocks and tree trunks. It was eerie to be in a forest but smell no natural odors. Nor could she hear any sounds of wildlife. The only sound was an oddly wailing flute far in the distance. Rachel had heard such noises in dreamland before.

"This is the southwest part of Roanoke Island," Rachel said. "I recognize those boulders and those standing stones, behind us." She pointed. "But everything else is wrong. There should be a field here, not trees. And here? There's a huge oak, not this tiny sapling. Something is definitely wrong." She turned to Nastasia. "Are you certain this isn't an overlap of two places?"

The princess looked concerned. "This is as it appeared to me. Maybe it's symbolic rather than meant to be an actual time and place?"

"Okay," murmured Zoë, looking at Rachel, "that wasn't freaky."

"Oh, I disagree," objected Valerie, holding up a finger. "That was most certainly freaky. Are you sure you aren't a computer, Rachel Griffin? Have you memorized the position of every stone on the island? How did you recognize this place?"

"She said it. I didn't." Gaius tipped back on his heels and whistled innocently.

"It's because she's a freaky dwarf genius," Lucky said proudly.

Rachel rolled her eyes. "I was here a little over a week ago. This is where we fought the barghests. One of the Agents had left something on those boulders."

"Okay," Gaius admitted. "That makes sense. Even I might have recognized a place under those circumstances, and the standing stones are an obvious hint. I've noticed them myself."

"Now that we have all admired Miss Griffin's mnemonic prowess, perhaps we can proceed with my vision?" Nastasia asked primly. She met Rachel's gaze, her eyes sparkling with good humor. Rachel smiled back, glad someone did not see her as inhuman.

Nastasia continued, "This vision occurred the afternoon after the Masquerade ball. I believe these young men snuck off the island after the dance."

Before them stretched a forest in twilight. It covered the same territory as the snowy field where Rachel and the Agents had fought the barghests. There was no sign of the docks or Bannerman's Castle. Through the trees, they caught a glimpse of a rowboat moored to a boulder by the shore. The eyes painted on the prow of the rowboat seemed to glow in the dimness.

Suddenly, two boys came running pell-mell through the trees. They ran flat out as if the wild hunt were on their tail. They were young boys—Rachel guessed them to be between eleven and thirteen—dressed in a jacket and pantaloon garment popular in the eighteenth century, a garment saddled with the unhelpful name of skeleton suit, due to how it emphasized the slimness of those who wore it. These particular skeleton suits were dark green velvet with golden ornamental buttons down the front and open white ruffled collars.

Silver moonlight spilled through the fingers of the boy in front. He shouted over his shoulder without pausing his breakneck speed, "Gasp, Run!"

The two boys kept running as if their lives depended upon it.

Near the shore waited a third boy, slightly smaller and with the pre-adolescent pudginess some boys develop before their growth spurt. He stood next to the rowboat, holding its lead.

"Firehawk! Gasphawk! Hurry!"

"Coming!" shouted the front boy, presumably the one nicknamed Firehawk, as he had called the other boy Gasp. All three boys spoke with British accents. "Make sure there's water between the shore and the boat!"

The smaller boy drew the rowboat away from the shore, water swirling around his black Hessian boots.

"They're being pursued by something fey," murmured Gaius under his breath, turning around and peering behind them as if hoping to catch a glimpse of whatever was chasing the boys.

Rachel gave her boyfriend an admiring glance. Many supernatural creatures could not cross water. She was impressed with Gaius for having picked up on that so quickly.

Valerie lifted her camera and then sighed and lowered it again. "Do we know any students with nicknames like that? Firehawk? Anyone in Drake?"

Gaius shook his head. "These boys are too young for the upper school."

Something clumped through the forest behind the boys—something bigger than a human.

Firehawk shouted, "Forget holding the boat, Dare! Pull it away from the shore and jump in. Those boats go on their own. Just tell it to wait there, a little ways out! We'll get to you!"

The scene froze, the boys paused in the act of running.

Nastasia turned to Gaius, her voice frosty. "So your prince is behind this!"

"What?" gaped Gaius, taken by surprise.

Rachel glanced away, regretting not having warned him.

"I received this vision the morning after the dance where Mr. Von Dread had an altercation with the elder Mr. Starkadder," replied Nastasia. "The gem the boys are carrying—we shall see it more clearly in a moment —is the same size, and cut in the same distinctive manner, as the Kadderstar. Our current theory is that Mr. Von Dread stole it as an act of petty revenge after he was unable to steal my sister from her fiancé. Do you know anything about this?"

"That may be the craziest theory I've ever heard," Gaius barked out, half laughing, half angry. "Literally. Not an exaggeration."

"It wasn't Von Dread," Sigfried declared. "Dread is Ace! Dread is best! He wouldn't steal a stupid gem. If he wanted it, he would beat Starkadder in a duel! All hail Dread!"

Gaius snapped, "Why would Vlad steal your sister? He's all but engaged to Rachel's!"

Nastasia, Valerie, Zoë, and Joy turned and stared at Rachel, all crying out at once:

"Is this so?"

"What?"

"*Hontou?*"

"And you didn't tell us?"

Rachel's cheeks burned. *That was a secret!*

Facing her friends, she nodded solemnly.   "It's not official yet. Vladimir proposed, but Sandra refuses to say yes until my father gives his permission. So they have asked us to keep it quiet."

"Boy, Rachel," cried Joy. "I can't believe you never said a word! To us! Your friends!"

"Not even a whisper. Impressive secret-keeping, Griffin. Didn't know you had it in you," said Zoë. "Did you know this the time we snuck into his room?"

"No," said Rachel. "I found out more recently."

"You snuck where?" Nastasia looked back and forth between Rachel and Zoë. "Whose room? Did I know about this?" She waved a hand. "Never mind. That's neither here nor there."

"But...." Gaius shook his head as if trying to shake away the craziness, "I am rather sure we would know if the Kadderstar were missing. I believe there's only a five or six percent chance of Romulus keeping that quiet."

"Maybe he does not wish his enemies to know he is without it," countered Nastasia.

Valerie offered, "Maybe it was replaced with a conjured stone. The ball was on the night of the full moon. The perp could have conjured it that night and degossamerized it long enough for it to last a month. If so, Starkadder would not even know it was gone until it vanished when it wasn't set out under the next full moon. Right?"

Siggy and Lucky both nodded simultaneously. They looked at each other and nodded again. Then, they looked back at the others and nodded a third time.

"How many full moons do you need for a conjured object to become real again?" asked Valerie.

Rachel answered, "Three to be stable, thirteen to be solid, and a great year—which is a hundred and one—to be real."

"You Wise and your crazy terminology," Gaius muttered under his breath. He turned to Rachel. "NASA defines a great year as the time it takes the equinox to make an entire period around the ecliptic, which is roughly twenty-five thousand eight hundred years. That would be a lot longer than a hundred and one months. What you Wise are describing is called an *octaeteris*, and it would only be ninety-seven or ninety-eight moons long."

"All very well, Mr. Scientific Genius," Rachel crossed her arms. "But a-hundred-and-one is traditional. If you have made it that far, why not be absolutely certain?"

"This whole conversation is not to the point!" objected Gaius, throwing up his hands. He scowled at Rachel. "Do *you* think Vlad was involved with this?"

"Of course not!" Rachel cried back aghast, hurt that he would even suspect her. "The very idea is ridiculous, and I told them so!"

"But you didn't warn *me* about this?"

Oops. "Th-the idea's absurd! I know what you two were doing that night!" she cried, casting around for evidence of her innocence. "I-I brought you along tonight, didn't I?"

The anger drained from his face. "Sorry. It's... harder to stay calm right now than usual. Maybe I am only eighty-nine percent awake. Maybe even only seventy-six percent. I hate it when people accuse Vlad of acting in bad faith."

"I understand." She reached out and squeezed his hand. He pulled her closer.

"Look at that jewel," Gaius stated more calmly, gesturing at the young man whom the other boys had called Firehawk. "It glows silver! How's that the Kadderstar? Romulus's ring is purple."

"Perhaps for the same reason this landscape is not quite as Rachel remembers," Nastasia countered calmly. "This silver jewel may be a symbolic representation of the Kadderstar. It has the same unusual cut. Nonetheless, let us examine the evidence. Jenny Dare serves your prince, does she not? Do you deny the other boys called the boy by the rowboat by the name of Dare?"

Gaius blinked, startled.

The princess continued, "Does Miss Dare have a younger brother at the lower school?"

"She does not," Gaius replied. "She has an older brother."

"A cousin, maybe?" asked Nastasia.

"That... I don't know," admitted Gaius.

"Can you guarantee that Miss Dare did not contact a relative at the lower school on the night of the ball and ask him and his friends to do a service for Mr. Von Dread?"

A shiver ran up Rachel's spine. Could Vlad be involved after all? Jenny Dare was definitely one of his people. Would she have acted on her own initiative?

"Can we get a better look at the jewel?" asked Joy. "I-I know this boy's name is Dare, but I don't think that's the Kadderstar. In fact...." Her voice trailed off, a strange look on her face.

"Let me see what I can do," said the princess. "There was a point in the vision...."

The scene seemed to jump ahead slightly, so that the boys were now closer to the shore. The boy in front opened his fingers and glanced at the gemstone on his palm. It looked like a silver twin of the Kadderstar—a silvery gem slightly larger than a grape, fashioned into a spherical cut with many glittering facets that struck Rachel as somewhere between a round brilliant and a Portuguese.

Nastasia froze the scene with the young man's hand still open. Joy rushed over to stand in front of the lead boy and stared at the jewel intently.

"This isn't the Kadderstar," whispered Joy. "I'm sure of it."

"If it isn't," Gaius said tersely, "then you ladies owe Vlad an apology."

"Very well," acknowledged the princess with a gracious nod.

As Rachel glanced at the boy holding the gem, her attention was drawn to the expensive leather Hessians on the twelve-year-old's feet. She examined the fancy, lace-edged, ruffled collars, the authentic dark green velvet suits, which looked well-worn in the very way that costumes never did. Who went to such trouble for a masquerade?

Zoë walked up and stared into the face of the other running boy. She called over her shoulder, "What would lower school children have been doing at the masquerade?"

"These are not masqueraders," Rachel replied softly, staring at the boys.

"Then why are they in costume?" asked Nastasia.

Rachel glanced at the sapling where the two-hundred-year oak should be and the empty slope where Bannerman's Castle should stand. *Dare, Gasp Hawke, Fire-hawk.* An eerie horripilation began at the top of her scalp, ran to the soles of her feet, and then back again as the boys' nicknames took on new significance. Realizing what she would see, she stepped forward and looked into the face of the boy holding the silver jewel.

With an audible gasp, she pressed her hand against her mouth. He looked entirely different and yet exactly the same: the same eyebrows already growing untamed, same imperious, commanding manner. Then she could not see his face through the welling of tears.

"They weren't at the masquerade." She blinked to clear her sight, calling on her mask of calm to keep her voice even. "Those are their school uniforms."

"What makes you say that?" asked Valerie.

"This event took place two hundred years ago," Rachel pointed as she spoke. "The docks and Bannerman's Castle were not built yet. The trees that are now venerable were saplings. These three boys were students then —the lower school had not been built yet, and the rules as to age qualification were not as rigid. The boy in back," she pointed at the one called Gasp, "is Jasper Hawke—he would have married Dean Moth if he had lived. He died in 1888." She paused for a hair's breadth, startled. She had not realized that their formidable dean was so old. "The one by the rowboat—"

Joy interrupted excitedly, "Is he one of Jenny Dare's ancestors?"

Rachel shook her head. "He's not a member of the Dare family at all. Dare's short for Daring or Darius. That's Darius Northwest."

"Our Daring Northwest?" Gaius asked, startled, examining the boy. "The author of *Kallikantzaroi and Their Cousins* and *Domovoi, Kikimora, and Other Denizens of the Forest*?"

"And *The Not-So-Long-Ago Dream Time: A Comprehensive Study of the Bunyip*?" asked Nastasia, moving to get a better look at the smaller boy.

Rachel nodded. "The very same."

"Who is Firehawk?" asked Valerie. She snapped a photo of the last boy, who stood with the silvery light, like living moonlight, escaping between his fingers.

"'Fire' is a nickname for *Blaise* and 'hawk' for Lord *Falcon*-ridge." Rachel's voice shook only the tiniest bit. "That's my grandfather."

Chapter Sixteen:
Three Coat Racks
and a Steeplechaser

From behind the running boys came a crash of splintering wood. Something big smashed through the forest, pursuing them.

"What's that?" Gaius spun around.

"I do not know," the princess admitted. "It's whatever the boys are running from, but it only appears in the vision at this one point. I couldn't see it clearly."

"The angel has clarified the vision for you, right? Let's take a look." Gaius backtracked along the boys' trail. Rachel nearly cried out for him to be careful. She clamped her mouth shut before she embarrassed herself. This was a memory of a vision of something frightening. There was no real danger.

A large shape stomped through the trees. The vision only skirted near it, but for one moment, a face appeared. It was a great, brutish face with small beady eyes, bright with malice. It had horns, tusks, and stony skin. The mouth was an enormous gash across the ugly features. The thick topknot of black, oily hair was wrapped around a wide bone.

Gaius took a surprised step back, nearly stumbling. "What in Jove's name is that?"

"It's Mambres!" cried Rachel.

"The ogre!" shouted Sigfried, grabbing the dream knife from Valerie and running forward. "Come on, Snakeasaurus Six! We killed him once. We can kill him again."

"I'm on it, Bossaurus Twenty-Two! Burnination coming up!" Lucky drew back his head.

"Please, Mr. Smith," the princess spoke politely, "do ask your dragon not to breathe fire all over my vision. The real ogre is still dead."

"The boys are fleeing from the ogre?" asked Valerie. "That confirms the theory that this didn't take place a week ago. The ogre was dead by then. Did they steal the gem from it?"

"What about that statue, boss?" asked Lucky.

"Right, Luckotops Sixty-Twelve! The ogre's cave had a statue in it, a big one, Egyptian looking. It had a setting in its forehead that would fit a big gem, but the gem was gone. I remember because we looked around for it, in case it had fallen onto the cave floor."

"When were you in the ogre's cave?" Valerie turned on him accusingly.

"Oh, just some time," answered Siggy, nonchalant.

Valerie gave him a long, sardonic look, but she did not ask more questions. Rachel knew it had been back in February, when Sigfried snuck out during the lockdown.

"We took what was ours before adults could kype it," said Lucky, with great satisfaction.

Gaius shook his head, bemused. "Mr. Smith, you never lack for surprises."

"The only other thing I remember about the statue," continued Siggy, "was that some boys had carved their initials into it."

"What makes you think it was done by boys?" asked Joy, still back by Rachel's young grandfather, staring at the silver jewel.

Siggy shrugged. "Who else carries a knife and carves initials into things?"

"Good point," Joy pouted. "Girls would have painted their initials with nail polish. That's what my sisters and I do to mark our stuff. Only Mercy likes to carefully paint over everyone else's initials, so your stuff becomes her stuff. She says nearly any letter can be made into an *M*."

"Sounds as if she's without mercy," quipped Gaius.

"She is!" Joy declared energetically. "Patience's patient with her, but Charity's got no charity for her at all!"

Gaius smirked. "Ah, Mercy's not so bad. She's one of the best scholars I know."

"That just makes her betrayal all the more cruel," Joy said with mock sadness.

Rachel asked, "How many sets of initials were carved into the statue, Sigfried?"

"Three. Two with two letters, one with three. Lucky and I debated what they most likely stood for and came up with some sound suggestions. What were they, Luckster?"

"Dumb Nothing," Lucky began, running his claw down his crimson beard as he thought. "Juicy Hippopotamus. I picked that one!" he added proudly. "I can't remember the other."

"Were they DN, JH, and BLF?" asked Rachel, "as in Blaise, Lord Falconridge?"

"Oh, right!" cried Sigfried. "Bavarian Liberation Front!"

Gaius gave a humorous snort. "Is the front liberating Bavaria for Vlad? Or from Vlad?"

"Why in the world would the boys have carved their initials into the statue? Isn't that like standing up and waving your arms and admitting you're the perp?" asked Valerie, astonished.

"You just don't understand boys," replied Siggy, confidently.

"I understand criminal boys," she shot back. "I just don't understand show-off boys."

Gaius stayed quiet as if he was not sure which side of this argument he agreed with.

Rachel walked around her twelve-year-old grandfather. "I don't understand. It said in the portion of his file that I read that he had been expelled for leaving the island without permission. He was accused of theft, but it could not be proven, so he was never officially charged."

"How could they possibly not be able to prove it," objected Valerie, "if he and his friends *carved their initials* into the statue that used to hold the gem?"

Zoë shrugged. "Were the people investigating the crime allowed into the ogre's cave?"

"Oh, good point," murmured Rachel.

"As to their initials," said Nastasia, "maybe the ogre himself did not understand what the marks meant. They weren't hieroglyphs, after all. Shall we continue?"

Rachel looked at twelve-year-old Blaise Griffin again. He looked so much like her memory of her beloved grandfather and yet so young, even younger than Rachel herself. She glanced at Jasper Hawke and her hero, Daring Northwest. She had known these three were friends, but she had not known that they had gone on an adventure together as children—stealing a jewel from an ogre and running away from school. *Why had they done it?*

And why had he never told her about this? Or about the death of his first family? She loved him so much! Why had she been shut out of such important parts of his life?

Rachel felt it as a palpable pain: that she had not been there, running through the forest with him and his friends. If only she could have known him then. Seeing him, proud and commanding—cool as ice and fierce as a tiger—and not being able to join his adventure was like finding the long-lost door to paradise and then discovering you were not allowed to enter, that you would be stuck, forever, outside in the cold, looking in through barred windows.

She did not speak or breathe, for fear that whatever came out would betray her agony.

Nastasia walked up and slipped her arm through Rachel's. "I remember you showed us a memory of him. This boy does look much like a younger version of that man."

"Yes." Rachel managed a smile. "The day I said 'boo' back to him." She wiped absently at the corner of her eyes, which were unexpectedly wet, and then took a long, unsteady breath. "That was the first time I was ever important."

"Let's see what comes next," said Valerie, taking her dream knife back from Siggy, to his dismay. He kept trying to form a knife out of the dream matter around them, but his knife kept dispelling back into dreamstuff.

The ogre did not reappear. The three boys jumped into the rowboat. The eyes painted on the craft's side glowed in the gloom, though the sky seemed to be growing lighter. The point of view of the vision followed them as the boat glided forward. The island the boys were leaving looked familiar, but the waters they floated upon were not the Hudson. Ocean waves crashed against the shore.

"Ah!" Joy jumped as water rushed around her feet. "Oh, it's not wet! Weird."

Rachel found herself standing in the dream water. She took a few steps back until she was out of the vision. Gaius came over to stand beside her again.

"This isn't the Hudson," said Valerie. "It's a coastline. Could be Maine. We have a lot of rocky coasts."

"Back then, the island was still floating," Rachel said.

"Then it could be anywhere," concluded Valerie.

Ahead of the boys was a rocky coastline beyond which lay rolling hills. As the boys glided closer, they rounded a small promontory. There, the coastline split, forming a deep cove. Two small, rocky islands lay between them and the inner part of the cove.

Rachel's lips parted in surprise. She recognized this place.

"It's Cornwall," she said. "Real Cornwall back in England, not Cornwall-on-Hudson."

"No way!" objected Joy. "You've memorized all the coastlines, too?"

"That's too freaky," muttered Zoë.

Nastasia peered at Rachel as if to see if she were joking. "Of all the shores in the world, you recognize this one? This seems extraordinary. Are you sure you aren't mistaken?"

"Actually, I recognize it, too." Gaius slipped his hands into his pockets. Everyone else turned towards him. He shrugged. "It's a major tourist attraction about an hour from my home."

"Okay," Valerie quipped. "We'll give you a pass, Griffin. *This* time." She peered at the approaching sloping rocks. "Looks like slate, at least without a hardness test."

Siggy said to Lucky, "That's my gal, the rockhound."

Lucky replied, "Why shouldn't she be a rock dragon?"

Siggy nodded. "Rock dragon is good."

"Looks like New Zealand, too," observed Zoë. "Not where I lived with my funky shaman relative, Aperahama Whetu. That was forest. But near the port town where I first arrived."

"Did you arrive by ship?" asked Valerie, surprised. "That's quaint. Do they still do that in the World of the Wise? They don't take a plane?"

Rachel and Joy and the princess all turned and stared at her. The princess clearly struggled not to smile at another's ignorance. The other two were not so restrained.

Nastasia said gently, "We travel by travel glass. It takes minutes to walk from New York to Paris or Cathay. Or New Zealand. The only people who fly are those who live far from a glass hall. And they would travel by broom, umbrella platform, or flying ship."

"Oh. Right." Valerie blushed.

"Yeah, nah," said Zoë, "there weren't any glasses where I was being shipped off to, so my father thought it would be cheaper to literally ship me off. He arranged for me to work my way to New Zealand, on a freighter owned by a distant relative, Captain Oceanus Moth. I was okay with this. Sounded exciting. Only turns out, they don't let pre-teen girls work in the boiler room or even the kitchen—though being a cook would have been sweet! Think of all the treats I could have flogged! I spent the voyage working in the laundry. At least, I'm now a mean hand with a shirt iron!"

"I guess that is some kind of benefit," murmured Valerie, stunned.

Rachel realized Valerie had not heard many of Zoë's stories about her crazy family.

"Can we get back to the vision?" Joy stomped her foot.

"Well, don't you have your panties all in a twist," said Zoë.

"Enough of you." Joy hip-checked her roommate, who took a stumbling step and then hip-checked her back. "I want to find out what happened to it!"

The boys glided into the cove. A rocky shelf stuck out into the water. Behind it was a small beach. They pulled the boat ashore. Then they started up the hill beyond the stony beach.

At the top of the steep incline, a girl waited for them. She wore a high-waisted calico gown and a large matching bonnet. She would have looked quite elegant, except that her skirt had been tied up to one side so that her pantaloons showed as she made her way down the steep slope. She waved both arms to draw the boys' attention. She had bright eyes full of laughter and an intelligent gleam. Something about her reminded Rachel of Laurel, though this girl looked more intellectual and less zany than her sister.

"Oh, good, you've come," the young woman called as if she waited for young men who arrived by rowboat at dawn every day. "Everything is prepared. I left crumbs from treats all over the cave and an empty bottle of my father's second-best Scotch."

"What did you do with the Scotch?" called Jasper Hawke.

"Poured it in the sea," she replied haughtily.

"Waste of good Scotch!" he complained.

"Still, it's all in the cave, just as you asked. Anyone who comes will think you lot came here and cavorted about." She gave them all an arch look.

"Enough of that," stated twelve-year-old Blaise Griffin. "Milly, where are the brooms?"

"Blaise Pellinore Griffin! How many times have I told you not to call me Milly!" She made a mischievous face. "That's Hon. Amelia to you."

"Stone the Crows!" Rachel cried, shocked. "That's my grandmother!"

No wonder the girl reminded her of Laurel. She looked a bit like Peter, too. The idea that this bright, spirited girl was the same person as her stiff and disapproving grandmother was almost too much to bear.

"What does she mean by 'On'?" asked Valerie.

Gaius answered airily, "Hon. is short for Honorable—a title, similar to 'lady' or 'your grace.' Probably means she is a baron's daughter or some such."

Rachel nodded in agreement. "Only she's teasing him. No one ever speaks hon. aloud. Titles of that sort are only for envelopes."

"Ah," Gaius gave an amused snort. He made a wide gesture. "Toff humor."

Amelia Abney-Hastings ran up the slope a few feet. Stooping, she held up three long straight brooms with narrow tail slats set a bit apart from each other, much like the teeth of a comb. They were an early bristleless design, colloquially known as coat racks, though they looked more like leaf rakes. Amelia waved them in the air and then, stooping again, lifted and waved a fourth broom, a steeplechaser.

Rachel and her girlfriends gasped in surprise.

"Is that Vroomie?" asked Valerie, peering carefully.

Rachel shook her head. While the design was similar, the coloring was different. This one had an oak shaft and tail fans of ebony and teak. And yet, it looked so much like hers that Rachel wondered if the two brooms had been made by the same craftsman. Until that moment, it had never occurred to her to wonder why her family had given a twelve-year-old girl something as complicated as a steeplechaser. Now she knew. Her grandmother had flown a steeplechaser, too.

The boys scampered up the hill, silver light still shining through Blaise Griffin's fingers. The Honorable Amelia handed the coat racks to the three boys and jumped on her steeplechaser. The four of them flew off to the east.

The vision ended. Rachel and her friends stood in the curve of a mist ribbon under the velvety, starred sky in dreamland.

"That was all." Nastasia looked disappointed. "I thought I was receiving important information—perhaps about an attack on the Kadderstar. But apparently not. This is most frustrating. I have no idea why I was shown this."

"I know," said Joy.

Everyone turned and stared at her.

"I do," she repeated. "Remember how I track prophecies? That was the gem from the prophecy. The prophecy that never came true about the Terrible Five finding something important—so important that, twenty-five years ago, they dug all over Roanoke Island looking for something they never found? That was it! The Heart of Dreams!"

"You think this vision's about finding this heart-thing?" Zoë asked as they sat down on some dream rocks at the edge of the evergreen forest.

"Perhaps," Nastasia replied dubiously, "but why would that matter?"

Rachel's heart was awhirl with a myriad of emotions after all that they had just seen. Donning her mask of calm, she said, "It means my grandfather and his friends stole the Heart, back when Roanoke was floating near England, probably 1824—That's when he was sent down. It was off the coast of England then, and Grandfather would have been twelve. They brought it to Cornwall and then flew east. Possibly toward Dartmoor, where my family lives. I don't know."

"Sent down?" asked Joy, puzzled.

Gaius drawled casually, "That's Brit talk for expelled. Though usually, it applies to universities, not primary school."

"And the ogre chased him," said Siggy.

"And accused him," said Gaius, "but they couldn't prove it? Or maybe the ogre didn't accuse him, and he got in trouble for leaving campus? The ogre must have made some accusation, however, because the school knew something had been stolen."

Rachel nodded. She realized she had not told Gaius about the heist and peeking at her grandfather's file. She was not sure he would approve. He was a virtuous young man.

"But why show this to me?" asked Nastasia. "Why now?"

"Fey come from dreams, right?" Gaius looked around as if expecting to see a fairy flit by. "Maybe this Heart of Dreams could help solve the problems brought by the death of the Heer."

"Of course!" Rachel jumped to her feet, her heart pounding. "Of course! That's why you had the vision! It happened the very afternoon after the Heer died. There must be a clue here that will help us find the Heart! Siggy and I can look over the holidays. He'll be in Devon with me. If we find it, maybe it will help Nighthawk and the Grand Inquisitor repair the broken covenant!"

She did not add that this vision had probably occurred soon after her conversation with Jariel. She recalled how the Raven had looked off to the east—towards England. Had he offered to arrange for her to help with the matter of the fey because he knew that the Heart, which could solve the problem, was in a place where she could find it over spring break? If so, was it he who had arranged for the princess to have this vision?

"Maybe," said the princess uncertainly, "but we should not jump to conclusions."

"When did your grandfather leave Roanoke Island?" asked Valerie. Again, she reached for her notebook and scowled, remembering yet again that she was in dreamland.

"February twenty-fifth," — Rachel glanced at her memory of her grandfather's file—"eighteen-twenty-four."

"So you were right about the year." Gaius smiled at her.

"Two hundred years to the day from when I had the vision," Nastasia observed. "So the vision might merely have been some kind of commemoration."

"Let's research this Heart thing. Maybe we can find some clues," said Valerie.

Joy pouted. "I've been researching it all year. I've found almost nothing."

"Me, too," Rachel sighed. "I even searched the libraries at home, but no luck." She paused and then added, "But I have seen it before."

Gaius's head snapped up. "You know where it is? Did your grandfather take it home?"

"No. I saw it in a vision—the one Nastasia had when she touched Vladimir."

"In the vision *about Vlad?*" Gaius asked, startled.

"Here." Rachel closed her eyes and concentrated, recalling the princess's vision from back in September. When she opened them, four figures on horseback stood on a hillside—a gaunt figure on a black horse holding a balance; a fierce soldier with a sword on a roan horse; a kingly figure wearing a seven-pointed crown of gold on a white steed; and a hooded figure with a scythe on a horse that was of a pale color.

"There," she pointed at the kingly figure. The crown upon its head was set with seven gems that twinkled like stars. These jewels were the same size and cut as the Kadderstar and the silver gem. One was the exact shade of purple as Romulus Starkadder's ring, and another was the moonlight silver of the gem her grandfather had been holding in the princess's vision.

Zoë jumped back in terror, shouting, "The Four Horsemen! Run! Oh… wait. Geesh! Rachel, don't do that to me!"

"You recognize them?" Rachel asked, astonished.

"From my former life. They were pretty famous." Zoë stepped forward and peered at them. "Never got to see them up close, though. Isn't that the Septentrion Crown on Pestilence's head? That's famous, too. It was supposed to be Adam's crown."

"Who?" Rachel leaned forward to hear better. She did not recognize the name Adam, though Jariel had once mentioned the Four Horsemen.

"Er… nothing," muttered Zoë.

"It's definitely the Septentrion Crown," said Rachel, "or at least that is what the Horseman with the skull face called it in Nastasia's vision."

Zoë stepped closer, examining the crown on the kingly figure. "You're right. Those gems look like the one we saw tonight."

"If nothing else," said Valerie, "it shows that other gems get cut that way. I think we can rule out, with certainty, the theory that the gem in the vision was the Kadderstar."

"Could you please send them away?" asked Joy, shivering and holding up her arm between herself and the horsemen. "They give me the creeps. It's like they are watching me."

"They did turn and see me in my vision," said Nastasia. "I, too, would prefer if you dispelled them, Miss Griffin."

Rachel stopped concentrating, and the four figures dissolved into mist.

"There was also an amazing building," Rachel added, "like nothing I have ever seen. It had gemstones in the windows and arches and buttresses and gargoyles."

"Gemstones?" Zoë looked skeptical.

Rachel concentrated on the building from the princess's vision that had so struck her. It was built of granite, but it was not square and solid like most stone buildings. A wonder of arches, buttresses, and spires spread behind twin towers. Statues of what she now knew to be angels graced its walls, along with statues of gargoyles and those of bareheaded men in robes with what looked like rope belts. The windows shone with brilliant colors—blues, reds, greens.

"Oh, that's a cathedral," Zoë said dismissively. "And those aren't jewels, just colored glass. That's called stained glass."

"I say," Rachel asked suddenly. She stopped concentrating on the majestic structure, and it vanished. "This Heart of Dreams, what does it do? Is it like Zoë's shoes, allowing a person to go in and out of dreamland?"

"I have no idea," said Joy, "though that makes sense with what little I've found."

"Why do you ask?" asked the princess.

Rachel said, "When Astrid and I were harried by pixies—"

"When were you harried by pixies?" asked the princess and Siggy and Gaius together.

"During the skating party," she replied. "Didn't seem worth mentioning after the ogre."

"I see," Nastasia nodded understandingly. "Go on."

"The pixie knights wanted to kidnap Astrid and me and take us to a place where no one could reach us, '*not unless they have in hand the star from the crown of the First of Kings.*'"

"Where exactly are these pixies?" Gaius asked, twirling his wand.

"I thought maybe they meant King Alilum of Sumer," said Rachel.

"That would be Adam," Zoë murmured. "The First of Kings, I mean."

"They then said it had been '*stolen nigh these two hundred years from our Heer! Let us punish these children for the crime of those!*'" Rachel repeated the pixies' lines with the correct intonation for their sweet, high voices.

"Two hundred years!" cried Joy. "I bet it's the same! And 'those children' are the ones we just saw, right? Your grandparents and their friends?"

"Why from the Heer?" asked Zoë. "Looks like it came from the ogre."

Gaius said, "The Heer was not anywhere nearby at that time, though I think the island did pass by New York before it went to England if I am remembering the path that Roanoke Island followed correctly. Could the ogre have stolen it from the Heer, and the children from the ogre?"

"If the Heer, who was a fey creature, had a way of moving in and out of dreamland, that might make sense," said Rachel. "Or maybe the ogre was guarding it for the Heer."

"We just don't know," Zoë shrugged. "Back to this vision. What was that place those boys rowed to?" asked Zoë. "Gaius, you said it was a tourist attraction near your house. I didn't see anything there. Has it changed a lot?"

Rachel said, "It is quite similar today. It's Tintagel, approaching Merlin's Cave. Our family friends, the Saps, live near here. We've gone sailing with them a number of times."

Siggy had been wrestling with Lucky. He suddenly stood up. "Tintagel! As in the castle where King Arthur was conceived? Is that Sap as in Gorlois Sap, Duke of Tintagel?"

"You remember someone's name, Siggy?" Joy gawked. "You?"

"An Arthurian name!" Siggy objected.

Rachel nodded. "Yes. The title is Duke of Trevena now, but that's another name for the same place. Gorlois's family still holds the title."

Gaius looked at her in surprise. "There's a *Duke* of Trevena?"

"It's a title of the Wise, one of the Peers of the Round Table," said Rachel.

Gaius echoed, "There's a Round Table?"

Sigfried cried, "There's a Round Table? How do I become a knight of it?"

Rachel smiled apologetically. "It's not a knightly table anymore. It's the ruling body of the Wise of Great Britain."

"I thought the Parliament of the Wise was the ruling body of the Wise," said Valerie.

"The Parliament is in charge of international matters, rules and principles of how to deal with the Unwary," replied Rachel. "The Round Table decides local British matters."

Siggy asked, "Could this cave of Merlin be where the sword from my dream is?"

Gaius shook his head. "Not if the cave we saw in your dream when we picked you up tonight is what the sword's home looks like. Merlin's Cave is quite different."

Rachel, who had visited Merlin's Cave once, nodded in agreement.

"Still, might be at least worth a look," insisted Sigfried.

"We can go over spring break; maybe with Gaius if he can get off from his chores." Rachel threw her boyfriend a fond look. Suddenly, she turned to Zoë. "Is it after midnight?"

"Yes, it is," said Zoë."

Rachel spun around and threw her arms around her boyfriend, rising onto her tiptoes and kissing him on the cheek. "Happy birthday, Gaius Valiant!"

Chapter Seventeen:
An Exchange of
Birthday Presents

The next evening was the long-awaited Knights of Walpurgis election. Rachel met up with Gaius after they both caught an early dinner. She walked up smiling, holding his present behind her back. Gaius was wearing new robes, not a patch in sight. Rachel was delighted for him, but she also felt embarrassed. Buying him something he actually needed, such as new robes, had not occurred to her.

"How did it go with William telling O.I. about Amber?" she asked.

Vlad and Gaius's best friend, William Locke, was the son of one of the two owners of Ouroboros Industries. It had fallen upon him to inform his father of the security breach in the form of Amber and Lucky.

Gaius shrugged glumly. "He was disappointed. So was Vlad. But William said his father and Mr. Moth were rather glad we found out about the leak."

"Better to know than not." She was quiet and then asked coyly, "So, have you been having a happy birthday? I mean since last night and since last time I asked you, at lunch?"

"I have," he replied, smiling gallantly down at her. "Rather."

"I have a birthday present for you," she announced. It was heavy and holding it behind her in such a way that he could not see it—or could not see most of it, anyway—was tiring her arms. So she was looking forward to pulling it out from behind her and showing it to him.

"And I for you," he replied.

"Me?" she asked, surprised. "It's not my birthday!"

"Ah, but your birthday is during the spring holidays, and my present for you is here at school. So I figure I should show it to you now."

"You couldn't bring it home and meet up with us over spring break?" she asked plaintively. She so hoped to see him over the break.

Gaius's eyes sparkled with humor. "No, I rather could not. You'll understand when I show it to you. What do you have for me?"

Rachel pulled his present from behind her back and held it out. It was a brand new O.I. Starling Flycycle wrapped in the long pale paper that Marlowe Hall kept available for murals.

Gaius's jaw dropped. "A bristleless? A real one? I can't accept that!"

"Why not?" Rachel cried, hurt.

"Rachel, those are expensive."

Her bottom lip trembled. Was he going to reject her gift just because he had a commoner's idea of expensive? She wanted so much for him to have it.

She spoke very quietly. "Not for me."

Gaius winced. "Don't look at me that way. What young man could bear that? Okay, let me at least see it."

He tore off the paper. Inside was a shining black bristleless with a blue racing stripe. It had handlebars, a seat, and foot pedals—footrests really—like a bicycle. The main shaft swept upward a hand's span towards the rear, ending in an elegant metal fan consisting of four medium-sized blades that stuck out behind the device like a horizontal peacock tail.

His eyes grew large. "Wow. That's... wow."

"It's a bit shorter and more maneuverable than a Redbird, but it is quite simple to fly, no complicated levers. But this here," she tapped a ring on the front of the sporty black shaft, "turns on becalming enchantments. I had them upgraded by Mr. Chanson's family. They're the best."

Gaius examined the handsome device. He swallowed. Was it her imagination, or did he look just a tiny bit teary-eyed? "You had the Chansons soup up a broom for *me?*"

She gave him her brightest smile. "I want you to be able to fly with me. Think of it as a present you are begrudgingly accepting on my behalf."

"That is still a princely gift." Gaius bowed deeply. "I thank you, Lady Rachel."

"You are welcome, Mr. Valiant." Rachel beamed and curtsied.

Rachel showed Gaius how to ride the Starling. She wished she had brought Vroomie, so they could take his maiden ride together, but that would have been a lot to carry. She could not leave her dorm window open, due to the cold weather, so she could not summon it with the *varenga* cantrip. She wondered if using a cantrip to call her steeplechaser from a distance counted as part of the now-forbidden "flying in and out of buildings"? and made the executive decision that it did not. It would be terrible to lose access to both her secret hexagonal room where she had left the plushy lion Sandra had given her and the trick of calling her broom to her through an open window.

Gaius must have taken flying in P.E. too, when he first came. He did not embarrass himself, but he did not excel either. Again, Rachel thought about Mr. Chanson's compliments regarding her flying process and wondered how she had come to be so good so quickly. Was it because she had recalled the moves of the Pinswallow Broom Ballet every night before she went to sleep for years? Maybe that was it.

"So, what is this present for me?" she asked after Gaius had successfully flown around the commons three times and turned on and off the becalming enchantments twice.

Gaius hopped off the bristleless, picking it up in one hand. He looked embarrassed. "Um…. I didn't have the money to buy you something—"

Rachel cut him off with a wave of her hand. "Don't be silly. I don't need things like that, but you said you had a present that required being at school. I must admit, I am quite curious!"

"I didn't buy it," he said again, "but I did have to spend time figuring out where it was, and I think there's a ninety-eight point six-seven percent chance you'll rather like it."

"Then let's see it!"

"Come this way!"

Gaius put his new broom away. Then, he took her hand and pulled her along with him. They ran into Roanoke Hall, up three flights of stairs, down a hall, up two more flights, to a different side hall than their usual haunt. Partway down this hall, he stopped and pointed up. Above them was a folding ladder and a trap door. Rachel stared at it blankly.

Gaius grinned. "Made sense to try to get in from this side."

Rachel stared, puzzled. Then she shrieked with joy. She jumped up and down and clapped her hands. "My secret room! You found the way in!"

He reached up and pulled down the ladder. Dust rained upon their heads. Once it stopped, Rachel gazed dubiously at the wooden rungs, hoping they would hold. She could not recall a trapdoor in the floor of the hexagonal room, but she did remember that a spot on the floor, under the rug, had produced a hollow *thud* when Gaius had stomped on it.

"I would go up first to test the ladder, but I'm probably not strong enough to push up the rug on the other side of the trap door. Do you want to go up, and I'll catch you with *tiathelu* if the ladder breaks?" She raised her hands, ready to cast *tiathelu*.

Gaius nodded and stepped forward chivalrously. "Let me go first."

He climbed the ladder, which, to Rachel's relief, did not break, and pushed on the door. It did not budge. He climbed down and shooed her away. Then he pointed at the trap door with his wand. With a soft *boom*, the door flew open, and dust showered down. He hopped out of the way.

After the dust cleared, he said, "I think that did it."

Rachel giggled and followed him as he climbed up. The ladder turned out to be solid, all her worries unfounded. She peeked eagerly above the floor at her first opportunity. Sure enough, the hexagonal room situated in one of the many turrets of Roanoke Hall met her gaze.

It was her room! He had done it! It was all there: the sofa covered by a peach damask slipcover, the large cream and peach quilted comforter, the two giant satin throw pillows, creamy with bright iridescent blue and green peacocks whose tails trailed off the fabric, and the plushy lion Sandra had bought her in London with its large red bow. She bolted up the last few rungs and ran to her plushy lion, hugging it. Then she sat on the couch, her arms still around the big stuffed toy. The room smelled a bit musty, but the lion still smelled fresh. Gaius moved the rug so it would not impede the trap door in the future.

"Oh, Gaius! This may be the best present ever!"

The edges of his ears grew pink with pleasure. "Glad you like it."

She patted the cushion beside her and looked up invitingly at Gaius.

"Just for a moment?" she asked.

"That sounds like a good idea."

He sat down next to her, very close. Rachel curled up against him. He gave her a light, feathery kiss. She wondered if she could convince him to lie down beside her. Was that not every young girl's dream, to curl up with the boy she fancied, snuggling side by side?

To her delight, Gaius sat down, legs across the sofa, and pulled her to him so her head was resting on his chest. His gold and black tassel fell into her face. He put his mortar cap aside and ran his fingers over her hair and whispered how happy he was to have her in his life and how this was the best birthday he had had in many years. Rachel hugged him tightly and made a soft, purring noise. She felt so very, very happy.

After a time, she spoke. "Oh, Gaius, you are the best and sanest part of my life. I don't think I would have made it through these last six months without you."

"I am glad I could be here for you." Gaius smiled down at her, still stroking her hair. "And that the giant amount of information you've given me hasn't caused me to lose my mind."

"I'm glad about that, too," she giggled. "It would be beastly if you kept me sane, and I drove you bonkers." Then she lay back and sighed contently. "That was amazing last night, seeing my grandfather as a boy. And my grandmother! What a shock!"

"I imagine so," mused Gaius. He paused and then asked carefully, "What did you mean when you said it was the first time you were important?"

Oh, he had heard that, had he? She probably should not have said it aloud.

"In my family," she tried to explain, "everyone has their favorite person—the person that, if they have been away, they run to greet first—the person that matters most to them. My grandmother went to my father first. Mother would run to Peter and pick him up, back when we were little enough. Father always went to Sandra. Laurel doesn't really have a favorite person, but she was a troublemaker and that gained her a great deal of attention."

"And you?"

Rachel bit her lip. She spoke hesitantly, not wanting to malign her family. "I was a good child. I remembered what people told me, and I obeyed. They loved me; they were always kind to me. But no one ran to greet me first. And, because I could remember things other children most likely forgot, I could also remember...." She sighed and then repeated flatly, so that her intonation would not give away anyone's identity, "'I need you to take Rachel.' 'Oh, wait. Who is going to watch Rachel?' 'See if you can't distract Rachel, while I....'

"Don't misunderstand," she continued. "It was in no way a bad life. No one was cruel. Nothing was lacking. I just wasn't important. I didn't mind. I didn't know it could be different." She paused. "The only time I was the center of attention was when I had done something bad, and they all scolded me."

"Maybe that's why you're so afraid of being the center of attention," said Gaius.

"Oh!" Rachel had never considered that. "Maybe."

"Then, that day," her voice grew quiet, "everything changed. Suddenly, *I* was the person Grandfather looked for first. When he entered a room or came back from some important function—he was the duke then, so he went to many important functions—it was always, 'And how's my little Rachel?'" She smiled, blinking away tears. "I was important. I was his most favorite person. And he was mine."

"That's rather sweet," Gaius said. "I don't think I've ever had anything quite like that. Maybe my mum before she died, but I can hardly remember." His expression faltered.

Rachel squeezed his hand. She could not imagine the pain of losing a mother.

Or maybe she could.

"And then he died, and it all went away," she whispered. A month ago, she would have told Gaius that he was now her most favorite person, but, alas, it was no longer true. The Raven had taken his place.

Gaius said, "Oh. I'm sorry, Rach. That's rough."

"Thanks." She gave him a wan smile. She leaned her head against him. He put his arm around her shoulder and held her tightly. She thought about her grandfather, how he had been when she knew him, how he had been when he was young. *Where was he now?*

"Gaius, what happens to us when we die?"

He shrugged. "Nothing."

"What do you mean, nothing?"

"Nothing. That's the end. We cease. What happens to flowers when they are picked? They're there for a time, and then they are gone."

Rachel shivered at that. Had her grandfather and Illondria and all those who went before been snuffed out like a candle? But if that were so, why had Illondria's shade needed Nastasia to take her home?

"B-but what about ghosts?" she asked.

"Residual memories," replied Gaius. "Like a psychic recording. An impression left upon the universe. Usually, an impression of a moment of high emotion—that's why so many ghosts say or do the same things over and over. They are a memory of some dire or drastic thing that happened to the person in life."

"What about the Terrible Five? Couldn't they all come back from beyond the grave?" Rachel asked. "Wasn't that why they had been turned to stone to begin with?"

Gaius shook his head. "They just had magic that kept them alive. Koschei did not die because his soul was in an egg in a rabbit in a dog on an island. That's not life after death. That's the magical equivalent of an advanced medical procedure. Aleister Crowley was merely possessed. After he died, it was the demon who was immortal, not Crowley. And in the same vein for the other three."

"But…." Rachel frowned. "What about Percy Cornelius Taylor? He didn't act like a recording. He seemed as alive as you or me. Same with the other musicians from the *Titanic* that we met at the Dead Men's Ball."

She expected Gaius to offer some glib retort. When he did not, she glanced up at him. He was frowning, uncertain.

Slowly, he said, "You're right. I… don't know what to make of them." After a moment, he asked, "How old were you—when your grandfather died?"

"I was ten. It's coming up on four years ago."

Gaius shivered. "Er, sorry. It's bad enough realizing that, for the next three or so weeks, I'm seventeen and you're still thirteen, without the reminder that, three years ago, you were ten."

"Oh." She had not thought of their ages in those terms. Thirteen to seventeen seemed a much larger gap than thirteen to sixteen. Suddenly, she could not wait to turn fourteen.

She asked, "Does it bother you when people tease you about me being so young?"

"You mean about me, er, let's go with robbing the cradle? Nah. I hear a lot worse."

"Tess Dauntless once told me that you get teased mercilessly. Is it true?"

He shrugged. "I'm rubber, and they're glue and all that."

She smiled slightly, happy.

He pulled himself up a little and looked down into her face, seriously. "A more important question is: Does it bother you, Rach?"

"Me?" Rachel cried.

Gaius nodded. "Do people's comments upset you?"

"Are you daft?" Rachel exploded with laughter. "Gaius. I'm a *girl*. Girls *live* to hear people gossip about them and their boyfriend. It doesn't matter what's said—good, bad, or indifferent—we get a thrill just from hearing our name linked to that of the boy we fancy."

Gaius frowned. Then, he gave a bark of laughter. "I believe you're serious."

"Of course, I'm serious. I'm telling you one of the great secrets of girldom. I would not dare misrepresent such a thing."

He tipped his head back, chuckling. "I am reminded of the time that one of our farm hands was arrested for some minor thing—drunk driving? Fighting in a pub? Something. When the story appeared in the news, his mother was so excited that her son's name was in the paper, she didn't care that it was for something humiliating."

Rachel nodded knowingly. "It's a bit like that."

"Glad to hear it." He closed his eyes and tightened his arm around her. "Glad I can serve my girl by being horribly maligned on her behalf."

Rachel giggled. She curled into the warmth of his body and let herself relax. Part of her wanted him to kiss her, but the other part was glad that he did not, as she felt so safe just snuggling against him. Her lids grew heavier. Then, she was riding her dream unicorn across a wide, green plain with warm breezes blowing. They rode past Vladimir and the Guardian playing chess on a marble chessboard among broken pillars. The Raven winked at her. Vlad looked annoyed at the game. Next, they went by Rachel's old rival, Cydney Graves. She was crying by a river, looking frail and tiny. They passed the Master of the World. He had Amber perched on his wrist like a hawk. She whispered something in his ear, and he reached for Rachel.

Rachel woke up, shaken. *What a strange dream!* She lay still, warm against her boyfriend, her embarrassment growing in proportion with her wakefulness. Hopefully, no one would ever find out that she had allowed herself to fall asleep with a boy who was not her husband. She could practically hear the ghost of her august grandmother dressing her down for her indiscretion. For just a moment, she hoped there really was no afterlife. Though, somehow, now that she had seen Amelia Abney-Hastings meeting boys at dawn, in bloomers, with her skirts tied up, her mental ghost of her grandmother lost just a little bit of its daunting authority.

Opening one eye, she saw that Gaius was awake and staring at the ceiling thoughtfully. She could tell he was concentrating, his eyes darted to and fro very quickly as if he were reading.

"You're awake," he said suddenly, smiling down at her.

"How did you know?"

"Your breathing changed. How are you doing? Feeling rested?"

"Much better. I had all sorts of funny dreams about unicorns and chess. How about you? You look pensive. What are you thinking about?"

He said, "A number of different things. Haven't figured them out yet. You'll be the first to know when I have." He looked at his watch. "Oh! Almost time for the Knights' meeting! If we don't get going, we'll be late!"

Together, they headed down the ladder. At the bottom, Gaius had Rachel practice pulling the ladder down and putting it back up again with *tiathelu*. Then, hand in hand, they set off for the Knights of Walpurgis.

The commons was crawling with proctors and Agents, more than had been there the last two weeks. As they walked to the gym, Rachel left Gaius and ran over to speak to Mr. Fuentes.

"Miss Griffin! Glad to see you're safe." The handsome proctor flashed her a smile.

"What happened?" she asked with concern.

"A student was attacked."

"Oh, no!" Rachel gasped. "Who was it?"

"Amaranth Kyle, from Spenser Hall. A sophomore, I think?"

"She's a freshman, but she's not in any of my classes." Rachel felt terribly sorry for Miss Kyle. Yet she could not help feeling a wave of relief that it had not been one of her friends or siblings. "What happened?"

"She strayed outside the new boundaries—the fences we spent so much time setting up and marking." Mr. Fuentes winced. "Poor kid. She was severely mauled."

Mauled? Rachel's face went pale. She dug her fingernails into her palms to steady herself. Mr. Fuentes saw her distress and laid a comforting hand on her shoulder.

"Don't you worry, Miss Griffin. The main damage has already been healed. The nurse promises that Miss Kyle'll make a full recovery."

"Thank goodness." Rachel curtsied and then, with a goodbye wave, ran back to Gaius. She told him what had happened.

"That's a shame!" He, too, looked distressed. "I've never spoken to that girl, but I've seen her wandering. She wears a coat and boots of fur and moves very quietly through the woods. Took me by surprise one day. I am happy to say that I did not embarrass myself by yelping, but it was a near thing. Glad to hear she'll recover."

"Me, too!" cried Rachel. "Poor girl."

She thought back, but the only thing she could remember about Amaranth Kyle was Hildy Winters, in Music class, claiming that Miss Kyle was unusually pretty for a Spenser Hall girl but that her hair was always a rat's nest. That did not seem very flattering to the poor girl.

As they continued across the commons, Gaius spoke in a low voice. "You should be a little more subtle about talking to him in the open."

Rachel turned to him, surprised. "Talking to whom?"

Gaius glanced over his shoulder at Mr. Fuentes, who stood alert, making sure students stuck to the gravel paths that ran between the buildings. Leaning closer, Gaius said, "Months ago, Vlad asked me to find out how you all are figuring things out—what info-gathering method you're using, besides the dragon who can turn invisible and the visions of the princess. We suspect you have a Wisecraft contact, other than your father. Vlad suspects it's the proctor, Fuentes."

Rachel walked calmly beside him. Then she started to giggle. She might have resisted, but she still felt jittery from the after-effect of the news of the recent attack. The giggles got the better of her. Then, she was laughing openly. Gaius watched her, puzzled but intrigued.

After a while, she gasped, wiping her eyes, "I can't believe that worked."

Von Dread and his group thought she had Wisecraft connections because of all the information that she and her friends had learned when they spied on the Agents using Siggy's amulet. She had deliberately set out to mislead them when she decided to befriend Carlos Fuentes. The fact that it had worked tickled her tremendously.

Gaius raised an eyebrow and then suddenly cried, "Wait. Oh, good grief. You played us!"

Rachel just continued laughing.

"Tell me, Miss Griffin," Gaius crossed his arms, bemused, "from where did you learn these subtle arts of misdirection? I assume through reading? I don't think even Dread suspects you were talking to Fuentes to throw people off. That makes it much harder to narrow down your Wisecraft contact. Or if you are even the one with the contact. The princess knows the Grand Inquisitor, but I doubt she could use that connection to get classified secrets."

Rachel just grinned. "Poor Fuentes. I've used him quite cruelly." She sighed with mock wistfulness. "Not that he's suffered. He did get hot chocolate out of it."

She had subscribed to news glass services to learn about flying polo, so she could discuss his interests in an intelligent manner. The truth was some time ago she had stopped thinking about her ulterior motive in befriending him. What had started as a stratagem had become a true friendship.

Gaius, however, was still stuck on the previous topic. "You do know that many proctors are going through the first trial period of Agent training, right?" he pressed. "Be careful about setting one up to look foolish or like he's a leak. It might boomerang back on him badly. They're supposed to be quiet about what they know."

"All I've done is talk to him about flying polo and bring him hot chocolate," objected Rachel. "And I do like him quite a bit. He saved me from Cydney and her awful friends back in September. As to being careful, Gaius!" Rachel laughed gaily, "No one except you and Vlad could suspect him of slipping us information. No one else knows that we *have* information."

Rachel laughed all the way across the commons.

As Gaius opened the doors to the gym, she was struck by an awful thought, and her laughter died away. Could Amaranth Kyle have been attacked by the barghest Rachel had spared? A sick feeling stole over her. Should she confess to someone? Or did it not matter, considering that the Agents were now as alert to such dangers as they could be?

Why had she done such a thing?

Chapter Eighteen:
For He's a Jolly Good Fellow

As they entered the gym for the Knights of Walpurgis meeting, Rachel passed Mylene Price, who was coming from the pool, accompanied by her otter. As Rachel and Gaius walked by, Mylene called out behind her, "Rachel, wait up!"

"I'm going on ahead," said Gaius, "in case Vlad needs help with setting up. You talk to Price."

He gave Rachel a kiss on the cheek and sauntered off. Rachel turned toward the pale redhead in pigtails, who gave her a big smile.

"How are you feeling, eh?" Mylene asked in her light Canadian accent.

"Much better, thank you," Rachel replied. "You were a great help."

"I'm so glad. You did me such good—I'd been so ill for so long! I'd like to think I could do something for you."

"I was overjoyed to help." Rachel smiled kindly. She paused, recalling her conversation with Mr. Tuck, and then asked casually, "Has your father learned any more about how that wraith managed to move about undetected?"

Mylene's expression became grim. "We haven't been able to find another one."

"Isn't that a good thing?" asked Rachel.

Mylene leaned forward, lowering her voice. "Don't spread this around, but we don't yet know if we can detect them. And by we, here, I mean anyone—my father, the Mounties W Division, the Wisecraft—anyone!"

Rachel nodded slowly. That was in keeping with what Mr. Tuck had told her.

Mylene's expression grew more serious. She asked, "Rachel, do you know why you could see the wraith preying on me, when no one else did?"

Rachel did know, but she did not want to say. She looked wide-eyed and said nothing. After a moment, she asked, "How about Dr. Mordeau's cloak? Were those wraiths, too?"

"Yes, but a different variety of wraith than we have ever seen." Mylene's already pale face grew paler, showcasing her freckles. "This is the one thing my father's tremendously concerned about: how what happened to me might happen to others if we can't find a method for detecting these new varieties."

Rachel shifted her weight uncomfortably. If she did not tell now, she might be putting others in danger.

"Your shadow was askew," she said. "It didn't fit your body. I must have noticed it earlier, but it didn't really sink in until I thought about it that night." She blurted out the last part quickly as she did not want to have to explain why she could recall things later that she had not noticed the first time around. She did not like to reveal her perfect memory to others.

"Shadow askew, eh? All right! I bet my father can work with that. After all, when it comes to wraiths, he's the best there is! No wraith can get the best of him forever. Thank you."

"Does your father have any leads?" asked Rachel curiously.

Mylene frowned. "Not really. Or rather, no leads that make sense."

"Oh?"

Mylene leaned close again and spoke in a hushed voice. "He says both the invisible wraith and Dr. Mordeau's cloak remind him of the work of the Necromancer."

A chill ran along Rachel's spine. The hair on the back of her neck stood up. "Claudius Stark? My father and James Darling captured him!"

"I know." Mylene grinned. "That raid's famous. My favorite issue of *James Darling, Agent* comics." She lowered her voice, which wobbled slightly. "Do you think Stark could be commanding these wraiths from beyond the grave?"

Rachel thought about this. "I don't think the Necromancer's dead. I believe he was sentenced to Thero-Pen."

"The Thero Penitentiary?" Mylene's pupils grew wide. "I would not wish that on a sick tick."

"The Wisecraft didn't dare kill him," explained Rachel. "It's thought he had access to Morgana La Fay's copy of *The Book of Going Forth by Day*. If so, he might be more dangerous dead than alive."

She thought but did not add: *Don't worry. Gaius says there's no afterlife, so you're safe.*

"So it's not him. That's a relief," said Mylene. "But then, who sent the wraiths?"

"I don't know," said Rachel, "but I can tell you one thing. Do you remember from your favorite comic who the Necromancer's partner was?"

"Of course, the Serpent Master, Eliaures Charles. But he was captured, too, right? During the same raid?"

Rachel nodded. "I wonder if Mr. Charles left something made by the Necromancer in the hands of his daughter. It would explain her cloak."

"His daughter?" asked Mylene.

Rachel spoke grimly. "Our old math tutor, Dr. Melusine Mordeau, is the Serpent Master's daughter."

The Knights of Walpurgis met in the gym. The enormous chamber was brightly lit and smelled of freshly laundered sheets. To one side were dueling strips—long foam mats separated by wooden posts imbued with protective enchantments. The Knights sat on the other side around the massive wooden table, long enough to seat at least forty. This was the first meeting of the Knights since the confrontation between the crown princes of Bavaria and Transylvania on the dance floor at the Year of the Dragon Ball. Everyone watched Dread and Romulus closely, hoping for some hint of how things stood between them; however, neither prince so much as glanced at the other.

Vladimir Von Dread called the meeting of the Knights of Walpurgis to order, noting that they would not meet the next week, due to spring break. He reminded everyone that this evening they would finally be voting on who was to replace the graduating Urd Odinson as his second-in-command. The candidates were Freka Starkadder and Gaius Valiant.

Von Dread sat at the head of the long table, his black leather-gauntleted fingers steepled in front of him.

"When deciding for whom to vote," Von Dread declared, "do not allow your choice to be swayed by sentiment or by baser motives. The Knights of Walpurgis exists to help us grow stronger by sharing our knowledge, because knowledge is power. Power is needed if we are to protect the weak and keep our loved ones safe. Pick the candidate whom you judge to be more able to banish chaos and uphold order. The future of the Knights depends upon your choice."

Lacy Farnsworth, a pale ginger whose family owned the multi-million dollar Full-Moon Fabrics, raised her hand. She spoke with a Texas twang.

"Your highness, are the rumors true?" She gazed down the table toward Romulus. "Are you free of your engagement and on the market again?"

Romulus responded with grave indifference. "I am not a commodity, Miss Farnsworth. But it is true. I am no longer engaged. Our families felt we did not suit and arranged a match between my sister," he gestured at Freka, "and my former fiancée's brother."

"Music to my ears." Lacy gave Romulus a long come-hither look.

"Can I have back the good cheer I wished you?" quipped Bernie Mulford, the son of friends of Rachel's parents.

Rachel stared at the grains of wood of the table. She was so embarrassed for the young woman she could hardly breathe. *How could anyone display their feelings so blatantly and live?*

People offered congratulations to Freka, who gave a very pretty reply. Rachel's heart suddenly fell. She had been delighted by Freka's engagement, but she had forgotten the effect this might have on tonight's election. With Freka as the only candidate standing against Gaius, any goodwill caused by the excitement over her engagement was bound to work in her favor. How was Gaius expected to win against that?

Rachel sighed. She had wanted to help him. She had made such wonderful plans. She had decided to meet everybody and subtly try to influence them to Gaius's side. But her first try, Michael Cameron, had been an unmitigated disaster. He had stomped out of the Knight's meeting after talking to her and never returned. After that, she had changed tack and spoken with Freka herself, thinking that if Freka wanted to alter something about the club, Rachel could talk up to others how bad such an alteration might be, since Gaius, as Dread's man, represented the *status quo*—only Freka had not wanted to change anything at all.

Rachel's plots had failed miserably. Social influencer was not a talent she possessed.

"Let us return to the matter at hand," stated Vladimir. "Before we turn to our elections, a development has occurred. This spring, there will be a two-day event celebrating the Twenty-Fifth Anniversary of the Battle of Roanoke. The faculty and the Sacred Days Club have notified us that the first day will fall on the thirtieth of April, which, as you hopefully," he shot those present a skeptical look, "all know, is Walpurgisnacht. They asked if the Knights of Walpurgis would take charge of the games. It is our duty to serve our institution in whatever way needed, so I have accepted upon our behalf."

Salome looked up from where she had been filing her nails. She sat between Carl, the younger of her brothers, and Sigfried. Next to him were the princess, then Rachel, and then Gaius. Since students were not encouraged to bring their familiars, lest the creatures get hurt during the dueling portion of the meeting, Lucky was not visible, but Rachel could feel him occasionally as he snaked back and forth under their feet, invisible.

"Games?" Salome asked. "Why would a twenty-five-year anniversary celebrating a battle need games? Is that the best way to celebrate the time a group of kids saved the world?"

Romulus turned to regard her, speaking in his customary regal manner that always struck Rachel as a mix of lack of interest and pomposity—"I wish to address the notion that children saved the world. Popular stories, such as *James Darling, Agent*, have misled our generation about the Battle of Roanoke. Many now believe that Darling and the Musketeers single-handedly ended the Terrible Years. Their contribution should not be overlooked. They did eliminate the Terrible Five—a notable feat. But even after the masters were destroyed, the enemy's forces remained.

"General MacDannan and General Griffin of the UEA, General Towers, head of the united armies of the Americas, General Ko leading the alchemists of Cathay, and King Ludwig IV of Bavaria arrived at Roanoke and destroyed the remaining troops."

Von Dread nodded. "Correct. Bavarian troops were among those that fought here that day. The success of this united effort is why this battle is being memorialized this spring."

"Really?" Gaius leaned forward. "There was a real battle here? With armies? Not just the students attacking? I had not realized this."

Rachel had not realized it either. Her grandfather had been at the Battle of Roanoke? *Why had this never been mentioned to her?*

"Even in defeating the Terrible Five," Romulus continued, "the Musketeers had help."

"Why do you say this?" Rachel asked, quite curious.

Wanda Zukov also looked at him with great interest. Rachel recalled that Wanda's father had been a high lieutenant in the Morthbrood during the Terrible Years. He was now in jail.

"Six college students discover the weaknesses of the Terrible Five, which Cain March and the rest of the world had been unable to discover?" asked Romulus. "They defeat the Five with talismans the likes of which have not been seen before or since? I mean no disrespect to Mr. Fisher, whom I respect as a fine tutor, but if he could have made the Tarnhelm, the Tarnkappe, the sword Nothung, or the shield Svalinn on his own, why has he not made many other equally powerful talismans in the years since?"

Rachel's lips parted. She had not thought about that. Siggy began to object, dismayed by this insult to his favorite tutor, Mr. Fisher, but Nastasia stopped him with a hand on his arm.

"The prince is right," she whispered. "They had help. Auriel told me. I will explain later."

Rachel and Siggy exchanged glances, agog with curiosity, but as the princess would say no more, they had no choice but to wait.

Meanwhile, Von Dread replied, "Yours was a fair question, Miss Iscariot. I shall pass it on to the person who has offered to chair this activity. Miss Dare?"

Grinning like the Cheshire cat, Jenny Dare jumped up and sat on the top of the long table around which they were gathered. "Hello, Miss Iscariot, you're a freshman, right? So you may not be familiar with Reality."

"I've heard of it," Salome yawned. "It's a year-end party, right?"

"In part," said Jenny. "In eighteen eighty-six, Roanoke Island was floating off the coast of Greece when the Olympic Games were rekindled. The students voted to have their own yearly Olympics, which they called the Real Olympics. This became the seed of the event we now call Reality —a party to celebrate that we will be leaving the protection of our beloved institution and going back into the reality of the outside world. Or maybe to remind ourselves that what we have here is reality, and what's out there, well... it isn't as real as this!"

Jenny jumped off the table and began pacing back and forth. "Reality is ordinarily held the last weekend of school. It's a time for games and libations. This year, the faculty and the Sacred Days Club decided that— rather than run two campus-wide celebrations in May—the two events will be combined. The Real Olympics will be held on the thirtieth of April. The memorial of the famous battle will be held on May Day, along with normal May Day festivities."

A long conversation ensued over which games to play, with both serious and spurious suggestions offered. After a lively debate, Jenny summed up what had been decided.

"Spartan Madball, the Battle of Salamis in boats out on the Hudson, Sisyphus roll, epicycle race — that's my favorite! — zap ball, flying polo,

fencing, stone skipping, rock, paper, and scissors, friend carry, and croquet. That's eleven," she said. "We need one more."

"You've been in the actual Olympics, Mr. Von Dread," called Salome's
brother, Carl Iscariot. "At which sports do you excel?"

"This is not about me, Mr. Iscariot," Vladimir replied dismissively.
"We are looking for activities that the whole school might enjoy."

These comments created a stir. Up and down the table, members
of the Knights watched their leader speculatively, wondering: *What game
would convince the elusive Dread to play?*

During his four years at the upper school, Vlad had participated in
the school's intramural sports and had been on the intercollegiate fencing
team, which had gone on to win, in a large part due to his prowess, both
national and international titles for three years in a row. He had also taken
off most of one fall and winter to compete in the Winter Olympics. Upon
entering college, however, he had dropped out of the sports program entirely, citing a desire to concentrate on his studies. The only time in recent
history he had participated in any sport had been the impromptu hockey
game during the skating party. The members of the Knights were eager to
see him play.

"Mr. Von Dread," Lacy blurted out, waving her hand, "are you dating
Sandra Griffin?"

The chamber went entirely silent, with every pair of eyes, except for
Rachel's, staring at Vladimir Von Dread. Rachel gazed straight ahead, not
daring to so much as breathe.

Miss Farnsworth continued in her Texas twang. "You arrived at the
Year of the Dragon Ball together, and there are rumors that you were seen
kissing her late that night. Are the rumors true? Are all our hopes of winning your heart in vain?"

"That question has no relevance to our meeting," stated Dread.

"But, oh, it does!" cried out the ever-impertinent Bernie Mulford.
"We congratulated Mr. Starkadder on his engagement. Shouldn't we con-
gratulate other members upon their conquests, ahem, er, relationships?"

Dread did not look pleased with the younger boy's choice of words.
His eyes narrowed. Quite a few members glanced away, cowed.

"This is not a gossip club, Mr. Mulford," replied their leader evenly. "I
recommend we stick to Knights' business."

Sigfried ordinarily nigh-worshipped Dread, but at the moment, he
was frowning. Her blood-brother was sick of secrecy, Rachel realized, even

when it came from his hero.

"Why are you keeping it secret?" Siggy demanded angrily. "Are you ashamed of her?"

Dread's color heightened, but his voice remained entirely calm. "I am not ashamed, Mr. Smith, but neither have I been given me leave to discuss the matter of whether Miss Farnsworth's rumor is true or false, so I shall not." He turned towards Jenny Dare. "Jenny, if you would care to continue with our legitimate business."

"Right!" Jenny smiled brightly. "One last game?"

"Irish Road bowling?" Bernie Mulford pantomimed bowling a ball.

"No roads here," objected Gaius. "But if you want Irish, what about hurling? It's a ripping game."

"Hurling?" asked Carl. "That's not a real game. It's from fairytales."

"Isn't the King of the Daione Sidhe supposed to play hurling and something else — chess, I think?" asked the Knight's secretary, Naomi Coils. "I'm with Carl. I believe it's mythical."

"Not mythical!" replied Gaius, "Even the Unwary play. It's Irish, but we play it in Cornwall, too. Near me are standing stones that are supposed to be hurling players who held a game on some sacred day and were punished by being turned to stone. Great game, hurling."

"What's it like?" asked Bernie Mulford. "When you're not being turned to stone."

"Something like hockey," red-haired Fiona Finnegan, the daughter of an Irish marquess, spoke with a lovely accent. "Field hockey and football crossed with lacrosse. 'Tis said hurlers need the skills of hockey players, lacrosse players, and baseball players, plus a few more."

"Fairies do play it," murmured a green-eyed goth girl with lavender glitter lipstick and a black choker, who sat alone with an empty chair to either side of her. She had not come to the meeting when members were introduced, so Rachel had never learned her name. "For what it is worth, I second the suggestion. Hurling is exciting, both to play and to watch. Much more interesting than the other stupid games humans play."

"Fastest game on grass," quipped Gaius.

"Fast, eh? That sounds," Bernie wiggled his eyebrows, "intriguing. How many men on a team? We don't want another four-man team, like flying polo."

"Then hurling's your game," Gaius grinned. "You can't beat fifteen men to a team! Lots of room for everyone who wants to play."

Siggy looked up from where he and Salome had been feeding French fries that Sigfried had snuck out of his pocket to the invisible Lucky. "We have another hurling player on campus, too. Seth Peregrine mentioned he's good at hurling."

"Isn't that the freshman kid who's so amazing at hockey?" asked Gaius.

Several of the others nodded.

"The MacDannans would probably play," Rachel spoke up. "I've seen them play hurling. Conan's top-notch."

"But could we field two teams?" asked Carl Iscariot. "Sounds like the game takes at least thirty people. Who would play?"

A number of people raised their hands.

"I'd play," said Joshua March. That caused a bit of excitement, as he was known to be one of the top hockey players on campus.

Jenny frowned reluctantly. "Teaching at least thirty people? That's a lot of work for games where anyone is supposed to be able to join."

Gaius leaned forward. Rachel realized how much he wanted them to pick his suggestion. Looking around the table, she suddenly had an idea.

Leaning close to him, she whispered, "Bet they'd be for it if Vlad would play."

Gaius grinned. He leaned back and drawled casually, "I'm sure we could find enough players. It'll be fun. William, Vladimir, would you two play?"

"I would be happy to," replied William.

The Knights of Walpurgis turned as one and looked at Von Dread.

"If you like," Dread replied.

"Very well." Jenny wrote with a flourish. "Hurling it is!"

The whole room cheered. Gaius gave Rachel a victory wink.

"It is now election time," announced Vladimir Von Dread. "Any last speeches?"

Both Gaius and Freka stood and made a short speech. Rachel thought Gaius gave a good accounting of himself. Freka also spoke well. Vladimir asked Naomi and Randal Graves to serve as tellers and gather the votes, which would be counted in front of the officers of the club, plus Romulus, if he cared to participate. The Transylvanian prince nodded his agreement.

"Any last comments before we begin?" asked Dread.

Rachel's hand shot up.

"Miss Griffin?"

Rachel stood and spoke shyly, "I just thought, before we started, we might wish happy birthday to my boyfriend, Gaius Valiant. Today is his birthday."

She expected a polite spattering of applause. Instead, the table went wild, cheering Gaius and wishing him many returns of the day. Carl Iscariot and Bernie Mulford stood up and led the entire meeting in a round of "For He's a Jolly Good Fellow."

Gaius won the election. A number of people congratulated Rachel for having chosen to announce his birthday in such a timely manner, claiming this contributed to his win. Rachel, who had failed utterly when she had tried to help her boyfriend, only to succeed when she had not intended to, merely sighed. Still, she was very happy for Gaius.

Chapter Nineteen:
Do You Know Him, Too?

The Knights' meeting came to an end, and Rachel, Sigfried, and Nastasia walked back to Dare Hall together, passing proctors and Agents patrolling the commons with glowing *lux* balls hovering over their shoulders. The March night was chilly but no longer icy cold. Overhead, the stars shone crisp and bright. The night air smelled fresh with only the faintest hint of wood smoke. The gravel of the path crunched under their shoes.

The two girls hooked their arms and strolled together, with Sigfried circling around them, as he and Lucky pretended that his wand was an incoming missile.

As they walked, Rachel asked, "Nastasia, you mentioned Romulus was correct about the Six Musketeers having outside help. What did you mean?"

"I must say, I am embarrassed I did not tell you about this right away," replied the princess. "I guess we were all tired after the ball, and you were in the infirmary. Really, you should have called us on the card to tell us where you were."

"I was asleep much of the time."

Nastasia nodded solemnly at that and then gave Rachel a kind smile. "I guess that's only to be expected, under the circumstances."

"What did Auriel say?" asked Rachel.

"Oh, right." The princess composed her thoughts. "Auriel helped the Six Musketeers directly. Wendy MacDannan had the Second Sight—visions similar to mine. Only she was also given specific weaknesses of the enemy and instructions on how to build weapons to stop them."

"Ooooh!" Rachel breathed. "So they *didn't* just do better research than other people."

"No. That was a cover, though apparently, they were quite thorough and competent."

"Wow. And Romulus figured it out. That was smart. Too bad he's such an *eejit.*"

"You may repeat that as often as you like," Nastasia replied, a smile crinkling around her eyes. "He behaved deplorably toward my sister."

Rachel flashed a returning smile. Then, she grew serious as she thought about what she had just learned. "I wonder if Finn and Agent Darling ever told Mr. March or my father any of this, or if the Six Musketeers kept it a secret all this time?"

"Auriel did not say," Nastasia replied.

"Who are we talking about?" asked Sigfried.

"Auriel," said Nastasia, "the young man with very blue eyes I spoke with at the ball." She looked thoughtful. "The other angel I spoke to back in September had very blue eyes, too."

"Other angel?" Rachel cried. "In September? You never mentioned this!"

The princess nodded, "I did not mention him because I thought at the time that it was a dream. It was while I was being observed in the Halls of Healing, after the Lightbringer and Zoë both left."

"What did he look like?" asked Rachel.

Nastasia frowned slightly. "He had golden curls and startlingly blue eyes, but...." She took a deep breath. "He was dressed in a business suit, with a sword on his hip, and carried a briefcase from which he took a large magnifying glass."

"That sounds like a dream," scoffed Sigfried.

"Exactly why I never mentioned it," the princess replied primly. "This second angel, Auriel, appeared more as one might expect."

Rachel pressed her lips together and did not explain about Auriel having been in disguise.

"Ace!" Siggy cried, swooping around the two girls. "Princess, is your angel-servant going to start sending you visions like those, too? I want to make super-powerful weapons!"

"Everybody needs superweapons!" cried Lucky.

"Auriel is not my servant, Mr. Smith," replied Nastasia serenely.

Rachel asked, "Did Auriel say anything about what happened to Wendy?"

Nastasia nodded sorrowfully. "The Terrible Five discovered she was the source of the 'leaks'. They cast a spell on her. She lost her grip on sanity and never recovered. Without her, the Six Musketeers lost their source of supernatural information and advice."

"Poor Wendy," Rachel murmured.

The princess continued, "Auriel also told me something on a different subject."

"Does it involve superweapons?" asked Siggy. "Because if the answer is no, I'm not interested. Why would a supernatural creature come from a super realm if not to talk about superweapons. Why would he come to say boring stuff?"

"Maybe it's a form of torture," said Lucky. "Say things so boring that blood spurts from your ears. Keep saying 'em unless the person relents."

"Recants," said Siggy.

"Retracts," said Lucky.

"Retreads," said Siggy.

"Isn't that where you put new treads on a tire?" asked Nastasia, puzzled.

"Tires might be tasty," offered Lucky, "though they smell bad when you burn them."

Siggy nodded sagely. "Remember the time...."

"We showed that lorry who was boss, boss," Lucky confided.

"That lorry will never nearly hit any boys ever again," declared Siggy.

"Or girls," offered Lucky.

"Or inchworms," declared Sigfried.

"But, boy, did the burning tires smell bad," finished Lucky.

Picturing a dump truck going up in flames, Rachel struggled not to giggle lest she encourage them. She murmured, "That poor lorry driver."

"He nearly hit me!" objected Siggy. "Just like a girl to take the other bloke's side!"

"Girls are not as loyal as dragons," Lucky observed.

"Some are," replied Siggy, "but girls have feelings, emotions. It confuses them."

Rachel just sighed.

Nastasia, for once, ignored Siggy. "Auriel also told me a little about the angels. Apparently, they come in three kinds."

"Three?" Rachel's head snapped around. Everything about angels fascinated her.

"There was a great war, long ago, a civil war between the servants of the Emperor of All Things Seen and Unseen," said Nastasia.

"That's the guy who made me!" said Siggy.

"He does quality workmanship," said Lucky.

Nastasia continued, "A third of his servants remained loyal. A third deserted. A third rebelled. The first group of servants is called angels. The last third are called demons."

"What about the second third?" asked Rachel. "The deserters?"

"Auriel did not give me a specific name. Apparently, many of them are now gods and Guardians, though some of the deities men worship are devils, and at least one is an angel."

"Which one?" asked Siggy.

"Athena. Auriel said she was loyal," replied Nastasia, "which means our Guardian must be part of the second group, the Deserters, which makes him quite despicable."

Rachel bit her lip, a lump forming in her throat.

As they drew near Dare Hall, Nastasia asked, "Did Amber mention to you that the angels—the good third, the ones that stayed loyal—had deserted the previous emperor, my great-grandfather?"

"Amber did not care for 'angel magic'," Rachel said sadly. "She said they went away in the middle of a battle—left without a word."

The princess nodded. "Auriel explained it. The angels 'deserted' when the World Tree's fruit, the worlds, began to drop off. The angels were needed to save them. Millions of worlds were brought by the angels up into," she gestured upward, "wherever it is they live."

Rachel looked upward at the night sky. *The place where the angels lived? She wanted to go there!* There was something about angels that drew her like a moth to a bonfire. It burned inside her like the voice of the sea calling to a selkie. The feeling was so powerful and so unexpected she missed part of what Nastasia was saying.

"Wait," Rachel cried, trying to catch up. "So the worlds themselves were saved, carried up? To the stars? What is this angel place like?"

"I don't know," Nastasia replied, "I only know millions were saved. They brought them to a place. I think it may be called Heaven."

"So up into the sky? Where the stars are?" Siggy pointed at the night sky. "Are those shiny lights we call stars the million worlds?"

Rachel spoke slowly, remembering. "This angel place, is it the one Mortimer Egg meant, when he said, '*We shall strike a dire blow against Heaven*?' Did he mean that he thought killing the Keybearers would harm the Country of the Angels?"

"I know not what Mortimer Egg intended by his words," replied the princess.

Siggy stretched. "So, the worlds were all saved? Brought up to this sky-home?"

"All but ten thousand," replied Nastasia. "Ten thousand worlds were too heavy and sank into the darkness, and fifty remain upon the fallen tree —including ours."

"We're living on a *fallen* World Tree?" Sigfried asked, startled.

"What does too heavy mean?" asked Rachel.

"Yeah," Siggy asked, "Were they too heavy because not enough angels came to save them? Or were they bigger than the worlds that were saved? Like gas giants?"

"I believe it was a moral heaviness, Mr. Smith," replied the princess. "The people were too wicked for the angels to be able to lift."

"Wow...poor worlds," Rachel murmured, her eyes unexpectedly pricking with tears. "Entire worlds? Like ours? Billions of people? Times ten thousand?"

The princess hung her head. "I do not know."

"What was that?" Sigfried stiffened, suddenly alert.

"What was..." Rachel began, but then she froze; she heard it, too.

The night was extremely dark, but something moved through the underbrush beyond the temporary ward-fence set up west of Dare Hall, something large—not as large as the ogre, but definitely bigger than an opossum or a raccoon. A deer, maybe? A large dog? A familiar?

"It's a lizard thing. With horns," said Sigfried, without even turning in that direction.

"The Mexaxkuk!" cried Rachel and Lucky together.

"Which one is that?" asked the princess.

Rachel replied, "Local American supernatural creature, feasts on human flesh. It's been on the northmost part of Pollepel Island since before the Roanoke Island moored here."

"Bet that's what hurt that girl," said Siggy.

A shiver ran through Rachel. He could be right. If so, it was not her barghest. She felt a bit better, but she still regretted not calling the Agents' attention to the beast.

"Knew I should have crisped that scaly bully when I had the chance," murmured Lucky.

"Come on," Sigfried said, drawing his Bowie knife. "Let's get it!"

Siggy and Lucky moved toward the fence. Rachel wished she had her steeplechaser; though if she tried to fly over the temporary wards, she would fall out of the sky again.

"Mr. Smith!" the princess's voice snapped. "Are you mad? We are freshmen with less than a year of experience. This is a job for a proctor or an Agent."

"Yeah, well, where are they?" Siggy replied. "We can solve this now!"

"Right there," the princess pointed at a figure standing guard where the path left the forest to cross to Dare Hall, maybe two hundred feet away. She ran toward the Agent. Siggy dashed toward the fence as if to get to the creature before the Agents stopped him.

"Siggy!" Rachel cried. "If they find you outside the wards, you'll be suspended!"

Siggy slowed down, scowling. He and Lucky looked the way the princess had gone. He sighed. Turning to his familiar, he grumbled, "Guess I'll have to stay here. Stupid adults."

Rachel smiled slightly. "The adults aren't so bad, Siggy. I think that's Agent Standish."

"Standish's okay. He's cool," Sigfried admitted grumpily, still disappointed not to be attacking the Mexaxkuk. Scowling, he slid his Bowie knife back into its hidden scabbard.

"*Lux*," called Nastasia, making the gestures that accompanied the cantrip.

When a ball of light appeared, she waved it back and forth as she ran until it caught Agent Standish's attention. The Agent sprinted toward them. Nastasia met him and explained. Standish thanked her and called for backup. Then he headed over to the fence.

On the porch of Dare Hall, the large wolf who often slept there had stood and looked to be in the act of coming down the stairs. When it was clear that the Agent was taking over and Sigfried was not heading into the darkness, the wolf lay down again. Rachel, who knew this wolf was Wulfgang Starkadder, wondered whether he had been planning to stop them or to join them. As she entered through the thick oak doors, she smiled at him.

The wolf winked at her.

The Agents did not catch the Mexaxkuk that night, though Lucky did manage to singe its tail before it gave him the slip. As Siggy had predicted, when Amaranth Kyle recovered, she identified the horned lizard as the creature that had mauled her, much to Rachel's relief. Not that she wanted anyone mauled on any account, but she felt a bit of peace of mind in knowing that the attack had not been her fault. So many other things were.

Siggy grumbled that if he had gone after the creature instead of waiting for the adults, between his amulet and Lucky, they could have found and incinerated it. Rachel allowed that he probably was right, but the princess remained adamant that telling the Agents had been the correct action.

The weekend passed quickly, with everyone working hard to finish their assignments before Spring Equinox Break. Saturday night, there was an impromptu skating party on the reflecting lake, with the Ginger Snaps and some tutors taking turns providing the music. Rachel had a wonderful time drinking hot chocolate with her girlfriends while they skated figures and watched the boys, and Zoë, play hockey.

Monday, Rachel had a free period following Art. She stayed behind after class to speak to their tutor, Mrs. Heelis, once known to the world as the famous children's author and artist, Beatrix Potter. Mrs. Heelis's ancient cat lay asleep in a pool of sunlight on the center of the long table around which class was held. Motes of chalk dust hung in the beam of sunlight shining through the high windows.

"Mrs. Heelis," Rachel asked plaintively, "I have been working with the books you recommended, but there are things I can't seem to master. Can you take a look?"

"Of course, my dear," said Mrs. Heelis. She was an old woman in high-necked red and black conjurers' robes. She had round glasses, and her white hair was pulled up into a bun. "What seems to be the problem?"

Rachel went straight to the point. "I am having trouble with perspective and also with drawing hands. They always seem… well, wrong."

"Hands are very difficult." The art tutor nodded. "They have so many planes and dimensions. Even expert artists struggle with them. One trick is to compose your picture so they are out of the way. I do, however, have a good book specifically on drawing hands and fingers. Would you like to borrow it?"

"Oh, yes! I'd like that very much!" Rachel cried.

Mrs. Heelis found the book and handed it to her. Rachel put it with her drawing pad.

"Come sit here, child," said Mrs. Heelis, taking a seat at the table. "Let's see your drawings. You can show me the trouble spots."

Rachel took out her drawing book, and they began paging through it. Her pictures were still cartoonish and awkward; some elements, such as hands and ears, were outright deformed. The spatial relations portion of her perfect memory balked at the obvious inaccuracies in the lines of perspective, yet she did not know how to fix them.

Mrs. Heelis complimented her on how her skill had improved since the fall and gently pointed out ways she could improve further. They flipped through her drawings of familiars, classmates, and landscapes. Rachel turned a page, and Mrs. Heelis gasped. On that next page was a drawing of a gigantic black bird. Rachel had colored the eyes with a red colored pencil.

Mrs. Heelis stared at the drawing, her face pale. "Do you know him, too?"

Rachel nodded, delighted. "You've met him?"

"Once, long ago. Twice, actually."

Rachel made a split-second decision. "Do you know what he really looks like?"

"He's not a bird?"

"No." Rachel turned the page.

On the next page was a drawing of Jariel sitting beside her bed in the infirmary. The drawing showed an eight-foot-tall man with enormous black feathered wings and a coronet in his hand. While she had hardly done him justice, Rachel had caught a hint of his beauty and his eeriness, enough to make the drawing haunting.

Mrs. Heelis pressed her hands against her heart. "Oh, how beautiful. I never knew."

Rachel wanted to ask about how Mrs. Heelis had met the Raven, but she knew people hesitated to speak of such things. As she contemplated this, an inkling of a suspicion came to her. Before she could pursue the subject, however, there was a matter she needed to clarify.

"I have a question," Rachel asked. "An encyclopedia I read said you were born in eighteen-sixty-six. But my grandfather was already in his fifties by that time. Did you know him when he was young? Or did you meet him later?"

Her grandparents had looked young in the photo Mrs. Heelis had shown her, but the Wise could look young for decades.

Mrs. Heelis smiled kindly. "Your encyclopedia must be from an Unwary publisher. I was born in eighteen-fourteen. When my books began to sell, my family thought it would not do to tell the mundane world my true age. We picked a date in keeping with my appearance."

"How old were you when you met my grandfather?" asked Rachel.

"I was ten," Mrs. Heelis smiled. "Funny thing was, Amelia and I lived close to each other—or rather her family's house in London was not far from my neighborhood—but we met during a family outing in Salisbury. Or was it Glastonbury? No matter. She introduced me to the others, and my life was never again the same."

Rachel smiled happily at that. "And you also met the Raven."

"Twice. But I have heard him many times, whenever I was about to say something he would rather I not—anything regarding the first time I met him."

Rachel recalled early in the school year when Mrs. Heelis had paused while speaking about Rachel's grandfather and looked warily out the window. It all made sense now.

She smiled sadly, "I was going to ask, but I guess if you can't speak of it...."

Mrs. Heelis nodded firmly. "No. I cannot."

Rachel sat quietly for a moment. Then, she met the old tutor's gaze boldly. "Did it have to do with the Heart of Dreams?"

Mrs. Heelis gasped, her jaw dropping. She made an effort to shut it twice, not quite able to do so, before she recovered enough to press her lips together again. Then, she quickly looked out the window as if expecting a dark shape to fly by. "H-how did.... How *could* you know that?"

"Nastasia told Dean Moth, so it's not a secret. So I don't mind telling you."

Rachel described Nastasia's vision of the three boys and her young grandmother. By the time she finished, tears poured down Mrs. Heelis's old, wrinkled face. The Art tutor dabbed at her cheeks with a cambric handkerchief, edged with handmade lace, and sniffed.

"For so many years, we kept this secret," she said, staring off into the distance as if she could see back through the years. "The boys followed the Raven's instructions to get the Heart and take it from the island. Amelia met them in Cornwall with bristlelesses. I met them later that day, and all five of us brought the Heart to its final destination."

"The Raven's instructions!" Now, it was Rachel's turn to gape.

"Blaise, Daring, and Jasp were expelled," Mrs. Heelis continued. "Only by the efforts of the duke, Blaise's father, did Roanoke take them back. The duke made a fuss when the evidence Amelia had planted in Merlin's Cave was discovered, claiming that the boys had sneaked off the island for an afternoon of carousing and had not been involved in the crime. And since the Heart was not found in the cave—where they believed the boys had spent the day—they had to drop the charge of theft.

"Poor Amelia. Her father discovered the missing Scotch. She had to confess, to keep a beloved family servant from being sacked. She couldn't say that she dumped it over a cave and into the ocean to hide a crime the boys had committed, so she announced, with all the flair for which she was so famous, that she had drunk the entire thing. For years,"—a flicker of a smile passed over Mrs. Heelis's lips—"the adults feared she was in danger of becoming a lush. They watched her like hawks at social gatherings, until she came of age."

Rachel gave a little laugh. "She seems so different from the grandmother I knew."

Mrs. Heelis nodded sadly. "Once upon a time, she was a fun-loving free spirit. Then, the man she had loved desperately her whole life, though she often did not let on to him, threw her over for some pretty young thing —that is the one thing for which I shall never forgive Blaise—and, of course, she then went through years of rigid discipline as a Vestal. What little of her old spirit that had survived died with Emrys."

"Uncle Emrys," Rachel whispered softly. "Why did she wait so long— after the death of Myrddin and the others—to marry Grandfather?"

"Well," Mrs. Heelis said sadly, "pride is a hard thing to bend. Besides, by then, she had taken her vows with the Vestals."

"What changed?" asked Rachel, who longed to know everything about her beloved grandfather and could not help being a little curious about her grandmother, too.

"There came a time when Blaise was deathly ill. I am afraid I do not remember if the cause was an injury or an illness. She took a leave of absence from the Vestal order to nurse him back to health. I am not certain of the details. I had mainly lost touch with her by then, but I was invited to their wedding." She smiled faintly at the memory.

"For almost two hundred years," she added, "I wondered why the Raven had sent the boys to steal the Heart. Then came the Terrible Years.

The Five came here, to this island, digging everywhere. Only then did I understand. Only Blaise, Amelia, and I knew why."

"And where it's hidden?" whispered Rachel.

"And where it's hidden." Mrs. Heelis nodded firmly. "Finally, it made sense. Still, it's strange, asking a group of children to hide such a powerful talisman and so many years before the danger."

"Maybe you were the ones who were capable of getting it to the place where the Terrible Five could not find it," said Rachel.

The old tutor's face became very still. "Yes. That makes sense."

Rachel thought of the princess and her impatience over her visions. She thought of her own impatience on many topics. If the Raven sent people to carry out missions to accomplish things that would not be needed for two hundred years, maybe she and her friends would need to develop more patience.

Aloud, she said, "You said you saw Jariel twice?"

"Jariel?" Mrs. Heelis asked alertly. "Is that the name of the Raven?"

Rachel blushed. "No. I just made it up so I could call him something."

Mrs. Heelis glanced down at the drawing of the statuesque angel with his black wings.

"He is very dear to me," Rachel whispered, lowering her lashes.

"Is he? How strange," mused Mrs. Heelis. "He's so frightening to me."

"It's a pretense," Rachel said softly. "You have to look through that to see him."

"I saw him once at a distance," the old tutor explained. "After that, he only came to stop me from speaking. Except for once, and that one time did not make him any less frightening."

"What happened?" asked Rachel.

"It was many years later, the early twentieth century." She stared out the window again. "I was debating whether to marry Mr. Heelis. Suddenly, the Raven landed on a branch. With no preamble, he told me Darius would not be coming back, and then he flew away." She dabbed her eyes again. "You see, before that, there was some hope, even after all those years, that maybe...." Mrs. Heelis stopped talking and covered her face with her hands. Rachel laid a comforting hand on her arm. After a time, the tutor sniffed, wiped her eyes again, and smiled.

Rachel asked, "I don't suppose you can tell me where you hid it? The Heart, I mean. After Nastasia's vision...maybe it could help fix the troubles between Roanoke and the fey."

Mrs. Heelis blew her nose. "Oh, I am certain it could and a whole lot more," she said sternly. "I would not tell you, young lady or anyone. It's not a thing to be taken lightly."

"This Heart of Dreams?" Rachel leaned forward. "You know what it does?"

"Child, you know how we conjure things and dispel them again?" As she spoke, the art tutor whistled. Her ancient cat perked up its ears. Mrs. Heelis reached up, performing the cantrip used for conjuring. Her cat had its gaze trained on something Rachel could not see. Jemima Puddle-Duke appeared on the table in her little blue bonnet, quacked once, and then puffed into mist as Mrs. Heelis dispelled the conjuration. When Rachel nodded, the tutor continued, "It did that, but it did it to everyday things: horses, chairs, people."

"What?" cried Rachel, aghast.

"It made unreal things real, and *real* things unreal."

"If the Terrible Five had found it...." Rachel gasped in horror.

The art teacher nodded grimly. "There would have been no stopping them."

Chapter Twenty:
Have Prince, Will Travel Again

Spring Equinox Break finally arrived. Rachel packed a small trunk and ran downstairs with Vroomie and her wand in one hand and her cat Mistletoe in his carrying case in the other. Her trunk floated before her, carried by a lifting cantrip from her wand. She was inordinately proud of herself for being able to pull this off all the way down the staircase.

She met her siblings in the foyer, ready to go. However, even using cantrips, it took six strong college boys to move Sigfried's four trunks, large black steamer trunks, each four feet high and five feet long, bound with silver clasps, into the foyer.

"What are these?" asked Peter, as he and Laurel came to meet Siggy and Rachel.

"Treasure," said Sigfried.

"Siggy's gold," Rachel guessed.

She pulled out her wand and tried to lift one of his trunks. She could not even budge it.

"Here, let me." Peter cast the *tiathelu* cantrip. He, too, could hardly lift a single trunk. After a few seconds, he lowered it again, panting. "I say, are you sure you need all this?"

"It's gold, Peter," Rachel explained. "He can't leave it here. Who would guard it?"

"It's a dragon hoard," Siggy said proudly, "plus a few things that came from the ogre."

"Wait." Laurel's jaw dropped. "Siggy *actually* owns four steamer trunks of *treasure*?"

"Three and a half," replied Sigfried. "The rest is my entrenching tool, two shirts, and a few other things."

Two shirts? He only owned *two* shirts? And one must be the thing without sleeves Valerie gave him. It had not occurred to her, however, back when she had ordered clothing for him, to buy street clothing. He had not owned shoes then either. So maybe he did own only two shirts. It was no matter; he could borrow some of Peter's until they could go shopping.

"How are we going to get these home?" asked Laurel.

"Maybe Forrest would lend us her backpack," suggested Sigfried.

Rachel shook her head. "It wouldn't help. We couldn't fit these trunks into the opening of the backpack. Or Nastasia's house, for that matter. The trunks are just too big."

"I'm not sure I know anyone with a larger-aperture kenomanced bag," said Peter. "I only have my pouch and a small carry-all. Do you, Laurel?"

"Nope. Just my backpack. My friends have jewelry boxes that hold three times as much as expected. Not cargo space." Laurel knocked on a trunk and then jumped up on it, one leg crossed over another as if posing. Lucky snaked around her, hanging over her like a furry boa.

Rachel glanced at the trunks. They were not as large as a horse. "I know someone."

A few minutes later, a knock came on the heavy oak front door of Dare Hall. Peter opened it and scowled. "You're not welcome here."

"Sorry, Griffin," Gaius sauntered in, smirking at Peter, "we're here to help *you*."

"We?" Peter asked stiffly.

The door opened wider, and Vladimir Von Dread shouldered it aside. Peter took a rapid step back, startled. Laurel snorted with amusement. Dread turned and regarded her, where she was poised like a pin-up girl atop a trunk, her bare calf showing beneath her skirt. Laurel's own smirk died away. She jumped down and readjusted her garments.

"Dread!" Siggy grinned maniacally. "All hail, Lord Dread!"

"I don't think you have to go that far," Gaius replied airily.

"Thank you for coming, gentlemen," Rachel said properly, ignoring her crazy relations.

"No problem, Rach." Gaius kissed her lightly on the cheek. "It's only a step or two out of the way for me, and even Vlad has to go through London."

"Happy to do our part." Vladimir's voice was so much deeper than the other boys. It sent shivers through Rachel.

Gaius was wearing a blue parka and jeans. Vlad was dressed in dark traveling suit cut in the Bavarian style, with shoulder braiding and a tuxedo collar, over which he wore his black dreadnought coat trimmed with wolverine fur. From an inner pocket, he pulled out his black swan-feathered cloak. The cloak's bright blue lining had a seam down the middle, which opened into a large inner space. Rachel recalled watching him throw it over the wayward water horse, after she and Laurel and Gaius had finally managed to capture it, so that he could move the dangerous *each-uisge* off campus and back to its marsh. This was why she had asked him to come help with Siggy's gold.

Vlad threw the cloak over the first trunk. The black feathered garment floated to the ground.

"My gold!" Sigfried lunged at the cloak. "Give it back!"

Lucky shot from the trunk where Laurel had been sitting, through the opening in the cloak lining, and into the space within.

"Mr. Smith," Vladimir looked faintly amused, "I assure you I will not be depriving you of your property. I do not need gold." He took in the panicked expression on Siggy's face and, stooping, held up the cloak. "If you wish to travel with your trunks, be my guest. Step to the side until the rest of them are inside and touch nothing."

Siggy followed Lucky into the space inside Von Dread's cloak. Rachel stepped closer to Gaius and slid her arm through his.

Her boyfriend smiled down at her, patting her arm. "Ready to go?"

"I have only the one trunk." Rachel gestured. "It's light enough for me to float it."

"Is this the same girl who could hardly float a doorstop at the beginning of the year?" Gaius grinned. "You have come a long way, Rachel Griffin."

His praise made her glow. "Thank you, Mr. Valiant."

The five of them made their way to the docks, with Lucky and Siggy inside the cloak, which Dread put over his shoulders, so that he now wore the swan-feather cloak over his dreadnought coat. Laurel walked with the glowering Peter, both floating their own trunks and cat carriers. Rachel chatted with Gaius, the two of them strolling together. Despite Rachel's increased prowess with the lifting cantrip, Gaius, who had only a backpack, gallantly insisted on floating her trunk, leaving her hands free for Vroomie and the cat carrier. Dread strode behind them, towering over the rest, even Peter, who was quickly gaining on their father's height.

They walked across campus, down the stairs of Bannerman's castle, and to the docks, where William Locke met them. Together, they boarded the *Pollepel II*. As the green and gold ferry made its way across the Hudson, Dread stepped aside to speak to Captain Zephy. William followed him. They were soon joined by the three Schmitt triplets—dark-haired beauties who were descendants of the famous Black Forrest Witches—and Wanda

Zukov, the redheaded freshman from the Knights. After a minute, Gaius squeezed Rachel's hand and went to join them as well. Rachel sat down on a bench next to Peter.

"Why's he doing this?" Peter glared over at where Dread stood.

Rachel said simply, "Because we're friends."

"He is *not* your friend, Rachel." Peter's voice snapped.

Rachel said nothing for a moment. Her brother's rejection of this simple truth hurt more than she had expected. It was strange how opening up and sharing what she actually felt so often led to pain while lying kept her safe and seldom got her into trouble.

"Oh, give her a break, Peter," Laurel objected. "She's dating his minion. Why wouldn't he help?"

"It's important Rachel understand what kind of person he is," Peter said sternly. To Rachel, he said, "He is a male who lusts after our sister. He's playing up to you because that's what bounders do. They play up to the little sister. When Sandra eventually dumps him, and she will, he'll drop the pretense of caring about you. I don't want you to be too disappointed."

Rachel clenched her fists. She knew he was wrong. She knew it. Vlad's kindness towards her was sincere. Half a dozen examples leapt to her mind—times she and Vlad had spoken or done something together—but she no longer desired to share their relationship with Peter. It seemed too precious.

Instead, she said, "Why would Sandra dump him? She loves him!"

"Because she's Sandra," Peter said as if that were self-explanatory.

"What does that mean?" asked Rachel.

"It's Sandra," Peter said wearily. "She longs for refrigerators and gas ranges. She wants to live in a smart London flat and work for Daddy and be a spy. The last place she wants to live is another 'moldering pile of rocks,' as she puts it." Peter made quote marks in the air. Straightening, he looked directly at Rachel, "The only female in our family who likes 'moldering piles of rocks' is *you*."

After disembarking from the *Pollepel II*, the group entered the Roanoke Glass Hall. William left immediately, heading for the Detroit walking glass, while the rest—including the Schmitts and Wanda, stepped through a travel glass to New York and then again to London. There, Vlad paused to take his leave of the four Bavarian women, assuring them that officers of his father's would be waiting in Bavaria to escort them to the glasses that would lead them home. He nodded to the triplets, who all gazed up at their prince with nigh-hero worship, and briefly lay a comforting hand on Wanda's shoulder, where she stood hugging her miniature polar bear. Then he rejoined Rachel and her party.

From London, they traveled to Exeter and then to Gryphon's Nest Pub in Gryphon-on-Dart. When Peter pressed his hand against the private door with the ducal seal, it sprang open, and they all walked through to the glass that led to the gatehouse at Gryphon Park. Gaius, who had not been there before, looked around with interest.

Once in the gatehouse, Von Dread offered to take Sigfried's belongings to the house, but Peter stiffly refused. Dread walked through the gatehouse to the gravel driveway and deposited the four trunks there, along with Sigfried and Lucky, who were both clinging to the trunks.

Peter and Laurel said goodbye to Dread and Gaius, Peter stiffly and Laurel with a cheerful wave. Rachel and Gaius walked arm-in-arm back to the glass that would return him to the Gryphon's Nest.

"It's a hop, skip, and a jump for me from here," he said casually. "I can get to Liskeard and, by that point, I'm almost home. I can walk from there if I need to. It's about five miles."

"Wonderful." Rachel grinned at him pointedly. "Now you know your way back *here*."

Gaius winced. "Not sure if I am going to have any free time between chores and homework, but we can talk on the bracelets, right?"

"Right!" Rachel gave him a bright smile that hid her disappointment that he did not seem more eager to spend time with her. Surely he could slip away for a few minutes.

He hugged her and kissed her goodbye very nicely and, with a wave, stepped through the walking glass. Rachel turned to find Dread looming over her with his arms crossed. He looked unexpectedly forbidding. Rachel's heart skipped a beat as everything Peter had said came rushing back. Had she disappointed Dread in some way? Was he cross with her?

Vladimir Von Dread dropped down to one knee, so that his head was closer in height to Rachel's. Reaching out, he took hold of her right arm and drew it toward him. With his other hand, he tapped the black bracelet around her wrist.

"Miss Griffin," he said sternly, "I gave you this for a reason. Do you recall what it was?"

"S-so we could keep in touch?" Rachel answered hoarsely, feeling frightened indeed.

"I gave you this device to keep you out of harm's way." His dark eyes bore into hers. "Not only did you not call me when you were attacked by barghests—even though I was right across the river—but also when I escorted you back to school, you neglected to mention that you had been wounded."

"Oh." She swallowed.

It had not occurred to her, with her father and the Agents there, to also call Dread.

"You did not even call me when you were about to be staked by the overly enthusiastic Mr. Van Helsing." He crossed his arms and stared at her.

Oh, he had heard about that? Rachel recalled why she had not called him and turned rather pink. Dread raised an eyebrow at this response.

"I... you were at Sandra's," she blurted out with the daring that occasionally overcame her when she was speaking with Dread. "I didn't know if you, well, might not be wearing pants."

He blinked twice, processing this information. Were the tips of his ears turning pink?

"Miss Griffin," he replied stiffly, "I assure you I treat your sister with all courtesy. I do not remove my trousers in her presence, much less my pants."

"Oh," she murmured.

Her face grew redder. Having lived in New York for six months, she had casually used the word *pants* in the American manner, which meant the same thing as the British word *trousers*. But he had taken the word in the British sense, meaning *underthings*. This made her comment far more risqué than she had intended. Still, inside, her heart sang, delighted that Vladimir was such an upright young gentleman and showed such concern for her sister.

"You should not hesitate to call upon me, Miss Griffin," he said more gently. "Whether or not you believe me to be..." he pursed his lips, "...wearing pants."

She nodded wordlessly.

"Very good," he stated, "because I assure you, my consternation, should you be harmed, will far outweigh any imposition you might make upon my time."

Her fear began to drain away, and she managed a wan smile.

"FB, I wish you would call me Rachel," she blurted out, using the nickname he had agreed to allow her to address him by. FB was short for FB-I-L —Future Brother-In-Law.

"All in good time," he replied evenly.

Suddenly, she realized that they were alone, entirely alone.

"Vladimir." Her eyes sparkled with pixie-mischief.

"Hmm?"

She glanced around. "There's no one here."

Vladimir, still on one knee, looked left and right. "So there is not."

"You told me not to hug you in front of other people. May I get a proper goodbye?"

The moment the words were out of her mouth, Rachel felt a stab of pure terror. What had possessed her to say something so daring? When he rejected her request, it was going to be a great deal more painful than Peter's rebuke.

Vlad gave her a genuine smile, such a rare sight, and opened his arms welcomingly. With a little cry of gratitude, Rachel threw herself against him. He hugged her tightly.

"I will not ask you to avoid danger entirely," he murmured beside her ear. "After all, you are Rachel Griffin."

"True." She laughed against his shoulder.

"But do take care of yourself, Miss Griffin."

"You, too, FB," she whispered back.

Stepping away, she kissed him on the cheek. Vlad kissed her cheek; then he rose until he towered over her again, nodded once, and departed through the glass without looking back.

When Rachel walked outside, Peter and Laurel were gone, but Sigfried stood gawking at the stone bridge of the gatehouse where it arched over the gravel drive.

"Is this where you live?" His eyes were rather wide.

"No." Rachel sighed. She took him by the shoulders and turned him a quarter turn until he faced down the gravel drive toward the manor house. "That is where I live."

"Where?" Siggy looked around. "I don't see a house."

Rachel looked. The house was right there, at the end of the drive. One could not miss it.

"What do you see?" she asked, puzzled.

"Um. Some trees and grass. And a museum or something that looks a lot like Dare Hall."

"That museum or something? That's my house."

"Your family's dorm rooms are in there?"

Rachel hid her smile. "Something like that."

Chapter Twenty-One:
The Overly-Ample Homecoming of
Sigfried Smith

Rachel convinced Siggy and Lucky to leave the gold at the gate-house and walk down the drive since no one could move the trunks, much less steal them—and since he would be able to see the trunks at any time with his amulet and could send Lucky if anyone approached them. Once they reached the house, workmen could be sent to fetch them.

Ahead, the gravel driveway stretched through lawns and formal gardens filled with topiary figures: green foxes, rabbits, hounds at chase, deer, dragons, centaurs, and even leafy birds, shaped as if in flight. Every fifty feet, green gryphons cut from yew trees stood on guard to either side of the drive. To the north, the lawns and paddocks opened onto rolling moors, spotted with wild ponies. Farther away to the left rose Gryphon Tor, the ruins of the family's original Saxon castle looming upon its peak. To the south and west, the lawns bordered on forest.

In front of the house, a wide stone platform complete with gardens spanned the moat. Handsome stone gryphons flanked this hundred-foot-wide bridge. From there, it was only a short distance to the manor house. The main wing of the house had been designed by the architect who built Dare Hall. It had a domed and peaked turret on each side, stylized gables, stone gryphons, and three domed and peaked turrets at the center—two shorter ones flanking a taller one that had a cupola, like a bell tower, which held the Gryphon Park obscuration lantern. To the right, abutting the main wing, rose the ivy-covered Old Castle with its even taller four towers. The west and south wings of the house were not visible from this angle.

Siggy and Lucky gawked at the grounds and the mansion. Their heads craned up as they stared at the cupolas and crenelations.

"How many people live here?" asked Sigfried.

"Six. Well, more like twenty-four, if you count the servants."

"You have servants?"

"You cannot run such a household without servants," Rachel replied.

"Many of them are descended from families who have served us for generations. Most of the work's done by fey—*bwca, bean-tighe*, hobs, fenodyree in the barn, and all the rest—but we have a butler, a housekeeper, a cook, maids, a steward, a horsemaster, a stable boy, hordes of gardeners, *et cetera*. Not all live here. Some come for the day, such as some of the gardeners or Father's steward or the seamstress—who is a distant relation."

Siggy stared at her as if she were a gibberish-spouting fountain.

"There must be much more than twelve rooms in there," he said. "If each of you has your own room, who uses the rest of the rooms?"

Rachel shrugged. "Nobody."

"You have empty rooms," he breathed, awed. He was too shocked by this revolutionary notion even to suggest lighting them on fire or blowing them up.

The front door opened, and the duke and duchess emerged, followed by Tennyson, the butler. Rachel's father strode towards them and shook Siggy's hand. The two gazed at each other with interest. Rachel realized suddenly that they had never met.

The duchess came forward, shy and smiling. Rachel thought her mother looked particularly pretty in her dress with its creamy bodice and dark plaid skirt; a black velvet belt emphasized the narrowness of her waist.

Siggy walked forward, smiling, to meet her. Then, he just stopped in his tracks, frozen, his gaze drawn, like a magnet, to the absurdly generous proportions of the tiny but voluptuous duchess. Rachel recalled something similar had happened back in September, when Siggy first met Rory Wednesday. Rachel's cheeks began to burn. She wondered if she might combust from sheer embarrassment.

She glanced at her father's impassive face and caught a twinkle of amusement in his eye. The Duke of Devon had long ago grown used to men's reactions to his lovely bride, but, in all the years they had been married, no one's reaction had been quite so dramatic as the young orphan boy, who just stared openly. Usually, men who were ill-bred enough to not behave like gentlemen either made untoward comments or attempted to ogle her mother discreetly.

Siggy just gawked, stunned.

Rachel's mother blushed, but as the stunned Sigfried continued to stare, The Duchess of Devon began to smile. It was a sweet, embarrassed smile, but one filled with mirth, too. Rachel's father, on the other hand, merely looked more amused, almost as if he were hiding a smirk. Rachel still felt acutely embarrassed, so much so that she dearly wished she were somewhere else, anywhere but here; however, when Sigfried just continued to stand there, staring at her mother's chest, she, too, began to smile. She met her mother's eyes, and they both struggled not to laugh.

"Siggy," Rachel said quite properly as if nothing were amiss, "this is my mother."

"Mother!" Sigfried yanked his gaze away and looked at the upper stories of the mansion. He very carefully did not lower his gaze. "She's someone's mother? You must respect mothers! Mothers are the most wonderful thing in the world. She's a mother," he repeated, almost to himself. "Someone's mother."

"Mothers are holy," said Lucky in his gravelly voice. "They lay eggs."

Slowly, Sigfried lowered his gaze and met the warm brown eyes of Ellen Griffin. He kept his gaze steady, not lowering it a single millimeter from her face.

"Welcome to Gryphon Park, Mr. Smith," said the duke.

The duke sent workmen to bring Siggy's trunks, after assuring Lucky that they would be very careful with the gold. Meanwhile, Rachel and her mother led Sigfried into the house. They walked into the enormous entrance hall, the central feature of which was a magnificent sweeping staircase with a red stair runner. Gorgeous murals, showing famous scenes from Arthurian legends, graced the upper walls and ceiling.

Rachel headed across the black and white marble floor toward the staircase that led to the next story, but Sigfried had stopped moving and stood frozen in the doorway. Sighing, she went back and pulled on his arm.

"Where are we?" His eyes darted back and forth.

"In the entrance hall. Of my house."

"This... is a house? Palaces are not as big as this. This is bigger than the gymnasium." He turned toward her, a crazed look in his eyes. "Who are you?"

"I'm The Lady Rachel Griffin, the daughter of The Duke of Devon."

"Your father's a *duke?*" He scrunched up his face and tilted his head left and then right.

"I've only said it a thousand times," Rachel sighed.

"Did you actually count?" asked Rachel's mother with a little smile.

"No." Rachel laughed, because counting how many times they said a thing was something she and her mother occasionally did. "But it has come up quite a few times."

"I don't listen to you," objected Sigfried. "You're a girl."

"Even if you said it ten thousand times, the boss would not care," Lucky said loyally.

Rachel burst out laughing, partially because she was not sure what that meant. She should be annoyed at Sigfried, but she knew he did listen when it mattered. Her mother looked taken aback but not offended. She kept gazing at Sigfried as if he were the sweetest boy in the world.

He stood still for a moment, scratching his head. Then, he said slowly, his voice full of amazement, "When you said you had plenty of room and I wouldn't get in anyone's way and I wouldn't have to live in a broom closet, you actually meant it. All of it."

"I did," Rachel replied.

He looked back and forth around the entrance hall again. "You could fit my entire orphanage—all twenty-eight boys—in this room alone."

In the end, she managed to drag him up the stairs to the next floor.

"Okay, so these are bedrooms. Peter's that way. He lives in the west wing. There are ghosts there. I think he finds them comforting." Siggy's face had begun to turn green. She had forgotten that the otherwise fearless boy was afraid of ghosts. She quickly grabbed his arm and pulled him in the other direction, through the main house toward the east wing. "And bedrooms in the main wing. You can pick any room on the second floor. My parents live on the first floor—first floor up, that is, not the crazy American habit of referring to the ground floor as the first floor. You probably don't want to be too close to them."

"Where do you live?" asked Sigfried.

"Third floor. That's the girls' floor."

Sigfried nodded as if that was as it should be. Rachel pointed at the corner, before the main hall turned into the Old Castle or one had to turn left to reach the east wing. "My room is exactly above that one. If you took that one, I could wave to you from my balcony. Well, if you came out on yours."

"I could have a balcony..." Siggy murmured. "I think I'm dreaming. Are we still in dreamland? Where's Wheels?"

He looked around as if Zoë would suddenly appear out of the wallpaper.

Rachel walked over and opened the door. "Take a look."

Sigfried stuck his head in the room and was quiet for nearly a minute. Finally, he leaned out again. "How many people do I have to share that room with?"

"No one."

"It's all for me?"

"All for you," Rachel smiled. "Well, and Lucky."

Siggy did not reply. When Rachel finally glanced his way, his face was wet with tears.

Siggy picked the room under Rachel's. It was tastefully decorated in white and blue with a medieval theme. The furnishings included a suit of armor, a large four-poster bed, and an attached dressing room, for Lucky and the treasure, Siggy said, and its own bathroom. That was what astonished him the most. It had not occurred to him that it was possible for a person to have a bathroom to himself. Rachel wondered if she should point out that, with his wealth, he could theoretically buy an even bigger house.

Siggy kept grabbing her and pointing, with great excitement, at things she had taken for granted. She found it amusing, but it also made her appreciate what she had all the more.

Her father had Siggy's treasure brought up. There was some concern about the strength of the second floor. Her father cast several cantrips to reinforce the house to ensure nothing would collapse under the weight of the gold. Then, Rachel went through Sigfried's clothing and confirmed that he did indeed own only three shirts—the one he was wearing and two others, one of which was sleeveless with gold lettering that spelled *I flexed and my sleeves exploded*. She informed her mother, and a shopping trip was planned.

Later that evening, she tried to show him around the house. The flying cupids painted upon the ceiling in the lesser ballroom proved too much for him. He spent an hour crouched between the fireplace and an urn, too nervous to move. Rachel eventually lured him out with promises of food, but even after a snack, he still seemed to be in shock. After that, she decided to pick a single drawing room they could make their own and show him how to get there from his room. The house had dozens of drawing rooms, but there was only one Rachel was absolutely certain no one else was using. Taking him by the arm, she led him to the Castle Room.

This drawing room had belonged to her grandfather, and he had decorated it. No one else in the family liked the chamber, not even her grandmother. They all felt it was oppressive. No one, that was, except Rachel. Even Rachel, however, no longer spent much time here. It felt lonely without her grandfather, and it did not have the cozy warmness of his library, nor all the books. So since his death, she had spent her free time in the tower library, not in the Castle Room. But Sigfried would like it. Of that she was certain.

She opened the door, breathing in the familiar scent of leather polish and furniture oil, with the slightest hint of pipe tobacco. The air was cold, and there was none of the cinnamon odor that accompanied salamanders. Dark walnut paneling covered the walls, and the heavy furniture was upholstered in dark brown leather. Huge hearths filled much of the north and south walls.

Within the chamber itself stood an old-fashioned globe in an oak stand and three orreries. The smallest one, beside Grandfather's favorite chair, was an open orrery with the planets, each of precious stone, on poles. In the center of the east wall, between two massive armchairs, stood one of mahogany and brass with circular gears and the zodiac symbols around the twelve sides; and in the far corner, near the southern fireplace, was a tower orrery of walnut, stone, and brass with nine planets, twenty-two moons, and a central sun globe that lit up, surrounded by a shimmering armillary sphere. Several handsome swords hung on the wall opposite the door, immediately drawing Sigfried's attention.

The most glorious part of the chamber, however, were the two gigantic murals, one above either hearth. Both fireplaces were empty. Rachel made a mental note to ask Tennyson to assign a salamander to one of the hearths and to have a pile of wood brought in for the other, so Lucky could enjoy lighting it himself.

"What's that?" Siggy asked, coming up beside her. He stared up at the mural on the south wall. It portrayed a huge gray castle draped in ivy. "That looks familiar."

"It should." She smiled. "That's Beaumont. You've been there twice."

"In Transylvania?" He cocked his head sideways. "It looks a little different."

"This was before the carvings of serpents eating children were added," she said wryly.

"Oh, yeah, that small thing," Siggy muttered. "Why did they add that?"

"Because demons were in charge of the castle." She paused a moment. "Of course, it doesn't look like this anymore: one whole tower fell down."

Siggy blinked oddly. "Didn't something bad happen to me? Why don't I remember?"

Rachel looked at him. He had never noticed not remembering a thing before. "You nearly died. Flops-Over-Dead-Chick flopped over and saved you. Only, it let Morax in."

"The bull with a human face that Amber saw stuck in that caramel candy stuff, right?" asked Sigfried. "The one we fought at that Greek temple."

"Carthaginian temple, but yes."

"Carthaginian, Shmarthaginian. The place with the crazy child skeletons." He shivered. "I still have nightmares about that one."

That was odd. Rachel had hardly thought of it in months. It was not that it had not been terrible. It was just that there had been so many other terrible things.

"We should go back and burninate them, boss," Lucky said in a low, tense voice. "So no one else can ever disturb them."

"Not sure if it works that way, Lucky," said Rachel, troubled by the idea of burning the child skeletons.

"Where are they keeping those demons—the ones Amber saw?" asked Siggy. "We could go there and burninate them."

Rachel did not answer. She did not feel it was her place to reveal what few secrets O.I. had left. She plopped down in one of the heavy leather armchairs. Sigfried chose another.

"What do you want to do tomorrow?" she asked.

"What could be more interesting than exterminating demons?" he replied.

"That's not an option," said Rachel. "We could hike up the tor. Go rowing on the lake. Visit the stables and the kennels. There's a new litter of puppies. Take a trip to town. Play billiards at the pub. Play snooker here —which is even better than pool. Visit the sweets shop and the library. Go riding on the moors—horses or brooms. If so, we could visit Wistman's

Wood or perhaps the Giants' picnicking spot. Or there's always exploring the house."

"There are giants?" Sigfried cried, eyes alight.

Rachel wished she had not mentioned the giants. "Yes, but they're not friendly, and they are often not there—at their picnic table, I mean. A few years ago, some schoolboys from Exeter School of Enchantment broke the obscuration on one of the chairs, and the Unwary could see it for a few years. Eventually, the Agents took that one away. We could at least fly by."

"I want to do that!"

"Brooms or horses?"

"I don't have a horse."

"We'll give you one. Remember? We can pick one from the herd, or we can look for one on the moors. Though a wild pony would take too long to tame." Remembering the last time they had discussed this topic, Rachel turned to Lucky, "And no eating the horses! Or the dogs. Or the sheep. Or people's ducks and chickens. Or the swans on the lake."

Lucky darted close to Sigfried. "Boss, that's a lot of things not to eat."

"We can get you your own flock of chickens if you wish," Rachel added, more gently.

"His own chickens?" Siggy's eyes grew large. "This place is paradise."

Rachel pressed her lips together to keep from laughing. "Sigfried, you do realize that you have even more wealth than my family? You could buy all these things any time you want."

"That just makes it all the more amazing that you are willing to give them to me." His eyes began to look suspiciously shining. "No one's ever given me things."

"Welcome to Gryphon Park." Rachel smiled.

As they stood up to leave, she paused to gaze at the other mural, the one on the north wall. Looming over them was her favorite of all the murals in Gryphon Park. A huge black castle stood on a high mountainside under a stormy sky. The castle, built of solid basalt, was surrounded by a defensive fortress. Within the outer walls, however, rose a fairytale palace, complete with crenelations and tall black towers. Other snow-capped mountains rose in the background, with the hint of the spires of a city in the lower left corner.

"Ace! What's that?" Sigfried asked, impressed. "Lucky, we should get ourselves a place like this! We would not have to worry about our gold if we put it in there!"

"That's right, boss! We could breathe on thieves before they got in," chimed Lucky.

"Or drop boiling oil on them," said Siggy.

"They'd show up against all that black. We could spot them and eat them."

"Unless they were ninjas," opined Sigfried.

"I bet ninjas taste good, too, boss."

"I don't know where it is," Rachel admitted, staring up at the massive black castle, her heart filled with an emotion she could not name. "When I was very young, I assumed it was in Scotland, but now, I'm not sure it's a real place."

"I have always thought Scotland was fake, too," said Sigfried. "Men wear skirts and toss logs. Can't be real."

"Scotland's not fake. I've been there. It's quite charming. And they're not skirts; they're kilts," she said, adding, "When I was little, I thought this was Magnus's castle."

"Whose?" Sigfried walked closer, examining the mural more carefully.

"Magnus Ridel, the Duke of Caledon," Rachel replied. "He's a Scottish duke. Very tragic and romantic. All the older girls love him." When Siggy began to roll his eyes, she added, "You would like him, too. He's the only person I know, other than you, who's fought a dragon."

Sigfried looked more interested. "And that's his home?"

"No." She shook her head. "I've been to his home. It doesn't look like that."

"So what is this place?"

"I think it is just a fanciful painting. Or maybe it's intended to portray some place Underhill," Rachel said thoughtfully. "Some place magical and lovely."

"The dark side of the moon?" offered Lucky.

Rachel smiled at that. She gazed up at the painting a while longer. Looking at it always filled her with a wild longing, as if, should she wish, she could step into the painting, enter the castle, and run through its halls, or fly her steeplechaser around the tall towers, racing the storm winds.

"Maybe," she murmured, "somewhere Beyond the Fields We Know."

"It's awesome," stated Sigfried. "Can I kype the picture and put it in my room?"

Rachel laughed, "I don't think the mural would fit, but I am glad you like it. My sister Sandra hates it. She feels it's oppressive and represents everything from which she wishes to escape. Laurel couldn't care less, but Peter rather likes it. At least, I think he does."

And I love it with all my heart, she thought but did not say aloud. After Peter's rejection of her claim of friendship with Vlad, she felt protective of the things that mattered to her. She loved this castle more than all other castles, and she loved many castles. She even loved this one more than Beaumont. It reminded her of her grandfather. Not only because she had gazed up at it so many times as she sat curled in his lap as he smoked his pipe and read news glass, but also because it was so easy to imagine him in such a place, just out of her reach. In a way, the black palace, as she thought of it, with its grandeur and its ancient strength, represented everything about the aristocratic life that she longed for and loved so much; the life she would have to leave forever if she married modern science-loving Gaius.

Gaius was a science boy who wanted to live in the world of Ouroboros Industries and scientific experiments. He probably wanted to live in a townhouse at some smart urban address.

"I'm with Peter," said Sigfried. "I like it, too. I bet someone King Arthur knows—like King Ban or King Vortigern—lives there."

Rachel nodded. "I like to think this is the sort of place my grandfather lives in the afterworld," she said softly. "I picture him on the ramparts or walking down the long halls."

"Do people get their own castle in the afterworld?" Sigfried asked, interested. "Ace! Lucky and I want a big one!"

"Filled with gold," said Lucky, "and more gold."

Rachel laughed. "I don't know if they do, but they should."

CHAPTER TWENTY-TWO:
THE CRY OF THE DART

Early the next morning, Rachel bounded from her pink canopy bed. She settled at her desk, near the hearth where her mottled bronze and black salamander lazed, to write letters on her pale green and lavender stationery. Mistletoe came padding over, rubbed against her leg, and then curled up upon her feet. First, she penned a thank-you note to Vladimir for helping Sigfried. Then, she wrote chatty letters to Nastasia and Astrid. With a sigh, she wrote quick notes to Zoë, Joy, and Valerie. Finally, more carefully, she wrote a short letter to Juma O'Malley, inquiring how he had been. She had not heard from him in some months and wondered how he was doing now that his mother was trapped in O.I.'s demon-containing substance. She addressed the first six and put the last in an envelope, hoping her father could arrange for it to be delivered to the safe house where Juma now lived.

Her bedroom was a huge chamber of dark wood with a ceiling that slanted along with the line of the roof. There was a giant fireplace, a walk-in dollhouse, a rocking horse, and a collection of stuffed animals neatly arranged on a trunk at the bottom of her bed, including Mr. Muffin, Splashdown the Dolphin, Alfred the Crocodile, and Torture the Penguin. Around the walls were four stalwart walnut bookshelves and a pretty window reading nook that looked out on the hedge maze. French doors led to a balcony, from which, on clear days, she could see the back lawns, including albino roe deer, an elephant herd topiary, paddocks of Friesian and Gypsy Vanners—surely two of the most beautiful horse breeds in the world. Beyond the lawns lay the forest to the west and the moors to the north. Gryphon Tor rose above the moors, the ruins of the family's original keep visible atop it. If she went out on the balcony and looked straight down, she could see a stone statue of an unknown giant carrying a child.

Outside her window, rain poured down. Mist covered the grounds. It was so thick she could hardly see the hedge maze, a hundred yards away. The noise of the rain, pounding against the stone of the house and running down the gutter in the corner, where the main building met the east wing, was rhythmic and comforting, as if the weather itself were welcoming her home.

It was the Ides of March, and, that evening, her father would be officiating the celebration of Anna Perenna, the goddess of the year. Rachel, who had felt uncomfortable about attending sacrifices ever since she had almost been sacrificed herself, had bowed out, claiming she wanted to show Siggy the grounds, and they would just be in the way. She almost relented when she was offered the role of Anna, where the goddess pretends to be the virginal Minerva and then throws back her veil to laugh in the face of the god of war, but Laurel had previously played that role with such flair that Rachel felt it would be a crime to rob her of it.

She chatted with Gaius over her black bracelet for half an hour, while he performed his morning chores, watering cows and feeding chickens. She lay on her pink canopy bed as they spoke, her eyes half-closed as she imagined their future life together, once they were married and living in Bavaria, where Gaius worked for Dread. She liked that mental image better than living in Detroit so he could work for O.I. though, of course, with glasses, there were many places they could live and he could still commute. Still, Bavaria with its stark Alps and green valleys was her first choice.

Once he went in for breakfast, she jumped up and put aside her Victorian flannel nightgown in favor of a black and white checkered A-line dress with a lacy Peter Pan collar. She also donned a pair of black pantaloons beneath her dress—in case she needed to ride her broom—and ran down in hopes of meeting up with Sigfried at breakfast.

Sigfried arrived at the breakfast hall with her mother, who had found him lost, wandering the corridors. He had a look of blissful joy on his face as the duchess led him along, arm-in-arm. After their first meeting, he had treated the duchess with nothing but cordiality, but he believed a mother was a magical thing, a being of infinite comfort. Every time Rachel's mother performed a motherly act, especially towards him, a little happy smile came over his face. The thought of his growing up without a mother, and what it must be like to suddenly have someone gently looking out for him, almost brought tears to Rachel's eyes.

Siggy walked up and down the breakfast buffet, gawking at the sheer amount and variety of food. No matter how often Rachel insisted he could have as much as he wanted, she could not keep him from filling his pockets with honeycake and scrambled eggs. He also filled his plate to overflowing, though Rachel noted that he did not touch the kimchi that she and Peter and their mother had so liberally scooped onto their own plates. Sitting down between her mother and Laurel, he tucked his food away at an astonishing rate.

Rachel looked around at her family and smiled. She remembered her revelation in the infirmary that she had shared with the Raven—the idea that an Amber raised by her parents might have been even a better weapon against the gathering darkness than the death doll Amber. She could not know if it were true, but as she looked around at her parents, Laurel, and Peter, all smiling and talking together, she felt particularly grateful to have been born part of this family.

"What's everyone's plan for today?" asked the duke, as he finished his French toast and took a sip of coffee. He had taken the day off to complete his ducal duties for the Ides of March.

"Nothing!" Laurel stretched, first one arm bent behind her back and then the other. "I plan to do nothing. Well, other than laugh in the face of the god of war. That's worthy of getting out of a chair."

Peter made an amused noise of disapproval. "I plan to spend the free portion of the day knocking off some of my schoolwork. If I get it done now, on this rainy day, I can enjoy the later portions of the holiday more freely." He paused and then smiled wryly, "Of course, that's bound to be rainy, too."

"People do homework while on holiday?" Sigfried asked, horrified.

"Only dorky people," Laurel murmured.

Peter ignored her.

Rachel said, "I plan to give Sigfried a tour of the house."

"That sounds boring," said Sigfried, "unless you think we might get lost and have an adventure. Are there people wandering inside the house we could rescue? Traveling tinkers, maybe? Trying to sell their wares but they can't find their way back out? What if we don't find our way back? We could be trapped in the wrong drawing room for months, and Lucky would have to light all the furniture on fire."

"I'm not sure furniture is good to eat, boss," whispered Lucky, who sat between his boy and Rachel's mother. "But maybe we could eat a few tinkers."

"We would all live longer if we did that," Siggy nodded his head sagely, "but humans are not just creatures of expediency. There is also a matter of honor. I don't think knights eat their dead. What would King Arthur say if he returned and found them at it?"

Peter, an enormous King Arthur fan, gave Sigfried an approving nod. Rachel's mother, meanwhile, was sneaking Lucky tidbits off her plate. Lucky gazed up adoringly at the duchess. She gave the dragon her shy pixie-smile, which Rachel's father had once claimed was what had caused him to fall in love with her, and scratched the top of his golden head, between his horns. Lucky made a deep, happy noise and kicked his back foot, like a dog when its belly was rubbed.

Rachel's and her father's eyes met, and they both smiled, thinking the same thought: The duchess had made a friend for life.

"I thought we would *look around*." Rachel put an extra emphasis on the last two words, giving Sigfried a telling look. "You know, see what *my grandfather* might have left."

Sigfried gaped blankly. Then, his face lit up. "Oh, you mean look for the eart-Hay—"

"Sigfried!" Rachel cut him off. "My parents speak Pig Latin."

"Can they?" Siggy gawked, shaken to the core. "I thought adults weren't allowed."

"Here at Gryphon Park, we have many unexpected talents," her father replied dryly.

"But, yes," Rachel said primly to Siggy, "exactly."

"Great," said Sigfried. "Luckster Sixty-Thousand and I are ready!"

"Just as long as *being ready* doesn't involve moving," Lucky said happily, as the duchess petted his ruff.

Rachel grabbed Vroomie and lent Sigfried a red Sherwood Fast-Track from the broom closet. Sherwood Bristleless still made their brooms from pine and eucalyptus. The Fast-Track was a racer, which meant that it was less steady than a traveler. Sigfried was doing very well in Wednesday Broom Riding Class, so Rachel felt he could handle it. A traveler might be too long to corner in some portions of the house.

They flew through the mansion: the west wing, the main house—or north wing, as it had originally been called—the Old Castle, and the east wing. They traveled down long drafty hallways lined with giant urns and suits of armor; by crimson dining halls with painted ceilings and crystal chandeliers; along a long, narrow gallery filled with portraits of generations of family and a shorter, wider one containing statues collected from all over the world. They zipped through a huge library with long wooden ladders and painted ceilings, that again terrified Sigfried, and a smaller, darker library containing only novels, and then into the creamy marble ballroom with its wall of mirrors and statues and its large, arched windows that looked out on the rose garden.

Siggy peered through walls and inside pillars, searching for the shining silvery light of the Heart of Dreams. Flying beside him, Rachel swallowed. When they set out, no one knew the house better than she. She had spent years of rainy days exploring, fitting into spaces no one else had bothered to visit in decades, sometimes centuries. But one fly-around and Sigfried would see things with his enchanted amulet that she had never found. The thought made her heart ache. Then, she shook off her dismay with a laugh. When she was climbing forgotten servants' staircases and crawling through dusty storage spaces, hadn't she wished for a friend to share it all with? It was ridiculous to regret that her wish had been granted.

"If we can find the Heart right off," she told him, "it will free up the rest of our holiday. If not, I will start working on getting permission for an outing to Merlin's Cave."

"I want to visit Merlin's Cave anyway," said Siggy. "It's a cave that was Merlin's."

She nodded. "Oh, and we could go to Glastonbury, too, if you like. Arthur and Gwenhwyfar are buried there."

"Ace!" Sigfried crowed. He tapped his chest where his amulet lay under his garments. "Are they? After I go there, we'll know for sure."

That was a curious thought.

A while later, Sigfried grabbed his head. "What is going on with this house? Where is all the extra room coming from? We go ten feet, and there's two hundred feet of room inside."

Rachel gave a snort of amusement. "Do you know what *kenomancy* is?"

"Like Wheels' backpack and the princess's house?"

"Exactly," Rachel said. "I have an ancestor, the seventh duke, who traveled to Australia soon after its discovery and learned kenomancy from the aborigines—the people from whom the Wise learned conjuring. He became an expert kenomancer and went around kenomancing everything. So the house and the hedge maze contain extra room. His name was Uther Griffin."

"Uther like.... Wait. That boy we saw, your grandfather. What was his name?" Siggy asked slowly.

"Blaise." Rachel grinned because her blood brother had finally made the connection.

"Blaise like Merlin's teacher?" asked Sigfried.

"And my father's name is Ambrose...."

"... who some people think was Merlin's father's name," replied Sigfried.

"And my uncle was Emrys and my great uncle was Cadellan," said Rachel, not bothering to mention that the first member of the family to come to Britain, almost two thousand years ago, had also been named Ambrosius. For all she knew, maybe he had been Merlin's teacher.

"Both names used for Merlin," said Siggy.

"And my other dead uncle, the one who helped us at Beaumont, was named Myrddin."

"Merlin's original name," Siggy said. "Blaise, Ambrose, Uther, Emrys, Myrddin, Cadellan...."

"He's an ancestor of mine, you know," said Rachel. "Merlin, I mean."

"Really?" Sigfried gawked at her. He flew closer and poked her twice as if checking to make sure she was real.

"Truly," Rachel nodded. "We are descended from both Merlin and from Ygraine...through the Saps. My great-great-great grandfather Uther, whom I just mentioned, his first wife was a Sap. So we are related to King Arthur through Arthur's mother."

Siggy frowned thoughtfully. "What horrible twist of fate resulted in 'Peter'?"

Rachel burst out laughing. "My mother. She didn't like the Arthurian names."

"Your mother is the most motherly mother who ever mothered," he said solemnly, "but about this one point, she's dead wrong. What mother in her right mind would pick a dull name like Peter, when he could have been Gwain or Vortigern?"

⁓⌁⁓

By early afternoon, when the sun finally peeked out from behind the clouds, Rachel and Sigfried had found no sign of the Heart of Dreams. They went outside and flew around the house twice, in case there was some space Siggy's all-seeing amulet could pick up from the outside that they had not encountered from within, to no avail. If the Heart was in the house, either it was in a space they had not yet come upon, or it no longer shone with a silvery light.

Since they were already on brooms, they decided to fly around the nearby moors and save horseback riding to the giants' table for another day.

"Where would you like to go? We could head south and visit Raven Rock," Rachel said. It was a place name that had much more significance to her now than it had had before she left for Roanoke. "Or we could fly north and over the moors. Or, oh! I know! Luckey Tor!"

"They named a tor after Lucky?" asked Sigfried.

"Boss, they knew I was coming!" cried the dragon in delight.

"Let's go there," said Rachel.

In all directions, the brown and green rolling moors spread out beneath them, except for a few places where clumps of bare trees were showing the first faint hint of buds. Snow still coated the higher rocky tors. The lower valleys were spotted with shaggy-maned ponies and the yellow of flowering gorse bushes. Rachel slowed her broom until she drifted, drinking in the splendid view, so familiar yet so missed over the last six months.

Dartmoor stretched out all around them, gray stones protruding from rolling, brown, boggy moors and literally hundreds of tors, some topped with stratified rock formations or stone cairns. Rachel knew the name of every single tor. She picked out a few of her favorites visible from her current position.

"That's Aish Tor and Mel Tor and, look!" Rachel cried, "that one's Luckey Tor."

They flew above the rocky peak, surrounded by the spider-like, moss-covered trees so common on Dartmoor. The tall granite outcropping was a difficult climb from the ground, but from the air, they landed easily on the top, gazing over the surrounding landscape and down the dramatic plunge of Dart Gorge. Even in the barrenness of winter, the moss on the rocks and trees of the gorge shone a brilliant green below the bare branches.

Siggy looked over the surrounding moors and tors. "Ace! Which way are the giants?"

Rachel closed her eyes a moment and thought back. The obscuration hiding parts of Dartmoor from the Unwary popped, and the expanse before her doubled. The rough stone of the giants' towers now rose in the west and north. She pointed toward them.

"The giants live over that way, near Hound Tor. Their picnic area is a bit north of that. Some of them live to the west, too, near Vixen Tor. But that area is much more dangerous. There's a witch—or she might be a hag—who lives there and eats travelers. Though Levera eats travelers, too, and she's not too far from the Giant's table. She's another witch. Or maybe hag."

"Boss, if she can eat travelers, why can't I?" asked Lucky.

"She's not supposed to," Rachel explained.

"What's the difference between a witch and a hag?" asked Siggy.

"A witch is a human woman. A hag is a fey creature from Beyond the Fields We Know."

"Which fields do we know?"

Rachel chuckled. "It's just a phrase, like Underhill or the Wood Perilous. It means 'from the fairy world.'"

"Hag, fairy. Witch, mortal. I've got it," said Siggy. He paused. "We're witches, right? Or at least you? I guess that would make me a warlock?"

Rachel shook her head. "We practice sorcery. You're a sorcerer, and I'm a sorceress. Witches are something different."

"Different how?" asked Sigfried.

"Does one taste better?" Lucky asked plaintively.

"Does one have more treasure?" asked Siggy.

Rachel laughed, shaking her head. "That depends upon what you treasure. But as to how they are different...." She thought for a moment and then tried to explain: "Witches are, for the most part, an unsavory lot. They don't study the Sorcerous Arts we learn at school, but witchcraft, which is something else entirely, and nearly every single one uses black magic. Every generation or so, one might come across a legitimate white witch, but they're rare."

"Can we kill this hag?" asked Siggy. "I mean, if she's a hag and not a witch?"

"You would have to ask my father. Hags are part of the Unseelie Court, but they're not evil by nature. They oversee decomposition the way Pillywiggins watch over flowers. So there are a number of hags on Dartmoor, with all the bogs. Some have covenants with the dukedom; others have gone bad—broken their covenants—and are fair game."

"Fair game?" he asked, his eyes aglow. "Which fey can we incinerate?"

"Phooka are fair game. Brollachan, but they're nigh impossible to kill. There's Bengie Geare—the black pony phantom, who had once been the evil mayor of a nearby town. He killed my great-grandfather. We'd love to put an end to him. And barghests, of course. Dartmoor is famous for them. Really big ones. There was even—"

An eerie booming noise rang out from the gorge below. The dreadful sound of it rang through every bone in Rachel's body. She cried out in terror.

"No!" Rachel shouted, jumping on her steeplechaser. "No! Dart, no! There's only three days left! Not now!"

"What's that?" asked Sigfried, running for his racer and jumping on. From under his coat, he drew his Bowie knife.

"It's the Cry of Dart!" Rachel called back. Taking off with a running start, she dived off Luckey Tor, straight into the gorge, plummeting toward the river. Sigfried and Lucky followed.

"'*For the cry of Dart is the voice of doom,*'" she shouted over her shoulder, quoting an old poem. "That noise? That's the sound Dart only makes when she's about to kill!"

Chapter Twenty-Three:
Dart, Dart, Cruel Dart

RACHEL DIVED STRAIGHT DOWN INTO THE GORGE. NEARLY FIVE HUNDRED feet later, she reached the river Dart at Black Pool, just north of the Venford Brook, and hesitated. Should she go south toward Sharrah Pool and Horseshoe Falls, or north, deeper into the gorge? Where was the danger?

She listened and then sped northward, flying above the riverbed, over rapids, boulders, cascades, ledges, and wooded islands. To either side stretched ancient oak woodland. The branches were bare, but pale moss coated the trunks as well as the rocks and boulders. Ferns, lichens, sphagnum, and liverwort, all a mossy green, carpeted the forest, making it picturesque. Here and there, among the rocks, the last snowdrops of the winter bloomed.

She flew above dark waters as they danced over small waterfalls and rushing cascades. An otter sunning on a rock leapt, startled, from the lichen-covered boulder upon which it rested. As she flew on, the walls of the gorge became steeper, closing in around the river.

"Dart!" Rachel shouted as she flew. "Dart! No!"

But she was not her father. She did not have the duke's authority to command the river to appear. She flew, bent low over the shaft of the steeplechaser, urging her broom to go faster and faster. As she sped above the empty river, she began to fear she had gone the wrong way.

The booming cry came again from behind her, low and eerie, causing the hairs along the back of her neck to stand. Rachel spun around. Signaling to Siggy, she barreled back the way they had come, over the rapids, through the ancient oaks, past Black Pool and Sharrah Pool, and onwards.

Ahead, along the right bank, was a shelf of moss-covered stone. A Persian family climbed upon the rocks, two men, two women, and three children. One of the children, a little boy about five years old, had wandered from the others and played on a promontory of the rocky shelf that thrust farther into the river. Rachel looked back and forth but saw no immediate danger.

Roar! She heard it before she saw it. Behind her, a four-foot wall of water raced down the gorge, overflowing Dart's banks. The recent rains and the melt waters had combined to create a flood, and the floodwaters were thundering directly toward the little boy.

Rachel screamed, but over the roar of many waters, the family could not hear her. She wanted to move the child, but when she reached for her wand, she realized that it was back in her school robes. Without it, she would have to lift her hands to cast the cantrip, and she was going too fast to safely let go of the bristleless.

"There!" she cried to Siggy, who was behind her.

She threw her broom into a spin to counter her forward momentum. The steeplechaser spun horizontally at a tremendous speed, once, twice, three times, the landscape in three-hundred-sixty degrees flashing by in a blur. She flipped on the becalming enchantment, but ever since Vroomie had come back from Chanson's Quality Bristlelesses, the drag of the becalming enchantment was so reduced that her momentum hardly slowed. As the world rushed by, she made a mental note to speak to Mr. Chanson about that.

After her third revolution, she yanked her broom upward into a vertical loop, flipping over and coming parallel to the river again. This finally slowed her. She leaned back and came to a standstill... to find herself only just above the river's surface.

With that same roar of mighty waters, the flood struck her. Icy cold water crashed over her broom. Her chest seized up, refusing to allow her to inhale. She and her steeplechaser were thrown helter-skelter. She grabbed onto Vroomie with her knees, but the terrible power of the water caught the tail fan and dragged it, yanking the bristleless away from her legs. She still clung to the handlebars and held on with all her strength.

If she lost hold of the steeplechaser under the water, it would be swept away. Even if she held on, would it still fly? Did water hurt bristlelesses? She fought to shift so the current would push her toward her broom instead of ripping it from her. Her leg snagged the device. She clung to it as the torrent of water dragged her along. This brought a new terror: *Which way was up?*

Was she right side up or upside-down? She was not used to being disoriented. Usually, she would remember back and figure out where she was, but she had been tossed and turned so many times she could make no sense of it. This brought her much closer to panicking. She could not panic. There would be no hope if she panicked—for her or for that little boy.

Rachel drew on her mask of calm and opened her eyes despite the iciness of the water. Dark murkiness surrounded her. If she tried to fly the broom with great enough speed to break free of the river and she went the wrong way, she would slam into the bottom or into a boulder. The chance of escaping a broken neck was slim.

From her left came a flash of red and gold. *Lucky!* But he was swimming as he looked for her. Was he above her or below? Terror gripped her. *What should she do?* Rachel gritted her teeth. If she did nothing, she would surely freeze to death or drown. Better to act.

She kicked the tail fan and flipped switches with her numb thumbs. She threw her weight, willing the steeplechaser to move toward Lucky. For a very long second, nothing happened.

Suddenly, Vroomie engaged and shot upward. The water dragged her back, trying to pull her from the broom. Her fingers were too numb to trust. She hugged the bristleless, wrapping her arms around the shaft. If she hit a boulder like this, there would be no recovering.

With an explosion of spray, she emerged from the river. Silver droplets flew every which way. As she shot into the air, the shock of escaping the icy temperatures wracking her entire body.

She was free. Her muscles released, allowing her to gasp for air. The first breath she drew to fill her lungs felt so sweet. To her astonished delight, her broom righted, shed the water, and flew true. She wanted to collapse over the handle and pant in relief, but she could not. *What had happened to the little boy?* She flew upstream the fifty feet she had been dragged by the waters. Sigfried waved to her from where he hovered above the surface. Rachel suspected that he had been scouring the river, looking for her. Lucky emerged from the river, spraying water droplets everywhere. Ahead of them rose Dart.

Not the river. The river roared below them, overflowing its banks. Gone were the placid dark pools and delicate rapids; in their place, raging white water crashed and careened, slamming into boulders and bouncing off rocky shelves. Ahead, near where the frantic family cried out, the figure of a robed woman, made entirely of water, rose ten feet above the riverbed. Just as the river itself was always in motion, the liquid forming her body flowed up from the river, through her lovely form, and back down again. Sunlight glittered off the smooth surfaces of her watery shoulders and hood. In her arms, entirely engulfed, she held the struggling five-year-old boy.

As Rachel flew toward them, one of the men, presumably the boy's father, charged into the raging waters, desperate to reach his drowning son. Instantly, his legs were swept from under him, and he was dragged downstream.

Dart, beautiful Dart, so sweet and feminine when she came to greet Rachel's father on the Equinox, threw back her head and opened her mouth. It opened much wider than a human's mouth could. Her watery teeth were sharp as a fox's, sharp as a piranha's. She laughed, a sound like the gurgling of a river—a river filled with malice and hatred.

Rachel cast *tiathelu* and tried to pull the boy's father from the rushing waters, but the pull of the river was too strong. She could not budge him.

"Sigfried!" she shouted. "Save him!"

She barreled forward, toward Dart and tried to yank the little boy from the river nymph but could not get a grip on him. Her hands swished vainly through Dart's watery substance. Lucky leapt forward and breathed his red-orange fire all over Dart's watery hood. The river nymph merely batted the flame aside. It had no effect at all.

"Lucky!" Rachel cried. "Go get my father! He's the only one who can stop her now!"

The *lung* glanced at Sigfried and then shot off like an arrow, disappearing from sight. Rachel turned back to the watery lady and prepared to fight. She whistled the paralysis hex. Blue sparkles of light struck Dart. A tiny portion of her liquid, about the size of a dinner plate, ceased moving and dropped into the river, but new water sluiced up to take its place.

Rachel whistled a wind; the water hardly rippled. She cast a Glepnir band, but her band was far too small to encircle Dart. Her attacks were so weak that the river nymph had not even glanced her direction. It did not help that her hands were so numb that it was hard to form the gestures. Also, her teeth had begun to chatter, which made it harder to pronounce the cantrips.

The river nymph's regard stayed upon the struggling little boy, gazing at him as a mother might. Only her expression was eager and malicious as the child flailed, unable to breathe.

Siggy swooped down the river and yanked the bedraggled father from the water with *tiathelu*. He hauled him to the shore where the rest of the family gathered. One woman was holding the other two children high on the bank. The other woman and man crowded onto what remained of the moss-covered ledge. They reached helplessly toward the boy. This woman, most likely the boy's mother, wept piteously.

Siggy turned on Dart. Like Rachel, he attacked with all the magic he knew. He cast *bey-athe*, *nothor*, and *argos*. The warding shield did nothing. *Nothor* deflected the drops of water that sprayed his way. His Glepnir band was larger than Rachel's, but when it came near Dart, her watery substance dropped into the river, child and all, before the golden glowing band could encircle it, and then rose again, child and all, in a new spot.

Sigfried flew forward and stabbed Dart repeatedly with his Bowie knife, but she did not even notice. He stabbed her again and again and again, maybe twenty times. When that did nothing, he reached into the water to grab the boy. Dart casually slapped him away.

Siggy tumbled through the air and slammed into the mossy oaks on the left side of the river. *Crack.* The violence of the impact snapped the shaft of his borrowed bristleless. Siggy himself smashed into the trunk of two trees and fell to the ground.

Rachel screamed and flew toward him, but he stood up and shook himself off. He ran to the edge of the raging waters and continued to cast cantrips. Rachel breathed a sigh of relief, her limbs trembling, and not just because the cold wind coming down the gorge was cutting through her soaked garments. There must be something she could do.

She did not have her wand with its remaining charge of Eternal Flame. She did not even have her amethyst necklace, not that it would have helped. It annoyed her that just because she had thought herself safe in her house she had not put it on that morning. Had not she promised herself that if she ever was given a protection against being paralyzed, she would wear it always, even in the bath? *What else had she learned this year?*

Rachel faced Dart again and cast *turlu*, drawing momentum from the water forming the giant female figure and directing it into the river behind her. Either she did it incorrectly, or water was different from other things. Her target, Dart's left shoulder, lost its form and sluiced back into the river, only to reform, but the momentum she had directed away from the watery figure to a point behind her did not come alone.

A huge sheet of water crashed first over Rachel and then over Sigfried, where he stood on the riverbank. Even though Rachel was already wet and shivering, the icy cold shocked her. She cried out. Fortunately, her cantrip had drawn out a single sheet of water, not a constant stream.

"Thanks, Griffin," muttered a wet, dripping Sigfried.

"Sorry!" she called.

"What does the water lady want?" called Siggy. "What would she take instead?"

"*'Dart, Dart, cruel Dart, every year thou claim'st a heart,'*" Rachel recited the rhyme.

What did Dart want? Rachel thought about what she knew of the river, about Dart's desire to kill, about the covenant that bound her not to kill anyone, at least deliberately—there was always a chance of someone suffering an unfortunate accident—after the Spring Equinox ceremony. She strove to put something of the river's nature into words.

"She wants the shock of death. She wants everyone to mourn and pay attention to her. If she waits three days, she'll get it in the form of a ceremony, but she prefers the real thing."

"*Ahura!*" Rachel cast the cantrip that calmed men, beasts, and storms. No effect.

"*Lux!*" cried Sigfried, trying every cantrip he knew. Siggy's cantrip worked. A ball of light appeared in the air before him and hung there, glowing faintly.

Oh! Rachel did not have her wand, but she did have her black bracelet.

"Vlad!" she cried. He had told her to call him. "Vladimir!"

Siggy looked at her oddly. "Do you think he can hear you from here?"

She did not answer him. When Dread did not respond, she called William, whom she knew could also jump. She called much more softly, so Sigfried could not hear over the roar of the river. William did not answer either.

"G-gaius?" Her teeth were chattering again. The wind coming down the gorge was not helping her already chilled and soddened state.

"Rachel?" came Gaius's cheerful voice, and then more concerned, "Everything okay?"

"C-can y-you reach V-vlad?"

"Same way you can," he replied. "Though I may have a phone number somewhere that calls an aide-de-camp in his father's castle. He's visiting William, and they're doing experiments. They may have taken off their bracelets to make sure they aren't disturbed," he replied.

Phone number! Hadn't Vlad given her a business card with a phone number? He had said that if she crumpled the card, it would bring help.

Rachel reached for the pouch at her neck and then sighed. Her pouch was back in her bedroom, next to her necklace and her wand.

She said, despite chattering teeth. "C-can you a-ask V-vlad to call if you hear from him?"

"Sure," Gaius said, followed by, "Hey, are you okay? Is it important?"

"It's a m-matter of l-life and d-death," she replied grimly.

"Whose life?" Gaius asked, worried.

"Must go!" Rachel called.

She circled back to where Sigfried was still casting every cantrip he remembered: *obé, taflu, endro*. Rachel thought *taflu* was a good call. It banished supernatural things. It might have worked if Sigfried had had the proper authority. Supernatural creatures often bowed only to those who held the proper rank or carried the proper bloodline. Sometimes, sheer magical prowess could overpower the need for authority. Here on Dart's own river, it did not.

Dart still cradled the little boy, but he was barely moving. The three adults, the two men and the boy's mother, crowded together at the edge of the water. The men bellowed with rage; their eyes betrayed their raw agony. The mother screamed and wailed, tearing at her hair with both hands. Tears streamed down her cheeks. Rachel could not imagine watching helplessly as a loved one suffered and not being able to save them. Even the thought was too painful for her.

Dart tipped back her head and opened her mouth. Her terrible, haunting cry echoed against the walls of the gorge. Terror shot through Rachel. They were losing. The river was going to win. She absolutely could not allow that. She had to save the little boy. What else might she and Sigfried have at their disposal that she was overlooking?

Two recent questions returned to her: *What would Dart take instead?* and *Whose life?*

Realization ricocheted through her. There was one thing present that Dart desired more than the death of a random little boy, one thing for which the river would trade the child.

Rachel glanced back at Dart, her heart thundering in her chest. As she watched, the child's body went limp. *No!* She landed on the bank. Leaving Vroomie next to the path that ran along the riverside, she jumped onto the part of the rock shelf that protruded into the river.

Standing on the mossy rocks at the edge of the raging waters, Rachel drew herself up. She pictured her father, her grandfather, her imperious grandmother with her perfect bearing.

In her most commanding voice, Rachel called, "Dart! *Kefwyth*, Dart!"

She did not bother with the gesture that accompanied the summoning cantrip. She concentrated upon authority and bearing.

For the first time, Dart turned her head. Her whole form followed. Still holding the limp boy, she flowed across the surface of the river, a hooded feminine figure, beautiful and cruel.

"Dart! Return the boy!" Rachel spoke clearly and deliberately. "Take me instead."

Dart flowed forward, staring down with disdain. "And why should I prefer *you*?"

Rachel met the gaze of the immortal squarely. "I am the duke's daughter."

"Devon's daughter!" Dart flowed forward, cresting high above Rachel. "Oh, that will be a treat. Come forward, child!"

Rachel raised her chin. "Release the boy first!"

"How do I know you will come if I release him?" asked Dart.

Rachel drew herself up as tall as her four-foot-nearly-seven inches could go. "I am the daughter of the Duke of Devon. Do you believe, for an instant, I will not keep my word?"

Dart took one look at the limp five-year-old. Rachel's heart skipped a beat. *What if the child was already dead? No! He could not be!* The river nymph tossed the child heedlessly in the direction of its family. To Rachel's relief, she saw the trajectory of the small body slow as Sigfried used a cantrip to control its flight. The boy landed safely in the arms of his frantic father.

"What's the plan?" called Sigfried.

Rachel turned her head and met his gaze. "The plan is: Save the boy."

Sigfried nodded and frowned at the same time. "And you?"

"Um…. Hold my breath until my father arrives?" Rachel mouthed with a slight shrug. Then she took a deep breath.

Without a trace of hesitation, The Lady Rachel Jade Griffin stepped forward into the waiting arms of the river.

CHAPTER TWENTY-FOUR:
THE LORD OF DARTMOOR

THE WATERY NYMPH CRASHED OVER HER LIKE A WAVE. RACHEL BRACED for the terrible icy cold. Her legs swept out from beneath her. Then, everywhere was water. Now it was Rachel whom Dart cradled like an infant, gazing down with a sweet yet malicious smile. Rachel knew she should have felt trapped and vulnerable, but she did not. She merely felt joyful. She had put her mind to saving the boy, and, assuming that he was not already dead, he was safe. She did not think beyond that. Despite the coldness and the lack of air, she smiled back at Dart, who looked faintly surprised and perhaps disappointed.

Suddenly, Dart's attention moved to the shore. Through the blue watery veil, which bent everything outside strangely, Rachel could see Siggy shouting at the river nymph. He gestured and grinned as he strutted back and forth, crowing like Peter Pan. Rachel could hear the crowing faintly through the water. *What could he be doing?*

Dart surged, flowing toward the blond boy, and Rachel suddenly knew. For a split instant, she was more terrified than she had ever been in her life. An image of a pale, bloated Sigfried floated before her mind's eye. Valerie had already lost a friend to drowning. How could she bear losing her boyfriend, too?

Then, Rachel chuckled.

This proved a mistake; she lost some of her precious air; but perhaps, if Siggy had his way, she would not need to hold it much longer.

A moment later, she was not underwater anymore. Dart threw her at the riverbank and dragged Siggy into the water. Rachel sailed through the air, barely getting her feet under her. She landed on the slick moss and went sprawling across the rocks. Her knee struck the stone painfully. What breath she had knocked out of her as she slid across the mossy stone.

Gratefully, she gulped new fresh air.

It felt good to breathe. How had Siggy convinced Dart to make the switch? Had he told her how famous he was? That would have done it. Dart could not have resisted drowning the most famous boy in the World of the Wise.

"T-thank y-y-you!" Rachel called over her shoulder, suddenly aware of the cold.

Sigfried waved cheerfully from where he floated in the embrace of Dart. He did not look a bit discontented, not even by the icy temperature, which was the only thing Rachel was anxious about. She did not want him to freeze to death, but beyond that, she was not worried.

Siggy could breathe water.

Despite the pain in her knees, Rachel tried to rise. Her parka, her dress, her bloomers, and her stockings, soaking and heavy, made this difficult. The bow that had clipped back her hair had vanished, and her sodden locks hung free about her shoulders, sticking to her face and getting in her eyes. After three tries, she successfully climbed painfully to her feet. Her knee ached.

Dart smiled down at Sigfried, cradling him in her arms. Siggy rested in the water, his hands folded behind his head, looking cheerful. The river nymph scowled.

Teeth chattering, Rachel tried the cantrip that she had failed to cast in front of Agent Armel. "*S-ilu var-renga. Ta-a-f-flu.*"

No result. Her teeth were chattering too hard for her to make a decent go at it.

"*Si-l-lu v-aren-nga. T-tafl-flu.*" She tried again. "*S-silu-lu va-varen-ga-ga. Tafl-lu.*"

She drew herself up as she had when calling to Dart. "*Silu varenga. Taflu!*"

To her astonishment, the water on her clothing followed her *taflu* gesture, formed into a ball, and dropped with a splash into the river. *My, it felt nice to be dry.*

The sounds of crying and weeping rose above the roar of the river. The Persian family still gathered on the jut of rock shelf. Rachel ran up the bank, leaping across the surging waters when necessary, to where the three adults stood around the motionless boy. Up on the bank, the other woman still held the remaining two children, forcing them to look away. The little ones wailed, trying to get to their supine brother.

Drawing herself up again, Rachel cast the cantrip: "*Silu varenga. Taflu!*"

The water soaking the boy's clothing rose into the air, following her gestures. Even after his clothing was dry, a steady stream left his mouth.

The farther Rachel moved her hand, the more water came up out of his lungs. She kept concentrating until the liquid leaving his lips petered out. She moved the whole ball of water to the right and let it splash back into the river.

Gasp! The boy's chest rose as he struggled to breathe. The whole family went wild, sobbing and cheering and screaming with joy. The father knelt beside the boy. The short and squat mother leapt up and hugged Rachel tightly. Rachel hugged her back. Over by his father and uncle, the boy's eyes flickered open. He sat up, gazing at his family. His mother rushed back to him, weeping tears of happiness and crying, "*Jigar talâ! Jigar talâ! Jigar talâ!*"

Rachel smiled, a great surge of gratitude sweeping over her as she watched the family weeping and rejoicing, the little ones leaping and shouting with joy up on the bank.

We saved him. He's alive!

She looked around. Dart was gone. The river still raged, full of white water. She ran to the edge and peered into the choppy, opaque, froth, wondering where Dart had taken Sigfried.

A beam of light flashed between the heavens and the riverbank. Rachel's father stood on the rock beside her, tall and implacably calm. His Inverness cloak billowed around him in the breeze whistling down the gorge. In his hand was his stout staff with its diamond tip. Lucky was wrapped around him like a stole.

Ambrose Griffin glanced from Rachel to the little boy and back. "All is well, then?"

The dragon unwrapped himself, swooshed to the river's edge, peered down into the icy waters, and then dived.

Rachel shook her head rapidly and pointed at the river Dart. "Sigfried's down there. He went...." No point in making it too complicated. "... instead of the boy."

Her father arched one eyebrow and stepped to the river's edge, peering into the churning waters. "How long has she had him?"

"Um... I'm not sure. Not long. The water's very cold, though. I am afraid it will be bad for him to stay in it too long."

Her father shot her an odd look. "Has it been fewer than five minutes?"

"Yes, but that doesn't really matter. Sigfried can breathe water."

"Rachel," her father's voice was calm, but he spoke as if he were talking to a small child, "this is not your friend Ben. Sigfried doesn't have gills."

Rachel replied primly, "Breathes water. Familiar gift."

"Ah! Good. Then he will live another minute." The duke called out, "Dart!"

The boy's mother watched all this with eyes wide. She whispered, "Who's that?"

"The Duke of Devon," Rachel replied. "He rules these woods. Fear not. All will be well."

The river rushed and roared, leaping over boulders and slamming into banks. The Persian family gathered up their little boy and hurried him up the bank, where the other two children, one older, one younger, ran joyfully to meet him. There was no sign of the river nymph.

"Dart!" The Duke of Devon did not raise his voice, but he sounded unexpectedly forbidding. Rachel was glad such attentions were not directed toward her. Knocking the butt of his staff once against the stone beneath him, he called again, "Dart, come forth."

The watery figure rose up out of the river. She exploded from the riverbed like a geyser, towering in the air, over a dozen feet high. Her mouth gaped open even wider than before, revealing an impossible number of sharp, shark-like teeth. She howled like a raging wind.

Then, she saw who stood upon the riverbank.

The look of abject alarm upon her watery features was almost comical. A large part of her liquid substance sloshed away. She dropped five feet in height. Lowering her hooded head humbly, her fluid face again took on a lovely feminine cast.

"Your grace!" her voice tinkled like a stream tripping over rocks. "How unexpected."

"You have a lad, Dart," the duke replied mildly, power thrumming beneath his words.

"What if I do?" asked the river nymph warily.

"He is my houseguest," stated Ambrose Griffin.

Dart regained a half foot of her height. "I have my rights! He came willingly."

"Come, sweet Dart. Return the lad," the duke coaxed. "I can hardly allow you to drown my guests."

"I shall never give him back. It is my right," cried Dart. "He's my guest now."

The duke gazed at her calmly. "You know I can make things difficult for you. Shall I allow more bridges?"

"You dare not!" Dart opened her mouth, baring her sharp, sharp teeth again. "I shall sweep them away."

"Is that so?" The Duke of Devon leaned on his staff.

"See me rage!" Dart threw up her arms. "I will call storms! They'll fill me to overflowing!"

"With what water?" he inquired.

Dart drew back warily.

"You once claimed the life of my great-great-grandmother," continued Ambrose in the same conversational tone. "My great-great-grandfather remarried, a young Frenchwoman, right before their revolution. She convinced him to grow lavender, even though it is hard to imagine a worse place to grow a dry-weather crop than eternally drenched Dartmoor."

The river nymph stared at him, clearly as uncertain where this speech was going as Rachel was. The water that made up Dart's form began rushing up one side of her and down the other, so that her robe and hood grew frothy and white.

Rachel listened curiously. She had not known that an ancestress had drowned in the Dart.

"Well do I remember Uther Griffin," replied Dart. Rachel did not catch the nymph's next words, something like "Bound by Griffin night am I" followed by, "to only slay before Spring Equinox and then abide by ceremony."

"To keep the lavender plants alive," the duke continued, "my great-great-grandfather set a sorcerer's shield over a portion of land he enhanced with kenomancy. You say it is your right to keep my guest, for whom I am responsible." Ambrose gestured upwards toward the overcast sky. "It is my right to widen that shield, so that not a drop of rain falls across Dartmoor."

Could he do that? Rachel rather doubted it. But then, he had not said he could, only that it was within his rights.

Dart hissed, horrified. "You would not dare!"

Ambrose Griffin raised a single eyebrow and said calmly, "Try me."

Dart rose another foot. "The Unwary would not stand for their precious moor drying out."

Ambrose crooked an eyebrow. "And what, pray tell, could they do about it?"

"Take him back!" spat Dart. "He won't drown. I don't want him."

A whoosh of river water slammed over the bank, depositing Sigfried, shivering but grinning, his knife still in his hand. Lucky burst out of the water and flew to him, wrapping around him, as if he could ward off the cold. The dragon breathed out a plume of fire. His shivering boy leaned toward it, rubbing his hands.

"Thank you." Ambrose nodded to the river nymph. "I shall see you in three days."

"I want an enormous gathering this year," cried Dart. "A thousand mourners!"

"And you shall have it." The duke bowed.

Dart collapsed back into her banks, vanishing. Siggy waved a cheerful goodbye.

The duke smiled down at him. "That was a very brave thing you did, saving that child."

Sigfried glanced at Rachel, who suddenly realized that her father might not look kindly upon his daughter trading her life for that of an unknown boy. Siggy, at least, had known he would not drown. She met her blood-brother's gaze and gave a slow and deliberate nod. She did not need to tell him twice. He immediately began basking in her father's praise. Lucky wound tighter around Sigfried so that he looked a bit like a living maypole.

The duke crossed to speak to the family. He examined the little boy and spoke to the parents, the mother of whom thanked him in tears.

"He was saved by the little..." she began.

Catching the mother's eye, Rachel put her finger to her lips and gestured at Siggy, who strutted forward, taking the credit, as the puzzled mother thanked him. The boy's father rushed forward and shook Siggy's hand, telling Rachel's father how Siggy had also pulled him from the river. The duke listened, pleased. Standing by her broom, shivering but dry, Rachel met the wide dark eyes of the little boy up on the bank and winked.

"Let's get home," the duke returned to where she and Sigfried stood. "We need to let your mother know that we'll be hosting a large affair."

Rachel picked up her broom. Putting an arm around each of them, Ambrose Griffin jumped them home. Just before they departed, Rachel heard Sigfried, who was looking into his pockets, exclaim with dismay, "My scrambled eggs are soggy."

"Tennyson, round up the staff," the Duke of Devon announced as the three of them strode into Gryphon Park Manor. "We have an event to plan."

The butler nodded and called, at his grace's request, both the house staff and the grounds staff. The duchess arrived in the midst of this, dressed in a soft angora sweater and long woolen skirts, both of light peach, with her hair pulled back by a butterfly clip. Rachel loved how her mother always looked so picturesque.

"What is going on, Ambrose?" she asked, gliding down the staircase and to his side.

He kissed her lightly and told her what had happened. Rachel's mother pressed her hands against her mouth, listening in horror to the description of Sigfried underwater. She rushed over to the boy and hugged him. Unable to put his head on her shoulder, due to their height difference, Siggy rested his cheek on the top of her head and stared off into the distance with a happy expression, as if floating on a cloud. He looked surprisingly young, like a little boy.

He murmured dreamily, "It's almost like having a mum."

Rachel saw her mother blink away tears. The duchess glanced over at her husband, and the two of them exchanged a significant look. Rachel wondered what it might mean.

Her mother stepped back and touched Siggy's face. "That was something very brave you did, saving that little boy."

"Ah, not so very brave. After all, the water wasn't going to hurt me," bragged Sigfried, but he gave Rachel an odd look, almost as if he felt guilty accepting praise from her mother under false pretenses, even though taking the credit had never bothered him before.

He was still dripping wet. Her mother removed the water from him, using the same cantrip Rachel had, and sent for hot chocolate and blankets. She also asked for tea to be served in the Oak Drawing Room where they now gathered. She had him sit in a seat of honor while she and Rachel's father gave instructions to the staff—the duke to the grounds staff, and the duchess to the house staff—as to what needed preparing for the Spring Equinox ceremony.

"I am off to send invitations," said her father. "Getting to a thousand is going to take some doing. It's more than twice our usual crowd. I'm going to contact Bedwyn. If I can get some of the other peers to show up, would you object to us hosting the Round Table this year?"

"Not at all. That's a lovely idea," said her mother. "But won't they have their own events on the Equinox?"

He replied, "Magnus and Harry, certainly. Not sure about the others. Even so, some of their family members might come early. We'll hold the Round Table on the 20th and 21st."

He strode off, and the Duchess of Devon returned and sat beside Sigfried, encouraging him to describe the whole thing. He told it exactly as it had happened—leaving out Rachel's part in the middle. After hearing his description, Rachel's mother looked thoughtful.

"Mr. Smith," she said gently, "why don't we turn your knife into an athame? If we pick the right warding essences, you will be able to stab supernatural beings—like nymphs and wraiths—and do damage."

Siggy stared as if she had uttered the most wonderful words ever spoken. "You can do that?"

"Certainly," the duchess replied. She took his hand and patted it. "We have a nice alchemy lab. I'll take you down tomorrow, and we can discuss how best to accomplish this. I can teach you a few new elixirs, too."

Sigfried pulled out his Bowie knife and kissed it.

"That would be grand," was all he could manage to say.

CHAPTER TWENTY-FIVE:
GUARDIANS OF LOST WORLDS

"Lady Rachel, are you well?" Tennyson stood beside her, offering a warm comforter and a cup of hot chocolate.

Rachel started to demur, but her entire body was trembling. She could not tell if this was the aftereffects of the terrible cold of the water, which had drenched her three times, or if she were going into some kind of shock. She felt strangely lightheaded. She accepted, nodded her thanks to the butler, and slipped away. Peter and Laurel had come into the entrance hall and were exclaiming over Sigfried's exploits. No one looked in her direction. She grabbed Vroomie and flew—first down corridors and then up the center of a spiral staircase in the highest tower of the Old Castle —to her grandfather's library.

It felt so wonderful to emerge into the round, book-filled room, her favorite place in the house. She ran to the fireplace, pulled the cord, and whistled, until one of the great old salamanders came crawling up the shaft and into the hearth. It lay there, content, glowing the black and bright orange of embers and filling the chamber with the scent of cinnamon and a steady radiating heat. She paused by the delicate brass and wrought iron spiral staircase that led to the trapdoor to the roof, her hand resting on the banister, and considered sitting on the second step, a favorite place of hers for reading back when her grandfather was still alive, but the cold brass immediately chilled her hand. Abandoning that idea, she climbed into her grandfather's huge leather armchair and curled up in it, snuggling inside the comforter.

The sight of the familiar paintings and stacks of books cheered her. This was a sorcerer's library, cared for by an elusive book bogel. The volumes occasionally rearranged themselves, and sometimes, she came upon titles she had never seen before on these shelves that she had examined a thousand times.

As she sat curled in the chair, sipping hot chocolate and trying to stop her body from shivering, Rachel thought about what had just happened. She had not meant to lie to her parents. She had not explained at first because it would have taken too long, and Sigfried had still been in the icy waters. After that, it seemed too late to change the story. But it was more than that. Her family cheered for the plucky boy who could breathe water when he dared the cold to save a child. She suspected they would not have cheered upon discovering that their daughter—who could not breathe water—had put her own life on the line for a stranger. Rachel felt no regret. The little child had stopped breathing. If she had not acted, he would not have made it.

Saving him had been the right thing to do. Yet she felt shaken. She had spent a long time in the cold water, between various dunkings, and she had offered her life without any thought for herself. She wished she could talk to her mother about this, but now she had to pretend nothing had happened. It was her own fault, and yet....

She put down the mug and curled up in the chair again, wrapped tightly in the comforter, her head resting on the chair arm. The warmth felt good, and the cinnamon smelled sweet and welcoming, especially here in the field of flowers with Dream Gaius and her dream unicorn. They asked her how she had been doing, to which she replied she was well and could she please go for a ride. To which the unicorn replied, of course, she could. He loved giving her rides. It was what he was there for.

The three of them rode across the field of flowers. After a time, Rachel glimpsed a strange red cloud on the horizon. Then, she, Dream Gaius, and the dream unicorn stood on the edge of a precipice, gazing down into the reddish cloud, which seemed to be coming from an endless plain of rusty rocks and red dust.

Rachel slipped down from the dream unicorn and lay down on her stomach to peer over the precipice. Below, in the midst of the red rocks was a circle of black and white creatures—black and white creatures with bright red eyes of the exact shade and intensity of black, white, and red as the Guardian—and one silver one.

In a loose circle stood a Lobster, a Moose, a Bear, a Weasel, a Cat, a Swallow, and an Aardvark. The Moose was white except for his horns and hooves. The Swallow was colored like a reverse magpie, white with a black stripe across its wings and back. The Aardvark was entirely silver. In the way of dreams, as Rachel gazed at them, she became aware of the qualities each represented. Those that were mainly a single color emanated one quality; those that were a mix of black and white emanated two. The black Bear was solemn to the point of rigidity. The mostly black Cat was sardonic. The piebald Weasel was crazy and energetic. The Swallow was sweet and shy. The nearly white Moose was graciously somber. The silver Aardvark struck Rachel as compassionate.

"There's a Fox, too, right?" Rachel murmured, recalling the one she had seen at the Year of the Dragon Ball.

"Is there?" Dream Gaius murmured back, peering down.

She had seen a Wolf, too, but he was bigger than these creatures, save for the moose, and had a different feel about him. In the way of dream logic, she felt he was of a different order.

"What are they?" Rachel whispered.

The dream unicorn said, "They are the Guardians of Lost Worlds."

"Lost Worlds?" Rachel jumped to her feet and turned to look at her traveling companions. "You mean the worlds that fell into the darkness?"

"Or those that were entirely lost, broken, destroyed, frozen over, *et cetera*." Dream Gaius slipped down to stand beside her. He smiled down at her with his too-wide smile. Otherwise, he looked like the real Gaius.

"How do you know this?" Rachel knelt and peered down at the lost guardians.

"I overheard another dream talking about it." He squatted down beside her, his hand resting comfortingly on her shoulder.

"Can we go down there?" she asked.

"Absolutely not," replied Dream Gaius. "Look."

He picked up a dream pebble and some flowers that looked like forget-me-nots, except they had hands and feet and could dance. These he threw over the precipice. They twirled down into the space below. When they were over the red ground, they began to tremble and then shake violently. The flowers bloated and then turned black and wilted. The pebble imploded.

"This is the dreamscape of Mars. It is not fit for the denizens of Earth. Our dream stuff would be torn apart, and living creatures, such as yourself, would be damaged and go mad."

"Oh. Important safety tip. Don't go to Dream Mars," murmured Rachel.

"Miss Griffin?"

Rachel blinked awake in the armchair in her grandfather's library, though, technically, it was now her library. She looked around, but no one was there. She could have sworn she had heard somebody call her name. In her dream, it had sounded like Vladimir.

"Miss Griffin?" his voice came again, in her ear. Her black bracelet trembled slightly.

"Vlad!" She sat up.

"Gaius says you called me. That it was a matter of life or death?"

"Yes! I did. But it is all right now. We took care of it."

"I apologize for not being available when you had need of me. I did give you a card for such a purpose."

"Yes, but I had left it home. I never do that at school, but here I wasn't on my guard."

"I understand. Is everything well?"

"Yes. Both with us and with the little boy who was drowning. We saved him."

"I am glad to hear it."

"Thank you again, Vlad."

The bracelet stopped vibrating. Rachel smiled and sighed. She tried to go back to sleep, but she could not regain the dream about the dreamscape of Mars and the Guardians of Lost Worlds. It had been such a vivid dream. She wondered if there had been any truth to it.

The next morning, Rachel wrote a letter to Mr. Chanson, asking if he could forward a second letter, which she included, to Ma and Pa Chanson at Chanson's Quality Bristleless. In the second letter, she described the previous evening's events and asked if it would be possible to make an adjustable becalming enchantment so one could increase or decrease the drag.

She dressed in a red dress, with a Peter Pan collar and a large bow in the back, and ran down to breakfast. Arriving, she found her parents and Peter discussing the upcoming Equinox ceremony. Sigfried was not up yet. She filled her plate from the breakfast buffet and sat down in her customary place, listening carefully. She was impressed at how much progress her parents had made. Father had sent messages to the farmer tenants and the town's folk, asking them to come and many of them had already RSVPed in the affirmative. Mother had contacted her side of the family, as well as other ladies from among the British Wise.

"Enough for the moment." Her father smiled kindly at her. "What sort of plans do you have for the next two weeks, Rachel? Is there anything with which you need help?"

"Yes," she said. "We want to see Merlin's Cave and go to Glastonbury."

"I'm up for that," Peter said keenly. "I love both those places." He turned to their parents. "May I take them?"

"Certainly, Peter," their mother said. "That would be very kind of you, especially with all we have planned."

Rachel looked at her plate and sighed.

"Is something wrong?" her father asked.

"It's just... I was hoping Gaius would come when we go to Cornwall, but he and Peter despise each other."

"Maybe you shouldn't be dating a boy who despises your brother." Laurel stuck her tongue out at Rachel as she sat down at the table with her plate of food.

"Sandra likes him," Rachel replied.

"Well, that counts for something," said their father thoughtfully. Out of his sight, Laurel made a face. "Had you thought about when you wanted to go?"

Rachel considered this. "April first is our last day on holiday, but it's also Sigfried's birthday. I would love to do something special for him."

Peter said, "I tell you what. I'll go with you to Glastonbury on the first. If you can work out your own trip to Cornwall before that, all to the good. I've been to Merlin's cave loads of times. If not, we'll do that on the same day." He turned to their parents. "Sigfried has a girlfriend. Chipper little thing. Writes for *The Roanoke Glass*. Might we invite her along, for his birthday? I bet he'd like that."

"Oh, that sounds like a splendid idea," said their mother. She turned to Rachel. "Do you know this girl?"

"Valerie Hunt." Rachel nodded, squelching any disappointment at the idea of having to share her blood-brother for his birthday. He would definitely enjoy having his "Goldilocks" along. "We're friends. I can write to her if you agree." She turned toward her brother. "That's a rather decent idea, Peter. Thank you for thinking of it."

"Then it is decided," said her father. "For Sigfried's birthday, Peter will accompany you to Glastonbury Tor, and we will invite the Hunt girl." He frowned slightly. "Is that the daughter of Kenneth Hunt, the American policeman who was turned into a duck?"

"Goose," said Rachel. "Yes."

He looked thoughtful but then just nodded. Rachel wondered if he were remembering the bad things that had happened to Valerie.

Aloud, she said, "I have an idea for a present for Sigfried, too, but the price is steep."

"How steep?" her father asked curiously. "I am curious what you might have in mind that could possibly be more expensive than your allowance."

"You saw the problems we had getting his gold into the house. I thought maybe a kenomanced bag with a large safe inside."

"Oh, Rachel, that's a brilliant idea!" her mother cried. "He's such a dear boy. Yes. Let's do that, Ambrose."

Her father looked dubious. "Rachel's correct. That could get expensive. Can't he just put it in a bank?"

Rachel shook her head. "He won't part with it. He doesn't trust banks."

"That's unfortunate." Her father frowned.

"If we don't give him a bag, how's he going to move his gold back to school?" asked Rachel. "Unless you want me to call Vlad and ask him to help us again."

"That's quite all right," her father replied dryly. "I am sure we can manage without needing to inconvenience the Crown Prince of Bavaria."

Rachel giggled. "Speaking of crown princes, do you know what I recently found out—from the Crown Prince of Transylvania, of all people...."

"Oh, are you friends with him, too?" Laurel teased.

Rachel replied solemnly, "Wulfgang, maybe. Romulus, no. He was speaking to a group. I just happened to be present." She turned back to her father. "I found out that the armies of the Terrible Five were not defeated by college students. In fact, Gra—"

But then she stopped, because her father had given her a very strange look. He made a negating motion with his head. Luckily, she was saved from having to think of something else to say by the commotion of Sigfried's arrival. In her family's eyes, he was still the conquering hero.

A bit later, after everyone had finished, Siggy pulled Rachel aside. He said in a low voice, "I'm out of Ziploc bags. Do you crazy magic people have any?"

"Out of what? I don't think I know what that is."

"It's an Unwary thing. A small plastic bag you can seal up."

"Ah. No. We don't. We can go into Exeter today. For what do you need them?"

Siggy pointed furtively at the oatmeal with his elbow. "If I put that in my pocket without a plastic bag, it will leak all over my trousers."

Rachel gazed at the bowl of oatmeal for a full three seconds. Then, she grabbed Sigfried's arm. "Mummy, can you come with us? We need to show Siggy something."

Rachel guided her blood-brother by his arm; the diminutive duchess followed behind them. They tromped along corridors and down servant staircases until they came to the kitchens. The fragrance of baking bread reached them before they fully arrived. Siggy sniffed deeply.

"Sigfried," Rachel said pleasantly, "this is the kitchen. You may come here and get food any time you want. No one will stop you. Right, Mummy?" She glanced at the duchess who nodded serenely. "Cook, here, will tell you if anything is off limits to eat because she is saving it for an upcoming meal. Everything else, you may have."

She stepped around the corner and brought him into the kitchen itself. The room was enormous. Copper pots hung from a high, arched, pale brick ceiling. Underneath, three separate tables provided counters for food preparation. Each had a storage area beneath it for mixing bowls and measuring cups as well as room for spices and cooking sauces. Stoves and ovens lined one wall. Bags of flour and rice and potatoes leaned against each other. Across from this, ice boxes with their ice stick talismans and stay-fresh boxes, which could extend the freshness of bread and pastries via enchantment, lined the opposite wall. Beneath the big windows were two long sinks and a rack of washing wands. Beside this stood a large tub of kimchi. A doorway led to a pantry that had stocked cabinets reaching from its floor to a ceiling of the same height as the kitchens. In the center of the pantry, floating shelves bobbed well above head height, full of jars of canned fruits and vegetables.

In the center of the chamber, up to her wrists in dough, stood a cheerful, chubby woman of many, many years. She wore a simple red dress and a white apron. A white chef's hat sat on a small side table along with her handbag; she was not currently wearing it over her sparse, straw-colored hair. This was Cook, the grandmother of Rachel's friend Taddy.

"'Allo, there. What 've we 'ere?" Cook asked cheerfully.

"Cook,"—Rachel gave her a bright smile—"this is my blood-brother, Sigfried Smith."

"Sigfried the Dragonslayer?" Cook pressed her hand to her heart. "In me own kitchen? Fancy that!"

Sigfried normally would have thrown a new acquaintance a charming smile, but instead, he stood in the center of the kitchen, his jaw hanging open.

"The kitchen?" Sigfried breathed out in wonder as he turned slowly in a circle gazing at their surroundings in awe. "I have never seen a kitchen before. There's food here. Endless food. It's like a buffet, only it never ends."

"You've never seen a kitchen before?" Rachel asked in surprise.

"Didn't you raid the kitchens at school?" asked the duchess sweetly. "It was a favorite activity when I was a student."

"Banger raided the kitchen. Once." Sigfried stared at the copper pots above his head. "The nuns caught him and cut off a finger. After that, none of the rest of us tried it."

"Cut off his finger?" The duchess sat down, hard, on a bag of rice, her face a bit green.

"Just to the first knuckle," Sigfried explained to soothe her.

For a moment longer, Siggy stood absolutely still. Then, he went off like a top. He whirled around the kitchen looking in ovens, under tables, on stoves, opening bags, pots, and cabinets. Lucky, too, flew around, checking the places his master could not reach. The dragon snaked among the hanging copper pots, setting them ringing in a musical cacophony, and then he zipped up to the ceiling, where he carefully licked the pale bricks.

"The kitchen itself is not tasty," he reported dutifully, with obvious disappointment.

"That's too bad," Siggy mourned with him, "but everything else is! This is like a repository of good tastes, all in one place! And good smells, too! Did you know that carrots came with green fluff on top? Or bread actually does come in loaves, not just on the telly? What's all this weird, pale, floppy stuff?"

"That's chicken," Rachel said dryly, watching him repeatedly poke what was most likely that evening's dinner.

"Chicken?" Sigfried drew back in disbelief. "Where's all the oily, crispy goodness? Is this what they look like naked? Where's its head? This chicken is weak and flabby! Ah! These must be related to those horrible, tasteless boiled chickens they used to give us at the orphanage." He turned to the cook. "This chicken is not fit for consumption yet." He picked up a piece and flopped a wing back and forth. "See? Too weak! Send it to the gym!" He looked up at Lucky. "Are there gyms for chickens?"

"Don't know, boss, but I'd be happy to open one," Lucky replied from the ceiling. "I could find ways to motivate the tasty chickens. And if some of them were too slow and I had to chastise them by crisping and eating them, I don't think anyone would miss those few."

"Want to 'elp me, young man?" asked the Cook, smiling despite the force of chaos at loose in her kitchen. "I'll show ye 'ow to bake scones for afternoon tea."

Sigfried looked at Lucky in wonder. The dragon and the boy bumped fists.

"Yes! Show me everything!" Siggy threw up his arms, spreading them wide. "I want to view food in its natural habitat. Learn its ways. Seek out its secrets!"

"Me, too!" cried Lucky. "I want to push food around before I eat it, too! Or, better yet, I could just eat it directly, without mixing it or pounding it. As for heating it, I can cook it on the way down." He breathed out a plume of flame.

Cook eyed him thoughtfully. "We can put ye to work, too, young dragon. Come this way."

CHAPTER TWENTY-SIX:
HALF AN HOUR TOO LATE

Leaving Siggy in the kitchen, Rachel spent the next hour with the book on drawing she had borrowed from Mrs. Heelis. The book fascinated her, and she loved the doodles of mushrooms and moths that someone, presumably Mrs. Heelis herself, had done in the margins. She understood much of what she was reading, in theory, but she could not seem to translate the theory to her pencil. Frustrated, she put the book aside, carefully donned everything she normally carried—her neck pouch, her amethyst necklace, her wand—and went outside to visit her pony.

By the stables, she shared a happy reunion with her little silver bay Shetland. Widdershins was overjoyed to see her. He cantered across the paddock to her, neighing and cavorting. Rachel hugged him tightly and stroked his soft nose. As always, he was covered with mud, so Rachel washed him and curried him until his rich brown coat shone. Then, she saddled him and rode northward, over the moors.

Mist blanketed the rolling hills, limiting visibility. The fields and bogs looked so mysterious dressed in fog, that, despite knowing these moors her whole life, Rachel was not entirely sure that she had not accidentally ridden Beyond the Fields We Know. She kept a sharp eye out for phooka but saw only a stray sheep and a hawk.

It was wonderful to be home again, back where she belonged, where she fit into the landscape like the gorse bushes and the moor ponies. She felt welcomed, as if the dryads and flower fairies knew her step. It was not until she came back here, surrounded by the manor and estate she so loved, that she had realized how out of place she had felt at school—much as she loved Roanoke Academy.

Returning to the stable, she dismissed Oliver, the stable boy, and curried her pony herself, talking to him happily as she brushed out his straw-like mane, telling him about the last six months of her life, and breathing in the pleasant, clean wood-shavings and fresh hay smell of the barn. Widdershins's ears twitched at appropriate moments, giving the impression he was listening. Charmed, she fed him a peppermint stick from her pocket.

On her way back to the manor, she came upon her father making his Saturday rounds, checking on the stable and the kennels. The duke leaned on the fence, speaking to his horse, Passelande, a magnificent black Friesian charger. As Rachel approached, she heard her father apologizing to the stallion for not getting out to ride often enough and promising to remedy this. It pleased her that both she and her father talked to their steeds. Shyly, she came up beside him and fed Passelande a sugar cube. The black charger, with his tremendously long and wavy black mane and tail, struck Rachel as one of the most beautiful creatures ever to walk the earth.

"What would you like for your birthday?" Ambrose Griffin smiled down at his daughter.

Rachel answered without hesitation. "I want an hour of your time."

"My time?" Her father arched an eyebrow.

"Yes." Rachel nodded her head firmly. "I have been wanting to talk to you since the end of September, and every time I have tried, something has prevented it."

"I had no idea. Did I know this?" he asked. "Before I lost my memory, I mean?"

"I have no idea," echoed Rachel.

Her father looked faintly amused. "Well, you shall have it. On your birthday, I shall put aside an entire afternoon to spend only with you."

Rachel beamed. *Finally*, she would be able to tell him what had happened at Beaumont.

She stepped onto the bottom rail of the split rail fence and waved to Polly Simes, the daughter of the Gryphon Park master-of-the-horse. Polly worked in the house as a parlor maid in the mornings and evenings, in return for the opportunity to work with the horses during the middle of the day. Polly waved back from where she stood atop the bare back of Dappleheart, one of the Gypsy Vanners. The young woman leapt into the air, performed a perfect flip, and landed lightly on the mare's back, her arms outstretched. Rachel clapped, and the duke nodded approvingly.

Rachel's gaze moved from Polly to the Friesians and Gypsy Vanners. The two breeds had much in common; both were smaller draft horses, light enough for riding, with feathering over the lower legs and hoofs and absurdly long flowing manes and tails. The Friesians were black and lighter of frame, the Vanners black and white and solid enough to pull a gypsy's van or wagon. Rachel's grandmother had trained both breeds for dressage and show. The lithe Friesians were also favored for hunting.

Father rode a Friesian. Laurel's Wild Child and Peter's Feste were swift-footed Arabians. Laurel's was black with a white star on its forehead, and Feste was a bay with white socks and a white blaze down his nose. Starbeam and Snow Princess—Mother and Sandra's steeds, respectively—were Vanners. Grandfather's Warlock and Thunderfrost—the ghost horse who kept watch over the family—were also Vanners, with tails so long they dragged on the ground. Grandmother had ridden several horses; her favorite had been a little gray Arabian mare named Dido.

Rachel stared at the beautiful horses and sighed. As a child, she had dreamed of riding one of these great beasts. The Gypsy Vanners were the most beautiful, but Rachel had yearned for her own Friesian, so charmed was she by the wavy, Rapunzel-like locks of the sleek black horses. Now, she feared she might never be tall enough. Her parents would probably just give her a larger pony, maybe of the highland variety. Still, it was a joy to watch them.

"Aren't they magnificent!" Her father leaned against the paddock fence, watching the horses run through the mist. "Like liquid motion."

"And solidified joy," Rachel murmured, standing beside him in a similar stance.

Ambrose Griffin smiled down at Rachel. "We must give you something tangible, as well. Your mother will never be satisfied with my spending time with you being your only present. In some respects, she clings to her old middle-class sensibilities. She needs something to wrap. Would you like a kenomanced bag? As long as I am commissioning one for Sigfried, I could get you one as well. A room in a bag, useful for keeping things?"

"Oh, that would be lovely!" Rachel's face lit up.

"Consider it done," he said. Then, after a pause, he added in a mock serious voice, "I mean, of course, no, we can't do that. Forget it was ever mentioned."

She grinned and said airily, "I have no idea what might be coming. But if it were the thing that I couldn't forget if I wanted to, but we are both pretending that I have, I would be grateful."

Smiling at her, the duke laid a fond hand on her shoulder.

"Father," she asked earnestly, "why did you stop me at breakfast? When I tried to ask you about the Battle of Roanoke?"

"Ah, yes. That." He squeezed her shoulder and released it. "I can tell you about that. When I am done, you will understand why we do not speak of it in this house."

Her father set off for the kennels. Rachel fell in beside him.

"There's a reason your grandfather never mentioned the Battle of Roanoke," her father began. "I had graduated the year before, and your mother and I had been married that spring. Emrys, however, was four years younger. He was still at school. Like you, he had gone to Roanoke a year early. He was a freshman at the college."

They reached the kennels, and any conversation was drowned out by the excited welcome the dogs gave their master. Border collies bred for shepherding; English Springer spaniels for detecting game birds, pheasants, partridge, and grouse; foxhounds for fox hunts and deerhounds trained to track down phooka all competed for attention. The Griffins also kept a single Irish wolfhound, an enormous, shaggy dog that Rachel found intimidating, and a breeding pair of black Belgian Shepherds, which had been given to her parents as a gift. These last two were Rachel's favorites. She dropped to her knees to hug them, laughing as wet noses and tongues found her face.

She spent a few minutes visiting the new puppies. Then, leaving the kennels, she and her father walked toward the outer paddock, where their moorland ponies grazed. Laelaps, the male Belgian Shepherd, trotted beside the duke, sniffing the newly thawed grass.

Her father continued, "The Wise had been making strides against the Terrible Five. Cain March's draconian methods were working. He had ferreted out three of Veltdammerung's bases, which were then attacked by the combined armies of our allies. That forced the Terrible Five to retreat, which is when they seized Roanoke."

"The Terrible Five were retreating?" cried Rachel. "I'd never heard that."

Stopping before the outer paddock, his hands resting on the split rail fence, her father stared off over the misty moors beyond, surveying his estate, perhaps assuring himself that all was well. Rachel watched the shaggy moorland ponies, which she so dearly loved. They looked so windswept and sturdy. A few were descended from the fairy ponies that occasionally appeared on Dartmoor and were endowed with unearthly beauty and wisdom.

"Might I have a fairy pony when I outgrow Widdershins?" she asked suddenly. A magical steed might make up for the loss of the beauty of the Friesians and Vanners and yet keep the charm of a mount descended from one of their own moorland ponies.

Her father frowned. "Why would you ask such a thing?"

"Isn't that what every girl wants?" she asked, puzzled. "A fairy horse?"

"I've chosen horses for all your siblings… well, the three who grew up with us. None have asked for a fey steed. They're dangerous, you know."

Rachel recalled how just standing near her Elf had caused her and Sigfried to fall into strange dreams and sighed.

The duke pushed off the fence and headed down the path to the lake. The air was warmer among the trees. Branches swished and swayed in the March wind. The trees were oaks, maples, birches, larches, and poplars, tall and straight—a proper forest, which was unusual on Dartmoor—a forest that did not appear on any Unwary map. As soon as one headed up the tor or crossed the river Dart, one was again among the kind of wood-lands that were common on Dartmoor: short, twisted oaks covered with moss or straight evergreens.

Rachel loved this forest. It was so solemn, so dark and majestic. They passed her favorite riding tree, a birch that grew sideways before it went up, leaving a perfect place to sit. She had not taken Sigfried out tree riding yet. It was not safe until after the gentling of Dart. As soon as the Equinox ceremony was over, she would bring him at dusk to see the dryads. She waved at her favorite tree. It might have been the wind, but it seemed as if a lower branch waved back.

As they walked, her father said, "Cain questioned everyone he had reason to suspect under the *Spell of True Recitation*. We might not like his methods, but he gained a great deal of intelligence about the enemy, which, in the months leading up to them taking Roanoke, had begun to pay off." He shot Rachel a wry look. "In fact, in the last twenty-five years, he has continued this policy, questioning everyone of whom he has any reason to be suspicious, with one single exception."

They arrived at the lake. Mist rose from the surface, making the boat house and the island with its gazebo nigh invisible. The two of them stood gazing out at the icy surface, the mist, and the swans. The black Belgian trotted down to the shore and lapped at the waters.

"Oh? Who's that?" Rachel asked.

"Your young friend. Your extremely tall young friend."

"Vladimir?"

"After the King of Bavaria nuked Syria, Cain decided to let that one slide." Rachel's father glanced from the rowboats to the boathouse, confirming that all was well. "Though I gather Darling and Scarlett went ahead and questioned him this fall, in the matter of Mordeau."

Rachel nodded and then added, "Oh! That's why you sent Sandra to seduce him!"

"I did what?" The duke paused, startled. "What makes you say that?"

Of course, that would have happened during the period he had forgotten.

Rachel said, "Sandra said you suspected someone at the school of being the Veltdammerung agent—the agent who turned out to be Dr. Mordeau—and you had sent her to investigate. I thought... I thought she meant you asked her to investigate Vlad."

"Ah. Well. That does sound like an idea I might have come up with. But as it happened within the last two years, I don't remember if I did or no," her father replied with a sigh. Straightening, he added, "But that's hardly asking her to *seduce* him."

Rachel rolled her eyes. "You cannot send a pretty girl to finagle secrets out of a seventeen-year-old boy, however impressive, and not acknowledge that she is seducing him."

"You make a fair point," he allowed. "I can hardly complain he fell for my daughter if I sicced her on him." Ambrose lowered his voice. "It may be I owe the young man an apology."

They continued down the path that led deeper into the forest. The dog barked happily and ran in circles around them. They walked quietly for a time, her father throwing sticks for Laelaps to fetch. The dog loped through the trees, passing one of the mysterious obsidian pillars that stood at various points inside the forest. He hunted down the stick and brought it happily back to his master. In this manner, they eventually reached the place where the trail branched. With a whistle to the dog, the duke took the right-hand fork, heading toward the wooden bridge arching over the river Dart and onto the lavender farm. The left fork led up to the tor and the ruins there.

"Back to the Battle of Roanoke," her father continued.

"Hold on," Rachel, who had been thinking about his story and all she knew about the related time period, held up her hand. "I have a question. Where were you during these events?"

"I was in London, fighting undead serpents coming out of the Thames."

Rachel blinked, startled. Then, her eyes widened. "You were fighting the Necromancer and the Serpent Master! But this was a few years before you and James Darling and Scarlet MacDannan finally rounded them up, right?"

He chuckled. "You heard about that, eh?"

"That raid is famous!—The one where you caught Claudius Stark and Eliaures Charles, I mean. I've never heard about you fighting undead serpents. That's the raid that got you into *James Darling, Agent* comics!"

Her father burst out laughing. "You mean the introduction of the character Merlin Thunderhawk? My claim to fame, I gather?"

"Of course. You've been immortalized." Rachel grinned and then continued more thoughtfully. "Did you know that Eliaures Charles, the Serpent Master, is Dr. Mordeau's father? That's why she hates you so much."

The duke raised an eyebrow. "Hates me? I know that she does; she told me so many times. But how do you know?"

"Many times?" Rachel thought back. "Was that when you were trapped in the Wisecraft building together last fall, and she was also threatening to do bad things to me?"

"How could you possibly know about that?"

"I could claim 'no secrets can be revealed.'" She threw her father a quick grin. "But this time, Sandra told me."

"Ah. She should not have frightened you," he said mildly. "Yes. Melusine Mordeau does not like either of us, I am afraid." His face took on a grim cast. "I wish we could find her. I am beginning to suspect she may be hiding in the one country the Wisecraft's not allowed to enter."

Rachel pressed her lips together and said nothing. He meant Bavaria; she was not going to give him the satisfaction of an opening to complain about Vlad's homeland.

"Returning to my father's story," the duke said as they continued to stroll through the forest, "the Terrible Five were on the run. They needed a new base of operations, and they chose Roanoke. They seized the school, killed seven members of the faculty—the seven strongest sorcerers—and let the rest of the tutors and staff flee. Then they held the students hostage and started digging.

"Immediately," the duke continued, "the armies began gathering. General Yrgwas MacDannan—the head of EUA, the European United

Armies—called for a combined attack. Snireth Ko, at the head of the Asian Armies, answered the call. However," he sighed, "this is where things began to go awry."

"What happened?" asked Rachel.

"General O'Keefe, the grandfather of your friend Joy and head of the United Americas—both North American and South American forces—had been killed at the Battle of Detroit," her father said. "The new head of the forces for the United States of America was General Towers; however, he was a very young man. Many of the other generals didn't trust him. So when he called the armies of the United Americas to gather, the South Americans didn't show.

"It took him three days to convince them. During those three days, your grandfather had moved into position," explained the duke. "He had his men encamped in the hills around Roanoke. With the help of selkies, he slipped travel glasses onto the island. This way, in addition to those who came by boat, he could move men directly onto the island at a moment's notice."

Ambrose continued, "Your grandfather wanted to move immediately, without waiting for the United Americas. General MacDannan received word the Americans had finally come to an agreement, however, and would be there within half a day. Roanoke Island was on their territory, so he asked my father to wait."

They stepped out of the trees to regard the lavender farm. There was not much to see this time of year, just round green-gray plants growing in straight rows. High above the lavender was an odd shimmer, like looking at the sky through badly cut glass. Rachel realized this must be the sorcerer's shield her father had mentioned to Dart. She noted that this was the only place she had visited today that was not shrouded in fog.

"Keep in mind," the duke added, "when you hear this story, none of these generals knew what we know today. They didn't know about the Six Musketeers. They didn't know that the YSL had been preparing for months to fight the Terrible Five. They didn't know about Crispin Fisher's talismans. So they had no compelling reason not to wait a few hours."

The black Belgian Shepherd ran down one of the rows, trotting back along another row. The three of them then headed back along the other leg of the horseshoe path that stretched from the lake to the lavender farm and back through the southern wood.

"Your grandfather then received a message," her father said. "It told him the students had begun their attack. He passed this information onto General MacDannan, announced that he was going in, and signed off before his superior officer could countermand his decision.

"He and his troops attacked," he continued, "defeating the now leaderless Veltdammerung—the Six Musketeers had already defeated the Terrible Five. General MacDannan and the others soon joined him. Together, they secured the island."

"And saved the day," Rachel smiled.

"Yes," her father replied sadly. "Only.... It was then, after it was all over, that my father learned that he had arrived half an hour too late to save Emrys."

"Oh," whispered Rachel, stricken. "Poor Grandfather."

Her father walked silently. The path through the southern wood came out behind the stables. Her father headed for the back paddock that held the Arabians.

"That day," Ambrose continued finally, "my father resigned his commission. He had been a soldier almost his whole life. He never again served. To my knowledge, he also never spoke to Yrgwas MacDannan, even though—up until that day—they had been fast friends."

"Oh, no!" cried Rachel.

"It gets worse. Much worse," her father said quietly.

How could it get worse? Rachel's heart wept as she imagined her grandfather's frustration at delaying his attack only to discover that, had he gone a half an hour earlier, his own son would have lived. What could be worse than losing his own child?

They reached the paddock where their master-of-the-horse, Dunstan Simes, was exercising the Arabians. Rachel, who had loved these short, swift horses, particularly since she read *King of the Wind*, paused to watch the brown, black, and white steeds racing across the mist-covered fields. They ran, turned on a sixpence, and ran again, their tails held high like streaming banners. Despite her sorrow at her father's story, watching their effortless grace filled her with an unspeakable joy.

The duke rested his foot on the lower rail of the fence and gazed at the Arabians. "The message your grandfather received," the duke passed his hand over his face, "came from your mother."

"From Mummy?" cried Rachel, astonished. "But she wasn't even at school then!"

Straightening, he turned and walked back across the misty lawns. Rachel hurried to keep up with his long strides. Green leafy topiaries loomed ahead, barely visible through the fog: a winged horse and an elephant herd with young—all painstakingly clipped from yew and maintained by Donald Wellsey, their albino groundskeeper, and his donkey familiar.

The duke continued, "Your grandfather was proud that his new daughter-in-law's timely news had saved so many lives and said so. When he praised her, a week later," her father's voice filled with pain, "your poor, sweet, innocent mother let slip that Ambie Benson had told her about the attack an hour before Ellen called my father, but Ambie had sworn your mother to secrecy."

"No!" whispered Rachel, who knew well her grandfather's opinions regarding loyalty.

They headed into the hedge maze, the same one Rachel could see from her window. Rachel's father grabbed the dog and snapped a lead onto its collar. Occasionally, they had lost sight of a hound in the maze. The dog would run down the many branches of the labyrinth as they searched, trying to choose the paths that led to the voice calling its name and going the wrong way. It sometimes took hours to find the creature.

Rachel's father took a turn that led into a clearing with a stone bench. He sat down, running his hand along Laelaps's sleek black fur. He smiled down at the dog, and it licked his face. Rachel sat beside him.

Ambrose said sadly. "After deliberating, your mother decided to tell her new father-in-law the secret her best friend had shared with her. When she told him the whole story, she thought this news would demonstrate her loyalty to him—that she had broken her word to her dear friend Ambie and cleaved to him." He paused for a long time, "It didn't work out that way."

"He...." Rachel swallowed, hardly able to speak. "He blamed her for Emrys's death?"

Her father nodded gravely. "Father saw it as a betrayal. He felt, had your mother been loyal to him, his son would still be alive. Your mother went from savior to murderess, responsible for the deaths of her brother-in-law and her best friend, in his mind—and in hers."

"Oh, no," whispered Rachel. She pressed her hands against her face.

Laelaps nudged her thigh. Dropping to one knee, she hid her face against the black dog, burying her nose in its fur. The dog nuzzled her ear;

Rachel hugged it tightly.

Ambrose laid a hand on her shoulder. "It was a horrid time for your mother. Her previously doting father-in-law now saw her as the enemy, and the dear friend she had been so loyal to—the one she had stuck up for when she delayed in reporting the attack—was dead."

"Poor Mummy," whispered Rachel, her eyes wet with unshed tears.

"You see why I did not want to discuss it at breakfast."

Rachel nodded wordlessly.

Her father rose. She stood and took his hand. They left the maze and headed back to the house. The thunder of deer hooves sounded through the fog as something spooked the white roe, and the herd changed course. Laelaps scented the air in their direction but left the deer to themselves when his master gave him a disapproving look.

Rachel stared at the misty winter grass beneath her feet as she walked. She felt so sorry for her grandfather and for her mother. How unkind fate had been. She tried to imagine what it had been like, in that first year of her parents' marriage, when her grandfather had been fond of her mother and how painful it must have been when that changed.

As they reached the bridge over the moat, a thought struck her. She and Sandra had learned their mother's dissembling techniques in part because their mother had taught them, but mainly because they had observed her in action, hiding her emotions from her disapproving in-laws. How different might Rachel's own life have been had she lived in the world where her grandfather had doted upon her mother? Would that version of her grandfather even have chosen a little girl to be his favorite if he had been on good terms with his daughter-in-law or if Emrys had lived? Would Rachel even have a mask of calm?

It was disorienting to realize that the only difference between these two distinctly separate realities was half an hour.

Chapter Twenty-Seven:
Immortal Memories

SIGFRIED FINALLY EMERGED FROM THE KITCHENS, STILL COVERED WITH flour, to find the Duchess of Devon and her two younger daughters standing in the vast entrance hall dressed in aprons.

"Cooking is wicked awesome!" Siggy declared gleefully. "It's wizard! It's like doing alchemy. Only it doesn't taste like lizard."

"That's why we love alchemy," added Lucky, "'cause it's edible."

"Glad you enjoyed it," Rachel laughed. "Would you like to join us for Spring Cleaning?"

"This is usually done after the Equinox," the Duchess of Devon said in her bright red apron, "but with guests arriving, it seemed wise to clean a few days early."

"I thought you said you never clean?" Sigfried said to Rachel.

"We don't, really." Rachel smoothed her peacock blue apron. "It's ceremonial." She held up a plum-colored crystal atomizer with a peach squeeze bulb. "We search for things that need fixing and mark them by spraying with this. Then the *bwca* and other domestic fey see to it that the work is done."

"Walk around and find stuff for other people to clean? Ace!" Sigfried declared. He gave Rachel a significant look. "I'm good at looking for things. What're we looking for?"

"Old houses need constant attention." Laurel managed to look as if she was about to do something naughty, even when cleaning. She was utterly fetching in her red and white polka-dotted apron. Siggy was momentarily stunned. "All sorts of things try to tear them down: woodworms, deathwatch beetles, carpet beetles, dry rot, and mold. We need to hunt them down and annihilate them before the house comes crashing down around our ears." Laurel raised her blue crystal atomizer and, squeezing the sky-blue bulb, spritzed twice, filling the air with a minty fragrance containing a touch of lavender.

Siggy rubbed his hands together. "Come on, Lucky! Let's hunt for bugs."

The four of them, along with the housekeeper, Mrs. Webber, the three maids—the parlor maids, Mary and Polly, and Tennyson's granddaughter Molly, who acted as a lady's maid for Rachel and her sisters when there was need—and an assortment of domestic fey set about searching the house high and low. They paraded through a hundred-sixty-two bedrooms, the seven studies, the twenty-six drawing rooms, as well as libraries, attics, kitchens, pantries, craft rooms, nurseries, dining rooms, galleries, staircases, the chapel, the snooker room, the alchemy lab, and the wintergarden.

Rachel found a spot of mold down in the music room in the basement, near her great-grandmother's alchemy lab—which was now her mother's alchemy lab. It surprised her, as she walked through that and other chambers, how many places reminded her of her grandmother, though she did not mind quite as much as she had before seeing Nastasia's vision. Laurel found beetles in the carpet in the Ruby Drawing Room, near the door to the rose garden, and her mother found where mice had made a nest in the Fairy Queen's Bedroom. Mrs. Webber and her girls also discovered a few spots.

Sigfried found twenty-seven instances of insects or mold or dry rot. The duchess and Mrs. Webber were astonished, praising his cleverness in thinking to look in so many out-of-the-way places. Rachel, who knew he was using his amulet, was grateful he was able to do so much for the preservation of the house, but she was disappointed, too. This was now the second time they had been through the manor, and there was still no sign of the Heart of Dreams.

"Do you think," she whispered, falling in beside him, "that I should ask my father?"

"About what?" asked Sigfried.

"The Heart.   I bet he would be interested in hearing about the princess's vision—about his father and mother," she said.   "Maybe my grandfather told him where they put the Heart."

Sigfried stroked his chin, pondering. "On one hand, telling adults, always unwise. Very unwise, Griffin. On the other hand, we are out of leads. Might be a necessary evil."

Rachel replied, "Let's wait a little longer. We can search the stables, the kennels, the boathouse. If, after all that, we still can't find it, I'll ask him on my birthday. He's promised to spend some time with me then. That gives us just a little less than two weeks."

Once they finished checking the house, Rachel's mother disappeared into the alchemy lab with Sigfried to work on turning his Bowie knife into an athame. Rachel walked back upstairs to find three weather-beaten men in loden cloaks and plaid kilts speaking to her father in the entrance hall. She sidled up to Tennyson, who stood nearby, ready to serve, and inquired about them.

"Your father asked Lord Caledon to send members of His Majesty's Royal Watch to patrol the river Dart until the ceremony can be performed."

"You mean they're Watchmen?" Rachel observed the men with interest. The Watch was the local force that guarded Great Britain against dangerous magic and fey. Rachel knew a few Watchmen, but these three were strangers. She shyly approached one of the men.

"Aye?" He spoke with a thick Scottish brogue. "What can I do for ye, wee lassie?"

"Please, if you go out along the river, our guest crashed one of our bristlelesses yesterday, and we left it where we ran into Dart. Do you think you could look out for it?"

"Aye, we could." He nodded.

She described where they had left it and departed with a grateful wave goodbye. She was pleased later that evening to see that not only had it been returned, but also it had been repaired.

Tuesday, the nineteenth of March, dawned rainy and gray, but that did not stop twelve hundred people from turning out at the duke's request. The Spring Equinox event was held on the field at Spitchwich, next to a stretch of the river Dart that was often used for wild swimming.

A great crowd had gathered under the floating umbrellas. They surrounded a central dais where the duke stood next to a priest of Oceanus, Father of Rivers. The old priest would be performing the sacrifice of the lamb and dribbling its blood across the straw effigy, which, this year, with the addition of golden corn silk hair, had been made to look a bit like Sigfried. The crowd included townsfolk, subjects of the duke — whose Round Table territory, as one of the eight Peers, extended across the entire southern coast of England from Devon to Canterbury—and other aristocrats who had answered her father's invitation including several of his fellow dukes as well as a number of earls, viscounts, and barons. Also, quite a few tricorne hats were visible, suggesting that a number of the off-duty Agents had chosen to attend.

Peter stood beside their father, a bit pale-faced but composed. Laurel and Sigfried looked on with eager glee. Rachel and her mother, on the other hand, huddled behind the dais with their backs to the ceremony, covering their ears to block out any squeals from the lamb. The umbrella above them occasionally bobbed out of place, allowing cold drizzle to coat their hair and slide down the back of their necks.

Her mother squeezed her eyes shut. "This is the worst part of being duchess."

Rachel leaned against her mother sympathetically. She would have pressed her arm, but she was using both hands to cover her ears. It still did not block out all the sound.

"But this is why we need a duke and duchess," Rachel called back. "For these moments—when we are dealing with the Wood Perilous."

"Tsk." Her mother laughed. "A mayor or alderman could do just as well."

"What?" Rachel was so shocked that she lowered her hands, just in time to hear the last high-pitched bleat of fear, a sound that would haunt her nightmares for weeks. "How can you say such a thing?"

"Other towns have elected officials perform such offices." Her mother lowered her hands.

Rachel's mother had grown up as a middle-class girl in the modern world. The future duchess's family had not been Unwary, but for reasons no one would explain to Rachel, Grandpa Kim and his father had decided to abandon the World of the Wise and live as mundane mortals. The only reason her mother and her sister, Aunt Melissa, had gone to Roanoke was that their great-aunt Ye Jin had paid their way.

This meant that, while Ellen Kim Griffin was an exemplary duchess, occasionally, her commoner roots showed. There were certain aspects of the aristocratic World of the Wise that seemed to escape her.

"No, Mum!" Rachel shook her head rapidly. "You're confusing play-acting with reality. You mean Unwary towns—which perform a ceremony where they pretend to placate the invisible world—might have elected officials officiate. But they aren't really interacting with the immortals, Mummy. They're just carrying out a tradition."

"What's the difference?" asked her mother.

"The difference is Dart," Rachel stated. "Their traditions are a myth. Dart's real."

"Why couldn't an alderman toss a straw dummy to Dart?"

"Because there is so much more to it than that. Do you think a different person every few years—some qualified, some not—could keep Dart's trust?" Rachel sought the words to explain something that seemed so plain to her. "Take that little boy! He would not be alive today if Father were not the duke."

"Silly, it wasn't your father who saved that boy. It was Sigfried."

Hoisted on her own petard. Rachel pressed her lips together, wishing she had told the real story from the beginning. She thought of explaining, but it would just derail this conversation.

"Mummy," she said sadly, "sometimes, I think you don't love the family."

The duchess cried out, shocked. "Of course, I love you! I love each and every one of you very much. How could you doubt—"

"Not *our family*," Rachel interrupted her. "I know you love me and Peter and Laurel and Sandra and Daddy and... A-amber. No one could question that. You are the sweetest mother who's ever lived. No, I mean *the family*. Us, but also Grandfather and Grandmother—"

"Oh, well, then." The duchess sighed.

"When Dart said, 'How do I know you will come if I release him?' I gave my word as the daughter of the Duke of Devon."

Her mother looked at her carefully. "You didn't include that part of the story."

Rachel worried that her mother might ask more questions, but she did not. Perhaps she assumed it was Sigfried who walked forward.

She pressed on. "Because when I said 'Devon,' you can be sure Dart was not thinking of Father. He's officiating this ceremony today for only the third time. She was thinking of Grandfather—who was duke for more than a hundred-and-seventy-five years—and of his father and his father and *his father*, Uther Griffin, the Seventh Duke—who was the one who bound her.

"And the Fourth Duke, Myrddin Griffin," Rachel continued rapidly, not giving her mother a chance to interrupt, "who had twenty children;

the Third Duke, Lamorak Griffin, who married Lunette, the descendant of Merlin—the original Lily, from the 'Lily, Lark, and Thorn' song, and of the Tenth Earl of Falconridge, Manawydan Gryphon, who became the First Duke after being granted the dukedom from King Edward III."

"Don't you think—" Ellen began.

Rachel pressed forward. "And Athelward Gryphon, the First Earl, who received Gryphon Park from King Alfred the Great himself, as a reward for his valor. Athelward fought and defeated the Danish wizard Hjorvarth, whose magic had protected the Vikings from Saxon arrows. Athelward's victory allowed the king's troops to win the day."

"Rachel," her mother said gently, "these things happened long, long ago. Nobody remembers these people."

"Dart does."

Her mother started. She glanced at the watery figure of Dart rising from her riverbank.

"Dart knew them," Rachel repeated, "and it's because of their integrity —as a group, as a family line—that she honors her agreements today. She knows a Griffin will keep his word."

Her mother was quiet, thoughtful. Rachel took advantage of the moment of silence to ask her mother the question that had been weighing on her mind so much the last few weeks.

"Mother, where are all the old dukes and earls? Where do people go when they die?"

"Oh. Didn't we ever tell you?" her mother replied sweetly. "There is an ocean of life, lamb. We come from it when we are born, and we go back to it when we die."

Rachel blinked. She had not heard that before. "Do we... remember who we were once we go back?"

"I don't know, lamb." Her mother shrugged, and then smiled kindly, smoothing her daughter's hair. "We'll find out when we get there."

Rachel frowned, not sure if that was comforting or creepy. The umbrella bobbed to the left and cold drizzle fell on the right side of Rachel's head and shoulder, dampening her face.

The duchess pressed Rachel's hand. "You make a good point about Dart. Still, you must admit there's a great deal of pomp and ceremony we could safely do without," her mother said gently. "And all these horses. Without your grandmother here, we should probably sell most of them. Nobody needs four herds!"

"Mother!" Rachel cried in horror, struck through the heart.

"Rachel, we are maintaining four *herds* of horses, and no one uses them," Ellen said. "You and your siblings already have mounts. Sandra took an interest for a few years, but she's too busy now. Without your grandmother to ride and show them…." She spread her hands.

"B-but…" Rachel sputtered, "which ones would you abandon?" She yearned to find a way to share with her mother the love and devotion she and her father felt toward their noble steeds. "The Friesians? Friesians have been used by the Dutch as war horses for over twelve centuries."

"Maybe but they have hardly been here that long. Didn't your grandmother buy them?"

"Certainly not!" Rachel cried. "Our family has been raising Friesians since 1689. Uther himself brought them over from Holland when he accompanied William of Orange on his voyage to assume the throne of England. William's army landed here in Devon, at Tor Bay. Uther arranged for five horses—two stallions and three mares—to be brought to Gryphon Park by a servant, while William and the army proceeded to London, where the Dutch prince was crowned King William the Third. We've been raising Friesians for over three hundred years."

"I hadn't realized they'd been here so long." Her mother frowned slightly.

"What else? The Vanners? W-Warlock was a Vanner! You ride a Vanner!" Rachel cried. "Grandfather's father, the Ninth Duke, bought the first Vanners from actual Gypsies, the week before he was killed by Bengie Geare during the draining of Cranmere Pool."

"Of course, not the Tinker's Cobs," her mother said soothingly, using a traditional name for the breed. "They must truly be the most beautiful of horses."

"The Arabians then?" Rachel asked. "One of our Arabians won the Ascot a few years back, and quite a few of them have placed in less prestigious races."

"Horseracing is an unpleasant affaire." Ellen Griffin shuddered. "So hard on the horses."

"Some of our Arabians are descended from horses that the Eighth Duke brought back from Egypt in the eighteen hundreds," Rachel said, "but others are descended from horses that the sixth earl raced at Smithfield Track in the eleventh century. He received them from his father-in-law, Robert, Earl of Mortain, the half-brother of William the Conqueror."

"Really, so old as that?" Her mother's voice rose in surprise.

Rachel nodded. "That leaves the moor ponies. They've been here longer than we have."

"There will always be moor ponies here," her mother agreed, "though I don't see why we have to pay for their upkeep. Why not just let them go wild, with all the other moor ponies?"

"But our moor ponies depend on us!" Rachel objected. "We've looked out for some of ours for more than a thousand years. Peat Moss and Buttercup are descended from Thoos, the first earl's moor pony, and Coaldust, the shaggy black mare, is descended from Sorrel, who Lunette Willt brought with her when she married Lamorak. Coaldust's also descended from the fairy pony that Sir Calidor Moth gave to Lynette—Grandfather's aunt—when he married her."

"Where did you learn all this?" her mother asked. Then she smiled and brushed Rachel's hair out of her eyes. "Your grandparents told you, didn't they?"

"Some of it," Rachel nodded. "Some came from Oliver and Horse Master Simes. Their families have lived here and taken care of our horses for many generations."

Her mother sighed. "Maybe Sandra could take the Friesians if she becomes Queen of Bavaria. They might do well there."

"Maybe," Rachel agreed hesitantly. Her mother might be right, but Rachel could not bear the thought of losing them. "But it's sad to think of how poorly posterity will regard us."

"How do you mean?"

"Two or three hundred years from now, Peter's descendants will look back and ask, 'What happened to those handsome Friesians for which Gryphon Park used to be famous?' And someone will say, 'Oh, the Eleventh Duchess dropped the ball, you know.'"

Ellen Griffin gasped and drew back as if she had been slapped. Rachel met her mother's gaze evenly. Maybe it had not been a nice thing to say, but it was true.

Then her mother's eyes went wide, and she pressed a hand against her mouth. "Merciful stars! *I'm* the duchess!"

Rachel stared at her oddly.

"I know, obviously," her mother laughed. "I mean I'm the old woman now!"

"I… have no idea what you mean," admitted Rachel.

Her mother touched her forehead to her daughter's, smiling, and then leaned back. "When I married your father, I was twenty-one. For the next twenty-one years—half of my life—I was Lady Falconridge, the young lady of the manor, who brought a breath of fresh air, blowing out the stuffy ways of the old set—or so people told me. Well, those who didn't mock me as 'the middle-class Unwary girl who rose above her station.'

"But now, I'm the Duchess...." Her mother sat up straight, struck. "*I'm* the one who must uphold tradition, or it will not be upheld. I no longer have the luxury of being a breath of fresh air. I have been so busy during these last three years, since your father inherited the dukedom; I have never thought through the ramifications of what it meant that the old despot, er, I mean your grandmother, was gone."

Slowly, Rachel began to understand what her mother meant. As a middle-class girl marrying the son of a duke, her mother had been under a great deal of scrutiny. A great deal of it had been negative, but Ellen Griffin had also been praised for her sweetness and her innovative ways.

The duchess pressed her palm against her cheek. "Oh, you're so right, Rachel! I do need to learn to love the whole family. I can't let your grand-mother's coldness rob you and Peter and your offspring of all that belongs to them. Where do I start? What do I do?"

"Well," Rachel looked up at the bobbing black umbrella and the gray, swirling sky beyond, considering. "Did anyone ever tell you who all the portraits in the gallery are?"

"Once or twice, but I've never thought about it."

"But you remember," Rachel said, stating the obvious.

"Of course," agreed her mother.

"Then, every day—or once a week—go into the gallery, look at a por-trait, remember everything anyone ever told you about that person. Start with Ambrosius Terminus Gryphon, our first ancestor to come to England, in the year 44. If you can't remember enough about any given painting, ask Father, or Peter, or me, or Tennyson. He probably knows more than any of us."

"He probably does," the duchess agreed. "All right! I will. I may prefer modern ways to old, but when I married your father, I swore to do my duty by his family and his people."

She gave Rachel a very sweet and warm smile. Rachel hugged her, resting her head on her mother's damp shoulder.

"You have an understanding of these things beyond your years." Her mother stroked her hair. "And you appreciate them in a way your sisters and I never will. Too bad it wasn't you who fell for a prince, and Sandra who fell for the young, Unwary-born scientist."

Oh, I wish!

Not really, Rachel quickly told herself, blushing with embarrassment.

Aloud she said, "I do love the beautiful old places, but I would rather marry Gaius."

"Marry? Oh, dear one," her mother continued stroking her hair, "you are far too young to be thinking of such things."

Rachel burst out laughing. "Too young? I've heard nothing else my whole life. On the third day I can remember, when I was two, you announced I'd inherited your family's gift, and Grandmother's first remark was,"—Rachel changed her intonation to echo her grandmother's elegant tones—"'Splendid. That will greatly increase her chances of making a good match.'"

"She talked about marriage all the time." Rachel gestured broadly, indicating her siblings and other children of Peers of the Wise among the crowd. "Will Peter marry Reela or Neens? Will he marry Lady Olivia? Grandmother would have *loved* that. Lady Olivia's undisputedly the best young horsewoman in Britain. And if Peter doesn't marry her, will Lady Olivia marry Magnus? Will Sandra marry Magnus? Remember when Sandra had a huge crush on him and used to follow him everywhere? The family was so hopeful, but that didn't work out, did it?"

"Magnus?" her mother objected hotly. "He's in his early forties!"

"So?" Rachel shrugged. "That didn't matter to Grandmother. She would've said, the Wise live long lives. At forty and sixty, or a hundred and forty and a hundred and sixty, what difference will a twenty-year gap make? Or a thirty-year gap?"

The duchess sighed. "I'm still not used to thinking like an aristo."

"Even Father would have been happy if Sandra, or one of us, married Magnus," Rachel reminded her. "Magnus was Uncle Emrys's best friend."

"I guess you're right."

"But it won't happen. Sandra and Laurel have solid boyfriends who want to marry them."

"You know about Laurel's boyfriend?" her mother asked. "I thought that was a secret."

Rachel winced. She should not have mentioned that. At least, her mother already knew. "She told me after I tried to arrange a marriage between her and Ivan Romanov."

"The prince?" her mother stared at her wide-eyed.

"He's my best friend's brother. I thought it would be lovely if she and I could be sisters. He was interested, too. Poor man."

Her mother looked flabbergasted. "So *that*'s how that happened. His parents did speak to your father, but Laurel said no."

So Ivan had been serious! Rachel's heart leapt with joy. She had *known* he was serious. This made her feel very good. It meant he had been serious when he had implied he might offer for her. He seemed awfully old to her, even though he was a year younger than Vladimir, but then, compared to the twenty-year gap of which her grandmother thought nothing, what was five or six years?

"I even asked her first," Rachel said sadly. "Or rather Ivan asked her first. Only she thought Ivan was teasing, so she said yes, to humor me."

"Oh." Her mother drew out the 'o' sound to be very long indeed.

Once the effigy was sanctified, the crowd lifted it, passing it overhead down to the river. Some of the young lords, friends of Peter's, raised the straw man and hurled him into the river.

Dart rose higher and seized the offering, embracing it like a lover. Rachel shivered. Once upon a time, she had thought Dart's treatment of the effigy was charming, almost romantic. Having seen the river nymph smile so maliciously at the little boy, she now felt otherwise. Still, from this point until the end of the year, the river nymph would be a gentler Dart, and while the river was never entirely safe, it would be safer.

Dart dived back into her river, bringing the offering with her, and the crowd began to mourn. They wailed; they screeched; they cried. Some screamed and tore their clothing. One of the loudest mourners was Rachel's Great-Aunt Ye Jin. Jin Cavendish was dressed in a mannish suit and carried a lit cigarette in a long cigarette holder. Great-Aunt Ye Jin yowled and swayed and carried on in a most convincing manner, but she did it all with no expression whatsoever upon her face. This was the great-aunt who had taught Sandra *kumihotoushi*, the family's dissembling arts and who had paid her mother and her aunt's way to Roanoke Academy.

Rachel screamed and wept along with the rest. It was easy to weep. She had only to think of the bad things that had happened in the last six months: the death of her Elf, whom Rachel seemed to miss more with each passing day; the harm that had befallen her friends, particularly Valerie, Nastasia, and Zoë; the abduction of Amber; even the death of the Heer of Dunderberg, much as the storm goblin had been a menace. Soon, real tears ran down her face, and her whole body was wracked with sobs. She cried so hard that her mother leaned over and pulled her close, hugging her tightly.

Rachel leaned against her mother, and they rocked back and forth. Rachel was grateful for the comfort. She was also grateful they wept for a fake Siggy of straw and not a real little boy.

When the crowd finally began to disperse—some heading home, others heading toward Gryphon Park and the promise of refreshments—Rachel slipped away and ran to her great-aunt. Jin Cavendish stared down at her from beneath the ancient black Hanway umbrella that bobbed above her head. She had penciled eyebrows and dark red lipstick and a fierce, piercing gaze that fixed one in place. She carried her cigarette holder everywhere, gesturing with it as she talked and pointing it at people with a short stabbing gesture when she wished to emphasize her point—everywhere except to family gatherings that included Rachel's mother's father, Grandpa Kim. More than once, Rachel had seen Grandpa Kim yank the cigarette holder out of Great-Aunt Ye Jin's mouth, throw it down, and stamp on the lit cigarette, declaring that it brought shame on the family for a woman to smoke in public. Rachel had once overheard her grandmother, the previous duchess, comment that had anyone other than Ye Jin's younger brother tried such a trick, it would have been the last thing he ever did.

"You are Ellen's youngest, no?" Ye Jin said in her surprisingly deep voice, possibly from years of smoking.

Rachel nodded.

"You are the one with the gift?"

Rachel hesitated only a moment before nodding again. She was reasonably sure Great-Aunt Ye Jin referred to their shared gift of perfect memory.

"What do you want?" Great-Aunt Ye Jin asked bluntly.

"Please," Rachel asked. "Can you tell me about your mother?"

"My mother?" Ye Jin looked faintly puzzled. "You mean Grandma Kim?"

"I mean Kim Sun Li," Rachel blurted out.

Ye Jin's penciled brows rose high on her forehead. She stared at Rachel silently, an intimidating stare. Rachel fought the desire to flee. Her curiosity about her great-grandmother, whose portrait she kept under her bed, forced her to meet the old woman's gaze. Ye Jin gave a curt nod and began to speak. She spoke for several minutes, her eyes never leaving Rachel's face; however, she spoke in Korean. Then she gave one sharp nod, turned, and walked away.

Rachel stared after her, knowing no more than she had before. But Great-Aunt Ye Jin knew Rachel would remember what she had said. If Rachel could learn Korean, or find someone who spoke it, she could discover what her great-aunt had said about her long-dead mother.

Chapter Twenty-Eight: Twilight Excursions

"We're going to ride a what?" Sigfried asked, flying beside Rachel on yet another borrowed bristleless as they headed for the forest beyond the lake.

"A tree."

They had spent the afternoon helping her parents entertain the crowds; or rather Rachel had spent it helping her mother in the duchess's capacity as the hostess—to her delight, she had been assigned to entertaining the young children—and Sigfried had spent it showing off Lucky and signing autographs for those who were fans of the famous dragon-slaying boy. He retold the story of how he slew the dragon at least three times, telling it slightly differently each time. Fortunately, except for Rachel, none of the people listening to any one of the retellings heard the others.

It had taken some clever planning to slip away, especially as sunset would be at six twenty-eight, and dinner was to be served at six. However, Rachel had been entertaining the children near the refreshment table all afternoon. The splendid high tea laid out there had included the family tea blend, Double Devon cream, homemade whortleberry jam, Cook's best Devonshire honeycake drizzled with oodles of buttered honey, plus stacks of cucumber sandwiches, trays of newly-baked scones, fresh fruit grown in the Gryphon Park wintergarden, local Sharpham and Devon blue cheese, and much more. So her claim of having already eaten too much was accepted. She promised the still-hungry Siggy that they could visit the kitchen when they came back from their excursions. This was enough to convince him. Sigfried now loved the kitchen.

"Tree riding. That'll be exciting," Siggy groused. "Oh, look. There's a rock. And, ten minutes later, yep. Same rock. Half an hour. Yep. Still there. Same rock. Woohoo."

Rachel could not help it. She started giggling. Soon, her shoulders shook with glee.

"At least Lucky can set the trees on fire. That'll break up the tedium—

for a few minutes."

"Oh!" Rachel frowned, uncertain.

"What's it now?"

"I'm not sure Lucky should come."

"Why not? Where I go, Lucky goes. I'm not going if Lucky can't go."

"It's just the trees are a bit afraid of fire. I'm afraid he'll scare away the dryads."

"Hmm. That's a problem." Siggy stroked his chin.

"I could go fly up to Luckey Tor," offered Lucky. "If you need me, I'll rush right back."

"I guess that'll work," Siggy said, looking glum as Lucky snaked off into the sunset. "You can drop many rocks into the gorge while I'm stuck sitting on a tree, staring at one rock."

The sun was low over the moors, filling the sky with peach, gold, and dark rose. They flew by the kennels and the stables and then by the lake. Dogs barked; horses whinnied; a tawny owl hooted mournfully. Siggy wanted to take a boat to the island. Rachel promised him they could do it another day and pressed on until they were in the deep, majestic forest.

"This is my favorite riding tree," she announced. "See how it grows sideways for two feet before it grows up again, making a place where you can sit? You need to find one like this. There are several, there, there, and there. Peter usually rides that poplar. Pick the one you like best."

Rachel leaned Vroomie against a mossy boulder. Then, having had the foresight to put on sweatpants under her dress, she climbed up and straddled the tree, a downy birch. With its white bark and black eye-like markings, the moor birch looked much like the paper birches visible out of the window of her dorm room, back at Roanoke, except the bark of the paper birch tended to peel off in long parchment-like strips. She put her arms around the vertical rise of the trunk. It was cold and hard, but it shivered beneath her palms. She loved the feel of the trunk, but the temperature was falling fast. She wondered if she should put on her mittens.

"What about this?" Sigfried pointed to a massive beech. Technically, it counted, as it grew sideways and then up, but the truck was enormous, far too wide to encircle with one's arms.

"I think that's too big. You might fall off."

"Fall off? At least that would be more exciting than staring at a rock."

Rachel hid a smirk. "Sigfried, this'll be nothing like staring at a rock. At precisely five minutes before sundown, something amazing will happen. It is quite important you hold on."

"Hold on, schmold on," scoffed Sigfried. "I'll be fine."

They sat on their trees for a time. Siggy reported upon a boulder as if it were a sporting event. Rachel ignored him, awaiting the approaching Twilight. She would not let anything disturb her joy. Then, it happened. The sun formed a golden line along the horizon. The forest grew hushed. The tree trembled.

"Hey, this tree is moving! Is that the wind?" Sigfried looked around, frowning when he saw that none of the branches above him were waving.

"Shhh!" Rachel put her finger to her mouth and then grabbed the tree again. "You have to be utterly silent, or you'll scare them. Trust me and wait. This is worth it! And don't stop looking around, especially at the other trees!"

"What about—" Siggy began.

Rachel cut him off. She leaned forward and said softly, "Hush. You will behold wonders."

Her tree trembled. It jerked violently. In a silence that felt like a dream, the tree drew its long roots out of the ground and stretched them like awkward limbs. Sigfried swallowed a shout. He looked over at her, his eyes huge. Then, a gleeful grin spread across his face.

Rachel held on with all her strength. Her tree began to run. It sped forward, its roots moving beneath it like snaky whips. Over on the huge beech, Sigfried clung to the tree, his eyes enormous. The trees that ran at such extraordinary speeds through the forest were not the most amazing part of the twilight ride. Rachel caught Sigfried's eye and pointed at an old oak. The great tree appeared translucent. Inside, a beautiful tall woman, with arms like branches and hair like twigs and leaves, smiled and waved at the two of them as they rode by.

Dryads. Not every tree had a dryad. Not even one in fifty, but enough dryads lived in the forest that they saw at least half a dozen. The oak dryad wore a garment of rough bark. The poplar dryad wore a bell-like gown, orange at her waist and greenish-yellow below, resembling the tulip-like flower of the poplar tree. The birch dryad wore birchbark with a crown of birch leaves. The beech dryad dressed in silvery gray and wore a crown of two-toned purple flowers. Each turned and waved when the two young people rode by, some cheerfully, some shyly.

Rachel loved the dryads. She waved back, sharing with each one a secret smile as if this twilight excursion were a private mystery they would never share with another soul. Unfortunately, Sigfried did not grasp this secrecy. Overcome with astonishment, he whooped like a cowboy.

Instantly, his beech bucked. Siggy held on, but the tree bucked harder. To Rachel's alarm, Sigfried went flying. She had never seen someone thrown off a riding tree. She had no idea what would happen; however, she dared not let go of her own tree until it was again safely planted in the ground. The entire twilit ride never lasted more than five minutes. She would have to trust Sigfried would be all right. Still, a spasm of relief passed through her when she heard him whooping and shouting somewhere in the forest behind her.

Rachel's birch sped on, past a forest of translucent trunks. She passed Dart, who rose out of her riverbed and pulled back her watery hood to watch as Rachel raced by, and a huge, dark seventy-two-point buck, much larger than their roe deer, who watched with deep, stormy eyes. When she looked back, a graceful doe stood there, pure and silvery amidst the trunks. The doe was surrounded by tiny, glittering, yellow-gowned daffodil fairies. The deer and her fairies went by so quickly that Rachel might have been convinced she had imagined them had she not been able consult her memory to confirm what she had seen.

A shiver ran down her spine. She wondered what these animals were and how they came to be in her family's forest. It was possible she had spotted a random buck and an ordinary roe doe, but she doubted it. She had never seen a buck on Dartmoor that was so large, such a dark color, or had antlers over six-feet wide. The doe, too, did not look like a roe. She was taller and slenderer, and her coat was silvery, not white like the Gryphon Park herd. Oh, and she glowed. None of the family's roe deer shone with moonlight.

Then the tree returned to its starting place. The birch dug its roots back into the ground, and the ride was over. Glancing to her left, she saw the large beech had returned, though there was no sign of Sigfried. All around her, the forest was solid again. Sunset was over for today.

Rachel grabbed Sigfried's bristleless and flew to where he had fallen. She found him running through the forest toward the tor. She tossed him his bristleless, and he jumped on.

"Lucky says there are people on the moor—at some circle of rocks," he said, flying beside her. "They're dancing around."

"Probably a Spring Equinox ceremony. Are they Unwary or Wise?"

"How do you tell?"

"Are they wearing Unwary clothing or proper clothing? Also, are they performing a sacrifice—do they have an animal in a cage or such? Or are they just lighting candles and laying flowers? The Unwary don't usually do real sacrifices. Lucky them."

He was silent for a moment, most likely communicating with Lucky. "Their clothing is a mix. Also, they have a troll."

"A troll! That sounds like...." Rachel's eyes grew wide. "Morthbrood!"

"What, who?"

"We've been over this before! Morthbrood. The ancient order of evil sorcerers who used to serve Morgana Le Fay."

"The guys trying to destroy the world?"

"No. That's Veltdammerung. Morthbrood just want to take over and rule the world their way—though," Rachel frowned, "there does seem to be some overlap. I think Dr. Mordeau might be in both groups."

"She's evil, and she wants to destroy the world?" asked Sigfried.

Rachel nodded. "Right."

"And they have two normal people," Sigfried continued, "People in normal clothing, I mean, who are tied up and look confused. One of the Morthgoon's sharpening a big knife. Oh, and now two others are arguing about how they 'should have done it' at sundown 'for the greatest effect.'"

"No!" Rachel cried, leaning forward and shooting upward above the trees to fly unobstructed. "Let's go! We must get there before the Morthbrood perform a human sacrifice!"

Twenty minutes later, Rachel and Siggy sat hunched with their backs to one of the many boulders that spotted the moors; to their left, a large gorse bush covered with yellow flowers hid them from view. Twilight was falling quickly, and the temperature was approaching freezing.

"You should have told me they were so far away," Rachel murmured, shivering. "We're at Grey Wethers. That's over ten miles from home, maybe fifteen! I could have returned home for Father in much less time, and he could have jumped here instantly."

Siggy shrugged, "Far, shmar. How'd I know distances? Lucky zips around super fast."

"Maybe you should give my father one of your calling cards. That way we could call him when we have need of him," suggested Rachel.

Sigfried touched her forehead with the back of his hand, as if checking for a fever. "Have you moved entirely to Bedlam? If an adult had one of our cards, they could 'check up'"—he made quote signs with his fingers—"on us. Then what would become of our life of crime and adventure?"

Rachel sighed. "It doesn't matter now. We're here."

She peered at her calling card. Siggy's amulet was showing the wide moors behind them. Night was approaching, but torches and a bonfire provided flickering light. She could make out the two circles of standing stones, one north, one south, with a short distance between them. The stones were different sizes. Most stood a foot and a half to two feet tall. A few were larger.

"You should've mentioned there were two circles of standing stones," she said. "I would've known it was Grey Wethers. It's the only double circle in the United Kingdom."

"Whethers? Whether what?"

"Wethers like sheep."

"Weather likes sheep? Why?" asked Siggy. "Because sheep look like fluffy clouds?"

Rachel rolled her eyes. "Wethers are to sheep as oxen are to cattle or geldings to horses."

Siggy drew his legs together. "Not another word. Girls. Always trying to unman us! Let's change the subject!" His voice rose an octave. "Quickly."

Rachel snorted. "Those rocks were once sheep, but dark magic turned them to stone."

Siggy frowned. "They don't look like sheep. They look like rocks."

"It was a complete transformation." Rachel shrugged. "Okay, looking at the gathering here, the big hulking thing must be the troll. You say Lucky can take him?"

"Yeah. Luckster Thirty-Nine says no problem."

"Very good." She peered into the card at the dancers, lit by the bonfire and standing torches. The nine celebrants, not counting the troll, completed their dance. Five wore black robes with high cowls; the rest wore normal garments that looked old-fashioned to Sigfried. With them were two Unwary locals with dazed expressions, their hands secured behind their backs.

"I know them! George and Margery Hobson! They own Berrydown Farm, south of Gidleigh. Such a nice couple. They've been bedazzled from the look of it. We must save them!"

"On it!" Sigfried jumped up. "Luckosopher Five-Seventy-Two and I are ready!"

"Sit down! They'll see you." She yanked on his trousers until he sat down. "Don't let them see you until we're ready! I don't suppose you have any chameleon elixir?"

"Nope. Left it back in my room," Sigfried said, adding, "Listen up! They're talking!"

In the glass, the celebrants moved the Hobsons to between the two standing circles.

"Will this ritual bring back Fair Morgana, our dear mistress?" asked a high scratchy voice, possibly an old lady. "Will we learn tonight whether the Cauldron is ready?"

"No," said a male voice. "To reach Morgana, we need more blood. A large quantity of blood. The upcoming May Day event should provide enough. Tonight, however, if we're fortunate, we'll be able to cross the void enough to see her and receive new orders."

"And if we cannot?" asked the old lady.

"We continue with the current orders: heed Melusine, prepare for the event, and kill the Keybearers. If there are any changes, Browne will inform us."

A shiver ran down Rachel's spine. Melusine? They must mean Dr. Melusine Mordeau!

Had their evil, erstwhile math tutor taken over the remnants of the Morthbrood? Rachel had thought she might be a member, but now it sounded as if she were in charge. And Browne? Could they mean Daniel Hanson Browne? Maverick Badger had said that Dr. Mordeau had broken her former Agent-turncoat accomplice out of jail. Browne had been another member of Mordeau and Egg's cabal that murdered families in front of the eyes of their most innocent member. It was Browne who had introduced Sandra to Mortimer Egg—a.k.a. the demon Azrael—back when Rachel's sister had infiltrated Veltdammerung.

A heaviness settled over Rachel. She herself had known Browne. He had always been nice to her, entertaining her with funny games. The thought that he had gone on to betray not only her father and the Wisecraft but the entire human race made her queasy.

"Let's get this over with," a younger man's voice said impatiently. "The slaughter of our fellow human beings is distasteful. Let's not draw it out."

"Patience. All must be done in the proper order, or it is as nothing." The first male voice replied. "We wouldn't have to do this if you had not released our borrowed barghests directly into the path of Agents of the Wisecraft."

The younger voice objected, "Who could have imagined that the whole pack would be wiped out at once! And before they could locate the penny-whistle player."

Rachel's jaw dropped. Did they mean the barghests *she* fought? And *borrowed barghests*? From whom did one borrow barghests?

"Keybearers must be our main target," said a deep, grating inhuman voice, perhaps the troll.

"And the identity of whoever helped Jacinda capture Melusine," insisted the old lady. "Finding out who that was! That's a top priority."

A shiver ran down Rachel's back. They were after *her*.

"It might be a priority for Mordeau," said the male voice. "But we can't be expected to find one man across the ocean in America based solely upon the fact that he plays a pennywhistle. Melusine and Browne will just have to pick someone else for their Great Sacrifice. As to the Keybearers, Belial removed the original leader. Azrael's servant damaged the new one; Crokel did a number on the Dream Thief." He paused. "That leaves Smith. He's the greatest danger."

"Destroy Smith," repeated the deep, gravelly voice. "Drink his blood. Drink all their blood. Hurry. Finish the slaying. I hunger for the flesh of our mortal captives."

Rachel swallowed. They were hunting *her* and *Sigfried*. She squeaked out, "Is that troll planning to *eat* the Hobsons?"

"That's about the sound of it," said Sigfried. "I say we eat the troll."

"We could stop the troll by eating these Hobsons ourselves," Lucky offered helpfully.

"We must save them!" Rachel replied, adding in the hope that it might gain Lucky's approval, "The Hobsons once bought me an ice cream cone after I dropped mine." It had been hot, and she had flown her broom to Gidleigh by herself. She had bought a cone with the last of her pocket change and wept when she dropped it on the hot gravel. The kind farm couple had replaced it. She added aloud, "I have a duty to see they come to a better end than my ice cream."

Lucky nodded in full agreement, but Sigfried gawked at her as if she were crazy.

"Are you babbling on about ice cream while the troll is eating your friends? Let's go! If we don't save them, they won't be there to buy other people ice cream!" declared Siggy. Then, he frowned. "Keybearers. Haven't I heard that before?"

"They mean you and the princess!" Rachel replied, chaffing her arms against the cold. She grabbed her broom, ready to go. "I don't know who was removed by Belial. Isn't he the demon Amber killed? Must be someone who died before Amber killed him. But I know who Melusine is. That's Dr. Mordeau. Morgana, of course, is Morgana Le Fay, the member of the Terrible Five who killed my father's brother. She's dead. Apparently, they're hoping to bring her back? Dr. Mordeau also said that resurrection of the dead was their goal."

"Isn't resurrection a good thing?"

"Depends how it's done, I suppose. Resurrecting one of the Terrible Five, definitely not!"

"Oh. Right." Siggy looked at the Hobsons in the calling card. "When they say 'Smith,' they're talking about me, right?" he asked, pleased. "I'm the greatest danger? Ace! That's one prophecy that will come back to haunt them. Let's get them!"

"Hold on! Before we go!" Rachel peered at the celebrants, her heart pounding rapidly with fear for the farm couple. "We need to figure out what we can do to help. What do the Morthbrood have? I see flutes and lutes and such. Can you move the view closer? Are any of them wearing rings of mastery? I don't see any. I wish we knew if one of them had a wand or a ring of mastery."

The point of view moved so rapidly that Rachel had to glance away. She stared back the way they had come. It would take far too long to get her father and come back. By then, the Hobsons might be dead. *What should they do?*

"Nope," stated Sigfried. "No wands. No big, jeweled rings like the tutors wear. Unless one of them has a bigger-inside pocket I missed. They each have an instrument but no wand or dueling ring."

A smile began to spread across her face. "If they don't have wands, we can take them."

Suddenly, she did not feel anxious. She felt entirely certain.

"Great! Let's go!" Siggy started to jump up but paused, "Why do wands matter?"

"Here in England, most of the sorcerers are just enchanters or conjurers. A few are both. Even the aristocrats, like my brother's and sisters' friends, who go to the most exclusive school on the island, the Lake District Conservatory, only learn enchantment," she said. "This means they aren't likely to have a *bey-athe* shield or use *nothor* or *taflu* to defend themselves."

"So we just have to protect ourselves from sparkly music magic?" ask Sigfried.

Rachel nodded. She did not know why she felt confident, but it was the same feeling as when she had known that she could take Cydney Graves in the duel, back in September. She just *knew* that saving the Hobsons was the right thing to do. It was as if some beautiful wise voice were whispering to her heart:

Go! Now! Save them! Do what must be done. And all will be well. Fear not.

She considered calling Dread but decided against it. Asking him to help against barghests or fey was one thing. Inviting a crown prince of another country to attack British citizens was quite another. But thinking of Vlad gave her a good idea.

"Right, and I know how to do it!" her eyes sparkled. "I once saw Dread and William Locke dueling a group of Dr. Mordeau-crazed students. Dread threw spells while William maintained the shields. We can do that! You be Dread, and I'll be Locke!"

"I get to be Von Dreadful! Ace!" Sigfried grinned maniacally. He drew his wand and his trumpet and then frowned at his knife sheath. "No time like the present! Let's go in!"

Rachel and Sigfried mounted their bristlelesses and flew to Grey Wethers. In the near darkness, they approached unnoticed despite flying over open ground. The Morthbrood were too caught up in their preparations to look out into the dark. The students flew toward the double stone circles, wands ready. The Morthbrood were in the closer, southern circle. Rachel hoped to arrive unseen, but Sigfried flew forward and landed while blowing his trumpet.

The Morthbrood all turned at once. With a burst of red-orange flame, Lucky dove from the night. He breathed fire onto the face of the troll, who stood on the east side of the southern circle. The brute let out a bellow of anger.

Rachel did not land. She hovered behind Sigfried, casting shield cantrips in front of him from her wand. Torches burned around the circle, and the bonfire blazed brightly to the west of the circle. This flickering illumination was not enough to make out the shimmer of the *bey-athe* shields. She would have to trust that the warding shields were there.

Sigfried pointed his wand. A powerful wind blew across the moors. It picked up a robed figure and threw him into two others, knocking all three to the ground.

"Woohoo!" Sigfried crowed. "Perfect strike!"

Across the circle, the troll bellowed. It threw punches at the dragon. Lucky ducked and wove. He breathed out long gouts of red-orange flame. The troll's head and tunic caught fire. It screamed, the odor of scorched hair filling the night.

Sigfried lifted his trumpet and played. With his other hand, he fired spells from his wand. He used a technique Gaius called 'spray and pray.' During the Knights of Walpurgis meetings, Gaius had instructed the freshmen never to do this. Duelists could not keep track of the number of spells stored in their wands if they fired indiscriminately. It also resulted in many wasted spells. Siggy, however, did not care. Not only did he not track the number of spells he cast, but also he did not even look. Bursts of blue or silver sparkles flew from his wand—some striking their opponents, some flying free over the moors.

Rachel aimed her wand precisely, firing hexes. Blue sparkles shone in the darkness. The scent of evergreens chased away the stink of burnt hair. She smiled as each shot struck home, freezing three in as many seconds. Siggy had knocked over another and left one wandering aimlessly, most likely bedazzled. *This was going to be easy.*

A frozen figure moved. The bedazzled man straightened and grabbed his accordion.

"Oh, no, they have a canticler," she cried.

Sigfried briefly lowered his trumpet and called, "What makes you think canticler?"

"You can't undo enchantment with enchantments," she called back, still firing hexes. "It takes the Word of Ending."

"Neutralize the canticler! Right!"

The troll stooped, perhaps ducking the flames. Rising, he swung a club at Lucky, like a batter swinging at a ball. He struck his target. The dragon was sent flying into the darkness, flipping in circles. His flame trailed around him, forming a spiral. The troll dropped to the ground, rolling on the damp moor to extinguish the flames burning his head and chest.

Maybe this was not going to be easy after all.

"Lucks!" Siggy cried, followed by, "He's all right. Get back in there, Lucky."

In the circle, the Morthbrood recovered from the initial surprise and formed ranks. The four in the front played hexes. Behind, three performed longer pieces: inspiring and entrancing enchantments. Behind them, healing spells streamed from the clarinet of a woman in a long gown. The green sparks surrounded those affected by Sigfried's wind blast. A final member stood to one side, bowing silver sparks from a viola. His breezes swept in front of the gathered Morthbrood, catching and carrying away some of Sigfried and Rachel's incoming spells.

The music of the varied enchantments merged into a cacophony. Sweet and pungent scents mingled in the night air. A barrage of sparkles struck the shields: blues, reds, purples. *Purple?* Rachel swallowed. The Dorian mode entrancing spells were bad news—geases and hypnotism. She glanced uneasily at the purple sparkles heading toward Sigfried. *Were her shields holding?*

An idea struck her. She cast a *bey-athe* a foot ahead of the current ones and then another, a foot ahead of that. Then, she waited. Silver sparks struck the foremost shield, winking out, then blue, another swirl of blue, and a ball of red sparks. The next stream of blue sparks winked out a foot closer. Rachel grinned. As long as she staggered them, she could tell when they gave way.

Spells came so fast and furiously that it took all her effort to keep up the shields. When she had decided to put fifty charges of the *bey-athe* cantrip into her wand, it had seemed like a huge number. Now she was not sure they would last through the fight. If she had to cast them directly, without her wand, it would take a lot longer.

What would happen if they lost? Most likely, the Morthbrood would sacrifice them. Would they recognize Sigfried as the Smith they were looking for and realize how fortunate they were? Should she and Sigfried retreat? If they did, who would save the Hobsons?

With a shake of her head, Rachel cleared her thoughts. No time for that. Under the sudden haze of fear, she could still feel that calm certainty. She made the decision to trust it.

Siggy still played his trumpet with one hand, a rather eerie song. With his other, he waved his wand, knocking over the accordion player, a flutist, and the healer. Across the circle, the troll held up its burnt hand, expecting it to regenerate. Its face, too, was severely burnt, and its hair was entirely gone. When nothing changed, and it realized that it would not recover from damage dealt by Lucky's flame, the brute let out a hair-raising *yowl*.

Lucky dove down again, blasting the brute with flame. It let out an ear-piercing scream. Turning, it pelted away across the dark moors. Fire streamed from its head and shoulders like living red-gold hair. Lucky dashed after it in pursuit.

Sparks danced, lighting the darkness, their glow magnified by the rising mist. A myriad of odors mingled together: evergreen, mint, vanilla, cherry, and wood smoke. The Morthbrood's spells came swiftly, with eight enchanters casting simultaneously. When a large swirl of red sparks rocketed their way, Rachel leaned around Sigfried. Instead of wasting a shield, she redirected the spell toward their opponents with a *taflu* gesture, duelist-style. The spell swerved and flew back toward the Morthbrood. Red sparkles streamed behind it like a comet's tail. It struck a tall hexer in robes, who dropped his violin and crumbled to the ground, weeping piteously. Red sparks meant inspiration enchantments. That one must have inspired incapacitating sorrow.

Rachel parried more incoming spells, sending them back. Those struck by these redirected spells fell asleep, wept piteously, threw themselves around in a frenzy, were suddenly covered with ice, or went into a trance. Unfortunately, the Morthbrood's canticler continued to undo Rachel's good work. Fortunately, she spotted him, the tall robed figure playing the viola. Now they knew who he was; it was just a matter of stopping him.

A tingle ran along the back of Rachel's neck. She glanced around. Mist was rising up around Grey Wethers. It slipped between the standing stones and obscured the torchlight. Rachel realized that it came in response to the song Sigfried played. Something about his tune seemed off, but she did not have the leisure to think about it.

"Why mist?" she called, hexing an opponent.

"Makes it harder for them to see us," said Siggy, lowering his trumpet, "or hit us."

As he spoke, he continued to attack. His wand work wasted many spells, but it did delay the enemy. Two of the opposition were swept from their feet. Vines constricted a third.

"Doesn't it make it harder for us to see them, too?" asked Rachel.

"Not me. Mist doesn't stop my amulet," her blood brother replied. Then he added with a shrug, "Also, I remember how to play it."

"Ah." Rachel pursed her lips. "Maybe you should stop. Try playing air blasts or hexes? I think we have enough mis...." She never finished.

A strong wind struck her from behind, sending her flying.

CHAPTER TWENTY-NINE:
MORTHBROOD ON THE MOORS

RACHEL FLIPPED THROUGH THE AIR, SPINNING END OVER END. SILVER sparkles glittered across her body. She gripped both Vroomie and her wand with all her might. Then, she slammed into something and dropped to the ground. She lay panting on the damp earth, winded and surrounded by mist. The breath had been knocked from her. She gasped, attempting to catch some of it. Where she had struck the standing stone, her back ached with fiery pain.

With a groan, she sat up. Her heart leapt into her mouth as she felt the length of her bristleless. A gasp of relief escaped her lips when she confirmed that the steeplechaser had not been damaged. Still aching, she rolled onto Vroomie and shot back towards Sigfried.

She had left him unguarded! Sigfried lay slumped on the ground. A hunched woman moved out of the fog toward him, knife raised. Rachel had no time to aim her wand. She was breathing too heavily to whistle. Instead, she flew directly at the attacker, slamming into the woman's abdomen shoulder-first. Rachel was not traveling fast, but she hit hard enough to knock the woman to the ground.

It turned out that she had struck fast enough to knock her opponent over but not fast enough to get away. As the woman toppled, she grabbed the haft of Rachel's broom, pulling it down with her. They ended up on the ground together. The woman lifted her knife and plunged it toward Rachel's face. Rachel twisted her wrist, pointing her wand at her assailant. Blue sparks struck the woman, accompanied by a burst of fresh-smelling pine scent.

The assailant froze in place, knife still raised. Rachel rolled out from under the blade and jumped to her feet, yanking her steeplechaser out of the woman's frozen hand. She also took the attacker's knife and flute for good measure. Then, she leaned over her blood-brother, terrified. *Was he still breathing?*

Zzzzzzzzzzzzzzz. Sigfried was snoring, probably a sleep hex.

"*Obé.*" Rachel raised her forefinger in the Word of Ending gesture.

She cast more *bey-athes*, this time remembering to place some of the shields behind them. No one would sneak up on them again.

Siggy jerked awake. He leapt to his feet just in time. Their opponents surged toward them, emboldened by the gap in Siggy's spray of spells. The Morthbrood moved closer. Sigfried had dropped his trumpet, but he waved his wand from one side of the group to the other, firing spells indiscriminately.

Of the four people rushing them, two were thrown back, one was wrapped in vines, and one ended up—somehow—surrounded by a Glepnir band but hovering horizontally four feet off the ground. Rachel had never seen that happen. The person must have tried to jump out of the way and had dived into the band instead. Rachel paralyzed one of those who had been thrown back before he could rise again. The remaining Morthbrood backpedaled. Rachel again noted the canticler behind them, freeing the frozen from hexes.

The stone circles were thick with mist now. Rachel could hardly see their attackers. Her stomach tightened as she spun to check on the Hobsons. When she made out the shape of the dazed couple through the fog, she released her pent-up breath in a *whoosh*. They still stood where the Morthbrood had left them, motionless between the two circles.

A hush was falling over the landscape. The hair on the back of Rachel's neck rose. Something was happening. It felt almost as if something were leaking through from the other world, as if Grey Wethers were suddenly Underhill. She looked left and right but could not discern the cause of this sensation. Close at hand, the Morthbrood still struggled against their spells. There seemed to be more figures in the stone circle than there should have been, or maybe the mist was playing tricks on her eyes. In the distance, the fiery form of the fleeing, burning troll moved across the rolling moors. Rachel could still smell the lingering odor of charred meat.

The fight continued. Rachel and Sigfried were protected on all sides, but she wished they had a proper ward. That would have stopped a lot of these attacks. However, it was too dark to draw a circle on the ground, and Lucky was off fighting the troll. Perhaps she should study warding and carry a pouch of iron dust as Xandra Black did.

Something pale moved out of the corner of Rachel's eye. A luminescent feminine figure danced through the circle. Then two. Then four. Suddenly, Rachel realized what had been wrong with Sigfried's trumpet playing and why a hush had fallen over the moors. Sigfried had not played the song for raising a mist. He had played the song for summoning *mist sprites*.

That was not good. Fey were dangerous.

Toward the far side of the south circle, two of the Morthbrood stepped close to one another and began to play their instruments. Their music combined. Red and blue sparkles swirled around each other, forming a single multi-colored spell. Rachel gawked. She had never seen that done. Then, the spell was speeding toward her. Worse, the casters had somehow directed it upward. It flew along a parabola, rising and then dropping. The far end of the parabola would land directly atop Rachel and Sigfried's heads.

Rachel swallowed convulsively. She had not put a shield above them. She did not know how to cast a horizontal *bey-athe*. She did not know if it were possible. The cantrip seemed to produce a vertical shield.

The red and blue sparkles raced towards them. Only a split second remained. Rachel dropped into the state of mind she used to make flame-flicker-fast decisions while flying. An idea came to her, a daring idea.

Months ago, when Gaius had returned her grandmother's wand to her after William studied it, her boyfriend had mentioned vestal wands had the unique property of being good at catching and storing incoming spells. She had only practiced this a few times, and she had only succeeded on half the tries. *Should she try it?* Or should she hope the warding shield cantrip would work if she cast it upward? There was not time for both. Closing her eyes, she raised her wand above her head. She drew a little circle in the air and then thrust upward, as Gaius had shown her. Then, she squeezed one eye and peeked with the other.

Red and blue sparkles swirled out of her wand, like a giant upside-down unicorn horn of sparks. No, they were swirling *into* her wand. The entire unknown spell sunk into the diamond tip atop her wand like glitter sliding down a drain.

From across the circle came a collective gasp.

"Who goes there!" cried the masculine voice they had heard over the card. It seemed to be coming from the canticler in the back.

"Sigfried Smith, the Dragonslayer!" Siggy shouted back gleefully. "You think I'm the most dangerous one, do you? Turns out, you're right!"

Another collective gasp rang out.

Carried away by Sigfried's cheek, Rachel announced in her most-posh English, "You have stepped upon land that is under the protection of the Duke of Devon. Surrender now or face the consequences!"

"Wait! What?" cried a young woman. "Roger, you didn't tell us this was Devon's territory! He's the Agent!"

"Wisecraft! Flee!" cried the high voice of the old lady.

Of the Morthbrood, some ran forward; some drew back; and some outright fled. From the corner of her eye, Rachel caught sight of mist sprites darting this way and that through the circle.

"Oh, no you don't!" Sigfried ran after those who fled.

"Siggy! No! Stay behind the shields!" Rachel cried. Then she sighed. "Ah, well. We had a good strategy while it lasted."

Sigfried pelted toward the remaining figures, firing spells. Plants sprang up and entangled the old lady. The canticler barreled toward them. He ducked around Sigfried and ran headlong toward Rachel. Rachel lowered her wand and smiled. He ran directly into whistling range.

There was just enough light for them to see each other. The man, heavy set and blond, drew back when he saw her. "You're not an Agent! You're…."

Rachel whistled. Blue sparkles danced over his body. He froze.

A moan of dismay came from the remaining Morthbrood. Without their canticler, they had little chance. Rachel relaxed. Their opponents would retreat or surrender now.

They did neither. Instead, the remaining three pulled together. One, a woman, began to play a soft, soothing song. White sparks rose from her instruments.

"Oops!" murmured Rachel.

"What?" Sigfried called back as he continued to shoot. Now that he was paying attention to his targets, he was doing much more damage.

"White sparks mean spells of binding," she whispered. "They're a subset of protection enchantment. They may be able to protect themselves from some of our magic."

Sure enough, the white sparkles formed a circle, similar to a *Sacred Ring*. Rachel made a mental note to add protective circles to her wand. She and Siggy continued casting, but the spells did not cross the white circle, not even the cantrips. Rachel thought this odd until she made out a small form near the feet of the violin player, a cat or dog. One of them must have called a familiar for a more substantial ward. The three Morthbrood moved forward together, advancing on them. The cat ran around them again and again as they moved forward.

"What do we do?" whispered Rachel, floating forward to come beside Sigfried. They were inside the south stone circle now. She cast a shield ahead of them. "Retreat?"

"Are they trying to come toward us physically?" Sigfried snorted. "Two can play at that game! Get 'em, Lucktastrophe Nine Thousand!"

Like a comet falling from the heavens, Lucky dropped from the night sky. The white sparkling circle stopped spells and evil spirits, but it did not stop physical attacks. Lucky hovered just outside it and breathed huge gouts of flame, setting hair, clothing, and wooden instruments ablaze. Screaming in pain and panic, the remaining Morthbrood scattered and ran.

Sigfried sprinted after those who fled, Lucky close beside him. Rachel flew forward and paralyzed those who had been unable to run, including the man hovering above the ground, still trapped in Siggy's Glepnir band. Then, she sauntered up to the frozen Roger the Canticler.

"The Keybearers will triumph." She stared him straight in the face. "Your upcoming event will be a bust, and your mistress will remain dead. You might want to turn over a new leaf. You've picked the losing side."

Siggy, meanwhile, ran forward to free the Hobsons.

"Don't remove the bedazzlement!" Rachel called to him. "Leave that to the Agents. They will need to decide what to tell them."

"Why can't we just tell them the truth?" he complained.

"Because they're Unwary. They won't believe the truth. You'll just terrify them more."

"Kidnapped by crazy, murderous cultists. What's hard to believe?" Sigfried stopped before a slim pale figure. Blue sparkles still glittered and danced around her. "What's this?"

Rachel moved to look and gasped. "Oh, no! You caught a mist sprite!"

"I'll let her go." Sigfried pointed his wand.

The ruby at the tip glinted. The pale shimmering feminine figure twitched. She made a soft moaning noise, like wind blowing through branches. Moving almost too fast to see, she slapped him across the face, her misty fingers trailing across his eyes. Then, she was gone.

"Wow!" Siggy looked left and right. "It just got a lot foggier, didn't it?"

"Lucky," Rachel called, "Can you go get my father? We'll round this lot up."

With sky-high flashes of light, Agents appeared. Rachel and Siggy had already freed the Hobsons from their bonds and checked on the remains of the half-burned, still smoking, troll.

"Good thing." Siggy nodded at the twisted lump of blackened flesh in approval. "He was going to eat me."

The arriving Agents pointed their staffs at the sky. A huge ball of *lux* light burst into brilliant radiance, illuminating the entire Gray Wethers. As Rachel and Siggy stood, waiting for Agent Griffin and his people to finish securing the area, gather the prisoners, and send the Hobsons home, Sigfried touched Rachel's arm.

He pointed off into the darkness, "What's that?"

"Where?"

"Over on that hill. Funny how much less mist there is over there than here."

"Probably because you didn't summon it there."

The mist was lifting. Rachel did not think the difference between the circles and the open moor was that significant anymore. She peered at the shape in the distance.

"I can't quite make it out."

"Hold on. I'll put it on the card."

The card showed a shape, blacker than the hillside. It was wolf-like, a very large wolf, which made no sense, as there were no wolves on Dartmoor. A shiver ran down Rachel's spine.

"Is it the Hound Tor Beast, do you think?" she asked excitedly. "Or maybe the Dartmoor Black Dog? It's not Bengie Geare. He looks like a black colt when he's not in human form."

"Don't know, but it isn't a normal animal. I can't see inside it, and it has red eyes."

She peered at the card. Then her lips parted in surprise. "Oh! Hold on! I recognize that one! I saw it at the Year of the Dragon Ball. Let's get closer."

Grabbing Vroomie, she flew close enough to make out the creature. The *lux* ball did not reach here. The moon was not up yet, but the stars were bright, an unusual occurrence on the oft-overcast moors. The Wolf was huge and darker than black. She felt sure it was the same one she had seen at the ball during the Hour of the Angels.

Rachel landed her bristleless and cautiously approached the beast. "Hallo?"

The great black Wolf turned toward her. Even in the dark, she could see the glow of its red eyes. She did not sense any hostility.

She asked hopefully, "Are you perhaps a Guardian?"

Grrrrr! The enormous Wolf leapt straight at her throat. Rachel threw up her arms and screamed. Only it never struck her. The entire Wolf passed through the space that contained Rachel, but their bodies did not touch. It was gone.

"Where...." Her breath came in gasps, her heart hammering. "Where did it go?"

"Don't know," Sigfried gaped. "Looked like it leapt straight through you."

"How strange," Rachel shivered. "Yet again, I appear to have said the wrong thing."

Rachel's father took them home. He asked many questions about what had happened and what they had seen. Rachel explained they had thought there was not enough time to return and get him if they wished to save the Hobsons, which was true. She even included the fact that the place Lucky had seen turned out to be farther away than they had first thought. She merely neglected to include that they had been on the estate when they set out. Her father listened carefully. He thanked them and promised to see to it that the information they had overheard reached the correct people. He even commended them on their presence of mind.

Rachel's mother brought her flute and healed Rachel's back where she had slammed into the standing stone. It had not bothered her much while she was caught up in the heat of the moment, but it began to burn quite painfully when she sat down at home. Sigfried, however, continued to complain that everything looked foggy. The duchess led him away with a quiet smile. After fifteen minutes, however, Ellen returned to her husband.

"Ambrose," she laid a hand on her husband's arm, "I can do nothing. I suspect a curse."

"How did this happen?" Rachel's father asked Sigfried.

"Siggy called mist sprites instead of mist," explained Rachel.

"Mist. Mist sprites," shrugged Siggy. "What's the difference?"

Ambrose Griffin gazed down at the orphan boy from his considerable height. "Young man, the difference between *mist* and *mist sprites* is similar to the difference between pulling out a *bobby* pin and pulling out a *firing* pin."

Rachel did not quite understand, but it made an impression on Siggy.

The duke led Rachel and Sigfried to a seldom-used, round room in the turret at the left corner of the main hall. Inside, the chamber smelled musty with hints of less pleasant odors. On the floor were inscribed a circle and a pentagram.

Rachel's father sucked in his breath and frowned. He stood in the door for a moment and then closed it without entering. "I dislike thaumaturgy. Let us do this the old-fashioned way."

He took them back downstairs and then outside. There, he asked Rachel and Sigfried to be entirely silent. He made a *tk-tk* noise and then stood quietly while Twilight, his lithe black and white cat, walked around them three times widdershins. Once they were properly warded, he stuck his staff into the ground, butt first, and conjured a violin.

He paused a moment to tune the new violin and began to play. Silver sparks came from the strings, accompanying the same melody Sigfried had played earlier on his trumpet. Siggy had done a passable job, but the duke brought to the song a life and beauty that Siggy's rendition had lacked.

Mist crept up. Three feminine mist sprites moved and swayed just beyond the ward created by the duke's familiar.

The duke said, "What offense has my guest committed that you have blinded him?"

A mist sprite swayed forward. "It is our right."

"He accosted our sister," said another in their whispering singsong.

"I request of you to release him from the fog obscuring his sight," stated the duke.

"We demand recompense."

"What kind of..." Siggy began.

Ambrose cut him off, thrusting his hand in front of the young man's mouth, fingers held in the *taflu* gesture. This would keep a supernatural creature from hearing him, or at least, they were required to pretend that they had not heard. "If I allow you into the lavender garden for twenty-four hours, from midnight to midnight, will that suffice?"

The mist sprites swayed back and forth. They seemed to move in and out of each other. Now there were two, now four.

"Yes," they all spoke together, a sound like wind sighing through the marshes.

"Done." Ambrose Griffin turned to Sigfried. "How are your eyes?"

"Hey! I can see!" Siggy cried. "Normally, I mean!"

"As it should be." The duke nodded and sent the mist sprites away. With his food, he scuffed the ward created by his familiar. "Sigfried, please return to the house and let my wife know I'll be gone for some time. I have to dispel the shields at precisely midnight. Rachel, run to the stable and rouse Oliver. Ask him to saddle Passelande. I'm off to the kennels to get Mòrcù."

"I can do it!" Rachel cried.

She ran to the stable. Rather than disturb the stable boy, who lived with his uncle, their master-of-the-horse, in the living quarters in the back of the massive stables, she grabbed Passelande's tack, slipped on his bridle, and saddled him herself, using a stool to reach his back.

As she finished, her father came in flanked by Piercer and Mudder, two of their deerhounds—one brindle and one sandy with a white chest—whom Rachel greeted warmly, and Mòrcù—the gigantic blue-gray wolfhound as tall than she—who made her nervous. Her father tried the girth and, finding it properly snug, gave her an appreciative nod. Then, mounting up, he rode off, flanked by the three dogs, heading for the lavender garden.

Chapter Thirty:
Peers of the Round Table

"Those aren't knights," Sigfried objected the next morning. "They're old!"

Rachel and Sigfried peered out from behind a topiary dragon—a huge serpentine creation involving numerous yew trees—on the lawn in front of the Gryphon Park manor house as they watched the arrival of the Peers of the Round Table. Siggy crouched with his back to the drive, presumably examining everything with his amulet. Rachel knelt beside him, peering through the bushy green branches of the yews. They watched an immensely old Irishman, whose long, tangled beard still retained a hint of its original red-gold color, totter from his carriage to the house. Two of his numerous red-haired progeny flanked him as he walked, ready to prop him up.

"Not all of them," Rachel replied, "though I'll give you the Duke of Tara. He's two hundred and thirty-nine."

"Two hundred-thirty-nine?" Siggy echoed. "Didn't know geezers could get that geezy."

"The Wise can. Two hundred is about the limit for most, but some live to three hundred."

"That's... really old."

Rachel paused. "Why are we crouched behind a bush?"

"I wanna look before they see me," replied Siggy. "People act goofy when they meet me for the first time. They ask for autographs and want to know all about the dragon I slew. I want to see the knights before I have to answer questions. I thought there'd be armor."

"Armor's crunchy," offered Lucky. "Not tasty at all."

Rachel shook her head. "They're not knights; they're peers."

"How are they the Round Table, then?" Sigfried lay back on the grass.

The day was unusually warm for March and unexpectedly sunny. It had not rained in over a day, unusual for Dartmoor, so the grass was dry. Looking down at him, lying so comfortably, Rachel found it disorienting to remember that Sigfried could see just as well while lying on his back as she could peering through the greenery, probably better.

"The Round Table is our ruling body of the Wise," said Rachel. "They meet around the Round Table, which is the same one King Arthur used. The Round Table meets once every seven years. Lords and knights—men with the title sir, not armored warriors—and even a few elected members come from all over England, Wales, Scotland, and Ireland. In some cases, if a lady or a dame holds the title in her own right, then she comes. During the other six years, the business of the Round Table is conducted by a council of ten. Those ten include the Peers—the eight highest ranked lords: seven dukes and a marquis—and two Visitors."

"Visitors? Like tourists?" asked Sigfried.

"Do they pick a new visitor every year?" asked Lucky. "Did someone eat the old one?"

Rachel sighed. "Sorry, Lucky, no one's eaten them yet."

"That's a shame," Lucky replied so seriously that Rachel laughed.

She said, "The two Visitors represent the monarchy and Underhill."

"Underhill?" Siggy asked. "That's fairies, right? Are we going to see a real fairy?"

"A fairy knight, even," Rachel smiled, "but he's not here yet."

"Are the fairy knights small or big? Bigger than a mouthful?" Lucky looked hopeful.

Rachel shook her head. "He's one-quarter human."

"One-quarter the size of a human?" asked Siggy, "or one-quarter of him is human?"

"The second," Rachel replied. "He's big."

"Giant big?" Siggy asked hopefully.

"Not that big," she said apologetically. "Just not tiny sized."

Siggy scowled. They still had not been to see the giants, and it bothered him. "I thought the Parchment of Coffee decided what happened to the Wise."

"I assume you mean the Parliament of the Wise in Cathay?" she said, after thinking for a moment. "Parliament decides large matters, policy that affects all the Wise. The Round Table decides British issues."

"Like what?"

"Well." Rachel thought back to newsglass articles in her memory library. "How much strangeness are the Unwary allowed to witness? What to do with Unwary who can see through obscurations? Those sorts of things.”

"What happens to Unwary who can see the Wise?" asked Siggy, sitting up.

"Sometimes, they are invited into the World of the Wise. Sometimes not."

"What happens if not?" asked Lucky, trying not to look too interested or too hungry.

"I don't know," she said softly. "I suspect their memories are wiped."

She was quiet for a moment. At some point, she realized with a heavy heart, she would have to outright admit she actively disapproved of the way the Wisecraft treated the Unwary. She had not yet entirely reached that point. It was hard to condemn the Agents whom she so admired.

She continued, "The Peers deal with things like what to do if the fairies overstep the terms of their covenants, or how to handle supernatural beasties that act up. For instance, the big black wolf last night. Imagine if an Unwary saw it. If it happened in an area known to have grims or black dogs—such as here on Dartmoor—nothing would be done. But if there were no local legends, and something stirred, that would need to be addressed. Also, the Peers adjudicate quarrels between members of the Wise, and they appoint judges to the Faire Court. That sort of business."

"Aren't all courts supposed to be fair?" asked Sigfried, laying back again.

Rachel chuckled. "The Faire Courts are the traveling courts that serve at country faires. And yes, courts are supposed to be fair, but it doesn't always work out. If someone has a complaint—that a Faire Court wasn't fair—he'd bring it to the Round Table."

Carriage wheels crunched over the gravel drive, and yet more guests, who had arrived by walking glass, approached on foot from the gatehouse. Rachel pointed out the Dukes of Trevena and Sherwood as they climbed from their conveyances, and the Dukes of Avalon and Caerleon, along with the Marquess of Logres, as they came from the gatehouse. Accompanying each lord were his lady and children, particularly those who were of an age with Peter and Laurel.

Rachel's siblings rushed to greet their friends. Peter greeted the grandsons of the Marquess of Logres: Lord Peregrine Scot, whom everyone called Peril; his younger brother Lord Freddie; Lord Edmond Ravenwood, who was the son of the Duke of Avalon; and Lord John Dymoke, son of the Duke of Sherwood. Laurel greeted her best friend and roommate, Muffy Calico, the granddaughter of the Marquess of Logres, along with Muffy's cousins, the Scot sisters—Lady Charlotte Scot, whom everyone called Reela, and Lady Xenia, whom everyone called Neens—as well as the daughter of the Duke of Avalon, the ever-elegant Lady Olivia Ravenwood, the best young horsewoman in England, with a shelf of awards to prove it.

There were no children Rachel's age. The youngest above Rachel, Lady Xenia, was sixteen and always tagged along with the eighteen- to twenty-five-year-olds. The next oldest child, after Rachel, was seven. Remembering how lonely these events could be, Rachel felt doubly grateful that Sigfried had come home with her.

"Who are the two blokes with your father?" asked Sigfried, pointing. "The ones the girls are all ogling?"

Rachel looked. Laurel and the other young women had formed a gaggle and stood with their arms linked, gazing raptly at where Rachel's father stood talking with Bedwyn Glyndwr, the Duke of Caerleon, and Lady Olivia's father, Harry Ravenwood, Duke of Avalon. Both Devon and Avalon possessed the striking good looks occasionally found among those descended from the blood of immortals, though Rachel secretly felt her father was the more handsome. Nonetheless, the Duke of Avalon, with his piercing blue eyes, was absurdly pleasing to behold. The fact that he was one of the most powerful men in England, in or out of the World of the Wise, in no way diminished his appeal. Caerleon, on the other hand, with his close-trimmed reddish beard, his rumpled tweed suit, and his beret, looked kindly and disheveled. He was her father's closest friend, after Agent Bridges.

"Friends of his. Distant relatives, too," Rachel explained. "The first one, the Duke of Avalon, also has a seat in the mundane House of Lords. The second, the Duke of Caerleon, is a descendant of Owen Glendower."

"Glendower as in *I can call spirits from the vasty deep?*" asked Siggy, impressed, adding, "That line's the only thing I remember from Sister Harridan's English class."

"The very same." Rachel grinned. "In the mundane version of *Henry the Fourth, Part One*, Hotspur replies, *But will they come when you do call for them?* But in the Wise version, Hotspur says, *When they do come, can you then send them back?*"

A motor car came through the arch of the gatehouse and down the gravel road. It was an old-fashioned vehicle, like a horse-drawn carriage but without horses. A royal crest graced its door showing a raven head protruding from a golden crown. The vehicle stopped and out came a man in a handsome royal livery.

"Who's that?" Siggy gawked at the man's navy-blue tunic trimmed with red and his similarly colored, tall, flat-brimmed hat.

"That's the Yeoman Warder Ravenmaster from the Tower of London," said Rachel. "He's one of the Visitors. He represents the king. He's a relative of Flora Towers Skaife, the Mistress of the Beast at school."

"You mean the woman who feeds Lucky chickens at the Menagerie?"

"Right. She's in charge of the Menagerie at Roanoke."

As Rachel peeked out from behind the topiary dragon to wave at the Ravenmaster, who had let her feed treats to his ravens when she was little, her father caught sight of her and beckoned. She ran to him, curtsying to the Dukes of Avalon and Caerleon, both of whom nodded at her fondly.

Her father gazed down at her. "Are you wearing the pouch your mother gave you?"

She nodded and pulled it out from around her neck. Ambrose handed her a small oval mirror framed in ornate silver with a green tint to the glass.

"Put this in your pouch. This calling card used to be your grand-mother's. Your mother and I have its match. Next time you need to rescue the Hobsons or face off with Dart or find yourself in Transylvania, you call me, hmm?" he said.

The handsome Avalon laughed as if at a witticism, but Caerleon looked at Rachel curiously.

"Thank you!" she chimed cheerfully, sliding it into her pouch. She did not add: *there goes Sigfried's cherished life of crime and adventure.* She also bit back the rather uncharitable *Vladimir Von Dread gave me a way to contact him back in November. What took you so long?*

"I have chosen a pony for Sigfried," her father continued. "Peter and Oliver evaluated his riding skills yesterday and found them nonexistent. Cummerbund is docile and will tolerate mistakes. He is also one of our larger ponies, though young Mr. Smith will outgrow him any day now. Bund will do, though, until the young man learns to ride."

Rachel nodded. "Siggy was a very quick study with a broom. It won't take him long."

"Good. You can give him pointers when you ride into town. Stop by the Needle and Dart and get that young man some shirts." He handed her a folded sheet of pale-yellow stationary Rachel recognized as her mother's. "Instructions from your mother to Marie Anjou."

Rachel curtsied again and ran back to Sigfried, who was still stretched out on the grass. He reached up, handing her five stoppered crystal vials. "Here. For you. Your mum helped me make them. I shared some elf-herbs with her."

Four of the vials had pictures of chameleons on the label; the fifth had a spider—four vials of chameleon elixir and one of spider-climb. She smiled and slipped them into her neck pouch with the oval calling card her father had just given her.

"Thank you."

The clip-clop of hooves sounded on the gravel. Rachel peered through the bushes to see the Duke of Caledon riding upon his highland pony, Gaoth. Laurel and her girlfriends struck pretty poses as they watched him arrive. He and the Adonis-look-alike, Avalon, were second cousins, but they looked more like brothers. They were both tremendously handsome with the same dark wavy hair and fierce blue eyes; but where Avalon had a ready smile and boyish good looks, Caledon was grim and weather-beaten. He wore an old leather coat and looked as if he had just come from tromping over the highlands on a particularly dreary day. One thing, however, gave the newcomer an immense advantage over his second cousin in the esteem of the young ladies. Of the Dukes of the Wise, only Magnus Ridel was unmarried.

"Who's that?" asked Sigfried.

Rachel whispered, "That's Magnus Ridel, Duke of Caledon."

Sigfried yawned.

Rachel leaned toward him. "Magnus's the one who's fought a dragon."

Sigfried sat up, more interested.

"Magnus's past is terribly tragic," Rachel continued, "which makes him romantic in the eyes of the unmarried young ladies, particularly Lady Olivia—the pretty one in the dark green riding habit. As a child, he was a distant cousin of the Duke of Caledon, but when Magnus was fifteen, the entire clan, nineteen members of his direct family, was slaughtered by the Terrible Five. Magnus was away at Roanoke, so he lived—and became duke at age fifteen.

"Two years later, his best friend, my Uncle Emrys, died right before Magnus's eyes while fighting Morgana La Fay. Later, Magnus married his childhood sweetheart, Lilidh Campbell. They had two little children.

Only..." Rachel's voice grew heavy with sorrow, "when the boy was four and the girl was two, the wife and both children were murdered."

"Wow," Sigfried blurted out in all sincerity. "Sucks to be him."

The postman came flying down the drive on his official Royal Mail bristleless. His post-box-red traveler had large panniers filled with letters and packages. Rachel stepped from behind the topiary and waved. He rewarded her by holding up a blue envelope. Rachel ran over and accepted it with a curtsy. She turned it over, curious, and then fumbled to open it with trembling fingers. *It was from Vladimir.*

The envelope contained a card with a picturesque Bavarian alp with a young woman standing amidst edelweiss. Inside, written in an elegant hand, it read:

> *Dear Miss Griffin,*
> *No thanks are necessary.*
> *It is an honor to defend someone so worthy of the effort.*
> *V. B.*

So worthy of the effort. Rachel felt suddenly breathless.

"Gaius," she cried with delight over the black bracelet. Her shivers of joy felt less disloyal if she shared her enthusiasm with him. "Vlad sent me a card. Isn't that nice?"

"That's not all he sent." Hearing Gaius's casual drawl sent a warm happiness through her. "Have you seen his list yet?"

"No, looking now." Rachel peeked into the envelope, pulling out a second folded page.

"Got to go. Chicks arriving. Over ninety-six thousand. Talk to you later!"

Ninety-six thousand? She knew Gaius lived on a commercial farm, and he had used that number before; but ninety-six thousand baby chicks was an exaggeration, *wasn't it?*

She unfolded the page Von Dread had included. The neatly typed sheet read:

```
    Please find below the results of my promised
    inquiry into the Morthbrood:

    1) You are correct; the Morthbrood are
       gathering.
```

> 2) They believe Morgana Le Fay is alive but
>   in some altered state or other dimension.
>
> 3) Baba Yaga of the Terrible Five was the
>   mother of Morgana Le Fay.
>
> 4) Their stated purpose is revenge, perhaps
>   for Baba Yaga's death?
>
>   PS: My father has approved this information
> to be shared with your father.

Rachel's jaw dropped. *Baba Yaga was Morgana's mother? Who was her father?*

The peers were heading into the house. She ran after them, calling, "Father! Father!" When he did not turn, she shouted, "Daddy!"

The Duke of Devon paused, frowning faintly. "I need to go, Rachel."

She shoved the paper at him. "You might want to discuss this."

He looked down at it, his frown deepening when he saw the Bavarian letterhead.

"What's this?" His pupils widened ever so slightly as he read the list and then the note at the bottom. "Where did you get this? From Sandra?"

"No! Vladimir sent it to *me*."

Ambrose Griffin looked up with his keen, searching gaze. "Why did he send it to *you?*"

Rachel allowed herself the luxury of putting her hands on her hips, puffing up her cheeks, and giving an exasperated sigh out of one side of her mouth. "Because I *asked* him for it."

"Good work." Her father nodded at her. He folded the page, slipped it into his pocket, and followed the others inside.

Rachel raced back to Siggy. "Come on! You can see for yourself what they discuss!"

They tried the music room, but the chamber with the Round Table was warded and stopped Sigfried's amulet. It occurred to Rachel that the ceiling of that chamber might not have been specifically warded. They ran through the house to the Dryads' Drawing Room, a green and silver chamber with furniture carved to resemble vines and leaves. It was a room that strongly reminded Rachel of her grandmother, who had once spoke to her here at length, but it was also directly above the Round Table. As Rachel had suspected, Siggy's amulet could look through the floor into the room below.

Rachel sat cross-legged on the wide sofa and gazed at her calling card. She could see the great table with its alternating triangular slats of green and white radiating out from the center like spokes of a wheel. It looked much like the reproduction that hung in the Grand Temple at Winchester, except it included no painting of an Arthur that distinctly resembled Henry VIII. Also, instead of a Tudor rose, white and red dragons graced the center.

The table was quite large. The eight peers and the Ravenmaster had gathered on the west side. The men held glasses of port, except for the Duke of Tara, who sat quietly snoring. Walter Pandoff-Sap, the Duke of Trevena, an elegant white-haired man who was the highest-ranking member of the table, leaned over to push on the snoring duke's arm, but Magnus Ridel waved his finger to stop him.

"Let the man sleep, Walter. He's too old to listen to us bicker. If we vote, we wake 'im."

"And what are we bickering about today?" asked the dashing Harry Ravenwood, the Duke of Avalon, as he clipped the tip of his cigar. He leaned back and smiled cheerfully at the others.

"Taxes," replied Bedwyn Glyndwr, the Duke of Caerleon, taking off his rumpled hat and hanging it on a hat rack. "What else do we ever discuss?"

Locksley Dymoke, the Duke of Sherwood, groaned. He was a dapperly dressed gentleman with a round face and a kindly smile. "No more taxes. Our people pay too many taxes. They pay mundane taxes and then, on top of that, they pay our taxes."

"His Majesty's Royal Watch is woefully unfit to meet the current need," growled Magnus, the Lord of the Watch. He had a light Scottish accent that grew heavier if he stopped paying attention. "What with all these strange new creatures and occurrences. We need men, and we need gear. We have money for neither."

"We don't need to expand the Watch," said Rachel's father. "Let your people call the Wisecraft for these problems."

The Scotsman slowly raised one eyebrow and crossed his arms. "Spoken by the man who nabbed three of my Watchmen not four days ago."

The left corner of Ambrose's mouth quirked upwards. He spread his hands. "You have me there, Magnus. The Wisecraft is spread mighty thin as well."

Avalon lit his cigar, his blue eyes blazing. "Ambrose, if the Wisecraft would help more, we could raise taxes. Can't you obscure more of our people from the mundane tax collectors? Why should they be paying for Unwary nonsense? If they could pay less to London, they could pay more for the Watch. And for the Wisecraft."

The Duke of Trevena shook his head ponderously. "We are still Englishmen, are we not? We must support king and country."

Rachel's father replied, "The obscurers can remove a town like Gryphon-on-Dart from the Unwary tax rolls, but they can't do anything with larger cities, where the Wise and Unwary mingle together."

"You could," Avalon countered, "if the obscurers put more effort into the Unwary side of things—computers and such."

"Before we continue our eternal bickering about taxes,"—the Ravenmaster poured himself another glass of port—"could we hear Devon's report on the recent troubles?"

They all looked to Rachel's father, who nodded mildly. "Last night, we brought in some Morthbrood who were about to sacrifice a local Unwary couple. They claimed they were trying to reach Morgana La Fay, who may still be alive."

There came a collective gasp.

Ambrose continued, "Their leader was Roger Walker, a member of the board of the APS, the Anti-Poltergeist Society. Used to be a respected organization, the APS, but they brought in a marketing expert. Now they're a glitzy operation, pushing their services on people who don't want them. There're a couple of lawsuits pending. We used Walker's arrest as an excuse to raid their Exeter offices this morning—something we've wanted to do for some time. Unfortunately, we found nothing of note. They may have been on notice.

"They did have a cauldron and supplies for brewing a virulent poison," he continued. "Most likely, this is the cauldron my daughter overheard them mention. We hope. We're still following up on other leads. Maybe one will provide us with the whereabouts of Dr. Mordeau. We've confirmed the local Morthbrood, at least, are working for her. Sadly, one of the prisoners was able to smuggle out a message before we secured him; she may have bolted."

"Did we intercept the message?" asked Avalon.

Rachel's father nodded. "Yes. *Drop the penny.* And, no. We have no idea."

"Drop the penny?" murmured Sigfried. "Obviously, a codeword for something big they intend to drop. An asteroid or a nuke."

"No one should drop pennies," Lucky objected. "It's disrespectful to wealth!"

In the chamber, Rachel's father was speaking again, "We also were able to confirm that it was the Morthbrood who set barghests against myself and two other Agents back in February. Among other things, apparently, the barghests were placed there to delay the Agents stationed on the Roanoke Academy campus from reaching New York City when Mordeau made her move."

"How did you confirm it was them?" Harry Ravenwood asked, curious.

Ambrose Griffin smirked ever so slightly. "We found an invoice for ninety-nine barghests and ninety-nine wraiths. They paid a pretty penny for them. They were not at all pleased that we demolished the pack."

"Invoice?" Trevena cried in astonishment. "From whom can you purchase barghests?"

The smile left Ambrose's lips. "Imelda Stark."

The soft sound of indrawn breath sounded throughout the chamber.

Magnus grunted grimly, "Claudius Stark's widow."

"Stark is not dead," Ambrose replied mildly. "He was merely sent away. But yes, Imelda is his wife, and she is apparently continuing his work and, most likely, working with the daughter of Stark's old partner —Dr. Melusine Mordeau."

"How's the Mordeau business going?" asked Locksley Dymoke. "Have you informed the public?"

Ambrose ran a hand over his face, covering any expression of frustration. "We would have announced it at the time, had it been up to me, but I don't set policy. The news has slowly leaked out. We briefed the dean and the proctors at Roanoke Academy immediately, of course, as that may be the Morthbrood's target. We're concerned they may be planning to disrupt the celebrations for the twenty-fifth anniversary of the Battle of Roanoke, which will take place on May Day."

"Any chance of canceling the event?" asked Locksley Dymoke.

Ambrose shook his head. "Too many bigwigs intending to attend. The plan is to make sure no unwanteds get in. Unfortunately, we're using so much of our forces guarding the school that we hardly have anyone left to hunt down Mordeau. Now that Roanoke's on holiday, Bridges has almost all our people on that case. We've quadrupled the guards on Zukov and Faust. They're the last major lieutenants of the Terrible Five still alive. If the Morthbrood try another jailbreak, this time, we'll be ready."

The door opened, and Molly and Polly arrived, dressed in their formal black and white parlor maid uniforms, carrying plates of sandwiches and coffee. To the dismay of Rachel, who was hanging on every word, the group paused for a short break.

"I'm bored." Sigfried jumped to his feet. "I want to meet my pony."

Chapter Thirty-One:
Needle and Dart

"You can open your eyes, Smith," Peter announced as he paraded Cummerbund before the flabbergasted younger boy.

Rachel had told Sigfried repeatedly that the family would give him a horse, but, judging by his astonishment, he had not believed her. Cummerbund was a bay pony with a long coarse mane that fell over his eyes. Rachel loved Bund, but she feared he was already too short for Siggy. Still, Bund would not bolt or buck. She did hope Siggy understood that, even though the pony was now his, he could not feed it to Lucky when he outgrew it.

Peter, Laurel, and their friends clapped as Siggy took the pony's reins. They crowded around, giving him advice about care and riding. While they talked, Rachel ran into the barn, grabbed a halter, and headed for the pony paddock where Widdershins grazed. Arriving, she found, to her dismay, that, yet again, her lovely little Shetland pony was filthy from head to hoof. Mud caked his legs, his tail, his back, even his mane.

"Oh, no! Widdershins!" Rachel cried. "Why are you always covered with mud?"

"'Tis the luck of the draw." Lady Xenia leaned against the fence, watching the moor ponies. She was a sweet young woman, blonde and aristocratic. She was not as astonishingly beautiful as many of the girls at school, but pretty in an airy way that seemed to go well with horses, whether she was in the stable cleaning a hoof or leading a high stepper into a show ring.

"Some horses love mud; some don't," Neens continued. "My Featherstar is fastidious. Other horses come in coated with mud, and he has merely a splash on one shin, but Peril's Rolling Thunder is like your little fellow. Always in the mud. Always."

"I don't mind washing and currying him." Rachel put the halter around the muddy pony and began leading him toward the stables. Neens fell in beside her. "I just feel sorry for Oliver. He has to do it when I'm not home."

"Ah, Oliver." Neens gave an exaggerated sigh. "He's so cute. When I want to annoy my parents, I tell them I'm planning to run away with Oliver the Stable Boy."

"Do you want to run away with Oliver?" Rachel asked, interested.

Xenia wilted like a bouquet left in the sun. "Oh, Rachel, you know the answer to that. Some people wear their hearts on their sleeves. I wish I could be that subtle. Mine is plastered across my forehead, along with an L for Loser."

Rachel did know. As far back as she could remember, Neens had been in love with Peter; however, Peter saw her as an amusing younger child, taking no real notice of her. Rachel gave her a sympathetic look. She understood Neens's plight much better than she had previously.

"Have you given thought to what you want when you outgrow your pony?" asked Neens.

Rachel felt faintly pleased that the older girl assumed she would grow. She nodded. "I wanted a Friesian, but I don't think I'll get tall enough. Looks like I'll be short like Mummy."

"Have you considered breeding the Friesians with the moor ponies?"

"I have," Rachel replied. "Or rather, at one point I looked into breeding the Friesians with Arabians—such beautiful horses—but crosses already exist, and they don't have the long, wavy manes that make the Friesians so extraordinary."

"What about applying Lloyd, Lord Fairweather's breeding techniques to keep the mane?"

"I hadn't thought of that," Rachel admitted. "I guess I could bring that up with Father."

Lady Xenia gave her a sunny smile and laid a comforting hand on Rachel's arm. "Don't worry. I'll have a word with him."

"Hey, look at me!" Sigfried sat atop his pony with possibly the worst form Rachel had ever seen. He pointed at himself and Bund. "Behold, I'm riding a steed! Like Galahad!"

"Like a whole bunch of Galahads!" cried Lucky, who was curled around him.

"Now all I need is a suit of armor. I already have a trusty sword." He pulled out his Bowie knife and swung it around. Apparently, he and her mother had finished their alchemical work on the blade, as it was now black in color. "Look at how gigantic my noble steed is. We never saw anything bigger than a dog or a rat at the orphanage."

Lucky announced, peering over his shoulder, "Some rats were bigger than the dogs."

"This pony is huge," continued Sigfried. "It's too huge to eat."

Lucky eyed the bay pony. "I could make a go of it."

"Not my steed! He's off limits, even for you, Luckerator Eight-Fifty-Two." Sigfried pointed toward the north. "Who's that?"

A horse raced across the moors. Or rather, it covered ground at the speed of a racing horse, but instead of running, it bounded as lightly as a deer, covering thirty feet at a time. The rider was a pretty young man with dark curly hair dressed in a green velvet jacket with long tails, beige suede britches, and high black boots. As it approached the moat, the steed did not so much as slow down. Instead, it leapt, sailed a hundred and fifty feet through the air, and landed gracefully on the other side.

Siggy's jaw dropped. "Even I know horses can't do that."

"That's a fairy horse," Rachel explained, smiling. "That's Sir Calidor Moth, from Underhill. He's the fairy knight."

They watched Sir Calidor, with his upswept brow and his pointed ears, as he rode toward the manor house. The elfin gentleman gave them a cheerful wave and sped on to the Round Table meeting.

"Where are we going now?" Siggy asked. "My war charger is eager for battle."

They had begun to ride. The usually docile Cummerbund kept pulling ahead. He even broke into a trot, leaving Rachel and Widdershins behind. Rachel's Shetland pony was significantly smaller than Sigfried's moor pony.

"Pull on the reins to slow down," called Rachel.

Sigfried pulled and kept pulling. Cummerbund slowed, then began to walk backward.

"No! Tug and then let up on the reins. He thinks you're telling him to keep going."

"How fast can he go backward?" asked Sigfried. "A good trot? A gallop?"

"I... doubt it." Rachel watched with concern as he continued to back up.

Peter came alongside Sigfried, took his reins, stopped Bund, and handed the reins back, showing him again how to hold them. Then, with a nod, he and his friends rode ahead.

"As to where we are going, we're heading to the Needle and Dart, so you can be fitted for new shirts," said Rachel, urging her pony to catch up. "It's a shame Mummy cannot come. I know she hates these formal affairs. She feels out of place among all the elegant, to-the-manner-born ladies, but as hostess, she couldn't get away. She did give us a letter for our seamstress."

"Will it hurt?" asked Siggy.

Rachel considered the question seriously. "Not physically. I have never known Marie Anjou to jab anyone with a pin, but it is excruciatingly boring."

"Sorry to hear that, boss," Lucky hung his head. "It's been good knowing you."

"Death by boredom," Sigfried frowned, dissatisfied. "Figured that's how I'd go. I don't get a cool death like dismemberment or tar and feathering or defenestrating."

"Or decapitation," added Lucky.

"Or dunked in boiling oil," said Siggy.

"Or broken on a wheel."

"Or eaten by rats."

"Or cats."

"Or bats," Sigfried nodded. "Eaten by bats would be a much better way to go than death by boredom."

Rachel sighed. Then, she sighed again as the usually plodding Cummerbund broke into a canter, nearly dumping Sigfried as she was left far behind.

By an unspoken agreement, the Griffin family only used the walking glass in the gatehouse when going to and from Exeter or London or some distant place. The rest of the time, they traveled to or from town via the road that ran from the manor to the town, winding its way among their tenant farms. They passed the farms of the Banks, whose children got into all sorts of scrapes; Farmer Hoggett, who went everywhere with his pig; the Rawlins, who had enchanted a four-poster bed to fly like an umbrella platform; the Claytons, who provided evergreen wreaths each year for Gryphon Park's Yule decorations and whose sons would line up by the fence to whistle at Laurel when she walked or rode by; and Farmer Sorenson, the grandson of the late Old Farmer Sorenson, who was young and unmarried and of great interest to the local girls.

Greyface Dartmoor sheep, with their long floppy wool and their black noses, grazed these fields. Rachel felt their expressive faces looked more like plush dolls than like real animals. Farmer Sorenson kept a few Hebridean sheep: the eerie beasts were entirely black with four horns, two that stuck up and two that curled downward. On the next farm, the Claytons kept Cotswold Sheep the color of hot chocolate with milk, a breed known for being particularly friendly. Rachel, who quite liked sheep—even before her boyfriend had joined their ranks, back in September, when Dread ended their duel by turning him into a... ram—waved to them as they rode by.

The farmhouses and most of the buildings in town were stone with thatched roofs. Squirrels or birds or even foxes made of straw perched at the edges of the roof's ridge, testaments to the thatchers' skills. Rachel loved the way these gray and weathered houses seemed to blend into the surrounding countryside as if they were almost part of the moors themselves.

The only buildings in Gryphon-on-Dart with tiled roofs were the stores and businesses on the town square, though the Gryphon's Nest pub was thatched. The pub stood at one end of the square, which was in truth more of a rectangle, and the Assembly Hall capped the other end. The green center of the square had a maypole, a fountain, and several picnic tables sitting beneath large shade trees, currently bare but with new buds sprouting.

The Needle and Dart was located on the square, on Newbridge Street, next to the library. The shop's proprietor, Marie Anjou, was a distant relative of the Griffins by marriage. The seventh duke—whose wife had been drowned by the river Dart—had chosen for his second wife a young Frenchwoman named Colette Anjou. It was she who had requested the lavender farm. When the French Revolution broke out, Colette's fleeing relatives had come to Gryphon Park, including an ancestor of Marie Anjou. Rachel's family was descended from the drowned wife, but there was a branch of the family descended from Colette. Were something to happen to her father and Peter, that branch would inherit the dukedom.

The shop had pretty gowns displayed on dress forms in the wide plate windows. Bolts of cloth lined the walls, along with ribbons and bobbins of thread. There were cutting tables, black and gold sewing machines that sewed on their own, and a wide oval mirror for fittings.

Marie Anjou was a stylish woman with an aquiline nose and her hair cut in a short dark bob. She stood at a cutting table, pins in her mouth and a measuring tape in her hand. As they entered, she put these things aside and rushed to greet them. Rachel handed her the duchess's note and then waited patiently while Marie conjured shirts directly onto Sigfried's naked chest. She conjured them tacked together, so when she decided that one was the right size, she merely pulled out the tacked thread, and she had a pattern, perfect for measuring the real cloth. Sigfried grumbled tremendously about the tedium of being sized, until he found out that Rachel's mother was paying for the shirts. Then he shut up and endured the process without a single complaint.

Afterward, they went to the library, to the sweet shop, and finally to the Gryphon's Nest for shandies and ginger beer. Siggy was astonished that the establishment allowed them entry. Apparently, Unwary pubs had age restrictions. Rachel explained to him that, here in Gryphon-on-Dart, the pub was a central gathering place that housed, among other things, the community talking and walking glass. Everybody knew everybody here, and the pubkeepers would never allow any local youngsters to come to harm. Besides, they would not have the gall to bar the door to the Duke's daughter.

Sigfried did quite well at darts, but Rachel could not hit the bullseye. She was lucky if she hit the board. She could see, with the spatial sense she used for flying, exactly how the dart needed to arc to hit the target, but she did not have the muscle control necessary. Sigfried, who hit the bullseye three out of four times, laughed at her.

"You suck at darts," he observed without rancor. "Are you good at any games?"

"One." Rachel glanced around the charmingly appointed pub with its dark wood and leather. Several locals were drinking stout or Doom Bar. They gave her a warm smile. Two were playing pool with a loud stranger who was bragging about his river rafting exploits on the Dart. Rachel gave his opponents a sympathetic smile.

"So that stuff your father was telling the geezers and not-knights," asked Sigfried as they sat down with their drinks, "that was related to last night, right?"

Rachel nodded. "Yes. I hope it leads them to Mordeau. That would be fantastic."

"And the person they wanted to call. Is that really Morgana La Fay, from King Arthur?"

"I'm afraid so. Rather sad, really—if Uncle Emrys died, and Morgana's not even dead."

"Who's Imeldtogehter Snark?"

"Imelda Stark? She's the widow of the Necromancer."

"The one they fight in *James Darling, Agent* issue seven?"

"I thought they didn't have *James Darling, Agent* in the Unwary world."

Siggy shrugged. "My roommate, Ian, collects them. I read some."

"Yes. That Necromancer. He must have taught his wife some of his art. Oh! I bet she's the one who is responsible for the wraith we fought in September! Mylene said that her father thought it was the work of the Necromancer," Rachel concluded. "She may have even made Dr. Mordeau's robe that had all those wraiths come out of it."

"Let 'er come," Siggy said confidently, tapping the top of his Bowie knife in its holder beneath his clothing. "I'm ready for 'em this time, thanks to your mum. Who's the Dream Thief?"

"You mean as in—" Rachel repeated exactly what they had heard the previous night, "—'*Belial removed the original leader. Azrael's servant damaged the new one; Crokel did a number on the Dream Thief. That leaves Smith. He's the greatest danger*'?"

"That's us, Lucks! The greatest danger!"

Rachel sighed, thinking, *Please don't let that go to his head. He's dangerous enough already.*

"They're afraid of burnination, Boss Five-Hundred-And-Two!" Lucky replied. "Or did you have a different code name?"

"That one'll do, until next time words come out of our mouths," replied Siggy.

The boy and the dragon nodded, acknowledging their shared understanding.

"Azrael's servant is probably Remus Starkadder," said Rachel. "We know he had made a deal with the demon—and the leader he damaged —" She frowned. *Did even the* villains *think Nastasia was in charge?* "—would be the princess."

"The princess was damaged?" Siggy cocked his head sideways.

"Remember when Remus Starkadder burned her with phantom flames? When she was under Drake Hall?" When he continued to look blank, she added, "You saw it with your—" she cut off speaking and tapped her chest.

"Oh, right! The blighter we beamed with the apple core."

"Apparently, that fire burns your soul. It harmed Nastasia, made her... more rigid."

"You mean it's not her fault she's so horrid?" Siggy looked skeptical. He crossed his arms belligerently. "I hope you aren't expecting me to weep for her. A real princess would know you can't fire a knight."

Rachel smothered a sigh. She did not want to get involved in the spat between Nastasia and Sigfried. She continued. "Belial, I recognize. That's the demon Amber took out, so whoever he removed must have been someone from before her time. Maybe there was an earlier attempt to gather Keybearers that failed?"

Over at the pool table, the out-of-towner jostled old Mr. Hodgeson's elbow as he prepared to take his shot. It was not clear if the act was on purpose or by accident, but Rachel did not like the expression on the man's face. The ball went wild, and Mr. Hodgeson scratched, the cue ball thumping as it fell into a side pocket.

"And the Dream Thief?" asked Sigfried.

"I've heard that term before...." Rachel recalled the little goat-legged urisk who had approached Zoë Forrest during the masquerade ball. A look of eerie horror had crossed Zoë's face when the term had been mentioned. Rachel did not know who Crokel was, but "did a number on" correlated uncomfortably with the scars on Zoë's body that had so frightened Joy.

"Zoë's the Dream Thief," she concluded slowly.

"She can steal dreams?" Siggy's eyes grew wide. "I thought she just walked in them!"

"It's just a guess." Yet Rachel felt certain. "Zoë must be another Keybearer."

Over by the pool table, the newcomer crowed loudly upon winning his game. Rachel's eyes narrowed at his boorish behavior. A farmer caught her eye, giving her a beseeching look.

"Hold a moment while I put that impertinent churl in his place," she said crisply.

Rachel put her hands behind her back and put on her sweetest simper. She wandered up to the pool table, batting her eyelashes. "Might I perchance be allowed to play?"

"Bug off, kid," said the loudmouth. He made shooing gestures. "Go."

Rachel straightened her back and raised a single eyebrow, adopting an imperious tone she would never otherwise use. "I want to play."

"Who is this?" the stranger asked the locals.

The farmer hissed in a loud whisper, "Better let her play. That's our duke's daughter."

"Oh, very well," the out-of-towner shrugged. "One game." He leaned toward her in a patronizing manner. "Do you know how to use a pool cue?"

"I believe I do." Rachel picked her usual cue from the wall. It was shorter than the others.

Over by the bar, Mr. Mather called to Mr. Downe, "If she beats him, I'll buy you a beer."

Mr. Downe replied, "If he beats her, I'll buy you a beer."

The out-of-towner laughed. "If she beats me, I'll buy all of you a round of beers."

Suddenly, the whole pub was paying attention. Many locals struggled to conceal smirks.

The stranger made three shots and then missed and turned the table over to Rachel. She stood gazing at the positions of the colored balls for what must have seemed to her opponent to be an uncomfortably long time. Pool was easier than snooker, her favorite cue sport. One did not have to hit the balls in ascending numeric order in pool, though she planned how to do so nonetheless. It paid to stay in shape. Possible motions of balls and the positions of the related ghost balls and tangent angles flowed through her mind's eye until she could visualize the entire game.

She picked up her cue. In a calm, clear voice, she called each shot before playing it. To make it more interesting for herself, she removed the balls from the table in ascending order, where possible. She utilized the imaginary ghost balls so as to line up tangent angle shots that put her cue ball exactly where she wanted it to prep the following shot. She was rather pleased when she hit the nine ball with just enough left spin to pull off an elegant plant shot and set up a very easy straight shot to follow. She even threw in a jump shot. In a very short time, she had won, leaving the stranger gaping and buying a round for the locals.

With a wink, she departed the pub with Sigfried and Lucky.

As they mounted their ponies—Sigfried did surprisingly well for his second time—he asked with admiration, "Have you hustled billiards before?"

"That was pool but yes. Loads of times. It makes the locals happy."

"You're very good."

Rachel chuckled. "Only compared to people who don't know what they're doing."

"How could you do that? Tell which hole the ball would go into?"

"Must be magic," said Lucky. "After all, she's a sorceress."

"Practice," she smiled. "My grandfather taught me to play snooker. The game was invented by his regiment, a Devonshire regiment, when they were stationed in India. He was not commissioned at the time, but when the officers came back on leave, they showed him the new game, and Grandfather loved it. He started me on it when I was four. Of course, all I did then was bump balls around. Couldn't even reach the table without standing on a box. At age six, I started trying harder—I wanted to impress him—and, suddenly, something happened."

"What happened?" asked Siggy. "Frogs? Snakes? Earthquakes? Did it involve food? Lucky would want to know." Lucky nodded in eager agreement.

"Sorry, no food," Rachel replied. "Something happened in my mind. I realized I could 'remember' where the balls would go. Ghost balls, tangent angles, stop, draw, follow, and stun shots. They're all predictable, so I could 'remember' how each one would play out." She paused and then added, "I realize now it's due to physics. Motion vectors and all that."

Her memory had not been enough to make her actually good at the game; however, the winter she was eleven—after her grandfather had died but before Vroomie—she had tackled the topic seriously. She had spent hours attempting to reproduce a number of famous shots, and she had mastered some but still had much to learn. For instance, she could not reproduce Efren Reyes' Z shot, the most famous single shot in the history of pool. Either she failed to get the ball all the way into the pocket, or she hit it with the force necessary to make the pocket and then scratched. She had mastered adding enough left spin to enable the wide angle needed to make the Z-shaped bounce reach the far end of the table, and she had figured out where she needed to strike the rail on the smaller English tables to achieve the correct angle, but she just could not yet manage the mix of speed and control needed to pull it off.

Of course, Efren Reyes had performed his shot in the thirteenth tie-breaking game of a race to twelve. Rachel had no illusions that she would play nearly so well under such pressure.

"Ooohhh!" Rachel straightened in her saddle, her eyes widening.

Suddenly, she understood the answer to a mystery that she had been wondering about since September. Mr. Chanson had exclaimed more than once over how unusual it was that she could fly so well when she had only been flying for two years, come the end of this month. Finally, she realized why. Calculating snooker and pool shots required the exact same motion vectors as flying. To impress her Grandfather, she had learned how to apply her perfect memory to recalling such vectors years before she picked up her first bristleless.

When she finally started flying, all she had had to do was apply this same mental process to the motion of the broom.

Cummerbund pulled ahead again. Siggy called back over his shoulder, "We had a pool table at the orphanage. A really old one. When Lucky was small, he used to hide in a pocket and eat any balls we sent into it. It was fun for him, but the nuns didn't replace the balls. Eventually, we ended up with only six. He also ate the cue ball one day when someone scratched. So we designated the five as the cue ball, because it was orange."

"Why orange?" asked Rachel, urging Widdershins into a trot in an effort to catch up.

"It stood out. We could tell it from the rest."

"But I threw one back up again," said Lucky, "so there were seven."

"Oh, that's right," Siggy nodded, "but it was pockmarked and rolled kind of funny."

Rachel covered her mouth, struggling not to burst out laughing. Bund broke into a canter, leaving her behind. As they passed the Sorensen farm, they saw Laurel and her friends by the fence chatting with the handsome young farmer.

Lady Olivia called out to Sigfried as he passed, "Stop trying to hold on with your heels. Your pony thinks you're kicking him to get him to speed up."

Oh! Poor Bund! No wonder he kept breaking into a canter! Rachel caught up with Sigfried, who was now going backward again. She reviewed for him both stopping and correct leg and foot positions. He was resistant to her guidance at first, but after a bit, he caught on. His seat improved considerably, and they rode their steeds back to Gryphon Park.

As they approached the barn, they came up alongside Magnus Ridel, who was walking his own pony back to the stables. Why he was bringing it back at this time, Rachel had no idea, but she enjoyed watching his pony. Highland ponies always looked to her as if they had been painted in watercolors. His stallion was a bay dun, a shade darker than buckskin but lighter than any other bay Rachel knew of, with black mane, tail, and legs, but its face and parts of its neck looked as if someone had spread a black paint wash over the reddish-tan. As usual, the sturdy steed wore a saddle blanket and a two-handled surcingle instead of a saddle.

"Duke, show us some tricks!" called Peril, from where he was leaning against the fence to the Friesian paddock.

"That's right," called Lord John. "Let's see a flip!"

"A scissor," cried Lord Edmond. "Or vault off the flank!"

"Och, off with ye lot," Magnus replied mildly, shooing them away.

Rachel slipped off her pony and walked beside him.

"Hallo, your grace," she said cheerfully.

"Squirt," Magnus acknowledged her with a curt nod. Then, he reached over and tousled her hair. "Ye've grown a wee bit."

"I work at it regularly," Rachel replied studiously.

"See ye keep it up." He gave a nod of approval and turned to look over Sigfried, who was still mounted. "Aye, is this the famous boy, then?"

Atop Cummerbund, Siggy drew himself up. "Sigfried Smith the Dragonslayer."

The Duke of Caledon waited as Sigfried slid awkwardly from his pony. Once the boy's feet were on the ground, he stepped forward and shook Sigfried's hand.

"Aye, we dragon fighters should stick together."

"Can you really do tricks on a horse?" asked Sigfried.

"Aye, that I can."

"Can you show us?'

The duke grunted. "If I must."

Magnus stood next to his highland pony and grasped a handle of his surcingle. Without effort, he straightened his arm and extended his legs until his body was perpendicular to his arm above the height of his mount. Then he swung his body over the top of his pony and landed lightly on the other side, his free arm raised. Rachel had seen him perform vaulting tricks all her life, but Sigfried looked severely impressed with the duke's arm strength.

The duke handed Gaoth's bridle to Oliver, who led the pony toward the barn, and turned to walk back toward the manor. Then he paused and spoke to Sigfried.

"I hear ye were the man of the hour, laddie. Saved a boy, did ye?"

Siggy squirmed. To Rachel's shock, under the discerning gaze of the Lord of the Watch, he broke and told the truth. "Rachel saved him. I just saved Rachel."

"Truly?" Magnus looked from Sigfried to Rachel. "That's not how I heard it."

Rachel swallowed, her mouth suddenly dry. "We didn't tell anyone."

"And why would that be now?"

"First, Sigfried needed help, so there was no time to explain. After that," Rachel sighed, "he was already being thanked. It seemed petty to claim credit."

"You saved the boy," Magnus gazed at her keenly. "You went into the river?"

Rachel nodded.

"And what would ha' happened if the Dragonslayer here had not saved ye?"

Rachel wanted to squirm, but she did not. She raised her chin with just a touch of defiance. "The *boy* would have lived."

Magnus Ridel stared at her for a long time. She met his gaze. It was tremendously difficult, but she refused to look away. They stared at each other eye to eye.

"Och." He nodded in approval. "Aye."

He turned away, heading toward the manor, but Rachel had recognized the look on his face as he grasped that she had risked her life to save a stranger's child. She had seen it on her grandfather's face the day she stood up to him, when she was three. Magnus was proud of her. More importantly, before this moment, she had been merely one of many children of whom he was fond. Now, suddenly, she was someone specific.

She had become important to the Lord of the Watch.

Chapter Thirty-Two:
The Fourteenth Birthday of Lady Rachel Jade Griffin

THE MORNING OF SATURDAY, THE THIRTIETH OF MARCH, DAWNED BRIGHT and clear. It was Rachel's birthday. Finally, she was fourteen!

It was going to be the best day of her life!

On the end table beside her bed sat brightly wrapped packages that had arrived from Astrid, Nastasia, Joy, and to her surprise, Zoë. Valerie had sent a card that played music, and there was even a birthday card from Vladimir featuring children in lederhosen marching in a parade. Recently received letters from Astrid and Nastasia, replies to her letters, lay beside them. There was also a package from her Great-Aunt Nimue containing a finely-crafted pair of silver and diamond earrings and, surprisingly, a short letter from Nimue's grandson, Blackie Moth. In it, he thanked her for the information she had sent to him about how to use the *turlu* cantrip on a lightning imp's javelin to create a tremendous force. Writing in the same brusque, clipped manner in which he spoke, her second-cousin let her know that her discovery had been the breakthrough he had needed for the success of his current project.

Included was a photo of Blackie in his Stetson, leaning grimly on his prototype rail-gun.

The previous week had passed quickly. The duchess had trimmed Rachel's hair so that it again just brushed her shoulders, and Marie Anjou had taken her measurements so as to begin on a new summer wardrobe, now that Rachel was a little taller. She and Sigfried had spent a portion of each day looking for the Heart of Dreams, to no avail. They had checked the stable and kennel, the boathouse, the hedge maze, the gatehouse, the grounds, the ruins on Gryphon Tor, and even the surrounding moors. They had tried the *endro* cantrip in case it revealed something the amulet could not, but nothing had come of it. Either the gem no longer shone, or the Heart of Dreams was not at Gryphon Park.

The rest of their days were filled with adventure. They visited different parts of Dartmoor, went to the butterfly preserve and to see the otters, rowed on the lake—everyone except for Sigfried staying dry—and climbed several tors. Some days, they even made it home by teatime.

Sigfried got into trouble with some giants. Rachel had to use all the spider climb elixir he had given her and three chameleons to get him out of it, but the ordeal had a silver lining. She had needed Gaius's help, and he had been able to spend a couple of hours with her, before he returned to the unending queue of chores his father had piled up for him. He did get time off the next day to accompany them to Merlin's Cave. There was nothing there of unusual significance; but both young men enjoyed the excursion, and Rachel was happy to be with them.

This morning, as she lay in bed beneath her pink canopy, she let her memories of the past year parade by, recalling the good and the bad that had occurred while she was thirteen. There was so much that was amazing and a good deal that was horrible. Rachel very much hoped that being fourteen would prove easier than being thirteen had been.

As she reviewed conversations from last fall, she noticed something she had missed the first time. She held up her arm with the black bracelet, waving it above her as she lay in bed in her white flannel Victorian nightgown.

"Gaius, do you have a moment?" she asked cheerfully.

There was something deliciously wicked about talking to a boy while she lay in bed in her nightgown, even if he was over thirty miles away. She luxuriated in it. It seemed like such a grown-up fourteen-year-old thing to do.

"Indeed, I do, birthday girl!" his voice spoke in her ear. He sounded quite cheerful "Welcome to your fourteenth year. Or... wait. You are fourteen, so it's your fifteenth year. Never mind that. Happy birthday!"

"Thank you very much, O' Best of Boyfriends." She grinned. "Um... I have a question."

"Fire away. I'm milking cows. By which I mean, I am attaching milking machine hoses to cow udders. Not particularly exciting but has to be done."

"They do that with a machine?" asked Rachel, not sure what to picture in her head.

"Everything can be done with a machine, me lovver, even printing food."

"You mean like writing on a cake?"

"Er... pay it no mind." He paused briefly to speak to a chicken. "Sorry, what were we saying?"

"Does your father mind that you are chatting with your girlfriend while you do your chores?"

"Um. I haven't actually told him."

"About the bracelet?"

"That I have a girlfriend."

"Oh." Rachel was quiet for a time. This news stung a bit.

"We don't talk about much that doesn't have to do with the farm and chores," Gaius said apologetically. "I had been planning to tell him when he asked about how school was going, but he hasn't asked yet."

"Oh! Okay," she said more cheerfully. Put that way, it seemed more understandable.

"What can I do for you, today?" Gaius asked gallantly.

"Oh, I just noticed: back at the beginning of the year, you mentioned, more than once, that, the previous year, someone had been helping your group with enchantments—and then, at least twice, you gave me an odd look as if you wondered if I might know something about this. It was Sandra, wasn't it? She was playing enchantments for you all to put into your wands."

"Yes, indeed. Only, I didn't know how open she had been with your family about her relationship with Vlad, so I didn't want to say too much."

"It makes sense now," Rachel said. She giggled. "I guess she was practicing for her new clandestine life as an undercover Agent. How did you meet her?"

"Sandra started hanging out with us my sophomore year. She brought Jenny with her."

"Oh, really! I had thought Vlad introduced Jenny to Sandra! If it went the other way, it makes a lot more sense that Sandra and Jenny had time to become very good friends." *And that Sandra had time to teach Jenny the family's secret techniques.*

"Hmm," mused Gaius, "they were in very different years and very different dorms, weren't they? I wonder how they met. Either way, they were friends when I came to school."

"How did Vlad's group come together?"

Rachel slipped out of bed and began getting dressed. Dressing while she spoke with her young man seemed even more decadent than lazing around in her nightgown. She blushed prettily as she imagined how embarrassed she would be if he knew. For her birthday, she chose a favorite dress: calf-length, green and black gingham with a Peter Pan collar, a panel of embroidered cream lace across the front, and a wide bow in the back. It was the perfect birthday dress.

Meanwhile, Gaius was saying, "Lucy joined this year. Jenny joined last year, and the year before that, Vlad snapped up Topher—the freshman with the perfect memory. I was his acquisition the year before that. When I joined, it was only Vlad, William, and Naomi—though, back then, Blackie might as well have been considered a member, too. William and Blackie grew up together, which I guess is sort of obvious since their dads run O.I."

Rachel picked up the photo of Blackie with his rail-gun and gazed at it. Sorrow gripped her as she recalled his memory loss. During the summer holidays the previous year, he had been investigating the area behind Roanoke Hall where vegetation barely grew and magic hardly worked—the results of some foolish experiment William and Vladimir performed their freshman year. When doing so, Blackie had learned a secret, Rachel did not know what, about the demon Moloch that the Raven thought too dangerous for any mortal to know. Jariel had tried to remove just that memory, but Blackie kept rediscovering the secret. Finally, the Guardian was forced to remove Blackie's entire memory.

Blackie never returned to Roanoke. He was now working at Ouroboros Industries. His scientific prowess remained intact. Last time Rachel had seen him, he had been part of a research and development team that was constructing a garlic-shooting rail-gun for the King of Transylvania—the project her letter had helped him complete. However, he had lost all emotional connection to family and friends. He had not recognized Rachel when they had met, nor did he recall that he had once been engaged to William Lock's now girlfriend, Naomi Coils. A small amount of good had come from this terrible turn of events; however, the umber substance that Amber had seen at O.I.—in which two demons and Juma O'Malley's mother were held prisoner—had been developed from the results of the experiments Blackie had performed on the area behind Roanoke Hall.

Rachel wondered how hard it had been on William, losing his lifelong friend. William Locke was so calm and collected; it was hard to remember he, too, could suffer pain and disappointment. Drawing a deep breath, she pushed the subject from her mind. She would not allow anything to steal her joy on her birthday.

"How did you come to be acquired by Vladimir?" she asked curiously.

"Are you sure you want to hear? 'Tis not a story that redounds to my glory."

"I want to know everything," Rachel replied gravely.

"Oh, that's right. You're Rachel Griffin. How silly of me." He chuckled. "Hold on, I'm going to shoot some milk into my cat's mouth before I hook up this cow."

This was followed by a few odd sounds and him speaking in a soft voice to, Rachel assumed, his feline.

"I didn't know you had a cat!" she said happily.

"In fact, I do. Her name is Mitten."

"Mitten? Not Mittens?"

"She has only one," Gaius explained. "Okay, so the first half of my freshman year, Vlad was away, preparing for and competing in the Winter Olympics. I had come to Roanoke an Unwary boy on an O.I. scholarship, and when I got to the Seven-Sided Room, I picked the wand because I thought you needed wands to do magic. What did I know?

"So I found myself a poor farm boy in a rich kids' dorm. It was not very comfortable, I can tell you. Both my dormmates and kids from the other dorms that did not like Drake kids—such as Dare—picked on me. Some older kids began mocking me, and what older kids do, younger kids copy, so my life was… less than pleasant, to say the least.

"One day toward the end of the winter, my tormentors went further than they had previously. They hung me Glepnired upside-down in the gym."

"Oh, no!" whispered Rachel.

Then, she wished she had not. Young men did not take kindly to being pitied, but she felt so bad as she pictured little Gaius, swinging by his legs from the gym ceiling. How adorable he must have been! Her heart went out to him.

"I was hanging there, contemplating my sorry state, when the door opened. This unknown tall boy strode in, who towered over my tormentors. He frowned at them, and they scattered like blown leaves; some of them actually shrieked. Only I had seen him before—in newspapers. He was the freaking Prince of Bavaria. The Olympic hero!"

Rachel burst out laughing.

"I mean," Gaius said, "it had only been two weeks since he had taken the gold in speed skating and skiing. And he had swept the previous Summer Olympics, with golds in fencing and septathlon, silvers in swimming and shooting, and a bronze in fulgurating. Everyone—magic and mundane—knew who he was."

Rachel noted that her boyfriend did not say Wise and Unwary, as she and her family would. She wondered if he found the terms insulting.

Gaius continued, "I thought, 'Oh, no. I'm in for it now!' I'd heard stories about his temper. He had a terrible temper back then—not like now. But he looked up at me and said," Gaius dropped his voice. "'I suppose you would like to come down.' And I said, 'Yes, please,' and he replied, 'My pleasure,' and got me down.

"Then, he turned on my tormentors and said, 'This was not acceptable.' They were backed into a corner, trembling, and Vlad asked, 'Which one of you cast the cantrip on this young man?'

"One of them confessed. Vlad blasted him with a cantrip, throwing him into the air, and then Glepnired him—so that he hung them for a bit. Eventually, Vlad let the poor bloke down and stated, 'Let that be a lesson to you. Those who abuse their power shall be abused.'"

"He sent them away. Then he turned to me and said, 'They shall not bother you again.' I was skeptical at first, but he was as good as his word. He took me under his wing, taught me to duel, and I never looked back."

"That's a lovely story," said Rachel, delighted. "Thank you for telling me. I must say, I am proud of both of you. Hearing this story is the most wonderful of birthday presents. When added to you finding my missing hexagonal room, it makes you a superb giver of gifts."

"You are most welcome. I aim to please," Gaius drawled charmingly. After a moment, he added more seriously. "By the way, I've been thinking about what you said about Percy Cornelius Taylor—about how even though he's a ghost, he seems like a real person, not just an echo. Not sure what to make of it. Maybe some people can stay around for a while without their bodies. But I think they dissolve eventually. Didn't you tell me that after you answered the question that had been worrying him, Old Thom dissolved?"

"What? No!" Rachel cried. "I said that it grew too bright for me to see. But I don't think he stopped existing. I think he went somewhere!"

"Where?" demanded Gaius. "Why would you think that?"

"I... don't know. But when Amber killed the Heer, I could see the ghost of a Dutchman, probably John Colman—he was the one whose ghost was said to have been part of the Heer. A beam of light came down from above. When I looked up, I could see what looked like a hole in the clouds, and some other Dutchmen—friends of his, I assume—waving and beckoning for him to come. Why would they be there if the light was not taking him somewhere? It was very similar to the light that came when Old Thom disappeared."

"You didn't tell me about this." Gaius sounded rather wry.

"Oh. I didn't, did I? I am sorry! That evening was followed so quickly by the attack of the barghests and all. There never seemed to be a good time to get back to it."

"Hmm. Yeah, I guess that makes sense," Gaius admitted, adding with his characteristic, casual drawl, "but it does make me wonder how many other secrets are locked in that pretty little head of yours that you neglect to let out. It's always an adventure, speaking with you, Rachel Griffin. Certainly keeps a fellow on his toes."

Arriving at breakfast, Rachel let out a shriek of delight. Standing at the breakfast buffet, filling a plate with eggs and toast, was someone who had not been home the night before.

"Sandra!" Rachel barreled into her sister, hugging her.

Sandra's lovely laughter filled the room. "Hallo, *dongsaeng*, happy birthday!"

Rachel's older sister put her plate down and hugged her back. Sandra had shoulder-length mahogany hair and extremely dark eyes with a hint of a tilt, giving them an exotic look. She wore jeans and a sweatshirt, which, to Rachel, added to her sister's general exoticness. No one at Gryphon Park dressed in mundane clothes.

The two sisters sat together, filling each other in on what they had done since they had last seen each other in early February. Sandra was on a new case, about which she could say very little. Rachel told her some of the events of the last few weeks.

The room filled as the rest of the family arrived for breakfast, with much wishing of happy returns of the day. Sandra spent some time talking to Sigfried and Lucky. They must have amused her because peals of laughter kept emanating from her direction.

After breakfast, Rachel was measured against the measuring wall, and it was discovered that she was now four-foot-seven-and-a-quarter, over two inches taller than she had been at this time the previous year. This was agreed by all to be a most worthy achievement. Then, the whole family moved to the Dilly-Dilly room—as the children of the family called the Lavender-Green Drawing Room—where they had last gathered the day Amber visited. It was an airy yet warm chamber near the center of the main wing that smelled sweetly of lavender, with a whiff of cinnamon from the salamander in the hearth. Paintings of the Gryphon Park Lavender Farm in bloom and dried sprigs of the flower pressed behind glass decorated the walls. Armchairs and divans upholstered in violet and green surrounded a hand-carved, two-toned Moroccan coffee table, upon which sat a cut crystal vase holding dried lavender blooms. In the southwest corner of the large chamber near the windows sat a six-sided Moroccan coffee table holding a chess set. An antique billiards table stood in the opposite corner, and a second antique, a lantern clock, sat on the mantel, ticking the time with its pendulum.

Once they were all comfortable, Rachel opened her gifts. She received stylish dresses from London from Sandra; a lovely, illustrated book of Dartmoor myths and legends from Peter; a bandolier of her own from Sigfried, filled with at least two of each elixir he had mastered; and, of course, the gift her father had promised—a large leather handbag with an easy-to-wear strap that contained a small, three-room cottage. Her friends had sent books, a spring hat, and a lovely painting of kangaroos in the snow, which Rachel put up in her new purse house. There were also a series of small gifts from servants, tenants, townsfolk, and neighbors, some of which were items—candles, tea, lip balm, or baked treats—from the Gryphon Park Lavender Farm Store.

The only embarrassing gift came, of course, from Laurel. Her middle sister had given her ladies' undergarments in three sizes, with a note that said that this, for sure, would be the year Rachel would finally need them, and while she would not likely need all three sizes in the same year, this way she would be prepared. Blushing, Rachel bundled the lacy pink garments into their wrapping paper and flung them into the new handbag before the boys could get a good look and be embarrassed or, worse, comment.

After the presentation of gifts, Sandra sat down at the chess table to do a bit of correspondence. The duchess sat in her favorite chair, with knitting needles and a basket of yarn, though she was not knitting but rather enjoying watching her family. Rachel also sat in her favorite armchair, facing her father, with Laurel and Peter and Sigfried all nearby.

Her whole family—well, minus Amber—plus her blood-brother, together in one place. Again, Rachel recalled her epiphany in the infirmary about how much good Laurel had done, just by being chosen as a vessel by the Lion's Father. Each of her family members had something particularly wonderful about them, she decided. She felt very grateful to be here with them. *It truly was going to be a perfect day.*

Laurel and Sigfried sat on a priceless Persian carpet teasing each other. They did so with ease as if they had known each other for years. If Rachel or Peter tried to join the conversation, Laurel and Sigfried both turned on the interloper.

"Little miss here knows everything, does she?" Laurel declared cheerfully, the next time Rachel tried to join in. "Turns fourteen and now the world's her oyster. I think you're getting a bit uppity, little sis." She turned to their father, grinning her Laurel's-up-to-something-naughty grin. "Daddy, did you know Rachel can whistle and produce the Prince of Bavaria?"

Rachel grinned. It pleased her to no end that Vlad had come and helped Sigfried move their bags. Her siblings had looked so impressed.

"Yes, as matter of fact, I do." Ambrose Griffin's eyes sparkled with amusement. "I've seen her do it."

Sandra looked up from her letter writing, intrigued. Their mother glanced up from the knitting that she was not really doing. *Oh, no.* For the first time, Rachel realized there might be a downside to her impulsive finger snap in front of the Agents. A frisson of fear crept up the back of her neck. *What if Sandra told Vladimir?*

Ambrose continued, "We'd been fighting barghests and needed to return to the office—"

Rachel blurted out the only thing she could think of that might derail this conversation. "Because Dr. Mordeau escaped?"

Sandra gaped at her. "How do you know about that, *dongsaeng?*"

"Information loves me. It comes and finds me," Rachel replied with confidence.

Her father and her older sister both stared at her. They looked at each other.

"What does that mean, Daddy?" asked Sandra.

"I am as mystified as you, dear," her father replied mildly.

Sandra wagged her finger at Rachel. "No distractions! I want to hear about summoning Vladimir."

Rachel waved her hands in objection, hoping her father would take pity upon her and stop. It was her birthday, after all; wasn't she supposed to get her way?

Her father's voice was tight with suppressed mirth. "I didn't want to leave her alone. Rachel suddenly announced she had her own escort back to campus. Calm as you please, your little sister raised her hand over her head and snapped her fingers, commanding: 'Dread!'"

"What happened?" Laurel asked curiously, looking up from where she was pulling on Sigfried's cheeks. Rachel could not tell exactly why, but Sigfried did not seem to mind.

Her father spread his arms. "A flash of light and Vladimir Von Dread appeared, in the flesh. Standish and Garbarino have been asking me ever since how she did it."

Her family was looking at her curiously. Sandra, however, had doubled over, her head on the desk, her shoulders shaking with mirth.

"Oh, my," she wiped tears of laughter from her eyes. "I can't wait to tell him about this."

"Oh, please don't!" Rachel cried, leaping to her feet. Humbling her pride, she clasped her hands together, and begged. "*Un-ni*, please don't! It's my birthday!"

The mental image of Vlad gazing down at her with contempt, as he contemplated how she had taken advantage of his chivalrous gesture for her own aggrandizement mortified her almost beyond the capacity for speech. Of course, that had not been her motive. It had been a spontaneous action, intended for the three Agents who had fought so valiantly to protect her. It would be a tragedy if something so charming and fun was the straw that broke the back of her friendship with the Bavarian prince.

Sandra raised her hand and waved it about like a drowning person about to go down. She was laughing too hard to breathe. "Sorry. Can't. Must tell. Oh, merciful stars! So funny!"

Maybe it was not going to be a perfect day after all. Slumping back in her chair, Rachel crossed her arms and sighed. As the family broke up to go their separate ways until lunch, Rachel's father called her over. Her parents were standing close together, looking rather serious. Rachel tried to maintain a cheerful casual smile, but her heart began to knock in her chest.

"Yes?"

"Your mother and I have a matter we wish to discuss with you, Rachel. It's serious, and we want you to promise to give us your true and sincere opinion. We have already discussed it with the others, and they were in favor; but as you are the one who would be most affected, we will not go forward unless you are entirely comfortable, too."

Rachel nodded twice. Whatever was coming did not sound terrible, and yet she could not imagine what it might be. Her parents exchanged glances, but they did not look angry. Her father had a pleasant expression, but her mother was practically beaming. The duchess looked sideways at her husband with a sweet, secret smile as if she were struggling to contain wonderful news.

Her father took her mother's hand and squeezed it. "We would like to adopt Sigfried."

"What?" Rachel cried, shocked, her hand flying to her mouth.

A thing so wonderful had never even crossed her mind.

"Do you not like the idea?" her mother asked, crestfallen. "We thought the two of you seemed so close, and you treat him like a brother. Did we misunderstand?"

Rachel launched herself forward and threw one arm around each parent, hugging them both tightly. They both hugged her back, so that the three of them stood in a mass hug huddle such as they had not done since she was a little girl.

"No! No! I mean, yes! Adopt Siggy! Yes! Yes! Yes!" She jumped up and down three times. "I can't even imagine something more wonderful. I didn't even know it was possible!"

Her mother's face lit up. "I knew I'd read you correctly. He's so sincere and so dear, and he so needs a mum." She spread her arms. "And we have all this room."

"Mummy, this is the best idea I have ever heard in my life!" cried Rachel.

Her father hugged her, too, tightly. "I am glad you think so."

"Can I go tell him?" Rachel cried.

Her father held up a hand. "It may not be possible. We will have to deal with the Unwary orphanage system. It can be quite sticky. I'll have to hire a mundane lawyer. I would rather not get the boy's hopes up. We should know in about six months. We'll tell him once it's certain."

Rachel nodded. Getting his hopes up and having it go awry would be worse than cruel. She whispered, her voice unexpectedly hoarse, "That's the best possible birthday present."

Seemed it was going to be a perfect day after all.

Chapter Thirty-Three:
A Long-Awaited Conversation

The promised hour had arrived.

Her father kept his word. She was to have a whole hour of his time, two if she wanted it. Finally, she could tell him all she had been waiting to say since September. She just hoped he would actually listen. He had not had time to listen after Beaumont nor had he had time over Yule. After the disastrous end to her previous attempt to speak to him in mid-January, when he wasted one of the two remaining charges of Eternal Flame in her wand to damage the world so that he could get Jariel's attention—which resulted in him losing his memory—she was understandably apprehensive.

She led him to the Castle Room. Inside was toasty warm. Rachel curled up in a heavy leather armchair in front of the mural of the looming gray castle. It seemed fitting as it was Beaumont about which Rachel wished most to speak. She sat back and breathed in, enjoying the mingled odors of cinnamon, leather, and a hint of old pipe smoke. It smelled like Grandfather. For just an instant, she could imagine that he was with her for her birthday.

"Here I am." Ambrose Griffin chose the seat across from Rachel's, next to the brass and walnut tower orrery. He gave her a kind smile. "What's on the agenda?"

"I want to tell you the thing I've been waiting to say," said Rachel, "but first, I have something else you may be interested in hearing."

"Very well," her father said patiently.

She told him about the princess's vision: how his father and the other boys had fled Roanoke chased by the ogre; how they had stolen the Heart of Dreams; how they had met her grandmother—his mother—and had all flown away to hide the gem.

Ambrose Griffin listened attentively. "My father was sent down from Roanoke—for stealing the Heart of Dreams? The jewel from the prophecy? The one for which the Terrible Five dug up the campus? And all that time, it had been spirited away by *my father*?"

Rachel nodded solemnly, though underneath, she thought: *point to Joy*. Joy had thought the Terrible Five were searching for the Heart of Dreams when they dug up portions of Roanoke Academy. Rachel had thought they might be searching for the demon Moloch.

"Thank you for telling me all this. I wish I could have seen this vision," he said. "I have no idea what my parents were like when they were young. I saw a daguerreotype once that a tutor had at school, of them when they were youthful adults, but when they were children? They told me very little about those times."

"You mean Mrs. Heelis's photo?" asked Rachel.

"Yes! How—" he frowned at her. "How could you possibly know that?"

"Mrs. Heelis came back. She's my Art teacher. She showed me the daguerreotype, too."

"I remember it had her and Mother and Father and two others."

"The other two boys from Nastasia's vision: Darius Northwest and Jasper Hawke."

"Darius Northwest. Yes. Father mentioned him often when I was growing up. He made Emrys and me read all Northwest's books."

"Aren't they the best!" cried Rachel. "That's what I want to be when I grow up! An adventurer-librarian like Daring Northwest."

"So *that's* where you picked up that idea?" Ambrose laughed. "Yes, I can see that might suit you."

Rachel grinned.

He added, "I don't know the other one."

"Jasper Hawke? He died fighting the same sorcerers who killed Grandfather's other family. He might have died in the same incident—the one where Grandfather bound Azrael into Crowley. Also, he was engaged to Dean Moth."

"He was?" Her father blinked at that. "I... had no idea. How do you know all this?"

"Information loves me," Rachel declared again solemnly. "It comes and finds me."

"Apparently," her father muttered under his breath.

"You said you would have liked to have seen it. Here's the next best thing." She pulled out her sketchbook and showed him some sketches she had done of the vision. Her father paged through the drawing, examining each one.

"These are good for someone your age, Rachel."

She ducked her head, pleased. "I've been working hard. My Art tutor's helping me."

She opened her mouth to explain why when she realized that, if she told him Mistletoe was not actually a familiar-grade cat, he would insist she choose a new familiar. She shut it again. When they came to the sketch of her young grandfather with light escaping from his fingers, Rachel looked eagerly into her father's face.

"Father, did he tell you where it was?"

"The Heart of Dreams, you mean?"

"Yes. I was hoping maybe you knew where he had stowed it."

Her father shook his head. "This is the first I've heard. He never mentioned it to me."

Rachel's shoulders slumped. Their holiday was nearly over. Asking her father had been her last lead. Apparently, she was not destined to find the Heart of Dreams.

She said, "Grandfather was following instructions from the Guardian."

"Ah." The duke considered that. "That makes sense. If my father was conveying the Heart as a courier, he would not have felt constrained to pass on the secret."

Rachel said, "We thought maybe Nastasia had the vision because the Heart might be an answer to the problem of the fey at Roanoke."

Her father leaned back in his armchair. "Possibly." He paused. "How strange that my parents were drawn into this. I had no idea. I'd heard the story of my mother and the bottle of Scotch, but no one ever mentioned what actually happened to the liquor. A number of stories I've heard through the years make more sense now. Thank you, Rachel, for sharing this with me."

Rachel smiled. Mistletoe padded in and leapt into her lap. As she petted him, she wondered why the black and white cat paid so much more attention to her here than at school. Maybe it was a cat thing, or maybe her roommates pampered him when Rachel was not looking.

"Oh, before I forget," her father said, "I wanted you to know that your good work at Grey Wethers the other night is not being wasted. I informed the Warders Association in Cathay of what the Morthbrood said. They have alerted Warner Smith."

"Who?" asked Rachel, confused.

"He's a member of the Warder's Association—those who carry the keys to the city."

Rachel stared at him for a full two seconds before she burst into laughter, pressing her fists against her mouth. "Not key holders! They were talking about the princess and Siggy."

"Sigfried?" Her father looked puzzled. "Why would the Morthbrood care about him?"

"Because he's a Keybearer. That's why Egg kidnapped him."

"Did I know this?" he asked, cocking his head to one side. "Before, I mean?"

"Probably," she replied with a shiver. "Sandra was present when Egg said it."

"There wasn't anything about Keybearers in your report from that event."

"Ah. That's precisely what I asked you here to talk about," said Rachel. "That report."

"I did read it," her father assured her.

"It doesn't matter if you read the report or not. All the important things are not in it."

"Why would you say that?" he asked, frowning at her.

Rachel's mouth felt suddenly dry. "I lied."

"So the important things were in the report?" He did not look pleased with her.

"No. I lied to Agent MacDannan."

"To Scarlet? You can't lie under the *Spell of True Recitation*, Rachel."

"*That* is precisely what I brought you here to discuss."

The duke leaned forward, gazing at her keenly. "I'm listening."

Rachel swallowed. Fear muted her as she recalled the argument in her father's office when he had not listened, but as her father continued to wait attentively, her voice returned. She drew a breath. Maybe this time would be different.

"Back at the beginning of the year, I met an Elf."

"Did I know about this?"

She shook her head. "No. Not only did no one know, except for Mr. Gideon, but also we were told that if anyone else found out, she would die."

Her father leaned back, frowning. "If that is the case, why would Mr. Gideon introduce you?" He paused. "Hold on. Was this Illondria, the

Queen of the Lios Alfar?" He leaned forward in surprise. "Did you actually meet her? I didn't even know she existed until after she died."

Rachel nodded. "It wasn't Mr. Gideon who told us she would die if we talked about her."

"And who did that?"

"The Guardian."

Her father's eyebrows raised. "He came and spoke to you?"

Rachel nodded. "To all of us."

"Is that how you became acquainted with him? When he came to speak to Amber, I could not help noticing that he seemed to know you." He frowned.

"Yes and no," said Rachel. "I can see him even when he doesn't intend to be seen."

"How?"

"By remembering."

"You remember that you saw him earlier in the day?"

"If I remember, obscurations break."

"Ah." His eyes narrowed. "Your mother taught you that, did she?" He muttered under his breath, "I asked her not to do that."

Rachel did not say anything to incriminate her mother. Instead, she said, "My Elf gave me a Rune that protects my memory. Can you see it? It's silver?"

She spread her hair around, trying to show him the Rune on the side of her scalp.

His voice took on a skeptical edge. "She did this without clearing it with me?"

"If we told more people about her, she would die—which we did, and she did," Rachel said sadly. "But we tried to keep her secret, at first. Later... I murdered her."

"You did what? Hold on. The Heer killed the Lios Alfar queen."

"That may be, but I murdered her nonetheless," Rachel stated gravely.

"Do you want to explain this, missy?"

"Later. I want to get to the other part first."

He did not look pleased, but he indicated that she should continue.

She took another breath. Where to start? "Did you know that the *Spell of True Recitation* works by interfering with your memory so that you remember only the true version of an event?"

"I did not."

"Well, it does. My memory cannot be interfered with. So, the spell no longer works on me."

"That's interesting, fascinating, even." Her father's hazel eyes focused on her face. "What worries me is: why did you *choose* to lie to Scarlett? Back then, she was an Agent. A duly appointed member of law enforcement. Why would you deliberately mislead her?"

"I was afraid if the Agents found out I was immune to the *Spell of True Recitation*, they would try another spell on me—and I might blurt out about my Elf, and she might die."

"You were trying to save a life?"

She nodded.

"Saving a life is a noble goal, Rachel. I commend you for that. But...." He fixed her with his steady gaze. "What I don't understand is how lying kept the Agents from discovering this. Wouldn't it be *more* likely they would discover the truth if you *did* lie, hmm?"

"That," Rachel replied simply, "is because you don't yet know what happened."

"Fair enough. Tell me."

Rachel moistened her lips.

"Hold on," her father frowned thoughtfully. "You're immune to the recitation spell. Wouldn't that make you also immune to geases?"

Rachel nodded, "If I had told the Agents I wasn't geased, they might have figured it out."

He nodded. "How did Serena O'Malley manage to geas you?"

"She didn't."

Her father regarded her for an uncomfortably long time.

"I just played along," Rachel offered by way of explanation.

"To keep her from doing worse? That shows wisdom," he allowed.

She decided not to explain about the Lion having sent her after the ensorcelled Sigfried and Nastasia or about how she had joined Serena O'Malley and her geased friends voluntarily. That seemed too much to ask of her father.

Instead, she said, "That's what I didn't want to tell the Agents. Because if they knew I wasn't geased, they could have figured out that the *Spell of True Recitation* didn't work on me either. And since nothing that happened after would have made sense if they didn't know that I was not geased, I could say nothing. So I just repeated what my friends had said."

He leaned back. "But there was more?"

"Much more. Much, much more."

"Very well, Rachel. Let me hear it."

"We left the place where the Agents were fighting Veltdammerung and jumped to Beaumont Castle." Rachel gazed up at the mural of the huge gray castle draped in ivy. Her father glanced up at it, too. "There was a many-colored fire burning there, like an obscuration lamp. Mortimer Egg —well, by that point, I think the demon Azrael had taken over—and Serena O'Malley laid you and Sandra and Siggy and Nastasia on the altar to be sacrificed."

"Sacrificed? Did they say to whom?"

"The *tenebrous mundi*."

Shadows cast by the glow from the salamander shifted suddenly as the Castle Room grew darker. The hair on the back of Rachel's head began to tingle. A shadowy shape appeared against the wall, like the shadow of a horned dragon.

At the exact same instance, both father and daughter shouted: "*Oyarsa!*"

The room grew brighter, and the shadows returned to normal.

Rachel's father examined her with interest. "Where did you learn that cantrip, Rachel? I can't imagine they teach that to freshmen."

"I heard you say it, the time I came up on the roof while you were adjusting an obscuration lantern."

He thought for a moment. "Surely not…. You mean when I was testing the new lantern before we had it installed in the cupola? You were seven!"

She nodded serenely.

"Of course." He ran his hand over his face. "You remember that as well as you would remember if I taught it to you today, don't you?"

She nodded again. He gave a short laugh and shook his head. "It's amazing how hard it is, after all these years, to remember that you and your mother are not going to forget. Well, it's easier to remember with your mother. She doesn't let me forget."

"It's good that I overheard it," Rachel said serenely, "because I used it to save the world."

"You didn't save the world, sweetie," he said almost by rote. Then, suddenly, he became very still. "Hold on. What was Azrael asking them to do?"

Rachel tipped back her head slightly and spoke directly from her memories, "He said: '*Come forth, O Vigilant Ones, Keepers of the Wall. Tene'*…

er, you know... '*I summon thee! I summon thee! I summon thee! It is my will you desert your post and tear down the Barrier that guards this world. Come accept your sacrifice and perform my bidding!*'"

Ambrose Griffin again leaned forward in his chair, a look of horror growing upon his face. "That would have destroyed our world."

"That's what I've been telling you."

The two of them stared at each other. Rachel waited for his reaction, but he gave none. Inwardly, she sighed. One reason she had loved her grandfather so much was that, while he was hard to impress, when she did something worthy of note, his reactions were marked. He would laugh or shout or scowl or grin in approval. She had known exactly where she stood. Her father was so calm that, while sometimes his reactions were gratifying, other times, she was left having no real idea of what his thoughts were. She wondered if Sandra, who worked so closely with their father, saw more in his face than she did.

"So, the..." he made a gesture towards where the dragon shadow had appeared, "... were there, and you dispelled them and waited for Finn to arrive? Or did he show up and save the day right then? Is that why Egg didn't stop you?"

Rachel just stared at him. "By the time Finn arrived, everything was over."

"Funny, that's what he says, too," her father frowned slightly. "That he did nothing. We thought he was being humble—which, come to think of it, would have been a first for him."

Rachel shook her head again. "No. He was telling the truth. As to what happened, there is more. Lots more. So as I said, there was a bonfire and the...." Now it was Rachel's turn to gesture toward where the shadow had been on the wall. "... were there. Egg wanted me to kill you all. He and Serena said the sacrifice was more powerful if fueled by pain and sorrow."

Her father breathed in sharply, but he did not interrupt her.

"So he handed me a wand." Rachel left out that Sandra had previously used a cantrip to silence her. She did not want to get her sister in trouble.

"And you used it on him instead? Good girl." He gave her a grateful look.

"No," stated Rachel.

"Then," he frowned, "why are we still alive?"

"I took the wand, stared him right in the eye, and said the master-word."

Her father's pupils widened. "Hold on. Do you mean *my father's masterword*? The one he set up to re-bind the spell that trapped the demon inside of its host?"

Rachel nodded solemnly. He blinked twice. She wondered if she had stunned him.

"Rachel, how could you possibly know that?" He actually sounded shocked. She resisted the desire to grin. He added, "Your sister Sandra told me she and I had spent hours looking for it last September and never found it."

"Did you think to ask the member of the family with the perfect memory who has read all Grandfather's Second World War journals?"

"I am gathering not?"

"You should have seen it," Rachel whispered, eyes alight. "The spell was magnificent! There were red, gold, purple, and black sparks. Have you ever seen black sparks?"

The duke replied, "It's possible to play a ward as an enchantment. Very difficult. Very rare. It would, however, produce black sparks."

Rachel continued, "The black and purple ones bound him up. The red and gold rose up into the air and made a wisp sculpture of a gryphon. Then, the gryphon attacked him."

Her father laughed out loud. "That sounds like Father's style."

Rachel nodded.

"What was it, if you don't mind me asking? The masterword, I mean."

"Myrddin."

"Ah." He nodded solemnly. "Of course."

"He came, you know," Rachel spoke very softly.

"My father?"

"Myrddin."

"I don't understand."

"He came with Thunderfrost." Rachel paused momentarily, recalling seeing the ghostly stallion with the ghost boy upon its back. "Thunderfrost ran down Serena O'Malley before she could kill me, and Thunderfrost's Boy tipped his hat to me."

Ambrose Griffin's astonishment carried him to his feet. This startled Mistletoe, who leapt up and ran from the room.

"Thunderfrost's Boy is my brother Myrddin?"

Rachel nodded. Her father shook his head in wonder.

"You do mean our Thunderfrost, right? The ghost horse that's the protector of our family?"

She nodded again.

He sank down again and stared off into an unseen distance. "So the time I was heartbroken over the death of Cavall—my lifelong dog companion, who had been given to me as a baby. We grew up together, this dog and I. At that age, I thought Cavall would live with me forever.

"But he died when I was ten, caught under a carriage wheel. I was heartbroken—I went to sit on the first rise to the north, overlooking the moor, and Thunderfrost's Boy came to sit with me, to comfort me—that was *my brother?*"

Rachel nodded again.

He shook his head again. "That would have meant so much to me, had I known."

He was quiet for a time. She bit her lip, chagrined. She had wanted a reaction. Now she had one, but she had not meant to distress him. She just wanted him to be impressed with what she had done, to be grateful that she had used her wits and saved him. Now she had to give him a chance to recover. Finding out that the family ghost was one's brother could be a shock. Rachel had an inkling of how he felt. She remembered how she had felt when she learned about the existence of Amber.

Eventually, he said, "Please continue."

"So then I had to send the...." She gestured toward the wall again. "I had to send them away, and I put out the bonfire."

"You did all that on your own?" He whistled with admiration. Rachel glowed. "And Thunderfrost was in Transylvania?" He shook his head as if he could not quite believe it.

"He protected me from being killed by Serena O'Malley."

The duke's head shot up, his face slack with horror. Then, her father was up and out of the chair and across the room and gathering her in his arms. He knelt down and pulled her tightly against his chest, holding her close, kissing her hair and cheek.

His voice cracked. "Oh, my precious, precious little girl!"

Rachel basked in the warmth of his embrace, her head resting on his shoulder, her eyes half closed. She could hear his heart galloping in his chest. He held her very tightly. A long time went by before he reluctantly released his grip and stepped back.

"And Finn came, after all that?" he asked as he returned to his seat.

Rachel was in the act of climbing into her chair. Instead, she jumped up again,

"Not yet!" she cried. "After the gryphon ripped off Egg's demon wings and dragged the red from his eyes, I broke his wand. I stepped on it and ground the gem under my boot."

"Ouch!" murmured her father, who spent hours every week on the upkeep of his fulgurator's staff.

"He was very angry at me, so he decided to kill you. I paralyzed him, but before I did, he threw you so that you were going to splat against the walls of Beaumont." She gestured up at the great gray castle. "Only I stopped you with *turlu* and saved you from falling with *tiathelu*."

Ambrose Griffin's brows leapt up. "Those are advanced cantrips for a girl who had been at school for a month. Are they teaching them to freshmen right off now?"

She shook her head. "I knew *turlu* because someone had used it on me. I knew *tiathelu* because Gaius taught it to me. In fact, that's how we met."

Her father gazed at her calmly, but the muscle at the side of his jaw twitched. "Are you telling me that the fact that I'm a bad father who lets my thirteen-year-old daughter—"

"Fourteen today!"

"—thirteen-year-old-at-the-time daughter date a sixteen-year-old thaumaturge commoner, *saved my life?*"

A smile danced back and forth across Rachel's lips.

He shook his head. "There's a lesson in there somewhere, I'm sure."

Rachel rose from her chair and crossed to his, slipping into his lap. He pulled her close, his arms wrapping around her, his chin resting on her head. Rachel cuddled against him. He smelled of lavender-scented aftershave and felt strong and warm and safe and powerful. She closed her eyes and basked in the joy.

Her father whispered, awe in his voice. "You actually did save the world."

"Yes," Rachel replied softly. "I did."

"And you saved your sister. And your friends. And me."

Rachel smiled, her eyes filling with tears. This was what she had wanted. This is what she had waited so long for. He knew what had happened, and he was proud of her. She leaned against him and fought the desire to cry.

Her father stroked her hair, continuing to hold her tightly. "I am sorry it took so long for me to hear this, Rachel. In the future, I will try to do better. I make no promises. Being an Agent is a time-consuming job, and that on top of being a duke, which is no picnic. I was very busy during those next weeks after this event, fighting the other demon and other things I can't recall now. I cannot be certain something that important will not occur again. But I will remember this lesson—assuming I can keep my memory this time—and do my best to make time for you if you tell me something is important." He gave her a penetrating look. "That is the best I can do."

"That should be enough." Rachel gave him a little smile. She snuggled on his lap for a bit within the circle of his arms, happy that her birthday wish had actually been granted.

Suddenly, he asked, "What did you mean, you murdered an elf?"

Sitting as straight as one could on a lap, she explained, simply yet precisely, how her friends decided to tell Valerie about the Elf and how she decided that if it was going to be done, she would take responsibility for it.

Her father actually growled, a low sound deep in his throat. "This idea came from your grandfather, didn't it? I told Father that six was too young to watch a horse die."

"But he was right. We mustn't put onto others the hard things that need to be done."

"Did your telling this young woman lead directly to the death of the Lios Alfar queen?"

"No," Rachel admitted reluctantly. "I took precautions. We found out later that it was someone else who spoke too openly." She decided not to mention Sigfried's part. There was no need to say anything that might possibly lower him in her father's esteem.

"Then you are not guilty of murder, Rachel. Your actions did not contribute to her death."

"You say that," Rachel replied evenly, "but if two people shoot at a man and he dies, is the one who missed less guilty due to his poor marksmanship?"

"No," he admitted, "but this idea came from my father, who blamed my wife for the death of my brother. I loved him dearly, but I am not keen on my family propagating his concept of guilt and blame."

Rachel nodded, acknowledging his words. Then, she asked, "Father, where is he?"

"Where is who?"

"Grandfather and my Elf. Where are they? What happens to us after we die?" asked Rachel. "I know Remus Starkadder was dragged down to a place of torment, but not everybody goes there, right? Where do good people go?"

"That depends on where you live," her father replied evenly. "On your family and your nationality. There are many underworlds: Annwfyn, Fortunate Isles, Hades, Hella's Kingdom, Valhalla, Xibalba, Elysian Fields, Yomi, Diyu, Happy Hunting Grounds, Naraka."

"Who decides who goes where?"

"That I don't know. Your grandfather had a Greek friend who moved to America because he did not care for the bleakness of Hades' kingdom, and he had heard that Americans got to pick from the afterlives of all the nationalities on their shores."

"Is that true?" Rachel asked.

"You mean do they get to pick?" He smiled and shrugged. "I have no idea. Your great, great-great-grandfather once asked Gwyn ap Nudd, the Master of the Wild Hunt—whom, as I am sure you recall, is a distant relative of ours—what he did with the ghosts he collected on the Wild Hunt. Gwyn ap Nudd replied that he returned them to their birthplaces, and the various local lords of the dead decided their fates."

"Will the Wild Hunt get Myrddin?" she asked, frightened for Thunderfrost's Boy.

Her father shook his head. "He's been with us for well over a century. I don't think he's the kind of ghost that is of interest to the Wild Hunt."

Rachel stayed on his lap, resting against his shoulder, for another ten minutes, warm and safe in the circle of his arms. Eventually, she kissed him on the cheek and stood up. He smiled at her with such love and fondness that she nearly burst into tears. As they prepared to depart, she paused to look up at the other mural, the one with the black palace she thought of as her grandfather's, though now she realized that this was but a childish notion. Yet, as always, the black palace filled her heart with a strange and wild longing.

It happened, she thought joyfully as she gazed at it, *my long-awaited conversation with my father*. And it had gone well. She felt giddy with gratitude and relief.

"Envying your sister?" her father asked lightly as he passed her.

"What?" Rachel turned to regard him, confused. "Which sister?"

"Don't you know where that is?"

"Is it a real place?" she asked in wonder, turning back to the mural.

"That's Svartschwanstein Castle."

What? The room began to spin. Rachel grabbed onto the back of a large armchair.

"B-but! I've seen photographs of Svartschwanstein!" she cried. "They didn't look like...." Her voice trailed off because there was a faint resemblance.

"Most photos show the front, facing the city of Verhängnisburg. This shows the approach from the Alps, the way your grandfather saw it when he arrived to liberate the city from Hitler's warlocks in 1945," her father said, adding dryly, "Why don't you snap your fingers and ask your friend Von Dread."

Rachel giggled at his comment, but, underneath, she felt so shocked that it was a lucky thing her knees did not collapse. She gazed up at the black palace again, her lips slowly parting. This was *Svartschwanstein Castle*, the royal residence of Bavaria? Her favorite place in the world was *Vlad's home?*

Suddenly, she did envy Sandra, very much.

Chapter Thirty-Four:
Guerre du Coeur

Ten minutes later, Rachel lay on her bed staring at the pink canopy, waiting for the thundering of her heartbeat to grow calm. It did not. *Why couldn't it be Gaius who lived in her favorite palace?*

After a six-month wait, she had finally spoken with her father and told him all that weighed on her heart. She had told him what truly happened at Beaumont and, wonder of wonders, the conversation had gone astonishingly well. She should be wonderfully happy. A moment ago, she had been. Why was she lying here, too stunned to think?

Once when she was eight, Laurel pulled a throw rug out from under her. Rachel's feet had flown up, and she had landed on her back, the wind knocked out of her. Before the pain, there had been a moment of shock, when she had been too disoriented to understand what had happened. She felt like that now, like the rug of her pleasant illusions had been yanked from under her feet, knocking the breath out of her idyllic dreams.

In her imagination, Dread stared down at her from a balcony of the black palace, his dark eyes imperious. He fit there perfectly. A sensation of exquisite agony traveled through her so powerful that it sucked away her breath. *She was in love with Vladimir Von Dread.* Not just a little bit, as she had been since the skating party, but completely and entirely in love. There was not anything pleasant about it. It did not make her feel happy. She felt utterly miserable.

Why wasn't Gaius enough? It might not have been as bad if she had fallen out of love with Gaius and then into love with someone else, but she did not feel any different about Gaius. She thought of her boyfriend, picturing him standing casually, smiling—so charming, so adorable, so adored. She loved him so much! How could she also be so drawn to this other boy? Before, it had been relatively easy to push aside thoughts of Vlad. Now, she felt like an iron filing fighting a magnet. *How could she be in love with two boys?*

Her room, usually so cheery, seemed gloomy and drab. The canopy bed she loved felt oppressive, as if she were trapped in a pink spider web.

Despair is a weapon of your enemies. They have embedded it deep in your heart. The Lion's Father had told her this, speaking through Laurel at the skating party. It was true. Despair was embedded deep within her. It felt like a sharp shard of glass cutting her inside. Whenever it reared its head, she fought it off, but when new bad things happened, it came crashing back, like a broken bone that had not fully healed and kept breaking anew.

The black palace danced before her eyes, mocking her. If it had a voice, she was certain it would be whispering: "You will never get anything you want. You will be tormented by unfulfillable desires until the end of time." *... embedded it deep in your heart.* Her heart was at war. It felt battered and bruised. How did one fight despair? How did one fight love?

Just love him.

Rachel sat up and looked around. "Hello?"

No one was there. She was alone in her room with her plushy bed buddies and her pink canopy bed. When she remembered back, the voice that spoke those three words had been in her head, but it was not her voice. It was soft and beautiful. Remembering it raised her spirits.

A frisson of pure terror spread through her. It could not be a good voice—telling her to desert her boyfriend and pursue her sister's almost-fiancé. It had to be something *very bad.*

It had not sounded bad. Rachel lay back and squeezed her eyes shut. The fact that she could not tell good voices from evil tempting ones left her feeling ill. It was that same lack of judgment that had led to her not being able to tell a familiar from a cat.

She jumped to her feet. She needed fresh air. She needed to get out of her stuffy room. She grabbed Vroomie, opened the French doors leading to her balcony, and flew out into the sky.

She flew over the lawns and the moat, over the kennels and stables. Landing, she gathered early spring wildflowers. Then, she flew to the south, away from the open moors and above the forest, until she came to the family graveyard. It was ancient and crowded, with gravestones, tombs, and a larger white mausoleum in the center. Statues—both marble and bronze—graced some of the tombs or stood between the gravestones. Here and there, daffodils bloomed.

Rachel landed and stood before her grandparents' graves, in the very spot where, almost three years earlier, she had made her now-famous (to her family—her sisters still mocked her over it) speech about how all the precious and beautiful things were fading and how it was their duty to protect them. Kneeling, she placed the flowers she had collected upon their graves. In the past, she might have put flowers only on her grandfather's grave, but it was not the bitter, old woman whom she honored today with snowdrops and marsh lilies, but young Amelia Abney-Hastings and her steeplechaser.

Rachel thought again of the black palace and blushed. Where had she come up with the childish notion that her grandfather might have his own castle in the afterworld? No fairytale or story promised such a thing. She felt so naïve and chagrined for having voiced such foolishness. But if he was not wandering the halls of some otherworldly black palace.... A cold clammy sweat broke out on her forehead and the back of her neck as a new fear assailed her.

"Grandfather, where are you?" Rachel spoke plaintively to his gravestone. Was he in the ocean of life? Flitting somewhere like a bat? Had he made it to the Elysian Fields? Had he been reborn as a baby? Swallowing sporadically, she whispered, voice quavering, "D-did you c-cease to exist?"

She shook off that fearful thought. Gaius's notion of ghosts dissolving was nonsense. Rachel had witnessed Colman going somewhere, and Remus Starkadder probably wished he had ceased to exist. She knew he was in a place of torment. Jariel had confirmed it. It made no sense that spirits would endure after death only to be tortured and not for a better fate.

Rising to her feet, she paced back and forth, walking past the great white mausoleum and various graves and statues, many moss-covered or green from patina. She paused at the graves of Margaret Sap Griffin, her great-great-great grandmother, whom she had recently learned had drowned in the Dart, and Colette Anjou Griffin, the young French wife Uther Griffin married after Margaret's death, the distant relative of their seamstress, Marie Anjou. Uther himself, of course, had no grave. His body had never been recovered.

Passing her grandfather's grave again, she noticed that right next to it were five markers sunk into the ground that she had not paid attention to before. They read: *Percival Lancelot Griffin 1886–1888, Morgana Charity Griffin 1883–1888, Lynette Moire Griffin 1877–1888, Myrddin Ambrose Griffin, Lord Falconridge 1874–1888, Vivian Iolanthe Griffin 1873–1888*. Rachel dropped to her knees before the fourth marker and ran her fingers over its smooth black stone. *Thunderfrost's Boy!* This was his gravestone. Tears welled up in her eyes. She took the best marsh lily from her grandfather's grave and laid it on Myrddin's.

Next to Vivian was a slender tombstone, different from the other heavy polished stone markers in the family cemetery. It was delicate and of pure white marble. On it was written:

The Lady Estelle
1888

Stars were carved into the marble around *Estelle*. Between her name and the single date was a bas-relief of a candle in an old-fashioned holder with a ring-like handle. At the foot of this gravestone, someone had laid a single long-stemmed rose ending in a bud. The leaves on the stem were green fading to brown, but the rosebud itself was golden. Rachel reached forward and touched it. It was as soft as a rose petal, but when she tried to lift it, it was as heavy as real gold. She dropped it and scooted back. Where had such a thing come from, and who had left it?

With a shiver, she put that mystery aside and continued her circuit of the graveyard, coming upon another Sap—the family name of the Dukes of Trevena—Margot Pandoff-Sap Griffin. Her grave lay next to that of her husband, Rachel's Great-Uncle Cadellan, her grandfather's younger brother who had died during the Battle of Roanoke. In front of them was the marker for their son, Aurelius Tiberius Griffin—her father's cousin Aurie—who had died at the Battle of the Somme in the First World War, over eighty years before the death of his father.

Rachel gazed sadly at this pruned branch of the Griffin Family line. What was the point of life if one strove and suffered and then, at its end, ended up lost in an ocean or flitting aimlessly around Hades? Was a life that ended thus worth living at all?

"A book ends." She spoke aloud to herself as she rose and continued her wandering among the family graves. She glanced at the weathered headstones of *Aethelflaed Griffin, Fifth Earl of Devon, 1171* and *Lamorak Griffin, Third Duke of Devon, 1473*. Beside Lamorak's grave was that of his wife with a lark carved into the stone: *Lunete Willt Griffin*—descendant of Merlin and the original Lark. She had died so young, barely thirty. Rachel paused briefly, blinking back tears.

"After the story is over," she continued her train of thought, "the characters never act again, and yet books are worth reading. At least, I find them to be. Does that mean our lives are worthwhile even if what comes next is of little account?"

The wind blew through the weathered stones and statues, but Rachel received no answer. She stared up at the blue sky with its puffy clouds. There must be something worthwhile — some purpose or good accomplished by each person's brief span upon this fair world, mustn't there?

"Please," she whispered. "Let there be something more."

Rachel suddenly glanced to the right and left. "Who am I pleading with?"

Not stars. Some stars were bad. She never wanted to ask them for favors again. Not gods, Greek or Welsh or such—they never answered anymore. Jariel had promised her another option, but he had not yet revealed it.

"Who is out there?" Rachel shouted upwards, over the treetops toward the cloud-spotted sky. There was no answer beyond an echo of her own words.

Returning to the house, Rachel did not feel like going inside. She decided to spend a little time on the roof; however, the roofs of Gryphon Park Manor were surprisingly cluttered. There should be plenty of room since the three sections of the house were each as large and long as a mansion in their own right, and there was also the Old Castle, which stood at the corner where the south side of the main house touched the west side of the east wing, but each was cluttered in its own way.

The front of the main house consisted of dozens of towers, buttresses, turrets, and carvings of gryphons. The central and tallest of these towers housed Gryphon Park's obscuration lantern. Behind this was a flat section of roof with an oval reflecting pool for *degossamerization*. This area seemed too exposed to her, and there was no good place to sit.

South of the main hall rose the four round towers of the Old Castle. They had flat tops with crenelations, over which one could lean to see the countryside in all directions. This was a favorite place of Rachel's, but she did not feel like landing there today. The east wing had an observation dome for tracking the signs and seasons as marked by the heavens and a porch-like area encircled by stone gryphons that peered over the edge like gargoyles. She loved that spot, but today, it seemed too confined for her current mood.

The west wing's roof was flat except for a square beige and green belvedere at the far end, with a bench, a short, stylized wooden railing around three of the four sides, and painted gryphons on all four corners. Rachel had no notion what the purpose of this last structure was; perhaps one of the earlier dukes had liked to entertain on the roof. All together, the three wings of the manor, along with the Old Castle in the southwest corner, formed three sides of a square, with the opening extending westward, away from the formal lawns and the gatehouse and toward the maze and the stables, the forest, the moors, and the tor. Within this open square lay the rose garden, a number of topiaries, and a flagstone patio with stone benches, tables, and shade umbrellas: perfect for enjoying sandwiches and lemonade on a warm day, but fully in sight of a full half of the house. Not what she was looking for today.

Finally, she flew to the belvedere at the far end of the west wing and sat down on one of the green benches, gazing out at the pony paddock, the moors, and Gryphon Tor with its ruins. Perhaps the sunlight and fresh breeze would lighten her mood. A shadow fell over her. Rachel looked up and to her right. Beside her, his black feathery hair brushing the roof of the belvedere, stood an eight-foot-tall, shirtless man with black wings. He wore black poplin pants and held a gold halo in one hand. His face was impossibly perfect, so much so that just looking at it caused her heart to ache. His eyes were red as blood.

"Jariel!" she cried. She wanted to rush and hug him, but she felt too shy.

"Happy birthday, Rachel Griffin," croaked the Raven.

Joy flowed into her, filling her up like water pouring into an empty vessel. Unable to bear the distance between them, she lunged forward and threw her arms around him, hugging him with all her strength. He embraced her in return, covering her with his warm dark wings.

"I'm so happy you have come," she cried. "That is a most wonderful present!"

"My visit is not your present, Rachel Griffin. I have but come to tell you that your gift will be ready tonight, at the stroke of midnight."

She stepped back, gazing up at him with great curiosity. "What is it?"

"Did I not make a promise to you when we danced?" he asked. The harshness had left his voice, which had become melodious to the ear. His eyes were now a beautiful rain cloud gray. "Tonight, it shall be fulfilled."

Rachel drew a sharp breath. "You mean I'll receive an answer to my question about whom to petition if it's unwise to wish on stars?"

Jariel nodded gravely.

Her lips parted in anticipation—a gift that promised exactly what she desired! Jumping with excitement, she cried, "Can you tell me now? What's going to happen?"

He smiled at her impatience. "You shall see."

She stopped jumping and caught her breath. "I saw a big black Wolf with red eyes the other night. Is he a Guardian, too?"

A great sadness passed over Jariel's face and then was gone. "He's of the same nature."

Rachel looked out at the countryside. "Jariel, are there Guardians of Lost Worlds?"

"There are." He regarded her strangely. "How do you come to ask such a thing?"

"Do they live in a red place that isn't like our dreamland: the dreamland of Mars?"

Jariel stiffened, his eyes widening in alarm. "How could you possibly know that?"

"I saw it in a dream."

"A dream?" He looked over her head and off into the distance, his eyes moving as if searching. "I cannot see what power brought that knowledge to you. Dream does not hold memory as does the waking world. I cannot track its origin. You should not have been able to see their sanctuary. It was hidden by my choirmate whose help is no longer available to me."

"Choirmate?"

"A fellow angel assigned to the same duties."

"Why can't this choirmate help you anymore?"

Jariel regarded her. He was silent for so long that Rachel thought he would not answer. A breeze passed by, blowing her hair around and rustling his feathers. When he finally did answer, he spoke precisely, as if choosing each word with care. "An unwise wager. Though I cannot complain because I was the one who first demonstrated the making of such wagers."

"Oh." Rachel was not sure what to make of that.

The Raven leaned toward her, gazing at her. "You seem despondent for a birthday girl."

Rachel looked away. It was hard to be sad when he was beside her, but her heart felt so heavy. "I am worried about what happened to my grandfather after he died, and I just found out my favorite place in the world is actually Svartschwanstein Castle. I had thought it was a fairy castle or a place in the land of the dead."

"Why does this second discovery distress you?"

"I don't want to be in love with Vladimir Von Dread!" she cried in anguish.

"Ah." He was quiet for a time.

Rachel wished she could ask him what happened after death, but he had said back at the infirmary that the subject was forbidden to him. She thought of asking again, perhaps in different words, to see if she might get some hint of an answer, but then her mouth snapped shut. A wave of utter terror seized her as she realized: *He knew*. The Raven *knew* the answer.

If it was something unbearable, she did not want to learn it on her birthday.

Instead, she said, "I feel so stupid. All this time I didn't recognize the palace. Why didn't I ask my grandfather about it? I just thought it was fanciful."

"That mural shows the real Svartschwanstein Castle from Lohengrin."

"From what?   You mean from Wagner?   I don't recall a Svartschwanstein in that opera."

A smile touched the Raven's lips. "Lohengrin is the name of Vladimir's homeworld."

"Oh," Rachel breathed. Her eyes became very round. "You mean that's a painting of a place on another world? How could that happen?"

"It came to the artist in a dream." He paused. "Sent by me."

"What is the difference? Between our version and the original?"

"The original is bigger, which is an oddity, as only two people ever lived there."

"Vlad and his wife from before?" She tried to keep the anguish from her voice.

"He did not marry."

"Oh. Good!" She blushed. "I mean.... Oh, Jariel! I wish I had someone to speak to about all this!" She blushed more, worried she might sound ungrateful. True, she was speaking with him, but she did not believe he wanted to stay and talk at length about the state of her heart. "I mean a woman with whom I could speak about these things. Like my dead Elf.

She would have listened. I am certain. Why am I in love with two boys? It's so unfair!"

He gazed off into the distance. Eventually, he said, "I foresee that you may learn the answer to that question tonight, too."

That stopped her cold, jerking her out of her despair. "There's an *answer?*"

He gazed at her with his storm cloud gray eyes. "There is."

This news stunned her. She stared off over the rolling moors again. In her mind, the sweet, light voice once again whispered:

Love him.

A shiver ran through Rachel from the hairs of her head to the souls of her feet.

"Jariel," she whispered, "what does it mean if we hear voices in our heads?"

The Raven regarded her speculatively. "Do they say good things? Or bad things?"

She replied in a small voice, "Bad things."

"It was not meant to be thus, but early on, your ancient ancestors disobeyed Our Heavenly Father. They ate something that gave my dark brethren access to your thoughts. Your first parents were given a chance to redeem themselves, but it went awry," his voice grew sad, "despite my best efforts."

"Could they be given another chance?"

"The one who failed was given another chance, but that went amiss, too. But because, this time, the fault was another's, one last chance will be granted."

"Is there anything we can do to help?"

He smiled as if pleased with her. "If there is, Rachel Griffin, you will be told."

Chapter Thirty-Five:
More Ghosts Than
You Could Shake a Stick At

RACHEL HEADED DOWNSTAIRS TO SPEND THE REST OF THE AFTERNOON with her family. As she descended the wide sweeping staircase with its red carpet runner, a young man waved up at her from the great entrance hall—a young man with dark skin, intelligent eyes, and a very wide smile.

"Ben!" she shouted with joy.

She raced down, taking the steps two at a time. At the bottom, on the black and white checkered floor of the grand entrance hall, stood Benjamin Bridges. It had been over seven months since she had seen him. Before she had left for Roanoke, her only real friends had been Cook's grandson, Taddy, and Ben. She still felt guilty about having opted out of the yearly Yule party, as normally, she and Ben would have spent that time together. Instead, she had chosen to pursue the secret of her lost sister by sneaking into her parents' room to get a look at the forgotten rattle hidden in her mother's jewelry box.

Had it been worth it? Did she really want Amber in her life? Rachel pushed away that offending thought as being unsisterly.

She hit the ground floor and slid into his arms. The two of them hugged and laughed.

"Rachie! I came for your birthday." Ben grinned at her. He gestured behind him. "Brought the whole family."

Sure enough, his little sister Yasmin, his mother, and his father, Agent Bridges—the current head of the Shadow Agency that Agent Griffin ordinarily ran—were with him. Rachel greeted them all cheerfully and introduced Siggy as he arrived. Her blood brother was an immediate hit with Ben and his little sister, or at least Lucky was a hit with eight-year-old Yasmin.

Yasmin, in turn, was a huge hit with Lucky. Ben and Yasmin Bridges both had gills and prehensile hair; though Ben kept his hair very short, and they both tended to keep their gills covered by collars and scarves. Watching Yasmin's hair fly about delighted Lucky, who flew up into the air to snake in and out of the dark, ropy locks.

Ben Bridges loved to ride; Gryphon Park was one of the few places where he had the opportunity, and there was just enough time for an outing before afternoon tea. Rachel ran upstairs to change into her riding habit, a lovely outfit of bottle green velvet with a smartly tailored jacket and a riding skirt with a golden border along the hem, full enough to allow riding astride—she wore her sweatpants underneath as she did at school. As soon as she returned, she and Ben headed for the stables, followed by their families. The three Agents, Ambrose, Sandra, and Templeton, walked together, discussing Wisecraft business, leaving Mrs. Bridges with Yasmin, and Peter and Laurel with Siggy. Rachel's mother seldom went riding.

As they crossed the lawns, Ben asked eagerly, "So, what have you read recently?"

Shame gripped Rachel. Reading had been her main activity before going to Roanoke and Ben loved stories as much as she had. She could not bear to tell him that she had read almost no fiction since she started school. He would not understand any more than she would have understood last year if someone said that they had stopped breathing.

But she did not want to lie to him.

"Sadly, it's been mainly nonfiction and schoolwork for me," she said regretfully.

He looked crestfallen.

"What have you been reading?" she asked quickly.

"I've finally got around to starting *Treasure Island*."

"Oh, I've read that one!" she cried, relieved.

"Have you? What did you think of Long John Silver?"

They talked about the book until the horses were saddled. Widdershins was, again, covered with mud, and Rachel had to scrub him down before she could saddle him, so the conversation went on for some time. Peter and Sigfried joined in, too, only Sigfried seemed to think the story featured a talking frog. A cheerful row developed on the subject of whether or not Long John Silver was evil. Eventually, they were all ready to ride.

As the group began to head out across the moors, Rachel's mother came around the corner wearing a new, rather fetching riding habit. She gave her husband a shy smile.

"Ellen?" Rachel's father sounded faintly surprised but pleased. "Fancy seeing you here."

"I thought I might join you all for the ride," she said shyly.

"A splendid idea," replied the duke.

As he leapt from Passelande to ask Oliver to saddle Starbeam—the duchess's beautiful Gypsy Vanner with its long fluffy mane — Rachel's mother gave her a wink. Rachel winked back and smiled. Maybe her mother could learn to appreciate the Gryphon Park horses after all.

They rode out over the moors, chatting happily and discussing favorite stories. The men rode together, discussing business, while Rachel's mother chatted with Mrs. Bridges. Rachel noted that her mother looked much more relaxed, speaking with her friend, than she had among the peers. Little Yasmin rode a tiny pony. She entertained the two mothers by letting her long prehensile hair stretch out from her head, expanding and contracting like a spring—to the delight of Lucky.

Rachel and Ben and Siggy and Peter discussed books until they came to a natural end of the current subject. Then, as they had since childhood, Rachel and Ben burst into song, singing a few of their favorites. Peter joined in with his nice tenor, and Siggy grumbled about not having brought his trumpet.

The boys began racing. Rachel and her little pony were left behind. She found herself riding next to Sandra, who looked fetching in a form-fitting russet riding habit that she had conjured for the occasion. Her boots were twins of Rachel's, which made sense since Rachel's had been a gift from Sandra. Still, it made Rachel happy to be a little twin of her beloved sister.

Ordinarily, Rachel adored her older sister, but right now, she felt slightly uncomfortable, remembering her father's parting words in the Castle Room.

Sandra glanced at her and chuckled. "Are there any other boys you can produce by snapping your fingers?"

"Oh, that's so unfair! Please don't tell him! Please!"

Sandra rolled her eyes. "So, how are you, *dongsaeng?* I can't believe you're already fourteen! How is Roanoke treating you?" She leaned toward her little sister and asked teasingly, "Has it gotten you over your obsession with moldy mounds of rocks and outdated ways of life? Finally ready to leave all that behind and embrace some new ideas?"

Rachel bit her lip. No wonder she so often found herself reluctant to share her innermost thoughts. When she did, the people she most cared about always seemed to use that very thing to pick on her. Why had she made her now-infamous speech about preserving precious old things in front of her family? She had been talking to her dead grandfather, upon the first anniversary of his death. She could have waited until no one else was present.

"I have not changed my mind," she replied quietly, not wishing to discuss the matter on her birthday.

Sandra smiled kindly. "You'll change your mind as soon as you get a taste of the wonders of Unwary living. Though some of their devices are so amazing that I suspect magic must be used to create them. O.I. certainly does. Like refrigerators. A brilliant invention that makes life so much easier. Once you've lived with one, you will never want to go back."

"We have ice sticks and stay-fresh boxes," countered Rachel.

"Ice sticks don't last very long," replied Sandra, "and stay-fresh boxes tend to dry things out. If you leave food in them too long, it becomes tasteless. That doesn't happen with a fridge. All that wonderful tasty goodness is preserved. Besides, *refrigerator* makes an excellent last line to any haiku:

> *"My little sister,*
> *Knows nothing of what is good.*
> *Refrigerator."*

Rachel counted the syllables in the word *refrigerator*. Sure enough, it was five.

"Let me try." Rachel drew in a deep breath.

> *"Please do not tell Vlad.*
> *He will flatten me with a*
> *Refrigerator."*

Sandra chuckled charmingly.

"Then you won't tell him?" Rachel asked hopefully.

"Too late. Already did."

Rachel let out a keening wail. Not only was she in love with her sister's boyfriend, but Sandra had cleverly arranged things so that he would never speak to her again. Sandra threw back her head and laughed gaily.

"*Un—ni*," Rachel asked plaintively, drawing out the Korean diminutive, "why haven't you brought Vladimir to speak with Father? Daddy said he was willing to hear him. Don't you want to get married?"

Sandra sighed. "*Dongsaeng*, it's complicated."

It was not to Rachel's credit that her heart leapt with hope. *How could it be complicated?* Vlad had said her father was the sticking point. Rachel had opened the way for them. Was Vlad's father now a problem? What else could stand in their way? Had Rachel been Sandra, she would have dragged Dread in front of Father before someone else sank her claws into him. Didn't Sandra realize how many girls were angling for her boyfriend, *including her own little sister?*

Hold on. No. She did not want Dread. She was happy with Gaius.

Any additional thoughts were cut short by a commotion in front of them. Gentle, plodding Cummerbund was on the run. He had the bit between his teeth and had taken off at a gallop. Rachel had not even known the chubby pony could gallop. Apparently, Siggy had forgotten and started holding on with his heels again.

Peter and their father urged their horses forward, but they were a distance from Cummerbund. Poor Sigfried had lost his seat and was sliding sideways. If he fell off at that speed, even a boy who could survive being pounded against the ice by an ogre might be injured.

Rachel watched helplessly as her brother and father attempted to converge on the hapless Sigfried. She reached for her wand to try to catch him with *tiathelu* as they had done for Jenny when she was stuck on the water horse, but by now, the pony and boy were far out of Rachel's range. At least, her blood-brother was not frightened. He was whooping and cheering even as he listed sideways, with Lucky flying right beside him.

The sun went behind a cloud, casting the rolling brown moors into shadow and gloom. Rachel's stomach clenched with fear. She urged her pony to go faster. How could this be happening, and on her birthday?

She heard the hoofbeats before she saw him. The hair rose along the back of her neck. She knew the sound of those hoof beats. *Surely it could not be....*

Across the moors, moving faster than any mortal horse, came a great stallion of moonlight and shadows. From his neck flowed a shaggy mane of mingled snow and black hoarfrost, and silky white feathering hid his hooves. He raced toward Sigfried and Cummerbund, passing Peter's Feste and Father's Passelande with ease.

Thunderfrost! Thunderfrost matched pace with the pony. Then, the ghostly stallion began to slow down. Sure enough, the smaller steed slowed as well.

On Thunderfrost's back sat a boy dressed in dark blue Victorian garments. He was faintly transparent, but she could make him out clearly. He leaned sideways, speaking to the runaway Cummerbund, soothing him. Soon, the pony dropped to a walk and just in time, as Sigfried slid off sideways, tumbling to the soggy cold moor, where he rolled and rose to his feet, smiling.

The entire riding party came to stop. The Griffins stared in awe at the ghost steed who was said to come when the family was in need. Rachel could not help wondering, did his appearance today portend Sigfried successfully joining the family? Or had he come because of her? Because it was her birthday?

Thunderfrost pawed the earth and snorted. Sparks flew where the ghost hooves struck the ground. Atop his back, Myrddin smiled into the eyes of Rachel's father, who gazed steadily at him. Beside the duke, tears streamed down the cheeks of his duchess, who was seeing the family's ghostly sentinel for the first time. Sandra and Laurel, who seldom spoke to each other, had reached out and grabbed each other's hands for comfort. Peter had a quiet smile on his lips as if all was right with the world. The four Bridges, who had heard of Thunderfrost but had not quite believed, stared open mouthed.

Thunderfrost's Boy glanced over his shoulder. He waved to Rachel. She waved back. Then, in a flash of silver and black, the stallion and boy were gone.

The clouds parted, and the sun emerged, shining off silver boulders and yellow gorse flowers. Siggy, who had been as cocky as a rooster at dawn during the entire debacle, gazed after the vanished horse in puzzlement.

Suddenly, he grew pale. "W-wait! W-was that a g-g-ghost?"

"Yes, and it saved you," Rachel cried, overjoyed.

She tried to encourage him, as did Peter and their mother, but to no avail. No amount of pointing out how beneficial the ghostly apparition had been would calm the nerves of the petrified boy. Ghosts were the only thing Sigfried Smith feared.

That night, at the stroke of midnight, Rachel found herself whistling along with a waltz she could not hear with her ears. She sat up and listened warily, whistling bits of the *Skater's Waltz*. Then, she hopped out of bed, grabbed Vroomie, and flew out the French doors, soaring over her balcony and upward. She rose over the lip of the eaves and found herself staring in awe.

The roof had been transformed. Roses the color of the face of the moon bloomed on the ordinarily ivy-covered walls of the Old Castle, filling the air with the most astonishing perfume. The flat flagstones of the roof above her room, between the rounded stone wall of the Old Castle and the reflecting pool to the north, were encircled by dozens and dozens of pots of a flower she did not recognize. It was a lily, but each blossom was at least seven inches long and shaped like a trumpet, with six points at the mouth that curled away from the opening. The lily itself was also moon-white, but inside each one glowed a stamen the color of candle flame. This pale golden light shone through the trumpet-like flower so that, while the roses were the color of the moon, the lilies seemed to glow with the soft creamy-gold of candlelight.

Seven will-o-wisps as large as her hand hung in the air high above these flowers, forming a circle that spun slowly widdershins. Unlike domestic wisps, they had faces, bright and pixie-like, that appeared and disappeared in the curls of their pale golden flame. Below, twelve smaller wisps, these the color of moonlight and about the size of the pad of her thumb, formed a larger circle and spun in the opposite direction in time to the music.

Rachel paused, charmed by the eerie dancing wisps. She could now hear the *Skater's Waltz* with her ears. The mingled scents of roses and lilies were so glorious that she would not have minded if she had never breathed anything else.

In the midst of the flagstone tiles, surrounded by the splendid candle flame lilies, played Wallace Hartley's orchestra. Ghostly figures in their Edwardian finery, these were the members of the band that had refused to abandon their post and had continued to play as the *Titanic* sank, even though it had meant their lives. And they played still, having vowed to remain until every single lingering soul abandoned the wreck of that great ship and moved on. Rachel recognized Hartley himself and her friend Percy Cornelius Taylor, who nodded to her while bowing his cello.

She landed in front of the band and put down her bristleless. It was only when her feet touched the roof tiles and felt the shock of the late March cold that she realized she was still in her white Victorian flannel nightgown, and her feet were bare. Young Mr. Hartley, her grandfather's friend, came forward, bowed, and held out his hands as if inviting her to dance. Rachel laughed and stepped forward. She could not feel the ghost's hand, of course, but she moved as if she did, dancing to the strains of her favorite waltz.

After circling the floor, so to speak, Mr. Hartley returned to his violin. Percy Cornelius Taylor rested his cello against his ghostly chair and came forward to take his place. Rachel stepped up to dance with him, delighted.

Percy Cornelius Taylor gave her a huge grin from beneath his wax-tipped mustache. "Welcome, Lady Rachel, upon this most holy of mornings."

"Today?" Rachel asked. She searched almanacs in the library of her memory but could find no special holiday associated with the thirty-first of March. "Sigfried asked me to ask you about the treasure ship you mentioned."

"Still quite cold up north, but spring is coming!" he replied. "August or September will be the best time to reach that ship."

"I will remember." She nodded. Then, she asked, pleading, "You told me that you and your fellows will keep playing until all the souls depart from the *Titanic* to go onto their next state. I know you said you cannot speak of what's beyond, but couldn't you tell me something? A hint? Rumors? Surely ghosts must talk to each other about these things."

"Alas, I cannot," Percy Cornelius Taylor replied, "for I do not know. We have been told that if we knew our future fate, we would find ourselves unable to remain here."

"Oh." Her eyes grew wide. "Never mind, then."

He gave her a brilliant smile. "I've heard there's something very nice in store for you."

"For me?" Rachel cried. "Can you tell me about it? Or is it a secret?"

He raised his hand, making the gesture as if to twirl her. Rachel obliged, twirling and spinning, and laughing with joy. Her white flannel nightgown, with its high collar, lacy front, and ruffles, flared out around her as she spun.

"I don't need to tell you, Lady Rachel," he replied, "It's happening right n—"

He froze. Everything froze—the silver and gold wisps, the music, the band. Rachel, however, kept spinning. She caught sight of something behind her—near where the roses climbed up the side of the Old Tower. As she continued to twirl, it came to be in front of her.

An unusually large Raven hopped on the roof tiles; his eyes gleamed red. To his left, towering over him, stood the Doe that shone like moonlight. It was the very same one that Rachel had glimpsed from her riding tree. Its eyes were lavender. On the Raven's right, the enormous black Wolf from the moors stood stiff-legged and hostile. Its eyes, too, were red as blood.

The Doe moved with an impossible grace and beauty. She spoke with a lovely feminine voice. "Hello, Rachel Griffin. I am Idunn."

Rachel curtsied. *Idunn? Wasn't that the Dryad of the World Tree, Illondria's mother? What had she been doing in the forest on Gryphon Park? Waiting for tonight?*

The Wolf grunted. "Hello, Rachel Griffin. I am Caziel."

Rachel's eyes grew wider. She curtsied again. "What can I do for you, ma'am? Sir?"

The Wolf stalked around her slowly, growling. It bared its teeth. "I did not come for you. I came for my brother." He looked at the Raven. "Zadkiel, you waste your time with this one. She will not be able to go. She has too much pain in her. Even now despair claws at her."

Fear stabbed through Rachel. *Despair? She felt so joyful! Was she in despair even when she did not know it?* Then, she blinked.

Zadkiel? Was that the Raven's real name?

The Raven croaked, "I will take it from her. For a time."

The Doe nosed Rachel's hip. "Child, you must give up your burdens if we are to give our gift to you. One very dear to me has asked it, and I would like to grant her last request."

The Raven shifted into an eight-foot-tall man with a crown of light and black wings. He reached up and took the halo from his head. It turned to solid gold. He knelt before Rachel so that he did not tower over her quite so much.

"I ask that you let me take your burdens for a short time." The Raven now spoke in his melodic angel voice, "so that we may show you something. It will be safe. You have my word."

Rachel nodded wordlessly. The Raven bowed his head and closed his eyes. The circlet in his hand turned into light, flaring brightly. He placed it over Rachel's head. The virtue of diligence spread through her, urging her to complete all duties required of her, earnestly and with persistence.

The Raven closed his eyes for a moment, murmuring, "All my grace is reflected, coming down from the Father of Lights, '*in whom there is no variableness, neither shadow of turning.'"*

The troubles weighing upon Rachel's heart melted away, draining from her the way water rushes from an unstopped sink. The red at the corner of the Raven's eyes began to drop like tears of burning pitch and splash on the flagstones. Rachel gasped, startled.

The Wolf growled, "Idunn, you must go now. I will hold this place while you are gone, and I will watch our foolish brother."

The Doe turned to Rachel. "*Sabriost.*"

Rachel recognized the word from the Original Tongue. It meant *mount up.* She reached toward the Raven, her fingers brushing the coolness of his cheek. Then, she climbed onto the back of the Doe, and they were off.

CHAPTER THIRTY-SIX:
FOR I AM WITH THEE

THE SILVER DOE RACED ACROSS THE NIGHT SKY, HIGHER AND HIGHER UP into the midnight darkness. Rachel bent over, her arms around her neck. Absolute blackness broke around them, as if they had stepped through a sheet of water. Then they raced through something far darker than night.

Where in the world were they going? Rachel looked back over her shoulder and gasped. The stars were no longer in their places in the sky. Instead, they had come together, each tiny point of silver-white light contributing to form a gigantic Tree. Larger than galaxies, this World Tree lay fallen, surrounded by roiling darkness.

In the distance, also made of stars and larger than the circumference of a solar system, was the jagged stump from which the trunk had fallen. Farther down, a stairway of enormous mushrooms led to an ornate opening in the side of the stump. Below that, a little fence made of stars surrounded the bottom of the broken trunk, and below that still, something so terrible that her eyes would not focus on it.

The Doe ran along a starry branch of the fallen corpse of the Tree. Here and there, a fruit dangled, silvery-blue or brilliant gold or deep green. Each looked like a gigantic version of the swirling balls of soul-light that Rachel had seen the Raven take from within her friends. Each ball, she realized as they leapt by, was a world. A single high branch reached up at a ninety-degree angle to the rest of the fallen trunk. The Doe leapt onto this and dashed upward.

As they climbed, the sky grew brighter and brighter. Far above shone a million, million stars—a billion, billion stars—and not pale silvery stars such as those forming the Tree. These were brilliant points of golden light, so bright that even a hundred-million suns could not compete, and yet this brightness did not pain the eye.

Near the very top of the highest branch of the Tree hung a fruit of swirling rose red and forest green. The Doe leapt into it and fell through the sky, Rachel still holding tightly to her silvery neck.

Idunn landed lightly in the midst of a wide glade. To one side, a massive wall of bark continued as far as the eye could see, leftward and right-ward and upward. This was the branch of the World Tree along which they had been running. In the other direction grew great rose trees, as tall as sequoias, with trees again as large growing out of the canopies of the first layer of trees and another level out of the second canopy.

The glade in which they landed contained stone benches and gardens overflowing with herbs and sweet-smelling blossoms. Arched trellises of climbing flowers—pale violet wisteria, bright blue morning glories, red, white, and yellow roses, and pink clematises plus many flowering plants Rachel had never seen—arced over the path of flagstones that circled around the gardens. Towards the far side of this arrangement stood two thrones, one almost three times the size of the other.

Rachel gazed at the many-layered forest. Astonishment gripped her so that she could hardly speak. She recognized this place; her Elf had shown it to her in a vision.

"Hoddmimir's Wood!" she breathed with awe.

She was on another world! Her shoulders sagged as she was struck with regret. She had come without Siggy! How was she going to tell him? He would be so angry that she had gone without him. He deserved to visit another world, too. Maybe she could convince Idunn to bring bring her back another time and Sigfried, too.

"True, child," replied the Doe. "This place once was my daughter's seat of power, from which she reigned over Lios Alfar and flower fairy alike. Await me here."

Rachel slid from her back. The Doe flowed like water, becoming a stately woman with silver wings and features as perfect as a statue. The angel had silver locks and a silver halo above her head that radiated gentleness and joy. As Idunn glided away, toward the great wall of bark, two willowy dryads with long green hair—one leaf green, one olive—stepped out from the bark wall to meet her. The three conferred together for a time.

Rachel turned slowly in a circle, gawking at the endless wall of wood and the trees growing out of other trees, wondering how this place was going to help answer her questions about wishing on stars. She approached the two stone chairs.

"Illondria's throne!" she breathed, "and this larger one. I wonder if it's Duneyr's."

"Indeed," replied a deep voice behind her, so deep that it reverberated through her body.

Rachel spun around and shivered, her limbs suddenly weak with fear. Looming over her was the antlered man whom she had once glimpsed in a dream. He was twelve feet tall with ears that came to points and the upswept features of an elf. Enormous storm-gray antlers sprouted from his head. His black armor bore feathered epaulettes. His storm-colored wings, which Rachel knew could spread to a span of over a hundred feet in either direction, rested against his back like a feathered cloak.

This, she realized suddenly, was the gigantic seventy-two-point buck she had spotted in the forest next to the Doe the evening of her and Siggy's tree ride. He had the same eyes. What had he had been doing in the forest of Gryphon Park? He was also the one who had brought Zoë back from Hell.

"Greetings, Rachel Griffin." His deep voice reverberated throughout her body.

"Hallo, Duneyr." She dropped into a curtsy. "Thank you for rescuing Zoë Forrest."

"It was my pleasure." Duneyr inclined his great, horned head. "Please tell my wife that my thoughts are with her, but I tarry here until my tasks are done."

Rachel's eyes filled with tears. "Shall I... shall I be able to tell her?"

"You will."

"Then I shall," she promised fiercely, though she could not imagine how such a thing could come to be. Was Illondria's shade still here, wandering in Hoddmimir's Wood? If so, why could Duneyr not tell her himself?

Idunn returned. She and the antlered man spoke quietly to each other. She again took the shape of a Doe and asked Rachel to mount. Then, they were off, racing through the sky.

They leapt out of Hoddmimir's Wood and left the fallen World Tree far behind, leaping through a vast empty space, moving toward the bottom of the sphere of golden light. Ahead, four silvery points hovered, above the Tree yet below the sphere of golden stars. With a sense she did not have at home, Rachel perceived these golden stars were the millions of worlds that had been saved when the World Tree fell.

The Doe touched down briefly on the first of the four silvery stars, which turned into a world globe when they approached it. She leapt off it, jumping on toward the next of the four. Peering down at the shimmering world-ball as they vaulted off it, Rachel received an impression of solemn white marble buildings with Grecian columns and trees growing together to form a ziggurat of living wood. Idunn leapt off two of the other three worlds as they hopscotched toward the golden sphere. Glancing down at the second world, Rachel glimpsed a snowy evergreen forest where a jolly white-bearded man in crimson robes spoke with a four-foot raccoon in a waistcoat. On the third world, two young men and a young woman on horseback, dressed in crowns and rich robes, cantered along a shining beach.

The closer the Doe drew to the gigantic sphere of golden stars, the greater grew the sensation of pure, unadulterated ecstasy. Joy flowed around Rachel, calling her to rejoice. Her soul leapt, eager to join the exaltation. Only there was more to her than just joy; there was fear, sadness, anger, and guilt. These qualities were reduced from their normal state, as if she had left behind a large portion of her guilt and fear. There was enough left, however, that Rachel found it hard to breathe.

The heavier burdens of her soul wrestled with the glory of the golden sphere. Whatever they were approaching was too magnificent for her. As Rachel and the Doe drew closer to the myriad stars, the disparate parts of her soul began to separate from each other, tearing her apart. Exquisite joy became pain. She gasped for air, fearing her heart would burst.

"Wait! Stop!" Rachel cried desperately, finding her voice. "I cannot bear it!"

The silver Doe slowed. "Do not be afraid. Nothing here can harm you."

Rachel gasped breathlessly. "I think I shall die."

"Do you wish to turn back?" asked Idunn.

Rachel stared at the glory shining ahead of her, tears streaming down her cheeks. She wanted to go on, but the pain from the joy of it terrified her. If she did not burst, she might dissolve. Nothing of her would remain. *But turn back?*

She reached up and grasped the halo, the diligence it shed strengthening her resolve. Diligence required perseverance. She could no more turn back than she had been able to stop practicing when she had been depressed and unable to eat. She let the emanation of the halo flow through her, calming the pain and turmoil within. Whatever was to come, she would face it.

Rachel swallowed. "Let's go on."

The Doe and the girl plunged into the golden sphere. Inside, the stars shone with a myriad of colors. Gritting her teeth against the internal pressures, Rachel looked around. The colorful points of light blended together to form images that filled her entire field of vision. The blue or green or crimson stars were bunched together into bright and jewel-like shapes of solid color that resembled the art form that Zoë had called stained glass. As the Doe and her rider moved, their relationship to the stars shifted, and new pictures formed. These portraits flashed by too quickly for Rachel to make out details. She would have to recall them later and contemplate them at her leisure.

Then, the golden sphere of stars parted, and they flew over a dark crystal sea. Ahead lay storm clouds such as Rachel had never seen. The ominous thunderhead formed a solid wall, stretching both upward and to either side as far as the eye could see.

Rachel tightened her arms around the Doe's neck, unnerved.

Forked lightning illuminated the storm-cloud bank, dark and pale gray swirling together. As was the way of clouds, shapes appeared and vanished—a dragon, a whale, a sailing ship, a skull. She could not tell if the cloud stuff truly formed shapes or if they were just tricks of the eye. The whorls and puffs appeared solid. She fancied if she touched it, they would have texture. Not that she wished to. She liked storms, but this one filled her with trepidation.

At the bottom of the expanse of storm was a narrow strip of black sand. It reminded Rachel of the beaches in Thulhavn, where her family went on holiday during the summer, except this one was strewn with golden pearls. The star-studded sky behind her lapped against this black shore, crashing over it like waves. Rachel wondered if the golden pearls were stars cast up out of the ocean-sky.

The Doe landed upon the black beach. Rachel slid off and took an uncertain step toward the wall of swirling gray cloud mass. Up close, it appeared even more ominous. The hairs on the back of her neck stirred and stood, and butterflies took up residence in her stomach. Then, she paused, staring at her body. Raising her arm, she gazed at her slightly translucent hand.

"Why am I see-through?" she asked, her voice catching.

"This place is more real than you," replied the Doe.

"More real?" Rachel examined her translucent hand, turning it this way and that. She had waited so long to visit another world. It had not occurred to her that it might be a place where she was as insubstantial as a ghost. Kneeling, she lifted a handful of the black sand, grateful that she was solid enough to touch it. The cool grains ran between her fingers, making a pleasant sound as they rained back upon the dark beach.

The silver deer flowed like water and took her human shape. Only now, her wings were white as newly washed wool, her hair was golden, and her eyes were the blue of a cloudless sky.

"You are no longer in the Shadowlands," said Idunn.

"I have no idea what that means," Rachel murmured.

Idunn smiled at Rachel, who felt suddenly lighter, as if something inside of her were so weightless that it was pulling her away from the ground.

Lightning flickered again through the cloud-stuff beside them. Rachel stumbled back, startled. She waited for thunder, but there was only a distant rumble. Still, her heart thumped violently.

"What is this place?" Rachel whispered apprehensively.

"Go forth and see." Idunn gestured toward the oppressive wall of storm clouds. "She awaits. I will meet you here when you wish to return, if that is how this ends."

"C-can't...." Rachel stared at the ominous grayness. "Can't you come with me?"

Idunn shook her head. "I can go no farther if I wish to retain my bond with the World Tree. So little life is left in it. I do not wish it to be damaged further."

Rachel nodded wordlessly. She stared at the storm clouds, flickering with lightning. Could she pass through it and live? The hammering of her heart suggested otherwise. The feeling of diligence lingered, however. Again, she reached up and touched the halo hovering above her, drawing comfort from it.

"I would not do that," Idunn warned gently. "Whatever grace you take from my brother's crown, you cannot return."

"*Oh!* Oh, no!" Rachel let go of the halo as if scalded. "I'm sorry!"

She took a step toward the swirling gray clouds. Its contours looked solid to her eye.

"It is just fear," said Idunn. "Walk ye through it."

"Fear?" Rachel asked, alarmed.

"Just fear. It cannot stop you." The angel gave her a gentle but firm push.

Rachel took a step forward, her arms outstretched. The swirling gray wall hovered before her. Warily, she reached toward it, but nothing met her except a clammy fog. Or, rather, nothing met her fingers; her thoughts were a different matter.

The moment she touched the Wall of Fear, thoughts burst into her mind like thunderclaps. *The lightning would strike if she walked forward. It would kill her.* Sure enough, a purple-bright flash illuminated the cloud-stuff to her left, coming uncomfortably close. She jumped. Fearful thoughts rushed through her mind, thick and fast: *Her family would never know what became of her.* She saw her father, head bowed in mourning, Sandra and Mother embracing in their sorrow over the loss of her. *Gaius would never know how his girlfriend had died, alone in a distant place where he could never follow.* She saw him sitting gloomily, inconsolable, as Vlad and William tried vainly to cheer him.

Trembling, Rachel shook her head and stepped forward until her nose touched the cloud stuff. *Being electrocuted would hurt. Every cell would be burnt from within.* Try as she might, she could not get herself to move. Her shaking legs refused her commands. Her jaw would not open. It was as if she stood upon a precipice of fear, and any motion might send her tumbling over the edge. She could feel the diligence radiating from the halo, but she dared not think about that, lest she somehow unwittingly rob the Raven. She did not know what actions might drain it. She only knew that she would do nothing that might hurt him.

But how could she force herself to go forward without its help? As she stared into the thunderhead, her heart galloping like a horse, Rachel suddenly remembered another storm—a storm in her mind that had attempted to push her away from a light shining beyond it. Ignoring her nigh-overwhelming desire to flee, she focused on recalling what had happened next. Beyond that storm, it had still been the first of November in the Memorial Garden at Roanoke Academy. The odor of ash from the previous night's bonfire still hung in the cold autumn air. At the foot of the shrine of the Unknown God had sat a tiny Lion.

The Lion gazed at her with golden eyes. *"Fear not, for I am with thee; be not dismayed."*

Rachel took a gulp of air. Closing her eyes, she pictured the little Lion walking beside her. With her eyes still closed and her hands outstretched, she walked forward. She trembled from head to foot. Her legs shook so badly that she could hardly move them. Yet, she did.

She opened her eyes. All around her was fog. She took another step. Lightning arched through the cloud-stuff, coming straight at her. She screamed.

The lightning struck her. Her chest seized up. She could not breathe. She was going to die, or worse, collapse burnt and helpless, in pain and alone.

Just fear. It cannot stop you. Would Idunn lie to her?

The Voice for Fear whispered: *You murdered her daughter. Maybe she wishes you harm.*

Rachel's limbs shook violently. She could not breathe. She tried to reassure herself. It was going to be okay. Jariel—Zadkiel?—had told her the way was safe. He would never harm her. *Not on purpose. Maybe he did not know Idunn's desire for revenge.*

Then, pain. Such pain. Every cell in her body screamed in agony. And yet, strangely, her mental conversation with herself continued unabated. *And Leander?* The Voice for Fear tried to tell her that she had only imagined the Lion speaking to her, but Rachel did not believe that. He had been real. *Fear not, for I am with thee; be not dismayed.*

A strange thing happened. In the same way that the whorls of the Wall of Fear had looked entirely solid but proved to be nothing but cloud and fog, the fearful images in her mind began to seem less significant. The pictures remained: her charred body, her father bent in mourning, an inconsolable Gaius; however, the color drained from them. She saw fear for what it was: false images formed upon mist and fog.

The pain vanished. Rachel looked down at herself. She was still a bit translucent but otherwise unmarred. The lightning had done nothing to her. It, too, was but a false shadow.

She strode forward. Lightning crackled around her, but she no longer feared it. When it came near, she reached out, allowing it to dance around her fingers. Dark images of harm and destruction still whispered to her, but now she dismissed them, brushing aside their cloudy substance. Then a sweet fragrance of cherry blossoms filled her nostrils, and it was not cloud-stuff that swirled about her but cherry petals—pale rose, peach, white, and a hundred other shades of pink.

Rachel spun around. Behind her lay the black beach strewn with golden pearls, the ocean of stars, and the inner curve of the golden sphere beyond.

No evidence of the Wall of Fear remained.

Chapter Thirty-Seven:
The Foothills of Heaven

Rachel turned slowly amidst the swirling petals, regarding the grove of cherry trees around her. It was as if she had lived her whole life in twilight, among muted hues, and only now stepped out into the sunlight and saw true colors. The flowering trees grew in rows so that their blossom-laden branches arched above an expanse of lawn, carpeted with shades of pale pink. Among the bark, flowers, grass, and sky shone new colors for which she had no names. Everything shimmered with an inner light. No shadows lay upon the petal-strewn ground.

She closed her eyes and inhaled. The perfume of the flowering branches engulfed her. A sweeter fragrance she had never smelled, not even amidst the roses and lilies on her roof. It made her feel simultaneously alive and at peace. Her thoughts were so calm, so quiet. The constant fears that plagued her, tearing at her and tormenting her, were gone. She could wonder about things, but no fears leapt forward to fill her imagination with horrors and trepidation. It was as if once she passed through the cloudy Wall of Fear, fear could no longer touch her.

She took a step forward and froze.

Oh.

She was wrong about shadows. There was one thing here that cast a shadow: *she herself.* She waved her hand and watched its shadow sway upon the pink petal carpet. Because everything shone with its own inner light, pale and diffuse shadows stretched from her feet in all directions, as if she were always at the center of a faint gray starburst. Idunn's words echoed in her thoughts: *You are no longer in the Shadowlands.*

"She meant it literally," Rachel breathed softly. "The land where there are shadows." Maybe Shadowlands was another name for what Jariel had called the Twilight Lands.

Then, she paused and cocked her head, listening. *Music.* At first, the song sounded dim and distant, but as she listened, she could hear more clearly: *Rejoice, Rachel Griffin, for you are fearfully and wonderfully made!*

Rachel's eyes widened. Who was singing? How did they know her name? And what did that mean? She looked around but could see no singers. The music seemed to come from everywhere at once as if every leaf and blade of grass were members of the choir. The trees, the branches, the petals: All were singing.

She walked forward, curious as to what lay beyond the cherry trees. What was this place? A breeze blew, shaking the branches and sending more blossoms flying. A whirlwind of pink spun around her. Ahead of her, in the midst of this petal tempest, someone was dancing. Swirling through the many shades of peach and rose and other unnamed hues, she caught a glimpse of hair—fern-green hair.

With a gasp of joy, Rachel ran forward. In the midst of the cherry trees danced Illondria. Her skin was even more luminous than Rachel remembered, like the smooth bark of a beech newly wet from the rain and glistening in bright sunlight. Her features were upswept, high cheekbones, slanted eyes, and fern-green brows. Her long locks of the same warm fern-green flew around her as she spun and swayed to the singing of the cherry grove.

It was her Elf! After all Rachel's tremendous longing to speak with Illondria again, *here she was!*

The seven-foot-tall Lios Alfar queen paused, eyes closed, head tilted, her hair slowly floating down to settle about her shoulders and hips.

"Do I hear footsteps?" she murmured. "That cannot be my Duneyr. It's too soon."

Rachel barreled into her, hugging her. "No, but Duneyr says his thoughts are with you, yet he tarries until his tasks are done."

Illondria's eyelids sprang open, revealing eyes that had starlight where mortals had pupils. She looked surprised. Her gaze focused on Rachel—whose head was more than two feet below her—and she laughed, hugging her back.

"Oh, my little one! You are here! You came." Her Elf sighed with joy. "If I did not feel you with my hands and see you with my eyes, I would not believe it. I do not think this is some sweet dream. I should think I know the difference."

Buried in her embrace, Rachel cried out, "Illondria! You're alive! You're all right! I didn't murder you!"

"Of course, I am all right. How could I be otherwise?"

"But you were dead! I killed you! How did you manage to come back?"

The elf queen's voice sounded both amused and chagrined. "I did not come back, child. Not in the manner you mean."

She hugged Rachel tightly and then held her at arm's length, examining her.

"You—" Illondria's hand reached towards Rachel's head but then drew back. "—have a halo. Rachel, how did you get here? You aren't…. You did not pass on, did you?"

"The Raven is making some kind of sacrifice to send me here," Rachel whispered back. The halo over her head was no longer a silver coronet. It had turned into a circle of light through which she could pass her fingers if she tried. She could feel the diligence radiating it. She was careful not to think too much about it. Of course, currently, she did not feel any need for its support. "He took away the terrible sorrow that weighs upon me, so I could come."

Illondria stroked her hair. "Oh, my little one. I am so sorry I cannot protect you. I wish…. I wish I had had more time to be with you. Though I must admit, it is nice to be able to rest again. It has been some time for me."

"Wh-where is this? Aren't you alive?" Rachel took a step back amid swirling pale pink petals. "W-why did you ask if I were dead?"

"This is a place for those who have completed their penance but who still carry burdens they have not yet laid down; or for those who wish to wait for another so that they might both enter that which lies beyond together," said Illondria.

"Wait. You mean," Rachel glanced back and forth rapidly, "this is the land of the dead?"

But it was so *beautiful*. It could not be. She must have misunderstood.

"Tell me," asked Illondria, "How have you come to be here?"

"It's my birthday," Rachel explained. "The Raven promised me answers to some questions. Oh, and I think your mother thought you would like to see me! She brought me here. Well, brought me to the shore of the Ocean of Stars."

Illondria brushed cherry blossom petals from Rachel's hair. "Only Rachel Griffin asks for the answer to questions for her birthday gift." She smiled fondly. Then, taking her hand, she added, "Come. Walk with me, and we can speak of all that is upon your heart."

They left the cherry tree grove, stepping through the branches and into a deep forest, more stately and more hallowed than any earthly woods. The trunks of these trees were straight as pillars and tall as skyscrapers. The branches high above met together in an elegant and awe-inspiring canopy, which was the reality that vaulted ceilings attempted to reproduce. The different trees had different-colored leaves so that a dappled many-colored light shifted above them as they walked, like a living kaleidoscope. Occasionally, through the trunks to the right, Rachel caught glimpses of a deep green field spangled with wildflowers that ran unbroken to the foot of rounded green mountains.

The subtle forest scents, of bark and leaves and pine needles, were so beautiful that Rachel felt as if these were the real fragrances of which the earthly equivalents had been but pale imitations. She breathed deeply, walking along a narrow path flanked by dark green periwinkle with its lavender-blue flowers.

Illondria smiled down at her. "It brings such joy to my heart to see you."

"Me, too," was all Rachel could manage.

She did not cry. It did not seem possible here, but she felt so full of emotion that, for a time, she could not speak. All of the beautiful and wonderful things that had happened in her life came to Rachel as strong, colorful memories. As for the bad things, she could remember them if she tried, but those memories felt as if they had happened long ago. They no longer held the power to harm.

Illondria was alive. Only she wasn't alive, or maybe Rachel was dead. Or.... Had Jariel's halo actually allowed her to come, living, into *the land of the dead?* If so... she looked left and right, lips parted in awe... it did not look anything like she had been led to believe.

Rachel turned in a slow circle. There were no shades, no flittering bats, no mindless ocean. It was, rather, more beautiful than any place Rachel had ever imagined. The thought that Jariel had arranged such a trip as a gift for her robbed her of her ability to speak. He was not just answering her question about wishing on stars. He was, in one magnificent package, answering all her burning questions: about wishing on stars, about the land of the dead, and—if he were to be believed—about why she was in love with two boys. What's more, she had wished to talk to her dead friend, and now she was! In all of history, had anyone ever done something so amazing for someone else?

Ordinarily, she might wonder if she were dreaming but such uncertainties were not possible here. She could not doubt that this was real.

Rachel and her Elf walked in companionable silence for a time between the columns of the great trees. They left the path and walked across the dark green groundcover. Rachel found she was so light she did not need to bend a single periwinkle stalk, but if her feet did touch the dark leaves, music rang out, a sound between chimes and singing.

"Everything is so peaceful here," Rachel said, feeling light and carefree. "Back at home, I'm tormented by sorrow and doubt. My mind attempts to fly away from me, as it did the time you saved me. Only you are no longer there." She sighed. "The Lion's Father spoke to me through my sister and told me not to despair, but it's hard."

Rachel lowered her head. She did not feel shame here, but she still knew what was shameful.

Illondria pressed her arm. "Do not let despair take you, my child. It is a trick. It is a weapon of the darkness that has no true blade. Everyone will be saved. This place"—she waved her hand around, indicating the exquisite beauty—"it isn't even the final destination in our journey. It is but a stop along the way to something even greater. The foothills, so to speak, before the Mountains. The Light shall win, my little one. It's just a matter of time."

Rachel asked, "Really? How could we know for certain?"

Illondria replied, "The Light... um, I think you know of Him as Leander's Father, the Emperor of All Things Seen and Unseen? He is the Creator. All things good come from Him and will return to Him. We are all His children."

Rachel stopped walking, astonished, "Even... me? I thought he just made Siggy."

Illondria laughed rather hard at that. She wiped her eyes. "Yes, even you, dearest one. He made all of us, and He loves us all. But He made us each differently. Sometimes, those differences can create... confusion. We are scared that others don't want what we do or will take what we think is ours. It leads to conflict. In this place and beyond"—she gestured toward the green mountains—"such conflicts are put aside. Here, we are closer to the Light and can feel His love upon us. In the face of that, no fear or confusion can remain."

"That's wonderful," Rachel murmured, trying to comprehend it all. Was that what the voices had meant when they sang that she was fearfully and wonderfully made?

"So you did not murder me," her Elf said kindly. "I am right here."

Rachel sighed and smiled. "I did murder you, but if you have forgiven me, I will not be too hard on myself."

Illondria squeezed her hand. "If that is the best I can get, I will accept it."

The majestic trunks opened into a glade filled with ferns and roses. The air here still smelled sweeter than any she had previously breathed, and it had a rarified quality that reminded her of the tops of mountains. Her family had climbed Schiehallion, the Fairy Mountain of Scotland, and Snowdon in Wales, and, once, when she was eight, they had visited Switzerland and climbed an alp. There was an exhilaration one experienced when standing on a peak that had nothing to do with oneself or one's own accomplishments. It felt like that here.

She fell silent, gazing at the astonishing beauty—the roses in colors never seen on earth, the azure sky, the perfect trees. Everything looked oddly different than she expected. Comparing it with images in her memory, she realized it was the lack of shadows.

At home, shadows gave objects definition. Forests were full of shadows, with the top leaves dappling the lower leaves and the higher branches overshadowing those below. Shadows were what allowed one's eye to distinguish one leaf, one branch, one tree from another. Here, each leaf glowed with its own light, so there were no shadows at all. Yet everything was distinct. In fact, she discovered that if she looked at a particular leaf, even a very distant one, she could see it clearly—its color and shape, its smooth surface, its delicate veins.

A stream tinkled over rocks to one side of the glade. Rachel knelt and ran her hand through the living water, which danced between her fingers. She cupped her hands and took a sip of it. It was pure and cool and amazingly refreshing. She closed her eyes a moment, savoring it, and breathed deeply.

Still kneeling beside the stream, Rachel turned to Illondria. "The Raven told me he would arrange for me to find the answer to a question. Can you answer it for me?"

"Which question is that, my dearest one?"

Rachel rose. "What should we do instead of wishing on stars?"

"Don't wish on stars!" Illondria said sharply. "Some of them work for the enemy."

Even here, a shiver ran down Rachel's spine. Both Amber and the Raven had said something similar, but it was still eerily disturbing.

Illondria continued, "Instead, pray."

"Pray?" Rachel tilted her head. "You mean make a petition to Apollo or Athena?"

Illondria laughed, a tinkling sound as lovely as that of the stream. The periwinkle flowers chimed with the sound of it.

"Praying is speaking to the Creator," the elf queen explained. "It is something you can *always* do. When He created you, He placed a piece of Himself within you. That spark is eternal. It cannot be taken from you. Ever. So when you speak to Him, He will always hear. Whether out loud or in your heart. And He will always answer. Always. Sometimes, far away. It is a whisper, though. You may miss it in the shadows."

"Interesting," murmured Rachel.

It sounded glorious but a little creepy — someone listening to her thoughts? At all times? She felt a bit skeptical such a thing could be true and was not entirely sure she wanted it to be.

She asked, "Can I pray for myself?"

Illondria nodded. "Of course, you can pray for yourself. You're supposed to."

Rachel closed her eyes. "Lion's Father, Creator of All, please give me peace of heart."

A wind blew by, rustling the branches high above. It smelled fragrant and was accompanied by a sound like high, sweet bells. As Rachel listened, liquid peace poured over her, like a summer rain. She felt loved the way she had the time she had touched the Guardian's halo, and he had allowed her to feel her father's love for her. The breeze ruffled her hair, causing her to smile.

She opened her eyes again, full of joy. Illondria watched her, looking slightly wistful.

"That was nice." Rachel's eyes danced. She felt uplifted, even though she was not exactly sure what had been accomplished. "Can we pray for other people?"

They began walking again, into the great trunks on the far side of the glade.

"Of course!" Illondria smiled. "If you are worried for others, ask the Creator to help you. He will reach out His hand and touch those for whom you pray."

Rachel considered this. "How powerful is prayer? What can and cannot it do?"

"It is the most powerful force in the universe," Illondria replied firmly.

"More powerful than sorcery?" Rachel asked, dubiously. "How could that be?"

"The Creator made everything, even sorcery," the Elf replied. Then, she winced. "He made *some* sorcery. Some comes from the lies of those below, but the rest is directly from the Creator, passed down from gifts He granted to your first father."

Rachel caught her breath, alarmed. "That doesn't sound good! Which part is which?"

"I do not know," the Lios Alfar queen admitted. "You'll have to work it out for yourself."

Rachel contemplated this as they strolled. The prayer part sounded too good to be true. She wondered if there were a catch, like how accepting wishes from genies almost universally went awry. Still, in this place of serenity, it was hard to doubt. She felt as if she could hear the truth in Illondria's words. She did wonder about which parts of sorcery came from the lies of the demons. Was it just particular spells, such as black magic? Or whole Arts?

"Okay, praying for others." Rachel felt such a calm sense of peace about the idea that there seemed no harm in trying it. "Like this?"

Rachel closed her eyes, thought about her friends, and said softly, "Lion's Father, Creator of All, can you help heal Nastasia from the damage done by the phantom fire?"

A vision unfolded before her mind's eye. She saw Nastasia sitting at a table looking out a window at a field where kangaroos grazed. Her face was sad and pinched. Within the princess, a little star shone. Its nature was one of *duty*. An ever-so-slight breeze blew through the room, gently playing with her golden locks. She smiled out the window at the kangaroos, looking less lonely and fearful.

Illondria nodded at Rachel. "I think you've got it."

Rachel prayed for Siggy and her father. Sigfried's spark was *fiercely loyal*. When the wind blew over him where he tossed in his sleep atop his pile of gold, he looked more serene and mature. Her father was in his home office gazing at a file marked *Amber Praetor/Griffin*, his jaw clenched, his eyes narrowed with anger. Within him was a star of *pure courage*. When the wind blew by, it ruffled his hair. He still gazed at the file, but he seemed less angry and more hopeful.

Seeing her father's anger startled Rachel. He always appeared so calm. What terrible damage the Master of the World had done to her family when he had taken Amber. Rachel prayed for him as well. The Master of the World might be sad, too. She prayed for him.

She saw him sitting by a tombstone at the edge of a cliff overlooking the ocean. Below was a great port city. Thousands of ships were in dock; many more spread out upon the sea. Andre Romanov rose and turned. She could see, stretching into the distance behind him, line after line of gravestones. Rachel bit her lip.

Within him shone a fierce spark. Its character was *ambitious*. A wind blew up from the sea. He nodded towards the many graves and looked a little less grim.

Rachel and Illondria came to a break in the trees. To their left, far above the towering forest, silver and gold lines of dancing, ever-changing light pulsed like a heartbeat in a dark purple sky. To her right, the sky was a brilliant blue. The field of fragrant wildflowers ran to the green mountains. As she gazed up at the green peaks, she caught a glimpse of something purple-blue high, high above them. She peered upward. Her lips parted in awe.

The green shapes she had taken for mountains were but foothills. Rising high above them—impossibly high—were the mountains themselves. They were the most beautiful, most rugged, most majestic of mountains imaginable, with slopes of silver, blue, and purple. Their white caps shone brightly, lit by a Source not visible from where she lay—a Light so beautiful that even the splendid landscape in which she currently rested seemed twilit in comparison.

Rachel recalled an evening in Scotland when she was seven. After a day spent hiking the slopes of Schiehallion, her family had headed back via walking glass to Loch Sidhe Castle. Rachel had been exhausted, but she walked proudly as they headed for the glass hall, her hand holding tightly to that of her grandfather. Twilight had fallen over the valley, but when she looked back over her shoulder, the last rays of the sun still struck the peak of the Fairy Mountain so that its east face shone with a brilliant golden light. Gazing upon these impossibly tall peaks was like that, only more so.

"What is that?" she whispered, pointing.

"Those are the Mountains," replied the Lios Alfar queen. "Beyond that's Heaven."

"The country where the angels live?" breathed Rachel, enraptured.

"We shall all live there someday."

"All of us?" Rachel turned to look at her. "Even me?"

"*Even you?* Especially you, my dear one."

Rachel looked toward the Mountains. Gazing at them stole away her breath, as if a world that had such peaks in it was more glorious than the one to which she had thought she belonged.

Chapter Thirty-Eight:
The Door to Saving Everyone

They walked out into the wildflowers, walking over warm yellow buttercups and purple clover. Rachel noticed that there were other people here. Far to the right, a redheaded woman and two little children ran through the flowers chasing butterflies. To the left, some distance away, a distinguished-looking man with a salt-and-pepper goatee sat in a chair by a wrought iron table reading a book; however, these people were far enough away that they did not impinge on Rachel and Illondria's privacy. The two of them sat down together on the fragrant clover. Rachel lay back, the motion producing a ripple of music through the clover. She stretched out beside Illondria, her arms crossed beneath her head, and stared up at the majestic Mountains. Then, closing her eyes, she listened to nature's symphony, the music of each blade of grass, each fragrant flower. She wondered if she, too, had her own leitmotif.

It seemed impossible that this was the land of the dead—or a land outside the land of the dead. Could anything so wonderful be true? How odd that it was so much easier to accept terrible things than glorious ones. It was easy to believe men lived short, brutish lives and then spent eternity fluttering about Tartarus like bats—unpleasant but easy. It was infinitely harder to accept there was a place more real and more magnificent than earthly life and that she and those she loved might someday be welcome there.

Would Gaius believe her if she tried to tell him about this place? Would he give up his notion that men ceased to exist once their day in the sun was done? What about those who faced life boldly despite its difficulties, such as her grandfather or Vladimir? Surely, if she tried to tell them about this, they would not believe it. They would probably point out that not everybody would get to come to this glorious place—Remus Starkadder, for instance.

Rachel sat up and gazed at the Mountains. Was her grandfather there somewhere, beyond those regal purple peaks? She fiercely hoped so. If he had been dragged down to the place of torment to which Remus had gone, she might not be able to bear it. What about Vlad? Would he make it to such a peaceful place? She wanted to think so, but....

"Lion's Father, Creator of All," she prayed silently, "please help and protect Vladimir."

In the vision that unfolded before her, Vlad was up late, seated at an elegant ebony desk in what might be his bedroom. The spark inside of Vlad was different. It had been damaged. Now, however, it had a piece of gold worked into it. Rachel recognized that gold. It came from the halo above her head—as if the Raven had fixed the damage with his own grace. It was unclear what Vlad's original spark had represented, but now it was *protective and lawful*.

When the breeze blew through the room where he sat, late at night, the pages of the book he was reading shivered in the wind. Vlad leaned back and took a deep breath, running his fingers through his black hair with its red highlights. Then, he glanced over at a silver-framed photograph of Sandra that sat upon his desk and smiled.

Rachel sighed. He was thinking of Sandra. That seemed a clear message. She needed to curb these unruly longings of her heart.

Love him.

Rachel glanced around, but no one was near besides herself and her Elf. She was sure she had heard a voice speak words out loud, but Illondria did not seem to have heard anything. The words rang in her thoughts like a promise, but they made no sense. Wasn't it her most base instincts that drew her toward the wrong boy? Shouldn't such voices be silent here?

"Illondria," she asked plaintively, "I have a problem and no one to speak to about it."

"You may speak to me freely," the elf queen replied kindly.

"I'm in love with two different boys... and it hurts."

"Two boys?" Illondria asked fondly. "So few?"

Rachel's jaw gaped.

The elfin woman's face broke into a chagrined smile. "My apologies. Those are boys whom *you* love."

Rachel nodded. "I love my boyfriend so much, and I picture a happy future for us. So why does my heart ache? I don't want to be in love with the other one. He is older and in love with someone else. I want to go back to just feeling hero-worship and brotherly affection.

"I just wish..." she leaned back and kicked her feet, "... that he would kiss me, once, really nicely, before he marries my sister. But I'm too young.

By the time I'll be old enough, he'll be married, and that would not be right. So wrong, in fact, that my imagination won't even imagine it."

Closing her eyes, she prayed silently: *Lion's Father, Creator of All, you can do all things. Mightn't I, somehow, against all logic, be old enough to be kissed—just once—before Vladimir marries Sandra?* Could the Lion's Father do that? It seemed impossible. A chill crept up her spine. Were there perhaps things for which one should not pray?

Her eyes suddenly flew open. "Oh! The Raven—is his name Zadkiel?—he told me there was an actual reason why I was in love with two boys and that I might find it out tonight."

"Yes, Zadkiel," Illondria's eyes twinkled with fondness. "As to the rest...." The Lios Alfar queen gazed off into the distance, the stars in her eyes shining brightly. Eventually, she sighed and said, "There is a reason, but it may be a hard thing for you to hear."

"No, please! Tell me."

Illondria took Rachel's hand and squeezed it. "Remember I told you I saw you establishing the Library of All Worlds?"

"Yes!" Rachel cried with joy. "I cannot think of a better future for a girl who wants to know everything!"

The elf queen nodded, smiling slightly. "If that is the future you pick, if you remain devoted to knowing everything, I believe you will find Gaius to be the perfect partner for you. His scientific curiosity and your desire for knowledge will blend together, and you will both be very happy."

"Oh, wonderful!" Rachel clapped, sending musical ripples through the surrounding grass and wildflowers. "And I'll just forget about... being in love with someone else?"

"*If* you choose that path, yes," Illondria said gently.

"I am so glad!"

"*If.*"

"If?" Rachel moistened her lips. She still felt calm and joyful—so joyful that she occasionally floated off the grass—and yet something inside her knew, had she been at home, this one word would have caused great trepidation.

"When I spoke to you before, that was the future before you, but now there is another possibility, another door."

"Where does this door go?" asked Rachel.

But even as she spoke, she knew the answer. It was the door the Raven had opened for her at her request, the door that would allow her to help the Keybearers in their quest.

Illondria replied, "It goes to an alternate path, a different future."

"Can't Gaius be in that future, too?"

"A future where you become the leader of the Last Harrowing."

Rachel rocked forward onto her knees and stared at her Elf. "I do... what?"

"One final step in the great plan that Our Creator prepared for salvation has not been carried out: the Last Harrowing of Hell. The Keybearers will descend into the depths and free all the souls that the demons have led astray over the millennia. '*And the sea gave up the dead which were in it; and death and hell delivered up the dead which were in them: and they were judged every man according to their works.*' The Keybearers will open the gates of Hell."

It seemed to Rachel that she heard bells ringing. These peals were far away, but, for a moment, she could not hear anything else. A strange sensation traveled through her, as if, somewhere, a door opened to a brighter, greater world.

She murmured, almost as if in a dream, "The door opened to *saving everybody?*"

Illondria nodded. "The mission of the Keybearers is the last action of salvation where created beings can lend aid. After that, all is in the hands of Leander—only He decides whose names are written in the Book of Life and who will meet... another fate."

The pealing of the bells grew louder, a sound both solemn and joyous. They seemed to reverberate throughout Rachel's entire being. She rose to her feet and gazed off at the snow-capped peaks lit by the distant Light beyond. Illondria looked towards the Mountains as well.

"What is that?" whispered Rachel.

Illondria replied, "Someone is entering Heaven. Those bells toll when someone leaves this land and enters Eternity."

They both were still, listening, until the deep and sonorous tolling faded away. The beautiful elf queen rose to her feet as well. She brushed her hand fondly over Rachel's straight black hair.

"If you choose the Library of All Worlds," Illondria said, "you will aid this venture by offering support, and you will find yourself in harmony with your young man. But if you choose the other path...."

"Can't I save people and love Gaius?" begged Rachel.

The starlight eyes of the queen of the Lios Alfar gazed directly into hers. "Can you?"

Rachel gazed up at the towering trees of the forest behind them. Then, she closed her eyes and imagined. It was easy to see herself as a gracious librarian, spending time with Gaius as he pursued scientific inquiries, searching the stacks with him in pursuit of knowledge, gazing up at him admiringly.

Then, she pictured herself stepping forward, leading her friends, being fearless, not letting anything stand in the way of breaking open the doors to the underworld and rescuing *everybody*. It did not matter to her what happened next, whether they were judged worthy or no. They would at least be free for a time, released from the prison to which the demons had dragged them. She could picture leading this mission with surprising ease, and when she did....

Rachel bit her lip. It was easy to picture herself, as the leader of her friends, working side by side with the Prince of Bavaria, coordinating their two groups as they prepared for what lay ahead. He would be an excellent working partner for such a project, but then, strangely enough, so might the Master of the World or anyone else who reminded her of her grandfather—any strong and powerful leader willing to cross worlds and take on the powers of darkness.

When she thought of Gaius from this position, however, he seemed strangely reduced — merely a follower of Dread's, no longer an equal. Rachel frowned, not at all happy. She opened her eyes again.

"But I *could* lead the Keybearers and stay with Gaius, right? I mean, if I wanted to?"

"Of course," Illondria replied gently. "The question is: would you want to?"

Rachel turned and gazed up at the Mountains, majestic and magnificent, lit by the Light from Beyond.

A flock of doves burst upward in a rush of wings. At least, she thought they were doves. They were so ethereal that when they flitted between the towering trees of the forest, they passed through the trunks. They were the purest white she had ever seen, except for one, who flew higher than the others and caught the Light from beyond the Mountains, which momentarily stained it with a pale golden hue. Rachel gasped at the beauty of their flight, and, even here, her eyes brimmed with tears. She felt as if she had lost something unbelievably precious, or perhaps as if it had just been returned to her. She had no idea why.

The Lios Alfar queen also fell silent, admiring the doves.

"So this is not about which boy I love," Rachel said slowly when the pale, ethereal birds vanished from sight. "It is about who *I* want to be: the girl-who-knows-everything or the girl-who-saves-everyone?"

"Yes. Very much so."

Rachel took a deep uneven breath. "But I don't have to decide right away, do I?"

"No, child," Illondria smiled. "You should have years. And remember: The librarian of the Library of All Worlds is an important position. Knowledge will be indispensable to the Final Harrowing. You mustn't feel you are required to lead. Not everyone needs to be out in front. I don't even understand how the path of your future could have been changed."

"Zadkiel did it," Rachel said simply, gazing at the majestic peaks again.

"What in the world possessed him to do such a thing?" the elf queen wondered.

"I asked him."

"You did?" Illondria cried, shocked. "Whatever for?"

"I wanted to do more."

"Ah," Illondria gazed at Rachel for a time, a slight smile curving her lips. "I see."

Rachel nodded once. She breathed the scented air and felt a buoyant lightness of spirit. Underneath, in the depths of her heart, the soft, sweet voice whispered to her, telling her that she knew the choice she would make, that there was no question which future she would choose.

Rachel ignored that voice. She felt it was suspect.

They walked across the symphony of clover again. The elf queen stared up at the Mountains, looking happy. "What your Guardian did for you was no small thing—giving you his own halo," she said. "I wonder…are you going to keep the gift he gave you? The grace he presented you with would allow you to remain here. You do not need to return. Going back down there would be very brave, but you must understand, the lightness you feel now will not be possible below."

"So all this joy, all this peace: it will all go away?" asked Rachel, not exactly sure what her Elf was saying.

"Only angels can dim their grace," said Illondria. "They can travel into the dark and not be affected by it. The rest of us rise up out of it as we become more pure, as we regain the joy of our Creator's love." She sighed. "I have to admit, my little one… I hope that you choose to stay. I would like to journey on to the Mountains with you and my beloved Duneyr. Time here is not the same as below. I do not think we would have to wait long for our loved ones to join us…."

Rachel hugged Illondria and looked off toward the Mountains with something more glorious than the sun shining upon their peaks. She wondered about the landscape beyond, overcome with sudden longing. "I would love to go on with you and see what comes next. I so want to see and know everything!"

But the longing was nothing compared to the sense of purpose that called her back to the world below. She might not know which of two fates she wanted, but remaining here would be turning her back on both of them.

"I could not possibly stay," Rachel said aloud. "There is so much for me to do down there, and I could not possibly take such a gift from Jariel and not return it."

It was beautiful here, but she could not wait to get home and tell Sigfried and Gaius and the others about all the amazing sights she had seen and the astonishing thing she had learned about the land of the dead. She imagined explaining to Nastasia about Heaven, telling Gaius how wrong he was about what comes next, and Vlad about the silvery, fallen World Tree, and Siggy, about, well, everything. She was fairly bursting with her eagerness to share what she had seen.

"Let me at least give you this." The Lios Alfar queen tapped her lightly on the forehead.

Rachel saw a flash of vision showing her a series of girls and one boy. She recognized Hope O'Keefe, Iolanthe Towers, Merry Vesper, Ameka Okeke, and Yolanda Debussy. She also saw an absolutely beautiful young woman, as lovely as Nastasia but wearing homespun clothing, and two younger children she did not recognize, a slender boy with a golden cat sitting on his head, and a slightly plump but bright and vivacious dark-haired girl. Somehow, she knew that their names were Caterina Caldwell, Odysseus Rune, and Iris Meadowsweet.

Illondria smiled. "I hope you don't mind this hint. I don't want to ruin all the pleasant surprises in store for you. But these people I have shown you, they may make nice friends."

Rachel could not imagine why the older girls, particularly a college junior such as Yolanda, would make good friends for her, but she nodded, noting their identities.

Eager to take in as much of this place as possible, she turned slowly. The sky beyond the forest was a deep, dark purple, almost as black as night. Silver and gold lines of light danced there, forming ever changing designs, like images glimpsed in the dancing flames of a hearth fire. It seemed to keep rhythm with Rachel's heartbeat.

The Lion stood beside her, larger than any earthly lion and more real even than this self-illumined landscape—as real as the Source of the glow that danced over the peaks of the snow-capped Mountains. His eyes were golden and seemed to shine with that same wondrous glow.

"How... how did I get here? I was—" Rachel turned slowly. She was back among the cherry trees, by the black sand. For some reason, she was holding a beautiful golden trumpet. Her voice rose. "I—I don't remember!"

"That is because it has not happened yet," replied the Lion.

"W-what?"

"Time does not run here as it does below. I have held aside a portion of your stay for you to use later, at a time of need."

"Oh," she breathed, blinking.

How could such a thing be? It made no sense, and yet, at the same time, it was supremely wonderful. *She would be allowed to come back, at least once more.*

She glanced up at the brilliantly lit white peaks, shining in such splendor. "Leander, is that... am I really going to be allowed to go there someday? Over the Mountains, I mean. Will I actually be able to come back permanently?"

The Lion stepped forward, towering over her, and gazed down at her with his great golden eyes. *"In my Father's house are many mansions: if it were not so, I would have told you. I go to prepare a place for you."*

"A place... for me?" Rachel's lips parted in joy. She was so surprised that her feet floated up from the ground. "Do you mean that I was right? People do have their own castles and such in the land of the dead?"

"If it were not so, I would have told you," repeated the Lion, which Rachel thought was an odd thing to say.

She ran and threw her arms around Him and hugged Him tightly, her body sinking into His silky flanks. Illondria, who stood nearby, rushed over and joined in the hug, as she had the time the two of them had hugged the Raven. Leander purred and licked Rachel's forehead, His huge, rough tongue combing through her hair.

Finally, drawing back, Rachel opened her mouth to ask if her grandfather would be there, too, on the other side of the Mountains, but then she shut it. If Leander were to say no, she would not be able to bear it, even here.

Illondria eventually drew back, smiling.

Rachel turned to Leander, "Is this visit… the blessing you promised me if I forgave others? I've been working very hard at forgiving people. Forgiving is very difficult… but it's not so very hard if you find something about the person to feel compassion for."

The Lion laughed, a noise like, and yet much more wonderful than, a roar. "No. Your reward is much greater than a visit. Your reward waits for you in my Father's kingdom. There is a place for you at His table. It is set, and the feast is already waiting. It shall be there later when you arrive. It is a place of honor awaiting you, one which is only given to those who choose to return to the shadows to help others."

He nuzzled her. "I will never ask of you more than you can carry, Rachel. And I shall not ask of you something I would not be willing to take on myself. As you have forgiven those who hurt you, so shall I forgive you for those things you did which hurt others. I shall take from them any pain they have when they remember you and leave them with nothing but memories of your light."

"I am so proud of you, little one. Please remember that you are in my heart always. I will pray for you," Illondria said.

"Do I need to leave now?" Rachel asked in a small voice.

The Lios Alfar queen said gently, "Though I am reluctant to say it, you should probably think of heading back. The part of the Guardian which is within you may be harder to release if you stay here much longer. And I am sure it is very tiring for him."

Rachel closed her eyes and said a prayer of gratitude for the Raven. In the vision that followed, she saw him standing where she had left him. His wings were looking battered. Some of the feathers had turned gray. The spark within him was more like a bolt of silvery lightning. Its character was *merciful*. A wind blew across the roof where he was and ruffled his feathers. He turned his head slightly, looking to the west.

Rachel gasped. Jariel's wings were damaged because of her. She did not feel frightened, but a sense of urgency seized her.

She cried, "Of course!"

"Oh! Rachel, please do me one favor," asked Illondria. "As long as you are bringing the trumpet to Sigfried, I wish to send something to Nastasia. When you return to Hoddmimir's Wood, ask Duneyr for my moonsilk gown. I think Nastasia will like it. It may be helpful; for it's stronger than it looks, and it has other virtues that could be useful to a Wayfarer. It can help keep her safe while traveling the Ways between the Worlds. I have nothing else I can give. My other possessions were passed to my children."

She hugged Rachel tightly and kissed her on the cheek. "I will see you again soon. Be brave, my little one. I shall pray for you. And remember, when you are in doubt, ask our Father."

Rachel nodded, gripping the golden trumpet—which was apparently for Sigfried.

Leander looked at her. "Are you ready?"

"I am ready," Rachel replied bravely.

"I will return you to the world below." Leander knelt beside her. "*Sabriost*."

Rachel gave Illondria one last embrace, climbed onto the Lion, and they were off. He bounded across the grass in great strides. Then they were loping through the sphere of stars, beholding again the star pictures that changed with each step. A stained-glass image showed a decapitated man holding his head. His expression was sorrowful but wise. Another step and the stars rearranged into a man pierced by many arrows. A third flashed by of a man in blue and gold robes holding large golden keys.

"What are these pictures?" asked Rachel.

"They honor those who put my Father's purposes ahead of their own," replied Leander. "That last, in blue and gold, is my right-hand man. He has the same name as your brother."

The next step revealed an older woman with a scarf over her head. She wore an old-fashioned costume with a vest and skirt.

"Who's that one?" asked Rachel.

"She was a mother to three children."

"Just that?"

When He replied, the Lion's voice was unexpectedly stern. "Isn't that enough?"

They plunged out of the golden sphere of stars and into darkness, back toward the silvery World Tree. Then they were in the garden on Hoddmimir's Wood. The antlered elf lord and Idunn were both there. Duneyr gazed at them, a slight half smile touching his lips.

"Hello, Leander. Nice little girl you have there."

Leander purred. "Yes, she is."

Rachel jumped down and curtsied. She told Duneyr briefly about her meeting with his wife. He listened with awe to hear about, as he put it, *these things of which mortal men know not* and thanked her for bringing such joyous news of his beloved. Rachel curtsied and asked about the gown. He nodded graciously and departed to fetch it.

Rachel smiled at both Idunn and the Lion. "Is there anything else you would like me to do? Other people who need messages or gifts?"

Leander and Idunn exchanged glances.

The Lion said, "Do not speak of what you have seen. If your friends ask where the gifts were acquired, answer that you are not allowed to speak of it."

"Oh." Rachel swallowed with some difficulty.

The Lion continued, "Speak to Nastasia Romanov. Ask her to point out to her grandfather that keeping the followers of my Father away has *not* kept demonic influence from entering the world. They have only pretended so they could slip in silently without fear of My interference. If you do this first and wait, the elder Romanov will rescind his order to Zadkiel.

"If you do not heed my warning and begin to spread word of what you have seen, Zadkiel may be forced to choose between harming you or breaking his oath. No matter which option he chooses, it will have a grave outcome."

Rachel gasped, horrified.

Idunn stepped forward and took Rachel's hands, her silver wings spread wide behind her. "Please, Rachel Griffin, do not risk my brother falling farther from grace than he has. I know you ache to speak of the wonders you have seen. Please contain yourself until my brother is safe."

The angel looked concerned, almost scared. The Lion cocked his head and gave Idunn a rather odd look. Rachel could not tell what it meant.

Rachel laughed happily. Maybe it was an aftereffect of the foothills of Heaven, but it had a lovely sound. "Idunn, do not be afraid. If it is a choice between speaking and harming the Raven, whom I love more than anything else or keeping quiet, that is no choice to me. I like knowing secrets, and I would do anything for the Raven. I have been waiting and waiting for a chance to do something for him. This... this is hardly even difficult."

Even as she said this, Rachel realized her words were not entirely true. Because she did not actually like *knowing* secrets. What she liked was *telling* secrets. Keeping silent about the wonders she had seen would be very hard indeed, especially when she was so eager to share all that she had seen with Siggy and Gaius. If it were for Jariel, however, it would be as nothing.

Duneyr returned with a white parcel, which he handed to Rachel. There was a rush of motion, and she was back on the roof at Gryphon Park. Even remembering back, she could not recall if it was Leander or Idunn who had returned her. The Raven was standing nearby. He looked weary but resolute. The black Wolf stood guard next to him.

The Wolf snorted. "Well, look at that. She returned. I owe you a guinea."

Rachel ran directly to the Raven, his halo in an outstretched hand. It had turned into a solid silver ring again that filled her with a sense of diligent certainty while she touched it. When she reached him, she threw her arms around him and hugged him.

He hugged her back. "Hello, Rachel Griffin. You smell very nice."

"Are you... are you okay?" She looked him over carefully, a lump forming in her throat when she saw a number of graying feathers in his black wings.

He bowed his head graciously. "I am well."

Rachel reached out slowly and touched a damaged feather, her face somewhat pale. "Is this... because of me? Why did you do that? Why didn't you tell me ahead of time that it would hurt you? Will they get better?"

She touched his face, laying her palm against his cheek.

He replied gently, "I will be fine."

The Wolf laughed. "Little girl, give him back his halo. While you ask questions, he grows weaker. And he's not going to ask for it. Give halo now. Ask later. Understand?"

"But I did!" Rachel cried. She looked at her hands. She still held the halo. He had not taken it from her outstretched hand. She thrust it at him.

Jariel took the halo. "Thank you."

The Wolf sighed. "We're done, right?"

The Raven nodded. "Thank you, brother."

The Wolf said, "Please... don't mention it."

It vanished before Rachel could open her mouth to say thank you. The Raven was gone as well.

Percy Cornelius Taylor was moving again. "—ow. How did you get over there? Oh drat, did I miss it?"

"Could... couldn't you see them?" Rachel asked, surprised.

He looked at her curiously. "See who?"

"How did you know a surprise was coming?"

"I just knew. We know things here on this side. And sometimes we hear whispers of things to come. All dreadfully mysterious." Percy Cornelius Taylor winked at her.

CHAPTER THIRTY-NINE: APRIL FOOL'S DAY

"Can we drop objects on the heads of the tourists?" asked Sigfried, as they flew their bristlelesses over the British countryside heading for Glastonbury Tor. Casually pulling a coin from his pocket, he made a motion with his arm as if he were aiming it at a man in a red jacket far below. The coin glinted golden in the April sunlight.

"I imagine they will forgive you for beaning them if they're allowed to keep the gold," opined Peter Griffin, from where he sat upon his red and blue racer.

"Boss!" cried Lucky, aghast, gazing at the gold coin as if at a long-lost brother, "not Wilberforce Wigglefoot Glintshimmer the Fourth! Spare Wilberforce, boss! Spare him!"

"Oh, of course! Right." Sigfried hastily returned the coin to his pocket.

"It's for the best," quipped Valerie, who had joined them for Siggy's birthday. She had borrowed a green Flycycle from Salome. It had handlebars like a bike. "This being April First, no one would believe them if they tried to tell the tale. Could ruin a person's whole life: 'Beaned on the head on April Fools Day, and no one would believe it.'"

"Do you have any idea what gold is going for these days?" asked Peter. "I should think their new fortune would make up for any discomfort. Or disbelief."

"Fortune?" Siggy frowned, puzzled. "One coin?"

"Glastonbury!" Rachel interrupted, pointing downward at the terraced green mount with a lone tower atop it. "There it is!"

"Looks like an upside-down ship," said Sigfried, turning his head to the side.

"Covered with grass," quipped Valerie Hunt, as she leaned forward on the handlebars of her bristleless. Her camera hung unused at her side. Instead, she held a small shiny object that looked like an overly thick, rectangular calling card that she waved back and forth as if it could somehow capture the landscape. "And sheep."

"An upside-down ship covered with grass," agreed Siggy.

"And tasty sheep!" offered Lucky.

"Nobody knows what gives it that ship-like shape—the scalloped, seven-tier sides—neither the Unwary nor the Wise," said Peter.

The four of them, wearing shadowcloaks thrown over their parkas to hide them from the Unwary, flew towards the stone tower atop Glastonbury Tor. Beneath them, mist clung here and there, between the rows of trees that separated one large square of farmland from another. Ahead lay Glastonbury. Rachel was always impressed by the way the green tor thrust up from an entirely flat countryside. Atop the green, ship-shaped hill stood the ruin of a stone building. Only a single tower remained, a rather handsome tower with arched doors on the bottom, on either side, allowing tourists to gaze straight through it to the emerald hilltop beyond. The tall, narrow tower looked quite eerie protruding from the top of the scalloped green tor.

It was a joy to be out flying with friends, though Rachel was glad it was such a bright day. Everything still looked a bit dim to her since returning from the brilliant light of the Foothills. The previous day, she had said very little. She was too full of the joy of her birthday visit to speak of anything else, and since she could not speak of that, she had hardly spoken at all. There had been nothing else she had wished to say.

That evening, she had come up with a clever way to give Sigfried the trumpet. She slipped it in with his birthday presents. Since he did not track which gift came from which family member, he never wondered who had given him an instrument to replace his battered school loaner. The whole family had been impressed by the angelic quality of its sound.

The family had given Sigfried his presents at breakfast. Having never had a birthday party before, he was a bit overwhelmed. He received books about King Arthur from Peter, a new wardrobe from the duchess, some personal items, such as a comb, razors, and a new toothbrush, from Laurel, and, from Sandra, a medieval surcoat of red and gold with a dragon on the chest that he immediately donned and was currently wearing. But the gift that had truly bedazzled him was the backpack from Rachel and her father. He had been utterly blown away at the discovery that he now owned a small house with an enormous safe. For a time, Rachel had feared he would never emerge again. When he did come out, it was so that he and Lucky could move their gold into the safe. After that, only the arrival of Valerie and the promise of the trip to Glastonbury had convinced him to reemerge. He wore the backpack now, as he flew, grateful to be able to keep track of his immense wealth at all times.

"Remind me again," asked Valerie, as they circled the tor itself. She peered at her rectangular calling card object instead of looking at the landscape, "what Glastonbury is known for. Why are we here?"

"It's part of the Arthurian lore," explained Rachel.

"King Arthur and Queen Gwenhwyfar are buried here," said Peter.

Sigfried tapped his chest where his All-Seeing Eye lay beneath his new red and gold dragon surcoat. "I don't see any bodies yet but.... Hey! There's a hallway inside the hill!"

"Does it lead to a barrow?" asked Valerie, peering downward with interest.

Siggy shook his head. "No, to an arched doorway. On the far side is a forest."

"There's a forest inside the mountain?" Valerie asked wryly, clearly thinking that she had misunderstood Siggy.

"Yes," said Sigfried.

"It's a big forest," said Lucky. "With castles and candlelight and monsters."

Rachel and Peter exchanged glances, exclaiming together: *"Underhill!"*

The four of them circled down toward the tower, Lucky following like a comet tail. They landed on the perfect green lawn of the tor. No one else was around. Sigfried walked into the tower and approached one of the stone benches set against the wall. When he lifted the slate seat of the bench, it revealed a staircase, leading downward, into the earth.

Rachel, who had visited this tower several times in her fourteen years, gawked at the hidden staircase. "Has it always been here?"

"Looks like it," Peter said, squatting down to examine the bench. "I see marks from where the seat has been removed before. They look quite old."

Siggy swung his leg over the rim of the stone box that was the base of the bench and descended. Rachel eagerly followed.

"Is this wise?" Peter asked behind her. "Fairyland can be dangerous. Maybe we shouldn't go any farther."

"And miss out on a chance to interview a fairy?" Valerie shot by him and came rapidly down the narrow stairs.

The others followed her. At the bottom of the staircase, a path led through a cramped, earthen tunnel to an arch made of ivory. Siggy and Valerie left their bristlelesses at the bottom of the stairs before continuing down the path to the ivory arch. Rachel and Peter held onto theirs. On the far side of the arch, an entirely different landscape awaited.

Beyond the arch, a silver path, much like the track moonlight leaves across water, stretched into the distance. The four of them walked warily along it, while Lucky flew overhead, eyes bright.

Lily-of-the-valley lined either side of the path. The bell-shaped flowers chimed like crystal bells, high and soft. Slender silver birches grew beyond the lily-of-the-valley. Beneath these saplings, bluebells stretched as far as the eye could see. In the periwinkle twilight, the bluebells—clusters of trumpet-shaped flowers on green stalks—shone a perfect sapphire and rang with a deeper chime than the "white coral bells" of the lily-of-the-valley. Here and there, among the bluebells, peeked snowdrops or a marsh lily. Only, instead of delicate white blossoms and elegant, curving petals of yellow, the snowdrops were of pure silver and the marsh lilies of shining gold.

What Rachel beheld was so dream-like and beautiful that she might have feared she had wandered into dreamland, except that the enchanted landscape, the lovely perfume, and the ringing chimes all remained in harmony. Had this been dreamland, the scents and sounds would not have matched. And yet there were strange noises in the distance that made her skin crawl and occasional whiffs of rotting vegetable matter. *The Foothills of Heaven, this was not.*

"Do not leave the path," Peter admonished sternly. "Fairies cannot harm us while we stick to the path. If we venture off, we are fair game."

"Don't leave the path. Important safety tip," murmured Valerie, drawing her mauve-handled butterfly knife and flipping it open. Siggy watched her do it with a happy, dreaming expression on his face. With her other hand, Valerie held up her Unwary calling card. "Do you think fairyland will damage my phone?"

Rachel knew about Unwary telephones. They were big, clunky things with dials or buttons. She was not exactly sure why Valerie called the device in her hand a phone, but then, she had heard that the Unwary were catching up and surpassing the World of the Wise in the communication department. Maybe they had invented electronic calling cards.

"No idea," replied Peter. "Magic and technology often interfere with each other."

Valerie reluctantly put away her phone and her knife and picked up her camera, which required two hands. A brilliant flash lit the twilight landscape. Tiny pillywiggins, with their dragonfly wings beating almost too fast for the eye to see, turned and gaped at her, terrified by the brightness.

"Look, fairies!" she gasped, charmed.

"Pillywiggins," Peter explained. "Flower fairies."

He pointed to a snowdrop fairy in her white shift with iridescent wings, and two bluebell fairies, each wearing one perfect blue blossom for a hat and a second for a smock. They hovered among the flowers, as if protecting them. Valerie made a noise of girlish delight, but her admiration for the flower fairies did not keep her from snapping several more pictures.

"Ace!" cried Siggy. "Can we catch one?"

He lunged forward, but Valerie leapt in his way.

"Don't leave the path, Sweetiekins. Remember?"

"I am not sure you should be calling me Sweetiekins in public, on my birthday," declared the now-fifteen-year-old boy.

"It rusts his dignity," declared Lucky.

"I think you mean ruffles or some such," Peter replied, looking this way and that very carefully, a hand on Rachel's shoulder to keep her from straying. "Dignities don't rust."

"No such luck," replied Valerie. "After some of the things you've called me, you're lucky I don't go for something much worse."

"Better suck it up, boss," warned Lucky. "Goldilocks means business."

They followed the silver path, walking amidst the sea of blue, punctuated here and there by a bloom of silver or gold. The lilies-of-the-valley chimed sweetly to either side. Rachel leaned over to sniff one and found her eyelids were suddenly very heavy. She even caught sight of her dream unicorn, offering to take her for a ride through dreamland. Quickly, she straightened and shook herself to stay awake. Valerie, too, nearly fell under the spell of fairyland. Walking while gazing through her camera, she would have wandered right off the path if Peter had not put a hand on her shoulder. She blinked, confused.

"Stay to the middle of the path," Rachel's older brother warned. "The pull of the fey is less powerful there." Then he added, "I say, Rach. I hadn't noticed that you were growing your hair out. Looks nice."

Rachel reached back and then ran her fingers over her straight locks. Her hair now reached the middle of her upper back. How could that be? Mother had just trimmed it the previous week. Was it a trick of faerie? No, thinking back, she realized that it had been a bit longer when she woke up on Sunday than it had been when she went to bed Saturday night—though not as long as it was now. How strange.

They walked on. A hush fell over their party, a sensation Rachel had learned to associate with the fey. Only this time, it was a thousand times stronger. The sense of anticipation was so powerful that it settled upon them like a weighty yoke, making it difficult to breathe. They moved closer together, sticking to the center of the path. Valerie and Siggy both pulled out their knives. Ahead loomed a dark forest. Beyond that, high on a hill, stood a fairy palace, complete with high white towers with blue conical roofs.

"Ace," whispered Sigfried, awed.

Valerie snapped a photo.

Ahead, to the left, candlelight twinkled between the trunks through the dark forest. As they drew closer to the edge of the forest, they saw two hulking shapes, like gargoyles, facing toward them, one hunkered down to either side of the silver pathway. They were made of stone, or at least, they stood as still as stone, but their eyes seemed to follow the newcomers.

Lucky dived down and wrapped around Sigfried. The five of them approached these guardian monsters warily. The hulking figures did not move as Rachel and her companions walked between them, but Rachel could have sworn she heard one of them growl as they passed.

They entered the forest. Even with the shimmering of the silvery pathway, it was surprisingly dark. The five of them moved even closer together.

"They can't hurt us if we don't leave the path, right?" whispered Valerie.

"That's the theory," replied Peter.

Valerie whimpered softly, and Siggy put a protective arm around her shoulder.

Suddenly, the sky above them burst into a thousand colors of light. Each glowing hue exploded overhead, raining down fiery dust, accompanied by a sound more like bells tolling than like a bang. The little points of falling flame spread wings and darted off in all directions, laughing gleefully.

"What the...." Valerie added her flash to the light and chaos.

"Is fairyland always like this?" Siggy gawked.

Peter shook his head gravely. "Today is the First of April, Fairy New Year. We are witnessing a New Year's celebration."

"Oh, of course!" cried Rachel, embarrassed she had not made the connection.

As the fairy fireworks died away, the forest that the silver path ran through seemed particularly dark. Ahead was a break in the trees. Grape vines blocked their view of what lay beyond, but golden lights, like a thousand candles, twinkled through the gaps in the greenery. This was the same candlelight they had seen from the path among the flowers. Huge black, horned monsters stood guard to either side of this vine-screened opening in the forest.

Siggy murmured, "What are those? Goth *Where-the-Wild-Things-Are* monsters?"

Valerie snorted, but Rachel agreed with Siggy's description. The monsters were similar to those from the children's book, but darker and scarier. Now, they turned their heads toward the party of young people and howled. In the next moment, hulking dark shapes with huge fangs surrounded the students, growling. There were monsters and monstrosities, fanged beasts, furry man-things with long prehensile tails, creatures made in part of shadow.

One particularly large, horned monster moved to block their way.

Peter straightened his shoulders and met the monster's gaze evenly. "We're on the path. What seems to be the trouble?"

Valerie stepped boldly forward and shoved her phone device out before her. "Hi, I'm Valerie Hunt with the *Roanoke Glass*. May I ask you a few questions?"

The beast blocking their way gawked at Valerie, as if not sure what to make of her, then it pointed a razor-sharp claw at Rachel's heart. "Not her."

The others turned towards Rachel.

"I say, sis," Peter asked, puzzled, "why are you so much brighter than the rest of us?"

Rachel looked down at herself. Peter was right. He and Sigfried and Valerie looked as if they were standing among dark trees, but her body was as bright as if she stood in... *the Foothills of Heaven*. In the same way that the glow of the Source Beyond had illuminated the white-capped peaks of the Mountains, the light of the Foothills still shone upon her.

"Ordinarily," cackled a hag who drifted forward from among the pack of monsters gathering around them, "we would slay you for such impudence, to bring such as that here. That light, that sweet scent. You do mock us with what can never be ours."

"Path or no path," a hyena monster crept forward, slavering, "let's eat her."

"I want to be interviewed by the mortal!" giggled a horned figure made of shadow.

"Stay on the path," Peter murmured under his breath, his hand still on Rachel's shoulder. He held his red and blue racer in his other hand as if intending to wield it as a weapon. Valerie stood in front of Peter. She pocketed the phone and lifted her camera with one hand, ready to ignite the flash if a distraction was needed. With her other hand, she flipped her butterfly knife back and forth. Sigfried had both his Bowie knife with its black warding blade and his wand, holding one in either hand. Rachel drew her wand as well, holding it tightly but not aiming it. In her other hand, she gripped Vroomie tightly.

The monsters moved closer. The shadowy things drifted the closest of all, hovering just at the edge of the silvery path. Snarling beasts opened thickly fanged mouths. The giant wild things flexed their claws and howled. The man-things swung by their prehensile tails, swooping dangerously close to the heads of the four students. The hag cackled, a disturbing sound that sent shivers up the backs of the listeners. The horned monstrosity, still the only creature standing on the path, took a menacing step closer; his growl rumbled like distant thunder.

Rachel took a step closer to Peter and Siggy, who now stood back-to-back facing either side of the path, with the two young women between them. Lucky stretched out and wrapped around all four of them. He sent a plume of flame at one of the swinging man-things. It withdrew, terrified.

"Should I go back?" Rachel whispered.

"We're not splitting up," announced Peter. "We go on together, or we go back together."

"We're on the path," murmured Valerie. "Is this a test? Or are they breaking the rules?"

"That's what I am trying to figure out," Peter replied, *sotto voce*.

The hyena-thing screeched, "Kill her, boys! Destroy her! Tear her limb from limb!"

Peter straightened his back. "It's got to be a test. Don't give...."

The giant horned monster took two ponderous steps forward. It reached out with its enormous hand and grabbed Rachel around the neck, lifting her into the air, pulling her right out of the loop of Lucky. His huge leathery fingers closed tightly around her throat.

Sigfried bellowed with rage and leapt forward, sinking his black Bowie blade into the monster's long, hairy arm. Peter lunged forward like a fencer and jabbed the monster in its round stomach with the haft of his bristleless. Valerie ignited her flash in the creature's face, causing it to reel back and throw its other arm in front of its face. Lucky swooped up and, with a huge breath of flame, set the creature's fur on fire.

Rachel tried to cry out, but she could not breathe. It was still holding her in its outstretched hand. In her surprise, she let go of Vroomie. She used this free hand to pull on the hand holding her neck, but she could not budge a single finger. She flailed with her arms and kicked her feet, to no avail. She still gripped her wand in her right hand, but what could she do with it? Freezing the creature in place would not help. It would trap her, too. She could call Vladimir. The bracelet would respond to her intention, but could a person jump from Bavaria to Elfland? If he failed, where would he end up? Descriptions of horrific jumping accidents involving mangled limbs and bodies stuck in walls leapt to mind.

The brute bellowed in pain from Sigfried's blow and from the intense heat of the flames, though Rachel wondered if it might have some resistance to fire, as she had seen Lucky's flame cause far more damage in the past. The monster raised Rachel higher as if to dash her to the ground. The edges of her vision began to go dark.

"Halt," cried a gracious, feminine voice.

The vines parted, and candlelight spilled out of the glade beyond. In the gap in the greenery stood a lovely golden-haired woman dressed in a gown of white and gold and wearing a crown of burning candles. She had lavender eyes and upswept elfin ears and brows. From her back spread translucent, glowing, golden butterfly wings. Fireflies danced around her, swirling about her head, shoulders, and delicate, pale gold slippers. Moths the color of a candle's flame circled above her crown of candles like a living coronet.

"Hark, Goineog," the lady chided gently, gliding forward, "hast thou fallen so far that thou wilt feast upon innocent mortal babes who have not even committed the offense of departing from the path?"

The monsters took a step back, perhaps to shield their eyes from her brilliance. The hyena-thing lowered its head and tucked its tail between its legs. The monsters and monstrosities turned their attention to this new-comer, growling and baring their teeth. The horned monster slowly lowered Rachel to the path and removed his great hand. Rachel's hand flew to her throat. She gasped for air, immediately grabbing Vroomie and hugging the steeplechaser to her chest. Peter rushed to her side, putting his arm around her. Sigfried slowly withdrew his knife from the monster's arm. It howled in pain, alternating between sucking on its wounded arm and trying to smother Lucky's flames.

Rachel drew a deep breath, nearly choking on the nauseating stink of burning fur. The fairy lady turned to the burning beast and made a come-hither gesture. The flames leapt off from the creature, formed a golden-red ball of fire, and floated over beside her shoulder. From within ball of fire, eyes opened and looked curiously around. Lucky's jaw dropped so far that it brushed the ground.

"'Tis New Year's Day," continued the lady. "Should not we show our famed fairy generosity by inviting these guests to share our festivities? Surely, ye would not have it bandied about that we fairies are less than gracious hosts? Yesterday was the most holy of days, the day when He who was dead lived again. Shall we not spare these in His name?"

Rachel looked at the lady curiously. Something about her face looked vaguely familiar. She searched her memory, but she was certain she had never before seen this person. It must be a family resemblance then, which was always harder for her memory to match. Rapidly, she brought to mind other golden-haired women she knew and then some blond men, but in none could she detect a resemblance.

When the fairy lady continued to gaze evenly upon the gathered pack of monsters, despite their growling and posturing, they began to slink back, looking wary, even frightened. The lady with the long golden hair and the crown of candles rested her gaze upon their faces. She sighed, smiling sadly. Then, she lowered her lashes and averted her face, feigning fear.

"Woe is me," she declared, her voice faint, her wrist to her brow. "The sentinels of my prison are such frightful beasts. I tremble at the thought. Alack, I must flee back to mine abode."

Her wrist still to her brow, she drew back the vines and gestured with her other hand, the blinking of fireflies outlining her motion. The silvery substance of the road flowed into the glade, forming a large circle within.

"Anon, children. I would fain have you accompany me to my bower. 'Tis safe for all as my glade now partaketh of the path. No harm shall there come to you."

The five exchanged glances. Sigfried still held his blade extended. It dripped with black ichor.

"Whose hospitality are we accepting?" asked Peter stiffly, eyeing the silvery circle beyond the screen of vines.

"Hath mankind so soon forgotten me?" the lady asked, looking faintly sad. "Dost thou truly know me not?"

As she spoke, she turned her head, and in a flash, Rachel realized who this fairy resembled and why it had been difficult to place her.

"Of course, we know you," Rachel replied with a deep curtsy. "How could we not recognize such a 'very influential fairy'?"

Chapter Forty:
The Gryphon Knight

Peter gazed at her with interest. "Are you the Lady Iolanthe?"

"Who?" asked Valerie.

Peter replied, "The subject of a famous operetta and an ancestor of our classmate, Iolanthe Towers."

"'Tis I!" The Lady Iolanthe clapped her hands for joy. "Thou dost know my namesake! Tell me: How faireth she? Doth she prosper?"

"She doth, er does," Rachel smiled. "She is training to be a fairy covenant negotiator."

"We have need of such," replied Lady Iolanthe. "All success I pray for her."

They followed her warily into her glade, now glowing with a silvery light in addition to the thousands of candles. In the center was an enormous willow tree. A throne of living willow wood stood under the tree's weeping branches, which surrounded the bower with a delicate veil of greenery. Chandeliers of delicately wrought gold hung from several of the larger branches overhead, each lit with a thousand candles. Moths the color of candlelight flitted hither and yon among the branches. Beyond the willow, a rushing dark river, curled around the outskirts of the glade.

The lady seated herself upon the throne of living wood. To either side were gathered *encantadas*, luminous fairies with the appearance of young women dressed in bright reds and oranges and yellows. Their hair was fair upon their head and then, as it descended, turned to amber and then to apricot or even tangerine, so that it resembled living candle flame. *Tisanieres*, who resembled pleasant old women with scarves over their heads and bright peasant skirts, sat nearby on large toadstools. These old-lady fey emitted a beautiful fragrance that perfumed the air of the willow bower.

The toadstools formed a semi-circle around a four-foot fountain of fire. The flame was the color of candlelight but made of thin darts of light that constantly burst into smaller and smaller starbursts before raining down like warm golden weeping willow branches. The fire fountain crack-

led pleasantly and smelled of newly struck matches. At first, it looked like fireworks, but then Rachel began to notice that the sparks formed lovely little feminine figures who danced within the sparkling flames. Several waved to her before their figures burst apart, reforming elsewhere in the fountain to wave again.

A pale crescent moon, glowing pearly white, hung in the upper branches of the tree. Three little fairy children with butterfly wings sat upon it, swinging merrily. They tossed tiny stars back and forth, as mortal children might toss a ball. Below them were tall figures in white whose appearance Rachel could not quite resolve. Was that large white shape a miter or a blossom-like head? Were those wings or giant flower petals? They reminded her of figures she had seen two years earlier when her family had attended the Platinum Jubilee Parade for the old queen, but she had no idea what they were.

Four knights with fanciful helmets shaped like mythical beasts, such as unicorn and minotaur, guarded the maidens and crones. The monsters who had confronted the four students before now slunk through the grape vines and surrounded the willow tree, careful not to step on the silvery glowing area or venture inside the screen of willow branches. They jeered and snarled at the candle-crowned lady and her attendants.

Valerie stepped forward, for some reason holding her phone up before her. "Valerie Hunt, Girl Reporter. I represent the *Roanoke Glass*. Do you mind if I write an article about you?"

The fairy lady laughed gaily. "Not at all. Though many mortals will not believe." Sadness came into her eyes. "They have forgotten us."

"The *Roanoke Glass* is read by the Wise; they remember. Though you are right. I grew up among what these guys call the Unwary. We had forgotten fairies," Valerie said sadly. Then, she gestured with her head toward the beasts and hags, "I can't help noticing your, er, escorts? Are you imprisoned here?"

A quick smile danced across the fairy lady's face. She leaned toward them conspiratorially, "They pretend so, but they could not restrain me should I desire to go thither." She gave the gathered shadows, monsters, and fanged beasts a fond look. "'Tis not of their own choosing that they have been given such an onerous task. I take pity upon them and pretend to be properly cowed."

Rachel pursed her lips. *So that was why the fairy lady had made a show of being frightened!*

"What is the reason for your supposed imprisonment?" asked Peter, stepping forward with a frown. He had a look as if, had he been wearing a sword, he would have placed his hand upon the pommel. Instead, he kept a tight grip on his bristleless.

With a sad smile, the lady replied, "They are sore afraid of me."

"Why?" asked Peter and Valerie together.

"They fear I will speak to angels," she replied gravely. "Or rather, they fear I will speak of angels, which, in our current clime 'tis countenanced the worse crime."

"Do you do that often?" Rachel asked. "Talk to angels, I mean?"

Lady Iolanthe replied, "Often? Not presently, but I am the high lady of the Seelie Court whose duty it is to do so."

"Wait. I don't get it," said Valerie. "Why is talking to angels bad?"

She turned in a circle, holding out her device. Then she switched to her camera and snapped a photo of the lady and her maidens, bathing the whole area in the brilliant light of her flash. The *encantadas* cried out with joy. As the flash faded, their incandescent gowns glowed brightly, but the darker monstrosities hissed and fled away from the light, slinking back slowly only once it had faded.

Lady Iolanthe replied, "The Emperor of Mankind decreed that this world forget Heaven."

"Why?" asked Valerie.

"I ken not, but rumor's foul tongue reports that a seer told him that, were it so, Hell wouldst consider us beneath its notice."

"That's what Amber said to the Raven," Rachel murmured to Sigfried, who nodded nonchalantly, not entirely paying attention. He was staring as if mesmerized at the figures in the flaming fountain, but his fingers tapped lightly on his chest, leading Rachel to suspect that he was actually using his amulet to examine their surroundings.

Lady Iolanthe continued, "The Gray Raven, in his great mercy, allowed us elves to keep our memories, but my fellow fey live in terror lest I upset this delicate balance, and we all be constrained to lose our memories, as mortals did.

"But enough o' my plight," she smiled kindly at her young guests. "Tell me, children: wherefore art you come?"

"What's that up there?" Valerie pointed in the direction of the palace on the hill beneath the fairy fireworks.

"The palace of my liege, Lady Cobweb," replied Lady Iolanthe.

"Lady Cobweb of the Five Elf Lords?" asked Rachel curiously.

Valerie asked, "They're the elves that make covenants with the Parliament of the Wise, right?"

Iolanthe nodded. Valerie asked more questions of both the lady and of her maidens. While his girlfriend distracted them, Siggy stepped beside Rachel and murmured, "It's here."

"What's here?" Rachel frowned.

"The thing," he replied. "The whatameguie."

Rachel blinked. That told her nothing.

"That we've been searching for," continued Sigfried.

Oh! Rachel's eyes grew wide. She suddenly recalled a great many things at once. Her Art tutor's voice echoed in her memory:

Your encyclopedia must be from an Unwary publisher. I was born in eighteen fourteen.

I was ten. Amelia and I lived close to each other... but we met during a family outing in Salisbury. Or was it Glastonbury?

Amelia met them in Cornwall with bristlelesses. I met them later that day, and all five of us brought the Heart to its final destination.

Mrs. Heelis was born in eighteen-fourteen. That meant that she met the others in eighteen twenty-four—the very year of the heist. *I met them later that day, and all five of us....* Rachel had assumed Mrs. Heelis meant that she had *met up* with her other four friends later in the day, but what if she had meant it literally? What if ten-year-old Beatrix Potter met Amelia Abney-Hastings and the three young men for the first time, later that day, *at Glastonbury?*

"Milady," Rachel curtsied to the fairy lady, "we are here for the Heart of Dreams."

Lady Iolanthe nodded. "Methought it might be thus. Gryphon Knight, come forth."

One of the four knights came forward. This one wore a helm shaped like an eagle but with lion paws to either side of his head—a griffin! He was grim of visage, with chestnut hair and a drooping mustache. Around his neck, a chain hung to the middle of his chest. In the middle of the chain shone the silver gem from the princess's vision.

Rachel looked up into the knight's rugged yet ageless face. It was a familiar face, one she had seen many times—in portraits, on the walls of Gryphon Park Manor.

"You're Uther!" Rachel cried, shocked. "Uther Griffin!"

"You mean our great-great-great-grandfather? The Seventh Duke?" cried Peter.

"Yes," replied Rachel, in shock.

"Didn't he wander off and get eaten by a giant or a frog or something?" asked Siggy.

"I think you mean a bog," Valerie called over her shoulder.

"I most certainly do not!" Sigfried replied indignantly.

"If he hasn't been eaten yet, I could do it for him," Lucky offered hopefully. "I mean, in case it's important that the legends be true."

"No good, Lucks." His boy shook his head. "You can't eat the blood-sister's relatives. We've been over this."

The fairy lady watched, her wise eyes crinkling with amusement. The knight searched their faces. "Are you Griffins? You do not have the family look."

Peter lifted his chin and spoke precisely. "That is because our mother is part Korean. I am Lord Falconridge, and this is my sister."

"I am Sigfried Smith, the Dragonslayer, and this is my lady, Valerie Hunt," said Siggy. "And this is my brother, Lucky the Dragon."

"A most curious brother for a dragonslayer," Lady Iolanthe said, her eyes dancing.

The knight's face took on a look of happy surprise, but then sorrow hijacked his features. "Ah. If you are Falconridge, then has Blaise finally departed the land of the living?"

"You mean Grandfather?" Rachel asked. "Yes. He died almost four years ago."

Uther Griffin hung his head in sorrow. "I am sorry to hear this." Looking up, he asked, "Did we know this, milady?"

"We knew," she replied solemnly. "Sir Calidor did inform us, but perhaps thou wert traveling, deep within our fair and perilous realm, when the news came."

Rachel looked from one to the other. "You knew Grandfather?"

"Yea, my almost-grandchildren, I did most certainly," replied the fairy lady sadly. "Once upon a time, Blaise Griffin was married to my daughter."

"Your d-daughter?" Rachel's jaw dropped. She recalled the marble gravestone with no birth date and the golden rosebud. "The Lady Estelle?"

Lady Iolanthe inclined her head. "My daughter Estelle became enamored of Blaise Griffin and asked for my blessing. She convinced me to allow her to venture into the mortal world. There tragedy befell her. Had it not, ye might have been my grandchildren."

Sir Calidor Moth must have left the bud for her when he came to attend the Round Table. No wonder it was so strange, made of gold yet living. It came from fairyland.

"Myrddin is half fairy?" she asked.

"A quarter fairy," the lady corrected. Her eyes twinkled. "Which maketh moot the question of whether the fey portion was his top half or his bottom half."

"Did you also have a son named Strephon?" asked Rachel.

Lady Iolanthe nodded. "I do. Sir William and Sir Arthur took many liberties with my life in their charming operetta. They changed the names of my late husband and some of the other peers, as well as adding details about fairyland, which they cut from whole cloth. At my request, no mention was made of Estelle. I did not want her name bandied about for the entertainment of mortals."

"Sir William and Sir Arthur," Valerie asked, looking between them. She pointed her phone toward Rachel.

Rachel leaned toward her, "Gilbert and Sullivan's first names."

"Oh," Valerie nodded. "Makes sense."

The fountain of flame crackled and popped. Gold-white spheres of light, almost the color of sunlight, appeared among the sparkling fire-fountain. Rachel blinked and rubbed her eyes. There was something strange and holy about the spheres, as if the Shadowlands dissolved for a moment when they appeared, and one looked directly upon some celestial glory.

She turned away from the fire and gazed at her lost-and-now-found ancestor in awe and curiosity. He was the great kenomancer who built much of the current manor and added all that extra space. It was he who had brought the Friesians to Gryphon Park and who bound Dart so that she was forbidden to.... *Oh!* Something she had not understood suddenly became clear.

When speaking to the duke, Dart had not said: *Bound by Griffin night am I to only slay before Spring Equinox and then abide by ceremony.* She had said: *Bound by Gryphon Knight.*

"Sir," Peter addressed their great-great-great-grandfather, "why did you leave? You had a new wife, a young son, in addition to your older children. You were renowned throughout the empire for your skills at keno-mancy. Why would you leave and come to live among the fey?"

The Seventh Duke of Devon regarded him with an expression that reminded Rachel of her grandfather. "I could not stay. I was no longer welcome in the sunlit lands."

"But why?" asked Valerie, snapping a picture of him.

Uther Griffin grunted in surprise, covering his eyes. He blinked for a moment until he regained his sight. "Why do you carry the sun in a little box?"

"Actually, it's a kind of talking glass," said Valerie. "It's just fixed on the sun. The shutter opens and lets the light shine out. It makes it bright as day. Just for a minute." She paused and grinned. "Then the leprechauns in my box paint a picture very quickly."

Sigfried regarded her, awed, "Are there tiny leprechauns in your camera, Goldilocks?"

Valerie snorted and punched him lightly on the side of his head. "No, you dunce. That last part was a joke. But it really is a talking glass that shows the sun. That's why it works on campus." She turned back to Uther Griffin. "I'm sorry. I should have warned you about the brightness. You were saying?"

The Gryphon Knight replied, "I would not allow my memory to be changed."

Rachel, Siggy, Valerie, and Peter exchanged glances. Lucky, who had drifted up to examine the chandeliers, flew down and wrapped around Sigfried as if to protect his boy from having his memory wiped. Rachel recalled how his great-granddaughter, her Great-Aunt Nimue, had repeatedly remembered Amber and how Blackie's memory had come back the first two times when the Raven tried to remove only the particular piece of information mortals could not be allowed to know.

"You mean when the whole world was made to forget?" Rachel asked.

Uther nodded grimly. "The world was different when I was young. Then, one day, everyone forgot… a great many things."

"What was it you were being asked to forget? Something called angels?" asked Peter.

Uther waved a hand. "I care not if I recall or forget angels. What would that affect? A few pieces of art? But I refuse to forget the Majesty of the Christ."

A hiss rose up from the monstrosities lurking beyond the delicate branches of the weeping willow. A few of them backed away, deeper into the darkness.

"I... don't know what that is," Rachel admitted.

Uther bowed his head in grief.

Rachel opened her mouth to speak, but she had such a poor track record for comforting people that she did not dare try. What's more, everything that wanted to come out had to do with the marvelous sights she had seen among the Foothills. She clamped her teeth down and, somehow, kept herself from blurting out all of it. When she returned to the conversation, Lady Iolanthe was addressing the monsters, some of whom had crept closer again.

"... surely best, for Good triumpheth over Evil even as Light banisheth Darkness. Doth darkness linger and struggle against light? Nay. It fleeth."

"Light," spat a shadow-being with ram horns. "Light is weak. It is a pathetic thing."

"Foolish Candle Queen, what we tell you 'tis true," cackled the hag. "Good is weak. As weak as rice paper that has been trampled in the mud. Do you not recall the tale of how the Angel of Light challenged the Demon of Darkness? They agreed to forget their immortal natures and live as mortals for a span. During their agreed-upon period, the Angel of Darkness conquered two-thirds of the country where he sojourned; the Angel of Light accomplished nothing. He fled into the desert and became a holy hermit—desperate to regain the knowledge he had abandoned." The hag laughed long and hard at this with her twisted, grating laughter. "Goodness is so pathetic."

The other beasts and monstrosities laughed with her, a chilling sound. A shiver ran up Rachel's spine. Was evil stronger than good? She closed her eyes and thought of the white-capped Mountains lit by the Source beyond and recalled how real and solid that place had been compared to here.

"Really, Rach." Peter shaded his eyes. "Can't you turn that down?"

Rachel opened her eyes. Her body shone so brightly that she could hardly see it. Lady Iolanthe rose from her seat and glided forward. She tapped Rachel on the forehead with two fingers. The shining glow dimmed until Rachel was only a little brighter than her companions. She looked down at herself and sighed, wondering what it meant that this seemingly charming fairy woman could dim the light of Heaven's Foothills.

Lady Iolanthe spoke kindly, "An abundance of life bringeth abundant growth. I have hidden this abundance with the gift thou hast been given. When thou discovereth that gift, the rest will follow, but this will give thee a little time in which to prepare thyself." She glided back and took her seat again. "Anon, children, your time here is nearly exhausted. Ye must away to the sunlit lands. Uther, bestow upon them the Heart."

Rachel blinked. She had not understood a single thing Lady Iolanthe had said—well, except for the part about the Heart. Sigfried was still staring into the fireworks fountain; Valerie stood beside Rachel, gazing with interest at the Heart. Peter, who had no idea what the Heart of Dreams was, watched warily.

Rachel curtsied, "Please, milady, we don't know how to use it. Can anyone instruct us?"

Overhead, the sky lit up again with fairy fireworks. This time, it was firebirds with their beautiful red, gold, and shining blue plumes, all flying in formation, forming flowers and starbursts and other intricate designs. Here and there, a phoenix of pure red flame burned amidst the more delicate and bird-of-paradise-like firebirds. Lady Iolanthe paused a moment to admire their performance and then turned back to Rachel.

"We are but custodians of the stone," replied the fairy lady, fanning her shimmering butterfly wings as fireflies circled around her "and would not dare touch it of our own accord. To master the Heart, thou must seek a fairy monarch: one such as one of the twin elf kings, Auberon and Erlkoenig, or King Finvarra or Queen Titania. Or Odin, perhaps, if he hath at last been found. Our portal to reach these most honored rulers hath been closed these many years. Our moonglass goeth only to and not fro. But perhaps ye canst discover a way to find one such exalted figure. Rumor hast murmured that the King of the Daoine Sidhe hath upon occasion been seen hither and yon, and I hear his associate, the Dream Thief, walketh abroad. That one knoweth secrets of which the rest of us can only dream."

The grim knight had pulled out his dagger and was prying the silver gem from the chain he wore around his neck. "Which of you shall carry it?"

Peter took a step back. "I am afraid I do not even know what this is. Heart of Dreams? Wasn't that mentioned in a prophecy? I think we read about it once in school."

Siggy said, "You'd better give it to Rachel. I'd just lose it."

"Boss!" Lucky cried, shocked. "We would never lose a piece of treasure! We could store it as snuggly as a bug in a rug. We could nestle it between Percy Peppershine the Fifth and Dewbert Doveshimmer the Twenty-Second. Our gold would not be offended if a gem moved in."

Valerie just shrugged and pointed at Rachel. Lucky wilted.

"Sorry, Lucks," Siggy said, "but if Goldilocks says the blood-sister, the blood-sister it is."

Lucky perked up. "We own the whole blood-sister, right? So storing treasure with her is just another way to own it, right?"

Siggy nodded sagely. Valerie punched him in the arm.

"Sorry, Slugger, Lucky. You can't own people," said Valerie.

Rachel stepped up and held out her hands, cupped together. "I'll take it."

The Gryphon Knight solemnly placed the shining silver jewel upon her palm. Rachel examined it curiously and then put it in the pouch she wore around her neck.

"Didst thou call her Rachel? Oh, I know thee!" The Lady Iolanthe clapped her hands in delight. "Thou art the Lady Rachel Griffin!"

"You've... you've heard of *me?*" squeaked Rachel, thinking back, she realized that she had never been introduced. Peter had merely said, "This is my sister."

"Is it because she's the Guardian's pet?" Valerie quipped wryly.

Rachel resisted the desire to sigh. She loved the Guardian, and she loved being associated with him; however, that was not a very flattering description of their relationship.

Lady Iolanthe replied, "Of that matter, I can say nothing. But I have heard tell of Rachel Griffin—she who saved the soul of my once-son-in-law."

"Wait..." Rachel gasped, leaning forward. "What?"

"A piece of Blaise Griffin died in the tragedy that ended the life of my Estelle. Another perished with his son Emrys. He became a mere cantankerous husk of the great man he once had been," said Lady Iolanthe. "Then, as if by a miracle, Sir Calidor Moth brought report that a child had come into the life of this, my most cherished son-in-law, and that his love for the child had rekindled his soul, undoing his perilous decline." She met Rachel's gaze. "Before thou camest into his life, I feared that, upon discarding his mortal coil, he would be dragged down to perdition, but by his love for thee was he saved."

Rachel opened her mouth and let it hang there. *Her beloved grandfather. She* had saved him? Had he made it to the country beyond the Mountains *because of her?*

Tears ran down her cheeks.

"Good for you, Rach," Peter clapped her on the back. "He still seemed rather cantankerous to me, but perhaps he used to be worse." Her brother reached into his pocket, pulled out a clean handkerchief, and handed it to Rachel, who wiped her eyes and smiled.

"Thank you," her voice shook, "for telling me that."

"This dreamstar has been here Underhill for some time," said Uther. "You must treat it with great care. It is a talisman of extraordinary power. Do not mention it to anyone you do not trust with all your heart, and do not show it to anyone at all until the time is right."

"How do we know when the time is right?" asked Peter.

The Gryphon Knight frowned. "Who sent you to fetch it?"

"The Guardian," said Rachel. "The Raven."

"Ah, the Gray Raven," said the fairy lady fondly.

"Ask him," said the knight. "It was he who sent it to us, to begin with."

Rachel asked curiously, "Why do you call him the Gray Raven?"

"Because he is as silver as the moon," Lady Iolanthe laughed gaily, "which is close enough to gray. Though truth be told, I am not privy to how he came to have that title."

"He's not silver," Rachel replied, puzzled. "He's black. Entirely black, except his eyes, which are red." She did not mention the damaged fathers. She hoped very much they would have recovered when she saw him next.

"No!" The fairy lady swayed. Her ladies ran to support her. "Art thou certain?"

"Without question," Rachel replied solemnly. "I saw him a day ago."

"'Tis dire news. If the Gray Raven hath fallen...."

The Lady Iolanthe covered her face, bent her head, and wept.

Chapter Forty-One:
Return to Roanoke

They headed back down the path to the ivory arch, the sky above them blue, gold, and silver with the latest festive display. Rachel lagged behind as they walked, distressed by the news about Jariel. She did not know what to make of it. The Raven did not seem *fallen* to her—whatever exactly that meant—quite the opposite. She wished she had heard this a day earlier, so she could have asked Leander, but maybe the tiny Lion would be in her dorm room when she returned to school.

A memory from February came back to her. Something the ogre had said as she stood in front of it, trying to delay it until Lucky could arrive to break its charmed life: *"The world has gone mad! Dark and awful changes have been made to the minds of men. They have forgotten all the truths that kept the darkness at bay."* Then, he had leered at her menacingly and jeered, *"Not so gray anymore, is he?"*

At the time, Rachel had had no idea what the brute had meant, but it was Jariel who had made the world forget, Jariel who Lady Iolanthe had called the Gray Raven. A shiver crept up her spine. *"Not so gray anymore, is he?"* Had the ogre been taunting the Raven for having fallen?

She sighed. She did not know why the Raven had done whatever he did, but he must have had a good reason. He always seemed to be encouraging her to do the best of things. Didn't that mean he was good? She remembered the slight smile on his perfect lips when the Lion came to help Zoë. *No, Rachel Griffin. You have done something very, very right.*

When the five of them reached the part of the path that was back in the mundane world again, Valerie stopped, eyes bright with excitement. "Psst. I found out something!"

"Oh?" Rachel moved closer. The boys did as well, Peter standing so as to keep a wary eye out behind them.

"I interviewed a bunch of the fey. They're pretty crazy and said a lot of inane things, but I did learn something important." She leaned forward eagerly. "Dr. Mordeau's been here."

"What?" Rachel cried.

"Great!" declared Sigfried. "Can she teach me how to turn into a dragon?"

Valerie swatted at him playfully and then exclaimed fervently, "According to the fey, she came down the path into fairyland with two other people, whom the candle lady fairies said were Daniel Hanson Browne and his sister. Some of the fey I spoke to thought Mordeau had departed; some thought she was still there, a guest at Lady Cobweb's palace. One creepy shadow-hyena thing—not a source that inspires confidence, I admit—claimed the humans had left but not the way they came. It said they departed through The Gate of Greater Slumber, whatever that is." Valerie paused and then added flatly, "Apparently, Mordeau didn't have that Jonah jerk with her."

Siggy ground his teeth and put his hand on his knife hilt. Peter, who had been looking behind them, gave him a quizzical glance.

When they reached the stairs that led back to the tor, Peter paused, a thoughtful look on his face. "Hold on a sec. I've a few family history questions I'd like to put to Great-great-great grandfather. He may know the answers to mysteries that the rest of the family have forgotten. I'll catch up in a minute."

Peter ran back the way they had come. Rachel was not sure he should go alone, but he was gone before she could argue. She waited until Sigfried and Valerie had climbed up to the top of the stone staircase before touching her black bracelet.

"Gaius, we found it!"

"Found wha.... Wait! You did? Wow, Rachel Griffin, you are amazing. I knew if anyone could find it, it would be you. Where was it? The garden? An outbuilding? Did you check the attic again after all? My money's on the attic."

"We found it in fairyland."

"Fairyland! Did you go to fairyland? Oh, wait. You were going to Glastonbury, weren't you? I wouldn't put it past fairyland to be in Glastonbury. It's rather that sort of place."

Rachel began telling him all that had occurred. She had just reached the appearance of Uther Griffin when Siggy's voice came over the calling card.

"Griffin! Calling Griffin! Mayday! Mayday! Who's this joker threatening my gal?"

"Oh, Gaius, sorry! Must go! Some kind of emergency!"

"You'd better go then. We'll see each other tomorrow," replied Gaius. Lowering his voice, he added, "Looking forward to it."

Shivers of delight radiated through Rachel. "See you then, Mr. Valiant."

She turned off the black bracelet and pulled out her calling card. It took her a moment to understand the situation from the images rapidly appearing in the card as Sigfried rotated the point of view, but her memory helped her piece the glimpses together.

Sigfried and Valerie were flying on their bristlelesses. Next to them, a dark-haired man stood in mid-air. A long-nosed, red, Japanese *tengu* mask covered the top of his face; the bottom half wore a scowl of impatience. His long coat and split *hakama* pants were woven with a thorny design. Real thorns wrapped around him; some appeared to be sticking into his flesh. Fastened at his hip was a long thorny vine wrapped up around a handle, like a whip.

A second figure stood in mid-air: a confused young Japanese boy with jade-colored eyes and shoulder-length black hair dressed in a bright golden kimono with a red obi around his waist. There was something familiar about this boy that Rachel could not place.

Then the image steadied. Seeing the scene properly, Rachel caught two important details she had previously missed. One was that Sigfried had his wand out and was pointing it at the thorn-wearing figure in the *tengu* mask. The other was that this stranger held a two-foot-long thorn like a sword, its point pressed against Valerie's stomach.

"That's the thorn demon who appeared at Stonehenge the time Leander helped Zoë," said Rachel. "He looks a bit different. That one had silver-blue hair, but I think what you are looking at must be a body he is possessing, or Jariel would have kicked him out already."

"Thorn demon, right," Sigfried called. "He wants me to drop my wand, or he'll hurt Goldilocks, and he turned Lucky into a little boy. Oh, and he says his name is Enkai Verrine."

That little boy was *Lucky?* Rachel examined him more closely. Yes, he did have a Lucky-like expression. *How extraordinarily strange.*

"Enkai," Rachel said aloud. "I've heard that name. Sak...." She paused. Considering the potential damage that resulted from hinting to Sakura Suzuki about her past, she thought it might not be wise to mention Sakura's name where a demon might hear it. "The person who mentioned him seemed to believe he had enough power to do things like rewrite history."

"Rewrite history?" Siggy actually sounded slightly shaken.

"I'm getting impatient," Enkai spoke with a clipped British accent. He pushed his thorn blade forward slightly.

"Ouch!" cried Valerie.

She tried to fly backwards, but Enkai kept pace with her. She did manage to pull far enough away that he was not poking her with the thorn-blade.

Sigfried ground his teeth.

"Sorry, boss," cried the Japanese boy. "I can't seem to breathe fire like this."

"Okay, Unkool, or whatever your name is," Siggy raised his hands, still holding the wand, "if I drop my wand, you will drop your sword, right?"

"Correct," replied the young man in the *tengu* mask.

"Then I am dropping my wand. Put down your sword."

Through the calling card, Rachel could see Sigfried's wand falling. She watched it with concern. Was he high enough up that the fall would damage it? Then, with a mixture of excitement and relief, she recalled what she had learned about praying. She took a moment to ask the Lion's Father to please make sure the wand was not damaged during the drop.

"Gullible fool," snorted the demon.

Enkai lunged forward, thrusting the thorn-blade through Valerie. It went into her stomach, pierced her body entirely, and protruded from her back.

Rachel screamed. Valerie screamed, but Siggy drowned out both of them. He bellowed louder than any bull, a noise of pure rage.

"But you agreed!" Sigfried shouted, as angry as Rachel had ever seen him. "That's unknightly! I can't believe I let you disarm me! Never again! *Argos!*"

Sigfried cast a Glepnir band at the figure in thorns, but Enkai floated away. When he did so, he pulled his thorn-sword free of Valerie. Blood spurted everywhere. Despite the pain, Valerie had the presence of mind to dart forward and stab him with her butterfly knife, but it skidded off, not even so much as scratching his skin. With a derisive snort, the demon wiggled his fingers goodbye and vanished.

The Japanese boy shook himself. His body flowed like water, and he was Lucky again.

"Boy, boss, that was weird! I didn't like it," The dragon looked eagerly back and forth. "Where'd he go? Gah! Boss, I think he escaped before I had a chance to burninate him!"

"Worry about that later," shouted Sigfried. "Help Goldilocks now!"

Sigfried soared towards Valerie, who swayed as if she were about to faint. Her eyes were rolling up, and she was sagging on her broom. Rachel ran up the stairs two at a time, wand out. She drew the calling card her father had given her and called her parents.

"Mum! Valerie's been stabbed!" Rachel cried, wishing that she knew any healing magic.

"No!" came her mother's voice. "How could that happen? Can you rouse your father?"

"He hasn't answered yet."

"How bad is it?"

"She was stabbed right through. There's blood spurting everywhere."

There was silence. Then, "I had better come right away. Let me get my healing bag. You're on Glastonbury Tor, right? Please stand in the grassy area away from the tower. I...." In the small image, Rachel's mother's face was white as a sheet. "I think I can manage the jump."

"A-are you sure?" Rachel's voice quivered as a rush of horrific images from jumping accidents again flashed through her thoughts.

Siggy landed and laid his bleeding girlfriend on the ground. Valerie cried in pain. Tears ran down her cheek, and blood gushed from her wound on both sides. It seeped through her clothing, spreading into a pool on the ground. Rachel pressed both hands against her mouth. Bad: back in September, when she had found Valerie on the bathroom floor, crying blood, she had thought it was bad. This was much worse. Rachel swayed slightly, afraid that it might be she herself who fainted.

"Griffin!" Sigfried shouted angrily. "Do something! Save her!"

Rachel's mother's voice trembled. "Please take Peter and go stand in the grassy area away from the tower. I should be able to picture that properly."

"Peter's not.... Oh, there he is!"

Rachel ran to Peter, who was putting the stone bench back over the staircase, grabbed his hand, and dragged her astonished brother onto the grassy tor.

"Now, Mummy!"

A beam of white light flashed over the grass beside Rachel and her brother. To Rachel's great relief, the light formed perfectly into Ellen Griffin clutching a black leather bag. Rachel's mother stumbled, nearly falling. Peter jumped forward and steadied her.

"I... I made it," Rachel's mother murmured, her voice trembling with gratitude. She gave her son a warm smile where he held her arm. "I lived."

The Duchess of Devon moved immediately to Valerie's side and pulled out her flute. Luckily, physical wounds were easy for an enchantress to heal. Within a minute—between her flute playing and some elixirs she kept in her bag to help with blood loss and to stave off infections—Valerie's wound had closed entirely, and she was able to rise shakily to her feet.

The next instance, a second column of light resolved into Ambrose Griffin. Rachel's father immediately took charge. He insisted they all get into Siggy's bag, so he could jump them home in a single trip. He did not want to leave anyone behind with a rogue demon in the area. Siggy swept Valerie into his arms and stomped into the backpack. Then Peter helped Rachel's mother down the staircase into the room below. The duchess gave him a grateful smile.

Ambrose glanced at Rachel, who held up a finger in a one-minute gesture and ran to the area of lawn above which Siggy had been flying. A quick search led her to his dropped wand. She retrieved it and climbed inside. As she headed down the stairs, she glimpsed flashes of light as other Agents appeared to secure the location.

There was no furniture within the bag, just a wooden floor and some white walls, plus the wall with the safe. They would have to work on getting some furniture next. It had that new bag smell that reminded Rachel of sawdust and ozone, with just a touch of licorice. As she climbed in, she saw Peter leave her mother and touch Sigfried on the shoulder.

Rachel wanted to ask Siggy how this had started, but he was so livid he could not speak.

Her brother inclined his head to Siggy's ear, murmuring, "Rage later. Girl now."

Sigfried straightened and nodded. He immediately moved to Valerie's side and put his arm around her, where she sat on the floor leaning against a wall. His girlfriend leaned against him, wrapping her arms around him tightly.

Rachel sat down beside Lucky, who was looking glum.

"I say, Lucky, what happened?" she asked, still holding Siggy's wand.

The dragon did a dragony shrug. "That loser came up and tried to mock me about stuff I don't care about—about how I had done something he thought was stupid before I was an egg. Then he put his hand on me, and I turned into a boy."

"You mean when you lived in the Japanese world with the cherry blossoms that the Princess saw when she first touched you?"

"Maybe," Lucky replied, uninterested.

"I wonder if Enkai is from the same world you came from," she said, rubbing her fingers up and down Sigfried's knobby wand, thinking: *Maybe Sakura and Enoch Smithwyck as well.*

Hold on, knobby? Rachel glanced at the normally smooth length of cherrywood in her hand and nearly dropped it.

"Mum"—her voice rose unexpectedly—"why is Siggy's wand growing buds?"

The next day, Tuesday, the second of April, they headed back to Roanoke bright and early. At least, it was bright and early by Roanoke's Eastern Daylight Time, which was five hours behind Gryphon Park. Rachel and the others had slept in, had a leisurely breakfast, finished packing—which was much easier for Rachel and Sigfried this time, as everything could go into their new housebags—before heading to the gatehouse with Valerie, Peter, and Laurel, to Exeter via the Gryphon's Nest, and then on to London, New York, and finally Roanoke.

Rachel's parents had accompanied them. Their first action was to take Valerie to be checked by the nurse, but Nurse Moth declared that the duchess had done a splendid job and merely gave Valerie a cup of water from the healing fountain, for blood loss. Reassured as to Valerie's well-being, Rachel's father set off to investigate the matter of what had caused Sigfried's wand to grow buds. He arranged for several wand experts in the Math department to examine it. The fourth one thought to come ask Sigfried about the spot where the wood was thicker and the gold tracery disrupted. Rachel and Siggy explained how the wand had broken, and the woodwose had repaired it. Her father was startled to discover they knew the woodwose through whose woods he and his brother used to sneak. He explained the woodwose must have somehow infused life into the dead wood. Father offered to get Sigfried a new wand, but her blood brother replied that they would have to pry the wand that grew leaves and flowers out of his cold dead hands.

Rachel made sure that she had filled her father in on everything they had learned, including that Dr. Mordeau and Daniel Hanson Browne had gone into fairyland through Glastonbury Tor but that they had never reemerged. Rachel's parents then departed—her father in search of the demon who had stabbed Valerie—and school life returned to normal. The first time Rachel found herself in her room when her roommates were out, she slipped the gown Illondria had given to the princess onto Nastasia's bunk. She wrapped it in brown paper and included a note reading: *This may be of use to you, especially when you travel.* Nastasia was utterly delighted with the dress, and much was made among the freshman girls of Dare Hall over who might have left it. Rachel did not venture an opinion.

Classes resumed. It was nice to get back to work, especially as all her classes were covering new material, which made the first day particularly interesting. After class, the Die Horribly Debate Club met in their clubhouse, along with a plate of cookies Joy's sister had sent along. They began sharing stories from Spring Break. The last three days had been so eventful that Rachel found herself feeling a bit dazed. She wanted to tell her friends everything that had occurred, but she could speak neither of her trip to the Foothills nor of the Heart of Dreams. Nor did she wish to speak of what had happened on the banks of the Dart. She remained quiet.

Sigfried did tell the Die Horribly Debate Club all about their battle with the Morthbrood at Grey Wethers. Rachel took advantage of this to quietly ask Zoë if she knew anything about the Dream Thief. Zoë shrugged nonchalantly and said she did not know anything, but Rachel felt that her friend was not being honest. She considered asking Zoë about Crokel, the name they had overheard when spying on the Morthbrood, but decided against it. If the "number" this Crokel had done on the Dream Thief was responsible for the scars Joy had seen all over Zoë's body, Rachel did not want to be the one to remind her friend of whatever had produced them.

She did casually ask Zoë if the other girl knew where the King of the Daoine Sidhe was. Zoë had started to turn away, toward where the others were discussing the Battle of Salamis and the various merits of greased watermelons, but then she turned back with another shrug and muttered, "How would I know? Hanging around somewhere."

To Rachel's delight, Nastasia seemed a little bit happier. Rachel wondered if it was due to time spent at home with her family or if her own prayers from the Foothills had helped. She remembered to ask the Princess to speak to her grandfather about the matter Leander had mentioned. The princess promised to do so but warned Rachel that she had not seen him since the day he brought Amber and did not know how to contact him.

Rachel kept her eye out, waiting for whatever might come next regarding the Heart of Dreams, but nothing occurred. She saw Leander every day, padding along with Kitten, but he did not reply when she spoke to him or asked him questions, though when she told him that she had asked Nastasia to speak to her grandfather, he purred. She did not see Jariel at all.

With the advent of April came spring thunderstorms. These April showers blew in extremely rapidly. The first one caught Rachel and her friends by surprise. One moment, the sun shone. The next, dark storm clouds broke overhead, drenching the lot of them. Joy squealed and leapt into the house inside Nastasia's bag, followed by Zoë and Kitten, who happened to be walking across campus with them. Sigfried was not there, as he was off committing alchemy. This left Rachel and Nastasia standing on the commons in the pouring rain.

"Almost sounds like music," Nastasia mused over the drumming of the raindrops.

"Isn't it wonderful?" Rachel called back, staring up into the downpour as water splashed off her face. "I mean being allowed to stay out in the rain. Not having to run inside at the first raindrop to escape the Heer."

Rachel glanced at her. Nastasia glanced back.

"We're wet anyway," Rachel murmured, eyes dancing.

"So we are," agreed the princess.

The two girls hooked arms and began to dance on the lawn. They performed the same Irish step combination from Riverdance as they had in the Watch Tower back in September, kicking and stamping in time to the rhythm of the raindrops. The downpour drenched them, plastering their robes and their hair, even Nastasia's golden curls, against their wet skin. Rivulets of water ran down Rachel's face and back. Neither of them allowed this to distract them from their footwork. Meeting each other's gaze as their feet flew, they grinned at one another.

As the torrential downpour lessened to a light spring rain, they slowed and then stopped, panting and laughing. As they turned back toward Roanoke Hall, they came face to face with Gaius Valiant, who leaned against a lamp post, watching them from under a dark green umbrella. He held a second umbrella like a cane.

Gaius bowed, an approving light in his eyes. "When we saw two such lovely young ladies caught in a cloudburst, Jenny conjured you two an umbrella." He twirled the one he held like a cane. "But apparently, no umbrella was necessary."

He came toward them, opened the second umbrella, and held it out over their heads. "I offer it in the spirit that it was created, despite the fact that it is obviously no longer needed."

"Thank you, Mr. Valiant. That was most thoughtful," replied Nastasia, who looked touched. "It appears I was wrong about you. You are a gentleman after all."

Gaius grinned, looking rather pleased. "I am honored you are big enough to admit it."

The princess's blue eyes crinkled. "I do not know that I am particularly big, Mr. Valiant, but admit it I shall. What is true is true. There's no point in pretending otherwise."

Rachel said nothing, but she was very pleased indeed.

Chapter Forty-Two:
The Day Before the Celebration

Spring soon arrived in all its glory. Flowers bloomed along the pathways. New couples strolled together or floated on the reflecting lake in the self-moving rowboats with their painted eyes. Rachel saw Joy's lovely blonde sister Hope walking hand-in-hand with Kitten's older brother Squirrel, his phoenix perched vigilantly upon his shoulder. Overhead, Norse god look-alike Donner Virgil could be spotted flying side by side with bristleless-flying sensation, Laura Diggle. They flew over Rachel's fellow Dare Hall inhabitant of Korean descent, Lionel Park, as he recited poetry to upper school senior, Priscilla Kim. She gazed back at him through her black-rimmed glasses, enraptured. This couple particularly delighted Rachel, as she had observed the beginnings of their romance during the Korean Lunar New Year ceremony the previous February. Rachel noted all these new developments with great interest. When it came to campus romances, inquiring girls wanted to know!

Rachel's own romantic life was... less romantic. She found she could banish her obsession with a certain Bavarian prince by contemplating the Library of All Worlds, but during those idyllic afternoons when other girls strolled with their beaux, Gaius was off teaching hurling. Once or twice, he did take out the new bristleless Rachel had given him for his birthday, with Rachel either flying beside him on Vroomie or hopping on behind him, so that she got to lean against his back with her arms around his waist, but for the most part, his time was entirely occupied. She still sat with him at lunch, saw him at the Knights meetings, and studied algebra with him on Wednesdays, but the rest of the time, he was busy. The Board of Visitors and Governors had decreed the sporting events should begin with a hurling exhibition game, and as the leader of the Knights of Walpurgis, Vlad had tasked Gaius with putting it together.

Or at least, she wanted to believe that was why he was not around as much, and that it was not because he still felt uncomfortable with their age difference, even though she had finally reached the exalted age of fourteen. Judging from his conversation, though, he was telling the truth, because all he talked about was hurling. Gaius reported that they had enough decent players to field two teams. A number of the students were shaping up into very fine hurlers, of whom Conan MacDannan and Seth Peregrine were the best. These last two played particularly well together, almost as if they were meant to be on a team. If he could only find another twenty-five or so like them, the hurling game would be the event of the decade.

Siggy was not around much either, as he had joined the hurling players. He explained that he did not care about the game, but his band couldn't practice without its other member, Seth Peregrine. Sigfried found that if he joined the hurling practices, he could grab Seth the moment practice was over and get in some jamming time.

As the month progressed, the Skunklaunchers even gave a concert on the lawns of the commons. The band consisted of Siggy on trumpet, Seth on bass, Misty Lark, whom Rachel had seen making objects float during the heist, on drums, and Salome in a black skin-tight jumpsuit playing the tambourine as she swayed to the beat. This last addition led their concert to be far more popular with young men than could be accounted for by the quality of their performance. Siggy, who had only begun playing that fall, was by far the weakest player, but the sound of his heavenly trumpet was so pure and sweet that listeners forgave his occasional missed or wrong notes.

Rachel would have enjoyed the concert more if they had played something that had more closely resembled music.

During the first few lunches after the break, Rachel had been on pins and needles, waiting to see if Dread would banish her from his table. Finally, after a week, when Gaius made a second trip to the kitchens, she gathered her courage and quietly asked the prince if he were angry with her.

"Angry with you?" Vladimir looked up, his fork hovering. "Whatever for?"

"Um... Sandra said she told you..." Rachel paused and then snapped her fingers.

"Ah, that." He regarded her. "No, Miss Griffin. I am not angry. Why would I be?"

"Um...." Rachel bit her lip, uncertain what to say.

She was saved from having to reply by the return of Gaius, his tray piled with sandwiches. Vlad nodded mildly and returned to his meal, but there was an odd tension around his mouth. Had he been anyone else, Rachel might have suspected that he was struggling not to smile.

Rachel and her friends soon fell back into their ordinary routines. The wonders and terrors of Spring Break drifted into the background, and the daily events of school occupied their time. In Language, they read Shakespeare's King Arthur work, *Emrys Myrddin*. They had reviewed it briefly earlier in the year, but now they read it aloud, each student taking a part. The play amused Rachel because nearly every character shared a name with a member of her family. In honor of a number of her ancestors, she volunteered to read the part of Lynette, the clever young woman who wins the heart of Sir Gareth. They also learned some Original Tongue word parts, such as *vo* (self or being), *or* (master), and *el* (spirit or magical substance). They also finally learned *varenga*, which Rachel had been using ever since last September when she had seen Mr. Chanson use it to retrieve a runaway broom.

In Math, in addition to completing Euclid, they learned that circles keep things out while angles invite them in, which was why thaumaturges, such as the cultists at Beaumont who had tried to summon Moloch, used summoning triangles inside of circles. They also studied stones with a hole in them and how they were useful for protection against solitary fairies and forest folk. In Science, she finally completed her quicksilver boots, though she was still dissatisfied with them. They hardly increased her speed; in fact, she was reasonably sure she went faster without them.

In Art class, they began learning to change the texture of the white ceramic-like substance they had been conjuring all year, making it rough or smooth. This made class extremely difficult for Rachel, because drawing a picture of the object did not help Rachel conjure the right substance. On the good side, inspired by the book Mrs. Heelis had lent her, and by her Art teacher's own doodles, she was beginning to develop a simple pen-and-ink style of her own that she rather liked. Here and there, she thought she had finally caught a hint of what she wanted to portray.

In True History, they finally made it to the agrarian revolution and began studying Ur and the other city-states. In Music, they learned the song for healing a runny nose and for dispelling red caps, which would have been quite useful a month or so back. Rachel worked hard on both of these, but they were too complicated for her whistling skills. She finally broke down and practiced her flute, but the only result was an increase in her dislike of the instrument.

The weather grew even warmer. Students began spending their free time outside, whenever the campus was not being drenched by sudden thunderstorms. Bristlelesses popped up all over, as did the new floating airboards, the operation of which resulted in so many trips to the infirmary that the dean decreed anyone who wanted to make use of the "glorified surfboards" had to wear a floating harness. Rachel found herself suddenly popular, as word spread that, as Mr. Chanson's assistant, she had a key to the broom closet where the floating harnesses were stored.

Rachel herself, however, was earthbound. After the first broom riding class, she had told Mr. Chanson about the problem she encountered during the rescue of the little boy from Dart when the becalming enchantments had not produced enough drag. He helped her write to his parents, describing the problem. A week later, they wrote back that they had just perfected a new ring that would allow a bristleless rider to increase or decrease the amount of drag. If she wished, they could install one for her. When she agreed, her boss had sent Vroomie off to them again. So she found herself on the ground, wistfully watching all the fliers enjoying the balmy spring air.

As April progressed without Vroomie, and Gaius and Sigfried were unusually busy, Rachel took advantage of her extra free time to work even harder on the things she was quietly practicing. She was now quite good at blowing her rock off the table, freezing it in mid-air for a moment with *turlu*, and then retrieving it with *tiathelu*. Occasionally, her timing was off, and the rock crashed to the floor, but the number of times this happened per practice session was far fewer than it had been a few months ago. She wished she could have several objects in the air at once so that she could practice the inertia transferring properties of *turlu*, but so far, she had not found a good way to accomplish this while practicing by herself in an empty corridor.

She did wonder what had happened to the plan for Wulfgang Starkadder to befriend Nastasia. Rachel had nearly gotten staked; Gaius had shared all their dangerous secrets with him, but Wulfgang had not taken the next step to speak to the princess. If anything, he had become more morose and private than ever. It was like Rachel's vain attempt to get her brother Peter to befriend the princess all over again.

She occasionally went down to the gym and practiced *turlu* with the tennis ball thrower that could put multiple flying objects into the air at the same time. She also spent time practicing on the balance beam. She was determined to learn to fly standing on a broom as Mr. Gideon had. Her balance was improving, but she still had a long way to go.

The other thing she did was study in the library. Relentlessly, she searched through everything she could find on the subject of elven rulers. According to both Iolanthe Towers and her ancestress, Lady Iolanthe of Underhill, these monarchs were the only people capable of pressuring the local fey into coming back into accord with the Roanoke Convent, and thus the best candidates to become the new owner of the Heart of Dreams. She read about the Five Elf Lords—or Elf Lords and Ladies, for Lady Cobweb and the Scottish Queen of Elphame were both members of the Five. Then, there were the Pixy Claves, the King Beneath the Mountain—who in some stories seemed to be the Heer and in others, a king of the dwarves—the Gnome King, her distant ancestor Gwyn ap Nudd, and more. She also read older stories about elf kings: the King of the Seelie Court, the King of the Unseelie Court, and the King of the Daoine Sidhe. Older stories still claimed that the Irish gods, Nuada and Bres, were variously the king of the Tuatha de Danann, but Rachel could not tell if the Tuatha de Danann and the Daoine Sidhe were the same group or not.

Some of the tales went into detail about the rules under which the fey lived, how they often solved problems through contests or chess games or other non-standard means, how they hated to turn down a challenge, how they seldom lied, but also how their words often had a second meaning.

She also looked in the multi-tomed *Compendium of the Wise*, which was enchanted so that the volumes with the information you sought glowed with light and opened to the proper pages by themselves. She researched members of the Wise whose names were the same as or similar to the fairy kings', but none looked promising. She even knew one of these possible elf king candidates, but Nastasia had checked that family back in the fall and reported they were all locals. Rachel was fairly certain that a fairy king would count as an Outsider.

She spent time tracing back the fey on Roanoke Island, trying to find from which tradition they originated. A few were native to the Hudson Valley, but the majority came from Europe. Not all, though: the kappa, for instance, was from Japan. Still, her research suggested that the only ones with the power and clout necessary to persuade the fey of Roanoke to reinstate the covenants were the three fairy kings and Queen Titania, three of whom Lady Iolanthe believed were locked out of their world. That left the King of the Daoine Sidhe. After weeks of research, however, she was no closer to finding such a figure than she was when she started.

To give herself a break, one day, she looked up Imelda Stark. Sure enough, she was listed in the compendium: *Imelda Stark, née Charles.*

Rachel straightened up so fast she sent her fountain pen flipping across the library table. Quickly, she began turning pages, and there it was:

The daughters of Eliaures Charles: Imelda and Melusine.

Rachel leaned back, astonished. Then, she penned a letter to her father, sharing this news in case he did not already know. The wife of the Necromancer—the woman who procured the barghests and, apparently, ninety-nine yet unused wraiths—was Dr. Mordeau's sister.

Senior Prank took place during the fourth week of April, with the college seniors disrupting classes and pulling the underclassmen out of their classrooms for an afternoon of games and fun. Since it was an unscheduled event, no one had any alternate plans. Rachel was able to spend a lovely afternoon with Gaius singing songs and playing games on the commons.

Several days later, she finally had an opportunity to keep her promise to Astrid from the night of the Year of the Dragon Ball. She took her roommate for rose cream sodas, courtesy of the Roanoke Bucks that were hidden in the red envelopes that had been hanging on the orange trees during the masquerade ball. It was now Monday the twenty-ninth of April, the day before Walpurgisnacht. The campus was breathless with excitement, anticipating the visitors and events that the next two days would bring as they celebrated the twenty-fifth anniversary of the Battle of Roanoke.

This worked out well for the two young women, as it meant that the Storm King Café was almost empty, and they were able to snag a choice table beneath the mural of the storm goblin facing off against Captain Vanderdecken of *The Flying Dutchman.* They sat surrounded by warm wood moldings, bright brass fixtures, and the large black and white squares of checkered linoleum floor. To their left, behind the marble counter, Faith O'Keefe and Xandra Black worked at the soda fountain, their little paper hats perched upon their heads (or in Xandra's case, on her hood). Through the open door behind Faith and Xandra, Fortinbras Thorn, the young man who worked at nearly every job on campus, could be seen aiding a small brownie in a tall white cook's toque, who stood on a wooden crate in order to reach and flip the burgers that sizzled on the grill.

Rachel shot Fort a smile. She had glimpsed him on the commons holding hands with Hekpa Tenatyee, the dryad's daughter. It was amazing that he could find time for a girlfriend, considering how hard he worked, but the couple seemed quite happy with each other.

Rachel and Astrid chatted as they sipped their sweet, bubbly, floral sodas and enjoyed the smell of fresh baking. They were finally able to wear just their robes and mortarboard caps, without bulky winter gear, though Astrid still wore her favorite blue silk scarf.

"So tomorrow is the twenty-fifth anniversary?" Astrid asked in her lovely soft voice. She spoke with a hint of a Southern twang from a childhood spent in Tennessee, even though she currently lived in New York City. She had tight black curls and caramel skin and sat sipping from her pink and white soda bottle through a straw.

"Technically, the anniversary is on May Day," Rachel replied. "Tomorrow is the warm-up. The actual ceremonies are on Wednesday. Are you excited about any of the games?"

"Do you re—." Astrid rolled her eyes. "Of course, you remember. What are the choices?"

Rachel took a deep breath and listed them. "Spartan Madball, the Battle of Salamis—in which we all take boats, rowing or sailing, out on the Hudson and try to be the first to capture a greased watermelon without falling in—Sisyphus roll, epicycle race, zap ball, flying polo, fencing, stone skipping, rock, paper, scissors, friend carry, croquet, and hurling."

Astrid blinked. "Um... those sound quite athletic. Couldn't they have thrown in Chinese checkers or maybe Mastermind? I think I could handle rock, paper, scissors. Maybe croquet. That doesn't sound too hard. Do we use flamingos?"

"There was some talk about offering those pink lawn ornament flamingos as mallets," replied Rachel. "But I believe they decided against it."

"I don't suppose they have competitive reading? Or math bee? I might have a chance at math bee—if William Locke didn't play," said Astrid. Then, her face lit up. "Wait. If I join in one of the more vigorous games, do you think there's a chance that your boss, our exquisite PE tutor, will be there? I don't like to feel envious, but I must admit I envy you your job."

"Are you sure?" Rachel replied quite seriously. She suspected that working for a person upon whom one had a crush would result in an exquisite kind of agony.

"Definitely," Astrid replied. She sipped her soda and sighed, closing her eyes as she enjoyed the subtle rose sweetness.

Rachel recalled standing in the foyer downstairs, staring into the salamander enclosure, and deciding that she needed a new best friend. She was not sure what to do with the list of possible friends her Elf had given her. She filed that away for now and regarded her roommate, feeling unexpectedly timid. Could Astrid be the one? Perhaps she could help the other girl overcome her crippling shyness and join in on some of the activities the others all did together.

Heavy footsteps sounded on the stairs. Three grown men tromped into the cellars of Roanoke Hall that held the mailroom, the talking glass rooms, and the café. They headed toward the café counter. The first was Agent Garbarino, with his wavy hair and his intense, dark eyes. The other two wore loden cloaks and had red hair and beards. Rachel recognized one of them. She stood and bobbed a quick curtsy, the sort one offered to a social inferior for whom one had fondness and respect. It was important for her, when dealing with Brits of the Wise, to recall that, to them, she was still Lady Rachel.

"Hallo, Watchman Adair, Agent Garbarino."

Garbarino nodded pleasantly.

"Hallo, Lady Rachel," Watchman Adair replied. He was a young man with coppery hair and beard, with a woolen sweater and plaid kilt beneath his loden Watchman's cloak. Rachel knew him from her family's occasional visits to Loch Sidhe Castle, where he worked directly for the Lord of the Watch, Magnus Ridel. "We've coom to buy some refreshment for the lads. It's hot and thirsty weark, what we're aboot oop there."

"What are you doing up there?" she asked curiously.

"Settin' up and wardin' a display of the treasures of the Six Musketeers: the Tarnhelm, the Tarnkappe, the shield, the sword, the dagger, and the ring. The sword's a reproduction, the real Nothung havin' bein' lost due to lack of degossamerization."

"Very good." The Lady Rachel Griffin nodded regally. "Carry on."

Adair nodded smartly and turned back to the counter, but Agent Garbarino's lips twitched with amusement at her presumption. He surreptitiously snapped his fingers, looked around, and then shrugged, as if disappointed that he had not yet mastered the Summon the Prince of Bavaria spell. Rachel's lips, too, began to twitch with humor. She knew he was merely teasing her, but she could not help picturing the look on his face were his finger snap to actually produce an imperiously scowling Vladimir Von Dread.

Rachel sat down again to find her roommate looking slightly stunned as she watched the nigh-inhumanly handsome Michael Garbarino. Astrid quickly ducked her head, blushing.

"I can't believe they've filched men from the Royal Watch," Rachel murmured softly.

"It's nice that we have so much security for the festivities," Astrid replied shyly.

"Nice. Maybe." Rachel pursed her lips. "But it's draining the resources of the Wisecraft and now the Watch. They're spending so many Agents keeping us safe. There's none to see to the problems of the rest of the world."

"Really? I never thought about how many Agents there might be."

"They were all wiped out twenty-eight years ago," Rachel reminded her. "They've mainly rebuilt, but they can only hire people who pass the Grand Inquisitor's stringent tests, so they are still a bit shorthanded, even on a quiet day."

"Do they think there might be an attack?" Astrid asked. When Rachel nodded, she whistled. "Why don't they cancel the events?"

"I don't know. They know the Morthbrood is up to something. Maybe they want to lure them out, using us as bait? I doubt it though. I'm not sure why."

"Do you think there could be members of these Morthbroods on the Roanoke Academy Board of Visitors and Governors, helping convince the school to allow the celebration?"

"Oh, that's a very good question," Rachel replied, startled. She took another sip and thought about it. "I suppose there might be."

"I guess they're looking forward to summer when they won't have to guard us," said Astrid. "How long do the Agents on campus need to stay? Will they be here again next fall?"

Rachel shrugged. "That all depends upon whether we can repair relations with the fey."

"Is there any hope?"

"There is." Rachel resisted the temptation to tap her neck pouch where the Heart of Dreams rested. She glanced right and left and then whispered, "I've acquired part of what is needed, but there's still a part I have not found. It's supposed to show up. So perhaps we'll resolve the matter and send the Agents back to work."

Astrid frowned. "Who told you it was supposed to show up?"

Rachel shifted uncomfortably. "Let's just say a large birdy told me."

"Would that be a large black birdy," Astrid asked dryly, "with red eyes?"

Rachel's eyes widened, but she nodded. Astrid nodded, too.

Agent Garbarino and the two Watchmen passed them again, carrying cases of Cheerwine and elderberry cordial. Watchman Adair waved, and Garbarino winked at the young ladies before lightly mounting the stairs. Again Astrid got a dreamy look. She fanned her face with her hand, before sighing and pressing the same hand to her heart.

"I say, he's handsomer than should be legal."

Rachel nodded. "It's because he's a selkie. They're like that."

"A selkie? You mean he turns into a seal?" Astrid asked, eyes wide. When Rachel nodded, she ran a hand over her face. "It's been almost a whole school year now, and the existence of magical things still surprises me. It's hard to keep track of reality."

Chapter Forty-Three:
May Day Eve

The morning of May Day Eve, also known as Walpurgisnacht or, in English, Witches' Night, dawned cool and bright. Rachel rose at the crack of dawn and rushed outside—by dutifully running down all the flights of stairs—eager to try the new variable air cushioning enchantments ring. Leaving Dare Hall, she leapt onto Vroomie and soared upward into the peaches and golds of the early morning sky.

Once there, she set about testing the new silver ring at the base of the right-hand brass handlebar. When she turned the becalming enchantments all the way down, there was almost no drag. She could detect the tiniest change, but only very slightly. On the other hand, when a turbulent breeze struck the broom, some of it got through the becalming enchantment, ruffling her hair and robes. So at this setting, there was almost no drag, but the protection was not as effective either.

Rachel turned up the gain on the becalming enchantments and did some experimental dives and turns. She had to pause to pin up her hair. It had not grown significantly since she came back to Roanoke, but it was still longer than she was used to. To her surprise, a number of people had complimented her on the new length.

Hair secured, she continued her experiments. When the ring was turned halfway, she reached the level of drag she had been used to before the Chansons worked on her broom the first time. Curious as to what came next, she turned it all the way to high.

Vroomie bobbed gently through the air, hardly moving at all. It was almost like drifting around in a balloon. She turned it off, flew up higher where there was more turbulence, and turned it on again. No matter how boisterous the wind grew, the air around Rachel remained placid. She slowly flipped upside-down and hung in mid-air, practically motionless. In fact, the only thing that moved was her wand, which slipped from its normal place due to gravity and began to fall. Rachel *tiathelued* it back to her with a hand-cast cantrip, turned right-side-up, and stuck it into her neck pouch.

She then spent several hours testing the new improvements in numerous ways. When she felt satisfied, she turned off the becalming enchantments and flew twice around the campus, floating over Roanoke Hall and the eastern dorms—De Vere, Drake, Raleigh, and Dee—over the infirmary, the gymnasium, the Oriental Gardens, the lily pond, the menagerie, the Monument Garden, and finally over the western dorms: Marlowe, Spenser, and Dare. Roanoke Academy was once again abuzz. Free of classes for the day, students milled about or played games. Workmen were setting out chairs on the commons, in preparation for the upcoming ceremonies. Farther south, visitors arrived, passing through a veritable army of Agents of the Wisecraft who performed a series of security tests, including making them pass before a bright light, before allowing them to make their way onto campus.

Rachel spotted a number of famous visitors she knew personally, such as General Yrgwas MacDannan, who had apparently once been one of her grandfather's closest friends until their falling out over the very battle being celebrated today. The grizzled but sturdy old man stood near the tree-shaped fountain in the Monument Garden, surrounded by his great-granddaughters, red-haired Oonagh and Colleen, and dark-haired Wendy Darling. There were also dignitaries she recognized from news glasses, such as the wolfish King of Transylvania, as well as some whose identities she could guess. For instance, the distinguished gentleman with Mylene Price was probably her father, the famous Canadian wraith hunter, and the dark-haired man in a uniform, with a veritable forest of bars on his sleeve, speaking to Iolanthe was probably her uncle, the supreme commander of the American Mage Army. This would be the same General Towers whose youth and unexpected promotion twenty-five years ago had caused the delay that had culminated in the death of her Uncle Emrys and the falling out between her beloved grandfather and her mother.

Next, she headed north, flying over the hemlocks. She flew almost to the wall of trees and back to the rocky outcropping in the northwest. Apparently, the makeshift wards had been pushed back for this occasion, allowing access to a larger part of the campus. She passed several groups of students scouring the woods in search of alchemical ingredients: a group of girls from Raleigh Hall, a second group from Raleigh of older boys, one of whom was trying to balance his black and white cat on his bristleless; and the three boys from Drake who had tried to play hockey with pickaxes during the skating party back in February. They had their pickaxes again and were putting them to use upon a mica-filled boulder. From there, she went due west and landed in front of the moss-covered statue she had found on her first day at Roanoke.

Rachel gazed at the statue, blinking back sudden tears. It looked so wrong, so bereft, without its wings. A burst of anger toward the Master of the World coursed through her. Yes, she had forgiven him for the harm that he had done to her family, but that did not mean that she was unaware of the damage he had done. She thought of Uther, stuck Underhill because he would not give up his memory. That was the Master of the World's fault, too. He was the one who had ordered Jariel to change their memories.

Perhaps, outside of her Elf's Foothills, forgiveness was something one had to work at over time.

As she thought back, recalling exactly how the statue had looked the first time she saw it, an idea occurred to her. Great-Aunt Nimue had been able to change the rattle she purchased for Amber. Rachel chewed on her lip. Could she....

Just as if she were breaking an obscuration, she thought back, recalling the winged version perfectly. Then she opened her eyes.

"I refuse to forget," Rachel stated aloud.

A staccato buzzing sounded in her ears. The air to either side of the statue, where the wings should have been, began to glow. For an instant, there were two versions of the scene in Rachel's memory, one with the wings and one without. Then a blinding light flashed to either side of the statue.

The statue Rachel remembered from September stood before her, wings and all. She clapped her hands with delight. This must have been what Great-Aunt Nimue had done when she unknowingly restored the *A* on the rattle she had commissioned for Amber just by remembering it— after the Guardian had changed it to *S* for Sandra to hide the loss of Amber from the world. Was this why her great-great-great grandfather, the Gryphon Knight, had been forced to retreat into fairyland? Had he, by sheer force of his personality, been capable of undoing the changes the Raven had made when he made the world forget—whatever it was that he had caused them to forget?

Above her head, a hemlock bough bounced. Upon it perched a very large black bird with eyes as red as blood.

Oh, no....

"Hallo, Jariel," she said, her heartbeat going triple-time. Shame and panic tumbled through her. What if she had just damaged the whole world? *Why had she not thought of that?*

She decided to brass it out. "Can you tell me what to do next with the —" she tapped her neck pouch where the Heart of Dreams was hidden "— with the you-know-what?"

The Raven croaked in his harsh voice, "There are better ways to draw my attention, Rachel Griffin."

Rachel wilted inside. She had not done this to draw his attention. *Quite the opposite!* She desperately would have preferred that he had not noticed. It hurt that he might think such a thing of her. Then she looked at the statue with its moss tears and dove wings. She was terrified of offending the Raven, but what came out of her mouth was truth.

"It looked so wrong. This is how it's supposed to be."

The Raven cocked its head and examined the stone angel. "Yet again, Rachel Griffin, you have done something that is right."

"May I call you Zadkiel?" she asked shyly.

"No."

Rachel lowered her head, chastened.

"As to the other matter, it will resolve itself soon." The Raven looked off into the distance. "Very soon indeed."

The black bird looked to the left, and his feathers ruffled in surprise as if he had seen something that disturbed him. Then, he was gone. Rachel sighed. That could have gone better. On the other hand, it could have gone much worse. It was his work she had undone when she restored the wings to the statue. Of course, he would be displeased. She should have waited to ask about his real name until a time when he was pleased with her. On the other hand, maybe there was a good reason why he did not want her to use it.

She flew eastward and then south, following the boardwalk that ran along College Creek. The bluebells were in bloom: their ethereal blue stretched up and down the river. She landed where the stream from the Oriental garden ran into the main creek. Just below, another stream merged from the east. As bluebells grew along all the banks, if she hovered over the place where the three waterways met, the eerie blue stretched in every direction, as far as her eye could see. She was reminded of their trek Underhill. Except that one expected blue forests in fairyland. Here, the color was so unexpected that the effect was almost more otherworldly than the other world.

She followed College Creek south. Enjoying the wonder of the blue-bells, she continued farther than was her wont. Ahead, she spotted the stone arch she had discovered during the first week of school. Through it, the lilies-of-the-valley that carpeted the forest floor, stretching beneath the great oaks, were in bloom.

Rachel landed and walked quietly among them, humming *White Coral Bells*. Everything was so idyllic, so peaceful, so far from the hustle and bustle of the upcoming events—events that would most likely remain peaceful. Yet, the thought that the Morthbrood had planned a bloody event for May Day and that they still had access to ninety-nine wraiths made her skin crawl.

How long ago, it seemed, that she had been in this forest garden for the first time? She recalled standing in this very spot, back during the first week of school, and running her fingers over a broad smooth-veined leaf while thinking that this glade, this very leaf, would be destroyed if the world froze or burned. She also recalled thinking: *If death was inevitable, she wanted to stare it in the face before it took her.*

That sentiment was still true, even if the situation was not so bad now. She was merely worried about the fey closing down the school. The Earth was safe and sound, wasn't it?

Or was it? A chill started in the back of her neck and ran all the way down her spine. Wasn't Dr. Mordeau, like Mortimer Egg, a member of Veltdammerung—those who wanted to destroy the world? Was Mordeau merely trying to get revenge on a few soldiers and statesmen who had captured her family members and allies? Or was she up to something more insidious?

Rachel recalled her exact thoughts from her previous visit. They had been: *the cool rushing rivers, the leaping waterfalls, the tall majestic mountains, the golden fields of the tenant farms and the gray stone of Gryphon Park, the thick dark forests of Roanoke—not to mention art and science and magic, and libraries, and all the good things of human civilization. Was all that at risk?*

A second chill ran up Rachel's back. *Was it?* She felt uneasy, as if something much worse than she had been anticipating was in the offing. She remembered how the Raven's feathers had ruffled just before he vanished and felt a tremor of cold fear. With a shiver, she leapt on Vroomie and headed away from the shadowy forest and back to the sunlight of campus proper.

Coming up from the south, Rachel left the creek and flew out into the sunny wide-open track and the green, oval playing field around which the track ran. She basked in the warmth, hoping it would dispel the chill that had fallen on her. Ahead, toward the western side of the track field, Zoë Forrest walked with her two friends Seth Peregrine and Misty Lark. Seth's hurley—a three-foot-long stick with a flattened, rounded end—bounced against his shoulder. He was dressed in what looked like a uniform of navy and silver.

Zoë had been practicing hurling as well, though Gaius would not put her on the final team because, he said, *girls play camogie*, which was apparently hurling but with less bashing people in the head with metal-banded hurleys. Metal bands, used in hurling since the eighth century, were not allowed in camogie; however, girls could still bash each other with hurleys of ash or bamboo.

She watched Seth swaggering across the field, along with the two girls. Rachel's core-group-mate looked Irish, though he was from Michigan. Or rather, he was from some otherworldly place where Zoë had previously known him. If Zoë were the Dream Thief and a former associate of the King of the Daoine Sidhe, perhaps Seth was, too. Of course, that did not help Rachel in her search for the fairy king since, unlike Zoë, Seth did not have his memories from his previous life before the Raven had brought him here.

Rachel ground her teeth. The Raven had promised she would soon figure out the mystery of how to use the Heart of Dreams to help the school. Yet she still felt as far from the answer as she had ever been. She had thought she was onto something when she concluded that Zoë was the Dream Thief—the little goat-legged fey had mentioned the name to Zoë; the Morthbrood had referred to the Dream Thief as a member of the Key-bearers upon whom someone had "done a number," which had sounded reminiscent of Zoë's scars; and Lady Iolanthe had believed that the Dream Thief was around and might know the whereabouts of the King of the Daoine Sidhe.

If Zoë knew, however, she was not telling.

Rachel thought back to when she had casually asked Zoë if she knew where the fairy king was and suddenly noticed something she had missed the first time. Right before Zoë made her comment, Rachel thought she had been about to turn back to the others, but that was not what Rachel's memory of Zoë's face showed. The other girl had started to glance furtively behind her. Then, she stopped herself quickly... as if she did not want to give something away.

What had been behind her? Rachel pictured the clubhouse room clearly. She imagined that Zoë had kept turning in a direct line in the direction that her eyes had moved. Each member of the Die Horribly Debate Club had decorated part of the clubhouse. Had Zoë kept moving along the same trajectory, she would have ended up facing the east wall, the one for which Zoë herself had chosen the posters. Maori punk rockers and Canadian hockey players hung there, plastered around a giant poster of....

An eerie horripilation ran along Rachel's limbs. The King of the Daoine Sidhe was famed for his love of two things, hurling and chess—hurling like Seth and Conan MacDannan, whom Gaius felt were the best hurling players in the school, as if they were meant to play on the same team *or as if they had been trained by the same coach?*—and his love of chess like Oonagh and Liam MacDannan, who had won the Dare Hall chess tournament during the lockdown and on Leap Day, in February. The King of the Daoine Sidhe also had something in common with another MacDannan, Red Ryder, the lead singer for the band *Bogus*, whose poster hung directly in the middle of Zoë's section of the clubhouse wall.

They were both named *Finvarra*.

Could the elusive fairy king, for whom Rachel had been searching all these weeks, be her family's friend, Finn MacDannan? On one hand, the very notion seemed ridiculous. Rachel had known Finn her entire life. He was the father of Siggy's roommate, Ian, and of Oonagh and Liam and Conan, her dormmates, and their youngest brother named Taliesin, who was not yet at school, but whom Rachel had known his entire life.

What's more, Nastasia had said the MacDannans were natives.

But had she checked them all? Rachel knew the princess had touched the MacDannan children, their mother, Scarlett Mallory MacDannan, and her fellow Musketeer, James Darling, Agent. All of these people were native to this world. Had Nastasia checked Finvarra, too, or had she merely checked his children and wife and assumed he would be like the others?

Finvarra MacDannan: He had been one of the Six Musketeers who killed the Terrible Five, and now he was a world famous rock star, whom even the Unwary adored. He was said to be the greatest enchanter in the world. She thought back to the moment during their fight against Velt-dammerung the previous fall when Finn showed up and the fate of the battle turned. If he turned out to be a fairy prince, would she really be surprised?

Rachel touched the pouch where the Heart of Dreams was hidden. Jariel had told her that this matter would resolve itself "very soon." Could this realization be what he had foreseen?

She pulled out her calling card. "Siggy!"

"Yeah, O voice speaking from a piece of glass? What is your wisdom, Dark Mistress?"

Oh, not that nonsense again! She ignored it and ploughed forward.

"Can you find Finn MacDannan and bring him to the track behind the gym? Tell him I asked for him."

"Finn... you mean *Red Ryder*? You want me to just casually walk up to the greatest musician on the planet and tell him where to go?" asked an astonished Sigfried.

"Yes." Rachel put her card away and flew up closer to her three class-mates. She said casually, "I say, Zoë, have you seen King Finvarra? Is he here yet?"

"He's on the commons, tuning his guitar," Zoë murmured, not really paying attention.

"So you are the Dream Thief!"

"I, wait…. Hey, you tricked me!" Zoë scowled.

Rachel smiled cheerfully. She landed and rested her steeplechaser against a nearby bleacher. "You may have just saved the school, and—Oh, look! Here he comes now!"

Zoë, Seth, and Misty all turned and gawked with identical expressions of hero worship at the tall, lanky figure with spiky red hair strolling toward them, accompanied by Siggy and Lucky. Finn MacDannan was dressed ca-sually, not in his stage outfit, which was said to be woven of fire and wa-ter. He wore jeans and a red tee-shirt that read: *Statistically, Six out of Seven Dwarves are not Happy*; however, he still wore his gold safety-pin earrings.

Still gazing starry-eyed at the aging rock star, Seth used his free hand to check his pockets. "Shoot. I don't have a piece of paper to get his signa-ture."

"You could ask him to sign your hurley," murmured Misty Lark.

"Do you think he would?" Seth looked delighted.

"Why not?" asked Misty.

"Here. I have a pen." Zoë held out a felt tip marker.

Finn came casually strolling toward them. "Hey, Mini Griff. You wanted somethi—." His expression changed. "Peregrine!"

"Boss!" Seth's mouth gaped open.

In a moment, Finn MacDannan had closed the distance and pulled the younger man into a bear hug. Then, he held him at arm's length.

"Look at you! You're alive!" Finn crowed.

Out of the corner of her eye, Rachel saw something move, but she did not want to look away from this reunion to see what it was.

"I... um...." Seth turned red. "How did I.... Why do I think you're my boss?"

"Because he is," Zoë sighed. "Or he was. Before. You didn't play hockey in our former life. You were one of King Finvarra's hurling players."

"The *captain* of my hurling players," Finn corrected her, slapping Seth on the back. He spoke with an accent that was part Irish, part Cockney. "And Lark!" Finn said a few things that were clearly swear words, though they were not in any language Rachel spoke, unless he was talking about damming a river, which did not make much sense in context. "You're alive! You're all right! Can you sing?"

He threw a quick glance at Zoë, who looked as if he had stabbed her. Zoë glanced away.

Misty Lark blinked. She stuttered shyly, "I-I...d-don't sing, sir. I-I play the d-drums."

"Drums?" Finn grinned at her. "That's new. Interesting."

"Should we be talking about this?" whispered Rachel. "Talking about lives before... here can break the world."

"She plays them and makes things float," said Sigfried as he walked up beside them.

"That's because she's from Nysa. Music makes things float there," Finn replied. He gave Zoë a lopsided grin and a light punch on the shoulder. "Hey, if it isn't the Dream Thief! How are you doing, Zoë? You look...." He paused and stared at her. "...young."

"That's me. Teen again," Zoë murmured.

Finn squinted at her. "You remember."

"Apparently, you do, too," she replied.

He scowled. "Stupid Raven should never have put me in a situation where my perfect-at-everything older brother was supposed to be my father. It was a stretch too far to be believed." He turned back to Rachel. "Is this why you called me, Mini Griff?"

Rachel shook her head. "I suspected you knew them, but I didn't know for sure. I called you about another matter entirely."

"Oh? Spill it."

Rachel took a deep breath. "I don't suppose you could be a dear and tell the local fey they have to reestablish the Roanoke Covenant?"

Finn MacDannan stared at Rachel. Then, he scrunched up his face into a scowl. Then he scrunched it up even more, into a deeper scowl. He was surprisingly good at that.

"That would be a no," he said finally.

"Please?" Rachel stepped closer to him and gazed up at him. "You have to help, Finn. There's no one else. I know. I've researched it."

"Are you out of your pretty little mind, Lady Rachel? What if my wife found out?"

Rachel opened her mouth, wordless.

"Isn't your wife our Math teacher?" asked Siggy. "Ian's mum?"

"Yes, and she has no idea that I am an immortal fairy king from another dimension. I'd like to keep it that way. Thank you very much."

"Are you a fairy?" Rachel asked curiously.

"No. I'm a Son of Adam." He shrugged, running a hand over his long chin, which had well over a day's worth of coppery stubble. "Or, actually, a great-grandson of Adam. I just ruled over fairies. You know. You beat a few up. Get them to behave. Next thing you know, they expect you to keep a whole bunch of 'em in line."

"Which is exactly what I want you to do," Rachel jumped in. "Beat up a few fairies, get them to behave. Keep them in line."

"No chance. Nada," Finn replied.

Rachel sighed. She had no idea what a son, or great-grandson, of Adam was—the first king of men Zoë and the pixies had mentioned, maybe?—but that did not matter now.

"And Seth?" Siggy pointed at his bandmate.

"Who, Peregrine?" asked Finn. "Nah. He's a fairy."

Despite still being star-struck, Seth had the presence of mind to roll his eyes. "Great."

"Zoë, too?" asked Rachel.

"Half," Finn replied. "Her mother was a mortal princess who rode a flying horse. Her father is..." he glanced at Zoë, "... a friend of mine."

"And Misty?" Rachel pointed at the other girl.

"Half-fairy girl from Nysa," replied Finn.

Rachel took a step back and let them talk as she considered what she knew about Finn MacDannan, trying to muster an argument that might convince him. She wished she had figured out his identity earlier and had had time to speak to her parents. They knew him quite well. They could have given her insights into what might motivate him to reveal his identity to the local fey.

Something brushed against her. She tried to step out of the way, but she could not. She seemed to be stuck. Alarmed, she glanced over her shoulder.

Gazing back at her were the dark eyes of the *each-uisge*.

CHAPTER FORTY-FOUR:
THE KING OF THE DAOINE SIDHE

RACHEL TWISTED AND SQUIRMED, TO NO AVAIL. SHE WAS STUCK FAST TO the water horse. The great black steed tossed its flowing mane, its gaze mocking. It shifted its weight, and Rachel's feet left the ground. Terror gripped her, but she forced herself to breathe calmly.

"Drop her, you oversized hobby horse," Finn MacDannan said casually.

"Ah, very good." Dr. Mordeau came gliding out of the forest, her dark cloak billowing around her. She was tall in a split-skirted gown of black and thaumaturge blue. Her silver-streaked black hair came to a formidable widow's peak. She spoke in cool and imperious tones. "You have captured the impudent chit. Just in time for the Great Sacrifice. Oh, look, Finn MacDannan. We'll kill him, too. Sacrificing one of the Six Musketeers would be the perfect cherry atop our successful afternoon."

Rachel squirmed, but she could not free herself from the black hair of the marsh kelpie.

"Lots of luck with that," Finn replied mildly. He stretched his arms slowly and then interlaced his fingers behind his head. He could not have looked less concerned.

Dr. Mordeau pointed her wand at Rachel. "I have a hostage, MacDannan. Don't try anything."

Finn yawned, patting his mouth with his hand. Sigfried was less cavalier. He scowled darkly and drew his knife and his wand, his eyes filled with a fiery hate. Rachel suspected he was recalling the demon who stabbed Valerie. She also noticed that, despite his casual demeanor, Finn was fully alert and was slowly maneuvering Zoë, Seth, and Misty behind him. He would have liked to get between Mordeau and Sigfried, too, but the younger boy would have none of it.

Siggy walked boldly toward Rachel.

"No closer!" Rachel called out, her voice more panicky than she wished it were. "This horse can elongate his neck, stretching to at least ten feet, and if it bites you, it makes you sick."

"Sick, schtick," scoffed Siggy. "I don't get sick."

Recalling the ogre bashing Sigfried's head against the ice, repeatedly, and how the boy was soon up again, Rachel wondered if there might be some truth to his statement. Still, she didn't want to test it under these circumstances.

Lucky rushed forward, breathing flame. Dr. Mordeau's wand glinted. Lucky ran into an invisible wall, most likely the dome cantrip; one the freshmen had not learned yet. The wall of the dome seemed immune to dragon flame. Lucky slunk back reluctantly and wrapped himself around his boy.

Siggy fired off a cascade of spells, all of which dashed harmlessly against the invisible barrier. He ran forward, knife blade extended, howling like an ancient warrior, but he could not pierce the invisible bubble. He stabbed it with his black Bowie knife over and over, but each time, the blade skidded sideways and slid off the invisible surface.

Dr. Mordeau pointed the sapphire on her wand at Lucky. "You killed my familiar. My pet. He had been given to me by my father when I was a little girl. *You* must die."

Finn tossed a harmonica into the air and caught it. "You cast a spell at one of these kids—or their familiars—and you're dead, Melusine. Just like that. No Dome of Protection is going to stop *me*."

Dr. Mordeau lowered her wand. Then, she raised a hand and gestured toward the forest.

A horde of fey poured out of the trees to flank her on either side. In addition to the *each-uisge*, there were ghostly women in white, tiny pixies, grinning red caps, a handsome young man in a seal fur cloak—who Rachel guessed was a selkie from the pod that had moved in recent years onto the little island off the western shore of Roanoke Island. A large rabbit with red eyes, a phooka, accompanied a man dressed in leather with long rabbit ears who Rachel did not know, though she recognized that he was dressed in the manner of the Lenni Lenape. Behind them, a shaggy, bark-covered spruce troll stomped nearly kicking several capering green-capped trow. A satyr-like creature accompanied the troll that Rachel recognized as a fachan. It had one leg, one arm, and one eye. They were followed by a hulking nine-foot shaggy man with long green pine needles for hair, which Rachel recognized from Daring Northwest's drawings in *Domovoi, Kikimora, and Other Denizens of the Forest* as a variety of leshy known as boruta. Above even the leshy loomed a gigantic green woman covered with fish scales.

The fey of Roanoke Island! A shiver traveled down Rachel's back. How had they gotten on campus? Had all the fey thrown in with Mordeau, just when Rachel had finally found the fairy king for whom she had been searching? Was that a bad thing? Or a good one?

Still stuck to the horse, which smelled unpleasantly of swamp, she could not reach her neck pouch to get the calling card her father had given her. But there was someone she could call. She shouted at the top of her lungs, while also activating her black bracelet. "Gaius! Vlad! William! Help! Mordeau!"

Dr. Mordeau snorted. "They could not *possibly* hear you."

"Rach, are you all right?" Gaius's voice sounded in her ear. "We're coming!"

Jenny's cheerful voice came next. "Sweetie, you don't have to be so loud. A mere whisper will suffice. You're blowing out our eardrums."

Dread's voice replied coolly, "If she doesn't shout, the enemy will be able to deduce the existence of our communication devices."

"How are we going to show up without letting on that we have a secret communication device?" asked Topher. "Won't it seem strange if we suddenly walk onto the flying polo pitch? A place we never go?"

There was silence, and then a noise that might have been a rather dignified snort of amusement, followed by Dread's voice stating calmly, "Miss Griffin, here's what you must do."

The fey were still pouring out of the woods. Following the leshy came a nut-colored being dressed in bark with wild hair like dried leaves. It stalked forward, grinning a maniacal grin... until it saw Rachel. Then it stopped and would come no closer.

"Spriggan." Dr. Mordeau gestured for it to join her. She threw a glance of annoyance at Sigfried, who was still trying to stab his way through her invisible barrier. "Do join us."

The Spriggan pointed at Rachel. "Let that one go."

"I most certainly will not. This little chit ruined my entire attack plan last time, and she interrupted the sacrifice that would have allowed us to commune with Morgana. We wasted an entire pack of barghests to hunt for the person who aided Jacinda Moth, when I knew all along that this one whistled her spells. Though, in my defense, who expects a freshman who has been at school for one week to be competent at anything at all? So, no. I won't let her go. I am going to keep her where I can see her, until it's time to sacrifice her to the powers Outside."

Oh. That didn't sound good.

The Spriggan shook its head and would go no farther. Rachel smiled at it, grateful that it had appreciated her returning its land enough to refuse to participate in harming her.

"Why would you want to bring in the Outside?" Finn scrunched up his face again. "You live here, too. There's no dream ocean anymore, not since the Tree fell. If you tear down the Walls, this little backwater world'll be ripped to shreds."

Dr. Mordeau drew herself, "True there will be some carnage at first, as the demons have their fun—but it will all be for such a good purpose."

Finn cleaned out one ear with his pinky and then leaned forward as if to hear what she said again. "Killing millions, maybe billions, will be for a good purpose?"

"The demons will rampage for a time, but then—" Dr. Mordeau raised her arms triumphantly above her head. The sun went behind a cloud, and a breeze blew only upon her, stirring her hair and cloak and the split skirts of her blue and black gown. Her voice rang out. "Our mistress, Morgana Le Fay will sweep in with her allies from the Uttermost Sea and restore order, bringing with her the Cauldron of Rebirth."

"Aw, not that *uth bo bruithing* rubbish again!" Finn let out a stream of what must have been swearwords, though Rachel recognized very few of them. "I thought we destroyed it!"

"It has not been fully restored yet, but the blood shed by the initial carnage should be enough to accomplish this. Then, what will it matter who has died, for they shall all be resurrected?"

"Lady," Finn scowled, "that Cauldron doesn't bring specific people back. It produces Cauldron wights, which have in common with real people exactly nothing," he made an O with his fingers, "zero, squat."

Dr. Mordeau made a dismissive gesture, grinning gleefully. "For the uninitiated, maybe. Mistress Morgana can coax it into producing the real thing."

"Who is it you wish to resurrect?" Rachel asked curiously from where she hung uncomfortably upon the side of the water horse.

Dr. Mordeau turned toward Rachel and the black horse. "My Francois courted me for three years before my father would allow us to wed. Three nights of marital bliss had we together. The fourth morning, he went out to draw water and was killed by a French Agent who mistook him for a marauder. He died in my arms." The manner of the tall, icy woman had changed. Instead of her arrogant condescension, she suddenly seemed young and vulnerable. Grief haunted her features. Her voice cracked with sorrow. "I wept tears of blood when our precious three nights did not culminate in the conceiving of a child. Nothing of Francois remained."

Dr. Mordeau straightened and raised her arms in spiteful exaltation. Again, the wind whipped her hair and voluminous black cloak. "When the Terrible Five slaughtered the entire Wisecraft—including the Agents who killed my love—I cried tears of joy. That day, I pledged myself to the service of the Terrible Five. I have never looked back."

Rachel worried her lower lip with her teeth. Her heart went out to Dr. Mordeau. She did not approve of anything the woman was doing, but her motives made sense, even if her actions were terribly wrong. Rachel wondered if her former Math tutor was as worried about the current whereabouts of her lost husband as Rachel was about her grandfather.

Still, her sympathy for this bereft woman went only so far. Rachel felt no desire help her destroy the Walls of their world, much less to volunteer to be the necessary sacrifice.

Dread's voice spoke in Rachel's ear. "We're in position."

Relief coursed through Rachel. She grinned inwardly and followed his instructions. She could not raise her arms, but she could move her hand.

"Dr. Mordeau, you will regret choosing to tangle with me," she said in her most imperious tone. Then she snapped her fingers. "Vladimir Von Dread!"

Dr. Mordeau looked from Rachel's hand to her face, puzzled. "Why would *he* help you?"

Dread strode out of the woods. "You called, Miss Griffin?"

He came forward, followed by William, Gaius, Topher, Naomi, Jenny, and Lucy, passing the fey who watched them warily. They all had their wands drawn, though Lucy also carried a parasol in her other hand, protecting herself from the direct sunlight. A thrill of delight ran through Rachel to see them come to her aid. Gaius winked at her.

The expressions on the others' faces were priceless. Mordeau's eyes widened in visible alarm. Siggy, Seth, and Misty gawked. Zoë looked suitably impressed. Even Finn gawked, though whether it was because she had performed a summoning by snapping her fingers—which he, as a master enchanter, would know was impossible—or because of *who* she had summoned, she did not know.

"You can really do that?" cried Siggy. "I thought Laurel made that up. Ace! I want to learn that spell!"

Gaius moved immediately to Rachel's side, careful not to touch the horse. Rachel gave him a grateful smile, feeling immediately braver. Dread and the others stopped slightly further away, but his keen eyes searched Rachel's face carefully.

"Are you well, Miss Griffin?" he asked.

"Well enough," Rachel replied, wiggling her fingers and her feet, which could no longer reach the ground, "for someone stuck to a supernatural beast." She added, in case they thought otherwise, "It snuck up on me."

"Bad horsey," murmured Gaius.

Vlad nodded impassively. He said nothing else, but he continued to examine the scene as if assessing the situation carefully.

"Okay, enough diddle-daddling. Give us back Mini Grif," said Finn. He turned to address the *each-uisge* directly. "Hey, there, you, Future Glue. What'll it take to get you to release her? What if I challenged you to a contest?"

The water horse's ears perked up. So did those of the red caps.

"We aren't here to play games with you, MacDannan—" began Dr. Mordeau.

A red cap cut her off. "It is within his rights."

"What do you mean?" Rachel's former Math tutor asked warily.

The red cap spoke to Finn. "What are the terms?"

Finn says, "You win, you keep the girl."

"Unacceptable." Dread's voice was dangerously soft. He crossed his arms.

"We win—" Finn began.

Rachel cut him off. This was too good an opportunity to miss! "And you lot agree to swear allegiance to the King of the Daoine Sidhe and to obey him in the matter of the Roanoke Covenants," she said. "Oh—and let me go."

The fey looked back and forth, one to another.

Mordeau said sharply, "We don't have time for this, and we aren't giving her up. We have a ritual to perform and a Wall to destroy. Seize them. Seize them all!"

"What kind of contest?" asked the selkie lad.

"Now that's the questi—" Finn began.

"Hurling," Gaius drawled, his eyes dancing. Rachel realized he had figured out Finn's identity, too. She had shared enough information from her research for him to jump to the right conclusions. He gestured toward the fey with a half bow. "A game of hurling. Winner takes Rachel."

Dread frowned imperiously at Gaius. "That's inappropriate, Valiant. What if Finn loses?"

"He won't," replied Gaius with confidence.

"I am not agreeing to this," stated Dread.

Over the bracelet, Gaius's voice said softly, "Obviously, we don't surrender Rachel. If we lose, we fight. But we will probably win, and then we won't have to."

"I cannot agree to a compact I intend to break," objected Vladimir over the bracelet.

Gaius winced. "Oh. Right."

Meanwhile, the red cap spokesman said, "Hurling is acceptable to us."

"Acceptable?" shrieked Mordeau. "Certainly not! We must hurry. Daniel and Susan are waiting. They cannot perform the Great Sacrifice without a suitable victim."

Susan? Daniel must be the former Agent Brown, but who was Susan? Could that be the sister the *encantadas* mentioned to Valerie when they were Underhill on April First?

The spriggan spoke to Dr. Mordeau. "The Morthbrood may call us, but they cannot change the rules of fairyland. The challenge is allowed."

Mordeau gestured with annoyance. "Very well. But you are all wasting your time. Do you see who I have here with me? Immortal red caps who have played hurling for centuries. What do you have? A has-been rock star? Some college students and a few who are still in high school? What chance do you have? Zero."

Rachel pressed her lips together. Mordeau did not know. Her former math-tutor-gone-rogue thought Finn was an ordinary human being. Rachel wished Mordeau had shown up just a few minutes later. She had not had time to tell Finn about the Heart of Dreams

"You heard it here, folks," crowed Finn. "A hurling game to be held in…" he glanced at the sun, "…half an hour. Get your team together."

The fey began talking among themselves. Finn gestured both to those around him and to Dread's people. Siggy reluctantly gave up trying to stab mid-air and stomped over to join him. Finn continued, "Okay, we need a team. And fast. Peregrine, who's good?"

"Your son Conan's our best player, other than myself," said Seth Peregrine. "Some of Conan's friends aren't bad—Van Helsing, Weatherby, Romanov. Valiant, here, is good, too."

"Not Romanov!" said Finn. "That's a can-o'-worms we don't want to open. Who else?"

Gaius said, "There are three seniors who are leagues ahead of everyone else."

Finn looked to Seth, who nodded.

"They're fantastic," said Seth. "Agravaine Stormhenge, Veli I-don't-remember-his-last-name, and the guy with the dragon, Donner Virgil. Also Dread, here, and Joshua March. March is like lightning on grass."

"Are you willing to play?" Finn asked Vlad.

"Yes, so long as it is understood that I will not agree to yield Miss Griffin."

A warm splash of sunlight lit Rachel from within. She knew Vlad could never face Sandra if he lost her, and he would probably do the same for nearly any student, but it still made her feel cherished.

"We need more," said Finn. "A team requires fifteen players, but whoever we pick has to be both an excellent player and discreet."

"That immediately eliminates the majority of the potential players," stated Dread.

Finn shrugged his shoulders. "Do your best. Gaius. Seth. Go. Pull a team together. Meet back here in ten minutes."

"Also," called Rachel, "can you call Iolanthe Towers? I think she'd like to be here."

Gaius said, "Seth and Zoë'll have to do it. I'm not leaving my girlfriend. In fact," he reached out and leaned on the black horse, so that one hand was now stuck to its back. "I won't be playing myself. I'm sticking with Rach."

Rachel melted inside. She leaned against him. "Thank you."

"Least I could do." He grinned down at her and kissed her nose.

"Wish you wouldn't, for all that I want you here," said Rachel. "They need you to win."

"Nah, they don't," Gaius replied. "There's a number of folks who are better players than I. I'm more of the strategy guy, and they don't need that with Finn here. Don't get me wrong. I'm not bad. I'm really not. But I'd never make professional. Now if it were dueling...."

Ten minutes later, the Roanoke team consisted of Finn, Seth Peregrine, Finn's son Conan, Conan's friends Abraham Van Helsing and Max Weatherby, Sigfried, Wulfgang Starkadder, Vladimir Von Dread, Joshua March, the three seniors: Agravaine Stormhenge, Veli Hirvela, Donner Virgil, and also Rachel's favorite proctor, Mr. Fuentes, who had walked onto the field while making his rounds and found himself drafted into the game. Rachel recalled that he had once considered becoming a professional athlete, and Gaius explained that Fuentes sometimes came out to play with them—alumni were allowed to play in the intramural sports at Roanoke—and that he had a solid understanding of the game. This left them down two players.

"Don't you have any other friends who can play?" Finn asked his son.

"I could ask Liam or Ian?" Conan suggested.

"No dice. Your brothers would tell your mother in a heartbeat."

Conan nodded as if he grasped the direness of that situation.

"Wait!" gasped Max Weatherby, a rangy dark-haired boy with a big chin and a ready smile. "Is that Red Ryder?" His eyes grew huge, and he began to stammer. "The l-lead singer of B-BOGUS?"

"That's him, in the flesh," quipped Zoë.

"But.... Bogus! Their *Putrid Nights* is the best. 'Last Sunrise: Today's the Day Everything Goes *Kaboom!*' was my absolute favorite song when I was eleven. I think I've listened to it ten thousand times!"

"Don't be a freak." Conan gave his friend's shoulder a light punch. "That's just my da."

Conan had that amused nonchalance of a kid who is used to people making a to-do over a famous parent. Rachel noticed that Max was not the only student awed by Finn MacDannan's presence, but he was the only one who displayed his awe so openly.

"But.... *Red Ryder.* Right here." Max stared at Finn with hero worship.

"That's right, kid," said Finn, "but we'll have to save autographs for later. Right now, we have a game to win. Now focus, people. We need one more player!"

"I'll play," said Zoë.

"Again, no dice," said Finn. "This isn't camogie."

"Hang camogie," Zoë snapped. "You need to win, and I can play. You know I can. I used to be on your team. Besides, they're letting the big green woman play."

Gaius called over Rachel's shoulder. "She's good. Zoë, I mean. I have no idea about the big green woman."

Finn scowled. "Moth can play. But I'm going on record as saying that I don't like it."

"Heard and acknowledged," said Zoë, rushing forward to pick a hurley from a pile that Finn had conjured.

"Moth," Seth looked confused. "Oh, you mean Forrest. Her name's Forrest."

Everyone looked at Misty Lark. Misty threw up her arms and crossed them in front of her face, saying hoarsely, "I'm a musician. Not a hurler."

No one argued with this, but Finn looked unexpectedly sad. Misty moved away and sat down on the bleachers to watch the match.

"We need one more player," said Seth.

"He's on the way," replied Joshua March mildly.

"Is he good?" Gaius asked.

"Very good," replied Joshua. "Very, very good."

"Oh, no." Finn tipped back his head and covered his eyes with his hand, groaning. Then, he proceeded to swear another blue streak.

"Why? What is the matter?" Dread asked calmly.

"That." Finn gestured toward the path that led from the gymnasium to the track.

Down the path walked Joshua's father, the Grand Inquisitor of the Wisecraft.

Cain March strolled onto the field. He must have been on campus for the Twenty-Fifth Anniversary festivities. The Grand Inquisitor was a lithe, extremely well-dressed man, handsome and bearded, with a Mediter-ranean complexion and eyes even more intense than those of his son, were such a thing possible. He had put aside his Inverness cloak, which he car-ried over one arm, for a simple gray pinstripe suit. In one hand, he held a fulgurator's staff with an onyx tip. Beside him sauntered his wife, Cassan-dra March, dressed in a skintight, off-the-shoulder, trumpet gown with a split on one side above the knee. The black satin clung to her curves as she moved, and at least half of the players, human and fey alike, paused to watch her walk by.

Iolanthe Towers also came running down the path. She paused, her eyes very wide, when she saw the fey. Then, she moved quickly over to Jenny's side. The two of them whispered together in quiet voices. Rachel could only catch the words, "Type three treaty."

Cain March and Finn MacDannan regarded each other for an uncomfortably long time. Then, they reluctantly shook hands.

"MacDannan."

"March. Kind of a Fourth-Gen reunion, is it?"

The Grand Inquisitor frowned, puzzled. Cassandra March spoke up. Her throaty voice always sounded as if she were resisting the desire to purr. "He doesn't remember."

Her husband gave her an odd look.

Finn grinned at her. "While you, on the other hand, never forget, eh?"

She lowered her lashes, smiling mysteriously.

Rachel gazed at Cassandra March with interest. The Raven had been loath to alter Rachel or her mother's memory, as he said it would change them irreparably. Mrs. March also had a perfect memory. Had Jariel altered Cassandra March when he brought her from Outside, or did she remember everything?

The majority of the players were gawking at the Grand Inquisitor. Mr. Fuentes, who hoped to work for Cain March's Wisecraft one day, looked stunned, but Wulfgang Starkadder appeared unaffected by the Grand Inquisitor's reputation. Rachel recalled Panther Fabian's comment that *fear of the Grand Inquisitor is one of the three certain signs of sanity* and smiled.

"Can he play?" asked Wulfgang, swinging his hurley over his shoulder.

"I can play." Cain March had a wolfish burr to his voice.

"He's not bad," Finn admitted. "He's better at hockey, but he'll do. It's show time!"

Finvarra MacDannan strode forward as if stepping onto a stage. He strutted back and forth, performing a slight dance-like hop before he turned. Glamour rolled off him like a shimmering cloak; he now fascinated the eye.

"Listen up, ye—." He glanced at Rachel. "—ye S's of B's! Do you know who I am?"

The fey had gathered into a team. It consisted of three red caps, the satyr-like peallaidh, a ghillie dhu in its outfit of shaggy leaves and bark, the selkie, the Lenni Lenape man with the long rabbit ears, two trow, the spruce troll, the one-legged, one-eyed fachan, the phooka, the leshy, the giant green woman with fish scales, and, strangely, the *each-uisge*, with Rachel and Gaius still stuck fast to it, who now held a hurley in its teeth. The rest stood off to the north, flanking Dr. Mordeau, who looked on with a cool and haughty demeanor. All their eyes turned toward Finn.

"I'm King Finvarra." Finn strutted, his teeth gleaming white, his spiky red hair dancing in the breeze like fire. "I was there for the first hurling game, over three thousand years ago. We played at hurling on the eve of battles, to toughen up our men and get them ready for the fight. After you've been bashed across the face by a hurley and kept playing, the clash of war is not so intimidating."

"Is that true," Gaius whispered to Rachel, "or is this Irish blarney?"

"He is King Finvarra." Rachel shrugged. "As to the rest, I have no idea!"

"I trained Cu Chulainn," Finn performed his hop-step-turn and paced in the other direction. "Heck, I made the hurley he used to kill the hound. But he took the mutt's place, so it all turned out all right." Finn paused and scratched his chin. "Assuming you think living one of the most tragic lives known to man, where you end up killing half your own relatives and die tied to a post, counts as 'all right'."

"As I said." Finn spun suddenly and slammed his hurley against the ground with a resounding *smack*. Half of the fey jumped. "I am King Finvarra of the Daoine Sidhe. If you are my subject, kneel."

The red caps, the trow, the phooka, the peallaidh, and the Ghillie Dhu in its outfit of leaves and bark all dropped to one knee. Dr. Mordeau glanced back and forth between the fey and Finvarra, confused.

"He is babbling," she cried. "He is bedazzling you with glamour. Don't fall for it!"

Finn tossed his hurley into the air and caught it behind his back. "If you are not my direct subject, but you recognize my authority and are willing to obey me, kneel."

The selkie knelt, along with the spruce troll, and the fachan dropped to its one knee. The black steed to which Rachel and Gaius were stuck took a step forward and lowered its head. Rachel was dragged along willy-nilly, but Gaius had to take a step along with the black steed.

Finn spun in a circle and then stopped, his arms spread. "Who among the rest of you is willing to acknowledge my dominion and obey me if I win this contest?"

The giant green woman and the nine-foot Leshy both knelt.

Finn stalked forward until he stood before the last member of Mordeau's team, the man with rabbit ears dressed in leathers. Finn squinted one eye and opened the other one very widely. He grinned a maniacal grin almost worthy of Sigfried. A number of the fey shuffled back a foot or two, away from him and the man with the bunny ears.

Finn leaned down, staring into the face of the shorter man. "Little god. Have you heard tell that I am the greatest Enchanter on the planet?"

"I care not for the Arts of mortals," the rabbit-man replied, meeting Finn's gaze undaunted. "Mortal enchanters can merely call. They cannot compel. What are you going to do, foolish mortal? Sing at me?"

Finn's spiky red hair flared around his head like a crown of living flame. It seemed longer than it had been a moment ago. Glistening glitter the color of starlight began to sparkle around him. Rachel leaned forward. The tiny sparks were exactly the same color as those that had appeared around Amber whenever she called up her butterflies.

"I don't think you heard me correctly, Moskim," said Finn, leaning very close to him. "I said, *Enchanter*."

There was something about the way Finn said that last word that Rachel did not comprehend. He was telling the small god something he did not want the rest of them to understand, but she could not fathom what it might be.

Tiny points of starlight shimmered all around him so that he twinkled like a child's toy, but the man with the rabbit ears, his nose twitching furiously, was staring at a point in front of Finn's face. Tiny flecks of the starlight glitter dust had begun to gather in front of Finn's eyes, exactly as they had with Amber, just before she captured and killed the red cap and the Heer.

Oh! He had *that* power! Rachel's heart beat against her ribs.

Moskim must have agreed with her assessment, because he gave a high-pitched scream and turned into a brown rabbit.

Finn leaned even closer, his hair still billowing in its own wind. "Do you agree?"

The rabbit nodded its head rapidly.

"Good." Finn straightened, suddenly just an aging rock star again. Moskim reverted back to a man with rabbit ears. "Then it's decided. If I win, you all work for me."

Rachel peered more closely at Finn. He did not look old, at all. In fact, searching her memory, she realized that he never had. Was his entire aging rock star persona merely a glamour meant to fool the Unwary?

"And if you lose?" asked the selkie. "What benefit is there in this game for us? Won't we have to fight the Dread Prince regardless?"

Vlad's brow twitched slightly. Rachel wondered if this was the first time he had been called the Dread Prince.

The Grand Inquisitor had been talking with Iolanthe and Jenny. Now he stepped forward. All the supernatural creatures took a step back.

Cain March said gruffly, "If we lose, you can have Roanoke Island."

Chapter Forty-Five:
The Fastest Game on Grass

"Hear me out." Cain March raised a hand, quieting the outcry from his own side. "I cannot continue keeping a major portion of my staff on babysitting duty. If we cannot re-forge the covenant, we're going to have to close down anyway or move the academy to a new location."

Iolanthe stepped forward, her silvery fox ears and tail showing. She tapped on the Grand Inquisitor's shoulder and said with a sweet smile, "I'll take it from here."

The Grand Inquisitor arched an eyebrow and gave her a skeptical look; Iolanthe was undeterred. Rachel winced at her presumption; then, she recalled that Iolanthe Towers was the person to whom Panther Fabian had addressed her comment about fear of the Grand Inquisitor and sanity.

"Hello, I am Iolanthe Towers. Daughter of Kuzu no Ha, and great-great-granddaughter of Lady Iolanthe of Underhill," she called out in a high sweet voice. "I will be your Fairy Parliamentarian today. Do both parties agree to the terms? I will repeat them."

Iolanthe held up a scroll from which she read. Rachel wondered where she had found one so quickly. Perhaps it was conjured.

"If the Roanoke team wins, Rachel Griffin goes free, and the fey of Roanoke swear allegiance to Finvarra MacDannan, King of the Daoine Sidhe. If the fairy team wins, the mortals will abandon Roanoke Island, and a fight will ensue over the fate of Rachel Griffin. Is that acceptable?"

One by one, each player—human and fey—agreed, though Rachel noted that nobody so much as asked her. As Iolanthe and Cain March went about securing the promises of the rest of the fey present, Cassandra March sauntered up to where Rachel and Gaius stood beside the water horse.

"Are you all right, Lady Rachel?" the Grand Inquisitor's wife asked.

Rachel nodded. "I am well."

Mrs. March turned and called to Dr. Mordeau. "Melusine, it will not do for her to be injured in the coming skirmishes. And your *each-uisge* will not be of much use to your team if it is burdened with two young people stuck to its side. Put them on top of the horse."

Dr. Mordeau coolly waved a hand, indicating assent. After a short discussion, it was decided that Rachel would be allowed to mount properly, so long as she kept both hands on the steed at all times. Mordeau wanted to stick Rachel's face to the horse, to keep her from whistling hexes, but Mrs. March would not hear of it, fearing that Rachel might be smothered.

Mordeau kept her wand trained on Rachel and Gaius while the steed partially released them. One of Rachel's hands was now stuck to the horse, but it could slide along the black steed's hide. With a little help, the two of them mounted and sat astride, with both of Rachel's hands stuck to the steed's mane, and Gaius seated behind her, his arms around her waist.

Gaius was then required to promise that he would not use his wand or otherwise interfere with the game. Again, no one asked Rachel. Her wand was right there, in her neck pouch. An idea began to form in her mind. In the meantime, however, there was another matter about which Rachel was curious. As they waited for the two teams to finish swearing, she whispered to the Grand Inquisitor's black-clad wife, "Mrs. March, you speak Korean, don't you?"

Mrs. March gave her an odd, sideways look. "What would make you think that?"

Rachel restrained the desire to blurt out *because the Raven has hinted that you are related to the Korean side of my mother's family in some way that he will not explain* and merely replied "Can you translate something for me?"

Cassandra March pursed her lips, amused by Rachel's persistence. "I can."

Rachel repeated the first sentence of Great-Aunt Ye Jin's reply to her question about Ye Jin's mother. At least, Rachel was pretty sure the part she repeated was a complete sentence. If her great-aunt had paused at some random place, this might just be a fragment.

Cassandra March's dove-like eyebrows rose. "Your grandfather said this, didn't he?"

Rachel shook her head. "My great-aunt, Jin Cavendish."

"Same thing," nodded Mrs. March. "What your great aunt said was: '*My mother was the most beautiful of the foxwives.*'"

Rachel's eyes widened, her heart beating oddly in her chest. Was she descended from a foxwife? And what was a foxwife? Was it the same as a fox spirit, like a kitsune or a *kumiho*? Or was it something entirely different? The Korean word she had repeated had not been *kumiho*.

"What made you ask if it was my grandfather?" she asked curiously.

Mrs. March, who had begun to saunter away, paused and glanced over her shoulder. "Because everyone knows the most beautiful of the foxwives is Kim Sun Li."

"All right," Finn announced, "Let's play—"

"Just a minute." Cassandra March crossed her arms and tapped her foot. "Surely, you are not going out there to bash each other in the face with sticks without wearing helmets?"

"Helmets?" Finn spat. "Woman, would you unman us all?"

"I can't be unmanned," said Zoë. "I'll take a helmet."

Mrs. March conjured a red helmet with a black racing stripe and handed it to Zoë. Rachel thought it was interesting that Mrs. March, famous world-wide for being the only conjured person who ever became real, could herself also conjure.

"People've played without helmets for three thousand years," objected Conan.

"They wear them in the official GAA games," Mrs. March countered.

"Only since 2010," said Conan.

Finn scoffed. "The Gaelic Athletic Association's gone weak. A broken jaw is a badge of honor in hurling."

"Are you ready to explain that to your wife?" asked Cassandra March, pointing at Conan.

Finn scowled. "Och. Very well. Coddle the lads if you must."

Smirking, Mrs. March pulled helmet after helmet from the air. Finn conjured one for Seth that had a peregrine on the top. It looked more like a knight's helmet than a football helmet.

"Ah, ah, ah!" objected Mrs. March. "Needs a faceguard."

Finn rolled his eyes so hard that Rachel feared he would hurt himself. The helmet he had just handed to Seth poofed into nothingness. He conjured an identical helmet, but this one had a faceguard. Wulfgang Starkadder conjured a similar helmet, except his looked like a wolf's head.

"Hey!" Seth cried, "how'd you do that? We've been in the same class all year. I've never seen you conjure anything that wasn't porcelain white. When did you learn this?"

Both Rachel and Siggy, who were also in the same core-group with Seth and Wulfgang, nodded their heads in agreement, astonished.

Wulfgang shrugged. In his normal sardonic, almost morose, tone, he said, "I just slum it in class. Less pressure that way. I've been conjuring for years. My mother is the foremost conjurer in the world."

"Yeah, she's hot stuff," said Finn. "I mean, as a conjurer. She conjures well. Though she is also a looker. Not as look-y a looker as Cassie March here, but then few can aspire to such a level."

Cain March glared at him. He glared very well. Rachel thought that the Grand Inquisitor might be a master glarer, perhaps one of the best in the world, almost as if he glared for a living, which, perhaps, he did.

His wife, however, merely chuckled as she slipped her arm through her husband's. She pursed her lips and gazed at Finn through half-lidded eyes. "All smoke. No fire."

"In your dreams, babe," replied Finn, leering. "And since you're a lucid dreamer, you'll enjoy every minute of it."

This evoked a cascade of silvery laughter from Cassandra March. Cain March murmured under his breath, "Can't kill him for that. I'll have him audited."

Gaius chuckled, too. He whispered softly to Rachel. "She's right, you know. Even among the Unwary, Red Ryder is famous for outrageous speech but chaste conduct."

Rachel leaned back slightly and replied, "He knows his wife would kill him. I occasionally fear she will blast Sigfried merely for being late with a Math assignment. Can you imagine if she found out her husband was carrying on behind her back?"

Mrs. March and Finn began conjuring helmets for the rest of the team. Vlad demurred and asked Jenny to conjure his, which she did, a snazzy-looking black and blue one with swan wings on the sides. He nodded to her, examined it, turning it this way and that, smiled slightly, and put it on. While this was going on, no one was keeping an eye on Rachel. She began slowly moving her shoulder and head until she was able to grab the strap for her neck pouch with her teeth and draw it out from under her robes. She considered asking Gaius for help but feared that might violate his oath not to interfere. So she did it on her own.

It was a difficult business. With her fingers stuck to the mane, there was little her hands could do to help, and she did not wish to take the chance that some other part of her might get stuck to the water horse's hide. Eventually, however, she managed to work open the pouch. Now, all she had to do was grab the wand in her teeth, and she could free herself.

Finally, everyone on the Roanoke team was wearing a helmet, except Finn himself. Goals had been set up on the north and south sides of the field, and Iolanthe had confirmed the rules of the game, making sure everyone was on the same page.

"Any more interruptions?" Finn called, looking around. "No! Play ball!"

Everyone moved forward at once. The students ran. The fey sprang into motion. The *each-uisge* leapt forward.

Two things occurred simultaneously. The first was that Seth Peregrine shouted out, "Hey, we forgot the sliotar! We can't play without one!"

Sure enough, there was no ball upon the field.

The second was that as the black steed leapt, Rachel was thrown forward over its neck. She could not fall off because both her seat and her hands were stuck to its sleek hide. Nor could she lose her wand, which was still wedged in, nor any of the light papers and the oval calling card, which did not leave the open pouch. The one heavier object stored within the pouch, however, continued forward with the *each-uisge*'s momentum, flying free and soaring away from her in a perfect parabolic arc—the Heart of Dreams.

Rachel gave a cry of pure horror as she watched the glowing moonlight gem arch through the air directly toward the gathered fey. Behind her, Gaius gasped. She had described it to him; he understood what was occurring. Across the field, Rachel's horrified gaze met Sigfried's, pleading. After all her careful searching, this precious talisman was about to fall into the hands of Mordeau and her fey.

All would be lost.

"Oh look," her blood brother yelled with a grin that would have put the spriggan to shame, "it's the ball!"

The nearest redcap smacked the Heart of Dreams with its hurley, sending it flying toward the south side of the field, and the game was on.

The game began in earnest. Students and fey sprinted across the field at tremendous speeds. Hurlers tossed the Heart of Dreams into the air, like a volleyball player setting up a serve, and then smacked the gem with their hurleys, sending it flying. Other players caught the silver sliotar in midair, ran a few feet, and then bounced it off their hurleys before passing it on. Even more amazing to Rachel was that players ran down the field at full speed with the Heart balanced on their hurley. It was like watching a high-stakes egg and spoon race.

Under ordinary circumstances, this was a difficult enough feat, but the hard, faceted gem, the size of a large grape or maybe a small apricot, was even trickier to balance than a real sliotar. The Heart rolled more freely. Rachel did not understand how it could be used at all; maybe some enchantment about the Heart was helping. Quite a few players on both sides lost the ball as it rolled off their hurley. Then a free-for-all would ensue until another player took control of it. Even Finn had trouble balancing the Heart at first, nearly dropping it twice before he got the hang of it.

Rachel began to develop an appreciation for why hurling was known as the fastest game on grass. With each play, the sliotar changed direction at tremendous speeds; it could move from one side of the field to the other in less than a second and a half. Watching the game might have been truly exciting for her... had there been an actual sliotar.

As it was, with each play, the Heart of Dreams—the talisman of eldritch power once so desperately sought by the Terrible Five—flew back and forth across the field, Rachel's eyes never leaving it. Her limbs trembled, so great was her terror that either it would break, or someone would recognize it. She could not imagine which one would be worse. The Heart had been entrusted to her by both Lady Iolanthe and the Raven. What would they think if she broke it or delivered it to the enemy? Each time it soared through the air, fear seized her anew. Her stomach felt as if it had gone straight through the top of her head and back up to visit Illondria.

When, after the first few good hits, the precious gem did not shatter into a thousand pieces, Rachel began to breathe more easily. She was still anxious. Real sliotars were considerably larger than the Heart. They looked a bit like large baseballs, though with more pronounced stitching. Sooner or later, someone might take a closer look at what was being used instead. If their erstwhile Math tutor or any of the fey realized what a treasure was here on the field before them, the whole struggle would be over—perhaps permanently, if the gem proved as powerful as rumored. Rachel tried to catch Finn's eye, hoping he would figure out what the ball really was before anyone else did, but his attention was fixed on the game.

Behind her, Gaius's body was tense as well, but he spoke to her cheerfully, keeping up a light banter about the game, as if hoping to calm her nerves.

"All right, so, the goal is to get the sliotar into the net. That's a score, which is worth three points. But if you can get it over the crossbar at the top of the net while still between the two vertical poles, that's a point. See, there goes Agravaine to score... oh, wait. No. Now the peallaidh has it. It can run rather fast with those goat legs of its, can't it? Impressive for a Scottish malevolent spirit that usually sits around haunting rivers and lochs. It looks like—Ah! Joshua has it, and he's passing it back to Vlad. Good man."

Vlad struck the Heart, passing it across the field to Abraham Van Helsing; only a redcap hooked Abe from behind and made off with the sliotar. The three redcaps passed it back and forth to each other, arching it over the heads of other players. Seth made a leap for it, attempting a block, the peregrine on his helmet bobbing, but the peallaidh leapt five feet in the air and kicked it across the field. Rachel glanced at Gaius, who indicated with a nod that kicking the ball was legal in hurling. The goat-legged sprite kicked it too hard; however, it whizzed over the heads of his teammates directly to where Sigfried stood in a midfield position. Siggy caught the Heart of Dreams and tossed it high into the air.

"Sigfried! Grab it!" cried Rachel, but he paid no attention. As it fell down again, he swung like a baseball player, batting the silvery sliotar clear across the field into the goal. He leapt up and down, triumphantly interlacing his fingers and shaking his hands over his head like a prizefighter.

A goal was nice, but he had forgotten in the excitement their need to retrieve the super-powerful magical talisman, or maybe he thought it did not matter now that the fey had agreed to serve Finn should the Roanoke players win the game. Rachel sighed.

"I wonder why no one objects that the ball isn't right," she mused, as the *each-uisge* leapt clear across the field after the ball.

"My guess," Gaius replied, grabbing her tightly as the water horse landed, "is that each side thinks the other requested such a sliotar, and they feel like total gits for not having specified the size and quality of the ball with the Fairy Parliamentarian."

"Is that a real thing, Fairy Parliamentarian?" asked Rachel, "or did Iolanthe make it up?"

"I have no idea," Gaius murmured.

The leshy guarded the opposing goal. His immense height gave him a great advantage. He could get to any part of the goal in a single step. He successfully smashed the sliotar away from the net on numerous occasions. But he was slow. Wulfgang Starkadder faked him out, pretending to go high, then reversing and smashing his shot downward, so that it flashed under the pine-man's legs and into the net.

The Roanoke team cheered.

"We're six points ahead!" Rachel cried with delight. "Oh, what a relief."

"Don't relax yet. Hurling can reverse fortunes more times than a game of *Sorry*."

"Oh," Rachel murmured, disappointed.

"Did you know," Gaius drawled lightly, perhaps hoping to cheer her, "that hurling requires a hundred and fifty different skills?"

"So many as that?"

"Yep. Basically, it requires the combined skills of lacrosse, baseball, and hockey. On top of that, you have to be willing to be bashed with a piece of wood and to risk being beaned with a ball that can move up to seventy miles an hour. Dangerous game."

"Played by fairies and Irishmen," Rachel quipped in the same tone one might use to repeat the old adage about mad dogs and Englishmen.

Out on the field, Seth Peregrine had control of the ball. He ran a few steps and then tossed the ball to his hurley. Here his excellent hurling skills got him in trouble. He tried to dribble the ball, but unlike a real sliotar, the Heart did not dribble. The gem plopped to the ground, and several players descended upon it.

"Pull it on!" cried Gaius, urging their players forward.

Rachel had heard that cry at other hurling games, on previous occasions when her family visited the MacDannans, but she had no idea what it meant.

"Ow! My, that looks painful!" she winced as, during the scuffle over who would take control of the ball, one of the red caps smacked Conan MacDannan so hard that something cracked, though Rachel could not see if it was Conan or the red cap's hurley. But maybe it was Conan, because a moment later, Jenny Dare came dashing across the field carrying her wand and her first-aid kit. Her face shone red from the exertion of all the running she was doing. This was the third injury so far.

Gaius murmured, "Poor Jenny. Many people kid that the person who does the most running in a hurling game is the medic. I'm not so sure it's a joke."

Rachel says, "Too bad we can't get closer to her. Vroomie's over by the bleachers. She could fly to the injured."

"That's not a bad idea," he said and proceeded to inform Jenny over the bracelet of the whereabouts of the bristleless. Rachel felt foolish for not having thought of that.

"That looks quite difficult," she added when Wulfgang grabbed the gem out of mid-air with a prodigious leap. He looked at it oddly, and a shiver ran through Rachel's entire body as she recalled how closely it resembled its purple twin, the Transylvanian Kadderstar, from which the Starkadder family took its name. But then he tossed it into the air and sent it flying with his hurley. "Can he grab the ball like that? With his hand?"

"Sure, and run up to four steps with it. Then you have to balance it or pass it," Gaius explained. "You can also bounce it off your hurley and back into your hand, but you aren't allowed to catch it that way more than twice in a given play."

The enormous green woman was not a skilled hurler and fumbled every time she had a chance to capture the ball; however, when it came to obstructing the Roanoke team, she excelled. The mara strode across the field, stepping over some of the smaller players on both sides and then stopping directly in front of a player who was in the middle of a promising run. Dodging around gigantic women was not one of the skills Gaius had covered during the practice games. Nobody seemed to know the best way to recover from coming face to face with her.

The mara blocked Siggy, who passed the ball to the left. The selkie ran in to hit it, but Finn moved in front of him, blocking his way. Zoë took advantage of this and hit the sliotar toward Veli; however, Moskim darted in, scooped up the Heart, and with a rabbit-like bound, leapt clear over the heads of both Veli and Joshua March, to land in a free spot twenty feet away, balancing the gem upon his hurley the whole time. Even Finn was impressed. The cocky Irishman mimicked tipping his nonexistent hat to the rabbit god.

Fuentes slipped up behind Moskim and hooked the sliotar. He then grabbed it with one hand and tossed it behind him to Vlad, who was coming the other way. The entire play was so seamless that Rachel wondered if they had rehearsed it, but when she asked Gaius, he said he could not recall Vlad and Mr. Fuentes even having been at practice at the same time.

Vlad passed it down the field to Zoë, who then lost the ball to Moskim, who leapt ten feet into the air and smacked the sliotar from there, sending it over the crossbar of the net but between the poles for a point. Cain March, who was playing goalkeeper, glared at the space more than five feet above his head, where the ball had gone, and muttered something about "no self-respecting goalie could be expected...."

This happened twice more, bringing the fey's points to three. The fourth time that the fey team passed the sliotar to Moskim, and he leapt high into the air, Donner Virgil ran forward and switched positions with Agravaine Stormhenge, who had been playing fight corner back. Rachel noticed that Donner's small, brightly colored dragon familiar now sat upon his shoulder. Looking back through her memory, she confirmed that it had not been there before. Donner bent his legs, leapt ten feet into the air, and smacked the sliotar Moskim had sent his way clear to the twenty-one-meter line.

Rachel cheered with the rest of the Roanoke team. Yet now that her initial fear was ebbing, a new fear rose to take its place. Moskim had scored three points, cutting their lead in half. *What if they lost?* Would the school really have to leave Roanoke Island? She suspected that if the Grand Inquisitor told them to go, the Board of Visitors and Governors would listen. But go where? Cathay, maybe? Would the school stay together? Or would it merely close, putting an end to the one academy in the world where the Arts fully cooperated? Would she still be able to go to school with her friends, or would they be split up and scattered to different local academies around the world? Nervously, she clutched the *each-uisge*'s mane, twisting her hands this way and that and wrapping them in the long, coarse hair.

The silver sliotar flew up into the air, with several players leaping for it. This annoyed Finn, for some reason Rachel could not grasp.

"One of ye!" Finn shouted.

Veli Hirvela snatched the Heart from mid-air, placed it on his hurley, and ran. Red caps swarmed him, as did the fachan and the spruce troll, but he pulled out ahead, running full out across the field. He outran the phooka and a trow and was drawing close to the opposing goal when the peallaidh came in from his left and whacked him across the back with his hurley, throwing Veli to the ground.

"Oooh!" Gaius winced. "Dirty pull!"

The spriggan, who was acting as the ref, agreed. Veli was offered a penalty puck.

"Puck? Does he get a new type of ball for that?" asked Rachel hopefully, straining to see over the players to where Veli stood twenty-one meters from the northern goal.

"Nah, in hurling, a puck means a certain kind of a shot. Usually, a free shot you get because the other side did something wrong."

"Odd," said Rachel, searching dictionaries in her mental library hoping to work out the connection between this and the round black object used in hockey, but she found nothing conclusive.

The leshy deflected Veli's shot, and the sliotar was back in play. Rachel sighed and leaned back against her boyfriend, who gave her an encouraging squeeze around her middle.

"So are you feeling better?" she asked over her shoulder, though her eyes remained focused on the Heart. She was eager to distract herself from the nail-biting pressure of the game and her concerns about both the Heart of Dreams and the future of the school—especially as she could not even bite her nails with her hands stuck to the water horse. "About us, I mean, now that I have finally reached the lofty age of fourteen?"

She glanced up at his face briefly, but Gaius's gaze was still trained on the game.

"Do we really have to discuss this now?"

Rachel's stomach, which still felt as if it had taken up residence up above in the stratosphere, flip-flopped. "Do you... is there something to discuss?"

"No. Yes. Maybe," Gaius said, his tone clipped. "Wow! That's an amazing move. Did you see that? The mara threw the entire phooka along with the sliotar! Is that legal? Um. What were you saying? Yes. Age. Look, Rach. This is not the place or time for a long discussion. I am glad you turned fourteen, but fourteen is still much younger than seventeen."

"B-but...." Rachel shut up until her bottom lip stopped trembling.

The black steed upon which they rode leapt clear over the heads of several players, landing on an entirely different part of the field. Rachel caught her breath and wished her hands were free to hold onto Gaius. The black steed swung its head, hurley and all, and knocked the sliotar clear across the field to land in the net. There was a collective gasp from the Roanoke team. Cain March, the Goalkeeper, frowned.

Now it was six to six. Rachel wished she had brought a watch. *How much time did they have left?* Had the two sides agreed to a time limit? She wished she had thought to ask.

She returned her attention to Gaius. "What does that mean? D-do... do you want to...."

"I don't want to break up." Gaius gave a short, good-natured laugh. "Give up the most amazing girlfriend known to man? Miss out on scenes like this?"

A grin began creeping over Rachel's face. "Very good, then."

Max Weatherby and Abraham Van Helsing raced toward the opposing net, trading the sliotar back and forth over the head of the three-foot-tall trow. A second trow dashed under Max's feet, tripping him. This did not keep Max from knocking the ball sideways, as he fell, heading toward the net. The leshy jumped in the way. Seth Peregrine rocketed forward and deflected the Heart, sending it directly into the far side of the net for a goal.

The Roanoke team whooped and cheered.

"We're winning again," Rachel cried, delighted.

"For this ten-second stretch," quipped Gaius. He returned to the previous topic. "I don't want to break up. I just want to make sure my behavior is entirely respectful. No more falling asleep in secret rooms without chaperones. That's just not.... We should not do that."

"Oh," Rachel's stomach dropped from whatever heights it had previously leaped to. She felt suddenly glum.

Gaius's arms tightened around her, his West Country accent creeping in. "Worry not, me love. This will pass. You will grow up, and when you do, I'll still be here. We just have to be... patient."

"Patient. Right." Rachel nodded sadly. Remembering what Illondria had told her about the futures that awaited her, she thought but did not say aloud, *but when that future comes, will I still want it?* She dearly hoped she would.

The game continued at a dizzying, violent whirl. The score was now nine to six, with the advantage to the Roanoke Academy team. The Ghillie Dhu hit the gem in mid-air and sent it flying directly at the far side of the goal from where Cain March stood. The Grand Inquisitor launched himself into the air, soaring sideways, to catch the sliotar with the flat end of his hurley and send it flying away from the net. He smacked headfirst into the bar of the net and fell to the ground, groaning, but he shook off the pain and staggered back to his feet, waving away the medic.

Rachel felt a wave of relief. They were still ahead. She again wondered what time it was. She glanced toward the path leading back to the gym.

Would the game be interrupted by visitors arriving in anticipation of the exhibition hurling game that was supposed to start off the festivities? She thought back over the visitors she had seen arriving earlier that morning, alumni seeking old haunts, parents greeting children, and....

A cold chill traveled up her spine. In her memory, something was wrong with some of these visitors, something that had not been apparent to her eyes. The individuals themselves looked normal, but the shadows stretching from their feet were oddly misshapen. They did not match the bodies.

Unless Rachel was entirely wrong, despite all the security that the Agents and Watchmen were providing, Roanoke Academy had just been *infiltrated by wraiths!*

Chapter Forty-Six:
The Heart of Dreams

"Gaius!" Rachel cried. "Dr. Mordeau! She brought wraiths with her!"

"What can we do?" asked Gaius, his voice full of concern. "Is there someone we could warn? I can ask Topher or Jenny to go?"

"Warn someone! What a good idea!" Rachel cried. "Yes, do that, but it will take them time to run back from here. Let me…." Leaning forward over the neck of the steed, which was thankfully standing still for a moment, Rachel called. "Lucky! We need you!"

Lucky the Dragon had been floating above the game, watching his boy. Now he flew across the field, undulating like a ribbon in the wind.

"Yes, brainy dwarf sister-creature?" the dragon asked in his gravelly voice.

Rachel cried, "Quick. Fly and find Mr. Tuck. Tell him that Rachel Griffin said there were wraiths on campus and that he should check the shadows of visitors. And then tell Maverick Badger. He might believe you, too."

She felt certain Mr. Tuck would believe her this time. He had promised he would. After him, the head of the proctors was the best choice, but Mr. Badger could be hard to find. Mr. Tuck would be on the commons preparing for the festivities, at which he was to be the Master of Ceremonies.

"On it!" Lucky shot off like a runaway bristleless, across the field and out of sight.

Meanwhile, Gaius spoke over the bracelet. Rachel saw William, Naomi, Topher, and Lucy take off, Lucy's parasol bobbing as she ran. Jenny stayed, as she was needed as a medic.

The game was still going strong. Agravaine Stormhenge tapped the ball into the air, but it went higher than he had intended. Both he and the mara spun around, searching for it, but even though the green giantess had reach on him, he caught it on his hurley as it came down behind his back and took off across the field with the Heart of Dreams balanced on his stick.

Gaius cheered, but Rachel gritted her teeth. This needed to end. Sooner or later, someone on the fey side might take a good look at the sliotar; or worse, the battering might be too much for the Heart, and it might shatter into a thousand fragments. If she could get the gem off the field, someone could conjure a real sliotar—which would be easier on the players. Rachel glanced around, trying to catch someone's eye, but none of the players looked her way. She breathed out a hiss of frustration. *It was time to take action.*

"Gaius," Rachel asked sweetly, "that silver bit poking out of my pouch. Could you be a dear and pull it out, turn it around, and put it in the other way?"

"Sure thing." Gaius did so. "Wait. This is your wand. We promised not to meddle."

"I didn't!" she said fiercely. "No one bothered to even ask me."

Gaius snorted with amusement and shook his head. Rachel twisted until her mouth was on the slender silver length. Then, she contorted her head until the diamond at the tip pointed downward at her hands. She fired off two Word of Ending cantrips. Her hands came free.

With a shout of exaltation, Rachel freed her bottom half from where it was stuck to the black steed and threw herself sideways.

She had not thought this through. She flew through the air pell-mell. The grass approached very fast. It was truly a shame that she did not actually have a cat familiar. Her habit of falling from things would be so much less alarming. Then, suddenly the ground was approaching more slowly. She rolled in the air and landed on her feet. Behind her, atop the *each-uisge*, Gaius surreptitiously slipped his wand back into his sleeve. Rachel drew her wand and pointed it at him, setting him free.

"Get down!" she called. "You didn't promise to stay on the kelpie!"

Gaius jumped from the back of the enchanted swamp steed. Rachel successfully wafted him to the ground—glad she had practiced *tiathelu* on heavy objects. The black horse turned its head and bared its teeth around its hurley, but then it charged off after the sliotar. Gaius moved toward the side of the field. Turning, Rachel ran across the field toward Finn, shouting and waving her arms.

"Finn!" cried Rachel, dodging players from both teams.

A near-miss collision with a red cap set her heart off at a gallop. She froze, terrified. The rapid motion of the players running in all directions disoriented her. She started to reach out to call her broom, but Jenny was using it. Rachel saw the older girl flying to help Max, who had been whacked in the knee.

Drawing a deep breath, Rachel closed her eyes for just an instant and pretended she was on her steeplechaser. Her mind went calm. As she opened her eyes, she felt her pupils widen. The three-dimensional movements around her now seemed clear and crisp. She balled her hands into fists, lowered her head, and dashed forward, moving in and out of the many players as she might trees in the forest.

It worked—for a time. Trees and furniture and walls and rooftops did not change their position. True, balls in snooker and pool moved, but they followed predictable trajectories.

Not so humans and fey at play. A hurley Rachel judged to be half a foot over her head passed by at two inches by the time she ducked under it. Then, the fachan moved right because Seth and Veli rushed in from the left, and suddenly, all four of them—Rachel and the three players—were all trying to occupy the same spot.

She slammed into Veli and the fachan and fell backwards, landing on the grass, staring up at the sky. As she waited for her head to clear, she had the dazed thought that maybe she needed to practice flying among moving targets. None of the players she had smashed into stopped to check on her; though, from another part of the field, Conan MacDannan shouted, "Clear off, Griffin! Pitch invasion isn't until the game's over!"

Dizzy and sore, Rachel struggled to sit up. Her knee and shoulder hurt, but nothing seemed to be broken.

"Capture her!" Dr. Mordeau screamed from the sidelines, pointing at Rachel. "She's getting away!"

"Get off the grass, Mini Griff! Are you out of your"—unintelligible—"mind!" shouted Finn, barreling across the field in her direction. Dread also sprinted in her direction, spruce troll, trow, and red caps scattering before him.

Rachel stared Finn in the face as he charged across the field toward her.

"Finn," she shouted. "Look! Please!"

Rachel dared not point, lest someone else notice. Her gaze darted to the gem and back. She mouthed as if each word were a separate sentence: *Heart. Of. Dreams.* She tapped her chest, above her heart, and then pressed her hands together by her cheek and tilted her head sideways, pretending to sleep. She did all this very rapidly.

Vladimir arrived and scooped Rachel off the grass and into his arms, holding her like a groom carrying his bride. Rachel wished she had the leisure to appreciate this, but her attention was focused on Finn, who squinted at her. He scowled with annoyance as he slowed and began to turn back to the game, dismissing her. Finn MacDannan was truly good at scowling, almost as good as Cain March was at glaring.

Then, Finn's eyes fell upon the moonlight-colored shining object, which the players were knocking around. His eyes bugged out, and his jaw went slack. He stumbled, almost falling. As he recovered, a fiery gleam came into his eyes. Rachel could not tell, but it might have been real fire. He leapt forward, jumped clear over a trow, and did a backflip.

In the middle of the backflip, he snatched the sliotar off another player's hurley.

With a whoop of triumph, Finn landed on the grass and thrust his hand upward, the Heart of Dreams clutched in his fist. Moonlight spilled from his fingers, forming longer and longer beams of silvery light. Rachel's jaw dropped.

Finn did not just know what the Heart of Dreams was; he knew how to use it.

Like waking from a dream, all the fey disappeared from the field, both the players and the spectators. One moment, they were there. Then, they were not. Dr. Mordeau, who suddenly stood by herself under the shadow of the hemlocks, gasped and spun around, alarmed. Many of the Roanoke players stopped, too, but not Sigfried, Wulfgang, Seth, and Conan. These four ran immediately to the opposing net and waved their hurleys, shouting that they were open.

Moonlight continued to stream through Finn's fingers. The red caps, trow, trolls, mara, phooka, and other fairy folk came back into view. Again, it was as if Rachel had dreamed that they were gone and now woke to discover she had been wrong.

Finvarra MacDannan stood in the center of the field with his arm outstretched about his head and silver light streaming from between his fingers. Rachel had never seen him look so like his Red Ryder poster.

"Bow down," he shouted the opening line of a famous poem, *"I am the emperor of dreams!"*

The fey of Roanoke bowed.

Fighting the tremendous temptation to put her head down on Dread's shoulder, Rachel looked up and met his gaze. "Wraiths came in on the shadows of visitors. William and Topher and the others have gone to investigate."

"Indeed. As they should. And I, as well." He put her down.

Rachel's showed no change of expression, but inwardly, she sighed. *Why couldn't she get a chance to snuggle up to the boy of her dreams—just for a moment—on a day when they were not under immediate threat of danger of wraiths sucking the life out of the entire campus?* Wait. Boy of her dreams. That was Gaius. Of course, now he did not want to snuggle up either. Some days, life was so unfair.

Rachel flashed Vladimir a quick smile and ran off in the direction of Jenny. The older girl had climbed off of Vroomie and was examining Max's knee. Rachel raced up, grabbed her steeplechaser, and leapt on.

"So long. Got to go!" She waved, preparing to depart.

"Wait!" Sigfried cried, running toward her. "Take me!"

Rachel paused until he jumped on and then rocketed down the path back to the commons.

Rachel and Sigfried burst out of the forest and into a war zone. Wraiths loomed and shrieked. Students ducked behind parents and tutors who were wielding wands or rings of mastery. Golden Glepnir bands and short glowing white darts floated and flashed.

Rachel halted her bristleless, blinking as she glanced this way and that, trying to make sense of what was occurring on the commons. She had been expecting a dozen wraiths, maybe two dozen. Instead, she realized that all ninety-nine that the Morthbrood bought from Imelda Stark must be here, black looming shapes swooping down on students and shrieking their horrible shrieks.

"Ace!" Sigfried's lips parted in sheer boyish joy. "It's a right regular battle! Now that's how to commemorate a previous battle! No boring lectures and ceremonies!"

"Siggy, some days, you are more boyish than should be legal," she murmured back, not really paying him much heed. She took in the battlefield. Some of the wraiths appeared as barely visible, flowing dark entities. Others were fully visible, eerie, gaunt creatures with skull faces.

"Why are there two kinds of wraiths?" she asked.

"Lucky," replied Sigfried.

"Who's lucky? Us or them?"

"No, the answer is Lucky. He's doing it. Look."

Sigfried pointed. Across the lawns, the red and gold figure of Lucky the Dragon snaked through the air, approaching a cluster of semi-visible wraiths. Lucky breathed great plumes of red-gold flame upon the dark shape. Instantly, the faint shapes popped, revealing the darker, more gaunt wraith beneath.

"Ooh! Lucky!" Rachel nodded. "He's breaking their protective charms. Right."

"Lucky," Siggy repeated fondly, "As in, we're lucky we have Lucky."

"So, what do we do?" Rachel looked around, trying to track everything, and failing. She frowned as she peered at the chaos more closely. "Where are the proctors? Where are all the Agents that were guarding the school?"

"What do you mean, what do we do? We attack!"

Sigfried leapt off Vroomie. Drawing his black Bowie knife, he charged toward a floating specter that hung eerily in the air like a living cloak, screaming as he ran. Lucky came barreling in like a living lightning bolt and breathed on the wraith. There was an audible pop. The dark shape now had sunken eyes, a gaunt face, and narrow bony hands.

Sigfried stabbed the wraith repeatedly with the warded knife that Rachel's mother had helped him prepare. The previous time they had fought wraiths, his blade had done nothing. Now, to his delight, the knife bit into the specter's substance. The wraith let out an ear-splitting screech. Steaming black ichor dripped from the wounds.

Rachel clapped her hands over her ears to protect herself from the screech. She recalled that noise vividly from the first time they had fought a wraith, during the first week of school. How strange. Back then, she had still been afraid of the Raven, thinking he was an evil omen. Of course, that had been in part because, back then, his presence reverted Lucky to an unintelligent state. How much had changed.

"Finish him, Lucky!" cried Siggy. "I've got to do a thing!"

Sigfried knelt and scooped up some of the dripping ichor in his hands. Rachel shrieked, objecting. Whatever that substance was, she doubted it should touch his skin. Siggy ignored her. He ran back toward Rachel, shrugging off his backpack as he came. Meanwhile, Lucky breathed flame all over the floating phantom, who shrieked even louder and fled, ablaze.

"Hey, blood-sis! Hold my bag! Oh, and can you open it for me?"

Sigfried dropped his backpack and held out his dripping hands. Rachel picked the bag up and stepped back, away from the strange, musty stench of the wraith ichor. She opened the bag. Sigfried took off at a run and dove into the opening headfirst.

Thump. Bump. Thump. The boy tumbled all the way down the stairs. Rachel looked on in horror, unable to slow his fall with *tiathelu*, as her hands were full. *Why in the world had he done this? Why hadn't he just walked down the stairs normally?* By the bottom, however, Siggy managed to tuck in his head. He somersaulted and leapt to his feet.

"I'm all right! All right!" he shouted. He stumbled but then righted himself again. "Must go commit alchemy!"

Puzzled as to why he would do this in the middle of a fight, Rachel could not help but notice that he had an entire alchemy lab set up in the room inside the bag. As she shifted the backpack to her shoulder and turned back toward the fray, she wondered how much of that equipment had been provided by her mother.

Ahead, she spotted Joy and the princess. They stood warily in front of a gaggle of freshmen and sophomore girls. The princess played her violin, and Joy was striking her bells with a little silver mallet, not having her xylophone handy. Sparkles of golden light surrounded the group, protecting them from the wraiths. Rachel saw a shadowy wraith float toward their position. It was repelled by the *Sacred Ring*.

Rachel flew over, pausing just outside the glowing golden sparks, which smelled of cedar. Now that she was closer, she could see that, at the far side of the cluster of girls, three older girls from Dare were playing their instruments as well. Unable to break through the circle of golden sparks, two larger wraiths drifted toward Rachel. She drew her wand from her sleeve and fired off a Glepnir band. Her aim was not very good, and the band missed; however, the wraiths judiciously backed away from her.

"Where are the Agents?" she called to her friends over their music. Her eyes tracked the wraiths. They seemed to be gathering more of their kind, perhaps to come back her way.

"At the docks," Nastasia called back. "Fighting the Morthbrood, who tried to attack the school. Do come inside the circle. Where have you been?"

Rachel was saved from having to answer by the re-emergence of Sigfried, who erupted from the backpack, crystal vials in his hands. Siggy did a flip, landed on the ground, snatched the pack from Rachel, and placed a dozen or so vials into her arms.

"Here. Take these," he said.

"What are they?" she asked.

"Your mother showed me how to make the Achilles elixir so you could prepare the whole thing ahead of time and just add the active ingredient from the thing you want to be immune to at the last minute. I added that wraith ichor, so now, these will protect a body from wraiths. Can you fly around and give them to people who need them?"

"Certainly!" cried Rachel, eager to help—and to avoid explaining to the princess where she had been. She wanted to give Finn time to talk to his wife before the story spread too far.

"Drink one yourself," insisted Siggy. "I don't want you to end up as wraith chow again."

Rachel put the vials into her robe pockets, grabbed one, pulled the stopper, and drank it. Instantly, she wished she had not. An eerily disturbing sensation slid down her throat. She shivered. Then, she turned and offered a vial to the princess.

Nastasia met her gaze with a little smile. "We're all safe here. I can keep this up for some time, and I am not the only one playing. Go give them to those in greater need."

Rachel gave her a quick nod and sped off in search of those under attack.

Chapter Forty-Seven:
Wraith Attack!

Rachel flew towards the center of the commons. A dozen wraiths, dark and cloak-like, streamed by her, heading eastward. Immediately, three of them swerved and swooped directly at her. She flinched and threw up her forearm. To her relief, the elixir worked. The phantoms rebounded from her, unable to gain any purchase. She was grateful these were the pre-Lucky wraiths, still in their cloak-like state. She was not sure if the elixir would protect her from a wraith grabbing her with its bony hand.

Rachel zig-zagged around another group of east-going wraiths, determined to find where Sigfried's elixirs would do the most good. With only a dozen vials, after she drank hers, she could not give one to everybody, nor did she wish to waste any on those who did not need help; however, there were plenty of students and visitors, maybe even tutors, out there who had no way of fighting a wraith. She needed to find those protecting such people and help them.

In some areas of the wide lawns with their occasional trees, the students, visitors, and faculty were forming defensive formations, based on the particular Art they practiced. Enchanters surrounded themselves with golden *Sacred Rings* or white *Walls of Protection*, while warders laid down circles of salt and iron filings, thus keeping the wraiths at bay. Alchemists shook charm bracelets, and thaumaturges wielded wands. Canticlers sheltered others under protective domes, such as Dr. Mordeau had used, while a second group of canticlers formed a circle and threw offensive cantrips to capture the specters or keep them at bay. One could not cast offensive spells from inside the protective dome.

On other parts of the lawns, chaos reigned. Students ran screaming. Conjurers from Marlowe Hall and scholars from Dee could do little against the onslaught of a supernatural menace. A visitor, an old lady, had fallen on her face, tears streaming down her cheeks as two wraiths ripped at her with bony claws.

Rachel rocketed forward, flying directly into the wraiths that troubled the old lady. The effects of the elixir Rachel had consumed threw them backwards. She paused to dismount, intending to help the old woman, but Skuld Odinson came racing across the grass, her fair hair streaming behind her, her fulgurator's wand bouncing in her hand.

"*Bestemor!*" Skuld cried, her face stricken. "*Bestemor!* Are you all right?"

"I am now," the lady replied in a strong Nordic accent. "This *unge damer* helped me."

"Thank you!" cried Skuld.

The elegant upperclassman hardly glanced Rachel's way in her rush to help her grandmother. Rachel suspected Skuld had no idea whom she had just thanked. Rachel recalled from an article she had once read in *Noble Wise* that this old lady was a member of the royal family of Norway. Rachel considered giving the grandmother and granddaughter pair an elixir, but while Skuld was a scholar from Dee Hall, she was also a Knight of Walpurgis and a top-notch duelist. With her wand in her hand, Skuld would be able to defend them both.

To Rachel's left, she spotted a promising candidate for a vial. Her Language tutor, Mr. Tuck, faced off against a pack of wraiths. Three of the dark specters were already restrained by Glepnir bands. The rest attacked him; some had already sunk their long, shadow-like arms into his body, draining his life essence. As she approached, he cast another cantrip, trapping yet another wraith, but his face was growing pale beneath his beard.

"Ah, Miss Griffin," he called, "a bit busy, but thank you for the warning. At least we got a bit of a drop on them."

Rachel sped toward him, holding out a crystal vial. "Anti-wraith Achilles elixir!"

"Indeed? That sounds… quite useful about now."

He turned back to his assailants and cast two more cantrips, trapping two more wraiths. Rachel used her wand to float the vial directly into his hand. He pushed the stopper out with his thumb and downed the contents of the vial with one gulp. The wraiths were instantly expelled from his body as if he had become solid to them.

"I thank you most sincerely," he rumbled, grinning as he caught another wraith in a Glepnir band with a gesture of his emerald canticler's ring.

"You can thank Mr. Smith," Rachel called over her shoulder. "He made it."

As she flew off, she heard him murmur, "Glad she didn't tell me that before I drank it."

Rachel chuckled as she soared on. Not everyone knew about Sigfried's prowess in alchemy, and even fewer were aware of his supply of super-effective elf herbs.

More wraiths soared eastward, but whether they were fleeing or seeking quarry, Rachel could not tell. She threw a vial of the elixir to a beleaguered-looking Art tutor who was trying to defend some students against a pack of the cloaked phantoms. The woman gave her a thumbs-up and downed its contents. Rachel threw her a second vial for her to give to another member of her group. Faith O'Keefe stepped forward and caught it, gulping down its contents. Then she swung into action, running at wraiths to drive them away from her beleaguered classmates.

Faith and her tutor were joined by Merry Vesper, who rode up on the back of her white reindeer. The lovely young blonde girl and her antlered familiar charged the wraiths, who moved rapidly away from them. Rachel could not tell why the wraiths were afraid of Merry.

Ahead, members of the Dare Hall Vampire Hunters Club surrounded other less able students, many of whom were underclassmen. Abraham Van Helsing, Conan MacDannan, and Max Weatherby had not yet returned from the hurling game, but the rest of the club—the Colt brothers, the Ferret brothers, and Alex Romanov—spread out around the cowering students, facing outward. They played their instruments, violins, a flute, and the odd rows of crystal triangle chimes played by both Colts. Several cats lounged nearby, watching intently.

As Rachel flew toward them, the two members of the Vampire Hunters Club Women's Auxiliary, Sarah Weatherby and Winifred Powell, came running pell-mell toward the rest. A bony wraith chased them, reaching for the girls with skeletal hands. Winny's familiar, a large seagull with gray wings and a scarlet line along the top of its otherwise dark beak, screamed its shrill cry. The brave bird beat its wings and pecked at the specter that heckled the two girls. A fluffy white dog loped beside Sarah, barking and growling at the wraith.

Rachel leaned back to throw a vial each to the two girls, but they reached their clubmates just as the young men succeeded in sucking a wraith into a white vase sitting on the ground at their feet. The two girls quickly joined the outward-facing circle, pulling out their instruments. The wraith that had been following them drifted rapidly away in search of easier prey. Rachel kept the elixirs and headed off in search of those who needed them more.

Ahead of her, the green-eyed goth girl who had spoken up for hurling at the Knights of Walpurgis meeting strode across the commons surrounded by a pack of snow-white Doberman Pinschers with blood-red ears. Wraiths fled before them.

Rachel watched, openmouthed. Those were hounds of the Wild Hunt, similar to the ones that had accompanied the Headless Horsemen, the time the phantom had chased Rachel and Gaius! Who was that girl and how had she managed to call up such dogs?

Then, Rachel hurried on, passing a warded group and a group protected by a Dome of Protection cantrip cast by one of the Language tutors. Among the protectors of another quite large group, she recognized some of the more prestigious visitors, Councilman Powers and Iolanthe's uncle, General Towers. These seasoned experts quickly captured or dispatched any wraiths who came near them. Beyond, her Music tutor, Miss Cyrene, stood side by side with a few others from the Music department, playing a *Sacred Ring* around a large group of students. One of the tutors, a short, dark-haired man with a pixie smile, who Rachel recognized as Mr. Kalkavage, the Sophomore Chorus tutor, paused his lute-playing to wipe his brow, only to be mugged by two wraiths when his section of the golden ring began to fray.

Rachel charged directly at the wraiths. One bolted. The second reached out a bony hand, grabbed the haft of her steeplechaser, and sent her into a spin. The bristleless rocketed sideways, hurdling toward a tall oak. Rachel tried to pull up or dive down, but she was spinning too fast. She could think of three ways of pulling out of such a violent spin, but none would happen before she and Vroomie attempted to occupy the same space as the tree. She threw herself against the spin, hoping to change her trajectory just enough to avoid a crash.

Suddenly, Rachel laughed aloud. Leaning into the spin, she twisted the new becalming ring to high. Instantly, a soft bubble of air surrounded her. She still floated sideways, but now she did so very slowly. She was almost embarrassed to escape so easily. Meanwhile, Mr. Kalkavage caught the offending wraith in a Glepnir band.

"Here," Rachel cried, righting herself and tossing him a vial. "Anti-wraith Achilles."

"Truly?" Mr. Kalkavage's eyes sparkled.

He gently put down his large lute and stepped deftly outside of the ring of golden sparkles, leaving his fellow tutors to maintain it. Miss Cyrene nodded, moving to the left, and the ring swiftly reconfigured itself.

He downed the elixir, shivering only once. After a glance at his lute, now on the other side of the ring of golden sparks, he withdrew a smaller, lighter violin from an inner pocket of his robe. Tucking it under his chin, Mr. Kalkavage began to play. White light swirled out of his instrument, surrounded a nearby wraith, swirled around it, constrained it, and tied the specter into a little package, complete with a bow. He did not even need a vessel as the vampire hunters had.

Rachel let go of Vroomie and clapped, impressed. The pixyish tutor winked at her and waltzed off to capture another wraith while saying something about bells.

Ahead, several dark shapes clustered together, leaning over a more solid shape. Rachel flew closer and gasped. Several wraiths had sunk their arms elbow deep in poor Mylene Price. Mylene's dark otter leapt upon one of them and seemed to be able to bite it, but the other wraiths freely harassed her.

"Mylene!" Rachel barreled into the dark, cloaked shapes, scattering some, and then opened a vial. "Anti-wraith!"

The young redhead lifted her head, and Rachel carefully poured the elixir into the other girl's mouth. Mylene drank eagerly, only shivering slightly at its unpleasantness. Immediately, the wraiths were expelled from her body. They drew back, startled, and then fled. Mylene grinned in delight. Then concern overtook her features.

"Can you get one to my dad?" Mylene cried plaintively. "The wraiths are mobbing him! They hate him because he hunts them. He went toward the moat, I think, hoping to draw them away and then cross running water."

"That should work!" Rachel shouted over her shoulder as she sped on. "But I'll keep an eye out for him!"

As Rachel flew closer to the center of the commons, her stomach gave an unpleasant lurch. Most of the students were safe behind the various protections put up by the tutors and parents who had been warned by Mr.

Tuck. Here, however, students had been caught unaware. They lay strewn across the grass where they had collapsed. In some cases, wraiths still bent over them, growing more solid by the moment. Rachel drew her wand and Glepnir-banded two wraiths as they preyed on fallen students. Then she landed and fed one upper school sophomore the contents of a vial, which repelled the creature preying upon her. Many other students, however, were unconscious and unable to swallow, though none appeared to be dead —at least, not yet. Among the fallen, Rachel recognized Dare sophomore Esteri Hirvela; Iolanthe's stout redheaded friend, Minnie Forthright from Raleigh Hall; Raleigh freshmen, Remington Black and Zachary Duff; and Laurel's best friend, Muffy Calico.

Rachel rushed toward where her roommate Kitten's middle older brother Bobcat lay stretched out across the grass just beyond the others, as he was attempting to sit up and thus clearly conscious, but Siggy arrived before her. Her blood brother leapt on the wraith and stabbed it with his knife, as well as gnawing on it with his teeth. The effects of the elixir apparently made it possible for him to bite the things. Rachel shivered at the thought and soared onward in search of someone she could actually help.

She handed out five more vials, two to tutors, one to Yolanda Debussy, the orange-haired Dare Hall College Resident who was also a member of the Brotherhood of the White Hart, and one to William Locke, which he, in turn, tossed to Topher. Naomi and William stood near Topher, firing cantrips at wraiths.

Just beyond them, Lucy Westenra had turned the hunter into the hunted. Her pupils shone a bright crimson, and her incisors had grown to twice their normal length. Three wraiths let out ear-splitting shrieks as they attempted to flee from the vampiress.

The fifth vial Rachel gave to John Darling. She could not track with her eye, but when she thought back, she recalled him briefly appearing and skewering a wraith with a sword. He looked immensely dashing, with his perfect fencer's form and his impressive Norse helmet, as he struck the specter through, causing it to screech and dissolve into tiny points of darkness. Rachel was so impressed she forgot she hated him and held out an elixir in his direction. He became visible, the faceplate of his helmet raised, drank the potion, and gave her a grateful nod before closing his helmet and vanishing again. Apparently, he had forgotten he hated her as well.

As Rachel flew over unconscious students she could not aid, a sense of helplessness began to creep over her. She still had one vial left, but that would hardly save all these people. She was not Lucky, who could remove the enemy's protective wards, nor Sigfried, who could stab them with his knife. She was not sure what more she could do.

She came upon her True History tutor, Mr. Gideon, standing amidst a large group of students with his hand raised over his head in a gesture that was not a cantrip. There were no wraiths nearby. Rachel looked around, right and left, but could not tell what he was doing to repel the attackers. Thinking back, she discovered that, in her memory, a yellow light suffused the whole area, making a faintly glowing dome over the entire large group of students. No wraith seemed able to penetrate this unknown yellow light.

Rachel quickly flew back to where Zachary, Remington, and a few other fallen young men lay. One at a time, she used her wand to lift the unconscious boys and fly them to the area protected by Mr. Gideon. As soon as she did so, students inside the invisible yellow glow ran forward to help them. Rachel did the same for Minnie and Muffy, but by the time she returned again, Esteri was gone, hopefully recovered or helped by one of her many sisters.

As she rounded a tree, she found the three boys from Drake with the pickaxes who she had seen out collecting specimens earlier in the day. The group consisted of Victor Travis, whom Gaius had once described as "a Black dude in sunglasses with stupid facial hair," South African Geoffrey Snork, the young man with the stringy red hair who had fought Rachel and her friends under Drake Hall during the first week of school, and handsome but creepy Herbert Sorrows, whose idea of humor was showing up at the Year of the Dragon Ball dressed as a Nazi. Travis and Snork had been Remus Starkadder's cronies before the second Transylvanian prince had been executed.

As Rachel flew by, Travis attempted to stop a wraith by swinging his pickaxe at a student with whom the wraith grappled. Rachel whistled, freezing him mid-swing. She did not bother speaking to the unpleasant trio. Snork and Sorrows could sort out Travis.

Another group of three wraiths broke off trying to attack some warded boys and flew eastward. Rachel followed them, curious where they all were heading. They floated down the path to Drake Hall, where more dark shapes hovered on this side of the moat, unable to cross the running water. Nearly a hundred people were gathered on the wide porch of the dorm, safe on the other side of the bridge. Rachel could not make out Mr. Price among the crowd, but she hoped he had made it here safely.

Some wraiths were not stopping at the moat but instead veered around to the south. Rachel still had about forty minutes of her hour of elixir left. She figured it should be safe to follow them. As she headed off, however, her eye fell on the wraiths clustered along the moat's edge—just lined up in a row. The temptation was too great.

Rachel drew her wand and rapid-fired Glepnir bands. She had 19 left, and she did not know what was still to come. She should not use them all, but she figured she could spare at least ten. Her year of dueling had done wonders for her aim. Her first seven Glepnir bands struck their targets, each glowing golden band of light encircling and trapping a wraith. By the seventh, however, the wraiths had caught on, and they scattered like startled birds. When her eighth band went astray, she held her fire after that, not wanting to waste anymore.

The startled specters mobbed her, which was both disconcerting and chilling. Rachel held her ground and her breath. One by one, the dark shadowy shapes were repelled by the effects of the elixir. Unable to devour her, they drifted slowly away, returning to the edge of the moat or circling southward. Rachel flew after the south-going group, curious to see where they were going.

"Rachel Griffin," called a high sweet voice. "My mistress has need of you."

Magdalene Chase's china doll stood on the gravel path that led southward from Drake to Raleigh, staring up at Rachel with its painted eyes. Rachel recalled the floating young woman with ropy hair whom she had met at the Dead Man's Ball, which was apparently the real form of the fetch that inhabited the doll. She swept down and lifted the doll, holding it on her lap.

The China doll directed her back toward the commons and down a flight of stone steps to the walled garden. Rachel's heart thumped loudly. She feared she would come upon Magdalene stretched out on the ground. Instead, she found the tiny, pale, dark-haired girl standing with her wand in her hand, defending half a dozen fallen students from six hungry-looking wraiths. Rachel recognized her old nemeses, Belladonna Marley and Charybdis Nott among the fallen. Two of the wraiths were constrained by Glepnir bands. Magdalene kept three more at bay. One, however, had eluded her defenses, come at her from behind, and sunk its head into Magdalene. The normally pale girl looked almost transparent.

Rachel charged into the fray. She tossed Magdalene the last vial, calling for her to drink it, and began firing at the wraiths herself. Her first two Glepnir bands went awry. She steadied her steeplechaser and caught one. She set her feet and continued to fire, now hitting with every shot. Soon, between her and Magdalene, only two remained.

Concentrating on one of the two remaining wraiths, Rachel did not see the bony hand that reached for her from behind. Its fingers sank into her hair. The wraith yanked her from the steeplechaser, which kept flying. Rachel dangled half a dozen feet above the ground, held by her hair, as the wraith floated upward. The elixir protected her from the specter's bony claws but not from the pain in her head—nor from the pain of striking the cobblestones when it dropped her.

Rachel lay on her back, moaning. She wanted to get up, but she felt dazed from the fall. The wraith could not hurt her directly, thanks to the elixir, but it now pried up a loose cobblestone, which it carried toward her head. Rachel called weakly to Magdalene, but the other girl was having troubles of her own. The wraiths could no longer sup upon Magdalene, but that did not stop the last remaining specter from going after their already unconscious classmates. Magdalene threw herself upon the other girls, to keep the wraith at bay. With a faint flicker of surprise, Rachel recognized Eunice Chase, Magdalene's cousin who had treated the small girl so badly, among those whom she was protecting. Magdalene cast a cantrip in the direction of the wraith attacking Rachel, but coming from her low angle, it missed.

The specter targeting Rachel drew back its arm to smash her head with the cobblestone. Rachel tried to raise her arms to block, but everything seemed to be moving slowly as the rock descended toward her temple.

Grrrrrr! A dark form sped from the forest and leapt onto Rachel's assailant, dragging the wraith to the ground. The newcomer was a large black canine. At first, Rachel thought of the wolf from the moors, but no, this dog looked thinner and rangier, more like a wolfhound.

The dark canine worried the specter, dashing it back and forth. Rachel pointed her wand at the distracted wraith as it flopped on the cobblestones. The diamond tip of her wand glinted, and a glowing golden Glepnir band encircled the wraith, trapping it. Rachel cheered, delighted. The creature released its jaws from the wraith's bony arm and stepped back. It paused for an instant, and a thrill of recognition electrified Rachel.

It was the barghest she had spared the time she and the Agents fought them.

The creature, now as solid as a dog, paused over her. Their gazes locked. It moved forward and licked the side of her face with its soft, cool tongue. Then, it turned and ran away, vanishing among the shadows of the forest.

"Rach! There you are!" Gaius came running down the stone steps toward the walled garden.

Rachel stumbled to her feet and raised her hand. "*Varenga*, Vroomie."

Gaius and Magdalene both looked suitably impressed when the steeplechaser appeared out of the sky and returned to Rachel's hand. Rachel allowed herself the slightest of grins.

"Nice work, here, Chase, Fetch." Gaius gave both Magdalene and the little China doll a nod of approval.

Magdalene looked pleased, and the expressionless little doll nodded in return. Gaius lifted all six of the unconscious young women with a flick of his wand and began floating them toward the commons.

"Better hurry," Gaius said to Rachel and Magdalene. "Mordeau's arrived."

Chapter Forty-Eight:
Facing the Dragon

Dr. Mordeau came striding out of the forest ahead of Rachel and Gaius, her black and blue split skirts flowing around her. There was no sign of the Roanoke fey, who had apparently departed, honoring their agreement with Finn, but trolls and solid wraiths flanked her.

At a gesture from the Morthbrood leader, a pack of ghostly wraiths flew through the trees toward the commons, making a beeline directly toward particular individuals. The phantoms poured into these students' throats. The victims' eyes turned black, and they looked to Dr. Mordeau as if awaiting commands. She gestured, and they turned to attack, moving jerkily as they fired their wands at students, visitors, and tutors alike.

Among the possessed students, Rachel recognized Duryodhana Patel, Nazir Neferet, and the Ishazuka brothers, all thaumaturgy students whom Dr. Mordeau had geased back in September. She wondered if the ex-tutor had kept hair or other personal items from the students who had originally been under her care, making it easier for her to cast enchantments upon them. Meanwhile, some of the defenders concentrated on the trolls. Rachel saw both Topher and Kitten's eldest brother, Squirrel Fabian, go down from a punch to the face before Mr. Chanson arrived and restrained the troll who had decked them.

Gaius swore softly under his breath, glancing from his friend Topher and the possessed students to the unconscious girls he currently held in mid-air. Over by Mr. Chanson, Naomi Coils showed up to help Topher to his feet. Gaius noted this and then ran toward the infirmary, the unconscious girls floating before him in an awkward pile. The effort of keeping them up, even with his wand to help him, must have been weighing upon him, because beads of sweat broke out across his forehead. Rachel and Magdalene followed, pumping their legs hard to try to keep up, Rachel's broom swinging in her hand as she ran. Gaius paused, panting, by the stairs, while Rachel ran forward to open the door.

"Who puts stairs on an infirmary?" he grumbled, while maneuvering the unconscious girls up the three brick steps and through the door.

Once inside, he lowered all of the young women to one bed, nodded at the nurse, who was leaning over a pale student stretched out on another bed, and headed for the door again.

Gaius called to Rachel over his shoulder, "I've got to go help my dormmates. They're mainly rotters, but really, they don't deserve this. No one does."

He took off at a run.

Rachel and Magdalene exchanged glances.

"I'd better stay with my sister and dormmates," said Magdalene, clutching her China doll.

Rachel nodded. "Take care of them."

Then, she turned, still clutching Vroomie, and dashed after Gaius.

Rachel pelted across the commons. The majority of the wraiths were gone, though many could be seen trapped in shining golden bands. Students and tutors were helping the wounded and fallen to their feet and moving them toward the infirmary or the gym. To her left, Rachel saw several proctors, including Maverick Badger and Coal Moth, running at full speed down the path that led from the docks toward the campus. Mr. Fuentes had returned from the hurling game and stood in the middle of the commons, directing people.

Rachel looked around, puzzled. Ahead of her, Gaius had paused, too. *Where was Dr. Mordeau? Was it all over?* Then she spotted Cain March sprinting around the reflecting lake toward the east side of Roanoke Hall, his Inverness cloak streaming behind his shoulders. She pointed. Gaius nodded, and they ran in that direction.

They ran hand in hand, paused once to pant and then continued onward. Rounding the corner of Roanoke Hall, they came upon an unexpected sight. Tutors, parents, and students faced off against a black and blue dragon that Rachel recognized as Dr. Mordeau. Only her dragon form was even larger than it had been in September. Nearly sixty feet long in its body alone, it dominated the area between the reflecting lake and the hemlock forest. It was a huge, scaled monstrosity, breathing an orangey-red flame that stank like rotten eggs. Spells and Glepnir bands flew furiously, some directed at the dragon, some at her human and inhuman minions. The air sparkled with multicolored sparks and smelled like a cross between a forest and a bakery.

"We have her!" cried the dean, who stood with her eagle on her shoulder. "Don't let up!"

"Fools!" laughed the dragon. "Do you think you have won? You know nothing! You should have paid more attention to your own campus."

"You are surrounded, Melusine," Dean Moth replied severely. "Surrender."

The dragon launched into the air and flew behind Roanoke Hall. The crowd pursued. Rachel and Gaius ran, too. The two of them came around the back corner to find the black dragon settling in the area of scrub and stumps directly behind the main hall, where plants still did not grow well.

Tutors and visitors and college students fired spell after spell, some at the dragon and some at the possessed students. Rachel caught a glimpse of William and Naomi among this second group. Mordeau's minions were getting the worst of it, but none of the spells seemed to reach the dragon. Streams of red or blue sparks or golden bands of light flew toward the great serpent, only to curve in mid-air and wink out before they reached the gigantic scaly beast.

Rachel skidded to a stop. "What sort of magic is this?"

Gaius shook his head. "I think it isn't magic. Rather quite the opposite."

"I... don't understand."

"It's this area here. Magic doesn't work well. Hasn't since the time William and Vlad blew it up, their freshmen year. What we're seeing is magic failing."

"But...." Rachel watched the scene, helpless, "what are we going to...."

Ding-dong! Dong-ding! The campus bells began to ring out from the six bell towers atop Roanoke Hall. They weren't ringing all at once, as they did for class. Instead, each of the six bell towers rang independently in a rhythm, no, not a rhythm, a tune. Rachel straightened up. She knew that tune! It was....

A solid wall of glittering gold spread outward from Roanoke Hall, pushing wraiths and trolls before it as an enormous *Sacred Ring* spread outward across the campus. Rachel recalled Mr. Kalkavage's comment about bells. He must be a carillonist, using the campus bells like an instrument to play the song of protection. The magical effect pushed back both the remaining independent wraiths and the trolls. The wraiths inside of students seemed unaffected, but at least the other menaces had finally departed.

Meanwhile, Mordeau-Dragon continued to roar and shoot flame. Those facing the dragon were falling back, out of range of its huge gouts of red-orange flame. Their spells were not effective, and they had no other way to attack. One figure, however, did not fall back.

Sigfried Smith strode forward, toward the dragon, a maniacal grin of glee on his handsome features. He was dressed in the red and gold surcoat with a dragon on the chest that Sandra had given him for his birthday. In his hands, he held a sword.

"Dragon Mordeau!" Sigfried waved the blade. "Fight me! You huge reptilian coward!"

The great black dragon turned its head. Screaming like a banshee, Siggy ran at the beast.

"Where did he get a sword?" asked Gaius.

Rachel laughed in spite of the growing knot of fear in her stomach. "That's Nothung. Well, fake Nothung. From the exhibit in the dining hall. Siggy must have filched it."

She watched as Dragon Mordeau breathed a huge gout of flame at Sigfried. Sigfried ducked, somersaulting across the rocky field and coming up to his feet. She breathed again. This time, Lucky blocked the flame by flying in the way and swallowing it. Sigfried ran forward and struck the beast's side, cutting into the flesh. The dragon bellowed and swatted him with its tail, knocking him from his feet. Sigfried fell backwards, but managed to turn the fall into a flip and land on his feet.

The dragon swatted him with one clawed arm. Sigfried struck the foot between two talons, but another talon caught him, raking across his face and arm. Blood ran down Siggy's face.

Lucky rushed forward, and the two dragons fought fire to fire. This gave Sigfried a chance to wipe his face and run forward again, striking the upper leg. The dragon let out a huge gout of flame. Sigfried dived to the left and rolled, barely avoiding being hit before Lucky again flew in the way.

"He's gonna get broiled," Gaius frowned. "Lucky can't protect him every time."

"What can we... oh!" Rachel swung her steeplechaser forward and leapt on. "Sorry! Got to go! See you in a bit!"

Gaius gave her a half salute as he sprinted off toward William and his possessed dormmates. Rachel waved goodbye. Then, she rocketed back toward the front door of Roanoke Hall as swiftly as her broom could take her.

Rachel flew directly into the empty dining hall, opening the heavy front doors with *libra*. She smiled slightly when the doors quietly parted. She had come so far from the thirteen-year-old girl back in September who could not manage the Word of Opening. She flew across the main hall and into the dining hall, directly to the display case that Agent Garbarino and Watchman Adair had mentioned. As she had suspected, the protective glass across the front had been shattered, and the replica of Nothung was gone. The Tarn Helm, which looked suspiciously like the helmet John Darling had been wearing, was also missing from the display.

Without even dismounting, Rachel floated the great red and white shield, Svalinn off its shelf and into her hands—the very shield that Scarlett MacDannan had been running to retrieve twenty-five years ago tomorrow, when Rachel's Uncle Emrys had leaped in front of her, saving her life and losing his own. Then she rocketed through the dining hall, out the open back door, across the field inside the square of Roanoke Hall, and up over the back of the building to where Sigfried still battled the dragon.

"Siggy!" she called, flying low behind where he danced right and left, ducking and weaving in his endeavor to avoid the great gouts of flame. "Here! Use this! If it protected Scarlett Mallory from Morgana Le Fay, it should help against mere dragon fire!"

She did not add aloud: *a talisman made from plans given to Wendy by the angel Auriel.*

Siggy threw her an eager grin and grabbed the shield Rachel wafted to him. "Now that's what I like about you, Griffin. No, 'You can't fight a dragon.' Just goes and gets a bloke a fireproof shield. Right. Back at 'er!"

Behind her, voices murmured, "Hey, isn't that the shield that was in the dining hall?" and "Wait? Can she do that?"

Rachel ignored them.

Sigfried ran forward, the shield over one arm, the heavy sword in the other hand. The weight did not slow him down. He charged, screaming, and stabbed the black dragon in the foreleg again, making a deep cut from which ichor flowed. The dragon bellowed and breathed another gout of fire. Siggy blocked the gush of flame with the shield—which, sure enough, kept the dragonfire at bay—and stabbed again. Lucky, freed from protecting him, flew back to breathing his own fire at the dragon's face. The black dragon bellowed again and counterattacked with its own flame.

Rachel backed away and hovered in mid-air. She glanced around for Gaius and found him beside William and Topher. They had been joined by Vlad. While tutors and visitors continued to attempt to fight the dragon with magic, Gaius and his friends were involved in a firefight with their possessed dormmates and Mordeau's supernatural goons. Sparks flew, plants grew, and ice glittered, coating the ground where they fought. Rachel could see the arrogant Duryodhana Patel and the gracious older Ishazuka brother bound with Glepnir bands, unable to do more than twist and turn, but a number of the others still moved jerkily, firing spells from their wands.

Rachel considered rushing over to help Gaius, but she was too worried about Sigfried to leave her current spot. If something went wrong, she wanted to be ready to come to his aid.

Agravaine Stormhenge, the captain of the Roanoke Fencing Team, tore around the far corner of Roanoke Hall, a rapier in his hand. He dashed forward and joined in the fight with Sigfried, also stabbing the dragon.

Dragon Mordeau breathed fire at him, Siggy jumped in the way, blocking the flame with the shield Svalinn. Agravaine backed up until he was out of the scrubby area. Then he pointed at himself and performed a gesture.

"Turpyr!"

Fireproof, Agravaine stepped out from behind the shield and returned to the fray.

Blue sparkles streamed toward Dragon Mordeau. When the strange effect started to deflect them, the number and strength of the sparkles grew. Following the sparkling blue line backwards, Rachel saw Finn standing on a stump, playing his guitar. Near him, she caught a glimpse of Gaius trading spells with the younger Ishazuka brother. Behind him, Dread hung in mid-air, ten feet above the ground, firing repeatedly at one of Mordeau's trolls as he descended. Rachel wondered fleetingly how Dread had gotten up there.

Finn's blue hex sparks snaked closer. The black dragon roared with rage.

"Hey," Sigfried shouted over his shoulder at Finn, "we're fighting here!"

The dragon reared back until it rested on its haunches. "Moloch! I call upon you. Know that I am your loyal follower and have committed many atrocities in your name! Utter devastation was once let loose here by two hapless freshmen. Come forth, Lord of Devastation! Protect this, your humble servant, from the slings and arrows of her adversaries!"

Rachel caught her breath then let it out slowly. Moloch could not come, right? All sorts of rituals were needed to summon him. She recalled that from her adventures last fall fighting his servant Morax. Merely calling the demons name would not cause it to awake.

Time stopped. All around Roanoke Hall, adults and students stood like a tableau, motionless in the midst of running or firing spells. A wind blew outward from a point just east of Roanoke Hall, near where Mr. Chanson had once emerged when the dragon had sent him flying through the earth back in September. The powerful wind blew back Rachel's hair and tossed her bristleless like a child's toy.

Rachel reached forward and twisted the new becalming ring. The wind parted around her, and she found herself drifting sideways at an odd angle, nearly upside-down. Carefully, she righted herself....

... and froze.

In the place from which the wind emanated stood a twenty-five-foot-tall figure with the head of a bull. He did not seem to be entirely present, more a shadow or a seeming of a distant figure than a solid being—almost as if one were looking through time at something that had happened long ago. He had four arms, one set of which ended in hooves. He extended all four upper limbs, sending an umber ripple over the scrubby area behind the school building. It was a familiar shade of umber, identical to that of the containment field that O.I. used to contain Egg and Morax. Rachel recalled that the O.I containment field had been created based on her cousin Blackie's research into the anomaly disrupting the magic in this very spot.

Moloch. A sensation colder than terror gripped Rachel. *He must be stopped, at any cost!*

The bull-headed being scented the air. He lifted his head and regarded Rachel, the only thing moving in his environment. She gazed back at him, too paralyzed with fear to speak.

Caw!

The seeming of Moloch crossed both sets of arms, bowed its head, and faded away.

Time restarted. Noise and chaos erupted everywhere. The blue sparks from Finn's spell twisted and turned, no longer making their way toward the black dragon. Rachel recalled the last few seconds. In her memory, she could still see the ripples of umber light forming a labyrinth across the whole scrubby area. The blue sparks from Finn's guitar appeared to be constrained to follow the contours of this umber labyrinth.

Rachel landed next to Zoë, who stood nearby, watching. As she stepped off her broom to stand next to the other girl, Rachel glanced to her left toward Gaius and the others, just in time to catch sight of a possessed Seymour Almeida bashing his fist directly into William Locke's face, sending William sprawling. Gaius jumped on Seymour's back, barreling him over, and both young men fell to the ground, where Topher kicked the hand of the downed Seymour, sending his wand flying. Vladimir Von Dread was somehow eight feet in the air. As he came down, Nazir Neferet, also possessed, snagged Dread's right leg in a loop of vine. As Vladimir landed upon the field of ice coating the ground there, Nazir yanked. Dread's leg flew out from under him, followed by his other foot. The back of his head hit the ice-coated ground so hard that Rachel could hear the *crack* where she stood.

"Vlad!" she screamed.

Dread lay motionless on the ice. Rachel leapt onto her steeplechaser to launch into the air, but Zoë grabbed her shoulder.

"Hey, Griffin, something's happening in Dreamland. Something bad."

"Oh?" Rachel longed to rush across the field to Vlad, but Dread's people were all around him, leaning over him. Already, she could see him stirring. Reluctantly, she tore her attention away and turned to Zoë. If there were more dire things afoot, Vlad would have to wait. "How bad?"

"End of the world bad."

"What?"

"Don't know. Can't be sure," Zoë said, gazing up at something Rachel could not see. "But I think the Wall of the World is coming down."

"That way." Zoë pointed as the two girls burst out of the mists of dreamland and into a wide field Rachel had never seen before. "Where that multi-colored fire is."

"Oh, no," Rachel covered her mouth in alarm. "Hurry! Jump on!"

Zoë mounted the steeplechaser, and the two girls shot across the open fields. Far to her right, Rachel could see the forests of the dreamland of Roanoke Academy. To her left, however, in midst of a great tawny plain was a huge, multi-colored blaze, with leaping flames of red, blue, and green.

Rachel's heart lurched. As she had feared, it was the same type of fire she had seen before—in obscuration lanterns and at Beaumont, burning beside the altar where Mortimer Egg had wanted her to sacrifice her family and friends.

Worse than that, the dancing, colored flames seemed to cast shadows, the great, dark shadows of horned dragons, which loomed over the bonfire, staring down at something beside it.

Rachel sucked in her breath. "It's the…" she bit off *tenebrous mundi* before she blurted out the word. "They're here! They've been summoned. This is… not good!"

"I don't know what that is," Zoë sounded unnerved, "but it doesn't look good either!"

Rachel looked off into the distance where Zoë was pointing and gasped. Against a pitch black and roiling background was a mile-high latticework of interwoven red lines. Or maybe it was more than a mile high. Maybe it curved around the entire world, and she was seeing just a small portion of it through a hole in the sky.

"That's the Wall, isn't it?" murmured Rachel. "The Wall that protects our world!"

Behind her on the bristleless, Zoë gave a low whistle. "I was really hoping you weren't going to say that."

As Rachel flew forward, she saw that all around this glimpse of the Wall were clouds and blue sky that looked as if they had been rolled back to reveal the red latticework. At the edges, the clouds seemed to be attempting to expand to cover the Wall again. Some force Rachel could not see impeded the progress.

In the center of the red lines of the Wall hung a pale golden moon with something black obscuring its face. No, as she looked closer, she realized that it was a large, flat, golden disk. At this distance, with no references, she had no notion of how large it was. What she could see of it suggested that the disk held an image, much like what one might find pressed into sealing wax. Too much of the image was blocked for her to make it out.

A crack appeared in the golden disk. The black shape moved, and the crack healed again. Then Rachel's mind resolved what her eyes were beholding, and her lips parted in shock. The object before the golden disk was man-shaped. The figure hung, or perhaps hovered, with dark-clad limbs stretched spread-eagle, as if trying to protect something precious.

To either side of him spread huge black raven wings, obscuring portions of the golden disk from sight.

Rachel pressed a hand against her chest to calm her racing heart, whispering, "Jariel!"

An ear-piercing scream of heartrending pain shattered the peace of dreamland. Zoë grabbed Rachel's arm. Rachel's heart began to flutter. There was something terrifyingly final about that scream. Trembling, Rachel seriously considered turning around and fleeing.

She straightened and dismissed such an unworthy thought. Leaning forward over the haft of her steeplechaser, she tripled her speed. Horrible as that sound had been, what if going forward could keep the same thing from happening again or to someone else?

She flew.

As they approached the multicolored bonfire, her newfound courage nearly left her. Standing beside the blaze was a tall, elegant man with handsome blond curls whom Rachel instantly recognized. It was former Agent Daniel Hanson Browne—Browne who had once shown her a trick where he pulled an egg out of Peter's ear; Browne who had taken Sandra under her wing when she joined the Wisecraft; Browne who had helped Dr. Mordeau and Mortimer Egg murder families, always leaving one member alive; Browne who was about to bring about the destruction of her world.

Next to the former Agent Browne was a tall post with a crossbar at about shoulder height. Tied to this device was the body of a woman with light brown hair. Her head lolled to one side, and her eyes stared vacantly. Blood ran down her chest from where her throat had been slashed.

A frisson of terror ricocheted through Rachel, followed by a flood of relief when she saw the dead woman was not anyone she knew. She paused just a moment to give thanks that she was not currently being sacrificed. Her relief was quickly followed by guilt as she reminded herself that while this might not be someone she knew and loved, out there, somewhere, was someone who did know and love this woman, and that person would be as bereft as Rachel was relieved.

"*Tenebrous mundi*, hear me!" The blond man raised his arms above his head. "Rip down the Wall! Destroy this pathetic world!"

CHAPTER FORTY-NINE:
THE WALLS COME
TUMBLING DOWN

THE SHADOWS OF HORNED DRAGONS GREW LARGER, MUCH LARGER. THEY reached up with clawed limbs and began to tear open the hole in the sky, revealing more of the red latticework. One of them ran its huge shadow claws along the latticework. Wherever the claws touched, the red lines dissolved, allowing the roiling darkness beyond to pour through the break. Bat-winged monstrosities burst from this darkness, spreading outward across the sky.

Three cracks appeared in the golden disk. As Rachel hurtled towards the bonfire, she saw the Raven lower his head slightly, as if concentrating. Slowly, though slower than before, the cracks began to heal. Rachel urged Vroomie to greater speeds, rapidly closing the distance between them and the former Agent Browne.

Daniel Hanson Browne stood with his hands raised, shouting, "Rain ruination! Bring devastation! Free Lord Molo—"

Rachel whistled. Blue sparks swirled around Browne, freezing him in place, arms still raised.

Behind her, Zoë murmured, "That was… surprisingly easy."

Rachel landed beside the red, blue, and green fire and jumped off her steeplechaser.

"*Oyarsa! Taflu!*" she cried, performing the hand gestures for the cantrips that had sent the *tenebrous mundi* away, both back in September, in the Watch Tower and Beaumont, and on her birthday with her father, when one had begun to appear in the Castle Room. "*Oyarsa! Oyarsa! Oyarsa!*"

She looked up hopefully, but the now-gigantic shadows of dragons continued to dismantle the Wall. More and more bat-winged demons broke through, followed by red imps with pointed tails and fat white maggot-like fiends carrying pitchforks. They spread out across the sky as if rushing off to the four corners of the Earth.

"*Oyarsa! Oyarsa!*" cried Rachel, to no avail.

"What are you trying to do?" asked Zoë, standing with one leg on either side of the abandoned broom, that now lay on the ground.

"Make them go back to their proper duties," cried Rachel. "But they won't!"

A familiar melodious voice spoke from the sky.

"Rachel Griffin, you have not the authority to dismiss them."

Rachel looked up. "Because the sacrifice has already been made?"

The Raven nodded.

Rachel thought rapidly about all that she had learned in the last eight months. "Who does have enough authority? A Romanov? Would Nastasia do?"

The figure hovering before the golden disk nodded once and returned to his task. Two cracks were gone, but the third had grown significantly while he paused to speak.

Rachel straddled the steeplechaser, lifted it up, and engaged it, raising the girls into the air. "Come on, Zoë! Let's go get the princess!"

They found the princess in the middle of the commons, comforting wraith victims as they waited for their turn to be seen by the nurse and her student assistant, Ignatius Moth. Joy moved around among the fallen, offering them cups of water from the infirmary fountain, while Nastasia stood in their midst playing the simple healing song they had learned in Music. She played it so beautifully that it seemed to be doing more good than expected. All around her, color was visibly returning to the faces of wounded students.

"Nastasia!" Rachel called as they landed. "Quickly! You need to come with us!"

"When I am done here, I will be happy to accompany you," the princess answered serenely. She looked so lovely with her golden ringlets falling around her head and shoulders as she bowed upon her violin.

Zoë grabbed her arm. "Princess. Now. The world is being destroyed —For real. Right this minute—and you're the only person who can save it."

Nastasia looked at the faces of her two friends. Whatever she saw there convinced her.

"Right." She nodded and called over her shoulder, "Joy, you are in charge here. Keep up the good work. I shall return shortly."

"You hope," Zoë muttered under her breath.

"Hurry!" cried Rachel.

She looked over her shoulder, wondering if Dragon Mordeau had been defeated yet, but a plume of red-orange fire flickering above Roanoke Hall confirmed that she had not. Rachel wished she could rush off and check on Sigfried and Vladimir, but if the whole world were destroyed, the fate of a single small battle would matter not at all.

"I don't think all three of us can fit on here," Rachel added to Nastasia. "We need Zoë to get back to dreamland. Might you get into your purse?"

The princess glided down the staircase of her own purse house. Joy ran over, leaping down the stairs before Rachel could stop her.

"No! I'm coming! Wendy and Sakura, you're in charge!"

Rachel sighed, grabbed the purse, and began flying, shouting, "Zoë! Go!"

It seemed to Rachel that they had been gone only a short time, but the whole sky above the tawny plain was now a roiling darkness being held at bay by a rapidly failing latticework of red lines. Only the smallest hint of clouds and blue were still visible in the far distance. The roiling darkness of Outside had broken through the Wall in multiple places, with streams of fiends entering at each break. Overhead, demons dived and swooped, cackling and shrieking.

Rachel rocketed toward the place where Daniel Hanson Browne stood motionless beside the dead woman and a multicolored bonfire. Reaching the bonfire, she landed and opened the purse.

"Quick!" she cried, pleading. "Before everything is destroyed!"

"Coming," the princess replied graciously. "I suspect you're overstating the threa—. Ah." Her voice warbled only the tiniest bit. "I see you are not."

Joy came out behind her, smiling. "Hi! What are we...."

Her voice trailed off as she stared at the body of the dead woman tied to the vertical pole, her arms stretched out across the crosspiece.

"That's not real, right?" squeaked Joy. "I mean, it—it's just a dream, right?"

"Oh, it's real, buttercup," snapped Zoë, grabbing her roommate's arm and yanking her out of the way.

Joy's face was very pale. She kept shooting furtive glances at the princess's purse as if she was considering retreating back into it, though, to her credit, she did not. Nastasia stared at the Wall and the stream of incoming demonic creatures. Her face also grew paler, but her back remained as straight as ever.

Joy pointed upward. "What are those?"

"Monsters from Hell," Rachel answered evenly, her dissembling mask firmly in place.

"Are they going to attack Nastasia if she tries to stop all this?" Joy squeaked.

Rachel swallowed despite her mask, her voice breaking. "They might."

Nastasia gazed up at the flocks of demons spreading out across the sky and then lowered her eyes to meet Rachel's. The two girls nodded to each other, entirely united in their willingness to give their all to save the world.

Joy grabbed Nastasia's arm. "No, princess! No! You could get hurt! Let's go back! Let's get a teacher or an Agent!"

Rachel replied tersely, "There's no time, and they couldn't help us anyway."

Nastasia reached out and laid a gentle hand on Joy's hand. "The foes arrayed against us are fearsome indeed, and the task before us is certainly quite daunting. But consider, even were I to shirk my duty and cower, how long would we last after the Wall came tumbling down? Both duty and wisdom require that I act. Therefore, act I shall. Will the enemy come against me? So be it,"

The princess lifted her chin, graceful and regal. Her eyes were bright, her expression determined, and her shoulders squared. She raised her voice and called, her voice firm, "Let them know that I, Anastasia Romanov, Princess of Magical Australia, shall stand against them until the last, and I will not falter, even unto death."

Then she faltered, glanced sidelong at Rachel, and murmured, "Zoë said I was the only one who could keep the world from being destroyed. However, I must confess this is not a situation for which I have previously prepared. What must I do?"

Rachel showed her the hand gestures and shared the cantrip. Nastasia gave the gigantic shadows of horned dragons one wary glance and then stepped up to the bonfire. Rachel drew her own wand, not sure what she would do if the demons approached but determined to defend her friend or die trying, However, none of the imps or fiends seemed to pay them any attention. They were spreading out as quickly as they could.

"*Oyarsa!*" The princess's voice was firm and commanding. She stood with royal grace, her head held high, her blond ringlets falling about her shoulders. "*Oyarsa!* Repair the Wall. Return to your proper duties!"

The great dragon shadows paused from where they were pulling back the sky and ripping down the Wall and turned their horned heads toward Nastasia. They bowed, once. Then, they began to move their claws along the holes they had created, knitting together the torn red lines. Nastasia's lips parted in surprise, as if perhaps she had not entirely believed in her own ability. She smiled ever so slightly, her eyes unexpectedly shiny as if with unshed tears.

"I can't believe you did that!" Joy whispered, hugging her. Joy's voice was nearly hoarse with fear and awe. "You're so brave!"

Nastasia endured this indignity and replied graciously. "Our world itself is in peril, but we can take comfort knowing that we are exactly where we ought to be: in the place where we can do our duty, to the best of our ability; the place where we can do what is right and just, in the face of terrible odds; the place where, if we fall, we fall not in vain, but doing what was required of us to preserve what was precious."

Rachel, Zoë, and Nastasia met one another's gazes and nodded. Joy swallowed and smiled wanly.

"I guess that wasn't so bad," Joy squeaked.

The horned dragon shadows began slowly repairing the damaged wall. The process was slow, however, and every moment, more demons burst through. Rachel glanced up at the Raven. There were numerous cracks in the golden disk. Again, the cracks were slowly healing, but their Guardian concentrated entirely upon this task. Rachel did not wish to distract him.

"Who is this... statue? Frozen man?" asked Nastasia. "Is he a dream or real?"

"That's former Agent Daniel Hanson Browne," said Rachel. "He's caused all this."

"The traitor?" asked the princess. With a flick of her wand, she floated the frozen man into her purse house. "We shall turn him over to the proper authorities. We must take this poor creature as well. We cannot leave her body here."

Nastasia fetched a blanket from her purse house, wrapped it around the dead woman, and began to try to get her down. Rachel and Zoë and Joy all rushed forward to help her. Nastasia then wafted the wrapped corpse down into her house as well.

"Hopefully, the dean or the Agents can discover who she is and return her body to her family," said the princess.

"She might be his sister, Susan," Rachel's voice cracked slightly. "The fairies told us she was with him when he passed through their kingdom to reach dreamland."

Part of that was guesswork, but Rachel felt reasonably confident she had jumped to the correct conclusion. The dead woman did look a bit like Daniel Hanson Browne.

"Let's get out of here!" Joy pulled on her arm. She stared nervously at the bat-winged fiends wheeling overhead.

"There must be something else we can do to help," cried Rachel.

"I do not see that there is more we personally can do," said Nastasia. She glanced up at the flying fiends. "These creatures are a threat far beyond our current abilities. But we can go for help. The battle against the Morthbrood at the docks has ended victoriously for our side. We can ask the returning Agents to come here and do what they can."

"Yeah, a great idea!" Joy lunged forward, pulled open the princess's purse, and began running down the stairs into the purse house. "Let's do that!"

Nastasia, too, turned to descend into the purse and then paused. "I must confess to being curious as to why you thought that only I could solve this problem, since Rachel was the one who knew the spell, but there is no time for that now." She laid a comforting hand on Rachel's arm. "There is still much good we can do below." She, too, disappeared down into the purse.

"I guess we go back," Rachel said reluctantly.

She bit her lip and glanced up at Jariel, who was still protecting the golden disk. His face was solemn with concentration. He did not look her way. Rachel noted with a ray of hope that the cracks in the golden surface now seemed to be healing more quickly.

She picked up the princess's purse, handed it to Zoë, and climbed back onto her broom.

As they sped off, Zoë asked, "Um...the Agents. They can't do anything, can they?"

Rachel glanced up at the writhing blackness and the flocks of fiends. She pictured her father and Cain March, in their tricorne hats and Inverness cloaks, pointing their fulgurator staffs at the fiends. She pictured them lying upon the ground, bloody and cut to ribbons, having accomplished nothing.

"No. I don't think they can."

"You know strange and amazing things," continued Zoë as they flew. "Do you know anyone who can help? Because I think our world is still in trouble. Real trouble. Do you remember how much damage one demon did through Mortimer Egg? Times that by thousands. They could be ripping up buildings and ravaging cities, even as we speak. Any chance of reaching that crazy-eye-beams sister of yours?"

"I have no way to reach her," Rachel replied as she flew away from the bonfire, waiting for Zoë to move them back down into the waking world. "The Raven could send all the demons away, I think—all the ones that haven't possessed anyone yet. But he seems to be busy protecting—whatever that gold disk is."

"A shame we don't know more like him," sighed Zoë.

Rachel halted the bristleless, hovering in place above the dream plain. "Actually, I do."

"Do you?" Zoë leaned forward intently.

"But they are supposed to be a secret."

"Griffin. We don't have time. Everything we know could still be destroyed. Everyone we've ever so much as heard of. We have no idea what these... monsters are doing to our world as we speak. If you know something that might help, now is the time to use it."

Rachel swallowed. "They were here, up in dreamland."

"Great. What did the place look like?"

"It was the dreamland of Mars."

"Hold up!" Zoë's voice actually shook. "You mean that reddish place *humans cannot go?*"

"Yes. They were there."

"And you think these Marslings might help us?"

"It's not that I think they will. Rather I don't know anyone else who could."

"Oooh, that gives me confidence," muttered Zoë. "What are they?"

Rachel hesitated just a moment, recalling her conversation with the Raven about the black and white animals she had seen in her dream. Jariel had implied their location should be secret, not their name. "They are the Guardians of Lost Worlds."

"Holy—." Zoë bit off whatever she had been planning to say. "Let's go!"

Rachel started flying forward again. "What about Nastasia?"

"What about her?" Zoë rolled up the top of the purse as if hoping that would keep it from opening. "What she doesn't know can't hurt her—or anyone else, right? She can hang out in the bag a little longer. She has Joy to speak to. And a whole house."

"Very good. Um... do you know the way? To Dream Mars?"

Zoë was quiet for a bit. Glancing back at her, Rachel noted with surprise that the other girl's orange tiger-spotted quoll was suddenly sitting on her shoulder, looking around deliberately with its bright beady eyes. "Yeah. I think I can get us there. To the edge of it, anyway."

They flew through mist and dreams, landscapes changing around them—trees, skyscrapers, castles, mountains. Rachel flew as swiftly as she was able, her sense of urgency growing with every moment. Muted sounds rang or sang out in the distance, but otherwise, everything was calm, as if it were an ordinary day. Somehow, Rachel found this more disturbing than if there had been evidence of chaos.

The *tenebrous mundi* had returned to their proper duties, but the Wall was still breached. Innumerable denizens of Hell roamed free, each set upon doing as much damage as possible. The world was still vulnerable. Her heartbeat pounded in her ears as she thought of all the people, billions of people, with no idea that today might be the end of everything that mattered to them.

The title of Max Weatherby's favorite Bogus song repeated itself in her head as if mocking her: *Last Sunrise: Today's the Day Everything Goes Kaboom!* Had this morning's broom ride been her last sunrise? Her eyes began to sting with the threat of unshed tears.

Rachel forced her attention back to flying. Under her breath, she murmured in time with her grandfather's cadence in her memory: *Think now, Child. Feel later. There will be time enough to mourn when you bury the dead. If you think first and mourn later, you might not have as many dead to bury.*

Behind her, Zoë asked, "That woman whose throat that creep slashed. Did you say she was that guy's *sister*?"

Rachel tried to swallow but could not. "Commanding the *tenebrous mundi* to destroy the Wall that they're duty-bound to protect requires slaying a loved one or someone important—something dramatic. Apparently when they couldn't sacrifice...." Her voice trailed off. Rachel could not bring herself to say that this woman had died in her place. "Without a victim family whose most helpless member they could terrify, apparently, Daniel Hanson Browne sacrificed his own."

"Poor lady," Zoë shuddered. "Ah. We're here."

Ahead was the familiar precipice from the dream she had dreamt after fighting Dart, when she had fallen asleep in her Grandfather's library. Beyond it, she could see only reddish clouds. Rachel landed, stepped from her bristleless, and ran forward. Kneeling, she stared over the edge, down at the endless plain of rusty rocks and red dust below. Below, among the red rocks, a group of black and white creatures with bright red eyes spoke together. The Moose, the Cat, the Lobster, and the Armadillo were missing, but there was a Squirrel, a Swallow, an Alligator, a Sea Lion, a Bear, a Weasel, and the Fox, entirely black except for a white tip on its tail, whom Rachel recognized from the glimpse she had caught of it during the Year of the Dragon Ball. Also with them was the enormous black Wolf from the moor.

"They are here," she called to Zoë. "Okay! Here goes!"

Rachel cupped her hands around her mouth and called out, but no matter how loudly she shouted, they did not respond. They did not so much as glance in her direction. Maybe they could not hear her. She tried throwing pebbles to get their attention, but the matter of the pebbles blackened and imploded well before it would have rained down to make a noise.

"I don't think air flows from here to there," said Zoë. "They can't hear us."

"But they're angels!" Rachel objected, her voice rising. "Shouldn't they be able to pick up on my intention? Jariel always seems to know if there's a probability of something changing."

"This is dreamland, Griffin. Anything you do here is like dreaming it. If you dreamed you were going to do a thing, would Mr. Scary Raven-Face know?"

Rachel hissed with impatience. "The world is in danger. We've come so close. Are millions of people all going to die because we can't get their attention? It's so unfair!"

"Life isn't fair." Zoë shrugged. "Look, Griffin, it's been nice knowing you."

Rachel stared down at the creatures, so close and so out of reach. There must be something she could do. The last time she had seen this place, she had been her dream self. Would being here in person change anything?

She drew two coins out of a pocket and dropped them, hoping the real matter from the waking world would last long enough to bounce on the red soil far below. For a few seconds, they spun downward. Then, they began to shake and vibrate just as the dream pebbles had, and both coins issued black smoke before imploding. Her only comfort was that the larger coin had lasted slightly longer.

Rachel glanced at the circle of black and white creatures hopefully, but none of them looked her way.

She paced back and forth along the edge of the cliff. According to an encyclopedia she had once read, if a man stepped out of a space craft without a protective suit in the depths of space, he could last about ten to fifteen seconds before lack of oxygen deprived him of consciousness. This had shocked her when she first read it, because pearl divers could hold their breath for many minutes; but apparently, one had to breath out when entering a vacuum, or the oxygen in one's lungs would boil. This situation reminded her of that, only the coin had not lasted ten seconds. It had only been four or five seconds before the damage began.

Yet four or five seconds was long enough to shout out a warning, or, if there was no air below, to wave her arms and think hard about intending to shout a warning, which should be enough to draw the attention of angels, if she were within their same frame of reference.

Was it worth the risk?

She looked over her shoulder toward where, in the far distance, she could still see demons—each one capable of unimaginable destruction—streaming in through the broken Wall. Zoë's words rang in her mind: *been nice knowing you.*

As she reached for her steeplechaser to return to Roanoke, an idea struck her. *No.* That was crazy. She could not do that. *She might die. She would almost certainly die.* But if she did not, who knew how many others would?

Rachel turned slowly to face her friend. "I'm going down there. Maybe if I get closer—into their frame of reference—they will hear me. Or at least, they will see me."

"What?" gasped Zoë. "You'll die before you get ten feet."

"I've got an idea. And if it doesn't work, well, maybe ten feet will be enough."

"Rachel, you might *die!*"

"Zoë," Rachel replied patiently, though she had to yank her dissembling mask into place to keep her expression and voice even, "we all might die."

"Oh. Right. Good point." Zoë suddenly looked much younger than usual. "Okay. Carry on."

"Can you get back without the bristleless?" Rachel asked. "I need it if this is to work."

Zoë swallowed awkwardly. She hugged Nastasia's purse close to her chest. "Yeah. Yeah, I can. Will take a bit longer, but...yeah."

"Okay." Rachel took a deep breath. "Here goes."

She mounted Vroomie and flew to the edge of the precipice, staring down. Her heart beat in her chest so violently that she felt as if a flock of birds were attempting to break through her ribcage.

Was she really going to do this? As she hovered above the edge, Rachel recalled the moment, back in September—her favorite moment in her entire memory—when Jariel had gazed down at her, choosing to risk her harming his world rather than damage her memory. He had given her life back to her. Every moment after that was a gift from him. Should she not use that gift to save the world they both loved?

Had she not vowed before him when they sat in the infirmary that she would do anything in her power to protect the world? She had come so close to losing the world at Beaumont, last September. Had not she promised herself that she would do whatever it took to see it never came to that again?

Peering downward at the red clouds, she recalled the expression of approval in Magnus Ridel's eyes when he learned that she had been willing to give up her life to save one little boy. *Would she truly do less to save so many more*

Raising her chin, Rachel twisted her new becalming ring to high and dove off the edge.

CHAPTER FIFTY: MORE POWERFUL THAN SORCERY

RACHEL DOVE, OR RATHER BOBBED, SLOWLY DOWNWARD THROUGH THE clouds of red dust. As she had hoped, on its new highest setting, the becalming enchantment formed a bubble of bluish air around her. The edges of the bubble sparked and blackened as she descended. The effect was creeping inward slowly, consuming the sphere of blue air, but she had a few minutes, or, at the very least, a few seconds.

Sadly, the same thing that gave her a chance of living endangered her. The broom descended so slowly that she might not last long enough to get the attention of the Guardian creatures before the deadly effects of the atmosphere of Dream Mars overtook her. *Should she lower the resistance and go down faster?*

Rachel shouted, hoping to draw the attention of the black and white animals below. "Help! The Raven needs you! Our Wall is breached!"

Nothing. They did not so much as look up. Should she descend lower? Or should she give up and return to Zoë while she still could?

Pop. Rachel glanced around wildly. To her horror, the air around her was dispersing. The front of Vroomie's walnut shaft began to blacken and twist.

Rachel screamed.

Watching her beloved steeplechaser disintegrate was more terrible than anything she had imagined. The last of the bluish breathable air was going, too. She shoved her terror and heartache behind her mask and shouted again: "The Wall is breached! The Raven needs you!"

She wanted to call out the Raven's name, his real name. Maybe that would get their attention, but he had told her not to use it. What if calling him somehow distracted him and made things worse? And then it was too late, because the air was gone, and she would never call out anything ever again. Everything went dark. She was dying, dissolving.

It hurt a great deal.

"Rachel?" From somewhere outside the pain came a cheerful voice she had never heard before, "What are you doing here?"

Rachel dreamed. She dreamed that a handsome young man dressed in robes of blue and red caught her up in his arms and smiled at her. With a touch of his hand, Vroomie was whole. It was a pleasant dream, a pleasant way to die.

She knew this young man, or rather, she had seen his face—on a poster that hung on Laurel's wall. It portrayed actors from a Chinese costume drama that Laurel had watched at the house of their mundane Kim cousins. The poster showed this young man with a cocky smile and a clever gleam in his eye. What was he doing in her dream?

The Wall. She willed her dream self to mention the Wall, but it was so hard to think.

Rachel opened her eyes. The concerned face of Zoë Forrest filled her field of vision.

"Griffin! You're all right!" exclaimed Zoë.

Rachel sat up. She looked at her hands and patted her chest and knees. Everything seemed to be intact. Her heart in her mouth, she spun about, looking for Vroomie. The steeplechaser lay beside her, good as new, except that the first few inches of the walnut haft were now black. She pressed the blackened area. It was smooth and polished like the rest of the shaft.

"Wha—" she stared up at Zoë. "What happened?"

"Um... your plan worked?"

"Did it?"

"Yeah. Kinda. You dived over the edge. You bobbed there for a bit. Then, you turned all black and imploded. It was frankly... Let's just say: if I never see that again, it will be too soon. Then, this kid jumped out of the red clouds, holding you. He laid you down, winked at me, and leapt away—like super ninja leapt away. I mean, exactly like wire fu." She made a gesture with her hand to indicate how lightly he leapt upward. "Then, all these black and white animals shot by, really fast. I could only catch glimpses of them."

"Who was the young man?"

"Don't know. I was going to ask you." Zoë turned and gestured. The dream stuff nearby formed an image of the young man of whom Rachel had just dreamed, the one who looked like the Chinese actor from Laurel's poster.

Rachel shook her head. "I don't know either."

"Creepy!" sang Zoë, helping Rachel to her feet. "Did I mention I'm really happy you're alive—and not a blackened crisp? If I didn't, I am."

The two girls mounted the steeplechaser and raced back. When they reached the tawny plain, things looked quite different. The red lattice-work had been repaired. All the roiling darkness was Outside now; no new demons were coming through. Almost the entire sky had been restored, only it was no longer blue and cloudy. Now it was the velvety blackness dappled with lopsided stars that Rachel recalled from the dreamlands of Roanoke.

Above them, the Guardians of Lost Worlds wrestled with demons, imps, and fiends. Some, like the Squirrel and the Swallow, struggled against them, but others seemed more than a match for a hundred bat-winged beings. The black and white Weasel moved at speeds too fast for the eye to track. It appeared for a moment in front of an attacker, hovering upside-down, knocked the fiend or imp out with a single punch, and tossed it onto an ever-growing pile.

There was no sign of a young man clad in red and blue.

As the two girls watched, the last crack in the golden disk vanished. The Raven lifted his head and looked with slight surprise at the other Guardians as they fought to protect his world. A very slight smile touched his perfect angelic lips.

"The Seal is safe. I go to repair the Wall and close any holes." His voice rang out from on high. Several of the other Guardians glanced his way and nodded. Then he was gone.

With his departure, Rachel could finally see the pale golden seal. It was round and convex. Upon it was an embossed image: a descending dove surrounded by seven trumpets. The image was simple, but there was something utterly beautiful about it in its simplicity A strange sensation went through Rachel as she gazed at it, as if her heart were suddenly too large for her chest. She blinked back tears, but she could not have said why.

"We're done here, right?" said Zoë. "Let's blow this Popsicle stand."

As they came out of dreamland, behind Roanoke Hall, Rachel was shocked to see that Sigfried and Agravaine were still fighting Dragon Mordeau. Almeida and Neferet both struggled in Glepnir bands. Vlad was still on the ground with Gaius and William and Naomi leaning over him, but Rachel was cheered to see that he had sat up and was speaking. Two other members of the fencing team had joined the fight against the black dragon, along with her True History tutor, Mr. Gideon, but otherwise, nothing had changed.

The bells atop Roanoke Hall playing the *Sacred Ring* still rang out across the campus.

"It's as if no time passed," Rachel exclaimed in shock.

"Basically, it hasn't. Time moves more quickly in dreamland. Remember? The only time that has passed for them is the two minutes it took us to get Nastasia to come with us."

Rachel recalled the experiments they had done where Siggy had gone into dreamland while Lucky remained behind. Lucky had mentioned Siggy seemed to be talking very fast.

She flew around to the front of Roanoke Hall and landed on the lawn next to the reflecting lake, letting Zoë off. As the other girl began to open Nastasia's purse and shout down to her that she could come out, Rachel touched her arm.

"Oh, and Zoë, don't tell anyone about that last part. Remember. They're a secret."

"Oh. Right." Zoë frowned. "What do I say to Nastasia, about going back?"

The princess emerged from the bag, followed by a nervous-looking Joy.

"Are we back?" asked Joy. "Is everything okay?"

"Yes. It's almost all back to normal. The Raven came down from that golden seal and went to fix the rest of the damage," Rachel lied blithely, though technically, what she was saying was true. She was just leaving out a great deal.

"Very good." Nastasia inclined her head. "I am grateful to have been of some real help."

"You were," Rachel said with absolute sincerity. "Without you, we would've been lost."

Nastasia gave a shy little smile. Then she pulled out her violin and gestured toward the wounded students still sitting on the ground around Wendy and Sakura. "Joy, let us return to our previous tasks. I see they still have need of our aid."

The two of them departed, heading back towards the wounded. Zoë gave Rachel a brief, four-fingered wave and sauntered after them. Rachel waved back. Then she flew up again and landed on the flat roof of the back leg of square that made up Roanoke Hall. From here, she could see Sigfried, Mr. Gideon, and the other members of the fencing club—there were five of them now—still attacking the black dragon with swords. Rachel recognized the other four fencers as Romulus Starkadder, Donner Virgil, Ivan Romanov, and an upperclassman girl from Drake Hall, Medea Volonski.

Sadly, Roanoke's best fencer still sat on the sheet of ice, holding his head, though Rachel was quite relieved to see Gaius and William begin to help him to his feet.

Dragon Mordeau swished her tail, the same tail that had sent Mr. Chanson through fifty feet of earth. She knocked over Medea and Ivan, sending them sprawling. Sigfried, however, leapt over the tail like a child skipping rope and stabbed her some more. His sword cut great gashes into her flesh. Black ichor dripped from these and other slashes along her lower body, but his three-foot-long blade could not cut deeply enough to reach her heart or her other vital organs. Those with rapiers similarly could not reach anything vital enough to stop her, though she was now limping badly.

"Melusine!" Dean Moth called severely. "It is over. Surrender."

"Never!" Dragon Mordeau laughed, an eerie sound. "You may have wrested the Roanoke fey from me, but it's only a matter of time before my troops arrive, and my minions are already among you, wreaking havoc. Your life, your world, is numbered in hours, possibly minutes. But before all comes to an end, I will have my revenge upon those who destroyed my father and put an end to our great plans!"

"Wrong, Melusine," the dean called back calmly. "Your forces have been defeated. See, the Agents have returned from their fight against the Morthbrood. Your wraiths have been routed, and the students you abused, restrained. You have nothing."

Agents and proctors were pouring around the corner, Inverness cloaks swirling about the first group. Rachel caught a glimpse of Agent Armel leaning over an Ishazuka brother and putting something on his tongue. A dark shape issued out of the young man's mouth. Someone caught it in a Glepnir band before it could escape.

To Rachel's delight, she saw her father among the newcomers. She waved, but having no idea she was on the roof, he did not look her way. No one ever looked up. She saw Scarlett MacDannan, who had been with the

Agents defending the school, kiss a grinning Finn on the cheek, but when she turned away, Finn grimaced. Rachel did not envy him the upcoming conversation in which he was going to have to come clean to his wife about being an elf king.

The Agents lined up, side by side. Their leader, Cain March, sauntered over and joined them. As one, they pointed their gem-tipped staffs at Dragon Mordeau. Rachel wondered if anyone had told the Agents about the magical dampening effect.

The black dragon roared. She drew herself back on her haunches, towering above even Rachel's position. Ichor gushed from her foreleg and side. The fencers all backed up, except for Siggy, who kept stabbing whatever part of the dragon he could reach, working through the scales and cutting out a chunk of dragon haunch, causing her to bellow in pain.

Mr. Gideon rose up into the air, while standing on his broom, but frowned as he did not seem to be able to move toward Mordeau in a straight line. Rachel recalled the meandering curtains of umber light she had seen when Moloch was present. Apparently, their anti-magical nature was impeding his broom as well, which was odd, because Rachel never had trouble flying there. Perhaps, Mordeau had increased the effect when she called upon the demon.

"If I am going to Hell, Jacinda, you're coming with me!" cried Mordeau. "We can join Jasper Hawke and his friends, where they burn in the everlasting fire!"

The black dragon raised its forelegs. Sigfried had seriously injured the right one. It dripped ichor, and large amounts of its inner flesh was exposed, but Mordeau was still able move it slowly. Her motions began to form a familiar gesture, one that filled Rachel with terror. She recognized that cantrip. Carlos Fuentes had cast it in a vision of the princess's back in the first week of September. It produced a deadly black flame only used by practitioners of Dark Arts.

"You might want to duck, kid," called a familiar, cool, flat Midwestern accent.

Siggy ducked.

Zwoom! Crack! The black dragon jerked backwards, a manhole-sized hole in her chest. Dragon Mordeau then fell sideways, slamming into the ground with a reverberating *bang*. Rachel spun around, looking to see who had struck down Mordeau. In front of the path through the hemlocks that ran to De Vere and the Watch Tower was a thick cloud of white smoke. Nearby, Finn played a riff and a gust of wind carried away the smoke.

Where the cloud had been, Blackie Moth leaned against his massive rail-gun.

"Well, look at that," drawled Rachel's second cousin, a tall, broad-shouldered young man with a black goatee, dressed in a Stetson and a half-caped great coat. He patted the weapon fondly. "The old gal worked."

Maverick Badger stalked over to where Blackie stood. The head proctor fanned away the remnants of a cloud of smoke near the weapon's muzzle. He frowned down at the large metallic device on its wheeled cart.

"How did you fire this here?" Mr. Badger growled. "Guns should not work on campus." He glared at the rail-gun. "Make that triple for weapons requiring massive amounts of electricity."

Rachel's taciturn second-cousin almost smiled. "A little birdie told me how."

As Mr. Badger turned away in disgust, Blackie looked directly up at Rachel, where she stood on the roof, and winked.

Rachel sat down hard on the roof. *Lightning!* He must be using *turlu* and a source of magical lightning, maybe even a lightning imp javelin. He had fired a gun on Roanoke Academy campus by using the idea she had sent him.

Rachel grinned from ear to ear. She had helped kill a dragon!

Sigfried was not as delighted. His shoulders slumped, dejected, and he slouched from the field, dragging the famed red and white shield in the dirt. His expression brightened a little when he was met by a kiss from a very enthusiastic Valerie Hunt, but Siggy continued to pout, dismayed that he had not been the one to live up to his dragonslaying title.

The body of the black dragon began to twitch and shrink. Rachel suspected this meant the dead sorceress was returning to her natural shape. She did not want to stay around to see her erstwhile Math tutor dead with a hole blown through her body. She launched off the roof and headed east. She still had about twenty minutes of her elixir left. It was time to follow the wraiths who went eastward and discover where they had gone.

She flew over Finn as he, looking as if he were on his way to face a firing squad, tapped his wife on the shoulder, as if asking to speak with her. Rachel gave him a sympathetic, encouraging grin and continued eastward,

chuckling as she went. She hoped his confrontation with Scarlett Mac-Dannan went well, but she could not help find the whole matter somewhat amusing.

She followed the path the fleeing specters had taken, listening to the peal of the Roanoke Hall bells. As she went, she recalled Mordeau's last words, about Jasper Hawke and his friends and their final resting place; a shiver ran down her spine.

Where was her grandfather? It was all very nice to have gone to the Foothills to see her Elf. Just remembering the peace of the vast forest lightened her mood, but.... Terror seized her. *What if he was not up there?*

Rachel reached the wall of golden sparkles that marked the perimeter of the *Sacred Ring* played by Roanoke's bells and passed through them. The sparkles tingled against her skin but the ring did not impede her. Through the trees, she heard voices. She flew toward them, approaching cautiously. A number of Agents, including Standish and Garbarino, stood in the midst of a devastation of wraiths. Skulls, ripped pieces of black cloaks, bony hand and arm bones were scattered over a thirty-foot glade. Someone had killed a great many wraiths here.

Rachel gawked at the sheer power of destruction that had been unleashed. She had seen many wraiths captured, but very few had been killed. Killing a wraith was hard work. Between this and Blackie's rail-gun, she found herself in awe of what sorcery had accomplished today.

"Hallo." Rachel landed and waved to the Agents. "Good work, gentlemen."

"We didn't do this, Lady Rachel." Agent Standish gestured around them. "Found it this way."

"Rachel, what are you doing here?" Agent Griffin strode out of the trees.

Rachel left her bristleless and ran to greet her father. He smiled and lifted her up and swung her around.

"You should not be here on your own," her father said. "There may be wraiths at large."

"Siggy gave me an anti-wraith Achilles. He made it with Mummy. So I'm entirely safe."

Her father chuckled and shook his head. Putting her down, he placed a hand atop her hair. "I am glad to see you safe." He turned to his companions. "Have we figured out what did this?"

"No, sir," replied Agent Garbarino. "No idea."

"Keep investigating. I'm going to take my daughter back."

Resting his hand on her shoulder, he began walking back the way he had come. Rachel pulled away, grabbed Vroomie, and then fell in beside him, trying not to step on dismembered wraith parts. She breathed a sigh of relief as they left the glade and entered the hemlocks.

Then, she stopped, horrified. She pointed at a leather sole sticking out beside a hickory.

"Wh-what's that?" she whispered, shaken.

"Looks like a shoe," said her father, unperturbed.

"I-I don't think it's a shoe, Daddy," Rachel whispered. "I think it's a foot."

Her father halted, suddenly alert. "You may be right."

They approached the shoe, Ambrose confidently and Rachel cautiously. Sure enough, there was a body attached to the foot, a grown man's body, dressed in a gray suit. Rachel's father squatted down and pushed on the man's shoulder with his staff, turning him over to reveal the very pale face of a distinguished-looking gentleman.

With a hiss of indrawn air, Rachel pressed both hands against her mouth.

"Oh no! It's Mr. Price," she gasped. "Mylene's father. He... he must have done all this." She gestured back toward the devastation-filled glade behind them. "That must have been why all those wraiths were heading this way. They were after him! Apparently, they found a place where they could cross College Creek."

"Price the Canadian wraith-hunter?" asked the duke, rising.

Rachel nodded numbly.

"He must have taken on more wraiths than he could handle." Her father shook his head sadly. "He defeated so many of them—scores—but they must have drained so much life from him before he killed the last of them that he collapsed before he could make it back to safety. Truly a pity. He was the best in his field. He will be sorely missed."

"Es-especially by Mylene."

Tears pricked Rachel's eyes. It took some effort to don her mask of calm. All she could think about was the plaintive note in Mylene's voice when she had asked for Rachel's help. Why hadn't she paused to confirm whether or not Mr. Price was on the porch of Drake Hall?

"I'll let the others know. Someone will collect his body," said her father.

"What if he's not dead?" cried Rachel, desperately clinging to hope.

"I am afraid he is, Little Dart."

"But what if he's not!" Rachel cried again, distraught. "What if he is in a coma? Or enough life remains to revive him? What if our leaving him now is what kills him?"

Her father drew in a breath and let it out slowly. "Very well, Rachel. Stay here. Watch the body. Dorian occasionally moonlights as a medic. I'll fetch him."

He took off at a sprint. Rachel reached wordlessly after him, holding out her steeplechaser, but he was already gone. She turned back to the prone Mr. Price. She did not know why the death of this man she did not know had hit her so hard. Maybe it was the culmination of this overly traumatic day—being caught by the water horse, the hurling game, the wraith war, the dragon battle, and witnessing the partial destruction of the Wall. Maybe it was her own near brush with death. Or maybe it was simply recalling her glimpse of him that morning walking peacefully with his daughter. Rachel recalled her mental image of her father and Mr. March, dead on the tawny dream plain. Tears began to fill her eyes despite her dissembling techniques. Magic, which only minutes ago had seemed so impressive to her, now seemed useless, empty.

Had not she been told there was one thing more powerful than sorcery?

Rachel kneeled down beside the prone body of Mr. Price and bowed her head. She spoke aloud, "Lion's Father, Creator of All, please give this man back his life."

Could He do that? Her Elf had said He could do anything. She waited.

"Hello, Rachel Griffin."

Rachel's head snapped up. An enormous Lion, at least twice the size of any earthly lion, stood among the trees near Mr. Price's head. Might and majesty radiated from Him as light radiated from the sun. Even though she knew it was Leander, a frisson of sheer terror passed through her. The Lion gave her a kindly look. Rachel managed a wan smile in return.

"I have something to show you," said the Comfort Lion.

Rachel nodded, not trusting herself to speak.

The Lion looked upward. "Behold."

The sky above Him opened, and clouds parted, showing the night sky. The point of view seemed to be moving very rapidly, passing through stars, and darkness, and more stars, and then the Wall of Fear. It passed over the beautiful forests and fields of the Foothills and up over the slope of the

Mountains. Rachel leaned forward, her breath bated. Suddenly, she was aflame with desire to know what lay beyond those majestic high peaks.

The view flashed quickly over landscapes almost too beautiful to comprehend, coming to stop on a castle atop a stately hill. It was not a castle Rachel had ever seen before, but it reminded her of Beaumont, of the Black Palace, and, particularly, of Gryphon Park, especially the Old Castle. The viewpoint zoomed into a rounded crenelated tower.

A dark-haired young man stood atop the tower, waving.

Rachel jumped to her feet, mouth agape. If she had not seen Mrs. Heelis's daguerreotype, she might not have known him, but he had the same confident gaze, the same bushy eyebrows.

"Grandfather!"

Her grandfather smiled at her, waving. Rachel waved back, tears streaming down her cheeks. *He was there! He had made it!!* Such tremendous relief rushed through her that her knees would have buckled, had she not been kneeling. Blaise Griffin spoke, but Rachel shook her head, indicating that she could not hear him.

A gleam of amusement came into his eye. He drew himself back. With a rush of excitement, Rachel knew what was coming. She imitated him, drawing back, too. More than a universe apart, grandfather and granddaughter leaned forward simultaneously, shouting, "Boo!"

The clouds rolled back, obscuring the view of what was beyond. Rachel was still kneeling on the ground before the Lion.

"He's there! He's all right! He… he even has his own castle!" Rachel cried, jumping to her feet. She leapt up and down, so filled with joy she did not know how to contain it. It overflowed as tears, streaming down her cheeks.

"Did I not tell you that there are many mansions in My Father's house?" purred the Lion.

"You did," Rachel smiled back through her tears, still not exactly sure what that meant.

The Lion stated, "He made it there because of you."

"Because of me?" cried Rachel. Lady Iolanthe had implied the same thing, but Rachel still did not understand. "But… I didn't do anything."

"You loved," the Lion replied gravely. "That was all that was required."

She looked down at the prone body of her schoolmate's father and then back at the Lion.

"Leander," she asked plaintively, tears cascading down her cheeks, "can you help him?"

The great golden Lion gazed down, His deep voice reverberating. "*I have come that they might have life and that they might have it more abundantly.*"

The Lion breathed out. All the hair on Rachel's arms and the back of her neck rose. A sense of awe came over her so powerful that Rachel feared her heart would stop. As the sweet-smelling cloud of His breath passed over the prone body, color returned to Mylene's father's face. Mr. Price twitched and coughed.

"Oh! Look! He's alive!" Rachel cried, overjoyed, but when she looked up at where the Lion had stood, no one was there.

Chapter Fifty-One: Breaking Through the Clouds of Gloom

"It is no bother, Ambrose. I am happy to reassure her." Agent Standish spoke in his lilting accent as he and Rachel's father approached through the forest. As they came into view of where Rachel was helping Mr. Price to sit up, Dorian exclaimed, "Oh! He *is* alive!"

The duke stopped short. "So he is."

Rachel wanted to run to her father and tell him the truth, but she had been charged not to speak of her trip to the Foothills until the Master of the World revoked his proclamation. There was no way to explain what had happened without explaining the things she had learned from Illondria. So she remained silent. Since neither Agent knew that Mr. Price had been dead, it did not occur to them that Rachel might have done anything, so they asked no questions.

"Mr. Price, we are most pleased to see you are still with us," said the duke, as he helped the other gentleman to his feet. "I am Agent Griffin. This is Agent Standish, and this young lady is my daughter, Rachel."

"You are Rachel Griffin!" Mr. Price's face lit up. "You saved my Mylene!"

Rachel blushed and ducked her head under the curious gaze of the two Agents. "It was my pleasure, sir."

"You shall have to tell me this story someday, Lady Rachel," Agent Standish grinned. "Come. Let us get this good man back to campus."

Rachel aided the two Agents in escorting Mr. Price back to the infirmary. She walked with confidence and her face was calm, but inside her heart was singing. Mr. Price was alive, and her beloved grandfather was safe in the House of the Lion's Father. Oh, and the world had not been destroyed. All other concerns faded as naught.

The infirmary was packed. Nurse Moth and Ignatius were treating those who had been supped upon by wraiths with glasses of water from the healthful fountain in the center of the room and sending them back to their dorms to rest, saving the infirmary beds for the more seriously injured. Even so, nearly all the beds were occupied. Recognizing one occupant, Rachel slipped away.

She crossed to where Dread lay behind a half-drawn flame-orange curtain, reading a book. White bandages had been wrapped around his head. Beholding him there, Rachel found herself overcome with a sudden longing to join the infirmary volunteers and serve as his nurse.

"Hallo." She smiled down at Vlad. "How are you doing?"

"The nurse reports that the bones of my skull are knitting back together properly. I should be out of here by tomorrow morning." He frowned slightly. "I am more concerned with discovering why I lost consciousness."

With a Herculean effort, Rachel managed to pull on her dissembling mask before she burst out laughing.

"Maybe hitting your head extremely hard against ice?" she suggested. "I heard the crack clear across the field of battle."

Vlad made a dismissive gesture.

"Get better soon," she instructed, struggling to keep the corners of her lips from curling.

Vlad's own lips twitched. "I had been planning on convalescing for weeks, but now that you have asked otherwise, I shall endeavor to recover quickly."

At that, Rachel did smile. She gave his hand a little squeeze and then ran off, calling over her shoulder, "Happy Walpurgisnacht!"

For the rest of the day, Rachel felt uplifted, as if the sweet peace of the Lion's breath lingered with her. Her steps were light, her smile bright. She spent the remainder of the afternoon helping clean up the campus. All official events had been postponed until the next day.

Blackie's rail-gun was a tremendous hit with the young men, who crowded around him on the commons. He calmly showed off the weapon to whomever inquired, but the faculty nixed his idea of demonstrating its power by blowing a hole through Storm King Mountain. Rachel did notice that the King of Transylvania stopped to speak with Blackie at length. She recalled that this weapon was a smaller prototype of a gun O.I. had been designing to fight Transylvanian vampires. From his expression, the king was pleased with their progress.

That night, however, Rachel's sleep was wracked with nightmares. She dreamed she was falling through a reddish haze, and her body was turning black and shriveling. Before her eyes, her hands twisted and cracked into pieces. It did not help that, when she woke up, these images were actually in her memory. To her conscious mind, it had been an instant between when the bubble of earthly air had popped, and everything went black. Her memory, however, had apparently captured every disturbing image.

Usually, Rachel looked forward to May Day, but today, it took tremendous effort to leave her bed. A cloud of gloom had settled over her, and nothing she tried shook it. It reminded her of the way she had felt back in late February, in the ladies' room and the infirmary, before her great realization about Laurel and Amber and the nature of ineffable joy. She was pleased to see her parents, to see Vladimir up and in the dining hall for breakfast, and to see her friends were alive and well. None of this, however, cut through the blanket of dreariness.

It did not help that the campus had been damaged, and many students had been hurt. Luckily, no one had died—or stayed dead, at least —unless one counted Daniel Hanson Browne's sister. Nastasia reported that she had handed over both the frozen Browne and the corpse of the dead woman to the dean. The dean had confirmed the latter to be Susan Browne.

At breakfast, Rachel and Siggy and Zoë put their heads together and discussed what to say about the hurling game. After a few hurried whispers, they decided to say nothing until the official story was released. It was possible that neither Cain March nor Finn MacDannan would want to admit that they had involved students—particularly the Crown Prince of Bavaria—in a wager game against fey. If so, Rachel did not want to be the one to blab. Sigfried declared that he would be telling Goldilocks the whole story later, privately. Rachel felt a rush of gratitude that she did not have to worry about whether or not to tell Gaius.

After the traumatic events of the previous day, it was decided not to hold the promised games, though a subdued maypole was offered for those who wished to participate in traditional May Day dances. After that came the ceremonies commemorating the twenty-fifth anniversary of the Battle of Roanoke, with speeches by General Towers, General MacDannan, and a number of other dignitaries, including a few kings. Rachel was disappointed that Vlad's father was not in attendance; she would have liked to have had a chance to meet him. Given how poor relations were between Bavaria and the Wisecraft and the Parliament, however, his absence was not a big surprise.

Proctors and Agents moved through the crowd with bright balls of lux light hovering beside them. As the light shone upon the audience, they carefully checked each shadow for hidden wraiths. The entire gathering breathed a sigh of relief when it was confirmed that no wraiths were present.

Watching them, Rachel wondered how the wraiths had gotten in to begin with. She had seen with her own eyes that the Agents had made the visitors pass by bright lights. As she remembered the incident, her eyes grew wide. At the time, all had looked normal, but in her memory, the shadows of some passing the lamps were misshapen.

Obscuration! The wraiths were hidden in shadows and obscured! When Rachel thought back and recalled seeing Mylene's shadow looking misshapen, it had not occurred to her that she might have been automatically breaking an obscuration, just by the act of thinking back. She moved quickly through the crowd, glancing at shadows and recalling her memory of them but was relieved to see no sign of trouble. She made a mental note to write Mr. Price a letter and tell him about the obscuration factor.

The highlight of the event, however, had been the announcement by Dean Moth that an agreement had been struck with the local fey, reinstating the Roanoke Covenant. Also, the fey of Roanoke, annoyed at the invasion of their territory, had agreed to help rid the island of the remaining wraiths. Credit for this excellent arrangement was given to the Grand Inquisitor and the lead singer of *Bogus*.

The Griffin children stood with their parents during the ceremonies, adorned in their dress robes, with the ducal crest embroidered in silver on the upper left breast. Ordinarily, Rachel would have been delighted to be with her family, but everything seemed muted, far away. She stood expressionlessly, even when a special ceremony was added to honor Nastasia for service above and beyond.

Only the briefest description was given regarding what the princess had done, but it was made clear that she had interrupted a plan by Veltdammerung to cause mass destruction. The matter might have been overlooked, except reports were trickling in from the outside world, reports of damage done: fires, explosions, floods, murders. Rumor said that the mundane news was offering mundane explanations, such as storms, gas line explosions, and water main leaks. The news of the Wise, however, included mentions of bat-winged monsters and mischief-causing imps. The news sources commented on how strange it was that all the disasters had occurred within the same two-minute period, with no reports of damage since.

Nastasia was presented with a plaque by no less personage than Snireth Ko, the Chancellor of the Parliament of the Wise. Snireth Ko was surprisingly tall and broad-shouldered for a native of Cathay. His immensely long white beard and hair were tied with thousands of magical, wind-controlling knots. It was said that if he should untie them all at once, the ensuing whirlwinds would flatten an entire city.

As Chancellor Ko presented the princess with her honor, Zoë stepped up and slipped her arm through Rachel's.

"Unfair. It's you he should be rewarding," Zoë said in a low voice.

Rachel, who was extraordinarily glad not to be the center of attention, shook her head. "It was Nastasia who stopped the Wall from coming down. All I did was help reduce the amount of collateral damage." She added, "You're the one who should really get the credit—for noticing the problem and drawing it to our attention."

Zoë shrugged. "Griffin, I saw what you did. I... I don't think I am a good enough person to do such a thing. That took amazing courage. Nastasia? All she did was repeat a few words you told her to say."

"Perhaps," Rachel replied, "but it was *her* repeating them that mattered."

Afterwards, the Die Horribly Debate Club met in the Storm King Café.

"You actually saved the world? The whole world?" Salome wiggled her neon blue fingernails at Nastasia. "Wow. You deserve that medal. Ordinarily, I would recommend my parents give anyone who saved the *whole world* a cash reward, but I know you're above all that."

Nastasia nodded regally as she stirred her Earl Gray tea. "I did my duty. No reward is necessary."

"I'm not above all that!" cried Joy, raising her hand. "I was there, too, and as the youngest of seven sisters, I take anything I can get!"

"You didn't save the world," countered Salome. "All you did was get in the way."

Joy looked as if she might cry. Rachel found that she felt quite sorry for her.

Sigfried gave the princess an accusing look. "Why didn't I know about all this world-saving?"

"You were fighting the dragon," Rachel replied.

He blinked, astonished. "The world was nearly destroyed *while* I was fighting the dragon? Between when you gave me the shield and when Bug-face Moth blew her up before I could strike the killing blow?"

"Yes. Exactly," said Rachel.

"Wow. That would have sucked."

"Yeah," agreed Lucky. "The world's where we keep all our gold."

"Griffin helped, too," Zoë elbowed Rachel. "She hexed the guy destroying the world."

"Did you?" asked Valerie, sitting down on Siggy's lap. "Good work!"

Rachel sighed. "It would have been a great deal better if I could have hexed him a minute earlier, *before* he began destroying the world."

Over the next week, Rachel's mood plummeted. Zoë's kindly meant comments had touched the heart of Rachel's quandary. She knew she had been unexpectedly brave, and bravery was commendable, but might Jariel have healed the golden disk and then kicked out the demons, regardless of what she had done? Was this like the incident with Dart all over again—where she had acted so bravely, only to realize that Sigfried was far more capable of solving the problem at far less cost? Or, worse, like the night she went looking for Wulfgang in the dark instead of waiting for morning— and almost got staked for her troubles? Was her father correct that she was headstrong and should stop rushing into danger?

She did not feel headstrong. She had risked everything, given all she had, out of a selfless sense of love and duty, but had she truly accomplished anything of value? Intellectually, she knew this idea was ridiculous, yet she could not shake the darkness that had settled over her. Her sense of gloom worsened as she recalled what the Wolf had said to Jariel on the roof. Did despair really claw at her? Was it so bad that the Wolf could see it even when Rachel thought she felt cheerful?

The nightmares did not help either. After a few days, they grew worse. She stood before the fence made of silver and gold spears that had troubled her dreams on Lunar New Year's Eve. The fence was beautiful but haunted by a terrible wrongness. She was trapped, or maybe someone else was trapped. Either way, she was desperate to get through, but when she opened the gate set into the fence, her hands blackened and cracked and disintegrated.

She woke up in a cold sweat, trembling with fear.

Rachel took a moment before going back to sleep to pray, asking the Lion's Father to protect her dreams. The nightmares continued for a few days after that, but somehow, she did not feel as frightened.

The next few weeks were very busy—for everyone except Rachel—which did not help her attempts to break through the cloud of gloom that be-deviled her. As everyone else crammed for their finals, Rachel, who had no need to review material she had read or heard once, spent time alone, contemplating the last two months—the soaring heights and the dismal depths. There was so much she longed to talk about that she could discuss with no one.

She did have things she had to do. She wrote her promised letter to Mylene's father, giving him the missing piece of information he needed to detect the obscured wraiths. Also, some of her classes would have practi-cals as well as written exams for their finals. For Science, the project could be completed ahead of time. Rachel had chosen a shadowcloak and had purchased, with her mother's help, a very nice quality, voluminous black cloak to use as the base. She had chosen shadow and black cat fur for her essences, along with darkness from a midnight sky, which had been a bit tricky to obtain. She was rather pleased with how it had turned out.

True History and Language would be written tests. As Rachel remem-bered every single word the tutors had said, she was not worried about those classes. Math would require demonstrating Euclid proofs, but she knew those by heart, too. Theoretically, Art should have been a problem for her, but as she had already memorized the shapes Mrs. Heelis was going to call upon them to conjure, she knew she would have no trouble passing that final.

That left Music, which meant that while everyone else crammed and studied for three weeks, the task Rachel should have been working on was mastering the piece required for her Music final. At this, she utterly failed.

She did come to an important realization. Not only did she finally ad-mit that she hated playing her grandmother's silver flute, but also she dis-covered that one of the reasons she hated it was that it was too big for her hands. Her tiny fingers had trouble reaching the wide holes. She would have to pick a new instrument if she wished to continue learning enchantment. She had a year to do it, however, since next year, they would have Sophomore Chorus, where they would learn how to perform group enchantments. She would not need to perform solo enchantments again until her junior year.

One nice thing happened during this period that poked a little hole in her blanket of gloom. A letter arrived for her, forwarded by her father, from her departed classmate, Juma O'Malley, to whom she had sent a letter during Spring Break. It was very brief, but he reported that he and his little elephant Jellybean were doing well, living with his aunt, and attending a local academy. Rachel was delighted and penned a quick reply.

The window of light in the gloom that Juma's note had brought closed again, however, when Rachel found herself wondering what had happened to Juma's best friend, young Mortimer Egg, Jr., whose mother had been killed by Juma's mother at the order of his father, who was now imprisoned in umber at O.I. That thought was enough to darken her entire day.

Two weeks before the end of the term, Vlad stood up in the dining hall and clinked a fork against a glass to draw everyone's attention.

"After much consultation between the dean, the Sacred Days Club, and the Knights of Walpurgis," he declared, his voice carrying across the entire hall, "it has been decided to hold Reality weekend after all. Or specifically the Real Olympics. The games that had been planned for Walpurgisnacht and May Day will be held at this time. Information and signup sheets are on the bulletin board next to the dining hall."

When Rachel and Astrid went to examine the board, they found a list of the games the Knights of Walpurgis had agreed upon: Spartan Madball, the Battle of Salamis, Sisyphus roll, epicycle race, zap ball, flying polo, fencing, stone skipping, rock, paper, and scissors, friend carry, croquet, and hurling. Recalling the comment Astrid had made the time they went to the café for rose sodas, Rachel glanced left and right. Seeing no one looking their way, she reached up and scribbled Chinese Checkers onto the list of games.

"I doubt they will honor that," Astrid gave Rachel a gentle smile, "but I am grateful nonetheless."

When the day came, so many people had signed up under Chinese checkers that Dread made an executive decision to include the game. Astrid was overjoyed. She took the honor very seriously and played her best. She tied with Rachel's sister Laurel for first place. Rachel recalled Astrid, curled up on her bunk, watching their other roommates play Chinese checkers during the lockdown and asked her if she liked the game so much, why had she not joined in. Astrid replied sadly that no one had invited her. Since Rachel herself had not been invited to play then either, she completely understood.

The exhibition hurling game was a big hit. The two teams, one in black and orange and the other in blue and white, ran across the field at lightning speeds, passing and dribbling and pulling and balancing. Rumors were beginning to circulate that a hurling game with the fey had been involved in reestablishing the Roanoke Covenant. This just increased interest in the game. Rachel overheard several of the intramural team captains discussing adding hurling to the fall intramural lineup.

After the game, Rachel finally had a chance to sit down and tell Gaius all that had happened on Walpurgisnacht—all that she felt she was allowed to say, anyway. He had been so busy studying for finals over the last few weeks that they had hardly had a chance to talk. She had already told him about the Guardians of Dream Mars over spring break, before she had discovered it was a secret. So the only part she omitted was the visit from the Lion.

Oh, and exactly what happened at the precipice overlooking Dream Mars. She merely said that she called down to the creatures below and left it at that. If she said more, either it would sound unpleasantly like boasting, or it might worry him to such a degree that they would not be able to continue their conversation. So she left that part out, but she told him the rest.

"It's a rather good thing that you found out about these Guardians of the Twilight Lands, because I think there is a ninety-seven percent chance that if you had not called upon them, things would have gone pear-shaped quickly for the rest of us rather quickly," Gaius said, as he sat beside her on a stone wall near the steps leading down to the walled garden. "Remind me. How did you first find out about these beings again? In a dream?"

"My dream unicorn led me to them."

"Your dream unicorn? Oh. Right. Is that a supernatural creature?"

"No. Just an ordinary dream unicorn."

Gaius's eyes sparkled. "Just an ordinary dream unicorn. Right. Does it fa—ahem." He put his fist to his mouth, clearing his throat. "Does it burp rainbows?"

"Certainly not," Rachel said. She put her nose primly into the air. "I do not believe that bodily functions are an appropriate subject when speaking with a young lady of quality."

Gaius burst out laughing. "Good thing I didn't say... ahem. Quite true."

He leaned over and kissed her on the cheek. "Rachel Griffin, you are amazing. I just wish I could have gone with you. All I got to do is save Seymour Almeida and Mark Williams from wraiths, two rotters I don't even like. Vlad feels even worse, I think. He would have been happy if he had been able to do even a tenth of the good you've done this year."

His words warmed her heart. It was true, no matter what she had actually accomplished, that she had been given amazing opportunities to help.

"You were there for the hurling game," she countered. "I called you for that."

"That only really worked because you had found the Heart."

"Shhh!" She looked this way and that, but no one was around. "I still don't think we're supposed to talk about that."

Gaius leaned over and kissed her lightly on the nose. "Maybe next time you're trying to save the world, you can snap your fingers and call me. Or does that only work on Dread?"

Rachel laughed gaily. For the first time since her nightmares had begun, she felt light hearted.

Gaius jumped to his feet, lifted her up, and threw her over his shoulder. Then he ran through the woods towards the playing field, with Rachel's feet kicking in the air as she shrieked with fear and joy.

Gaius and Rachel came in fourth in the upper school friend carry, which Rachel found quite impressive, considering how many of the young men had longer legs than Gaius. Siggy and Valerie came in first. Valerie was dressed like an old-fashioned starlet, with a polka-dotted sundress and her hair in ringlets. She blew kisses to all the boys Sigfried passed. The sight of her fingers moving away from her pursed lips, outlined in bright crimson lipstick, caused a number of young men to stumble and may have significantly contributed to their win.

When it came time for the college friend carry, the Dee Girls and Drake Girls mobbed Dread, begging him to join the race—and pick them. Vlad had participated in the exhibition hurling game, playing goalie for the orange and black team and doing a sufficiently good job that, while their opponents were able to make some points by sending the sliotar through the poles above the crossbar of the net, they were not able to actually score. Since then, however, he had remained in his chair atop the dais set up by the Knights of Walpurgis, keeping a watchful eye over the activities.

Young men then joined in cajoling him to participate, perhaps because they wanted him to pick a young lady so that they could approach the rest. Dread ignored them.

Standing between Dread and William, Gaius drawled merrily, "Maybe you should do it, Vlad. It's your chance to show everyone you've fully recovered from hitting your head."

Vladimir actually rolled his eyes heavenward, though he did it so rapidly that Rachel had to recall the event to catch him at it.

"Very well." He stood up, pushed through the crowd of waiting girls, and strode over to where Magdalene Chase sat hugging her China doll and chatting with her best friend, Rachel's old rival, Cydney Graves.

Vladimir bowed. "Miss Chase, might I borrow your person briefly?"

A blushing Magdalene agreed. Dread scooped her up and carried her to the starting line as if she weighed nothing at all. Cries of: "Wait, she's the lightest girl here!" and "No fair!" rang out among the other young men.

Gaius murmured wryly to William, "We may have created a monster."

William nodded gravely.

The race began. Vlad ran, his long strides leaving the other contestants far behind. He crossed the finish line more than fifteen feet ahead of the next runner. He deposited Magdalene gently back at her seat on the bleachers, bowed, and returned to the Knights of Walpurgis dais. After that, the other students left him alone. He spent the rest of the day observing the events, offering advice, and adjudicating disagreements.

Rachel was a bit surprised that all the games seemed equally popular, with students cheering and shouting with equal excitement over who would win rock, paper, scissors as over which crew team would survive the Battle of Salamis without a dunking in the Hudson. For croquet, it was decided that each dorm would furnish a team, with the Knights of Walpurgis providing the eighth team. To everyone's surprise, the Dee Hall team, captained by Laurel's boyfriend, Charlie Fairweather, won, followed by the Knights team, captained by Dee Hall's Skuld Odinson and with a strong showing by Dee Hall member Romulus Starkadder.

When Rachel expressed surprise to her sister — who looked quite lovely in her long dress as she swung the croquet mallet, which she held in hands clad in a pair of her Leap Year bounty gloves—Laurel laughed.

"Are you kidding? Croquet is practically the only thing Dee folks do. They have wickets set up next to their dorm and can be seen out there playing day and night. After all that practice, if they hadn't won, it would have been a crime."

"It's not important that Dare lost to Dee," Laurel crowed. "What's important is that we Dareians won our match against Drake!"

As the day continued, the dark clouds of gloom that had surrounded Rachel since the day after the War of the Wraiths, as students were now calling it, (the Agents called it the Walpurgisnacht Incident), began to lift. A buoyant sense of cheer slowly replaced the darkness that had oppressed her.

Only one incident marred her lovely day, but even that, surprisingly, did not dismay her. Conan MacDannan talked her into challenging graduating senior Kiki Diggle to a version of the epicycle race, which was meant to demonstrate Ptolemy's motion of the heavens, where two of the three runners were on bristlelesses, one flying around the first runner, and the second flying around the first flier. Rachel picked Siggy and Hildy for her team. She thought they had a good chance of winning.

They might have won, too, had Vroomie not failed her.

There had been signs, since they returned from Dream Mars, that something was off with her steeplechaser, but she had studiously ignored them, hoping whatever it was would go away. Vroomie looked good as new, except for the black around the tip, but underneath, something was not right. In the midst of the contest, as Rachel flew tight circles around Hildy, who was circling the running Sigfried, Vroomie began to react incorrectly to commands. Eventually, it stalled out altogether and dumped Rachel unceremoniously onto the ground.

So Rachel's team lost, and Conan moaned loudly. He had apparently wagered money on the match. Yet, even with this, it was a jolly day all around.

As Rachel headed to the broom closet, in the vain hope that oiling and polishing Vroomie would solve the flying issues, Iolanthe Towers fell in beside her. Her Australian shepherd, Angelo, trotted beside her.

"I just wanted to thank you, Miss Griffin, for inviting me to participate in the negotiations between Roanoke and the fey. I was able to contribute in a useful fashion. Having been involved in these negotiations is going to make a huge difference to my future."

"You're welcome," Rachel replied, delighted. "I had promised you that I would."

"You had," Iolanthe's eyes danced, "but I hadn't believed you. You would have been entirely within your rights to cast me off for my lack of faith."

"But then I would never have been able to show you that I had actually done it, would I?" Rachel replied with a cheerful smile.

That had not been her motive, but it did make the older girl laugh.

"True. True." Iolanthe gazed at Rachel for a moment and then seemed to come to some kind of decision. "Are you aware that, ever since Spring Break, you've had a beam of light from on high following you wherever you go?"

"Wha-what?" Rachel asked, taken aback. She looked up but saw nothing, not even in her memory. "What do you mean?"

"A beam of light. You aren't the only girl on campus who has this, but it's, um, let's just say it's quite rare." Iolanthe flashed a bright-eyed grin. Her silver fox ears popped out from the sides of her head. "I have one, too."

"Do you?" Rachel thought about this. She recalled the vision Illondria had shown her of a group of students whom the elf queen had stated might make good friends. "These other girls with light, would they be Hope O'Keefe, Merry Vesper, Ameka Okeke, and Yolanda Debussy?"

"Yes!" Iolanthe cried. "You can see it, too?"

"No, someone told me there was something special about them—and you were on the list, too. I just guessed."

"Yes! It's true! We all...." Iolanthe fell silent. "Um, I'm not supposed to say. But I tell you what. There's someone I can ask this summer. If this person says it's okay, I'll tell you in September."

"I would appreciate that," replied the girl who longed to know everything.

"You should call me Kit, short for *kitsune*, of course." Iolanthe kicked up one foot behind her as she departed and winked over her shoulder. "All my friends do."

Chapter Fifty-Two:
Last Sunrise—
of Freshman Year

On the last morning of her freshman year, Rachel rose at the crack of dawn and decided to risk a flight on her steeplechaser. She spent only a few minutes up in the air, enjoying the cool breeze and the pastel sky. After that, she flew rather low so that if the bristleless misbehaved, she would not have far to fall.

She flew south along the creek but landed and walked after Vroomie nearly kicked her off. She would have to send her beloved broom back to the Chansons. She should have done it first thing when she realized there was a problem, but she was afraid they might tell her that they were unable to help.

She walked south through the forest, carrying the steeplechaser, and then westward, back toward the campus proper. Her path brought her to the stone arch, beyond which lay the lily-of-the-valley, which, thanks to the magic of Roanoke Island, were still in bloom. Rachel walked under the arch and stood beneath the oaks, among the flowers. Recalling the content of her thoughts the last time she had been here, on Walpurgisnacht, before everything went haywire, she felt a tremendous rush of gratitude.

The world had not been destroyed. They had lived.

She had learned so much this year, discovered so many amazing secrets, and yet so many questions remained. Worse, it seemed as if each secret she discovered unfolded into more questions than answers. Where was Moloch? Would the Master of the World release her world from the interdiction he held it under so that she could share all that she had seen with Illondria? What were the Romanovs? What did Finn know? What was a foxwife? Was it the same as a *kitsune,* or something entirely different? And what was the relationship of Cassandra March—the conjured woman—to Rachel's family?

Where did Lucky come from? Where were Sigfried's parents? Who had written *Felicity* on the lantern that stuck to Sigfried's as they soared up into the night sky, and who was Felicity? Could that be the name of Sigfried's mother? Why had words disappeared from some lanterns? What did it mean that Vlad had received a message from his supposedly dead uncle? More importantly, who were the three hooded figures who opened the ward-lock during the skating party, and what was the strange mask of ice that the woodwose saw in a dream that summoned him to come to campus?

When would they get the treasure the musicians from the Titanic had offered to Sigfried? And whatever had happened with the plan for Wulfgang to befriend the princess? Why had his response to all the information they had shared with him been nothing at all?

Which Arts were the wholesome ones, and which came from below? So many questions. So painful for the girl who longed to know everything.

Knowing everything? Is that what you really want? Aren't you the girl who gave everything to save the world? Rachel ignored this thought. Anyone could choose to be brave in an emergency, even a librarian—especially an adventurer librarian. That did not mean that she had to lead the quest to harrow Hell. She wanted to know everything. She wanted to become a librarian, marry Gaius, and have six children—five great sorcerers and a librarian— or was it going to be four great sorcerers, a librarian, and a farmer?

She was not even going to think about the other boy—looking utterly handsome and vulnerable, lying in bed with his head wrapped up, needing someone to care for him…. Rachel sighed and pushed that thought away.

She thought back to her morning flight above the forest. How strange to recall her very similar flight on the first morning she was here, back in September. How full of hope she had been, how eager for the challenges she had expected to face. What would that girl have thought if she could have seen how the year would unfold?

Wonderful things had occurred, but frankly, all in all, some events had been a great deal more terrible than anything she could possibly have imagined that first day. She had expected trouble, but she had expected it in the form of tough tests, petty bullies, and unforgiving tutors.

She had not expected a Math tutor who turned into a fire-breathing dragon, to be kidnapped twice—once with her cooperation, once not—to fight an ogre, to discover a hitherto unknown sister, and to leap into nigh-certain death to save the world, not to mention the wonders of her trip to the Foothills or to discover a way Underhill. Looking back, these events merely seemed like part of her life, but what would her thirteen-and-a-half-year-old self have thought, back when she first arrived?

Rachel could not imagine.

She did recall, however, what her younger self *had* imagined: She had imagined the friends she might make, the adventures she would have, the secrets she might learn. She had wanted to study every Art the school had to teach; to entrap storm imps with her flute playing; to conjure roses; and to walk with dragons. She wanted to do daring deeds and accomplish marvels never before known to humankind.

And how had that worked out? She had definitely walked with dragons! She could not yet conjure a rose, but she had done a fine job during her Art final of making a circle, a triangle, and a square. She had even learned to draw. She had been given the opportunity to conjure an empty box and move to an advanced class the following year, along with Nastasia, Sigfried, Joy, and Wulfgang, all of whom had met this challenge. After a discussion with Mrs. Heelis, however, it had been decided that she was better off in the slower class. Also, she rather liked the idea of having a class with Astrid, without her other friends there to disrupt their budding friendship. Mrs. Heelis had even promised that the two of them could be in her own sophomore class. Coming back to one of her favorite tutors would definitely make facing sophomore year a little easier.

As to imps and flute playing, her flute playing still left a great deal to be desired. Passing her Music final had been a close thing. The required song was for summoning a domestic fey. It was far too complicated a tune for her whistling talents. Luckily, she had helped one of the dorm *bwbach* one day when it had a problem with some laundry. When it came her turn to play during the final test, the grateful little creature showed up with some of its friends.

Miss Cyrene knew she had not mastered the song, but the Music tutor let it go, admonishing Rachel to do what she could to improve. The tutor did, however, compliment Rachel on befriending the creatures she was attempting to summon, saying that the ability to do this was invaluable to the practice of enchantment. And so Rachel had squeaked by, which was a very good thing, because her musical family would never have understood had she failed Freshman Music.

So, no flute-playing victories, but she had learned how to make a powerful weapon out of lightning imp javelins. That surely must count for something. As to daring deeds and accomplishing marvels, Rachel allowed herself the tiniest of smiles. She rather had achieved that, hadn't she?

She knelt down and ran her fingers over the smooth leaf of a lily-of-the-valley. She shook the tiny stalk of white bells, but unlike the bells beside the silver path Underhill, no sound emerged—even when she thought back. Despite all her trepidations in September and in April, this plant, and the world it grew on, was still here. It was still here, in part, because she had been brave.

That was something to smile about. As to the friends she had made? She had....

There was a noise behind her. Rachel turned her head and started in alarm. Someone was standing next to the stone arch. She caught sight of a pair of black-clad legs and looked up and up and up until she beheld the inhumanly handsome face and black, feathery hair of an eight-foot-tall man with enormous raven wings stretching from his shoulders, wings that still bore a few damaged feathers from when he had lent her his halo. In one hand, he held that golden hoop.

"Jariel!" She leapt to her feet.

"Good morning, Rachel Griffin." His voice was melodious. His eyes were as gray as the wing of a dove.

Rachel rushed through the lily-of-the-valley to where he stood. The Raven extended his hand toward her steeplechaser. Slowly, Rachel held it out to him. He examined it, turning it this way and that. Then, he ran his hand over it, very slowly, concentrating as he went.

"This blackness on the top, shall I remove it? Or would you rather keep it as a memento?"

Rachel thought about this. "Keep it, please."

He nodded and continued, taking quite some time. Eventually, he smiled and handed it back to her.

"It should be good as new now."

"Thank you!" Rachel cried, tears of joy making it hard to see.

"The one who repaired it before is not familiar with the workings of broom spellwork."

"Who was he?" Rachel asked curiously.

The Raven looked slightly puzzled. "One of those whom you sent to help me."

"But, which one? Was it the Wolf I met on the moors? A different one?"

"He was not the Wolf."

"How did he know me?"

"Know you?"

"He called me by name, as if we were friends: 'Rachel, what are you doing here?'"

The Raven's wings rustled. "I will speak to him. Tell me at once if he troubles you."

"Troubles me?" Rachel asked, surprised. "He saved my life!"

Jariel did not answer. Rachel looked at his wings, and her heart skipped a beat. Among the jet-black feathers, a few pale ones still remained, like the gray hairs on the muzzle of an old black dog.

"Is that... is that still from my birthday present? Did it hurt you very much?"

Jariel smiled at her, his eyes filled with warmth. "I am not hurt."

"I don't think I have thanked you properly. That was a princely present. I learned so much—even if I cannot speak of it yet." She pressed her lips together and then blurted out. "Jariel, is it true that you used to be called the Gray Raven?"

He nodded. "Many did call me that."

The voice of the ogre echoed in Rachel's memory: *not so gray anymore, is he?*

"What...." Her voice failed. She tried again. "What happened?"

The Raven said nothing.

"Does it have to do with having made us forget?"

He nodded once. "It does have to do with that."

Rachel looked down, so sad for him. Then she looked up. "It was Leander, wasn't it? That you made us forget. Him and his father. Was it because a seer told the Master of the World that if we did not know about the master of the angels, no demons would come?"

He nodded again but then put his hand to his heart as if in pain. "More than that, I cannot say. I have been instructed not to speak of this matter."

A shiver ran up Rachel's spine. She thought of all the lost things, orphaned words, and who knows what else, all done to carry out a plan that had failed.

"What about the demon who stabbed Valerie? Has he been caught?"

"Enkai? He is not a demon, not exactly, though he has all the force and power of one." He gazed off thoughtfully. "His attention is far from here at the moment, though you all will no doubt face him again someday."

"We will? Why? I mean, why us?"

Jariel said nothing.

Rachel cocked her head and fixed him with a thoughtful stare. "Is it because he's from the same world as Lucky? And Sakura and Enoch, too, right?"

A hint of mirth touched the Raven's lips. "There is no hiding anything from you, Rachel Griffin."

He looked upon her kindly, but Rachel could tell that she would get no more from him on this topic. Recalling something he had said back in February, she asked, "And you said that Ivan the Magnificent would never have ordered you to do such a thing?"

The Raven's feathers rustled like cat's fur standing up in surprise. "I said no such thing."

"Yes, you did." Rachel frowned. "You said it to Amber." Rachel repeated his words back, complete with his intonation. "'*Ivan would not have asked such a thing of me.*'"

"Ah." The Raven nodded. "That I did say, but that is quite a different thing."

Rachel pursed her lips, puzzled. "Can you tell me more about it?"

The Raven said nothing.

Rachel looked at her steeplechaser. "Thank you."

"Thank you." Jariel went down on one knee so that his eyes were closer in height to hers.

"For what?"

"Saving my world."

"Nastasia did that. I wish I could have done more."

"You did all that was required. Nastasia would not have been there had you not come and discerned what was needed. When I was guarding the Seal, I searched for some possibility where our world survived, and I found only one." He reached out and touched her cheek, brushing away a stray lock, his gaze intent. "It was where I gave Zoë Forrest a dream of the place Browne had chosen while she was standing next to you, and then I trusted the fate of the world to you."

"To me?" she breathed.

"I did not know what you would do," he added, "but from that possibility came a hope of the Seal being saved, and the world surviving. All other avenues, the enemy had already cut off."

The idea that she had been a help to him, that he had trusted her, it was too wonderful to bear.

Tears ran down Rachel's cheeks. "Oh, Jariel!"

She rushed forward into his arms. He pulled her into his embrace, holding her tightly. He smelled of nighttime and the sea. She laid her head against his shoulder and wept.

After a time, she breathed deeply and asked, "What was that? The thing you were protecting?"

"The Great Seal of the Veiled World. It is what hides us from the demons."

"But there were lots of demons there. Doesn't that mean they know where we are now?"

He shook his head. "They came following a summons, but they cannot find us if someone here does not call them. If the Seal were lost, they could come any time they wished."

"Oh."

"Some two dozen demons remain, having possessed natives. I cannot move against them so long as they are in this state. But over twelve thousand were ejected. If you had not sent the Gray Hats to help me, nearly a thousand would have found hiding places before I could have spared the time to oust them. Three million and seven more people would have died. Possibly many more."

"Wait. Are you saying that *I* saved three million and seven people?" Rachel's voice rose unexpectedly.

"I am, Rachel Griffin."

"Wow. I... wow," she murmured, stunned. Then, after a time, "What's a Gray Hat?"

He looked faintly amused. "A term I picked up from Gabriel. The other beings like myself who were gathered on Dream Mars. Those who are neither heavenly White Hats nor demonic Black Hats."

"Gabriel?"

"One of my brethren. Possibly the best of us."

The Raven kissed her gently on her forehead. Then, he stood, inclined his head to her, and was gone.

Rachel stayed among the lily-of-the-valley for a time, hugging Vroomie to her chest. She was profoundly glad to have her steeplechaser working again. She had been terribly frightened that the Chansons would tell her it was beyond saving. Now, she could fly again without worry. She made a mental note to send a gift to the Chansons, to thank them for all their help, perhaps something nice from the store at the Gryphon Park Lavender farm.

She hopped on her broom and started back. If she were lucky, Gaius would be done packing, and the two of them could spend the afternoon on their bristlelesses, flying around campus together.

As she flew, she thought back. Where had she been? Oh, yes. Friends. *The friends she might make.* She had made friends, good friends, especially Sigfried, but also Nastasia—even if that was a work in progress—Zoë, Astrid, even Joy, not to mention the best boyfriend ever, and the imperious Crown Prince of Bavaria. And she had even, by some chance of wonder she could not explain, won the friendship of the Guardian of the World.

If this was what her first year entailed, she could not wait to see what next year would bring.

Even among the Wise, animals did not talk.

These two were talking.

Rachel Griffin awoke in her bunk bed in Dare Hall. It was the last night of her freshman year. The other girls in her dormitory room were asleep. She could hear their rhythmic breathing. Yet she distinctly heard voices.

Was this a dream? She had heard those same voices her first night at school. Was this a memory? She opened her eyes partway.

On the windowsill, sitting side by side, were a tiny Lion and an unusually large Raven. They stared out into the star-speckled night.

Presently, the Lion spoke again, "You take your work here quite seriously."

The Raven replied in his harsh, croaking voice, "If I have offended, I shall seek to make amends."

"You have not offended Me." The Lion cocked his head and glanced sideways at the large black bird with his golden eyes. "Tell me, my old friend. Do you ever regret your request?"

The Raven stiffened, his feathers ruffling. When he answered, it was not with the harsh voice of a bird but with the glorious, melodic voice of an angel.

"Never, my Lord and King," the Raven replied, "not for a single instant."

Here ends *Guardians of the Twilight Lands.*

Rachel Griffin will return for her sophomore year in
the Seventh *Book of Unexpected Enlightenment*:

THE YOUNG ANGELS' SOCIETY

Subscribe to the *Roanoke Glass* at https://goo.gl/UEdUKW
to be kept up-to-date on all things *Unexpected*
and the further adventures of Rachel Griffin.

For more information about the
Roanoke Academy for the Sorcerous Arts, see the school's website:
http://lampwright.wixsite.com/roanoke-academy
or join the Facebook group at
https://facebook.com/groups/RoanokeAcademy

Short Stories That Take Place During
Guardians of the Twilight Lands

The *Fantastic Schools* series of anthologies contains stories by numerous authors devoted to life at magic schools of all imaginable sorts. These include several stories from the world of Rachel Griffin, among them the following which take place during the events in this book:

"The Unexpected Rescue of Sigfried Smith"—Sigfried and Rachel visit the Giant's Table on Dartmoor during Spring Equinox Break. When Siggy gets too close to a phooka, things go wildly wrong. But the disturbing turn of events develop a silver lining when the rescue requires that Rachel get help from Gaius.

Found in: *Fantastic Schools Hols.*

"Rachel Griffin and the Missing Laundry"—When Siggy and Lucky burrow beneath Dare Hall, they open a hole into the tunnels that run beneath Roanoke Academy. There, Rachel comes upon a little domestic fey desperately in need of help. Aiding the little bwbach requires visiting each dorm. Is Dare Hall the right place for Rachel? Or should she consider pursuing a different Sorcerous Art?

Found in: *Fantastic Schools: Volume Two.*

"Rachel Griffin vs. The Real Olympics"—Rachel's position as a Knight of Walpurgis and the assistant to the gym tutor leads to a busy day as she runs hither and zither to support the end of the year sports day known as the Real Olympics. One of her tasks is to report cheating, but when the cheater turns out to be someone very close to her, she finds herself in a difficult dilemma.

This story will appear in the yet-to-be-published volume *Fantastic Schools Sports*, expected to be out by early 2024.

Cast of Characters

The Griffin Family

Rachel Griffin—youngest member of the Griffin family

Laurel Griffin—middle sister (Sophomore in the college)

Peter Griffin—a.k.a. Lord Falconridge: brother; heir to the dukedom (Senior at the Upper School)

Sandra Griffin—eldest sister (graduated; works for the Wisecraft in London)

Ellen Griffin—mother; also has a perfect memory

Ambrose Griffin—Duke of Devon, a.k.a. Agent Griffin: father (Agent of the Wisecraft)

General Blaise Griffin—the former duke, Rachel's grandfather, who died when she was nine

Amelia Abney-Hastings Griffin—his wife, who died when Rachel was six

Non-Human Characters

The Raven—said to be the Doom of Worlds

The Lion—familiar of Kitten Fabian

Lucky the Dragon—Sigfried Smith's familiar and best friend

Beauregard the Tasmanian Tiger—the princess's familiar

Mistletoe—Rachel's erstwhile familiar

Aardvark the Tiger-Spotted Quoll—Zoë's familiar

Payback—Valerie Hunt's Norwegian Elk Hound

Widdershins—Rachel's Shetland pony

Cummerbund—Sigfried's pony

Friends at School

Sigfried Smith the Dragonslayer—super rich orphan boy who grew up in the mundane world

Princess Nastasia Romanov—princess of Magical Australia

Valerie Hunt, Fearless Reporter Girl—freshman from Maine, grew up Unwary (Dee Hall)

Salome Iscariot—Valerie's best friend, grew up in the World of the Wise (Drake Hall)

Joy O'Keefe—Seventh Daughter of a Seventh Daughter

Zoë Forrest—well-traveled young woman with a New Zealand accent who can walk in dreams

FELLOW STUDENTS IN DARE HALL

Jane "Kitten" Fabian—English girl with a tiny Lion for a familiar

Astrid Hollywell—shy girl who is an excellent scholar

Brunhilda "Hildy" Winters—blond cheerleader from California, athletic and smart

Sakura Suzuki—Japanese student

Seth Peregrine—base playing friend of Zoë and Siggy

Enoch Smithwyck—Siggy's roommate, Japanese accent

Wulfgang Starkadder—a prince of Transylvania

OTHER STUDENTS

Gaius Valiant—cute yet mysterious older boy, senior at the Upper School (Drake Hall)

Vladimir Von Dread—Prince of Bavaria; head of the Knights of Walpurgis (Drake Hall)

William Locke—son of one of the two founders of Ouroboros Industries (Drake Hall)

Naomi Coils—Junior in college, Secretary of the Knights of Walpurgis (Dee Hall)

Jenny Dare—College sophomore in the Knights of Walpurgis (Marlowe Hall)

Topher Evans—Upper School sophomore in the Knights of Walpurgis (Dee Hall)

Wanda Zukov—Upper School freshman in the Knights of Walpurgis (Dee Hall)

Cydney Graves—(Drake Hall)

Belladonna Marley—(Drake Hall)

Charybdis Nott—(Drake Hall)
Zenobia Jones—(Drake Hall)
Arcturus Steele—(Drake Hall)
Ameka Okeke—daughter of a chieftain, soccer champion
Misty Lark—friend of Zoë and Seth (Marlowe Hall)
Magdalene Chase—little girl from (Drake Hall)
Michael Cameron—Knights of Walpurgis member (Marlowe Hall)
Jarius Knight—(Dee Hall)
Mortimer Egg Jr.—(Dee Hall)
Juma O'Malley—boy with a tiny elephant for a familiar (Dee Hall)
Ivan Romanov—college junior, the princess's eldest brother (Dare Hall)
Alex Romanov—a senior in the Upper School (Dare Hall)
Alexis Romanov—his twin sister (Dee Hall)
Ferdinand Meadows—Rachel's cousin
Arjuna Pandava—student
Romulus Starkadder—Crown Prince of Transylvania
Remus Starkadder—second prince of Transylvania
Fenris Starkadder—fourth prince of Transylvania
Carl Iscariot—one of Salome's older brothers
Rory Wednesday—second-most beautiful girl on campus
Eunice Chase—Knights of Walpurgis member
Xandra Black—a.k.a. Flops-Over-Dead-Chick; works at the Storm King
    Cafe
Faith O'Keefe—Joy's older sister; works at the Storm King Cafe
Jonah Strega—Dr. Mordeau's assistant
Yolanda Debussy—Female Senior Resident for Dare Hall
Urd Odinson—Second-in-Command of the Knights of Walpurgis
Randolph Graves—Knights of Walpurgis member, Cydney Grave's brother

THE SIX MUSKETEERS AND THEIR FAMILIES

James Darling, Agent—the head of the effort to stop the Terrible Five, now
    an Agent for the Wisecraft
Ellyllon MacDannan Darling—the Conjurer of the Six Musketeers, Sister
    of Finn, and the wife of James Darling
John Darling—their oldest son, captain of the Track and Broom team
Wendy Darling—his sister, a freshman
Michael Darling—their younger brother, not yet at Roanoke

Wendy MacDannan — the youngest of the Six Musketeers, was driven crazy by magic

Finn MacDannan—a.k.a. Red Rider; rock star with the band BOGUS; also works for the Parliament of the Wise; said to be the world's best Enchanter

Scarlett Mallory MacDannan — only person ever to get Seven Rings of Mastery from Roanoke Academy; currently an Agent of the Wisecraft

Oonagh MacDannan—A senior at the Upper School who plays a tuba

Liam MacDannan—A junior at the Upper School

Conan MacDannan—A sophomore at the Upper School, part of the Vampire Hunting Club

Ian MacDannan—Siggy's roommate and one of the MacDannan Clan

Taliesin MacDannan—youngest member of the MacDannan family; not yet at Roanoke

Crispin Fisher—the final member of the Six Musketeers, their Alchemist and a tutor at Roanoke

Marta Fisher—his daughter, a freshman at college

VAMPIRE HUNTING CLUB

Abraham Van Helsing
Conan MacDannan
Alex Romanov—the princess's brother
Max Weatherby
Sarah Weatherby
Winifred Powell
Andrew "Drew" Colt
Laurence Colt
Frederick "Efrick" Ferret
Richard "Arrick" Ferret

ROANOKE ACADEMY FOR THE SORCEROUS ARTS

DEAN

Dean Jacinda Moth
Mr. Gideon—Assistant Dean, Upper School
Miss Edwards—Assistant Dean, College

Tutors

Mr. Hieronymus Tuck—Freshman Language
Mr. Crispin Fisher—Freshman Alchemy
Mr. Archimedes Gideon—Freshman True History
Mrs. Beatrix Heelis—Freshman Art
Mrs. Miss Himeropa Cyrene—Freshman Music
Dr. Melusine Mordeau—ex Math Teacher
Scarlett MacDannan—Freshman Math
Nighthawk—Master Warder

Staff

Horatio Jareth Poole—Librarian
Mr. Roland Chanson—P.E. teacher
Flora Towers Skaife—Mistress of the Beast (head of the Menagerie)
Nurse Moth—School Nurse
Ulysses Burke—Gardener
Captain "Zephey" Zephyr—Captain of the Roanoke Island ferry called the *Pollepel II*
Umberto "Sarpy" Sarpento—Custodian

Proctors

Maverick Badger—Head of Security
Coal Moth
Carlos Fuentes
Matt Scott
Harvey Sanders
Roderick Stone

Wisecraft

James Darling, Agent — Canticler; familiar: tortoiseshell cat named Pyewacket
Agent Scarlet MacDannan — all Seven Arts; familiar: rat named Thorin Oakenshield

Agent Dorian Standish—Canticler; familiar: cheetah named Mwendo
Agent Melody Briars—Alchemist; familiar: oriole
Agent Miles Caldor—Warder; familiar: sheepdog
Agent Lily Follower—Conjurer; familiar: cat
Mortimer Egg—secretly member of Veltdammerung

WISECRAFT-LONDON OFFICE

Agent Ambrose Griffin—Enchanter/Canticler, familiar: black and white cat named Moonracer
Sandra Griffin—Conjurer, Warder, Enchanter, Canticler, Alchemist, familiar, cat: Starpaw
Agent Templeton Bridges—Scholar/Canticler, familiar: cat
Agent Michael Garbarino—Enchanter, familiar: seal
Agent Vicky Armel—Warder, familiar: magpie

PEERS OF THE ROUND TABLE

Walter Pandoff-Sap—Duke of Trevena
Ambrose Griffin—Duke of Devon
Magnus Ridel—Duke of Caledon
Locksley Dymoke—Duke of Sherwood
Lugh O'Clery—Duke of Tara
Harry Ravenwood—Duke of Avalon
Bedwyn Glyndwr—Duke of Caerleon
Peregrine Scot—Marquess of Logres
The Ravenmaster of the Tower of London
Sir Calidor Moth

THEIR CHILDREN (MENTIONED)

Lady Olivia Ravenwood
Lord Edmund Ravenwood
Lady Charlotte "Reela" Scot
Lord Peregrine "Peril" Scot
Lord Frederick "Freddy" Scot
Lady Xenia "Neens" Scot

THE TERRIBLE FIVE

Simon Magus
Baba Yaga
Koschei The Deathless
Morgana Le Fey
Aleister Crowley

OTHER VILLAINS

Morax—demon
Moloch—demon
Rupert Lawson—a Veltdammerung cultist
Serena O'Malley — Juma O'Malley's mother and an agent of Veltdammerung

OTHERS

Jasper Hawke—mysterious sorcerer who died over a hundred years ago
Darius "Daring" Northwest—an Adventurer Librarian
Thaddeus "Taddy" Orwell—grandson of the Griffin's cook, too young for Roanoke
Ben Bridges—Rachel's friend, too young for Roanoke; son of Agent Templeton Bridges
Ferdinand Meadows—Rachel's cousin
Aperahama Whetu—Maori expert of dream magic; made Zoë's silver sandals
Kenneth Hunt—Police detective and Valerie Hunt father
Cassandra March—Cain March's wife, said to be the only conjured human being

GLOSSARY

Agents—Magical law enforcement. Agents fight magical foes, both human and supernatural.

Alchemy—One of the Seven Sorcerous Arts. It is the Art of putting magic into objects.

Bavaria—A country that exists in the world of the book but not in our world. It is known to both the World of the Wise and the Unwary. It is ruled by the Von Dread family.

Canticle—One of the Seven Sorcerous Arts. It is the Art of commanding the natural and supernatural world with the words and gestures of the Original Language.

Cantrip—One word in the Original Language, *i.e.* a canticle spell.

Cathay—The Democratic Republic of Cathay, a country that exists in the world of the book but not in our world. It is known to both the World of the Wise and the Unwary. It is ruled by an elected council.

Conjuring—One of the Seven Sorcerous Arts. It is the Art of drawing objects out of the dreamlands.

Core Group—A group of students, usually from the same dorm, who attend all their classes together.

Dare Hall—The dormitory at Roanoke Academy that is favored by enchanters.

De Vere Hall—The dormitory at Roanoke Academy that is favored by warders and obscurers.

Dee Hall—The dormitory at Roanoke Academy that is favored by scholars.

Drake Hall—The dormitory at Roanoke Academy that is favored by thaumaturges.

Enchantment—One of the Seven Sorcerous Arts. It is based on music and includes a number of sub-arts.

Fulgurator's wand—A wand with a spell-grade gem on the tip that is used by Soldiers of the Wise to throw lightning and to hold other kinds of spells.

Gnosis—One of the Seven Sorcerous Arts. It is the Art of knowledge and augury.

Heer of Dunderberg—Storm Goblin locked up with his Lightning Imps in a cave in Stony Tor on Roanoke Island.

Jumping—A cantrip that allows the practitioner to teleport.

Magical Australia—A country that is only known to the Wise. It is ruled by the Romanov family.

Marlowe Hall—The dormitory at Roanoke Academy that is favored by conjurers.

Morthbrood—An ancient organization of practitioners of black magic. During the Terrible Years, the Morthbrood served the Terrible Five.

Mundane—Without magic. Refers both to the modern technological world and to those who cannot use magic. It is possible to be mundane and Wise, if one has no magic but is aware of the magical world.

Obscuration—A subset of Warding. It allows for the casting of illusions that hide things and trick the Unwary.

Original Language—The original language in which all objects were named.

Parliament of the Wise—The ruling body of the World of the Wise.

Pollepel Island—The name the Unwary call the island they see in place of Roanoke Island. It is also called Bannerman Island.

Roanoke Academy for the Sorcerous Arts—A school of magic on a floating island that is currently moored in the Hudson near Storm King Mountain.

Scholars—Practitioners of the Art of Gnosis.

Sorcery—The study of magic.

Spenser Hall—The dormitory at Roanoke Academy that is favored by canticlers.

Terrible Five—The leaders of the Veltdammerung, who terrorized the World of the Wise during the Terrible Years. They consisted of: Simon Magus, Morgana le Fay, Koschei the Deathless, Baba Yaga, and Aleister Crowley.

Thaumaturgy—One of the Seven Sorcerous Arts. It is the Art of storing charges of magic in a gem.

Thule—A country that is known only to the World of the Wise. It occupies the section of Greenland that is, in our world, occupied by the world's largest national park (larger than all but 32 countries).

Transylvania—A country that exists in the world of the book but not in our world. It is known to both the World of the Wise and the Unwary. It is ruled by the Starkadder family.

Tutor—The term used for professors at Roanoke Academy.

Unwary—One who does not know about the magical world.

Veltdammerung—Twilight of the World. The organization that served the Terrible Five during the Terrible Years. It consisted of the Morthbrood and of supernatural servants.

Warding—One of the Seven Sorcerous Arts. It is the Art of protecting one's self from magical influences.

Wise—Those in the know about the magical world (as in the root of the word 'wizard').

Wisecraft—The law enforcement agency of the Wise. The Agents work for the Wisecraft.

World of the Wise—The community of those who know about the magical world.

Acknowledgements

Thank you to Mark Whipple, John C. Wright, and
William E. Burns, III, who breathed the life into the original story.

To Virginia Johnson, Erin Furby, Brian Furlough,
Bill Burns, and Jeff Zitomer, who helped iron out the bumps,
and to my sons, Orville and Justinian for playing along and particularly to
Juss, for wearing a lightning imp under his cat.

To Erin Furby for slogging through the early drafts.

To Anna "Firtree" Macdonald for making it readable.

To Jim Frenkel for his brilliant editing,
for which Rachel will be forever grateful.

To Anthony Regan, Michael Putlack, Sue Sims, and Valerian Gallant.

And to my mother, Jane Lamplighter,
who listened for the last time,
at least this side of the Foothills.

About the Authors

L. Jagi Lamplighter is also the author of the *Prospero's Children* series: *Prospero Lost*, *Prospero In Hell*, and *Prospero Regained*. She is an assistant editor with the *Bad-Ass Faeries* anthologies. She is also a founding member of the Superversive Literary Movement and maintains a weekly blog on the subject. When not writing, she switches to her secret identity as wife and stay-home mom in Centreville, VA, where she lives with her dashing husband, author John C. Wright, and their four darling children, Orville, Ping-Ping, Roland Wilbur, and Justinian Oberon.

> Her website is: http://ljagilamplighter.com
> Her blog is at: https://arhyalon.livejournal.com/
> On Twitter: @lampwright4

Mark A. Whipple grew up in Croton-on-Hudson, which is not far from Roanoke Island. He then attended St. John's College in Annapolis, the mundane sister school to Roanoke Academy. Until recently, he has spent his free time, when not busy torturing Rachel Griffin, protecting the world from video game threats. Now, however, he volunteers with Stillbrave, a charity devoted to helping the families of children with cancer.

UNEXPECTED CHARITY: 30% of the authors' proceeds from the *Unexpected Enlightenment* series goes to charity. Current charities of choice:

Mark's choice: Stillbrave Childhood Cancer Foundation — helping families of children with cancer.

Stillbrave Childhood Cancer Foundation
6731A Edsall Road
Springfield, VA 22151
https://stillbrave.org

Jagi's choice: Mary's Shelter—sheltering women and their children

Mary's Shelter
1601 Princess Anne St.
Fredericksburg, VA 22401
http://marysshelterva.org